To Coach

Thank you so much for the continued support!

THE GETAWAY PEOPLE

Liam Cuddy (signature)

LIAM CUDDY

No part of this publication may be reproduced, stored in a retrieval system, or transmitted in any form or by any means—electronic, photocopying, recording, or otherwise—without prior written permission, except in the case of brief excerpts in critical reviews and articles. For permission requests, contact the author at lmcuddy98@gmail.com.

All rights reserved.

Copyright © 2021 Liam Cuddy

ISBN: 9798513490791

The author disclaims responsibility for adverse effects or consequences from the misapplication or injudicious use of the information contained in this book. Mention of resources and associations does not imply an endorsement.

To those who both inspired and encouraged
the completion of this book,

&

My Dad

1

Ray had decided he was ready to die. The skies, however, were not overflowing with rain or split with lighting as one might expect them to be on such a dark occasion. Instead, the clouds seemed to be spun with silk, the sun beamed down from the heavens, and every ounce of magic nature had in store was ever-present.

He exhaled as he slowly stepped into the water. Behind him sat the knapsack and walking stick that had accompanied him along his tiresome journey. The sun was now beginning to set, and it was time for his journey to end. The water was shockingly cool as he waded farther in off of the bank. He sank into the water until he could feel the muddy silt oozing between his toes. Despite the pleasant atmosphere, there was little hope to feel in the current pushing past his legs.

Ray arched his neck and examined his surroundings. The trees shed a spotted green light on his surroundings as the sun shone through the various leaves above. He glanced at the rocks and thought about how they were formed in their perfectly round, imperfectly ridged ways through thousands of years of erosion. The thought of erosion flashed through his mind. It was a subtle thought of beauty, the idea that one stubborn rock could be made perfect over years and years of duress from the current. He looked at his green knapsack and how it blended in with the foliage surrounding it. He listened as the birds sang for their lost lovers, each one a new call, each one a sweet new melody of desperation.

Feeling the subtle current pushing around his body, he allowed himself to sink back into the water. It wasn't as cold now. As the water rose, it absorbed all the tiny droplets that had gathered on his skin. He laid back and the water flooded his ears as if to tell him that he better not listen to what was to come. The world went silent. He could no longer hear the birds, the trees, or the whispering wind; he could only hear the noise of rushing water swiftly carrying his body away. He drifted along the top of the water like a plank of dead wood.

Suicide was always built up to be the act of a coward, yet after heavy meditation on the subject, he found it to be quite the contrary. Being seen as such a taboo subject, he never had the opportunity to explore the real meaning behind it all. Yet after years of solitude and one heartbreaking mistake, he felt that he knew suicide as an acquaintance, the ultimate means to an end—a decision rendered easy without the burden of loved ones. Some saw suicide as a cry for help, yet Ray did not intend to seek help. He didn't intend to be found at all.

The rush of the water grew stronger as the curves within the river became less frequent, giving way to a straightaway. The noise became dense and lost any sort of pattern as the current pulled him effortlessly to the water's edge. Soon he would reach the cutoff where the water fell freely to the rocks below. The sounds got louder and louder, yet Ray's face remained expressionless. Before he had time to take his dramatic last lungful of oxygen, he was whisked off of the edge of the falls. For a brief moment, he could hear the sounds of the earth once more as his head lifted from the water, though he didn't focus on sound. He was too distracted from the sight of the sunlit sky growing further away as he plummeted to the rocky depths below.

There was a point, as he floated through the air, where he could feel the fear at his fingertips. All his life, he had felt he was a part of something bigger, yet here he was, bringing an end to it all. Every question that rattled through his mind was the same one philosophers had asked themselves for centuries. *What comes next?* And though the idea of bright lights and golden gates were comforting, with every thought of glory came one of darkness.

Ray's body smacked the water before any more questions could be contemplated. His body sank faster than he had imagined as his leg swiftly met the blunt side of one of the boulders below. A deep pain surged through his body; he moaned as he clutched at his upper thigh, depleting what little oxygen he had left. The rapids tugged him from side to side, violently throwing his body like a rag doll. He gripped his leg as he sank deeper and deeper before getting swept up in a different current and rocketing out of the chaotic whirlpool. He inhaled more water and immediately felt the pain in his gut. The plan for a painless death was now gone. The determination had been replaced with a fear of suffering. Before he knew it, his limp body was pushed out of the current as the stream met a quick, unexpected curve.

Swallowing another lung full of water, he made his peace, sinking slowly into the depths of the day. His insides trembled as he tried to resist the temptation to reach for air. He felt the weight of his thick clothes drag him deeper and deeper to the rocky floor. Looking up to the surface of the water, he saw what he could only imagine heaven to be as his vision began to blur. The fire-red sun was beating down on crystal waters, casting an unforgettable burning glow that rippled across the surface. He watched as it grew further away, his life running between his fingers like sand. His struggle quickly subsided, and with another lungful of water, his body went numb. His panic was quickly replaced with an odd euphoric aura that blanketed him as his back met the muddy floor.

As the beautiful scene began to fade, a rather small object plunged into the water above, creating a series of fiery ripples. His heaven had been vandalized. The object began to squirm and eventually gained direction as it proceeded to move straight toward him in a rhythmic pattern. The closer the object drew, the clearer it became despite his fading consciousness. It took only a moment for him to recognize the movement of arms and legs frantically making their way toward him. He wanted to tell them to stop; he wanted to tell them to leave him alone. He wanted so badly to explain that this was meant to be, that his life as he knew it was over. Yet despite his depressive thoughts, despite his desire to die, he found himself reaching out to them with all the strength he had left. Their nimble fingers interlocked with his as his vision faded to black.

There was no tunnel, no light, no mystical being. There was, however, an ache of disappointment upon not seeing his life flash before his eyes like a movie specifically tailored for him by the forces that be. Instead, he pictured a small boy, no older than the age of eleven. The boy was running through the front yard on a summer evening. His skin hot and sweaty, his arms pumping back and forth like a locomotive charging forward in full force. The boy had dark brown hair and eyes to match. His smile was tinged yellow, but he wasn't ashamed in the least. He just kept running, and running, and running. He didn't have a destination, nor did he have a care in the world. He was just running because that's what he was meant to do at that very moment.

He watched the boy run wide circles in the tall grass, wondering if he too could partake, wondering if this was what eternity was. Ray stepped forward and tried to speak, yet he couldn't form words. Inch by inch, he was pulled backward away from the boy, away from where he wanted to be. A blunt, rhythmic force kept pulling him back, further and further away. The pressure left by the disappointment in his abdomen becoming more prominent by the second. The force grew tighter and more direct and left a sour taste in his mouth. Before he knew it, his vision was ripped away from him and replaced with blurry visuals. A concoction of earthy colors bombarded his vision and spun faster than they did on his most intoxicated nights.

He was alive; it was wrong. Ray finally came to in the act of hurling himself to his side and allowing all the water to drain from his body like a spring. It was all followed by the feeling of incredible weakness, his arms trembled, and his fingers shook within the prints they left in the pebbles he lay upon. Nearly all of his attention was focused on his throbbing leg and the sting in his back. He squeezed his shoulders tight as his pale body lay shaking on the rocky bank. The water drifted by him effortlessly as if it hadn't nearly been the cause of his demise moments prior.

The silhouettes of feathered scavengers circled in the sky above him. Ray blinked to clear his eyes of any remaining water. He was lying still upon the riverbank, far from where he had last entered. He dug his hand into the fine pebbles that lay next to his beaten body. The pain slowly began to creep up his bones, aching as deep as the marrow.

There was a rustling out amongst the trees. Something was moving along the brush. He closed his eyes and listened as best he could, trying desperately to take his mind off of his throbbing leg. There were definitely voices, many of them. It wasn't long before he could make out each individual person. He needed to flee but knew it was a pointless undertaking. He began to move his right leg in, but the pain was crippling to the point of exhaustion. He ground his teeth as he once again attempted to move his body. It was no use; he was stuck on the bank, captive to whomever it was coming his way.

He thought about how there wasn't supposed to be anyone else out this way, how that was the whole idea of living off the grid in the first place. The idea of sanctity and privacy were two things he held dear, especially at the time of his decided passing.

The movement grew louder and more prominent; the voices were now distinguishable and clear. They had spotted him and were now moving quicker. Ray closed his eyes and tried to stifle all noise, hoping that maybe they'd decide he wasn't worth the trouble.

A woman led the group, followed by a rather disgruntled male counterpart. The others kept to themselves.

"There, there he is, Tobias," she gasped.

"Look at him. The guy stands no chance, Luna. You saw him moving?" replied Tobias.

"He was. I tried getting the water out of him. He's hurt, though, hurt real bad. His leg may be broken," said Luna. She quickly ran up to him and pressed two cold nimble fingers against the side of his neck, slightly adjusting them as she felt for a pulse. She turned to look at the others and nodded before placing a hand on his cheek in a comforting manner. "*I've got you,*" she said in a reassuring way.

Tobias sighed and cursed under his breath. "Grab the damn stretcher," he ordered as if it were a chore he wasn't willing to do. "Let's get him back to Corazon. Maybe Maple can work her magic."

"We're really bringing him back?" one of the others asked, sounding surprised.

"Elliot would have had mercy on him," Luna chirped in defense. "It's only right that we do too," her hand remained on Ray's cheek.

Tobias sighed, clearly uncomfortable with the entire situation. "Luna, we need to talk…"

The gentle hand left his cheek as she stood up. "We'll talk later; we need to get him back now."

There was a pause as everyone exchanged glances.

"Like right now," she said, this time in a more demanding tone.

He was suddenly surrounded. He could feel the presence of many eyes staring at him from above. They set a stretcher next to his body.

He could feel a pair of hands running up and down each of his legs, carefully feeling for a burn or serious abrasion.

"It's the right leg," Tobias stated as he ran his hand along a sizable lump near his upper knee.

"Well, what are you waiting for then? Get him on the stretcher," said the raspy voice to his left.

"We need to be careful!" Luna snapped. "He's hurt enough; we should roll him."

There was no retaliation following her careful insight. They rolled him onto the stretcher and counted down from three. Ray felt his body leave the earth as he was lifted up and carried through the woods. The people beneath him grunted and stumbled, yet there were no words spoken. It felt as if he were levitating for ages. He opened his eyes and watched the pines, still wet with dew, pass over him from above. Each minute presented a new challenge as he felt his body slowly deteriorate. It wasn't long before he noticed his back was damp with the blood pooling beneath him.

It seemed as if it had been hours by the time the team stopped to rest. Ray opened his eyes slightly in order to see where he was headed. They all walked under a massive wooden underpass, which had something etched into the wood.

Soon new voices came into play. Outsiders gasped as he was carried through what sounded to be a hushed crowd. *Who is that? Where did he come from? Is he alive?* He heard children scampering underneath him, winding themselves in between the bodies of his rescuers like frightened little snakes.

"Knock it off," Tobias said bluntly. "Go prepare Luna's hut; we're bringing him there."

The scampering of the children quickly took a new direction. He wanted to look around; he wanted to open his eyes and see. Part of him was far too afraid of what he might find. He was taken into a small enclosure; it was dark and smelled of mud and wood. They rolled him off of the stretcher and onto a platform. He lay still, recognizing that he still had several pairs of eyes watching his every movement. He could practically hear them breathing, waiting for him to move or speak. A few more people came into the enclosure.

A large man threw back the tarp that hung at the entrance of the hut. It was Constantine, an individual who was as pompous as he was insecure. He wasn't used to sudden excitement, and his every move wreaked of subtle insecurity. "Let me see him."

"He's unconscious," someone spoke.

"Lily, we can't keep him here; we don't know anything about him. What if he was being hunted? What if he carries a disease? What if—what if he was sent here *looking for us?* It was wrong for us to have taken him in," Constantine said. "Just wait until Elliot finds out."

"Well, we can't just discard him. He's a human being." Lily stressed. "Where is your code, where are your morals? *Mother* would be *so disappointed*," she said, emphasizing each and every word.

"How dare you make this a matter of my creed," Constantine hissed. "I'm looking out for the good of the community. This man could be—"

Constantine was cut off when a voice from the doorway chimed in. "He was not being hunted, and he doesn't have any disease that we know of. I saw him, I watched him get taken under. He was… just walking. Must've accidentally fallen in and got caught in the current. He is no more dangerous than you are judgmental, Constantine." Luna said, not quite knowing whether she was out of line in speaking up. The air was saturated with tension.

"How dare you talk to me that way, Luna. Have some respect for a Disciple. I am trying to be logical here. If Felix were here, he'd expect us to ask these sorts of questions. Our community is fragile, we must take the proper precautions to protect it," he said as if he were trying to rally the masses. Nobody seemed to be taken up with his words.

"Oh please," said a new voice, an older woman by the sounds of it.

Luna tried to intervene. "Maple, don't involve yourself, he's my prob—"

"I'm not involving myself; I'm just wondering why nobody has asked him any of these questions yet!" she shouted. Everyone seemed to simmer down as Maple and her elderly wisdom took control. "The man is in pain, we can use that to our advantage. He won't be going anywhere on that leg anyhow."

"He's unconscious, we can't interrogate him," Tobias stated in an attempt to reclaim authority.

"You don't know what you're talking about, Tobias." Maple replied. "He's not unconscious, he's been listening to us this entire time. And you're no Disciple, so don't think you can bark orders the way you're carrying on. Make yourself useful and go get this man some water. I'll have him wide awake in a second or two."

Ray felt a tingle run down his spine as his skin broke out in goosebumps and a cold sweat accumulated on his forehead. The room went silent, Tobias stormed out.

Maple approached him and rested her hand on his wounded leg. "Constantine, please hand me that cup right there. We'll refill it once Tobias gets back." There was a scuffle amongst the people. The woman grabbed the water and took one more step so that she was standing just above him. It felt as if he were standing under the shadow of a tower. "Watch and learn. We old folks aren't completely useless," she said with a smirk.

Maple turned to Ray and rested her hand on the throbbing lump on his leg. Even with her gentle touch, pain seared up and down his body as if his blood had just caught fire. He lurched forward and grabbed her hand as he gasped for air. "Stop!" he pleaded, "stop!"

Maple quickly placed a strong hand behind his back so that he couldn't lay back down. "Shhh, easy there. Stay up, stay with me. Here, drink. It's water," she said, lifting the tin cup to his lips.

Ray hesitantly sipped from the cup while simultaneously glancing at the figures surrounding him. His head was pounding as his eyes adjusted to the light as the room spun around him. Maple held him up and snapped her fingers in front of his face as everyone else in the room watched diligently.

"Focus," she ordered as she snapped her fingers again. "Focus! What is your name? *Your name.* What is it?"

Ray panted heavily. His headache was so tremendous he could barely make out her words. "Your name," she said sternly. "Tell me your name." The woman lifted the cup above his head and let the water spill out onto his damp hair. He felt the cool rivulets run down his face and back, perking him up.

The water seemed to whip him back into a hazy reality, one in which he could hear the lady and her orders. He opened his dehydrated lips and began to speak. "Ray… my name is Ray."

The lady continued to snap her fingers in his face, "All right, Ray, do you know where you are?"

"No… I don't know where I am," he muttered, being completely honest.

The woman they referred to as Luna spoke quickly from the doorway. "He's in a lot of pain, Maple. Please, let's just give him something! You and I can work on his leg once we put him under."

Even while dealing with the excruciating pain, Ray was able to connect the dots. The old woman's name was Maple, and they may be able to fix him, though it sounded as if it would come with a price.

Maple sighed and spoke swiftly, "Luna, you know we don't have the resources to spare."

"When else would we use them, Maple? Even the crippled lamb will be swaddled in Mother's arms! Right from the lips of Elliot himself, this man is suffering!" she yelled.

"I admire your dedication, but that was for followers of Elliot alone. This man is not one of us!" Maple shouted back. Another fast silence swept through the room.

He wanted to speak up and tell them to leave him as is, but the pain spoke for itself. He could feel a cold sweat running down his face. He ground his teeth and clutched the edges of the bed frame.

Maple looked deep into his wincing eyes. She slowly began to nod her head before looking at the small curious crowd accumulating behind her. "Get out. All of you, now! Luna, grab the pills. We'll need something heavy for him, and quick! Thomas, get my kit while you're at it, the one under my bed, Musgo will know where it is." The crowd began to disperse as Luna bolted out the door.

"You're in good hands, just relax," Maple said as she began to pat his forehead with a cloth she swiped from the bedside table. She eased Ray back onto the bed, he calmed down and attempted not to squirm. He was fixated on what she was doing, feeling every fiber of the cloth brush against his pounding head. "Shhh," she said. "Be still, be very still." She looked up toward the ceiling and placed her bare hand on his sweaty forehead. She closed her eyes and began to speak in what seemed like an incantation.

"In the name of Elliot and all things sacred, please oh great, oh powerful, oh merciful Mother, grant me the power to bear this burden upon my back. Bless me that through your eyes, I may see, through your ears I may hear, through your hands I may work, and through your heart I may feel. Grant us these gifts in hopes that we may one day join you in eternity. In the name of Elliot and all things sacred. Bless us."

Ray studied her face as she spoke the phrases over and over with determination and haste. And for a moment, lost amongst her cryptic chanting, all the pain surging through his body seemed irrelevant. In an instant, it was back and worse than before.

Maple continued to recite her prayer as he curled up his free fist and slammed it down on the table where he lay. Upon bringing his fist back up again, he noticed the blood running down his wrist. The table was wet with the blood, still pooling beneath him. He felt an immense pressure weigh down on his chest; perhaps they hadn't noticed. *Perhaps,* he thought to himself, *perhaps this is it.* An unnecessarily prolonged death sentence, botched from the very start.

Luna dashed into the room holding a bag that seemed to overflow with medical tools, gauze unspooling out of the outside pocket. "Soak the rag, hurry!" Maple said sternly. Luna did as she was told, taking a moment to remove a large mason jar and dousing a rag in its liquids. She handed the rag to Maple, which caused her to cough and stabilize herself on the bed frame. "My dear, too much! Far too much!" she coughed as she took the rag and wrung it out over the open jar.

Maple took her free hand and wafted the remaining fumes to check the potency. "That should do. Luna, hold his arms down," she ordered, nodding toward his arms. Luna quickly leaped to his side and grasped his wrists. Maple stood directly above his face and leaned over. "Sweet dreams, Mr. Ray," she said, pressing the cloth firmly against his mouth and nose. He winced as he initially inhaled the pungent fumes, but there was no struggle. His vision began to ripple, and his fingers went numb as he continued to inhale the intoxicating fumes. A wave of euphoria washed over his body, his vision blurred, and soon he was asleep.

2

The idea of floating over water was calming, lingering somewhere between what was real and what was his drug-induced dream state. He saw bright blue skies and large swaths of wheat reaching far into every direction. He walked through the fields of wheat, stopped to look at the sun-soaked clouds, and walked some more. Everything was just right. Then came the crickets, those six-legged pests. There was always something about the cricket that carried with itself a sad undertone. It was not like any other insect. He often admired how they called out into the dead of night, searching for a mate of their own.

His dreams and reality slowly began to fuse as his visions were engulfed in black, yet the sounds of the crickets remained. There was a numbness in his right leg, and his head still ached. Nothing held a candle to his indescribable hunger, though. He furrowed his brow as he tried to recall the last time he had eaten. His efforts were cut short when his attention was directed to the sound of mason jars clinking against one another in the corner of the room. Ray blinked as he tried to adjust to the flickering warm light of the fire that burned silently on the dirt floor. He could see much better now.

There was a woman standing with her back to him. It wasn't Maple; he knew that much. This woman was taller and more slender. Her back was lit up, illuminated by the small fire in the center of the room and the lantern at the foot of his bed. She wore a beaten-up white shirt that she kept tucked into her worn-out jeans that had seen better days. A thick leather belt was wound tight around her waist. Her feet were bare, and her hair blonde. He couldn't yet see her face, but she exuded a kind of natural beauty. It was the way she stood, relaxed but determined.

Ray licked his flaking lips and tried sitting himself up. As his torso left the top of the table, he felt as if parts of him remained stuck to the surface. The spent blood was now sticky, acting as an adhesive that kept him glued to the bedsheets. He winced as he reached around to his back. The woman was startled by his voice and hopped to his side.

She placed a hand on his chest and slowly guided him back down to the table. "You don't want to do that," she said with an alarmingly subtle panic in her voice. "You're still a long way from healed, and we need to make sure you don't lose any more blood." Her voice sounded so familiar, kind, but mysterious. "You must have gotten jabbed with one of the rocks from the fresh outcropping. They aren't big, but they'll cut deep if you hit them right. The bandage has to stay on until your wound scabs over, then we'll talk about recovery."

Ray nodded as he felt for the bandage on his back. There it was, heavy and soft. He then looked up at the woman who knew so much about his condition. With one look, he took every detail of her face in. She had pale blue eyes that seemed almost *too* blue. She had round pebble-like cheekbones that sculpted her face. Her features were so sharp and exact, giving her a very cunning and intellectual aura. She looked directly back at him, unblinking. She was mirroring him, dissecting his appearance, trying to figure out who he was before the interrogation even began.

"Do you understand?" she said, snapping out of their mutual trance.

"Yes, yes. Don't move. I understand," he said reassuringly.

She studied him for a few more moments before going back into her corner. She fiddled around with a couple more items and then turned to him, holding a tray prepared with a cup of milk, bread, and a variety of fruit. Ray followed the tray with his eyes. She slowly walked toward him, being careful not to spill any of the milk, and set the tray down gently on the stand next to his bed.

"I don't think you realize how badly you're hurt. It's not often someone survives a fall like that. Your leg is definitely broken, but we think it's just a fracture. We can set it and put it in a splint for the time being," she said, nodding toward his right leg. There were two planks of wood spanning from his ankle to the middle of his thigh. They were placed on each side of his knee and were wound tightly together in certain spots with what appeared to be wire.

"Aside from the wound, your back is just bruised up. And nobody falls that far without a good concussion. You're lucky to be alive," she said, looking at him through the corner of her eyes.

"Am I?" he asked with a sigh. "I didn't ask to be saved."

She seemed angered by his passive remark. "Would you rather me have left you out there? I can always have that arranged. The wildlife around here doesn't care if your heart's still beating or not. Food is food."

The tone of the room shifted, causing him to reflect on what he had just said. She was irritated and quite worked up. Her jaw was wound tight, and her arms now folded. She did what she knew was right. He couldn't judge her for that. "I'm—I'm sorry. I shouldn't have said that."

"Blame it on the painkillers while you can. You have enough running through your blood to numb an elephant right now," she said as she pulled a thick wool blanket over his legs and abdomen. "You're lucky, too. I had to beg them to break out the emergency stash. You were shaking quite a bit, writhing in your sleep. I'm no doctor, but I know a seizure when I see one."

He imagined what he might have looked like *writhing in his sleep*; it wasn't the most comforting of thoughts. "Why are you doing this for me?"

"No living thing deserves to feel that way. Ever. End of story. These painkillers are part of what's keeping you alive right now," she said, rattling an orange pill bottle on the stand next to his head.

That would explain the euphoria. Ray's mind began to race again. "I've got a lot of questions."

She rolled her eyes as she set the pills down and began to fiddle with the various instruments at the other side of the room again. "I'm sure you do."

"I have *a lot of questions*," he repeated in between coughs. She turned to him as she leaned up against the brown wall next to his bed.

"What's stopping you from asking them?" she asked, shaking her head and shrugging her shoulders. She stared at him with wide, tired eyes. She clearly hadn't had the best of nights either.

He cleared his throat and turned his head to her. Suddenly all of the questions seemed to disappear, drained from his lips. She held his stare and eventually raised her eyebrows in sarcastic anticipation. He had to say something. "Who are you?"

"My name is Luna," she said quickly. Ray looked at her, expecting more. When he realized that was the end of her sentence, he quickly tried to make up lost time.

"Okay, Luna… where am I?" he asked.

Her face changed in the slightest of ways. It almost appeared as though she were trying to conceal a smile. Luna grabbed a stool and set it down at the side of his bed. She let out a tired sigh as she sat down and leaned in, resting her elbows on her knees. "Well, the general answer? Colorado. But I'm going to assume you already knew that." She waited to see if her sarcastic jab lightened the mood; he remained as stoic as ever. She continued, "But if we were to get into specifics, you're currently in Corazon. A place untouched by the evil and greed of the world you knew."

Ray's face tightened. He was out in no man's land. "Never heard of it," he said plainly.

"That's by design. More people means more diseases to worry about, more controversies that arise, more mouths to feed. We find that life is better lived lost."

"What type of a city is this?" he asked, as confused as ever.

Luna sat up straight. "*Corazon is no city. We are a united group of selected individuals brought here to carry out the deeds of Mother through simple, modest work and through the daily praise of The Prophet.*"

Ray began to smirk in hopes that she, too, would break her stern composure. He desperately wanted her to laugh. He wanted her to give him something more than that cryptic description. But she remained stern, unmoved, and slowly his smile faded. He couldn't decide on whether it was more intriguing or unsettling.

"So um... I've got a few more questions," he muttered.

She responded swiftly and with a sting. "All of your questions can be answered in the morning, but for the moment, keep your mouth shut and do exactly as I say, understand?"

"I'm not trying to cause any trouble, I promise," he coughed.

"Great. Then eat. You're no good to anyone dead." She retrieved the tray from the far table and made her way to his bedside. She tore a piece of bread from the loaf and held it to his mouth.

He looked up at her. She once again held his stare. It was almost as if she was wearing an unbreakable mask upon her face. He reluctantly opened his mouth, allowing her to place the bread upon his tongue. He chewed and swallowed before she brought the tin cup to his lips, letting him sip on the milk. This process continued through the entire loaf of bread and into the fruit.

"We're a self-sustaining community, all of our food is homegrown, all of our drinks purified and distilled right within the community. No preservatives, no currency, no debt," she said as she pushed a crisp apple slice into his mouth. "We have been this way for over fifteen years. I'm sure others will fill you in on Corazon's history. All of us were rescued by the Prophet himself. Chosen by the hand of Elliot, Mother's one true Prophet. He lives up in the mountain with a few of his closest Disciples. He decides who stays and who goes."

Ray chewed his food as long as he could; it was the only action that could keep him from showing his true bewilderment. He eventually mustered up the courage to speak. "You know I have been living in a cabin not too far from here. Thirty or forty miles, if I had to guess. I thought that was secluded, but…"

He was cut short when Luna seemed to belt out, "Why did you leave?" An awkward silence slowly ensued as Ray found himself at a loss of words. It seemed as though she, too, realized that her tone was too aggressive. It was too late; the damage had been done. "Why did you leave, Ray? What brings you thirty or forty miles away from home?" She stopped to let him think for a moment but decided to push further. "Why would you go all that way just to end up at the bottom of a river? I need to know. If you're in some sort of danger, and you brought it here, then…" He was caught off guard by her sudden outburst.

She could see he was growing flustered and continued to push on, hoping that he would give her something to work with. "It was your home. Why would you leave your home like that? Do you have a family waiting for you?"

"Enough!" Ray shouted, elevating his head slightly. The air was thick with a heavy wet haze, and the growing tension wasn't improving a thing.

Luna stepped back. She angled her head and narrowed her eyes as she looked down at him. What started as a startled expression turned into one of intimidation. "I apologize," she said as she wiped the juices from her hand. "But you must understand that you're not the only one that's confused here. When you live in a community that hasn't seen a new face in years, and all of a sudden you show up, well... "

"Well, what?" Ray said through his teeth.

"Well, it's bound to bring trouble," she replied softly.

❊❊❊

The two of them sat in tension-ridden silence for a few minutes. He distracted himself by looking at the dying fire while she began cleaning up after herself.

"Here, swallow this," she said as she put a white capsule to his lips. He opened his mouth and accepted it without question. She then gave him water to wash it down. "It's just another painkiller. This should get you through the night." She glanced at him again, the dying light flickering upon her face. He wondered what she was looking at, whether she was still giving him a threat assessment. What did she see with those deep blue eyes? Whatever it was, it was more than he was willing to show.

"So what now?" Ray croaked from the back of his throat. She moved about the room taking care of the leftover food and water. Each piece of fruit had its own respective bowl. She even carefully funneled the milk back into the carton that sat in a pail of ice.

"Now? Now you rest. Your body won't heal without sleep. Lay back, you'll be out in a minute or so." She pulled the blanket to the base of his neck and brushed the sweaty strands of hair off of his forehead. She had a tender touch for someone so defensive.

"All right then," she muttered as the fire went dark, the embers shining like stars on the dirt floor. "I'll see you in the morning." She then laid down below Ray on a blanket she had rolled out for herself earlier.

He tried to get a glimpse of her, but he simply couldn't move his body the way he wanted to. "You're not sleeping on the floor, are you?"

"Nowhere else to sleep," she stated.

"There isn't room for you anywhere else?" he asked, sounding a bit worried.

"I fought to let them keep you here. I'm not going to leave your side," she whispered. This time there was a certain undertone to her words. He didn't know what it was, but it was reminiscent of fear in nearly every way. Something about that made him feel something he hadn't felt in years. Who was this woman lying next to him, and why did she care whether or not he lived? With little thought or hesitation, he came to the conclusion that whatever was about to happen was not within his control, and he was willing to accept certain consequences.

"Good night, Luna," he said, barely opening his mouth. He waited for her answer. He wanted her to say it. The tips of his fingers began to curl as he realized he was not going to receive the same evening send-off. He couldn't help but wonder if he had just crossed some imaginary line. She did, after all, save his life today.

It was most certainly dangerous territory when it came to expressing the slightest feeling with a simple *good night*. He winced as he immediately regretted his demonstration of minor affection. They both lay there silently, eyes open, staring at the ventilation hatch on the ceiling, the same hatch that let the subtle glow of moonlight illuminate the earth around them.

"Good night, Ray."

And just like that, everything was all right.

If only for a moment.

3

The day before Ray came into her life, the day before he showed his dishonest face, the day before everyone's life changed, Luna woke according to her daily routine. She opened her eyes to the warm sun casting itself across her face. The smell of ripe pine lingered in the air, and the midmorning chatter of the other followers could be heard in the common area. Though something was off, there was a certain buzz in the air that refused to be ignored. Suddenly there was a commotion, a rumbling amongst the masses. Outside of the solid foundation of sheet metal, plywood, and tarp she called home, something was off.

A woman let out a scream. Luna leaped out of bed and darted outside. It wasn't until she saw the pleasant faces of the other followers that she realized it was not a scream of terror but rather a scream of excitement. It was because of this that she didn't rush herself to get ready. She retreated back to her hut and took a deep breath in. She made her way to the corner where a small bowl of water lay. Kneeling down, she closed her eyes and cupped the still water in her hands. Bringing it to her forehead, she let the water run down her face, christening herself for a new day.

"In the name of Elliot and all his glory, we welcome this bountiful day. Bless us, oh great, oh powerful, oh merciful most high."

With another quick breath, she was back on her feet, moving over to the dirty mirror that was propped up against the wall next to her bed. It had a large crack right down the middle, but she didn't mind; it was a luxury all the same. She dressed herself and did some basic stretches before responding to the commotion. Throwing back the canvas flap that gave her a certain amount of privacy, she left her hut and strode into the outside world.

The sun seemed particularly bright, a gift to them all. She then made her way to the common grounds, the local gathering place used for worship, discipline, and daily chatter. The earth was trod upon to the point where grass no longer grew, and the huts and dwellings of the other followers seemed to be pushed back to give way to a massive boulder that doubled as a stage when necessary. Some followers spread out blankets, while others herded into clusters of people avidly discussing the recent news. Luna was greeted by several others from the community, all also trying to see what was going on.

"Morning Luna," spoke Tobias, a brawny middle-aged man built like a lumberjack with broad shoulders and thick arms forged by manual labor. There was a certain spring in his step that was more cheerful than usual as he lifted his entire boot off of the ground instead of shuffling along amongst the mud and twigs. His face seemed more chipper than it had been in days past. His otherwise intimidating fixed scowl gave way to a much softer, almost approachable demeanor. He looked at her with delight in his eyes as he handed her a vibrant flower. A long silky green stem with an explosion of yellow and purple petals. Luna took the flower from his hands and looked at him, one eyebrow raised.

"What's the occasion?" she asked, her smirk over-shining her skepticism.

"Maybe I've had a good week, maybe I'm trying to fix things." He paused briefly, trying to get the message across. She tried to break his eye contact, pretending to notice the children playing by a fire. "Maybe I don't need a reason to pick a flower for my best friend," he said, his fingers gracing her forearm.

She smiled and smelled it once more. "It's beautiful, thank you." She slid it behind her ear so that it sprouted up between her golden locks. She hopped forward and began to walk toward the growing crowd. His hand fell back to his side.

"What's the hurry?" he asked, jogging to catch up to her. "No exercise this morning?"

"Seems to be more important things going on," she observed. Two young women dashed past them both; Tobias quickly drew a bit closer to her side, hiding behind the excuse of staying out of the way.

The two began to walk side by side, allowing their hands to brush up against each other in between swings. Tobias cleared his throat and practiced the old-timey voice that made him sound knowledgeable and official. "Elliot has blessed us with another beautiful day!"

"That he has," Luna responded, "Praise be to him, do you know what all the screaming is for?" she asked curiously.

Tobias shook his head, "No clue, but I did see Brooke in her white dress, the one she usually keeps tucked away. Best guess—"

Luna looked at Tobias in astonishment. "You don't think…"

Tobias smiled, "I do. The Prophet may be ready to take another companion… I could be looking at the *next Angel*."

Luna attempted to keep her smile to herself, but her efforts were poor. She covered her mouth with her hand. "I'm embarrassed to admit I still get excited."

Tobias laughed, "I don't blame you, there is something in the air today." He shook his head in disbelief and gently grabbed her arm, stopping her in her tracks. "I'm not even in the running, and yet—" he stopped and faced her, "—this could be your year."

Luna shook her head. "Stop it."

Tobias touched her on the shoulders and lowered his head to match her gaze. "Luna, it could be. You just need to pray, have faith. *It's a matter of faith before beauty.* Remember that. Rumor has it that Felix is returning from the mountain. He's been appointed the High Disciple, next in line to rule."

She stepped back and turned her back to him, tossing her arms up in the air. "I'm not going to let myself get all worked up over a rumor. Let me go ask around, I'll decide whether or not it's worth getting dressed." She looked back at him with a sly smirk as she walked away. He once again jogged to catch up with her.

The two of them made their way around the foliage and into the center of the community. There was a sizable crowd of about forty people, both men and women, gathering in the middle. A heavier man with a patchy beard pulled himself onto the boulder. He looked out over the crowd and clearly reveled in the idea of standing out amongst them all.

The man spoke bold and true. "Yes, yes! Everybody remain calm! I will repeat the message as soon as I have silence!"

Everyone began to simmer down, all eyes glued to the man on the rock. He obviously knew he had a captive audience. He tried to appear humble, but the look in his eyes told everyone else that he felt more power in that very moment than he ever had before. He dressed in all black. A black button-down shirt and black jeans that were muddy near the ankles. Black boots and the ceremonial black cap reserved for only the most loyal of Elliot's Disciples. He smiled as he looked at the crowd. He tried to convey his humility through his silence, but it was clear there was not a humble bone in his body. He soaked up the attention like a sponge. After holding the audience captive for a few more moments, he continued speaking.

"I, Dante, loyal Disciple to the one true prophet Elliot, have been sent from the mountain by his hand to deliver a message. You have all been working hard to keep this community sustained, and it is now time for one of you to be met with *reward!*"

Whispers wound through the crowd in anticipation of what was to come. "Elliot has made up his mind. Soon, our High Disciple Felix will make his return and speak on behalf of the prophet himself, he has told me that it is time for another Angel to rise!" The whispers in the crowd grew louder. "The others will be left to continue his work down here in our humble community. Prepare for his presence! Best clothes, best attitudes, best spirits! And praise be to Mother!"

"What about Elliot himself?" shouted a woman somewhere near the back of the crowd. "When can we expect his return?"

Her inquisition was met with more curious rumblings. Dante seemed angered by how his moment of glory was stifled with curiosity. "You all are well aware that our Prophet is still in deep thought. We feel his grace, and he will be here in spirit. We are still living in peace, are we not? It is not up to us to question his actions, but accept them in good time."

The response was far less enthusiastic; Dante's face dropped ever so slightly, disappointed by the now lackadaisical response.

Slowly they dispersed, breaking up into chunks as they excitedly fawned over the idea of hearing who the next Angel would be. Dante was left standing on the large rock. He nodded and scratched his scraggly, patchy beard as he watched them disappear into their respective living quarters. He leaped off the rock and rested his large arms on his hips. He saw everyone continue going about their day, but with an exceptional hop in their step. He smiled his signature tobacco-stained smile before turning toward the path that led up the mountain.

Luna walked away with her eyes wide and her mouth ajar, her mind consumed with thoughts of being an Angel. Suddenly she felt a set of short arms wrap themselves around her chest as a blunt object hurled itself into her back.

"Luna!!" shouted the girl, "Luna, he's coming! Did you hear? Elliot's sending his High Disciple to choose the next Angel!"

Luna scooped the excited girl up in her arms and set her down in front of her. She then took a knee and pressed her forehead against hers. "Easy there, Beatrix, don't get too worked up just yet, you're still a bit young."

Beatrix rolled her eyes as she propped her short arms on her hips with a hefty dose of sass. "Age is just a number in the eyes of Elliot."

Luna leaned back and ruffled her hair. "Well, age is definitely a number to me. And I think you're too young."

Beatrix mockingly leaned in and reciprocated her gesture by messing up Luna's hair. "We'll see about that."

She shot back and spun around in place as she fantasized about the moment of the choosing, "Can you imagine? Me? An Angel?"

Luna laughed, taking in Beatrix's excitement with her own. "I think you will make a lovely Angel one day Bea… you just aren't ready yet."

Bea's whole demeanor seemed to sink. Luna quickly bent over and whispered into her ear. "That doesn't mean we can't make ourselves pretty, though," she whispered with a subtle wink.

Just like that, her vibrant smile returned. Beatrix flicked her curls out of her face. "Well, you have a good shot at being chosen, at least… the High Disciple always chooses the prettiest, smartest woman, and… well, one day I'll be there too."

Luna stopped and grabbed Beatrix by the shoulders. "Bea, listen to me… you may be too young, but Elliot loves us all. So what if you don't get chosen this time around? There are plenty of other choosings that will happen in your lifetime. Keep your head up, there's no time for frowning today."

Beatrix nodded her head, agreeing with her logic as she pushed some dirt around with her toes. "Come on, Bea," Luna whispered, ruffling her frizzy hair once again. *"Let's go make each other pretty."*

Beatrix smiled with big rosy cheeks, revealing a slight gap in between her two front teeth. She giggled and took Luna by the hand. The two of them ran off amongst the flowers.

4

The women of the community scavenged the surrounding area, looking for twigs and flowers to hold up their hair. Luna and her little companion skipped through the trees, picking flowers and clovers and showing them off to each other.

"I don't know if we should be out here this far…" Bea said, looking side to side.

"Well, this is where the best flowers are, so you have a choice to make," Luna replied.

Beatrix was getting noticeably more nervous. Her hands began to wrestle with each other as she slowed down. "I saw the monster out here the other day Luna. He was looking right at me."

Luna patted her on the back. "There's no such thing, Bea. I promise."

"No, it's true! Clover saw it too!"

Luna smirked. "Of course she did. Clover's just trying to frighten you. She's a little troublemaker. Don't forget that."

Bea disregarded Luna's warning as she nervously looked all around, but the concern melted into a look of wonder as she spotted a small treasure sprouting from the earth. She ducked down and picked it. "Do you think this is good enough, Luna? Do you?" Beatrix said, shaking with anticipation. She held out a mutilated flower she had accidentally crumpled due to her growing excitement.

Luna took the flower and slid it through her hair, "I think it's an excellent choice, Bea."

Bea hopped up, "Come on! Clover found a patch of these last week! I'll show ya where they are!"

The two of them wound through the wooded area until they came upon the bed of flowers. They were slender and white with delicate brushes of red staining their petals in the best of ways. Elegant with a hint of sass. "Bea, these are beautiful…" Luna said as she knelt to pick some.

The joyful moment was quickly dampened by a nearby presence. Luna could hear them approaching from behind. It was in their walk, in the way they nearly floated above the leaves, one could smell their superiority complex from miles away.

"Good morning, Luna…" one of them said slowly. Luna stood up and faced her. The woman had olive skin and long slender legs she was never shy to show off.

"Good morning Aria. How are you?" she asked, putting on as kind of a face as she could muster. Luna tried to hide the fact that she simply didn't care, giving Aria a chance to perhaps show a brighter side. Aria had proven herself to be an inherently selfish woman, and the community was well aware. Whether Aria was there to gloat about her latest sexual exploits or spread community gossip, Luna had no desire to listen.

"Those are some nice flowers," Aria said sarcastically, "although I hate to tell you that rumor has it, Elliot has already made up his mind." She pulled her hair back behind her ear.

"I guess we'll see for ourselves soon enough," Luna replied, gesturing for Beatrix to wrap up her flower picking.

"Yes, yes we will," Aria said, clearly not satisfied with the sting of her words. "I just know that he tends to prefer women with experience, someone who knows what she is doing."

Luna let out a deep sigh and shrugged. "Have you got something you wanna say?"

Aria touched her chest, pretending to be alarmed by Luna's subtle volatility. "I just hope you're not getting your hopes up. I don't think Elliott is interested in… well, like I said, he prefers experience," she said, eyeing Beatrix as she stood behind Luna.

Luna stepped forward, hands curled into red hot fists, feeling foolish for even letting Aria say her piece. "Leave her alone, Aria," she said with a vicious stare.

Aria took a small step back and let her hand dangle limply in the air as she pretended to ponder her current situation, "I'm sorry, is there a problem?"

Luna held her ground, trying her best not to say exactly what was on her mind. "There wasn't until you showed up."

A thin smile spread across Aria's face. "Tell me I'm wrong then, Luna. You've been here longer than I have. You must know the type of woman they prefer." The two women standing on either side of her began to giggle. They weren't much of an entourage, but they gave Aria all the egotistical fuel she needed.

Taking a deep breath in, Luna unknotted her balled-up fists and relaxed her shoulders. "I suppose if they're in the mood for a slut, you're in luck."

The tall, brawny woman to Aria's left forced a scowl and began to step forward. Aria held up a hand, stopping her in her tracks. She seemed rather amused. "Oh honey, you just don't get it, do you? Mother blessed me with this beauty so that all of the men and Disciples of Elliot would have a *proper reward*. I am their reward. You see," Aria began to walk on her toes, circling Luna and Bea like a predator casing its prey before attack, "I have everything that they want. I don't have *thin hair* or—or *filthy clothes*. I don't have *a messy past*. I don't have *self-doubt, and I know when it's my turn to listen*."

"Well, if we're adding to the list of things you don't have, how about self-respect? I don't feel the need to come running every single time a Disciple's had too much to drink. I'm not going to apologize for having standards," Luna said through clenched teeth.

"Is that it? Or is it because Mother *didn't* bless you with the beauty of an Angel?" The two women standing behind Aria began to laugh. "Let's be honest, Luna, when's the last time you actually slept with a man? How long has it been? Certainly looks like you scared Tobias away. You would think after a while you're doing something wrong, wouldn't you?"

Beatrix popped out from behind Luna and pushed Aria's legs. "Hey! Leave her alone you… *bitch!*"

The three women continued laughing. "Oh honey," Aria sneered, "Luna might not have a chance right now, but if she actually put some effort into her appearance, who knows?" Aria turned back to the women who stood behind her. "Look at the little thing, picking flowers like she actually has a chance. Bless her heart."

Luna took another step forward and grabbed the collar of Aria's shirt, spinning her around and pulling her close. "This is not how Elliott would want us to behave, Aria. We're supposed to love each other. Now get the hell out of here before I disappoint him."

Aria smirked, "What are you going to do? Beat me up? What'll they think of you then? You're smarter than that."

Luna slowly relinquished her grip. Aria smiled and walked past her. She bent over and plucked the rest of the flowers from the patch. Aria brought them close and buried her nose in the petals. "Delightful, aren't they?" She turned back toward her entourage and walked away. "Best of luck to you both!" she shouted in her high falsetto.

Luna ground her teeth and squeezed her eyes shut. If there was one person who could get her to such a state of frustration, it was Aria.

"Luna?" Beatrix squeaked from behind her. Luna turned to Beatrix, whose nose was now running as tears slipped down her face. "Luna, is she telling the truth? Am—am I ugly?" Beatrix stared at Luna, trying hard not to cry.

Luna knelt down to her level. "Oh Bea, no... no, you're not ugly. You are the prettiest, most talented, beautiful girl I have ever met. And it's the beauty in here that shines the most." Luna patted her heart as she tried to fight back her own tears. "You're not stuck up like a lot of the other girls who think Elliot blessed them with outer beauty. Because he doesn't care about outer beauty, he cares about the way we live and what we do with our inner beauty. That's what really counts."

Beatrix began to sob. "Wh-wh-why do they say that, Luna? I—I—I try to be nice! I try to be friends with them! They're s-so mean to me—."

Luna squeezed Beatrix tighter than ever before, "Bea, listen to me. Listen to me closely. You do not want to be friends with those people. People like that don't have friends. They don't care about others, they only care about themselves." Luna looked up to the sky because she, too, was starting to get emotional. The sun reflected off the tears welling up in her eyes. She couldn't cry in front of Beatrix. She wouldn't let herself.

"Bea... Bea, you have me, and you have *Jojo* and *Kai* and *Clover*. We are your friends. We are the only ones who matter! Forget about all the rest of them. Mother will judge them for who they are in the next life. You can't pay any attention to them now!"

Beatrix continued to cry, "What if nobody likes me? Wh-what if nobody thinks I'm pretty? What if I stay ugly forever and—and none of the Disciples want me!"

"Bea, do not worry about that yet. Do you hear me? You are still growing! Look at me!" she said, turning Bea's doubtful head back toward her. "You are still growing! Don't worry about looking pretty so the men will lust after you yet. It's not time, *it's not right*. Aria is just trying to get in your head. You're perfect the way you are!"

Luna leaned back so she could be eye to eye with Beatrix. She pushed her hair behind her ears and repositioned the crumpled flower before grabbing her by the shoulders and whispering, "*You're perfect just the way you are.*"

Beatrix took a moment to clean up. Luna helped wipe away the tears and fixed her hair. Soon, the two of them were off, heading back to the community.

They walked hand in hand, but as they approached her hut, something was off. They pushed past the canvas cover and were startled by Tobias.

"Tobias!" Luna shouted as she gripped her chest.

Tobias turned to her and laughed. "My apologies Luna, I just came over to see how things were going? Hi there, Beatrix! I like your flower!" he said, gesturing toward her hair.

"Thanks, Tobias," Beatrix murmured, still wiping at her eyes.

Luna shook her head as she walked toward her bed. "Those conceited little whores."

Tobias was taken back by her sudden outburst, "You ran into Aria?"

She remained still, furious as she stood over her bed, her arms crossed.

Tobias rubbed the back of his head, "Beatrix, wanna give Luna and me a moment?"

Beatrix rolled her eyes and left the hut. Tobias poked his head outside to see if anyone was listening. The community was still abuzz with speculation. It may as well have been a holiday. He ducked back into her hut and turned to face her.

"What has gotten into you?" he said, confronting Luna. She avoided eye contact. "Luna, what is going on?"

She looked up at the ceiling, trying to hold herself together. Tears began to roll down her face.

"Hey..." Tobias said as he wrapped his arms around her, "tell me what's wrong."

Luna reluctantly allowed him to hug her. "It's nothing. Aria and her little crew are always so damn mean to Bea and—and I want to kill them sometimes. I can't stand it. Why don't they leave her alone?"

Tobias held her tight. "Sometimes nerves can get the best of us, and uh—"

Luna pushed Tobias back, "Like you don't know who I'm talking about..." she said, trying her best to collect herself.

Tobias looked around, holding his arms out to the side. "Luna I—"

"Tobias, it's not a huge community... word gets around. I know you've slept with Aria and most of her crew. Don't play stupid with me!" she said, using both arms to shove Tobias bluntly. "Not to mention the fact that you live right down the lane, not even thirty damn feet away! I'm not deaf!" she shouted as she turned her teary face away from him.

Tobias shook his head in disbelief, "I don't get you, Luna! Ever since I knew you, I've looked out for you. I am there when nobody else is, and you know just how much you mean to me. I don't know what more you want from me."

"It's not what I want, it's what I *wanted*!" she said, raising her voice. "Stop pretending like everything between us is all right because it's not. I *wanted* to be with you, I *wanted* to trust you, I *wanted* to know you were always going to be there for me. That's not what I want anymore."

"Elliot says that the only true way to salvation is through love!" Tobias preached in rebuttal. He raised his hands and began to walk back and forth as if giving a sermon. "Spiritual love, emotional love, physical love. We won't achieve salvation unless we abide by his teachings. This is what Elliot wants, instructions given to him by the lips of Mother. I'm only doing what is right. We weren't created as monogamous beings! Elliot has told us that the best way to promote love is through connection and—I'm only living as my Prophet instructs me to!"

Luna turned her back, not willing to entertain him with an argument, "Get out."

Tobias lowered his hands, "Listen, Luna, I know that sometimes we—"

"I said get out," she muttered bluntly.

Tobias sighed as he tried to think of how he could un-dig the metaphorical hole he found himself in. She remained with her back to him, her shoulders shaking out of frustration. He turned and walked out of her hut.

Luna cleared the tears from her eyes and went to her mirror again. After eyeing herself for another moment, she walked over to her bed. She knelt down and placed her face on the dusty floor, then extended her arms and felt for the bin she kept under the tattered drop cloth. She pulled out the bin and peeled back the dirty rags. Inside was a small pink box that sat on top of a larger, sturdier wooden box. The wooden box, when unfolded, revealed a fully functional battery-powered CD player, her most valued treasure within the community. She flicked the switch and allowed the fuzzy static of the radio to fill her room, hoping that maybe by chance she would get some sort of reception. There was nothing, but the static did its purpose in drowning out the other noise, and just for a moment, she felt alone.

She took a deep breath in and exhaled into the space around her. "Relax," she told herself, "just relax." She flicked off the radio and slid it back under her bed frame.

She undressed and once again made her way to the mirror, a task she found humbling from time to time. She examined her naked body, running her slender fingers up and down her arms. Turning around, she ran her hand along the many scars she had on her back, the very scars that brought her to Corazon, cryptic markings that would often manifest themselves in the dreams of the nights where she would barely rest. She quickly snapped out of her daze and focused on the task at hand. In the corner of the room sat a chest that held all of her clean clothes, things she only considered for the most special of occasions.

She quickly put on her best, most colorful dress that was seldom ever seen. It was long, silky, and stretched down to just below her knee with vibrant blues, greens, and pinks all mixed up into a floral pattern. Her golden locks of hair fashioned slight natural curls that she teased ever so slightly.

Once she was all done preparing herself, she made her way out of the hut and toward Beatrix's home. She walked proud, keeping her head high. As she walked, her eyes made contact with Tobias, who was also wearing his best clothes, a dark pair of jeans, clean boots, and a button-down tweed shirt. He wore a look of dismay on his face as if he knew he had done something wrong and wanted to fix it, a problemed dog looking for some form of redemption.

Nevertheless, she continued to walk. She knocked on the frame of the hut. "Bea! You ready? Felix is arriving in ten minutes!" There was no answer. "Bea!" she said a bit louder. "Bea, come on."

To her surprise, it wasn't Beatrix who pulled back the canvas; it was another one of her adult friends Willow. Beatrix knew Willow through her friend Clover, who often spent nights in Willow's hut. Beatrix was always playing with Clover, making puppets out of the skin of the dead animals they would find around the woods, drawing on each other's faces with smashed berries and dirt clumps. Clover and Beatrix got along quite well despite the fact that Clover was a social outcast amongst the other children in the community. Most people, including Luna herself, tried to steer the youth away from her.

But she knew Bea had made up her mind. Clover was a good friend to her, and that was that.

All of the puppets, exploration, and curiosity fashioned Clover into something of an outcast, but she held her head high. Even Willow tried to instill in her a desire to be found attractive by others, but it was apparent Clover couldn't be any less concerned with that idea. This caused Willow and Clover to butt heads quite often, yet at the end of the day, Willow would always be her mother and offer the two girls a place to sleep for the night.

"Willow, how are you?" she asked politely.

Willow smiled her signature, warm smile. "Good morning Luna. I'm wonderful, how are you doing? My, you look lovely."

"You're too kind. Is Bea here?" she asked eagerly.

Willow took Luna by the hand and drew her away from the hut. "Luna…" she said quietly. "I don't think Beatrix will be attending the ceremony."

Luna's face grew troubled, "Why? It's not because of what happened when we went flower picking, was it? Willow, I swear I am going to—"

"Hush now." Willow said quickly in her deep, calming voice, "You will do nothing. Mother and the Prophet will always have the last word, and they see us for who we really are; never forget that. Now I know you must be angry, but let things take their course. These sorts of things will always work themselves out."

Luna tried to calm herself, angered by the idea that Aria's words had hurt Bea more than she had originally imagined. "Can I at least see her?" she asked.

"I don't think that's a good idea right now, dear. She is in a very fragile state."

Luna looked toward the sky again; she was already getting worked up.

"Go to the ceremony, get yourself chosen for the Prophet, prove those self-centered women wrong," Willow said, in her infinite wisdom.

Luna nodded and began to walk toward the main square where the ceremony would be taking place. A horn rang out in the distance, a sign that the choosing would soon begin.

"And Luna!" shouted Willow from behind her. "*You do look lovely!*"

Though Willow's kind words put a smile on her face, it couldn't take away from the determination in her eyes. Luna picked up the pace, heading toward the others at the center of the village.

5

She pushed her way through the outskirts of the crowd and occasionally stood on her tiptoes to see where the other women were headed. There was a small line forming at the center of the crowd. All of the women giving themselves up for the Prophet's choosing stood shoulder to shoulder like soldiers at attention. She kept pushing until she, too, was positioning herself in that line, her toes aligned with the women on either side of her, two women about her age who also resided within the community. One of them nervously stroked a crumpled piece of her blouse. The other kept her hands clasped tightly behind her back and kept scanning the crowd.

"Afternoon, Luna," said the one looking over the others.

"Afternoon, Brooke," she responded, not necessarily begging for conversation.

Brooke went back to looking at the others but couldn't resist trying to strike up a conversation. Anything to keep her mind off of things. "I'd be shoveling compost right about now, but… here we are," she said, her true excitement spilling out onto the earth in front of her.

Luna tried to keep her excitement from shining through, but Brooke seemed to be just as worked up as she was. Despite wanting to remain reserved, Luna deemed it all right to let her guard down in front of Brooke, who seemed even more excitable at the current moment. "What do you think it's like?" she asked, sounding hurried and out of breath. "Up there, on the mountain?"

Brooke thought long and hard. "I've heard it's electric," she said with a gasp. "Food prepared on command, entertainment in the blink of an instant. Enough love to go around, just as Elliot and Mother intended."

"Seems nice," Luna replied in a melancholic tone as if she were dehydrated, looking at a mirage in a distant desert. Though her hopes were high, her dreams of one day residing on the mountain with Elliot and the Disciples seemed to be just that, a dream. "Do you think Elliot is actually coming down today? How long has it been?"

Brooke shrugged, "I haven't seen him since his last blessing, but… that seems like it was ages ago."

"About two years." Luna followed up.

"I'm willing to bet he sends Felix. Did you hear he's now the High Disciple?" Brooke asked, raising her brow in disbelief.

Luna nodded, "It worries me. You don't think…"

Brooke stopped her before she could finish. "I think anyone in his position would eventually grow tired. I think Elliot is alive and well. I can feel it in the air, it's his presence… I know you feel it too."

"I do," she nodded, hoping to summon a fraction of the faith Brooke had in that moment.

"See?" Brooke said, taking a deep breath in. "You feel that? The warmth? The grace? Nothing to worry about."

Luna nodded in agreement, but her look of worry didn't evaporate the way Brooke would have thought it would. Thinking on her feet, she quickly resorted to what Brooke was known for, community gossip. "People have been talking about settling down for the winter.

It's a little premature, but… still fun to mention here and there. What have you been up to?" she asked. Though she already knew Luna was a hunter at heart, there would be no revelations there. "Or should I say who have you been up with?" she asked giddily as she tugged at Luna's arm. This got her attention.

Luna smirked, "Oh, you know me, Brooke, I never kiss and tell. But if it puts your curiosity to rest, trust me, I'm not that interesting."

"Oh, but Luna, I've heard things… Tobias has eyes for you. I've seen the way he looks and acts around you. Sure he may be a little rambunctious from time to time, but I know a good man when I see one. He has such a way with… well, I don't need to be telling you, do I?"

"Tobias? It's a bit complicated. I'm starting to think I'm too boring for him. Besides, I want security, and for the moment, he's anything but."

"You make it sound like there's something wrong with experience… After all, it's what our Prophet demands of us. Share the love, no? Sin breaches the heart with coveting and lust. No restrictions. No designated partners, just love for—"

"Yes, I am well aware," Luna said blatantly. "Brooke, I'm just laying low for a while. Tobias and I just… it wouldn't work. I understand what you're saying but, it's just not time, not now."

Brooke began to scan the crowd again, nervous upon noticing that several pairs of eyes now rested on her. "You know my mother always told me never to turn a blind eye on something while you have it. Suit yourself, but I don't know how long a guy like that will be around…" her eyes narrowed, and her lips curled at the ends, fashioning a thin smile as she looked to Luna through the corners of her eyes. It was the sort of smile that said *I know something that you don't.*

Luna didn't know how to respond to that; she just stared into the distance, where noise began to pick up. There, coming down from the mountain, was a caravan of sorts. At the front of the caravan were two Disciples who trampled over the flower pedals that were thrown at their feet. Their faces were ruddy and flawless, their eyes fixed in the distance, trying their best to stifle their ever-growing messiah complex.

"This is it," whispered Brooke with the utmost excitement. "*He's here!*" she muttered as if the words were spilling right out of her.

Luna's hands shook ever so slightly at her sides; she didn't know what to say. As the procession drew closer, the crowd began to part, giving way to the twenty women standing at attention in the center of the square. If they were to be chosen, the rest of their life would be lived serving the Prophet and his Disciples in the fabled *holy house on the mountain*.

All of them walked barefoot, twigs crunching under the calloused soles of their feet. The well-kept men dressed in traditional purple garb, long cotton material cloaking their bodies, the tails of the robes floating effortlessly over the earth. They walked in unison. It was less of a march, more of a collective stride. They held their noses high and nodded at members of the community as they passed, each nod doubling as a blessing in its own way. They were too noble for common chatter but too kind to ignore.

In the middle, surrounded by the fifteen Disciples, was Felix, the newly appointed *High Disciple*. He was a bit taller than the rest and appeared to be at one with the surroundings. There was a sense of Zen that followed him, a loud silence. His hair was kept up in a loose, peppery bun, his beard trimmed so that it was a fine, uniformly thick bristle. He had a slender, meek build. His arms were long and drifted back and forth with each stride, his eyes were tired and kind, welcoming in every way. He pivoted his head and glanced over the crowd. A silence had washed over Corazon; even the wind ceased to blow.

Children were brought to the front of the pack, some of them perched atop their parents' shoulders for a better view of the High Disciple. The women held themselves together, trying desperately to think of something to say if a conversation were to be initiated. The men stood tall and true, trying to prove themselves as worthy candidates for future Disciples. The men clasped their hands tightly behind their backs, their thoughts somewhere between deep-seated respect and a certain degree of jealousy.

The crowd parted as they made their way into the center of the village. They all began to break away from each other, each of the Disciples finding their own respective places amongst the crowd. There was Dante, who, even on the most sacred of days, came off as unkempt and disorderly. From his blackened teeth to his general order, people knew it best to stay on his good side. Orwell proved to be one of the more reasonable of the bunch, speaking in a low, calm voice, always favoring compromise over chaos. Next was Constantine, a quiet yet rambunctious younger man, who seemed cool and collected on the surface, but had been heard having outbursts on the more silent of evenings. Simeon followed in Orwell's steps, always seeming unsure of himself. He was the newest Disciple and often appeared as more of a shadow than a figure of authority.

The other ten Disciples found their place in the crowd leaving Felix to stand alone, facing all of the possible candidates. He was dressed in all white, his robe was pressed and clean, emanating a warm presence indistinguishable from sitting beside a small fire on a starry night. He was the only one to wear white, the purest of the colors. The white brought out the tones of his deep brown, understanding eyes. His hair had grown to about shoulder length; he often knotted it up behind his head. His hair was brown, with streaks of gray tossed up amongst his voluminous mane, though nobody had the courage to actually acknowledge it. His face was beginning to age as well. He gazed at the candidates as he held up a hand, somehow making the already quiet crowd completely silent. Nothing but the sound of oak leaves drifting effortlessly to the ground could be heard.

Felix looked around, showing off his tan face with his beard beginning to grow back in. He made his way toward the rock Dante had stood upon earlier that day. The audience took in every moment as he was escorted up there by Constantine while one of the village children laid down flower petals before him.

He cleared his throat and raised a hand slightly above his head. The eyes of everyone in the community were now fixated on him and only him. "*My people...*" he spoke softly. "I've been thinking of things to say to you all for the past week. I debated simply asking our Prophet to supply me with his words and allow him to speak through me, but it didn't feel right. No... it didn't feel right." He paused and looked over the crowd, then angled his gaze toward the sky as if to read his sermon from the clouds themselves. "And then last night, as I was thinking on my past sins, I felt something."

He exhaled and held his nimble hand up, curling his fingers into a fist as he formed his next words. "I felt it deeply; I felt it within *my bones*. I felt it within my very being, within the earth I walked upon. I felt the grace of Mother, I felt her touch, her love, her eternal wisdom. And that's when I knew... the people of Corazon deserved more."

Heads began to turn as the community exchanged glances. This was not the typical sermon they had grown accustomed to. Felix continued, "I could write a sermon. I could tell you that everything is going to be all right. I could tell you Mother has no more trials in store for our precious community, but that wouldn't be enough because that wouldn't be the truth." He nodded and looked back toward the people. He had accomplished his goal. Every single one of them was now in his grip, captivated by his rehearsed words. "The truth is... *something is coming*. What it is, I do not know, but it is hurtling toward us like a freight train on a path to uncertain salvation. And yes, I do mean *uncertain* salvation."

Luna glanced at Brooke. She was now wiping the sweat from her hands on her dress. For a moment, she took solace in the fact that she wasn't the only one made nervous by the words of The High Disciple. His tone began to rise, a pattern that always resulted in an explosive climax. "We are told we are sinners. The old world told us we were cruel, wicked, vile creatures in need of redemption. That was the old world before Elliot rescued us with Mother's grace. Now with the help of the Disciples, we are free from that burden. But I must remind you that just because we are free doesn't render that burden nonexistent." He touched his fingers to his lips as if his next words would be particularly difficult. "The old world is still alive and well. It still picks away at the wounds it has given Mother through years of pumping poison through her veins, breaking her bones, and stripping her of her identity. And we sit idly by, pretending there is no fire because we are not the ones lighting the match." He held out his arm as if he were choking the life out of a foe. It was clear he had reached the peak of his sermon.

His eyes widened as he nodded his head. "This path of uncertain salvation has an end; it has an answer. My question for you is whether you're strong enough to get that answer. This next year will test you all as you have never been tested before. And as the book of Elliot says… only faith will guide you to Mother's embrace." He took a breath as he allowed his body to relax.

"Please pray with me," he muttered, his words carrying their way over the heads of the community. He began to speak, and within moments the other followers chimed in. A mosaic of different tones and voices quickly rendered the air thick with unity.

"*In the name of Elliot and all things sacred, please oh great, oh powerful, oh merciful Mother, grant us the power to bear this burden upon our back. Bless us so that through your eyes, we may see, through your ears we may hear, through your hands we may work, and through your heart we may feel. Grant us these gifts in hopes that we may one join you in eternity. In the name of Elliot and all things sacred. Bless us.*"

Everyone took a moment of silent meditation as their heads hung low. Eventually, all eyes fell back on Felix as he looked up from his prayer. He began to pace upon the rock, his hands clasped tightly behind his back. "We Disciples work tirelessly to protect what we have here today, to protect the great community of Corazon. To protect all that Mother has given us. I may act through Elliot, but I do so while you are all able to reap the rewards."

He stopped and addressed the crowd directly. He spoke in his signature humble, modest tone. "For myself, being in the presence of the Prophet has been the greatest reward I could ever receive. It has filled my life with more light than any of you could ever imagine, and I am eternally grateful. But a Disciple's path in life is a difficult one, a lonely one. We are only able to keep peace, only able to keep order by enforcing what we hold sacred in Corazon."

Felix clapped his hands together, snapping those with a weaker attention span back into reality. "And where is their reward?" he asked, looking toward the sky as if expecting an answer. "Their reward lies in the relationships they have with the Angels. Our beautiful, talented, blessed Angels up on the mountain..." Felix's mouth twisted itself into something that resembled a smile. "The role of the Angel is oh so important. It is the Disciples who keep us sane, but it is the Angels that keep the Disciples on track, worthy companions for the worthiest of workers. We are coming upon difficult times. I know you feel it too. And whether it will bring with it great fortune or deep despair is beyond even Elliot's wisdom."

A solemn silence swept over the masses. This talk of what was to come was unsettling, but Felix continued. "We Disciples will keep things in order. Now it is time to find the chosen individual, the next Angel..."

Felix extended a hand, which Dante immediately took in his own, helping the High Disciple down off of the rock. Before them stood the women waiting to be chosen, all statues frozen in anticipation.

"Please bow your heads…" spoke Felix, looking down on them all. They all lowered their heads, averting any eye contact.

He began to pace again, taking small strides as he examined the women before him. "A simple, devoted life," he said softly, lifting the chin of Eleanor, a black-haired, fair-skinned candidate. He continued to walk down the line. "Immediate access into the afterlife, into the arms of Mother herself." His smile was slight as he passed by them all. "And a place in the home of our Prophet, Elliot."

He touched Luna's chin and gracefully lifted it up. There was something so polarizing about his gentle touch. He gazed at her with heavy, powerful eyes. She could feel herself beginning to sweat and made it a point not to look at him. She didn't want to come off as disrespectful. He smiled as he looked at her, his gaze lasting a bit longer than usual. "What an amazing feeling it is to watch you grow into the woman you are today," he muttered before releasing her chin and continuing down the line.

Felix reached the end of the line and let his head sink for a moment. All eyes remained glued to him. He paced back to the center of the circle and turned to face everyone. "I have had the opportunity to grow and love with all of you. It amazes me to see how far you've come," he said, nodding his head, revealing his age for just a moment. "A decision has been made. Before me stand amazing, smart, young, beautiful, fertile women. Never forget that, and never let the decision discourage you from serving in the name of Elliot because he knows each and every one of you deserves to be Angels."

"All I ask now is that our Prophet gives us a sign," his words sparkled with glee. He stretched his arms up to the sky and slowly angled them toward the mountain. On the mountain, there was a cliff that was positioned perfectly to overlook Corazon. Followers would often find Disciples perched there, watching the sunrise or taking a break from their daily activities, but there was something different this time.

Everybody froze in time, waiting patiently for the supposed sign that was to come. It seemed as if that moment lasted a lifetime as they all stood still with their eyes shut, waiting for anything that they could take as a so-called sign.

Everyone lifted their heads, still glued to Felix and his every move. Luna watched as Felix remained still, his attention still directed toward the mountain. There on the mountain stood Elliot, the Prophet, the creator, the miracle maker, looking over them all with pride. Within moments everyone was also looking toward him, their jaws wide, their eyes misty, their emotional state beyond words. It was a small gesture, but a sacred one all the same, a nod of appreciation, a visual check-in, a sign that everything would be all right. It was in his look. Elliot turned and proceeded to stride back to his quarters, disappearing over the lip of the cliff. The magic of his brief presence remained hovering over the masses even after he was gone.

A subtle breeze slightly stronger than any average gust blew past them all, causing a tingle to run through everyone's spine. Felix smiled. "Thank you for your generous blessing, oh merciful one."

He then nodded his head, knowing that the Prophet's brief presence would act as the force to make his decision that much grander. He made his way down the line of women, further and further away from Luna. It felt as if, with each step, he was driving a metaphorical knife deeper into her heart.

Felix extended a hand, which was quickly accompanied by the hand of another. "Welcome, Aria…" He said in that calm voice of his. Aria took a step forward, revealing herself to the crowd. She was trembling, scared that what she might say would ruin her chances of going up to the mountain. The Disciples dressed in purple began to surround both her and Felix. She looked back at all of the candidates as she was swallowed by purple. A look of pure shock remained in her eyes, a scared animal caught in the headlights.

The community gazed back at her, wondering why she didn't appear more excited. The blood ran from her head, and she took the hands of two men cloaked in purple as they slowly began to process back up toward the mountain. Aria looked back at the other candidates, still no sign of appreciation on her face. Her eyes made contact with Luna, who wore a look of pure disdain. Aria swallowed her ego, feeling that as an Angel, she was now beyond gloating. Everything had happened so fast, people had forgotten to clap. Slowly the applause picked up, and within a second, people were cheering and yelping. One woman began to pick away at her guitar, trying her best to string together a happy melody.

Felix took his self-righteous bows as he backed away, feeling the applause was solely for him. Dante lingered by his side, desperately trying to soak up any second-hand praise, his foreboding eyes slowly finding their way back to Aria. Soon they too turned around and joined the procession back up the mountain, back up to holy grounds where only Disciples and Angels resided.

The cloud of purple traveled further and further down the beaten path until it was swallowed by the greenery. Felix was gone, as was Aria, leaving them with a half-happy crowd and a lot of questions.

Luna stood silently as the crowd slowly began to disperse. Most of them did not know whether to resume daily chores or fashion a sort of celebration out of the circumstances. Luna stood still, her jaw clenched, her hands now hot balls of flesh and blood. She needed to move. She needed to scream. She needed to find a way to channel whatever she was feeling or she was confident she would explode.

Trying her best to remain calm, she walked herself back to her hut. She snatched the flowers out of her hair. She stripped herself of the finer clothing and pulled on the worn shorts and top she had on earlier. She threw water on her face in an attempt to clear her pores of any unwanted makeup, rigorously scrubbing at her face until all that was left was naked skin and red streaks of irritation. There was still so much chatter going on outside; she needed to be alone, she needed quiet, she needed an outlet.

Luna darted out of her hut and sprinted toward the open woods passing Tobias in the process. She didn't want to call any attention to herself. She didn't want to have any conversations; she just wanted to bask in the sanctity the woods never failed to supply. Tobias shot up and ran after her.

"Luna!" he shouted. "Luna, wait! Stop! Where are you going?"

The honest answer was that she had no idea where she was going. She just needed to be away for a while. She just had to run. Tobias may have bested her in nearly all physical aspects, but when it came to the purity of running, Luna had no competition. Tobias pursued her into the brush, he stopped shouting in an attempt to conserve oxygen, but it was no use. He trampled through the woods as fast as his thick legs would carry him, but his efforts were halted when his foot met a root, sending him rolling into patches of dirt and spotted leaves. He looked up and watched as Luna wound her way through the foliage with ease. "Luna, please!" he shouted again, "Where are you going?"

Luna ran further than she had planned, eventually making it to a riverside that she followed for quite some time. She focused on her heartbeat, trying her best to ignore the many questions streaking her mind. How could someone so vile do so well? She ran until her legs burned; her heavy breathing reduced to an airy whimper amongst the rushing waters. She found a spot with enough shade to allow her weary body to rest. Leaning her head against the smooth bark of the tree overlooking the river, she sank to her knees and listened to the various birds chirping above her. Sweat beads ran down her forehead and off the bridge of her nose. She felt alive, wired, ready to jump into action, but her legs throbbed and tried to tell her *no more*. She wanted to scream. She knew the river was strong enough to cloak her obvious frustration. Something told her to hold it in. All she could do was lean against the bark and let her frustrations drain from her body with her sweat.

It was at that spot that her life would change forever. As she let the sunset beat down upon her wet skin, she heard a noise. There, on the other side of the river, was a man. He stood awkwardly, his head craning as he looked up through the leaves into the broken sunlight. His shoulders were slumped, his clothes appeared quite clean. He had a weathered, tired look on his face as if he had seen better days, and his body seemed beaten down. He appeared to be lost, but he didn't seem *lost*. She didn't recognize him as a member of Corazon and hadn't seen a stranger in years. In her fifteen years on Corazon, she had never once seen an outsider make their way so deep into the forest. He hadn't noticed her yet; he seemed to be in a trance of his own. The man wore a standard, oatmeal-colored t-shirt with a pair of darkened jeans. He had a slight scruff, and his hair was messy due to the fact that it looked as if he had been giving himself haircuts for quite some time. He looked defeated as he knelt over a rock, his green burlap backpack weighing him down.

He then bowed his head and removed a necklace with a small shining medallion at the end of the thin chain. He placed the medallion on the rock he knelt on. He then removed the thick burlap back from over his shoulder and set it aside on the embankment. Then, looking up to the sky, he sighed. Without any further hesitation, the strange man then began to slowly push himself down off of the embankment and into the rushing water beside him.

Luna gasped as she watched him ease himself into the late spring rapids, the same rapids that had broken up ice blocks months earlier. Yet the man didn't even jump; he just exhaled slowly as he submerged himself. Using the trees as cover, Luna traveled downstream in order to get a better view. The rocks that were jutting out of the water could be used as an easy means to hop to the other side and question the man on his foolish actions. But something told her that her role as the silent spectator made things much more intriguing. He surrendered himself to the current and was quickly carried downstream.

Luna took the time to prance across the rocks to investigate what it was the man had left. She lifted the silver medallion from the rock and traced her fingers over the engraving that read *"Something More,"* a saying she had little time to interpret. Luna thought about why he would have left the medallion there and nothing else, especially when he appeared to treasure it so much. It all came together as she too stood under the broken pink sunlight. She quickly turned and looked for him. He had now gone around the bend and was out of sight.

"No…" She whispered as she began to pick up the pace seeing the approaching waterfall. "No… no! No, stop! Stop! Sir!"

It was too late. The man was submerged, muffling the sound of the outside world. Luna ran faster until she was parallel with him. She wanted to jump in and grab him, but that would be condemning her own life as well. She screamed for him as hard as she possibly could, but the roaring of the coming waterfall made it impossible for anyone to hear her. She sprinted ahead to the drop point. What was she to do? There were no objects long enough to reach him. She picked up a sizable stone and hurled it his way, just to have it land with a halfhearted plunk in the river inches from his torso.

Luna panicked as she scooped up handfuls of dirt and threw them at his floating body; it was all useless. She looked at the drop-off where the water fell and wondered if there was a chance he would survive. She came to the conclusion that if he had any chance at all, it rested on her tired shoulders. She couldn't let someone's life slip through her fingers. She had to do something. She ran ahead to where the falls broke and found her footing on the rock wall, a skill she had practiced diligently for the past ten years. With sure footing and a firm grip, she began to scale her way down along the falls, mist pushing up against her body, giving her the cool reassuring wave she needed. She felt the dirt beneath her toes and let herself drop to the earth. She looked up in time to see his limp body plummet into the depths beside her.

She began to quickly scan the water, looking for any sign of the man at all, though nothing but foam and turbulence broke the surface. Just when she thought all hope was lost, she caught a glimpse of the oatmeal-colored fabric drifting aimlessly through the rapids. She followed it like a hound, her eyes fixed on his shirt, her back hunched ever so slightly as she leaped along to where the current ended. The beige-colored shirt began to grow darker and less apparent as it sank deeper into the depths of the crystal water. Luna removed her shirt and thought about the best plan of action. Her mind raced as he continued to sink; within a moment, he would be gone.

Her heart was beating through her chest as she paced along the side of the river bend, trying to think of the safest entry point. "Just do it…" she told herself, her hands shaking as she ran them through her hair. With no further hesitation, she leaped off of the edge and dove into the water.

The cold was immediate, sending frigid shocks shooting up and down her body. She quickly made way for the strange man who had sunk to the bottom of the floor. She pulled her way down into the dark, nothing but the evening glow of the sun to guide her. She grasped around in the murky depths until she grabbed his wrist and tugged it as hard as she possibly could. She kicked as fast as her legs would allow, but it seemed to do nothing. Her neck strained as her lungs burned, begging her to take a breath. She let go of the man and resurfaced, taking in a half lungful of air before diving back under. She caught him before he reached the bottom and once again swam as hard as she could muster, finally breaking the watery surface. She gasped as she clawed her way toward land, his body dead weight and half-submerged behind her. Her vision nearly black with bursting spots, she blinked in an attempt to clear her view. She threw her hair back behind her head as she held the man by the collar of his shirt, dragging him up onto the bank like a wounded soldier.

Placing her two fingers on his neck, she could feel his pulse like a faint whisper for help. She didn't necessarily know what she was doing, but she had seen it done before. Luna placed two hands firmly below his chest and began to push down in a forceful, rhythmic pattern. The man gurgled and soon began to cough up water and mud. Delighted to see her actions might have actually made a difference, she kept giving him compressions.

"Come on! Come on!" she yelled. The man coughed and turned himself over, forcing copious amounts of water to drain out of his mouth and nose into the pebbles he lay upon. He then went limp without a word, his body shaking.

"Hey…" Luna said as she shook his shoulder. "Hey, are you okay?" she said, taking his pulse again. The beat was now more present.

"*Help… help, I need help,*" she sighed as she fell back and tried to catch her own breath. Within moments, she was back up on her feet, putting one foot in front of the other until she was running again.

On her way back to Corazon, she couldn't stop thinking about the events that had just occurred and how the community will react to a newcomer, let alone an injured one.

Within twenty minutes, she was stumbling her way into the community, completely out of breath, lungs ablaze. It only took a few seconds for Tobias to come running up to her. "Luna!" he shouted as he approached her. "Where the hell did you run off to? You had me so damn worried!"

Luna attempted speaking while still trying to catch her breath. "Tobias… there's a man… in the woods… he almost… drown… he's on the… he's on the riverbed…"

Tobias looked thoroughly confused. "What? Hey! Stop! Catch your breath and speak."

Luna took a moment to catch her breath, leaning onto her knees for support. "A man! I saw him get caught up in the rapids! He went over the falls—he'll die if we don't do something!"

"Wait, stop! Is it one of our men?"

Luna shook her head.

"Oh, Luna... no..."

"Tobias, he was dying! I had to do something! What else was I gonna do? Just watch?"

"You should've come back here and let us know! You should've stayed here instead of going out and throwing a temper tantrum! That's what you should've done! He could be *a Former,* for all we know!"

The statement humiliated Luna, who looked at her feet. "Tobias, there is a man dying out there. Former or not, if you don't pull a team together, then his life will be on your shoulders..."

Tobias looked betrayed. "You really wanna play that game?"

Luna responded swiftly, "You really consider a man's life a game?"

Tobias took a deep breath in before furiously walking away. He then yelled out, "Shawn! Akira! Sienna! Come with us!"

Luna hopped up and down, she knew time was of the essence, and she needed answers. Her curiosity had peaked. Today had spiraled into something completely different than what she had originally imagined.

Despite the sudden dramatic turn in events, Luna's mind was on other things. She thought about Tobias and how things weren't right. She thought about Beatrix and if she was feeling better yet, and most importantly, what was going to come of Aria.

Tobias was silent as the troop pushed their way through the woods. He was held captive in a state somewhere between fear and disbelief, a rifle slung tight over his shoulder. He wondered about what had gotten into Luna. She seemed panicked, more concerned than ever before. She was obviously upset about the ceremony and the fact that she hadn't been chosen, but there was something else going on, something more. He debated whether it would be wise for him to bring it to her attention, though he knew the truth would come out in good time.

His mind drifted to the dreams in which they had a life together, the same dreams he kept to himself. The ones where they shared a hut, where they had little children running around, the ones where he felt happiness like never before. The care they shared for each other, which was once something beautiful, though emotions and the community standards got in the way of any real romanticism. The care they had transcended anything sexual, though his case was one of curiosity and opportunity to act, those actions leading to the demise of what was once beautiful. That's just how it was, and that's how it would stay unless he began taking more chances. Either way, he had to figure out what was bothering her.

They came across the body within a good time. Few words were spoken, still, despite Tobias not wanting to take the man back to camp. He continued to look from left to right as his paranoid mind got the best of him. While some saw it as an act of charity, he saw it as a trap. His fingers remained within inches of the trigger. His eyes darted from covering to covering, convinced that they would be surrounded by predators of some sort at any moment.

He briefly considered another debate with Luna, but the troubled look on her face told him she was in no mood. Tracking back to Corazon was no easy task, but tracing back while carrying a body was far worse. The community was constantly reminded never to venture too far into the trees. Some were regaled with tales of monstrous men lurking in the shadows of the nearby trunks; some were just held back by the fear of getting lost. But for the hunters, for the trackers, stifling this fear was a daily task. The walk back to Corazon was silent and riddled with questions.

As they breached the gate, walking beneath the underpass, they were bombarded by the more curious members of the community, wondering the exact same thing.

"Get Maple!" someone ordered among the crowd. By the time they reached Luna's hut, the sheets had already been laid out on her bed, Maple was ready and as alert as ever. She, too, shared in their look of anxious anticipation. Could this be what Felix was referring to? *Was he the something that was coming?* Strangers usually bring with them good or bad tidings, but seldom ever both.

Luna bit at her tongue so that nobody could recognize her anxieties in the moment. She paced back and forth as she contemplated the next move, waiting to hear what orders Maple had for her. She didn't know who this stranger was, but something told her he was going to bring change.

6

Luna woke to the early morning air. It was colder than usual. If she were to leave her hut, she might even be able to find the occasional patch of frosted foliage. She considered it actually, though the idea was quickly abandoned in lieu of recent events. She stood up and looked at Ray's face. It was sweaty and thin; the blood had drained from his cheeks. His body was slowly shutting down, and there was nothing she could do about it. She took a cloth in her hand and wiped away the sweat accumulating on his forehead. She then ran her fingers through his thin wet hair. There was some sort of calming presence about his demeanor, even when he was completely unconscious. She continued to run her fingers through his hair, brushing it out of his face. She placed her hand on his hot cheek and sat with her thoughts. It was in moments like this where she noticed the quiet around her. Everything was still.

"Pull yourself together," she told herself, turning her back to him and retreating toward the corner of the room where she performed her morning rituals. Ray lay in the background, nearly motionless as she prayed to the Prophet for strength. Even though Felix chose Aria to accompany him and his Disciples on the mountain, he was still the High Disciple, Elliot's puppet.

Maple pushed her way past the entrance disrupting her morning ritual.

"Good morning Luna, how's our man doing?" she asked, striding over to Ray. Luna stood up and accompanied her. The two of them again looked at Ray and his nearly lifeless body. Maple immediately took a pulse.

"He's not doing so well. I was talking to him a bit last night. I even got him to eat food, but these cold sweats have got me worried. I don't know what else I can do," Luna said quietly.

Maple felt around to Ray's back. Her face shriveled up even more as she spoke. "Well, you can start by getting him a new bandage. He's already soaked through."

Luna didn't dare question Maple. She couldn't count how many times Maple had treated her and many other followers on Corazon. She retrieved the bandages and quickly helped Maple apply them, firmly wrapping the gauze in tape that spun around his core.

"How many more painkillers did you give him?" Maple said as she stretched the tape halfway across his back.

"The rest?" Luna asked, now beginning to question the dosage.

Maple shook her head without even looking at her; she didn't want to make her too nervous. "No, no, no, they were for the rest of today too. You should have spaced them out more. No wonder he's not waking up. *He's so high he won't even know which way is up.*"

Luna's eyes widened. "I didn't hurt him, did I? Maple, I'm so sorry! I—"

Maple put her hands on Luna's shoulders, "Shhh, my dear, nothing wrong with being a little *extra comfortable*. That's all. You did nothing wrong. I am a little worried about our painkiller stockpile. I don't know if we have very many left. I may have to make him go without them until Todd comes back with another supply run."

Luna nodded her head. "Yes, family first, of course."

Luna rested against Ray's bedside and let her head hang low, revealing her exhaustion. Maple walked around the room and admired the simple setup she had—a bed with a few boxes and chests under it, a prayer corner, and the cracked mirror Luna held so dear. Maple smiled as she looked at her reflection.

She placed her hand to her lips and began to speak. "You know… I will be eternally grateful for everything Corazon has done for me; nothing will ever change that. But I must admit, I miss the old world from time to time."

Luna looked over to Maple with astonishment. She never heard anyone speak of the old world and how they *missed* it.

"It's easy to forget how old I am in a place with so few mirrors," Maple said, chuckling as she set her hand on her hip, gazing at her imperfections on the glassy surface. "Age is catching up with me. I can feel it. Women's tastes mature with age, but—well, the older men here still try to convince themselves of their youth. I say, *let them*. Who needs 'em? My glory days are well behind me," she said, laughing louder.

"*Maple,*" Luna said, smiling. "Maple, you're beautiful. Nothing will ever change that. Mother and Elliot see our inner beauty as well. Don't ever forget that."

Maple smirked, "You're very kind, dear. But take it from me, enjoy it while you still can. Take in the love. There will come a day when they may not want to love you anymore."

Luna was taken aback by this remark. "What are you talking about? You of all people should know there is more than one way to show your love. Physical love is so valued here, but it's what comes after that I find the most valuable. The emotional connection, the spiritual bond. Maple, I'd think you of all people would see that."

Maple nodded. "Calm down, dear, calm down. Someone might hear us… I know that. I just… I don't know. Fifteen years ago, when

Corazon was founded. Well, I was having the time of my life. Things were just—different. I was so young and full of love and, well, not a moment was spared."

Luna laughed, "Well, I'm glad for you, but this isn't the type of information I need."

"You're not seeing what I'm trying to say, sweetie," Maple said, helping herself to the water Luna kept stored in the corner. Maple took her time as she sipped at the water, her elderly charm ever-present. "Finding the courage to say what you need to say is never easy." She finished the water and paused for a moment, keeping Luna in suspense. She then sighed.

"Luna, you know I love you like a daughter. And I want to look out for you, I care about you, I really do… I just…"

"Maple, just say it. I can take a little criticism." Luna leaned back against the bed, the smirk now absent.

"It's just that… When we are ready to begin repopulating Corazon, I want you to be prepared, have someone to help you grow Elliot's family. I know you were hoping to be an Angel, but I still think—"

Luna cut Maple off as she cleared her throat. "I know what you're saying. I really do. I'm not one to settle, but I'm certainly not going to sleep around either."

Maple leaned in, her arms extended, "Then how will you know he is the right one. You need to find someone so that when the time comes—"

"Yes, Maple, I understand. That's just not me. I need more than just a body. And, I've seen people, I just keep my personal life to myself."

Maple nodded her head. "Ah, yes. I see you're still stuck in the mindset of the old world. You forget we're further developed."

Luna's eyes rolled. She quickly tried to correct herself, not wanting to make Maple feel out of place. "Polygamy isn't further developed, it's a preference. I'm not cut from that stone."

"This is Corazon! We operate by our own rules. Our own religion. There are no limitations. No titles. No government to dictate what is socially correct or not. Isn't this why you are here? To live a life free of burden?"

Luna gestured toward Ray, who lay still on the bed. "I'd hardly call this a life free of burden. And that's not exactly what I was thinking… It just seems too easy. I don't want to be easy. Some of the other women in camp have a new man every night. There's no meaning to any of it. It's… it's just not what I'm looking for."

Maple smiled wryly, "Do I sense a little judgment? Jealousy, perhaps?"

Luna stood up straight and shook her head in defense of Maple's slight accusation. "Absolutely not. I just don't have the time to waste on frivolous momentary nights of passion. If they want to be with a new man every night, that's on them, but I want something more meaningful."

"And those women will be that much closer to Mother in the afterlife."

Luna paused, trying to choose her words more carefully. "Right… well, I follow Mother and her one true Prophet just as much as you or any other woman in Corazon. If you don't understand, then so be it, but you have my explanation."

Maple nodded her head as if she saw what Luna was saying. "So what about Tobias? That boy bends over backward for you. It's painfully obvious how hard he tries."

"He can be complicated sometimes…"

"That's another reason why the word of Elliot helps us all… no complications."

"No, it's complicated because there are supposed to be no complications… I was with Tobias a while ago. It's been years. He's a good man, he really is. Strong, fast, heart of gold and all. But no matter what I did, no matter how hard I tried, he would always end up finding another woman and expecting me to just welcome him back as if nothing changed. I made it clear that it wasn't like that with me, but apparently, he never got the message."

"But Tobias has been through so much…" Maple said, walking slowly toward Luna. "He's seen such bad things. When he came to Corazon ten years ago… he was in bad shape. He reminded me a lot of someone else I took care of." Maple bowed her head and looked Luna in the eyes, her gaze soaked in sympathy. "Sometimes you have to look past a person's faults and see where they come from… see what has brought them to that point."

"Enough," Luna said, turning to face Maple. "I've explained myself to you. That's just how it is. If I'm just some sort of reward to him, he'll have to work a lot harder if he wants any more chances. Simple as that. As for the other men… when someone who genuinely interests me decides to step up… well, we'll see what happens. But until that day, I will wait without an issue."

Maple had a sly look on her face. She looked deep into Luna's eyes, attempting to peer into her soul. It was a gift she had, yet seldom ever used, a stare that could cut through diamond. Luna had a stare that could kill, but Maple's stare played with death. She was one tough old woman. Luna knew she had something to say. She had one more card up her sleeve. It was just a matter of how she would deliver it.

Maple pursed her lips together in an attempt to hide her smile. "So what's the deal with this one then?" she said, nodding toward Ray's seemingly lifeless body.

"Well, you can probably tell me more about his condition than I can… what do you mean?"

"You know what I mean. Why'd you save him? You know resources are already tight around here. And I may be old, but I'm not stupid. Nobody is stupid enough to get caught in a current like that."

"What are you trying to say?" Luna coughed, clearing her throat.

"I'm saying my guess is he wanted to be carried to the gates of the afterlife, and *you* prevented him from doing that." Her eyes narrowed.

Luna's eyes widened, "How dare you insinuate that—"

Maple shot back with venom. "A life that was not yours to save! You do not *play God*, Luna! *Nothing good ever comes from playing God.*"

Luna began to sound bitter, "Why are you helping me keep him alive, then? I told you I wouldn't let a human die in front of me. But you? He'd be dead if you weren't here. Why are you allowing it? Nobody told you to help me! You could cut me off right now and let him wither away, *yet you came back. You came back.*" Luna stepped back and looked her up and down. She made it clear she wasn't happy. "So what is it, Maple? You act like you're the only one with questions around here! Why are you wasting resources on him!"

Maple's tolerance snapped, and she no longer held her tongue. She took Luna by the arm and yanked her so that the two of their noses were practically touching. Luna was so caught off guard her eyes widened, and her mouth hung open mid-sentence.

"*You wanna know why?*" Maple asked her through clenched teeth. "You wanna know why I am wasting our precious time and resources on some suicidal stranger, Luna?"

Luna knew the question was rhetorical, and Maple was not one to tamper with. She had clearly pushed her too far. Maple held her glass-shattering stare for a moment as Luna tried her best to hold it together.

Maple pulled Luna in closer so that her lips were now right next to Luna's ear. Luna closed her eyes, trying to think of how she could apologize for going off on her like that. Maple spoke in a whisper, breaking down Luna's walls of secrecy in the process. "*I am saving this man's life… because I saw the way you looked at him.*"

With that, Maple released Luna's arm and stormed out of the hut. Luna opened her hand to find a few more pills Maple slipped her during their brief embrace. She exhaled and stood still for a moment, trying to decipher what Maple was trying to say. She got the message, but she didn't think anyone else had actually noticed. She felt ashamed. She felt foolish. She felt like her private life was now an open book for the entire community to see. And she didn't like that one bit.

She looked back over at Ray's body still lying on her bed. This time her eyes were narrow, her brow stiff, a look of disdain more than anything else.

Sitting back in her chair, she contemplated her next move. Was she to leave and go confront Maple on her drastic assumption? Or was she to sit back and let things happen? Were Maple's assumptions even founded on solid ground? The act of contemplation resulted in her sitting longer than she had intended.

Cabin fever was a common issue in Corazon. The lifestyle of those in the community was a simple one full of modest work. Contribute to the community, pull your weight, and you will be fed, groomed, and welcome. It left little time for any other activities, particularly during the day. Having Ray sedated in her hut left her with few other options.

She wanted to move around; she wanted to hunt and taste the thrill that came with being the predator. She looked down at her feet and wiggled her toes. She then reached under her bed and retrieved a carpet. It was a cheaply woven rolled-up carpet, but it did the trick. Luna rolled it out onto the dusty dirt floor and began to stretch. After stretching for a bit, she began to go about with her daily exercises. His presence forced her to forfeit her typical run through the mountain trail, but basic calisthenics would suffice for the time being.

She did push-ups until her arms burned and she collapsed. Once she collapsed, she would immediately commence her crunches or sit-ups while her arms recovered, letting the sweat of her brow wash away her worries. Luna continued her exercises until the beads of sweat rolled from her forehead to the bridge of her nose and dripped onto the stained, ragged carpet. Once she was done, she rolled onto her back and breathed heavily.

"Knock knock." said a familiar voice. She sat herself up to come face to face with Tobias, peeking through the flap of the hut. Luna looked up at his dark skin accompanied by darker eyes. "Mind if I step in real quick?"

Thinking about it for a moment, she nodded and got to her feet. Tobias made his way to the bedside and looked down at Ray. "Listen…" He said as he avoided all eye contact with her. "… about yesterday morning…"

Luna shook her head. "Tobias, don't."

"No, you need to understand that my mind was in another place. When you went running into the woods, well… I didn't know what you were doing. I didn't know where you were going, and honestly, I didn't know if you were coming back…"

Luna scoffed. "Please, why would—"

"Let me finish," he said commandingly. "And when you came running back, I didn't know what to think. So when you started going on about a man in the woods and all that, well… you gotta just see where I'm coming from. It could have been a Former—hell, he *could still be a Former. W*e don't know anything. I didn't want to snap at you, but… you gotta know I only do it because I care." He let his words hang at the end of his sentences as he slowly moved toward her.

Luna saw what was happening and was going to try her best to avoid it. "I get it," she said, throwing her hands up. "He's not a Former," she said plainly.

"And how do we know that?" he shot back. "Orwell hasn't even seen him yet. He's the only one who can really tell us."

"Then go get him!" she shouted. Tobias was taken aback by her sudden burst of aggression. She crossed her arms and pulled it back in. "Look, I get it, I really do. I'm sorry for worrying you. I was just trying to blow off some steam. It wasn't the best day for me either."

"What? Because you weren't chosen to go up on the mountain? You do realize that nobody ever comes down. They stay and serve Elliot and his Disciples for the rest of their lives. You would have been *gone*."

"Gone in paradise. Besides, you're trying to tell me Aria deserves that?" she asked, her arms still crossed, eyebrows raised.

"That's not what I'm saying. What I'm saying is… If you're looking for happiness, maybe look for it down here instead. There are plenty of people looking to settle down."

"I am done having this conversation," she said, holding a hand up. "Take it somewhere else."

Tobias kept a blank face and quickly changed the topic. He wasn't trying to get her heated. "So what's the plan with this one?" he said, nodding toward Ray's body.

"Ray?" she said, thinking about it herself.

"Oh, he has a name now?" he said, raising his eyebrows sarcastically.

Luna shot him a look of disgust. "He's a human, Tobias. He has a life, a name, a story just like you and I. He didn't ask to be here. Don't take this out on him."

"Don't take what out on him?" he shrugged.

"Just because you're frustrated with me doesn't give you the right to hate an innocent man!" she hissed.

"Innocent man!" he laughed. "Sure, he's as innocent as I am an Angel. Luna, he was alone in the woods. What about that makes him *innocent?*" he shouted.

"What about that makes him *guilty?*" she replied.

Tobias angrily slung the bag from around his shoulder and opened it right in front of her. "*This!* This makes him guilty!" he said as he pulled out a dark metal object. He pulled it from the bag so fast she was barely able to make out what it was. It wasn't until he was holding it in front of her face that she recognized the shape of a revolver.

She stared at the handgun for a moment or two. "Where did you get that bag?" she asked, attempting to play stupid.

"I went back earlier this morning. I wanted to see what I could find, and…" he held out the gun again. She took it in her hands and flipped it over. It was heavier than it appeared.

"He may have been hunting," she whispered, trying to convince herself of his innocence.

"That gun is meant for protection. The only thing you can hunt with that is a human," he said, quieting his voice. "There was ammunition, too. A jar of some sort of food and uh—that."

She looked back over at Ray. "You really think he's a Former?"

Tobias sighed. "I really think we can't rule it out yet," he replied, taking the revolver back.

"Who knows about this?" she whispered, nodding toward the gun.

"Just you and me. And it's gonna stay that way, but…" he opened his mouth, but there was nothing more to say. It was clear the revolver had just complicated things greatly. "Just you and me," he repeated.

She nodded without saying a word. Tobias gently placed his hand over the gun and took it back. She watched as he slipped it back into the bag and slung it over his shoulder.

"So what is your plan? You didn't answer my question," he said, his tone now far less accusatory.

Luna took a cloth and wiped the sweat from her eyes. "Well, he has to stay here until he's better. He can't walk on that leg right now, and he's lost a lot of blood. He has a long road ahead of him."

"A long road home, I hope," he replied, keeping his eyes glued to her in an attempt to see her reaction.

Her reaction was more melancholic this time. "What's your problem, Tobias? Just say it. Why does everyone feel the need to tiptoe around these things? I'm here. You obviously have a concern, so go ahead."

He clasped his hands together and shook his head. "I just hope you don't think he'll be staying here for a long time. You know, make this place his home. Luna… it's a problem that he even knows about us. You know how secretive Elliot is. Do you think he even knows yet?"

"Word gets around fast in these parts… and I don't know. Is that what you want to hear? Because I really don't know. I don't know what I'm doing. I thought I was doing the right thing, but so far, every *fucking person* in Corazon has made me doubt myself. I saw a man drowning, and I saved him. That's literally as simple as it gets. But if you wanna be *real honest*, if I knew all this was going to happen, I don't know if I would do it again," she said as her face began to tighten.

"All right, all right, all right. Luna, settle down. I didn't come to stir things up. Don't fret about all this, the others are just scared, that's all. If anyone ever bothers you, you tell me."

"I can handle myself, Tobias." She was noticeably angrier now.

Tobias was quick to pull back on the reins. "I know, you're the most independent woman I know. Like I said, I can't help but care…" Lingering in front of her for another silent moment, he decided that a brief embrace was worth a shot. He leaned in, and to his surprise, she was accepting. They hugged each other, Tobias much more passionately than Luna. Her arms lowered to her sides, and he held on longer than he should have.

He drew back from his hug yet let his hands linger on her shoulders. He slowly began to lean in, bringing their faces closer inch by inch.

"You should go," Luna said abruptly, stopping Tobias dead in his tracks. "Ray, he um… he really isn't doing well, I shouldn't be getting myself distracted."

Tobias was irritated as he backed up and nodded sarcastically. "Right, of course… *Ray.*" He turned his back on her and threw back the tarp, letting himself back out into Corazon.

Luna sighed and buried her face in her hands. She screamed into her palms. Sliding her back down the wall of her hut, she thought about the mess she had made. Two of her closest colleagues had just stormed out of her hut within the hour. If only Ray knew what he was stirring up. He just lay in the corner doing absolutely nothing.

"Wake up," Luna said out of nowhere, cutting the eerie silence within the confines of her hut. There was no response. She stood up and looked down at him, still cold, still unmoving. "Wake up," she repeated. She thought about squeezing his knee like Maple did the night before, but that would just cause trouble, and why waste the painkillers?

7

A ball rolled in through the door. A tiny red rubber ball, a ball that Luna had played with many times before. She crossed her arms and watched the sphere bounce its way to the middle of the hut. She picked it up with a smirk and tossed it back outside. Knowing what to expect, she sat down on the floor, legs crossed. Within seconds, the ball rolled back in and gently ricocheted off the side of her foot. She smiled and tossed the ball back out, this time with a little more force. The ball disappeared through the doorway and this time was accompanied by a cute giggle. Luna giggled too before sighing and saying, "Come on in, Bea!"

Beatrix shot through the door and bolted toward Luna, launching herself into her arms and knocking her down with a great hug. As Bea squeezed her tightly, Luna noticed the shirt she was wearing. It was a pink and green button-down shirt that had colors so vibrant they were insulting at first glance. Everybody agreed it was the ugliest shirt they had ever seen, and the shirt had found its way at the blunt end of many jokes throughout Corazon, but they wouldn't dare tell Bea. She squeezed Luna harder than Luna had ever been squeezed.

Luna laughed as all of her worries evaporated for a moment. "What was that for?" Luna shouted in between laughs.

"I dunno. I just missed you," Beatrix replied as she removed herself from Luna.

Luna laughed again, "Bea, it's been a day and a half."

"I know, I know," she said, grinning, the gaps between her teeth ever-present. There was an awkward silence. Bea was always happy to see her, but they both knew why she was really there.

"You wanna get a little closer, Bea?" she asked, raising her eyebrows.

Beatrix didn't even look at Luna. She was fixated on the body lying on the bed. "Yes," she said as she began to move toward Ray.

"Careful, though. Don't get any blood on you," Luna said, getting herself up to accompany Beatrix.

"Is he dead?" Beatrix asked, poking his shoulder.

"No. No, he's all right. He's just having himself a nice sleep is all," she replied.

"Ohh…" Beatrix whispered, as if what Luna had just said was some sort of groundbreaking diagnosis from a renowned medical professional.

Beatrix picked up Ray's hand and let it drop to the table. "*Well… he looks dead*. Clover will know! She finds dead animals all the time. She tries to fix them too!"

Luna rolled her eyes. "And how successful is she with that?"

Beatrix shied away from Luna's double-edged question.

"Listen, I'm not saying you should stop hanging out with this girl but… maybe look for some new friends? Clover sounds like she's a bit too much sometimes."

Beatrix responded quickly. "*Well, I like her*. And you don't have to be jealous. Just because I have another friend Luna doesn't mean I'll stop hanging out with you." Beatrix looked up toward her with a sly smile, her way of telling Luna not to worry. She quickly looked back down at Ray. "He's sweating an awful lot. Are you sure he's okay?"

Luna ruffled the top of Beatrix's head, "I know he is. He'll wake up soon."

Beatrix took her ball and set it on his chest. She then watched it roll into the crevice of his arm. She continued to let the ball roll down his body until Luna gently shoved her on the shoulder. "Come on, Bea, have a little respect."

Beatrix left the ball in his clammy hand as she walked to the mirror on the other side of the hut. "So Aria won the choosing. She's the next Angel."

Luna walked over and accompanied her by the mirror. She placed her hands upon Bea's shoulders and balanced her chin on the top of her head as they looked on into the mirror. "She did, Bea. But that doesn't make her any more beautiful than you or me. That just makes her lucky. Nobody ever said that life was fair," she sighed and rested her chin in the nook of Bea's shoulder. "Aria is a jerk, and I don't care if she was chosen to join Elliot on the mountain, Mother won't have pity on her if she's that mean."

Beatrix nodded, "She is pretty mean. What do you think she's doing now?"

Luna paused and asked herself the same question. W*hat is* Aria doing right now, she thought to herself. "Well… I'd imagine she is keeping them company," she muttered, trying to convince herself that the job of an Angel was really that innocent. "We're better than that, Bea. We don't need that."

"But you wanted to be chosen *so badly*. Isn't that why you got angry afterward and ran away?" Bea asked as she stepped away to turn and face Luna.

Luna found herself completely caught off guard by Beatrix's blunt understanding of the situation. "You're right, I was mad, but I'm better now. I am thinking clearly now, and that's what matters."

Beatrix was a young girl with an insatiable curiosity. She thought for a moment and opened her mouth to further question Luna.

Before any words were spoken, the red ball bounced to the floor and rolled in between her legs. Luna whirled around to see Ray trying to sit himself up. "*Morning ladies…*" He muttered in a raspy, dehydrated voice.

"Oh… Bea, get a damp cloth! Hurry!" Luna said, rushing over to help support Ray. She put her hand on his back and helped hold him up while Beatrix soaked a cloth in some water.

"How long was I out?" Ray blinked, trying to adjust to the lighting that filled the hut.

"About fifteen hours or so. You're still weak. You needed it."

"Not arguing with ya there," he said, wincing as he tried to sit up.

Beatrix came over and applied the cloth to his head, mopping up all the sweat and leaving a cool coat of water on his skin.

Ray sighed in relief, "And who might you be?" he said, trying to force a friendly smile.

Beatrix looked up at Luna, Ray was still as good as a stranger to her, and she knew not to talk to strangers. Luna nodded slightly, and Beatrix spoke up. "My name's Beatrix! Who are you?"

"Neat name you got there. I'm Ray. Pleasure."

Beatrix smiled and looked up to Luna with wide eyes. A moment ago, she thought this man was dead; now he was showering her in compliments. "Nice to meet you too, Mr. Ray. Where did you come from?"

Ray's chuckle was followed by his hand moving toward his bruised ribs. "So the interrogation has begun."

Luna smiled, "It's better to be questioned by her than the alternative, trust me."

Ray nodded and propped himself up a little bit more. The splint on his leg was restrictive. "All right then, Miss Beatrix. I've lived a whole bunch of places, but for the past few years, I have lived alone, in Colorado."

"You don't have any family?" she followed up, cutting right to the bone.

Once again, Bea managed to ask the question nobody else thought to ask. He paused and looked at Luna, who appeared just as eager to hear his answer. "No, no family."

"Why did you fall off of the waterfall, Mr. Ray?"

Once again, he looked toward Luna, who was giving him no social cues. "I was hiking, and I fell in. I have a cabin quite a ways from here. I was planning on spending the night out in the woods for a few days, and um… I had no idea this place even existed," he said solemnly.

Luna chimed in. "Very few do. We like to *keep it* that way."

"*Message received*," Ray said sarcastically, saluting her.

Luna looked to Bea and touched her on the shoulder. "Bea, why don't you go find Clover and play outside? Leave the grown-ups to talk. I'll let you know if I need any help."

Beatrix nodded and proceeded to back away.

"Hey, Beatrix!" Ray shouted before she exited.

Beatrix spun around. "Yes, Mr. Ray?"

"I really like your shirt," he said honestly, giving her a quick thumbs up.

Beatrix's face lit up as she gave him a big smile, topped off with two great big rosy cheeks. "Thank you!" she said, slowly backing out, her glimmering eyes fixed on him until the tarp closed behind her.

Luna looked at Ray. "That was really nice of you."

Ray shrugged, "What? Me liking her shirt?"

Luna rolled her eyes. "Listen," she said, bringing the atmosphere to a more serious tone. "People are asking questions and getting scared. If you've got anything to say, anything to disclose, get off your chest, whatever it is… I need to know now. Because trust me, it will look a lot better coming from me, but I don't know how long that'll last." Her mind was still fixated on the revolver Tobias had found and how heavy it felt in her hand.

Ray paused and looked around. "That's a pretty broad question."

"I'm not messing around," she said sternly. "Is there anything you have to tell me?"

After another moment's silence, he opened his mouth to speak just as Tobias and a man dressed in purple stormed in through the opening of the hut.

"I heard the mystery man is up," he said, moving Luna out of the way as he approached the bedside with the man in purple.

"Tobias, stop. Now's not the time to act all macho, I was already—"

Tobias shot back with anger "Macho? Luna, I'm trying to step up and protect this community, I don't have time to play around. I'm taking care of business. Now back off!"

His words shut Luna down. She looked at the Disciple, who silently nodded. She slowly backed away, and he leaned in closer to Ray's face. Ray was stuck, unable to move or do anything about the large man trying to make him sweat.

"Listen, we just want answers. If I get anything else…" Tobias gestured toward Ray's swollen knee. "You know what happens."

Ray clenched his jaw. He was more than compliant when it came to giving up information; the unnecessary force was off-putting. The bald man in purple stood silently over him, examining his face.

Tobias exhaled, "So you were hiking? Who were you with?"

Ray shook his head. "Nobody."

"Were you running from something or someone? Are you wanted? Are you being hunted? Do you have *anybody* looking for you?"

Ray looked confused. "What? *No.* What are you—"

"Just answer the questions," muttered the bald man in purple, keeping a stoic expression, his voice deep and intimidating.

Ray tried to relax as the two men hovered over him. "No, I'm not in any trouble."

Tobias followed up his answers with quick questions; he was talking fast and loud, trying his best to be intimidating. "Why were you so far from home with so little supplies? Not very smart for a guy traveling alone now, is it?" Tobias sarcastically questioned.

"Jesus Christ, what are you? A detective?" Ray said, rolling his eyes. Tobias leaned in as he grew noticeably angrier.

"Oh, you think you're a funny guy, huh? Let's see how funny you are when I break your leg again," he said, raising his elbow.

"Tobias, stop!" yelled Luna from the corner of the room. "That's enough! No useless violence. This is obviously a job for a Disciple, not *some hunter*. I get it that you're angry with me, but you've gotta put that behind you. He has done nothing wrong!"

"I'm trying to figure out what he was doing, Luna! He didn't even have a vehicle! I mean who the—"

"I was trying to kill myself," Ray said plainly. "I was trying to commit suicide. God, a man is alone in the woods, miles from any sort of civilization, no company, no survival tools, just a guy and his backpack. I wasn't planning on walking out alive. I wasn't lost because I never wanted to be found, and now—somehow, I end up here. She knew from the start," he stopped and tried to cross his arms. They all stared at him, not knowing how to respond.

Tobias took a step back; he didn't see that one coming. "He tried... he tried to kill himself?" he asked, looking over to Luna.

She hesitantly nodded.

Tobias looked back over to Ray. "That's a sin. He's a sinner, Luna. Suicide, it's... not acceptable. This is a defective human," he gasped with his eyes wide. He looked over to the bald man in purple, who remained surprisingly calm through the whole ordeal. "Orwell... what do we do? We're dealing with a *jumper* now."

Luna cut in quickly. "You make him sound dangerous. The only person he's dangerous to is himself!"

"Orwell..." Tobias said again, ignoring her as he looked at the bald man in purple.

Orwell stared at Ray in an understanding way, his foreboding demeanor softening before his very eyes. "This man is lost."

Tobias turned to face Orwell. "What? What do you mean?"

"I mean, he's a lost soul. He's confused, hurting, alone. Mother brings all lost souls to the arms of Elliot and his Disciples. I'd expect you to know such things, Tobias. He doesn't need to be cast aside like a sick dog. What he needs is rehabilitation."

"Rehabilitation? What?" Tobias was thoroughly confused.

"Yes. This man is in dire need of healing. We cannot turn our backs on him now. The Prophet is well aware of what is going on down here. He has made us aware that this man must go under physical, mental, and spiritual healing through the power of Mother. Luna shall be in charge of all three."

Tobias turned to Orwell again. "Luna? She's already busy enough with the hunting and—"

"Are you questioning the reasoning of a Disciple, Tobias? The reasoning of your own Prophet?" Orwell asked, raising his eyebrows.

Tobias took a step back, bewildered. "No... no Orwell, I'm—I'm sorry, praise be to Elliot."

"Praise be to Elliot," repeated the other two followers.

Ray lay back, studying the three of them carefully, knowing full well his very fate lay in their hands.

Luna took a step forward so that she, too, could be included in the conversation. She knew what was going on, but never had she been summoned by one of the Disciples themselves. "Hold on for a second... if I may..." she put her hand to her head and scratched it for a moment. "So you want me to treat him? Make sure he gets better?"

"No, no," said Orwell as he turned to face Luna. "His life is now completely in your hands. His mental health, his physical health, and *spiritual health*... all up to you. Introduce him to the community and our way of life. Show him that there is more to live for. In order to heal your physical body, you must first go under a spiritual cleanse."

Luna exhaled. She wasn't ready for this kind of task. She could lend him her bed and home to use while he recovered, but a complete mental and spiritual rehabilitation? That was a task she wasn't sure she could handle.

"Orwell," she said softly. He looked at her directly as if there were nobody else in the room. "Orwell, there... there has to be somebody else. I have my communal duties. I have stuff to do, people to deal with... I don't think I can handle—"

"There is nobody else. You are the only one fit for this task. The Prophet has made it so," he said with certainty.

Luna's eyes widened slightly, "The Prophet has called upon me? Me, specifically?"

Orwell smiled, "Trust in yourself, Luna. This man needs someone like you," he said, nodding slowly.

Tobias looked perplexed. "Someone like her? What exactly do you mean someone like her? I can go outside right now and find another woman just as fit for the job!"

Orwell looked over to Tobias, "You may go now, Tobias."

"But I'm trying to—"

"You may go!" Orwell said in a tone more reminiscent of a demand.

Tobias left the room in a hurry. Luna looked toward the Disciple and then toward Ray, who was staring directly at her.

"You can do this, Luna. Consider this man your one job," he said slowly. "He isn't a Former. I would have known. Dante and I checked on it last night, and—he is all clear. Besides, someone would have recognized him."

Luna pushed her hair out of her face and placed her hands on her hips. "He would be another mouth to feed," she said, worried.

"I am confident in your ability to heal. Like I said, trust in yourself. You never know what you might find along the way."

Luna seemed speechless. She ran her fingers through her hair and took a deep breath in. What would the community think of her, taking in a man like this? Keeping him by her side and teaching him the ways of Corazon? It would be one thing if he were a newcomer recruited by Elliot. But there hadn't been any newcomers in years aside from the children born on site.

"Luna, may I speak with you privately for a moment?" Orwell asked, gesturing toward the exit.

"Yes, of course," she said, looking at Ray. He was just as silent as usual, lying on the bed like a terrified little lamb.

The two of them went outside into the pink of the setting sun. She hadn't realized she had been inside all day. Orwell began to walk down the open path leading toward the mouth of the woods.

"I know how you must be feeling right now," he muttered, holding his hands out in front of him as if he, too, were pondering the morality of the situation. "You're scared. You don't know what people will think. You expect them to actually believe you *stumbled* across a man in the woods and took him into your home at will? Cared for him and treated him like your own kin? Especially with all the chatter about the Former lately... Luna, this will surely be a scandal," he said bluntly. "People will talk. It's one of the only ways we can entertain ourselves. Watching the sunset will only take us so far. But you need to see it as a necessary deed."

Luna followed along, keeping her eyes glued to the path as gravity felt particularly powerful, each step getting heavier and heavier. Orwell looked at her and her body language and knew what he had to do.

He stopped in his tracks and turned to face her. "There is always *another option*," he said, looking around. Luna looked at him. He obviously had her full attention. "The other option would be the easier of the two. No doubt. We could always get rid of him. Drag him back to where you found him. It wouldn't necessarily be the *right* thing to do. We would make sure he feels no pain. I'm sure Mother would see you and your precarious position. She is merciful after all."

"No," Luna responded immediately. Orwell looked at her and smiled knowingly. "No, I'll take him," she said, looking back down at her toes. "I'll treat him, make him better."

"Physically, mentally, and spiritually? You're ready to take on such a task?"

"Yes. Absolutely," she said, straightening her posture.

"Very good then. I believe in you. *We* believe in you. Mother has seen and recognized your good deed, I'm sure. Take care, Luna. Praise be to Elliot."

"Praise be to Elliot," she muttered as he walked away from her.

Just like that, Luna was alone in the woods. She closed her eyes and lifted her chin so that her face could bask in the pink glow of the sinking sun. She took a few moments for herself before heading back to her hut.

As she walked toward her hut, she passed many others who glared, wondering what it was she was actually doing with the stranger. All of the looks were surprising, but none beat the look of betrayal shot at her by Tobias as he set up tables for supper. He stopped what he was doing and approached her.

Grabbing her by the arm, he pulled her aside. "Did he tell you anything about the Former?"

Luna shook her head. "He's all clear. Dante and Orwell already checked him."

"Did they know about the gun?" he asked, leaning in closer.

Luna looked toward her hut. "Did you tell him about the gun?"

Tobias backed up. "Not yet."

There was a drawn-out silence between the two. It was obvious that there were more than a few sets of eyes fixated on them as they stood off to the side of the community square. "Are we done here?" she asked, beginning to grow red in the face.

Tobias let go of her arm. "I'm just trying to look out for you, Luna."

"Well, you've got a funny way of showing it," she muttered as she turned back toward her hut.

❊ ❊ ❊

Ray had managed to sit himself up. By the time she was back, his splint was hanging off the edge of the bed. "What's going on? Listen, I can just go, I can leave. I swear I won't say anything. I'll forget all about you and your *community*. I—"

"Relax," she said. "Everything is going to be okay." She noticed he had one hand behind his back. "What's that?" she said, gesturing toward his hand while keeping her distance.

He slowly removed his hand from behind his back, revealing the tin cup that was on the nightstand.

"Is a tin cup usually your weapon of choice?" she asked, smiling.

"You never know," he said, putting the tin cup back onto the nightstand.

She rolled her eyes. "Get some rest, Ray. Tomorrow we put you to work."

Ray looked astonished. His world was spinning. So much had happened within the past couple of days, and he had no idea what to think of it. One moment, he was dead, and the next moment, he's working in a hidden community under the supervision of a mysterious woman. What had he gotten himself into? "Y-yeah, okay, sure… thank you." He took a moment to swallow his confusion. "*Seriously, thank you*," he said, feeling as though he had somehow dodged a larger bullet.

"Don't mention it," she replied, sitting herself against the wall. Ray lay back and swallowed the pill Luna had left by his cup. He let his tired arms sink to the bed and stared up into the ceiling. "Oh, and Ray…" she said, her eyes closed as she continued to rest. He quickly turned his head back to her. She had closed her eyes as she leaned up against the thick wooden beam supporting her hut. It was now apparent to him just how much she had already sacrificed in her attempts at charity. She could feel his eyes on her, and for the first time all day, she felt like she could breathe. "Welcome to Corazon."

8

No amount of sleep seemed to break his ever-present exhaustion in the midst of recovery. Luna frequently got up to check on him, yet her services were seldom needed. She would often try to fall back asleep, but her efforts were often rendered useless by her growing anxieties. A busy mind is never at rest. She thought about what Ray may be dreaming of as she tried to find a more comfortable position up against the wall.

He eventually opened his eyes to find her stretching in the corner of the hut. "Morning," she muttered as she knelt down, stretching her legs out. Her belongings had been shifted around, and her hut seemed clean and organized. Ray looked around, confused.

"I hate to ask so soon, but… do we have any more of those pills?" he said, squinting and moving his neck around. Luna twisted her back so that she could look at him through the corners of her eyes. She had an *are you kidding me* glare in her eyes. Ray quickly picked up on his mistake. "Oh uh, yes, good morning to you too. How was your night?"

She turned back to her mirror. She wasn't going to give him the satisfaction of having an answer. However, she could tell he was serious about the painkillers. "No, we need to ration the very few we have left. I will give you one this afternoon and another tonight, but that's all you get until Todd comes in with another shipment."

"Todd?" Ray said, trying to scratch the back of his nappy hair.

"Todd is Otto's brother. I'm sure you'll meet him eventually. He is the one outsider that is familiar with our way of life. He wants to be a part of our community, but he can't seem to let his old life go. He comes once a month and drops off all necessities. Sometimes it's food, medicine, solar panels, etc. He is a big help, as you can probably imagine." She saw the excitement her words fostered in his eyes. "He should be here in two days, and I'll put in an order for more. He won't be able to take a lot. He's bringing loads of jackets this time around."

Ray was speechless. It was easy to forget where he was and how they operated. He still had no clue how the people of Corazon ran the place, having just met the natives a day earlier. He tried to clear his mind by sparking up some small talk with Luna. "So you're my babysitter now?"

Luna twisted her back to look at him again. This time she was smirking. "Not quite."

"Then explain this little situation to me," he said as he ran his hand over the cotton white linen sheets.

"I watch over you to make sure you contribute to the community. I make sure you don't try to *off yourself* again and force you to look at this life of yours in a different way," she stated, turning back to her stretching.

"Look," he said, shaking his head. "Please don't try to shove all of that *value of life* bullshit down my throat. I looked for the value of life stuff a while ago, and it's a lot better at hiding than I am at looking."

Luna stopped her stretching and spun around to face him. "You obviously weren't looking in the right places."

Ray swung his legs off of the side of the bed, grinding his teeth as he did to bear through the pain. "If you're gonna try and tell me that

Corazon is what will turn me around, then you are mistaken." He held out his hands as if to reason with her. "I appreciate what you're doing and all, but to be honest…" he stopped and thought about his next words carefully. "I'm scared," he said, his eyes wide. "I don't know anything about you, or Maple, or mister macho Tobias, or anyone… I don't know anything, Luna… *nothing*."

Luna began to walk toward him. "Oh. Because I know *so much* about you, right?" Ray avoided eye contact due to her blatant sarcasm. "You need to realize that the only person paying for your mistakes is me. Just get that through your head. You're just some guy I happened to fish out of the river. I know nothing about you, who you really are, why you were trying to kill yourself, if you actually have any family looking for you, if I'm in danger, I mean… the list goes on."

Ray sat on the side of his bed with his head hanging low. "Well, if we're gonna be working together for a while, then… well…" he slapped his hand against the mattress as if he had sprung a brilliant idea. "Let's get to know each other. Every night, I ask you a question, you ask me a question. No bullshit. That work?"

Luna slowly nodded without saying a word.

He didn't speak for a few moments before eventually deciding to change the subject. "So what am I doing today?"

Luna took a deep breath. "You want help changing your clothes first? You've been wearing them since you got here. You look like you got trampled by a herd of buffalo."

Ray shook his head, "I'll worry about that later. I figure I'll be getting them dirty today anyhow."

Luna nodded, "As long as you don't pop a stitch, you'll be all right. A little sweat never hurt anyone." He remained still, awaiting his orders. "You ready to meet some people then?"

"As ready as I'll ever be," he muttered, unsure of himself.

Luna approved of his semi-sarcastic enthusiasm, "Let's get going then." She ducked outside of the hut and returned with two wooden crutches. She then gave the crutches to him and extended a hand to help him up. He took the worn-in support sticks in his hands and held them firmly.

"They're a bit short," he said, looking at her once he gained his balance. "But it'll do just fine. Thank you."

Luna pulled back the thick curtain allowing the natural light to flood the room, temporarily blinding him. He put his hand up to his eyes to allow himself to adjust to the light. He quickly noticed the dark silhouettes of the other community members stirring about, staring at him, waiting for him to introduce himself. He didn't know whether he should feel more honored or terrified.

As his vision cleared, their faces became more detailed. Old faces, young faces, the faces of children, all with eyes locked directly on him. Each face had its own separate characteristics. Some had looks of approval, some doubt, some had looks of love, and others hatred. Sparing himself any painful conversation, he decided to avoid eye contact altogether, staring at the earth he hobbled over.

The same went for Luna; she was not used to this much attention. All the people that she had come to know and love were here, staring at her as if she were a stranger.

Ray stood still; he didn't know what to say. He didn't know how these people functioned on a daily basis. He opened his mouth to speak, but nothing came out. He was far too nervous, and his hands began to grow clammy. It was becoming more evident that the crowd was waiting for some sort of introduction.

"This is Ray," Luna said, speaking boldly to the crowd. "Ray has been sent to us by the forces of Mother. She has put him on a path of redemption," she stated. The crowd began to clap. The claps slowly formed something of a half-hearted applause. Ray's mouth hung open, his throat still dry. This was the first he'd heard anything about a *path to redemption*.

The applause quickly broke as people immediately resumed their daily chores, some coming up to greet Ray in passing, introducing themselves and shaking his hand while giving him a slight bow in the process. Most of them wore friendly faces.

"Aye," Luna called to him, snapping her fingers. She was standing in a patch of grass that overlooked a field of shimmering wheat. He limped over to her, and she began to walk down the beaten path leading them further into the tall grass. The dirt trail led them to a small pasture with a handful of cows wandering aimlessly about, fenced in by a poorly constructed excuse for a fence. He noticed a few faces poking out from between the wheat. Some children ran along the tree line and hid behind the bark-wrapped giants just to get a better look at the two of them.

"So because of your fragile state, I think this is the best place to start," Luna said, gently guiding him toward the nearest cow.

"It's a cow," he muttered.

"How observant of you," she said. He didn't move a muscle. "Come on, get up there. She doesn't bite," she said, encouraging him as they stood before the large beast, peacefully grazing under the sun.

"Wait," he stopped in his tracks. "What are you asking me to do here?"

She raised one eyebrow as she crossed her arms. "You're being serious?"

He swallowed his pride and looked back toward the cow. "You want me to milk this thing?" he asked in an uneasy tone.

"No," Luna said, whipping out the small knife she holstered on her belt, "We want you to butcher two of them."

Ray's eyes widened. "Uh, I don't um... I've never really..."

She laughed and brushed the sweat from her brow. "I'm messing with you. Yes, we want you to milk them. You'll have some help, don't worry."

A young woman made her way around a few of the cows with a huge grin on her face as she carried two large pails under each of her arms. She was petite, much like Luna, though it was clear she was not as active. She wore her jet-black hair back in a ponytail and tucked her red polka dot shirt into her dirt-encrusted work pants. She seemed proper yet ready to work.

"Ray, meet Brooke. She tends to the cattle in the community," Luna said, presenting Brooke to him with an overenthusiastic wave of the arm. Ray looked at the approaching woman and gave her a gentle nod.

"Pleasure," he said, extending a hand to shake.

"Nice to finally put a face to the name," she said, winking at him as she shook his hand.

Luna rested her hands on her hips and nodded as if she approved. "Don't take it easy on him, Brooke. He's able to get out of bed by himself now, so he should be more than capable of milking a cow," Luna said, turning her back to them.

"You're leaving?" he asked, not wanting to leave her side as if he were a toddler being pulled away from his mother on the first day of school.

Luna chuckled. "You're not the only one with responsibilities, pal."

"Oh, so I'm a pal now?" he smirked. She was in no mood to bicker. She waved him off and continued walking. "Why can't you stay here and milk with us?" he asked, fully cognizant of his unwarranted attachment to her.

Luna turned to him and crossed her arms as she continued back into the field. "Not my detail. I'm a hunter."

Ray looked surprised. "Bow and arrows?" he asked earnestly.

Brooke laughed out loud from behind the two of them, "The man thinks we're savages, doesn't he?"

The two of them chuckled until Luna noticed his lost expression. It had been a genuine question. "I hunt with a rifle. We have a few guns and a whole lot of ammo lying around," she said, trying to make him feel less embarrassed. "I can take you out once you're mobile if you're up for it, but for now, stick to something more your speed."

He nodded. "Fair enough."

Luna continued to jog down the path. He watched her until she disappeared around the bend. Brooke watched Ray as he watched Luna and took it all in. Having a reputation as the town gossip, she was prepared to get any little bit of information that she could.

"Let me show you around!" she said with a wide grin. She escorted him through the pasture. "Milk duty is one of the more underappreciated jobs here in Corazon, but it's also the easiest. You get quick enough, you might even find some time for a book," she said excitedly.

"I gotta say," she spoke in more of a whisper as they continued to wind their way through the pasture. "When you first got here, everyone thought you were a Former," she said in a tone somewhere between a whisper and shout. "I did too until I got a look at you. You don't really fit the mold, if you know what I mean," she said, raising her brows.

"What is that, a Former?" he asked.

Brooke stopped moving and began to brush the nearest cow. "I suppose I'm moving a little too fast for you. I apologize, I'm sure you'll find out in good time."

He reached out and touched her on the shoulder. "Please," he said. "I can't be left in the dark here."

She looked at him and went back to brushing the cow. "A few years back, there was a… *fundamental disagreement* amongst the community. Some preferred a more traditional way of living; others refused to change. Eventually, push came to shove, and *The Former* were born. A Former is someone who *used to* live here in Corazon. Every so often, something happens, and we have to send someone into exile. They have two options, prove themselves through punishment, or leave. Most choose to leave. Hence the name Former."

Puzzled, Ray leaned in closer. "Where do they go?"

She stopped brushing the cow and turned to him. "Don't worry about any of that right now. Consider this your crash course in milking. Come on."

Brooke guided him through the pasture, introducing him to each one of the cows, telling him their names and all of their preferred habits when it came to grooming. She then carefully demonstrated how he was to milk a cow. For the next few hours, Ray set aside his crutches for a stool and learned the art that was milking. The udders were difficult to grasp, and he was always worried he might do something wrong that may cause the large animal to retaliate.

"Don't be so tense!" she chuckled. "Stop worrying. You're doing a great job!" Brooke said, encouraging him the best she could. Ray would fill pail after pail with the rich milk. Brooke, who was milking the cows three times as fast, would then take the pail and pour it into a larger container, which was then transported somewhere else by two men on the hour. He didn't know where the two men brought the milk; all he knew was that there were buckets that needed to be filled.

After all of the cattle were properly milked, Brooke instructed him on how to go about calming and nurturing each beast into a resting state.

"They must be well rested," she said, "You can't scare them. It does something to the milk. I couldn't explain it to you, I've never been much for science. But you'll taste it." Ray saw many flaws in her logic, but he was in no place to argue. "Just take this brush and run it along their side. They absolutely love it," she said, cheering him on.

"So you figure you'll be staying here long?" she asked, curling the ends of her sentences in a slightly flirtatious manner.

Ray looked over to her as he stroked the side of the cow with his brush. "No. No, I don't think so. Luna was talking with some guy last night… Orwell? I guess they are working on some sort of plan to help me get back on my feet. But until then… I'm here to help."

Brooke nodded. "Orwell is a Disciple, A higher up in the community. Great man, truly respected. I am not surprised he showed you mercy. He works with Elliot himself."

Ray stopped brushing and turned to face her. "Yeah, you know I was wondering about this Elliot guy. Who is he? A leader of some sort? Mayor of *Corazon* or whatever?"

She took a deep breath and looked toward the sky. "Elliot is the one true Prophet. He is the man that started Corazon. It is through him that we are summoned here," she said, angling her gaze toward the mountain in the distance.

"Okay, so I guess I get that. But one true Prophet of what? What does being a Prophet entail? What does it even mean?" he asked, leaning his elbows onto his knees in exhaustion.

Brooke set down her brush and met his stare. "Everyone here on Corazon worships and believes in our God. A God who goes by the name of Mother. Don't think of Mother as a person—think of Mother as a force, as the presence that surrounds us all." She took a deep breath in. "Everything around us. The air we breathe, the food we eat, the life we live. Mother is the energy that runs through us all," she exhaled. "You can feel it if you try," she said, lost in her own words.

"Mother is the all-powerful, all-great, all-holy force that allows this world to run the way that it does. And Mother speaks through Elliot. He can channel the energy and make things better. He knew that living a simple life on a commune in the woods was the best way to go about pleasing Mother. This colony is founded on the basis of love and not greed. We trade goods and services and act as one human body instead of separate insects fighting for a chance at survival. Elliot saved us all by preaching about the power of Mother and encouraging us to take that leap. If it weren't for him, who knows where I would be?"

Her words were unsettling, but not as unsettling as the way she seemed to evaporate before him with the mention of Mother or the Prophet. It seemed as though everything had just taken a turn for the worse. He had to ask more questions; he had to know more of the specifics. "So… how did Elliot preach this stuff. What is the good word of Mother?"

Brooke smiled, "Elliot traveled far and wide collecting his followers. He looked for those who were living in squalor—the poor, the lonely, the abused. He helped us back on our feet. He got us clean," she said as she turned her forearms to Ray, revealing the deep scarring left by the track marks on her arms. "He gave us food and shelter and taught us how to live as lovers. The word of Mother is *all around you*. The *proof* is all around you."

He squinted and tried not to smile. "Proof?"

Brooke held her arms out to her sides and looked at the horizon. "No sickness. No death. No disease. It's been this way for years, and it is all Elliot's doing. He brings Mother's power wherever he goes. He makes Corazon the haven we deserve. Meanwhile, the animals of the old world are still tearing each other apart over what? Land and political differences?"

Ray continued to nod his head, eager for more, enamored by the way Brooke just believed anything, wondering if she was alone in her beliefs. "So… can you outline some guidelines for me? I'd hate to offend Luna by accident."

Brooke smirked at Ray. "Of course you don't, honey," she winked. It was obvious she was trying to hint at something. "Well, to put it simply, *love*. Corazon is a community based on shared love. That love can come in many forms. Physical, mental, sexual, and so on." She seemed amused by his curiosity. "We are never supposed to be tied down to a single partner. It's only when we claim things as ours when jealousy and lust slip in. There is no owning another human being, not here. We are reborn with a new purpose in life. That's why we all change our names. By entering Corazon, we are ridding our life of sin. We are turning it completely around with the help of Mother and the one true Prophet. There is no unnecessary violence, no hatred, no misconduct of any kind."

"You change your names?" he said with a look of surprise. He had seemed to miss the fact that everyone had their own unique name.

"Yes, everyone is gifted with a new name once they become a member of Corazon. It is a sign of new life. We do not speak of our previous lives with our old names. That can be seen as a sin. It's somewhat of a trend to choose your new born-again name after something in nature. It gives tribute to all that Mother has given us. It's not necessary but encouraged. I'll be interested to see what you pick."

Ray tried his best to keep his face from twisting into something ugly. He didn't know whether or not he wanted to burst out laughing or crying. He decided to disregard the fact that Brooke had just actually hinted to the idea that he was even considering joining them as if it were even a possibility. "Is there a book? You know, like a bible? A code of some sort that I could reference?"

Brooke slowly nodded, knowing exactly what he was referring to. "*The Book of Elliot.* Legend has it that Elliot was once a normal man, a man looking for something more out of life. He wanted meaning." Brooke began to stroke the side of the cow with her brush again. "Mother first revealed herself to Elliot up on the mountain, *that* mountain. It is now a sacred place only fit for Disciples and Angels. Nobody else is allowed to go until they are cleansed of their sin. When Mother revealed herself, Elliot scribbled the teachings on the mountain's walls. He later recorded it in a book. Now, every time Mother comes to him, he writes it down. *The Book of Elliot.*"

Ray watched her facial expressions carefully. He couldn't quite figure out if she was trying to mess with him or not. Either way, he pretended to go along, better safe than sorry. "This is all... very interesting."

"Don't let it scare you, honey. I can see it in your eyes; everybody is a little hesitant at first. Once you feel the love, you'll never want to go back," she said, strangely confident in her words.

Ray chuckled but quickly held himself back when he saw that Brooke might have found it mildly offensive. The two of them went about their business, milking and grooming the cows throughout the day. The sun beat down on them both, causing him to grow uncomfortable after a while. After what would be one of the longest days of his recovery, he was thrilled to see Luna making her way back around the bend, rifle slung over her shoulder.

9

"Looks like Brooke worked you pretty hard, huh?" Luna said, brushing up against his shoulder.

"Felt good to get off that bed, that's for sure. Back is killing me, but I'll just soldier through it," he said, letting his tired head hang between his shoulders as he propelled himself forward with the crutches.

"Oh, I didn't know I was dealing with *Mr. Tough Guy* over here!" Luna laughed, poking fun at him. He smirked back. Truth be told, he was underplaying his misery, and Luna knew it just as much as he did. "Come on," she said lightly. "Let's get you some food. I've got some more medicine back at my place."

He followed her until they made it back to the main square that was swarming with locals. He looked around, finding it hard to believe that everybody there had bought into the idea of Mother and her one true Prophet.

He leaned against a sturdy oak as he thought about telling Luna about the conversation he had with Brooke. She seemed as though she had enough on her own mind, though, and he decided to keep it to himself. The sky was beginning to turn to a pinkish purple hue, the sun set beneath the pines, and the chilled breeze picked up, causing the trees to aimlessly whisper amongst themselves.

"Luna, Ray," a man said, passing by the two of them. He tipped his baseball cap in their direction as he walked by them. Ray gave him a nod back; he didn't realize he was already becoming a star. Some people even shouted from across the square to get a look of acknowledgment from the two of them. Ray couldn't remember the last time he had this much attention. He was even more surprised to feel a tingle of excitement in the back of his throat.

Luna pulled back the flap to her hut, and Ray made his way toward her bed. "Listen, Luna," he said, looking at her bed. "You look exhausted, I don't want you to sleep on the floor, I mean… the floors gotta be pretty uncomfortable. You can—"

Luna looked over at him, her mouth slightly ajar and curling up at the ends. "I'm not sleeping with you."

Ray threw his hands up and began to laugh a bit. "I was just offering you your bed back. Just trying to be chivalrous. I can take the floor. I wasn't—I didn't mean to—you know what I meant."

Luna smirked at him. "I know what you're saying. It's all right. You take the bed. You're in recovery. I'll be right back." She ducked out quickly.

He looked down at his hands, which were red and blistering from all of the work he had done that day. He poked and prodded at some of the bigger blisters but was careful not to let them burst. He then bent his neck and took in a whiff of his underarms. "Shit!" he said, pulling his head away. He smelled awful. All of the blood and sweat had soaked into his shirt and crusted over. The thought of a shower hadn't crossed his mind since he'd arrived.

Luna came back with a tray that had a bowl full of a brownish paste and another one full of mixed vegetables. "Oatmeal and veggies tonight," she said, setting the tray next to his lap.

"What? You're not gonna feed me tonight?" he said, in a poor attempt at being a wiseass.

"If you're strong enough to milk and groom cattle for eight hours, you're strong enough to feed your own damn self," she said in reply to his cheeky remark.

Ray began to pick at the vegetables as he sipped from the tin cup on the nightstand. "How did hunting go?"

Luna placed her hands on her hips, "You're eating oatmeal and veggies. How do you think the hunting went?"

He nodded. "Got it."

She grinned as she watched him crawl back into his shell. "We got a couple, but it was right before we came back. They won't be ready until tomorrow. We're also planning on letting some dry out too. We'll make some jerky for when we can't cover as much ground come winter."

"Very nice, very nice," he said, spooning the oatmeal into his mouth.

"Did you learn anything today? Brooke's got quite the mouth on her," she said. "If I had to guess, you spent more time listening to her than milking the cattle."

He shook his head as he swallowed. "No, you know… she just asked a whole bunch of questions that I wasn't ready to answer yet." Luna nodded as she sat back in the chair in the opposite corner of her hut and began to eat oatmeal herself.

The two of them talked about their experiences from the day. Ray commented on the various people who confronted him with questions of all kinds, and Luna remarked on their particular characters and whether or not he should worry about them. Luna explained to him all of the close calls she had when it came to prey in the woods earlier that day. She gave him exact details on *the ones that got away* just in case he were ever to come across them later on. They smiled and laughed at each other. The laughter was usually followed up by long, drawn-out moments of silence as they looked up at each other from across the room. The type of silence where one could hear the drawn-out hum of a harmonica or the rare pluck of some guitar strings in the distant evening air.

Luna went over to what she referred to as her *prayer corner* and opened up a small brass case. She removed a tiny red pill from the case and held it up above her head. She knelt on her small prayer mat and bowed her head, whispering a chant under her breath. She then brought her hands and the tiny red pill to her mouth and swallowed it. She dipped her hands under the glassy surface of the water bowl in front of her and brought her cupped hands to her soft lips. She drank slowly from her hands as she closed her eyes and let the life of the water surge through her body. It seemed as if it were a spiritual experience for her. She opened her eyes and let them slowly drift across the room until they fell on him.

"So, what was that?" he asked.

"All of the women in the community share their nightly ritual around the same time, as the sun begins to set."

"Right, but what did you just swallow?"

She smiled and looked at him, "Call it *communion*."

"You can call it communion, but I want to know what it actually is. At the end of the day, it's just bread and wine."

"Easy there," she said, putting him in his place. She picked up the brass case with one hand and brought it over to him. He took it in his hands and traced the angelic pattern etched into the surface of the top. He then removed the top and picked up one of the red pills. He held it up to his eye.

"C-17? That's birth control," he said anticlimactically.

"For you, it might just be birth control. For us, it's communion. Can't risk a pregnancy in this sort of environment. In a community where sex is almost treated as a currency, it's important to stay in control of the inevitable. We take this every night to keep Elliot happy. We know that we can barely afford another mouth to feed, especially a growing child. Todd brings it in with him every month or so."

"Yet here I am," he said, sounding somewhat ashamed.

"Yet here you are," she repeated quietly.

"So tell me more. This is the ritual for the women, what do the men do?"

She shut the brass case. "Well, the men are encouraged to experiment on all fronts. The hope is that one of them has a great awakening, but… so far, there's been no proof of luck."

"Well, that hardly sounds fair," he said in all seriousness.

She shook her head. "You don't understand. Women are held above all else here. We are the divine beings, able to bear children and spread the word for generations to come. The time for having children is just not upon us now. Sure, we all live in a male-dominated society, but that's only so we can be shown the respect we deserve. And if you haven't heard, our god is a woman."

Ray shook his head. "Who decides how much respect you deserve?" he asked, confused.

"Well, the Disciples do. They work through the power of Elliot, who works through the power of my God herself. If they tell me I deserve to go without a meal, if they tell me I deserve to stay inside for a night, if they tell me I should be ashamed, well then it must be so, but that's only because they hold me in high regard. They expect me to act as a woman should because women are the holiest of them all."

"So they put you down because you are held so high in their eyes? That hardly makes sense," he said with a chuckle.

"It doesn't have to make sense to you. You don't fully appreciate our culture yet. We have kept the peace for so long because we follow these exact rules and boundaries set by the Prophet himself." She sounded as if she thought she were making perfect sense. To Ray, it only spoke to how submerged she truly was.

He decided to just accept her answer and not pick at it any longer. Eventually, the two of them grew tired. The sun was setting, so Luna lit a small fire in the middle of her hut and kept the hatch on the ceiling open for ventilation. She looked over to Ray, who sat contently on the edge of her bed. "I'll be back in a few," she said, once again ducking out of the room.

Ray remained on the edge of her bed and smoothed out the wrinkles in the sheets on either side of his body. He looked over to the prayer station Luna had set up in the corner of the hut. It consisted of a prayer mat and a bowl of water. A few feet down sat a long mirror with a crack down the center. Ray pulled himself up to examine the prayer corner. He hobbled over to the mat. It seemed to be a simple yoga mat, no elaborate designs, no fine silk or fur embellishments, just a plain blue mat. The bowl of water was just that—a wooden bowl filled halfway with water. He would've bent down to touch it, but the splint on his leg forbade him from doing so. He looked down at the bowl of water and slowly began to slip into his dream state.

❈ ❈ ❈

He was no longer in Luna's hut, dimly lit by the dying fire. He was now standing along the shore of a lake. He wore cargo pants, a clean, pressed blue collared shirt, and sported a trimmed mustache slightly above his upper lip. He wore rectangular glasses and held an empty glass test tube in his hand. The wind blew back his hair as he knelt down and sunk the test tube under the surface of the lake. As the test tube began to fill up, he looked around at all of the life around him. He looked at the playgrounds and all the children inhabiting them. He looked down the beach to the roped-off section where swimming was allowed to locals. They splashed each other and laughed as they went about it. He looked at the lifeguards slumped over on the bench, pretending to look satisfied with their jobs. He smirked, knowing full well that he was in the same boat. He lifted the test tube from the lake and screwed the cap on tight. He then held it up to his eyes and examined it closely. He watched as the small black particles drifted from side to side as they floated gently to the bottom of the glass. He focused carefully on these specks as they aimlessly drifted about.

❊ ❊ ❊

He snapped out of his trance when he heard a noise come from outside of the hut. He was in no position to explore, though. He made his way over to the mirror and looked at his reflection. He gasped at how terrible he looked. This was, after all, the first time he had seen himself since he tried to commit suicide. He brought his hand up and ran it down the course stubble growing out of his face. He pushed his hair back and tried to make himself look presentable, though it was hard to see everything against the flickering firelight. His body acted as more of a functioning corpse than it did a living, breathing vessel of muscle and meat. He considered removing the bandage on his back, but it would've just torn the scab from his skin. It was in his best interest to leave it be.

He felt the crack in the mirror and then made his way back to the bedside, where he was to wait for Luna. After a while, she appeared back through the flap of the hut. She was different, though. Her hair was all wet, and she had it tied back into a ponytail. Her arms were up above her head, ringing out the thick wet tail of hair she squeezed tightly between her fingers. It was tied tightly so that no remaining strands could make their way to her face. Her face had been scrubbed and appeared more naked than usual. There were little water beads that ran down from her forehead and into the crevices within the smile lines on her cheek.

She looked up at Ray. "What?"

He shook his head, noticing that he may have been staring. "Nothing, um, nothing," Luna smirked and began to walk toward him. He noticed that she had a bucket of water with her. The bucket sloshed from side to side due to the volume of water inside it. "What's this for?"

She scoffed, "You smell awful. We need to get you washed up. I got a new pair of jeans and a shirt for you. *These clothes,*" she said, fluttering her finger toward the browning fabric that clung to his skin. "They need to go."

"I didn't know it was that apparent."

"Trust me… it's apparent."

Ray laughed to mask the embarrassment as Luna fiddled with the sponge below the bed. She wrung it out, soaked it, and wrung it out once more before leaving it to saturate in the water. She knelt to one knee and examined his leg. She poked at his knee really quickly to check his reflexes while he wasn't looking.

"Christ, Luna! What was that?" he said as his body jumped.

"Just checking up on it… I can't take your splint off yet. We should've taken off your jeans when we had the chance. I can try to cut around them, but you should probably wear these until you're ready to move without the splint," she said, looking up at him.

"Okay… okay, that's fine."

Luna stood up and began to peel his shirt off. He was caught off guard but raised his arms to make it easier for her. She lifted his shirt from his shoulders and threw it toward the fire. She then knelt down and brought the sponge to his chest. It felt strange. He was more than capable of washing himself.

He looked into her eyes as she focused on getting the built-up dirt off of his shoulders and chest. She was determined. That's just the way she was; whether it was washing him or rescuing him, she was determined.

He still had so much he wanted to ask her. Weirdly enough, he wanted to know her real name more than anything, but he was afraid that he might be treading on thin ice because of how Brooke had put it earlier. *Leave the past in the past,* he thought to himself. Though however much he told himself that, he could not resist. She silently scrubbed away at his shoulders and began to make her way to his back. He needed to say something to break the tension.

"Why are you here, Luna?" he said, biting his lip.

She stopped scrubbing for a moment to think. She then continued scrubbing and said, "Because this life is a whole lot better than the one I was living. I have friends that look out for me. They don't hurt each other here. They treat each other the way humans are supposed to be treated."

He tried to arch his neck so that he could see her. She stood on her knees so that their noses were inches from each other. "Is… is your family here?"

She held her dangerous stare for a few moments. "Corazon is my family. I have nobody else," she stated bluntly.

Ray turned his head away. He had no counter-question to that. At least none that he was comfortable asking right now. "Luna, you said Todd's coming in less than two days. How does he get here?"

She scrubbed gently around the bandages. "He drives to the nearest drop point and hooves it from there. He typically stays the night on the mountain."

"A truck?" he repeated after her.

"Yes. Why do you ask?"

"Well, you know… I figured it might be a good idea if I just go with him. It'd be smart. I'll leave you guys behind, I'll get proper medical attention, I'll… you know, I'll be okay."

Luna stopped scrubbing and sat back. "Ray… that could have worked, but…"

Ray's eyes widened as he looked directly at her, "But what? What do you mean *but?*"

She sighed and placed her hand on the back of his wet neck. "I tried to save you… I told them you fell in." She looked toward the fire as she finished. "Now that they know you tried to *kill yourself*, well… they feel responsible for saving you. They feel as though Mother has placed you in our hands for a reason, and they won't let you go. You have become our personal project."

Ray straightened his posture, making himself taller. "So you're saying that even if I wanted to, I couldn't leave?"

Luna looked back at him with a solemn expression. "No… no, you can't…"

Ray stopped talking and looked down at his leg. "*What the hell have I gotten myself into…*" he whispered.

Luna ran her hand from Ray's neck to his shoulder and rested it there. "It's all right, I'm looking out for you. Nobody's gonna—"

"If I can walk by myself, I can wash myself," he said, cutting her off.

"What?" she said, taking her hand away from his shoulder.

"If I can walk by myself, I can wash myself. No help needed. Thank you," he said, repeating himself. It felt petty and childish, but he no longer saw her as the pure ally he thought she was.

Luna took the hint and left him alone, leaving the sponge in the bucket. Ray swung his legs up onto the bed and turned his back to her. She stood there for a few moments hoping that he would turn around so that she might be able to explain herself a bit more. Upon realizing she wouldn't be getting any such satisfaction, she left the hut to wet the rag she used to smother the fire at night.

As she made her way to her hut, soaked rag in her arms, she caught a brief glimpse of Tobias, who was also retiring for the night. She wanted to go talk to him. She wanted to vent so that she could possibly feel whole again, though she knew he too would give her no such satisfaction. She took a few deep breaths before entering the hut again. Ray had turned around and was now facing the wall, his painkiller sitting alone on the other side of the room.

She gently placed the tiny pill on the wooden nightstand. She then sat down on the floor and pulled the covers up to her neck. She wrinkled her face as if to scold herself for what was about to leave her lips. "Good night, Ray." She waited for a moment. Was it now her turn to bear the burden of waiting for a simple two-word response? She lay there in the dark, looking toward the ceiling wanting so desperately to take back that foolish *good night* she had just delivered. She did, after all, just explain to him that he was being held against his will.

Ray lay on his side; his eyes were wide open. He still found himself at a loss for words. He was no longer a man being aided back to life. He was a prisoner, whether he liked it or not. Despite the obvious facts, he couldn't help himself. He wanted some form of warmth, and here she was, giving it to him on a silver platter. A simple form of acknowledgment wrapped in a disguise that read *good night*. As much as he wanted to open his mouth and scream at her, questioning her rationale and purpose behind keeping him here, the sheer brutality of silence said even more.

10

I have to get out of this place. I have to get out of this place. I have to get out of this place. Ray kept repeating the words within the confines of his head. He had somehow woken up before Luna, who still lay silently on the blankets below him. He didn't know what to say. She had, after all, just told him he was technically her prisoner. Luna finally came to and didn't waste a minute when it came to getting breakfast situated. Biscuits and more oatmeal with a side of leafy greens. He ate without saying a word. Luna looked at him as if she were worried for his well-being, but the more he thought about it, the more he felt she didn't even care.

He pulled on his new shirt and hobbled down to the pasture. His crutches readied a set of dry splinters to surprise him throughout the day. "Morning, Ray," Brooke said with a subtle curtsy. Ray acknowledged her with a nod as he grabbed his stool. The sun came and went with the hardening blisters on his hands. By the time he was finished, he was far too tired to eat. He crawled into Luna's bed and pulled the stained sheets up to his neck.

Luna came into the room with a bright smile on her face. "Hey there! I know the oatmeal wasn't the best, but I was lucky enough to—"

She looked over to him, his back still turned to her. She knew he wasn't sleeping, but it was clear he was in no mood to speak to her. She stepped back outside and went over to where the two deer she had killed earlier that day were hanging. They were strung up over a fire drying out, waiting to be devoured.

Someone placed a firm hand on her shoulder. "Well done. That was some good shooting today." She turned toward Tobias, who then took his hand off of her shoulder. He looked at her with intensity.

"Thank you," she said, still keeping her eyes on the deer.

"You know, you're really good with that rifle. You should consider joining the hunters full time again. We could really use your help. I'd hate to see a gift like that go to waste."

Luna rolled her eyes. "I'll be back soon enough. I have other things keeping me busy."

Tobias touched her arm, "Don't worry about him, he seems to be getting used to things. Plus, if he needs any help, I can talk to Maple and get her to help out. Seriously, I'm sure she wouldn't mind."

Luna turned to him. "I'll pass. I enjoy playing nurse every once in a while."

"That's a lot of responsibility. It's gotta be tiring. I can help you with that. You know I've got some extra room in my hut if you want to take a few hours away from it all."

"You really don't give up, do you?" she said, pulling her hand from him. She began to walk away from the fire and toward the woods, where she could have a few moments to herself.

Tobias stood still with a perplexed expression before deciding to pursue her. "No, I don't think *you understand*. I'm trying to be a nice guy here. I can still be your friend, can't I?"

"Yeah, oh sure. You can be my friend all you want, but we both know that's not what this is about. I'm not just some number. Leave it alone," she said, picking up the pace a bit as she drew further into the woods.

Tobias laughed as he pursued her closely. "I just don't want to see you work yourself to the bone! This isn't about my numbers. I can go sleep with anyone I want. It doesn't make any difference. I care about you. You should take this as a compliment!" he said with a broad smile as he caught up with her.

Luna rolled her eyes, trying to steer away from wherever he was trying to corral her. "If you can go sleep with any woman, go right ahead. It didn't stop you before, it won't stop you now. You can take your compliment and go give it to someone who actually gives a shit."

Tobias was taken back by her blunt remarks. He paused for a moment to take it all in before his facial expressions changed from cockiness to anger. "You can really be one stupid bitch, can't you? I think you forget how much I've done for you, Luna. I cared for you when you were sick. I was your friend when nobody wanted anything to do with you. Now you have all this attention because you find some crazy guy in the woods, and all of a sudden, you think you're too good for me? No. I don't think so. That's not how it works." He was getting noticeably angrier. "I came up to you to congratulate you on a good job hunting today. That's all!"

Luna kept walking silently into the night. Tobias wasn't dangerous; he was just annoying. Even if he was her friend, he certainly had a funny way of showing it.

"Are you even listening to me?" he shouted. "I want things to go back to the way they were. I get it; these past few days have been a little weird. Everybody's a little panicked. *Tensions are high.* I know you must be crushed knowing that Aria was chosen and all… but we gotta let that stuff go," he huffed as he tried walking with her. She just picked up the pace. "Luna, are you even hearing me?" She kept walking in silence. "Luna?" No matter what he said, her body language made it clear that she wanted him gone.

Tobias ground his teeth as he slowly tailed her through the woods. "Luna, listen to me!" he grunted as he snatched her arm and forcefully pushed her up against the closest tree. Her face scowled as the rough bark scratched into the thin skin on her back. Tobias grabbed both of her upper arms and pushed her up against the bark. He paused for a moment as if he didn't realize he had just assaulted her. She seemed shocked as well, Tobias had always gotten mad at her, but she had never seen anything like this. "*Are you listening to me now?*" he whispered after bringing his nose to her cheek and lifting his chin so that he could speak directly into her ear. He closed his eyes and pushed his body in closer.

"Tobias… *let go of me*," she said, avoiding eye contact. He pulled his cheek back. She felt his rough facial hair scratch against her cheekbones. He pulled back so that the tips of their noses were touching and tried to stare deep into her eyes. He was much too massive for her to put up a fight. He held her pinned against the tree with his strong hands.

"I just want you to—" he began to stutter and fumble about his words.

"*I said let go of me*," she said, much more sure of herself yet still avoiding eye contact. Tobias looked down at his hands curled like pythons around her arms. His grip was so tight his knuckles were white, but there were light red rings forming around his finger and pinky from the lack of blood circulation in her arm. He quickly let go. She looked up into his eyes with disgust as she dipped under his arm, setting herself free from being pinned between him and the rough bark.

She slowly backed away as she faced him and watched him carefully. She was looking for any signs of remorse or regret. All she saw was confusion and fear. She didn't say anything as she backed away. If anything, her lips trembled. She was, after all, truly afraid. Tobias had never been a violent man.

"Luna, I'm… I'm sorry, I… I'm sorry," he said, standing face-to-face with the tree he had just forced her against. She continued to silently back away, at a loss for words. She backed up until he was out of sight.

She didn't know what to make of that whole episode. She made her way to the table in the center of the community, where she was to collect her food. As she walked toward the table, she wiped at her eyes. The thoughts that buzzed around her mind were overwhelming, so much so that she found it hard to hide her emotional state. It would take more than one incident to break her, though. Tobias was different. He always had been.

She joined the line that led to a long, broad, collapsible white table where there was plenty of food set out. Behind the table were two Disciples, dressed in purple, portioning out the food to everyone. Luna stood in line and slowly made her way toward the table where the freshly cooked deer was to be served to her. She reached the table and eventually grabbed a plate. One of the Disciples came up to her from the other side of the table. It was the ratty-looking man who had announced that Felix was to choose another companion right before Aria was chosen.

"Evening, Luna. What will it be?" he asked bluntly.

"Evening, Dante," she said as she poked her head forward and scanned down the table. "I'll take the deer, the potatoes, and…."

"Easy there," Dante said, cutting her off. "We discussed it, and… one serving covers you and your little charity case," he said, nodding toward her hut.

Luna licked her lips and looked down at her feet. "I know. I'll stick with the venison and potatoes then," she said, looking back up at Dante. He smiled, revealing his blackening teeth.

"As you wish, dear." He stabbed a piece of venison with a knife and flopped it onto her plastic plate. "I talked to Aria yesterday," he said as he picked a few potatoes out of the big pot next to the venison.

Luna didn't want to respond to prove that she genuinely didn't care what Aria was doing on the mountain, but she was just too curious, and Dante knew that. He had her hooked. "How is she doing?"

Dante smiled at her as he handed her plate back to her. "Oh, she's doing just fine, just fine, dear." His black smile seemed to widen a bit. "She seems to really be enjoying herself, and the Disciples enjoy her very much as well."

Luna was both puzzled and disgruntled upon receiving half as much food as she needed. She leaned up against the table and looked directly at Dante, "Why are you telling me this, Dante?" she asked, trying to refrain from getting in his face.

"Oh, you know. I knew you two were pretty close, is all," he stuttered as he raised his eyebrows and popped a chunk of potato into his mouth. "Bye now!" he said sarcastically as he obnoxiously chewed on the undercooked potato.

Luna rolled her eyes and walked away, looking down at her food. This wasn't enough for her and a fully grown man in recovery. A strip of venison and a few potatoes wouldn't cut it, but it was going to have to do for the moment. She thought she could suck it up and deal with less than half portions for a while, but it had only been three days, and she was already hungry.

As she made her way back to the hut, an older man summoned her over to a fallen tree. He sat on the decaying log and looked at her with kind eyes as he waved his hand. He had dark skin and sprouted a long grey and white beard that stretched down to his chest. He was one of the older men in the community but also one of the nicer ones. He liked to be called Musgo.

Musgo was more of a non-traditional follower, one of the few that actually stuck around. Why he stuck around, few actually knew, but

Luna had a better idea than anyone else. He never seemed interested in the younger women. He knew he was old, he knew he had lived a life of servitude, and he knew Mother would notice him because of that. He didn't need to prove himself to others by seeing how many different community members he could sleep with. He was actually quite fond of Maple, and Maple of him. Yet they kept things hidden. They didn't care for their personal details to be exploited by the community. Because of these facts, Luna decided to answer his summons. There was never any shady business with Musgo. He was just a lonely, down-to-earth man, most likely just looking for a conversation.

She walked over to him and crouched down, sitting next to him upon the log. "How are you doing, Musgo?" she asked, looking at him with a grin.

Musgo licked his lips and bobbed his head up and down. "Oh, you know how it is, Luna, just *another day in paradise*," he said as he jerked his head around to smile back at her. "Say, how is that boy doing? You know the one?"

Luna set her plate of food down between them and stiffly set her arms to her side. "You know, everybody wants to know how mystery man is doing. He fell over the falls. It doesn't take a damn doctor to know he isn't doing well." She paused to roll her eyes and take a deep breath. Musgo held his tongue. It was apparent she had more to say. "He's here for less than a week and everyone's obsessed. I spent the last fifteen years of my life here, and nobody thinks to wonder how I'm doing."

She looked at him as if he were to have some sort of answer for her. His eyes were gray and cloudy, and his beard dirty and thin, but somehow, he appeared to understand her struggle. "And how are you doing, Luna?" he asked.

She turned her head for a moment. When she looked back over to him, her eyes were misty, her mouth fashioning a frown against her will. "*I feel like an outcast…*" she silently cried.

He stared into her watery eyes with a wise intensity, trying to see something deep within her. He licked his lips again and began bobbing his head. "You know Luna, I know we're not supposed to talk about our past lives… but I know what it's like to be an outsider. An *outcast*. And you know…" he paused to think for a moment.

"Through all my years of being an outcast, I learned something. Now, whether or not you want to know what that something is, that's up to you. If you want to skip the boring moral stories that old Musgo loves to tell, then you can just be on your way. I won't be mad. Promise." He spoke this with the utmost honesty in his voice. She really could just walk away and he would think nothing of it. That was why she loved Musgo. He was always going to speak nothing but the truth.

She smiled and patted the top of Musgo's knee. "Of course. I always have time for a good Musgo story."

Musgo nodded and set his plate aside, too. He looked up at the stars and admired them and all of their twinkling beauty. "You know, before Elliot found me, I was… I guess you could call me homeless. Most people do. Something happened where it all got taken from me," he said, brushing over years of his life with a wave of his hand. "The old world, it's corrupt, one moment you're finally getting onto your feet and then the very next, poof—you're lower than you ever were before. I was nothing. I had nothing. I once assaulted a police officer just so that I would have a cell to stay in, you know, to get out of the cold."

He silently shook his head as he reflected. "Well, when my life was ripped from my hands, I learned something. And this is something that I wished I had known much sooner… *It was only when I had absolutely nothing that I knew who my friends were*. Most of them ran away and hid from me. Some pretended not to know me at all. That hurt the most."

Musgo seemed to get caught up in his own story. He looked down at his hands, which were trembling. He stared at them for a few seconds and made them into fists as he looked toward the fire. "Know your real friends, Luna. Know who you can trust and know who is in your life for the wrong reasons. There's a saying: 'Keep your friends close and your enemies closer.' You ever heard of it?"

She nodded her head, and Musgo continued speaking. "Well, *forget* that expression. Keep your friends close and get as far away from your enemies as you possibly can. They can't hurt you if you're far away. But your friends, your friends will protect you. They'll watch your back. They'll stick with you through thick and thin." He grabbed her hand. "Maple… Maple is a friend, Luna. Don't chase her away. Your little pal Beatrix, she's a friend." Luna listened carefully to what he was saying as she looked out toward the food table where Tobias was collecting his portion. He looked at her briefly and immediately turned away.

"And Luna, I'm a friend." Musgo picked up his plate and scraped the remaining food onto Luna's plate.

She pulled her hands away. "Musgo, no, I can't," she said frantically, trying to stop him from giving her food.

"Enough," he ordered, pushing her hands away. "I know the deal, Luna, I know what the Disciples are doing to you, and I think it's horrible. You did your duty as a human being saving that man, and you're being punished for it. This is the least I can do." He finished scraping the last of the venison and potatoes onto her plate. "You're a good one. Stay that way and remember what I said."

Luna slowly picked up her plate. "Th-Thank you, Musgo," she whispered, wiping at her eyes again.

"Oh please, wouldn't be the first night I've gone without food," he said, winking at her.

Luna touched her heart and mouthed *thank you* as she stood up, not wanting to make a scene. Musgo nodded at her, and she walked back to her hut.

11

Luna approached her hut, carrying the food. Right as she got to the entrance, a little red ball rolled its way out of the middle of the flap and ricocheted off of her feet.

A giggling Beatrix shot out of the hut, scooped up the ball, and darted back in through the open flap. Luna stood there with wide eyes and a huge smile. Beatrix was laughing so hard it was difficult for her to speak. Luna pushed her way through the flap to see Ray sitting on the edge of his bed, sloppily bouncing the ball off of the back of each of his hands and finally bouncing it high enough so that it would bonk him on the head. When it bounced against his forehead, he would react as if he had just been hit in the head with a brick. Beatrix found this act absolutely hysterical.

"What is going on here?" Luna laughed as she looked back and forth between the two.

Beatrix attempted to stop laughing so hard so that she could explain to Luna what was going on. "Look! L-Look! Look at—look at Ray, Luna!! Look at him!! He-He-He's pretending to be a-a-a seal!!!" Beatrix burst into laughter immediately after speaking.

Luna examined the situation and saw how Ray would bounce it off of his forehead while making the sound a seal would make.

"ARF! ARF! ARF!" Ray barked as he managed to keep the tiny ball bouncing on his forehead.

Luna laughed, not at Ray, but at how hard Beatrix was laughing. She had known the girl for years now, yet she had never seen her laugh this hard.

"Ray," Beatrix squealed! "Ray st-stop! Ray, I can't—I can't keep laughing I'm—I'll pee if I keep laughing!"

"Whoa there, Bea! We don't want that happening now, do we?" he said, bouncing the ball off of his head and into his hand.

Luna kept giggling, "Well, what did I miss?"

Beatrix went up to Luna and gave her a big hug. "I came by to see if you wanted to play, but you weren't here. So I played with Ray!" Beatrix let go of Luna and looked over to Ray, who was sitting on the edge of Luna's bed. "We're friends now," she said in all seriousness, no traces of laughter left in her voice.

"Well, great!" he replied to her honestly.

Luna looked over to Ray, too. "I thought you were sleeping?"

"Nah, maybe just a little nap. It was a long day. A lot of milking," he said, pretending to yank on imaginary udders in front of him.

Luna laughed and held up the food, "Got us some food. Killed the deer myself!"

Ray leaned forward, "That's fantastic."

Luna gave Ray an over-the-top, elaborate bow, "Thank you, thank you."

Beatrix looked at the two of them and started to giggle.

"What are you laughing at, Bea?" Luna said playfully, shoving her to the side.

"Ohhh, nothing," she replied mischievously.

"So what did *you* do today, Bea?" Luna asked.

"Well… I went to go pick some berries with Clover and Jesse, and then… we saw a squirrel, so I tried to catch it because I want to be a hunter when I'm older, just like you! And then Clover and I made a little fort in the woods."

Luna blushed, clearly flattered by Bea's innocent statements. "So did you catch it?" she asked enthusiastically.

Beatrix twisted her foot around on the floor. "I chased it around for a long time. But then it got tired and climbed up a tree, and I'm not good at climbing trees, so…"

Ray chimed in, "So squirrel: 1. Beatrix: 0."

Beatrix held her fist up to Ray and snarled at him, "We'll see about that *next* time. Clover actually climbed the tree and got it instead. But I'm getting better. You just watch!"

The three of them laughed as Luna prepared Ray's dinner. "Venison and potatoes," she said, handing it over to him.

"Thank you, seriously," he said with a nod of appreciation. He tore some of the venison off with his teeth and chewed it. "And the deer. Five-star quality, I'm telling ya!"

"Oh, stop," she said, waving him off.

"No, I thought it was really good too, Luna! Honest!" Bea said, chiming in.

"Well, thank you, but I killed it, I didn't cook it. You can thank Maple for that," she said as she began to pick at a potato.

The three of them sat in silence as the two adults ate their food. Beatrix looked up at the hatch on the ceiling so that she could peer at the stars.

Once she finished her meal, Luna looked over to Beatrix. "Hey Bea, getting late, isn't it? Willow might be getting worried. Are you still staying with her?" she asked.

"Yeah, yeah, I am. I know. Can I come back tomorrow?" Beatrix asked in her young, sweet voice.

"Of course you can, young lady," Luna replied as she brushed some of the stray strands of hair from Beatrix's face.

Beatrix took her ball from Ray and marched out the entrance of the hut. "See you guys tomorrow then!" she yelled as soon as she realized she had forgotten to say goodbye.

Luna leaned up against the thick beam that kept her hut sturdy, looking at Ray to see if he was ready to talk. Ray knew exactly what she was doing; he just didn't know what to say. He was her prisoner. There was no denying that, and he was coming to terms with the fact that he could say nothing to change that.

He sighed and looked up to her, "Tell me something about yourself."

Luna scoffed, "That really narrows it down."

"Anything. Literally anything. Give me something that will make me feel better about… about all this," he said, waving his hand frantically in the air. "Listen, I know you're not supposed to talk about your past life and all… but please, Luna, give me something."

"Who told you about that?" she asked, surprised that he knew about the unspoken code of Corazon.

"Luna!" he said in a demanding demeanor attempting to get her to focus on the task at hand.

Luna took a deep breath and slowly walked over to the bed, taking a seat next to him. He focused on her. He watched her every move, trying to dissect any sort of body language she may be giving off. There was nothing, just emptiness.

"Before I came here…" she said, clinging onto every last syllable. She was trying her hardest not to say what she felt she was being forced to say. Ray could see she was uncomfortable, but he pushed on.

"Before you came…" he said, trying to coerce her into finishing her sentence.

Her lips trembled as she tried to find her very next words. Ray noticed that her hands were shaking as well. She was scared, afraid of the very words that were about to leave her mouth.

"Relax," he whispered, noticing that he had taken things a bit too far. "Luna, you can start with something simple."

She took in two full breaths. "I had a brother once," she stopped there, her words lingering in the warm air around them.

Ray paused and thought about what that could mean. Was her brother still alive? Did she just forget about him? Leaving him behind to join up with the cult in the woods? He looked at her, locked and loaded with a follow-up question. However, she was obviously troubled by this. He instead reached out and touched her gently on the back, right where her neck met her shoulders.

"Okay, there we go. That's a start, just what I was looking for," he removed his hand from her back. He expected her to cry; she seemed distraught. However, she just turned to him with a blank face.

"Your turn," she whispered.

He cracked a smile and shook his head. "I'm sorry, but I think I'm going to have to one-up you." He looked back up at her with an ironic smile. His smile seemed to lighten the heavy mood set by her barely telling answer. "I was married once," he said as if he were actually boasting. She angled her body to face him better.

"Really?" she asked, sounding surprised.

"Well yeah, don't act too surprised!"

Luna laughed a bit, "No, it's just that... well, we don't believe in marriage on Corazon, you know, free love and all that."

"Ahh," Ray said, smiling. "Well, it's a good thing I'm not married anymore then."

"You got separated? A divorce?" she asked, sounding very much interested.

Ray cleared his throat and quieted down a bit. "Well, I, uh—I don't know you that well. *Yet.* But there was a time in my life where

I couldn't be there for them the way I wanted to be. And when I was eventually ready for them, well… she had moved on. Had a new husband and everything."

Luna scooched a bit closer to Ray. It was becoming more and more clear that the story wasn't going any further. "You can't stop there!" she said, slapping him on the shoulder.

Ray laughed. "Oh! So all I get is *I had a brother once,* and you expect to get my life story out of it? I don't think so. You'll get more information when I do."

Luna scooched back to where she was before. "Be that way, then."

Ray responded swiftly, "I will. Takes two to tango."

"All right, all right. Later. We have to get rest. Hopefully, Todd will come in the morning. He has a whole mess of supplies for us. Which means more painkillers for you," she said, nudging him as she rolled off of the bed and onto the floor where she was to sleep.

"Luna, please sleep up here. Seriously, I hate seeing you lay on the floor. I really do feel bad," Ray said as he lay back on her bed. "Just come up here, I'll make room."

Luna smiled. "You know the deal. You don't get to know that much about me… *yet*."

The two of them smiled to themselves as they both lay back, letting the fire extinguish itself until it mirrored the stars twinkling above.

12

When the sun rose the next morning, Ray woke up feeling rather sprite and more rested than usual, though the gloom of imprisonment still loomed thick in the air. A dense ball of venison and potatoes digested in his stomach, his hunger finally subsided. He turned to where Luna had been sleeping to once again find her gone. He wondered where she might be. It was always something—hunting, fishing, gathering, building, or helping with one thing or another in the community. He pushed himself up, being very careful not to use his legs at all, relying on the force of his triceps to propel him backward till his back reached the wall. He winced as his splint got caught on one of the sheets, shifting it to the left a bit. His leg still hurt immensely, but the swelling was starting to go down, and he was slowly improving day by day.

He took a few deep breaths in and flicked a bug off of his shoulder. It was at this moment where he actually stopped to take in the architecture of the hut. It had always just been a place where he would rest and recover, but he actually stopped to take in the function of it all. There were thick wooden posts hammered deep into the ground surrounding him. The posts stretched about 12 feet high and were met with a series of different cross-hatched sheets of metal, with a hole in the center where a hatch had been placed. The hatch allowed for proper circulation.

The beams were cemented together with what looked to be some sort of mud mixture. Ray scratched at it and found it to be as hard as rock. There were, after all, tiny stones fitted into any small crevices that were left uncovered by the mud mixture. There was a small pit in the middle of the floor that made it possible to have a fire, and there were numerous battery-powered lights around the hut. In the front, there was a door that was essentially a rectangular gap in the woodwork. There were thick leather tarps draped down over the gap. Ray noticed that she always referred to that fixture as "the flap." There was another heavier structure that Luna always placed over the door every night. It was placed to the side of the flap whenever it was needed. It, too, was made out of tin bound together with sticks and twine.

He halted his admiring when he heard Luna accompanying someone else toward the hut. "He's *quite a character*," he could hear her say. He quickly decided to take that as a compliment. "Hold on. Wait here. Let me see if he's up yet. I can always bring him to you later, depending on if you're still here or not."

Ray sat up and brushed himself off as he waited for the company.

"Is it true?" said the man Luna was with, having must've stopped her before entering the hut. "You know, about the killing himself and all? Is he really being hunted by cannibals? I heard one of the kids mention *vampires*... I mean, what's this guy's deal?"

Luna laughed, "You need to stop talking to those kids." She took a deep breath. "No, no. Ray is a good guy. His story seems more complex, but we're still working on him. Haven't gotten too much out of him yet, but I don't see him as a threat."

"Interesting. Well yeah, let's get a look at him. Give him some of my goodies," he said as he shook a paper bag making a rattling sound. The two of them pushed past the flap and entered the room.

"Morning," Ray said with a partially authentic smile. "Let's see these goodies. You wouldn't happen to have any garlic on you, would ya? Wooden stake? Holy water?"

Luna and the man looked at each other and smirked. The man spoke up, saying, "Well, I don't know about all that, but I do have these." The man reached into the bag and held out a small orange pill bottle. "Morphine Sulfate. It's a slow-release morphine. A few of these should get you through the day just fine, and believe me, you'll be feeling pretty good, too." The man winked at Ray as he tossed him the pill bottle. "The name's Todd. I come in about once a month to deliver anything that the community, Elliot, or the Disciples might need."

Ray looked at the pill bottle and nodded. "This will be great. Seriously thank you, Todd. The leg has been a pain, to say the least. Those crutches can only do so much."

Luna came up behind Todd and rested her hand on his shoulder. "Todd has helped us out more than we can even imagine. There hasn't been a single thing he can't get us, even when we don't have the money to back it up."

He looked back at Luna and rested his hand on hers. This subtle action made Ray slightly uncomfortable. Luna was quick to pull away.

"Well, I'm here to help. You guys know that," he said with a cocky smile.

Ray opened his mouth. He was trying to find the right words to say. "So um, Todd… given my condition. Do you think I should probably get to a good hospital? Luna has been doing a great job," he stopped and looked at Luna. "You really have." He directed his attention back toward Todd. "But I need modern care. I need those whistling machines and annoying nurses. I need to get back—"

"I know the whole situation. Luna gave me the rundown." Todd pointed directly at Ray's chest and held his free hand to the sky. "And don't you worry, Ray. The power and eternal light of Mother will illuminate the dark soon enough. You'll see what I mean eventually. This is where you are meant to be. Mother made it so. Things will fix themselves if they need to be fixed. But something tells me you are right where you belong," he said with a wink.

Ray slouched over a bit, Todd was his last possible ticket out of this place, but it seemed as though he, too, were under the strange spell. Everything was Mother this and Mother that. It seemed as though all possible obstacles put in his path were personally put there by Mother to prevent him from leaving. What did they want with him?

"Right. No, of course. Thanks again," he said, slightly defeated. "These will help a lot," he claimed as he rattled the pill bottle in his hand.

Luna smiled, thinking that she had just introduced two new friends. "Well, I hate to pull you guys apart, but The Disciples need their delivery, too. If any of the kids are tampering with your truck, just let me know. They're just curious."

Ray immediately sat up, trying not to look too alarmed. "Truck?"

"Yeah, I bring my old jeep on these supply runs. How else do you think I get all of this crap to the middle of nowhere?" Todd said as he shrugged.

"Right." Ray didn't know what to say in reply. He briefly thought about how he could go about stealing the truck, but Todd had the keys strung up around his neck, and after little consideration, he came to the conclusion that it would be wrong to leave Todd stranded like that.

There was a brief pause before Luna spoke up. Slapping Todd on the shoulder, she said, "You wanna go see Otto before you leave?"

Todd blinked a couple of times and nodded before letting out a long sigh. "Yeah, he's still by the river, is he?"

Luna nodded, and Todd sighed again. "I'll go have a word with him. Ray, it was nice to meet ya. Take care. I'll see you in another month or so."

"Yeah, nice to meet you too. Good luck with everything," Ray said as he watched Todd swoop back outside. Luna was quick to follow but turned around right before exiting.

"Hey, I'll be back soon. We can take today off. I already told Brooke!" she said, sounding more excited than usual. Ray bobbed his head as she danced away, gone into the late spring sunlight. He thought about how happy she seemed in comparison to the first time he had met her. A certain spark seemed to only spread with his presence.

His mind bounced back and forth between various places. Never had he ever thought that imprisonment would feel this way. He looked back at the orange pill bottle in his hand and squeezed it tight. *There was more than one way to leave this place.*

13

Todd and Luna walked through the woods together in search of Otto. "How has he been lately, Luna? You can tell me, really, I have to know. If he has done anything… anything rash, please tell me."

"No," she said plainly. "He's just been very quiet. We leave him to himself most of the time. He likes the river. It seems to calm him," she said as she looked at Todd, who seemed to be growing more and more sorrowful with each step. "He's made himself a nice home out here. We rarely ever see him, to be honest. Maybe once a day for meals or something. But other than that, Otto keeps to himself."

"Doesn't surprise me," Todd grunted. "He's always been an outlier. Any luck with finding him a friend?"

Luna smiled, "He seems pretty content with the one he has."

"Mm-hmm," he responded, his eyes rolling. "Any luck with finding him a *real* friend?"

Luna shook her head. This time there was no sigh, just disappointment.

They eventually found Otto sitting by the riverside. He was a very skinny man with a clean-shaven face. His hair was grown to about shoulder length, and he wore a military jacket that had seen better days. The coat was a heavy-duty coat made of some kind of burlap that Otto wore all year round. It did him well in the winter, yet he kept it on right through the spring and attempted to keep in on through the Summer, though sometimes one might find him slipping it off on the hotter days of the year. That jacket was his constant. It made him feel in touch with a world in which he was otherwise lost.

Todd walked up to Otto and took a seat. Otto was unfazed by his presence. His hand slowly made its way up to Otto's back and remained there, hovering within inches of his spine. Todd seemed unsure on whether or not he should show any sort of physical affection. Luna watched carefully as Todd's hand found its way to Otto's back and rhythmically patted the back of the beaten-up jacket. "Hey there, Otto, it's Todd. How are you?"

Otto turned toward Todd and looked at him with cold, lifeless eyes, "Is that a question you really want me to answer?"

Todd repositioned himself and cleared his throat, removing his hand from Otto's back. "Well, what do you want me to—"

"How's Mom and Dad?" Otto asked in a shallow voice.

"They're doing, uh... well. They ask about you a lot," Todd said, avoiding his brother's eye contact at all costs.

"What do you tell them?"

"I say… I say I miss you, too. And I say how I would do anything to find you as well. They don't know anything, Otto. They're getting too old. They're learning to live with you being gone."

Otto nodded his head. It was hard to tell if he was pleased or concerned. Todd watched him with a worrisome look on his face. "Do you um…" He cleared his throat abruptly. "Do you still hear them?"

Otto looked toward the water and spoke with a certain level of hatred in his voice. His hands began to tremble as he flared his nostrils. "Every. Single. Day." He muttered under his breath. "But it's getting better. *She's really helped me a lot.*" Otto looked lovingly at the patch of grass of his left. "She's so patient and—and yes, things are getting better. Aren't they, Sarah?"

There was a silence. Otto stared at the space absent of any life for a moment as he nodded and smiled. "I hope—I hope you can be so lucky." He looked back to Todd, his eyes slightly warmer.

"Lucky, yeah." Todd looked back to Luna, who stood quietly in the background, her arms crossed. He then turned to Otto again. "You still don't want me to get you any—"

"No," Otto said, cutting him off again. "No medication. I told you that. It numbs my head. I can't feel my fingertips when I'm on that shit. It sucks my soul out of me, pill by pill. You know that."

Todd rubbed his brother on the back and got himself to his feet. "Okay. Well, I'll, uh… I'll see you next time then?" Otto turned away from him and began to whisper to himself. Todd looked as if he were in pain as he turned to Luna. She jerked her head in the direction of camp, and he clapped Otto on the back and stood up to face Luna. The two of them then started back toward camp.

❈ ❈ ❈

"He started having those episodes when he was fifteen," Todd said as he looked down at his boots, wet with dew. "It was only when Dad started to medicate him when he lost it. He became volatile. He kept talking about Elliot and all of his greatness. I thought it was just another one of his fictional characters until I met him and saw what it was all about. But I couldn't do that to Mom and Dad. I saw how losing one child was hard enough. I knew I couldn't leave, too. Besides, I'm not complaining. Monthly supply runs for a direct pass to Mother on judgment day? Fair trade, if you ask me," he shrugged.

"All that without having to sacrifice indoor plumbing," Luna joked.

Todd toasted an imaginary chalice in her direction. "It's the little things."

Luna shook her head as the two of them walked. "Mother is always forgiving. And Otto has done nothing wrong. Sure he might spook someone every once in a while, but he is *good*. And we all know that. He belongs here, Todd. Trust in Elliot and Mother. They will always deliver."

Todd nodded his head in agreement as they walked on in silence. After a while, he decided to speak up. "Yeah, so, those pills. One or two a day should do it. I got the prescription upped a bit, so the dosage is higher. They'll keep your man pretty comfortable."

"Wait," Luna said as she held a hand to Todd's stomach, stopping him in his tracks. "Do you have the pills? Tell me you took them with you!"

Todd searched his pockets and showed two empty hands in return. He shook his head. "I… I don't—"

Luna took off running as fast as her legs would carry her, bolting around tree after tree as she sprinted straight for her hut. Her skin broke out with little bumps as she thought about the dangers of leaving Ray alone with the pills. It was a certain death sentence for anyone committed enough. Luna ran, trying to pick up speed, faster and faster with each step. She panted heavily as she pumped her arms as hard as she could to gain momentum.

She whizzed by Tobias, who was picking away at a berry bush. He tried getting her attention as she ran by.

"Luna, where are you running?" he said in passing. She didn't answer him; she needed to conserve her breath. Tobias got to his feet and began to tail her, the gap between the two widening with every step she took.

Her lungs burned as she chugged along. The further she went, the more community members she began to pass. She was only a little over a mile away, but it felt as if it were a marathon. Sweat ran down the bridge of her nose and right off of her face as the wind pushed back her hair. No matter how hard she ran, it would never be fast enough. She pushed her way past Maple and a friend as she darted into the center of the community and made a beeline for her hut. She ran up to her hut and flew through the flap, immediately looking toward her bed.

There he sat, still as stone, propped up against the wall with a few dry tears staining his face. His eyes shot open as he looked toward Luna, who wearily stumbled to his bedside, panting as if it were her last breaths. "Ray…" she said in a deep breathy whisper as she placed both of her hands on either side of his face. "Ray!" she said again as she looked at the nightstand, seeing an empty pill bottle. Her sentences curled at the end as her face began to crumple and her eyes watered.

"Stop," he whispered as he sat up, bringing his face level with hers. He gently pushed her back so that he could bring his other arm up. He held out a clenched fist and turned it so that his knuckles faced the ground. Luna cupped her hands under his as he released his grip, letting all of the tiny white capsules spill into her palms. She collected them all and looked at them, counting to make sure they were all there. She then brought them to the nightstand, where she funneled them back into the bottle.

Luna turned back to Ray with a confused look on her face. She was so distraught, so shocked, so relieved all at the very same time. His lips trembled as he spoke, "Luna, I'm—"

He was cut off as Luna swiftly brought the back of her hand to the side of his cheek, sending a clap echoing throughout the hut. He turned back to her and took in a deep breath preparing himself for another one. She then pulled him forward and wrapped her arms around him, squeezing him tight. He returned her gesture, slowly squeezing her with the little strength he could afford to muster. They remained like that, suspended in time, holding each other as close as they would possibly dare.

Tobias looked with malice toward them both as he peered through the fold of the entrance of her hut, watching them as they embraced for a prolonged period of time. He eventually scowled and left them alone, dissolving back into the community under the baking sun.

14

"Some things you do out of habit," Luna said as she stared up at the hatch in the roof, letting the morning glow bask upon her face. "You wake up in the morning, you brush your teeth. You bump into someone, you say excuse me. Hear something funny, most people laugh. *It's all just habits*. I like habits. I like having a daily or weekly schedule. It keeps everything in order, and when everything's in order, it's hard to get out of control."

She took a generous sip of water out of the tin cup and handed it to Ray. "Every morning, I wake up and exercise. After that, I wash up and meditate. I do all of this before my working day starts so that when night comes, I sleep like a child. Going to the gathering is a habit of mine. I do it every week, and I can't afford to miss it. It allows me to feel closer to Mother," she said as she snapped a leather band onto her wrist, a flare of jewelry in an otherwise fashion-less void. "I'm assuming the others have explained the concept of our religion. It's hard to grasp, but once you accept it, well… magical things happen."

She looked toward Ray, who lazed out on the bed. "I'm not saying you have to go… but it would help with your spiritual healing. And once you heal spiritually, you heal physically. It may sound strange, but it's true." She then looked down at him blankly but with a hint of hope. It was a beautiful sight looking at her. She was dressed in all white; her golden skin acted as the perfect contrast.

He had his lips pursed together as if he were considering some million-dollar offer. He looked at her through the corner of his eyes. "Do you want me to go?" he asked plainly. He couldn't think of a good reason to go, yet then again, there was no good reason not to go. He could get a look inside the social culture, see how things work, and get a deeper feel for what he was living with. The villagers would surely be fawning over the idea of his presence.

She looked at him and shook her head. "It doesn't matter whether I do or don't want you there. It's whether or not you want to go, whether or not you are willing to accept Mother and her will."

Ray nodded sarcastically. "Right. Mother and her will." His sarcasm seemed to upset her as she turned away from him. He quickly tried to fix his attitude. "I just don't want to give people the wrong impression, I mean… I'm not here to stay."

"You're here to stay a lot longer than you thought. You might not have swallowed those pills, but it was enough to worry me. You know what's worse than living with regrets?" she asked, her tone still somber. He remained quiet, and she continued, "Not living to regret them. We're trying to help you, and if that means you staying here to be treated, then so be it. You just… you can't worry me like that again." She spat in frustration as she threw her hands down to her side. She was clearly distraught.

"All right, all right, I'm not arguing with you. Just tell me whether or not you want me to go. It's not too much to ask," he said, trying to calm her down.

"I think it would be good if you go," she said, giving a swift nod.

The two of them looked at each other in silence for a brief moment. "I want to hear you say it," Ray said, provoking her.

She held a stare with him, the kind of stare that asked, "*Are you kidding me right now?*" without coming out and saying it. It was a stare held in between the lines of anger and frustration. Two emotions that often acted as siblings. She turned her back to him and exited the hut.

"Wait, Luna, I was just—" It was too late; she was already gone. Blown away in the wind like a white wisp of smoke.

Ray threw his head back into her pillow and sighed. "Goddammit," he muttered under his breath as he pulled himself up and carefully swung his legs off of the side of the bed.

Luna joined everyone else as they began to walk the trodden path alongside the mountain. She jogged up to Beatrix and spooked her from behind. "Boo!" Beatrix's body jolted as she spun around and yelped. Once she saw it was Luna, she gave her a half-hearted smile and punched her in the shoulder.

"Hi Luna," she said, slowing up so that she could walk beside her.

"What's new, Bea?" she replied, rocking into her small friend's shoulder.

"Oh, not too much. I went for a run this morning. I'm gonna beat you in a race someday, you just watch," Bea stated, baring her teeth and trying to appear as ferocious as possible.

Luna laughed. "I don't doubt it for one second! I'm getting slower, I can feel it."

"Haha, yeah..." she replied, sounding a bit drearier.

Luna noticed this and tapped her on the shoulder as they walked in unison with the others. "Something wrong?" she asked curiously.

"Well... not really. Nothing's *wrong*," she said, stressing the syllables. "I guess... I guess something is just not *right*. I've been thinking about Aria lately. She was mean, I know that, but I can't stop thinking about her still. What does she do up there? Do you think she's enjoying her time? What if she gets sick? The more that I think about it, the stranger it seems, and the happier I am that you weren't chosen."

Luna reflected on what Beatrix was saying and how little she actually knew about the whole ordeal. She didn't know what Aria was doing, and she didn't really care, but she couldn't let Beatrix know that in all of her innocence. She decided to fall back on the only failsafe that could explain anything in their warped way of life, "She is serving Elliot and his Disciples so that she may pass into the afterlife immediately after her work is done. She has a free ticket, all is forgiven, which is lucky for her because she was… well, you know, Aria."

"She was a *bitch* is what you mean, right?" Beatrix said timidly, looking up to Luna.

Luna tried to hold in a laugh making an embarrassing pig sound by accident. Once she had control of herself, she whispered back, "*Yes, Bea, that's what I meant.*"

The two of them chatted while they walked until they took a sharp left, veering off of the main path. There, as they pushed through the coverage of the thick pines, was a small grassy clearing with a stone altar. They walked to a grassy patch that looked plush and got to their knees. There were two Disciples dressed in purple behind the altar. They both looked on toward the gathering crowd as they all knelt before the great stone structure and began to whisper prayers to themselves. The prayers they were whispering varied from person to person. Some people prayed for clarity; some prayed for answers; some even prayed for a different lover to be presented to them. Even the children prayed.

Luna looked over to Beatrix as she knelt next to her, the little girl she had grown to love as a daughter, and quietly prayed to become beautiful.

Luna felt a certain kind of pain when she heard this. Here before her was the sweetest, most innocent girl she had ever known, wishing to become more beautiful so that the other men in the community would lust after her. This pain was immediately followed by a melancholic feeling of confusion. This was, after all, what their God had intended for them. Mother wants love for all, and it is a tad more difficult to find love when you don't have the looks to accompany it. She then reflected on how her mind had been completely encompassed by her faith in the days of late. She hadn't questioned it so much as long as she'd been involved.

The fact that Aria, the most juvenile, foul-mouthed woman she had ever met, was just given the highest honor a woman could get just didn't make sense. Luna worked hard for the community. She bled for the community. She loved everyone and showed respect for the community. The one thing she wouldn't do was frivolously sleep around with the members of the community, and she was being forever punished on account of those actions. She was never very outspoken about these feelings, but they would somehow show through, and it was only the ones who knew her the most that would see it. People like Beatrix.

Her self-reflection was interrupted when one of the Disciples spoke out. It wasn't a Disciple that she knew very well. This particular man lived higher up on the mountain for most of the time she had been here. He rarely came down to the community like Dante or Orwell. They seemed to be the ones sent there to watch over people the most, even though they were relieved of their duties every other week.

The man raised his hands and spoke in a deep, bold voice. "Rise," he commanded. Everybody slowly got their feet. It wasn't all in unison like one might expect it to be, but it happened eventually. Once everyone was standing, all attention was directed toward the altar, where the service began. Everyone looked up at the two of them wide-eyed. The two of them looked back at the crowd. The white of their ceremonial clothing in beautiful contrast with the lush grass they stood on. The Disciples began their service. The two Disciples dipped their hands in a small bowl of water. "Oh great, oh prosperous, oh merciful Mother, please look down upon us and cleanse us of our earthly sin," they said together. The two men in purple then reached into the lining of their purple silk robes to retrieve a small white cloth. They each unfolded their cloth as the rest of the villagers admired them. Once the cloth was unfolded, they turned their backs to the massive crowd and rummaged through a bag sitting on the ground behind them. They then turned back around, holding an object that caused whispers to ripple through the masses.

The white cloth was meant to separate their human flesh from the holy Book of Elliot. The two Disciples held the seemingly normal journal up to the sun, then placed it gently onto the table. The journal was bound in cheap leather and had seen better days. The audience was so captivated by their actions; every detail was so delicate, so careful. The Book of Elliot, until this day, had been a mere fable, a text of mythical status. Elliot really had been given messages from Mother, and he had written them down. In their hands, they held the proof that reaffirmed the faith of so many.

❋ ❋ ❋

A familiar, warm voice spoke out from behind the masses. "Praise be to Mother; praise be to Mother indeed." Everyone slowly turned around to face Felix as he stood silently in the back of the grassy knoll. He gently stepped toward the altar in a graceful fashion. He donned a flawless white robe that dragged across the earth as he walked. It made it look as if he were actually floating. People calmly walked away from where they were standing to fashion a path for him to walk. Both of the Disciples stood aside as Felix made his way up onto the altar. He threw his long greying hair over his shoulders and stroked his beard of the same color. He observed the crowd with tired eyes and a faint smile. They all knew exactly why he was here. They just didn't believe it was actually happening.

"My brothers, my sisters, my children, my lovers," he muttered in a tone slightly more aggressive than a whisper. "I understand that we have a visitor here today. *A visitor here to stay.*"

Luna's eyes widened as she broke out in a light sweat. She had no clue Felix would be making a special appearance. If she had known, she would have never given Ray the option of staying. Now everyone would look at her as the woman who left the injured mystery man behind.

Felix spoke up again. "I have been up on the mountain for quite some time. Elliot has been speaking with me. He knows his days are numbered, just as all of ours are… but we need to keep that in mind from time to time. Because if we let these days slip by, we will have no life to look back on. And we can only pray that we look back on our days with fondness. Truth be told, I've been struggling lately… mentally, physically, and spiritually. But speaking with our Prophet provides me with some… clarity. I wanted an answer, I felt that I deserved an answer, and therein lay the problem."

He took long dramatic pauses as he scanned the crowd looking at them as if he understood all of their pain and struggles. "We feel we deserve these things that are luxuries that Mother so kindly supplies us with, and we often wonder why we don't have more. I felt that I deserved more guidance. I felt that I had been left behind." All eyes remained unblinking as they followed him across the altar.

"There have been times *where I, too,* considered taking my own life. But then something amazing happened. I saw the light that pulled me out of the abyss. That light was Mother. She saved my life just as she has saved all of yours." Some people began tearing up as they nodded their heads in agreement. "And Mother will save this newcomer's life as well. Elliot has said it himself!" he shouted, demanding a response. Certain sections of the crowd applauded while others waited for the real climax of his sermon. "It is our duty, as people of the most high, to watch over him. To welcome him, to take him under the wing of our community."

He stopped, and his eyes widened. "I know a new face is frightening. I know there have been rumors that—the Former have returned and that—this newcomer brings with him bad omens. But I come here today to ask you to welcome him."

He raised his arms into the sky. "Take myself as an example. Even at his lowest point, every man can be saved. Every man can find redemption. Every man can live and prosper as long as they accept the teachings of Mother into their life!"

Luna wiped at her forehead and turned her head, desperately scanning the crowd for any sign of Ray. Everything was beginning to spin. What would she say if he were to be called out and everyone saw he wasn't there? All eyes would certainly look to her, and then what? She decided to try and slip away before anyone pointed her out.

As Felix babbled on about finding himself through the acceptance of Mother, she began to slowly crawl her way around the followers too captivated to notice her. She accidentally knelt on Maple's fragile feet as she made her way through the masses. Maple shot her a dirty look before realizing what was going on. She allowed her to pass as the High Disciple was reaching the climax of his sermon.

"There is always a reason to praise! There is always a reason for being thankful! There is always a reason for life!" he screamed, throwing his arms up in the air. The crowd jumped in the raised grass as they screamed and cheered, making Luna nearly invisible as she crawled along.

Felix looked at the crowd; the meager old eyes of his had been replaced with bloodshot orbs making him seem as if he were wired on some sort of hard-core stimulant. There were veins popping out of his red-hot neck as he held a hand over everyone causing them all to grow silent immediately. *"Now, where is my sinner!"* he screamed over the heads of his people.

They all turned to each other, looking for Ray. Luna sped up her crawling, trying her best not to alert anyone. All of a sudden, she heard a gasp come from above her head. She looked up to see

Brooke looking down at her with her mouth slightly ajar. Brooke knew exactly what she was trying to do, and she wasn't going to let her.

"Luna!" she screamed, causing everyone to direct their attention toward them. "Luna knows!"

Luan grabbed two handfuls of the grass she crawled upon as she thought of what to do, slowly follower after follower looked to her. She now had too much attention on her to escape. She carefully rose to her feet and looked toward Felix, who stared right back at her.

"Luna, Luna, please come to me," Felix said, kindly extending a hand. She froze in her tracks. The *High Disciple* had just called out her name, summoning her to his side at a gathering. She hadn't felt so singled out since the day of the choosing. She didn't know what to do. Brooke placed her hands on Luna's back and gently guided her forward, pushing her to a point where she began to walk on her own, still wide-eyed, still unsure of how to proceed. She approached the altar and bowed her head, trying not to look directly at Felix.

"Come, child," he said in a soothing voice as he extended a hand. Luna looked at his soft, flawless hands and questioned the state of her reality. "Come," he said again, moving his hand forward in the slightest of ways. He took her trembling hand in his own and escorted her up onto the altar. Luna felt a knot forming in the pit of her chest. She felt as if she were about to pass out. All of the light around her seemed to blur together, with Felix being the focal point. He pulled her to his side, grabbed her on both sides of the head and gently kissed her on the forehead.

"Pr—praise be to Mother," she said, unsure of herself. The point where his lips graced her forehead was still tingling. Felix looked at her and noticed how she was looking down at her feet, too nervous to actually face him.

"Luna, dear," he said, tapping her on the bottom of the chin, signaling her to look at him. She raised her head, revealing her deep blue eyes. He gazed into them as he spoke, "Where is our sinner? He is here… is he not?" A vast silence washed over the crowd. The only things that could be heard were the mosquitos and crickets in the surrounding brush.

Luna's lips trembled as she licked at them, trying to find the right words to say. "Felix, he… well, I asked him to come, and—"

The crowd watched eagerly to see what the High Disciple would do when he found out that Luna wasn't taking care of Ray like she had been ordered to. No good healer would ever leave their patient alone. Luna repeated herself to elongate the time she had to let them down. She wanted to enjoy the last few moments of the seemingly eternal attention she was getting from the High Disciple himself before she blatantly embarrassed herself. "I asked for—for him to come and—"

"And I came," stated a voice from the back of the crowd. There stood Ray, hunched over on one of his crutches, sticking out like a sore thumb from the crowd dressed in shades of white. He sported a brown t-shirt and the same jeans he wore when he was brought to Corazon.

Luna closed her eyes and sighed in relief, a single tear ran down the side of her face, but nobody seemed to notice. Even Felix's attention was on Ray. He was sweaty and out of breath; it couldn't have been easy hiking the trail while on crutches. Felix looked at him and smirked as he held out his free hand. The crowd on the grass quickly moved, creating a path between the two. Ray looked around, bewildered by what he was seeing. Did he really expect him to just come to his side with a hand gesture? By the way the crowd looked at him, that was exactly the case. He saw Beatrix poke her head out from between two adults. She glared at him with a certain excitement in her eyes.

Ray was conflicted with his actions, but it didn't matter. He looked to Luna, who looked back at him with a painful stare. A stare that pleaded with him to do whatever it took. Despite his better judgment, he limped forward. The crowd went silent again as Felix spoke in a bold voice. "Come forth, sinner!"

This tone of his voice alone made Ray want to stop, yet still, he kept moving forward. All eyes followed him and seemed to fixate on each step, each drop of sweat, each wince of pain. He forced himself to the altar and was aided by the Disciples, who then discarded his crutches and lifted him off of his feet. They set him down in front of Felix and held him firmly under his shoulders to support him. Felix looked down at him and smiled. There were whispers winding their way through the crowd. "You are a sinner…" Felix quietly declared. "And sinners must *repent*. But before all repentance, first comes the *confession*," he said, as if having a personal conversation with him while simultaneously announcing it to the crowd.

Ray nodded his sweaty head and jerked it to the side so that he could flick the wet hair out of his eyes. "What do I do?" he asked, genuinely curious. Anything to speed up the process. He was never one for the spotlight, and here he was, pinned up like a rag doll in front of everyone.

"My child…" he said softly. "It appears to me that you've seen better days," he muttered with a modicum of enthusiasm.

Ray nodded and looked Felix directly in the eyes. "I would say that's correct," he replied in a deadpan tone.

Felix touched him on the shoulder and turned to face the people. He spoke to Ray but did so in a manner as though he was addressing the crowd. "Explain to all of us why you are a sinner. Admit it to them, and you will admit it to yourself."

"Admit what?" Ray replied, blinking the sweat out of his eyes and looking at Luna with a flash of concern. Felix smiled and brushed a hand down the side of Ray's face.

"My child, admit to them why you are *a sinner*. The truth will open the gates of paradise. Accept your faults, and Mother will accept you."

The two Disciples picked him up and made him face the crowd. As they turned him, the hefty one with the low voice leaned in on him, making his knee start to throb. It hurt immensely, but Ray knew what he had to do. Let them hear what they want to hear. This situation, however, seemed more serious than usual. Felix gave off this spiritual aura making him seem as though he were a human lie detector. "Tell them, my child. What have you done?"

Ray looked to the crowd, then back at Felix. "I'd like to keep my sins to myself, if you don't mind."

The crowd exchanged glances, and eventually, all eyes landed on Luna. She tucked her head into her metaphorical shell and hoped for the best. Felix smiled and squeezed Ray's shoulder. "I don't mind, my child. But Mother may, and if you can't wash your own sins away… then a baptism is in order. The choice is yours."

"Baptism? As in water, candles, and holy oil? I think I can handle that," he replied, sounding cheeky. His response was followed by a tense silence as a thin smile ran across Felix's face.

Felix turned to the Disciples and shrugged. "The sinner wants a baptism," he then dropped his head and thought for a moment. Turning to the crowd, he raised his eyebrows. "So it shall be." He then turned to everyone and walked off the altar. "Bring him," he ordered.

The Disciples reaffirmed their grip and dragged Ray forward as they followed in Felix's steps. The crowd exchanged glances and whispers right before they collected their belongings and followed them. Luna pushed by people as she hopped up and down, looking for Maple's nappy grey hair. "Maple!" she shouted, getting her attention. "Maple, what are they doing to him!"

Maple stopped in her tracks and grabbed Luna's hand. "He refused to answer the questions he was asked. Felix has called for a baptism."

Luna furrowed her brow and shook her head. "I don't understand. Why?"

Maple frowned as if she were delivering unwelcome news. "Well, the baptism is the initiation into the community, but... I fear that this isn't your typical baptism."

The two of them began to pick up the pace, keeping up with the bulk of the community. "What do you mean?" she asked, growing more concerned.

"What I mean is... they're just as scared as anyone else here. This won't be any normal baptism, dear... this is an *interrogation*."

Luna felt the deep-seated panic course through her blood. She let go of Maple's hand and ran ahead to where the Disciples escorted Ray as they followed Felix through the weeds. She wanted to jump ahead of them and stop them in their tracks, but she was chained back by her beliefs. You never interfere with the work of a Disciple. Never.

Ray glanced back as his feet dragged through the dirt. He caught a glimpse of a worried Luna right before the sound of the river pierced his ears. The last time he had heard that sound, he was lying on the side of a bank coughing up an entire lung full of water.

He faced forward and saw Felix wading into the calmer part of the river where the massive rocks acted as a barrier to the rapids around him. Felix walked in until he was thigh-deep. He turned to face Ray with a wider smile this time, holding out a hand and summoning him forward. Before he had time to think, he could feel the water forcing his pants to stick to his skin. The Disciples waded into the water with no hesitation, and the sound of various other followers could be heard, disrupting the hushed atmosphere.

"Come forth, and become blessed in the waters of Mother," Felix spoke with an unnerving amount of serenity in his voice.

Ray shook his head and thought of some sort of way to protest. Before he could speak, Felix was in front of him. Felix placed his smooth palm on Ray's forehead as his other hand wrapped itself around his jaw. Without any hesitation, Felix tightened his grip and immediately forced his head underwater. The Disciples loosened their grip and allowed Ray to be completely submerged. He thrashed about and tried to break free but, it only irritated his wounded body. Felix kept a firm hand on his face.

Luna lurched forward but was caught by Maple. The chains were no longer metaphorical. "Wait—just wait, Luna. Think about this," she said, not even sure how to proceed herself. The rest of the community stood silently on the banks as they watched the sinner's body move around under the thin surface of the water.

They watched in anticipation as Felix lifted his hand, pulling Ray's head out of the water with it. Ray gasped for air as he was immediately restrained by the Disciples again. Dante looked back at Luna with a certain malicious stare. Some of the followers began to leave with their children. There was no need to view such an act.

Felix continued, "Tell them, child. Repent, and tell them why you are here!"

"I don't know what you're talking about," he spat, still trying to catch his breath.

Felix shot a demanding look at the Disciples, who then forced Ray back underwater. They held him there until he began to thrash about again. He gasped for air as he broke the surface. Felix spoke up again, "Only those who cleanse themselves in these holy waters are welcome in our community. Just confess and—"

Ray found his footing and stood up with a certain rage in his eyes. "Confess to what!" he shouted. Felix stood there, unfazed by the sudden outburst. Ray looked at the crowd, who watched contently as he was drowned before their very eyes. "Confess to what? That—that I tried to kill myself? Because I—because I was done with life? Is that what you're looking for?"

Dante placed a firm, demanding hand on Ray's shoulder, a physical warning to tread lightly with the mockery in his tone. Felix remained calm and clapped his hands together. "Everybody is already aware of that, though, aren't they, brother?" he whispered, his eyes narrowing in on Ray.

Ray's facial features went soft. It was clear his defensive wall was disintegrating before them. "No," Felix stated, stepping forward. "I want to know why you tried taking your own life. I want to know why you chose this river, and I want to know why you haven't stopped looking over your shoulder since the day you arrived on that stretcher." He looked back up into his eyes and nodded.

Ray stared back with wide eyes and a dry mouth. "I, um…"

"Tell us, brother," Felix preached, raising his hand into the air. "Tell us all why you're running. Tell us all why you're trying to die…"

The grips on his shoulders tightened, and the Disciples leaned in on him. His knee began to throb, and the wound on his back was still tender. "Because…" Ray said, trying his best to keep the words from spilling out. "Because I'm a coward."

Felix's eyebrows raised. He seemed oddly satisfied with the half-hearted answer. "Louder."

"Because—"

"*By the power invested in me by the Prophet Elliot, louder!*" Felix shouted.

Ray winced as he was turned to face the crowd. "Because I'm a coward! Because things got difficult, and I ran. From everything. Because I don't deserve to live anymore. Because I'm a fucking coward!" he screamed as he began to break down. He prepared to be forced underwater again, taking deep breaths in with every exhale. His vision grew clouded, and his legs went numb. "Because I abandoned my wife, my boy! Because I was selfish, and—because I couldn't deal with the mistakes I made!" he exclaimed. He winced, once again preparing for the worst.

All of a sudden, there was a warm touch to his cheek. He blinked to see Felix standing in front of him again, this time with a more accepting expression. It was as if the monstrous man had transformed right before him.

"Your sins have been heard. And through admission comes reconciliation. May the current now pull them away, as Elliot welcomes you under his loving embrace. You have entered these waters as a sinner, but you shall leave a clean man. By the power of Elliot and all things holy, you are baptized." Within seconds there was an eruption of applause. The followers all clapped together; some of them waded into the water to shake hands with the Disciples. Others cleared a path. Luna and Maple rushed to Ray as Dante and Orwell let go of his limp body.

Felix was gone within seconds, and the crowd began to disperse into the woods when it became clear that the excitement was over. Luna cupped Ray's head in her arms as he blinked the water out of his eyes and took in deep breaths. Maple rested a heavy hand on her back in an attempt to console her. She glanced around and noticed a man lurking in the brush nearby. She turned to face him as her blood began to boil. "Was this you?" Maple shouted as she turned her back on Luna and Ray and faced the figure standing in the brush. "Was this your little recommendation? An interrogation disguised as a baptism?"

Tobias pushed his way out of the brush. He seemed smaller. His typical charisma had been washed away. He spoke in a low, collected tone. "He is not a good man, Maple. He may not be a Former, but he is not a good man."

"And who are you to judge?" she asked, her anger growing as she began to wade toward him. "You talk like you've never seen sin before. I know you better than that, Tobias."

"I never denied having seen sin. That's how I know he's lying. There's more to this story, and we shouldn't just let him into this community without knowing it first! He's a liability, Maple!"

"What is your fucking point, boy?" she exploded, throwing her arms into the air. "What if he's a liability? He's not going anywhere! He's crippled! He's sick! And we have tools to defend ourselves! I'd love to hear what you think this man is capable of because the way I see it... you're just intimidated."

Tobias's eyes shot open. "You don't know what you're talking about."

She nodded. "Believe me, Tobias. I know exactly what I'm talking about."

He stepped into the water with a certain hostility. "Think about the resources we have! We can't even afford to have children; resources are too tight right now. And you just want to welcome him in? He's just another mouth to feed Maple, he doesn't even contribute!"

"Bullshit! He's up every single morning tending to the cattle with Brooke. He works just as hard as you. Hell, he probably works harder! At least he always comes back with milk. It's never guaranteed you come back with meat."

Tobias closed his eyes and clenched his fists. "You're not seeing things clearly. Your age is catching up with you and—"

"I may not be seeing things as clearly as I could," she said bluntly. "But at least I'm not blinded by my love for Luna! You act as if none of us see it, but if I can see clearly enough to notice it. Anybody can."

His face went red with embarrassment. Luna turned to look at him as she cradled Ray's head in her arms. Tobias glanced at her and looked away as quickly as he could, his fists tight, his jaw clenched. "You better watch yourself, Maple," he said, trying to conjure up any sort of menace he had in him.

Maple took another step forward so that they were face to face. "What are you going to do about it? I guess I see a little more clearly than you thought."

"Hey!" Luna shouted as she began to drag Ray's body from the water. "Lock it up. He needs our help," she said as if she were captaining a ship.

Maple's eyes were ablaze with a certain kind of rage. She spun around and helped drag Ray onto the bank, where he continued to catch his breath. Tobias paced about on the wet pebbles, his bare feet leaving tracks in his path. "I just want to be practical about this. Felix said that change was coming and—well, it's my job to make sure that change is a positive one."

Luna turned Ray onto his side and rubbed his back as he hacked up what was remaining of the bitter waters. "And who made you in charge of change?" she spat, looking up at Tobias.

He froze and tossed his arms in the air. "Well, if I'm going to be a Disciple one day, I need to prove myself as a—"

"Oh!" Maple moaned. "Oh, listen to the poor thing," she shouted as she looked at Luna. "The man thinks he is going to be a Disciple but watches a member of his very community lie in discomfort before him."

"He is no member of my community. He's an outsider," Tobias exclaimed.

"Well, thanks to you, he's been baptized!" Luna shouted. "And that means you are required to care for him just as you would a loved one. I would hope any man of Corazon would recognize that, let alone one with hopes of being a Disciple."

Tobias prepared a hard-hitting remark to sling back at her, but he stopped himself before speaking. She was right. He had to uphold his duties as a member of the community. Luna held his stare as she continued to comfort Ray.

Ray placed a firm hand on the bank and pushed himself up with the aid of Luna and Maple. He looked at Tobias with sheer hatred now. He was beyond the point of questionable morals, now Ray knew he was a delusional, and that made him dangerous. "Just get me back to the hut," he said coldly.

Tobias looked to Luna, then to Maple, and eventually back to Ray. He took a deep breath and took a step forward. "Very well, then," he said as he knelt down and slung Ray's arm over his shoulder. "Let's get you back."

With one mighty grunt, Tobias stood up and forced Ray onto his broad shoulders and began to trudge down the path. Luna sat where she was and watched Tobias walk away, Ray slung over his shoulder, defeated, his arms still hung like that of a rag doll.

The two pushed on through the woods. Ray kept an eye on Luna and Maple and watched as they grew smaller and smaller. Luna hunched over on the bank, Maple trying her best to console her.

"Am I a bad person?" Luna asked, her voice beginning to break up.

Maple hushed her as she rubbed her back. "Not at all, child. Bad things happen to good people every day."

Luna wiped at her eyes. "He doesn't belong here. He doesn't even want to be here, I can see it in his eyes at night."

"Well, it's a good thing he has nowhere to go," Maple said, wondering whether her words were actually helping.

She leaned forward and pulled herself to her feet, turning around to look at the woods. Ray and Tobias were out of sight. "I'm worried about Tobias, Maple."

"Don't be. I'll make sure he doesn't harm our little friend."

"No, I know that won't happen, but… something is different about him. He just hasn't been the same lately."

"Blame it on the change in seasons. He may be confused, but I believe he's a good man." Maple looked over at Luna, hoping for some sort of nod in agreement. Luna remained fixated on the woods and began to follow in their trails.

The sun sank quietly that evening. A dense silence plagued the two of them as Ray lay still on the bed. It was now a matter of who was willing to talk first. Luna was just as sorry as she was skeptical. She wanted to know more about his boy, more about his wife. Ray, on the other hand, was willing to talk but still unwilling to trust.

The fire withered away to sparkling embers. She stared deep into the ash and decided to disrupt the pattern. "I know you don't want to talk," she spoke softly. "But I swear I didn't know that was going to happen. I couldn't do anything about it. I don't know—"

"Luna," he said, cutting her off, "there's something I need to tell you."

15

"I don't really know how to tell this story. It was one I never thought I would have to tell." Ray sat in his usual spot on the edge of Luna's bed. She leaned up against her wall and gave him all of her attention. She was weary and nervous as to what he was about to say. If he were about to tell her about his life, she was worried she'd be obligated to do the same.

"Before…" he waved his hand around the room. "All this… I had a wife. I had a beautiful son. I had a nice house in the suburbs. I had a mortgage. I had a steady job. I had a boss that I hated, and… well, I had everything I could have ever wanted," he mindlessly nodded, agreeing with himself. "So I still can't figure out why I had to go and fuck everything up."

Luna kept quiet. She wanted to see what he was willing to give her without any verbal poking or prodding. "My son, he had autism. He was such a good boy, but he would always get so frustrated with himself. I haven't seen him in years. I'll get to that part. Anyhow, he was a great kid, always has been and always will be. He had the funniest thoughts, he um… he was so creative." There was a glimmer in his eyes that she hadn't yet seen, something she could only imagine was a connection of pride and regret. "He thought that all squirrels were assassins. He would tell me stories about how there were gnomes living under the earth that would come out at night and steal candy from the candy drawer in our kitchen. My wife and I obviously knew it was him, but the attempt alone was so creatively absurd that we had to let him get away with it."

"His name was Martin. I called him Marty. Marty always had a tough time making friends, but for whatever reason, he had this one guy at school that was always looking out for him. The kid's name was Gary Robinson. He was like… he was like the last kid I would see ever hanging out with my little Marty. They were both outcasts, in a way. Gary was a strange one. Strange in the best of ways, though. The kid colored his hair green and still listened to cassette tapes. He was the kinda kid that loved everything about life. He walked around with a skateboard, although I really don't think he could ride it. I think it was something about being retro or something like that. But like I said, he would hang out with Marty. They'd go watch a movie or they'd go see a baseball game, they'd just *do* stuff together. It was really nice." Ray paused his story and grinned; it was a genuine grin, the type of grin that only his son could bring to his face.

"My wife was also just—incredible. I met her when I was in college. Her name was Jean. She was a bartender at this divey place my buddies and I always went to. She had just graduated and was saving up money for a car. She really just needed a way out of town. I was studying microbiology then. I graduated the next year, and we decided to stick around with each other. Seven years later, we had a son, a dog, and a house we could barely afford in the suburbs."

"We moved to a small city in eastern Colorado. It was nothing special, but it did the trick. Jean became a librarian, which was good because that meant she would be closer to Marty, and I managed to get a job as the county water inspector. Things were going so well. We were always a little tight on money, but at the end of the day, everything was all right. We loved each other, Jean and I, and nothing was going to change that."

Luna sat still, unsure as to whether she was expected to respond. Ray continued, "My job was simple. I would take a sample of the lake water every week, bring it back to the lab, run some tests and tell them everything was all right. That's all they wanted to hear. The lake I was taking samples from was a big deal because that's where everyone got their water from. It was called Lake Diane. People would just call it Diane, though. 'Hey, I'm heading down to Diane for the day. Do you wanna come?' That kind of thing. Every single week I would go to a different place in the Lake with my little kit and take a different sample, and every single week it would come back negative for any toxins. Then I would go home and eat microwave macaroni and cheese with Marty, and we'd call it a night."

Ray paused again and sighed. It was obvious he was getting to the part where everything went haywire, though she couldn't tell what was going to happen, not yet. He continued with his story, "So the bills were piling up, and we had to find a new school for Marty. He was beginning to get volatile. The teachers weren't giving him the time he needed on tests or quizzes and so on, and for whatever reason, the school didn't have enough faculty to spare, putting him in a separate room. There were also those odds and ends, chores around the house. We needed a new water heater, a new stove, a new car. We just didn't have enough to get by. Not to mention all the tutors that came in every week to help Marty with his classes."

"One day, I went to collect some water at a little lagoon off the end of Diane. I filled up my test tube and turned around to see some guy staring at me. He didn't say anything, but he was wearing a Nutrastay shirt. Nutrastay was this big company that had branched out into our town. I had tried to get a job there. They were rumored to have been doing some cutting-edge stuff, but everything was so locked down that it wasn't the sort of gig that you applied for. You had to be recommended. You had to have *an in*."

"Nutrastay essentially focused on chemically engineering foods so that they last longer. It was like preservatives but on some bigger scale. Imagine if you could make a banana go ten years without browning. That was the idea. There was a big upset when they moved into town because a lot of their food had been recalled. It was something about the chemicals they were using not being properly tested or something, but by the time word got out, they were too big to be taken down, and they were too new to be proven unethical."

"When I saw this guy on the beach, I knew that whatever he had to say was trouble, but I listened anyway. He essentially told me that something had gone wrong at the facility. A pipe burst or something, and that to get rid of it, they had to dispose of it quietly. I guess by quietly he meant by dumping the evidence in the lake. I knew it was wrong. *I knew it was so wrong*, but he made it sound so minuscule that, well, I didn't really think anything of it. He offered me $25,000 to fudge the test results. Make up something and sweep the dirt under the carpet. When I saw that money, well, I just couldn't resist. They even had samples of water from the lake taken before the incident. I didn't even have to lie, I just had to test old samples and say that everything was all right. At first, I was skeptical, but they promised me that it was just a little hiccup, that nothing would ever come of it. So I took the money, and I turned in false results."

Ray ran his hands down his face and sat quietly for a few moments, looking up at Luna to see if she had any input on any of it, but she stuck to her guns and let him finish by himself. He sighed and sat up, letting his legs hang off the edge of the bed. "With all that money, we were able to hire better tutors, move Marty to a better school, fix up the house, and… just so much. I went about doing my work, doing things like I always had, until one day, about two months later, I saw that guy again. This time the conversation was much faster. He gave me another 25,000 and another clean sample. I didn't even hesitate. Jean knew something was up, she was a smart lady, but I feel like she wanted to be kept in the dark. She didn't want that picture-perfect family image smeared by a dirty little secret. She started saying things like *be careful* when I went to work. I should've seen it coming, too."

"The man showed up more often. It started off as once a month, but then it became twice a month, once a week, sometimes even more than that. I was making so much money that the whole morality thing was out the window. And it wasn't like I could just stop. They knew who I was, and they had connections. They could ruin me for life. If the story were to ever break, it would be a small dent to their reputations, but it would absolutely ruin me. I was in their pocket, and there was nothing I could do about it. They even started lowering the price. I didn't mind, though, I was still making thousands a week on top of my county salary."

"It was kinda like those mechanical bull rides at the fair when you were a kid. At first, it goes easy; you think you've got control over everything. But then it bucks, and you're never ready. Except you don't stand up laughing in the real world." Ray stopped again and was growing more upset, his calm regretful demeanor turning to a scowl relatively quick as he carried on.

He broke into the next line with a remorse-riddled confidence. "People started getting sick. *Real sick*. Turns out, the shit Nutrastay had been putting into the water supply was toxic, but I mean… I shoulda known. No, I *did* know, I just didn't do anything about it. I don't care how rich you are; if greed can grab ahold of you like that, there's no escaping. Nutrastay packed up and left town right before things started to get too out of hand. More and more people started to get sick, and then some private companies hired people to take some tests of their own. I remember when the news story broke, it was pretty chaotic, there was so much pollution in the lake that they had to issue the water undrinkable for years to come. People depended on that lake, they lived off of that lake. Water is literally essential for life, and I just… stripped that right away from them."

He gripped the sheets of the bed. "Like I said, people were getting worse and worse, and by the time the water was issued undrinkable… people started dying. All fingers immediately pointed to the Health Department, and I knew it wouldn't be long until they figured out what I had done. I knew I had to get out fast, not because I was afraid of prison… I knew I deserved that. But if I didn't run, they might think that Jean was in on it, they might strip us of our house, and… what would happen if my son ever caught on? It was all too much to even comprehend. I got one of my friends to find me a place out in what we used to call the deep woods. It's where we'd go hunting every year. It was small, quiet, away from all the damage I had started, I didn't think anyone would ever find me. It took us about a week to stock the place full of non-perishable food, and within another week, I was gone. Just like that, my entire life, all that I had worked for, just gone. Jean was distraught; she was an absolute wreck. She knew what I had done, and she was disgusted. I know she loved me, but… how could you stay with such a coward."

Ray began to tear up a bit, and Luna lit the lanterns within her hut. She then sat beside him and debated putting her arm around his shoulder in an effort to comfort him. After a little internal debate, she decided to keep her hands to herself and let him continue.

"The worst part was hearing Marty as I was about to leave. He cried like… it sounded like nothing I had ever heard in my life. And I pray to God I never have to hear it again. He cried so hard he was ready to throw up; his eyes were so red. He ran up and down the hall and punched at walls. He was having a fit. I never even told him I was leaving. Jean and I thought it would be best if I just faded away. I found out later—"

Tears welled up in his eyes at a rapid rate and quickly began to overflow, sending rivulets streaming down his cheek. "I found out later—" he croaked, trying to get the words out. Luna decided to put her arm around him onto his shoulder. "He, um..." he said, still trying to get the words out. Luna stroked his shoulder in an attempt to calm him. He wiped at his wet eyes and took a few deep breaths in order to settle down. He finally gained control of himself.

"I found out later that… that Gary Robinson had uh… *passed away*. Gary had died due to the contaminated water. It was my little Marty's only friend, and I could've prevented his death along with the fifty-six others who died because of what I failed to do." Ray bit his bottom lip as if he were padlocking his mouth to prevent the wailing that was about to come. His face shone with a bright red hue as he tried his hardest to keep his cries contained. It remained this way for a few moments, then his cheeks deflated, and he resumed the story.

"I moved out into the middle of nowhere. I lived in a small cabin. Loneliness is just a word. But no word will ever depict how truly horrifying that feeling of being *alone* really is. I hated every second of it. I wanted to hibernate, I wanted to go to sleep and stay asleep for as long as it would take. As long as it would take to just make the pain go away. But it never left. Every day I would wake up, and maybe for a moment, just for a single moment, I could look out the window, and look at the clouds, and appreciate the view. But as soon as that mindless moment passed, my head would be filled with all that I had done. I heard Marty crying, I heard Jean screaming at me. I hear that man from Nutrastay telling me that it's *no big deal*."

"I stayed in that cabin for six, maybe seven years; I lost count after a while. I hunted, I climbed the walls of some nearby mountains. I hiked near and far, anything to keep my mind off of things. But nothing would take it away. After a while, I couldn't take it anymore. I couldn't find ways to keep myself busy. I realized I was never going to get rid of the guilt. It was going to stick with me like a disease until—well, until I did something about it."

Luna leaned in. She had finally figured out where this story was going.

He calmed himself and patted Luna's hand that rested upon his shoulder. "So I went back to my little cabin in the woods. I stayed there for as long as I possibly could, and one day I knew I had enough. I got up and decided right then and there, I knew I didn't deserve to live anymore. So I packed a bag, and I walked. I walked as far as I possibly could. I loved to hike, and I wanted to take in all that life had to offer in my last hours. So I just walked. I had no destination in mind. But then I saw that waterfall, and it felt poetic in a way. Die with my sins, you know?" He smirked and shook his head at the thought of the irony. "I took a few deep breaths, I got into the river, and I let the water drag me away." He wiped the tears from his face and looked toward her with a half-hearted smirk. "And then you decided to show up."

The two of them shared an ironic smile as they looked at each other, although both of them now had tears in their eyes. "I'm a sinner, Luna. Felix is right. I deserve to suffer; I deserve to die. This… whole thing. It wasn't part of the plan. Corazon, Elliot, Mother, all of this spiritual healing, *you*… It wasn't supposed to happen."

Luna took her free hand and touched his face. "I am so sorry about everything. But you made a mistake. You gave into the greed. But you can't hate yourself for being human. It's such an easy thing to do. You can't let your regrets consume you. You have been running for so long, I can feel your fear. Maybe this is life trying to teach you a lesson. Maybe this is its way of getting you back. You may not want to believe in my religion and creed but believe in something… some people call it fate, others call it destiny. You don't have to call it anything at all, but just know that it's there. You are here for a reason, Ray."

Ray seemed mesmerized by the words she said. It was perhaps the way in which she said them that kept him so hooked. Whatever it was she was saying, it made him feel some sort of comfort. It made him feel welcome. It made him feel something he hadn't felt in a very long time; it made him feel loved. There was no sort of sexual tension; it was more of just a feeling of warmth. The affectionate touch of another human being seemed to transport him into another state of being.

The moment of passion was cut short by the pitter-patter of small feet coming from just outside the hut. Beatrix poked her tired head through and eyed them suspiciously. Without any words spoken, she could tell her presence alleviated the heavy mood pressing down on them. She pushed past the tarp and cautiously tiptoed over to the bed, where she hopped up and rested her hand on Ray's shoulder, a gesture she had picked up from Luna. Her little fingers patted him with the utmost innocence as she tried to force a smile. He placed his hand on top of hers and smiled back.

"I think it's time for bed," Luna said, standing up.

Beatrix leaped up in protest and crossed her arms. "I don't want to go back. I saw the monster in the woods today. I know he's coming to get me."

Luna shook her head. "Bea, enough with the monster. You're a big girl now. You can't go around saying that sort of stuff."

"But Luna!" she shouted.

Luna held up a hand in an attempt to silence her. "You can stay here tonight, but promise me you'll stop talking about this monster?"

Beatrix nodded and began to make the bed on the floor. Ray leaned forward so that he could speak more privately with Luna while Beatrix nuzzled herself into the thick blankets. "At least let me sleep on the floor tonight, Bea, and you should take the bed."

Luna playfully pushed him away. "After today's events, you need a good night's sleep. Plus…" she looked over to Beatrix, who was already beginning to doze off. "I don't think she minds at all."

Ray backed away and noticed how she took hold of his hand. He felt the crushing exhaustion rush over his body again. She could feel it too. With little hesitation, Luna took his head in her arms as he fell back, his head positioned comfortably on her abdomen. She brushed his hair to the side as his tired body sank into a deep slumber.

16

The next day, Clover and Beatrix pranced about the woods a bit further than they should have. It wasn't the idea of being in the woods that was exciting, but being somewhere where they were told not to go, passing the invisible boundary, that gave them the thrill they desired. The girls pushed past each other and swung small sticks in the air, wielding them like long swords.

"Oh, come on, you want a piece of me? Huh?" Clover said through a grin, her lanky limbs and frizzy hair bouncing back and forth as she avoided Beatrix's advances. "Come on then, tough guy! Come on!" she flicked her stick in the air, gesturing for Beatrix to attack. Bea bit her lip as she lunged forward. Clover stepped to the side and whacked her friend in the ankle with one swift motion.

"Ow!" Beatrix shouted. "Watch it!"

Clover shrugged. "What's that saying Musgo always says… play with the bull, get the horns?"

Beatrix spun around and swung at Clover some more. "I never asked to play with a bull! You just gave me this stupid stick and started hitting me!" She gave one last mighty swing before she tripped on a root, somersaulting into Clover, knocking the two of them down.

Clover tossed the sticks aside with a smile and looked at Beatrix. Bea stared back with a certain wonder in her eyes. The two of them shared the quiet moment until Bea turned her head to the side. The entire setting seemed to change for the two girls in an instant, the place of wonder transformed into that of a nightmare as Beatrix let out a blood-curdling scream.

Clover jumped up and leaped back as she too saw the two filthy men standing awkwardly before them, half-hidden behind a large oak. One of them stood behind the other, his hands bound with wire that cut into his wrists, dried blood encircling his restraints, his eyes black and blue, his nose slightly out of place. The other man stood forward; he held the wire firmly in his hands like a leash. His hair was long and damp. He had a bleak complexion and eyes that seemed dead.

With no hesitation, Clover grabbed Beatrix by the collar and yanked her to her feet. Beatrix threw her stick at the two men as she turned to run. The man in front deflected the stick with his arm and turned back to watch the girls as they dashed through the woods, screaming as they went. The two men exchanged glances and continued to push forward.

"Clover, what—what was—" Beatrix tried to talk in between breaths, but Clover yanked her harder.

"Just run, Beatrix. Those were Former. They've come here for us!" she said, exhausted.

The two of them broke out into the center of the community. Clover caught her breath and let out a heart-stopping shriek. "Former! The Former are here!"

Everybody turned their heads. Sterling was the first to approach her, a rifle slung over his shoulder. "This better not be one of your games, girl, or I swear I'll—"

Beatrix piped up, "I swear, I swear they're right—" by the time she had spoken, other followers had poked their heads out of their huts.

Sterling looked around at the eyes that had accumulated. Soon Tobias was walking toward them, pulling a shirt over his head.

"What is all this?" he asked.

Sterling sighed, "Little girls think they saw a Former. I don't buy it. You know how they play their games."

Tobias glanced at Beatrix and Clover, taking note of the fear on their faces. "Game or not, the least we can do is look."

Sterling shrugged. "So be it. Gives me something to do."

Before the two of them could even take a step in the right direction, the two men walked out of the brush and into the open. Beatrix screamed and grabbed at Tobias's shirt. Gasps could be heard from all around as the two zombified creatures came into view. Sterling pointed his rifle at them and barked the first order that came to his head.

"Hands! Let me see your hands!" he yelled in his signature raspy voice.

The one with bound wrists raised his mangled hands in the air. The one who held the wire in his hands stuck his arms out to the side. "I'm afraid I can't do that, friend."

Sterling slowly lowered his sight as he glanced up at the man who had just spoken. "Benji?" The name seemed to fall right out of his mouth like the whisper of a legend.

The man holding the wire leash lowered his arms. "Quite the welcoming committee."

Benji brushed his long dirty hair over his ears and began to walk forward. His step carried with it an old-school swagger; time seemed to stand still. "I have a lot of explaining to do, friend."

Sterling held his rifle close. "Stop. Don't move."

Benji froze in his tracks, a slight smirk on his face. "Fair enough. Who do I have to talk to?"

Sterling began to show the cracks within his stoicism. "Are you being followed? Where is everyone else?"

Benji held his hands out in surrender. "Nobody else, friend. I knew how to get back by following the river. Once I saw Otto's cove, I knew I was home."

Sterling anxiously looked around at the various sets of eyes that were now on them. "Just—just stay back. Felix'll decide what to do with you. He came down from the mountain to check up on the others."

"As I said," Benji stated, taking a step back, "fair enough."

Tobias stood still, his gaze set on the prisoner bound with wire. Their eyes met with immediate familiarity. Benji noticed his gaze and nodded toward Tobias. "Tobias."

"Benji," Tobias spoke without taking his eyes off of the prisoner.

Within seconds Felix and Dante rushed toward the center square, both donning their purple robes, a small yellow armband on Felix's cuff to differentiate him from any normal Disciple. Dante rushed up to Benji and touched his face, wiping some of the dirt away from his eyes.

Felix rushed to the other man and looked him up and down before taking a few steps back. "So it is true…" he said, noticing that the other community members were starting to peer out of their huts.

The prisoner shrugged, "What would that be?"

Felix straightened his posture. "You found them, the Former."

The prisoner smiled, "Alive and well, Felix."

Felix looked toward Dante. "Get this man out of my sight," he stated.

Dante approached Benji, who held the wire that kept the prisoner captive. He grabbed the leash and tugged the prisoner away from Benji and Felix.

Felix walked over to where Benji stood. "You have some explaining to do, Benji."

Benji nodded, "Aye, I figured as much."

Felix looked him up and down with skepticism. "But first," he said, raising his voice so that the others could hear him, "somebody get this man some bread and water!" he called out. He looked back at Benji. "You must be exhausted. Come, I'll get a fire started."

Benji smiled, "I was afraid I had lost you all for good. Thank you, Felix. What about Samuel?"

Felix raised his eyebrows. "We'll figure that out. We've got a lot of catching up, you and I."

Benji nodded as he aggressively shook Felix's arm. "I see the robes; congratulations. Since when do they keep the high Disciple off the mountain?"

Felix rolled his eyes with a heavy sigh. "Since trouble showed up. Go get cleaned up. We'll speak later."

Orwell snatched the wire from Benji's hands. "I'll take care of him," he said, immediately walking back out toward the woods.

Felix wrapped his arm around Benji as they began to walk toward his hut. Benji stopped abruptly. "If um… if I could have some final words with Samuel?"

Felix rubbed him on the shoulder. "You'll have your chance to speak with him later. We must get you cleaned up first."

Once again, he stopped in his tracks. "If you don't mind, I'd like to find someone first."

Felix shook his head, "Of course, what am I thinking? Go! See who you need to see."

Benji turned around to see Tobias, still standing where he stood minutes before. "Everything all right, friend?"

Tobias looked at him with a brow furrowed by confusion. "Maybe you could tell me."

Benji walked up to him and wiped sweat from his forehead with his tattered sleeve. "Everything's better now… I'm home," he said with a wide-eyed smile.

Tobias watched as Benji happily shuffled toward Luna's hut. He then looked over to Felix, who was showing all of his excitement in telling other followers of the good news.

Benji pushed past the canvas of Luna's hut. He stepped into the room and immediately took notice of the man in her bed. Ray sat up and blinked himself awake. "Hey, can I, uh—can I help you?"

Benji looked around the room, confirming little details with himself. "I'm looking for Luna," he said plainly.

Ray tried to sit himself up a little straighter. "She should be right back, she was just—"

Before he could finish his sentence, Luna pushed past the entrance and immediately froze in place. She looked Benji up and down before throwing herself at him and wrapping her arms around his neck. He reciprocated her actions as they held each other in a strong embrace for what seemed to be minutes.

When they separated, there were tears in her eyes, but her face still seemed to be held in disbelief. "I thought… they told me…"

He grabbed her by the face and pressed his forehead against hers. "I'm not. I thought I was for—for a long time, but… but I'm not."

She grabbed his face as well. "What now? What happens now?"

He took a step back and shrugged. "They say they want to talk to me, hear my story. They may even bring me to Elliot."

Her eyes widened with her smile. He was exactly how she had remembered him.

"Looks like you've got a story to share as well," he muttered.

She turned to Ray, who watched the entire encounter in silence. She touched Benji on the back and smiled as she looked at him. "Benji, meet Ray. Ray… Benji."

He nodded to the filthy man as he stood limply in the center of the room. "Pleasure," he muttered, still off-put by his presence.

Luna took a deep breath in. "Benji is… *Benji is my brother.*"

Benji looked him in the eyes. "Pleasure is all mine, friend."

17

Benji took a seat by the small fire in the center of the hut. He gently took the bowl of water from Luna, who dashed about the hut trying her best to show every relic of hospitality she could muster. Ray leaned onto his crutches as he eased himself off of the bed and examined Benji, who sat still, slowly munching on a carrot. "Can I get you something more to eat? I can run to Maple, see what she's got in the greenhouse?"

Benji shook his head. "Not necessary, Loon. Can't eat too much too fast. Last thing I need is a belly ache," he said with a cheerful wink that Ray didn't know what to do with.

Luna sank to her knees as she began to wipe away the dirt on his face. "You're all skin and bones, Benji…"

"That's what happens when you starve, Loon," he said calmly.

She sat back, her eyes wide. "So it is true… the rumors."

He shook his head. "Still blows my mind how fast rumors run around here."

She continued to wipe away at his forehead. "They're all talking about it by the altar. Everyone. They tried to keep it quiet, but… is it true? Samuel?"

He nodded his head. "Wish it weren't. They're real. They're all real. The Former are somewhere out there," he said, nodding toward the exit. "Thriving among the trees."

She stopped mopping up the dirt again, entranced by his words. "What did they do to you?"

He winced as he took the cloth from her and began to clean himself. "I wouldn't dare tell you half of it, Loon. Some details are best left alone."

"I'm sorry—" Ray muttered, cutting in. "But I'm trying to piece things together here and—"

"Trust me, friend," Benji said. "You're not the only one."

Luna got to her feet and began to pour fresh water into the bowl. "I can explain everything later, but… I suppose we begin with the divide."

Benji finished wiping the muck out of his eyes and glared at Ray with a silent intensity. "Ah yes… the divide. *The great divide.* The most significant event to ever affect the least significant people."

"We really don't have to get into this right now if you don't want to," Luna said solemnly, returning to his side.

"Nonsense," Benji choked as he crawled to the exit and reached his hand out into the open world, pulling back in a dried stick. "Never a bad time for a bit of history." He snapped the stick into smaller portions until there was a variety of uneven wooden chips.

"What's all this?" Ray muttered, carefully eying Benji as he sat on the floor, picking apart the stick.

"It's not about what it is… it's about what it was," Benji said with a hefty dose of mystery.

Ray rolled his eyes, "I'm tired of all the metaphors. A simple explanation will do."

Benji nodded, "An explanation *will do*. But a story? A lesson? *That'll stick*."

Luna squatted down next to Benji and nudged him in the shoulder. "Get on with it then."

Benji let the wood chips fall to the floor. "This *was* a living thing. This was a tree. It was a functioning part of the ecosystem around us. But things happen, and certain parts of the ecosystem are rejected, dried-up sticks and branches. This is us," he said, circling his finger around the small pile of woodchips. "We're the rejects. We're the dead stick."

Ray watched as Benji carefully swept the chips into a neat pile. "The rejects got together one day and said, 'Fuck it, we're on our own. We don't like the world we live in, we can't change it, so let's make a new one, away from the chaos.' That's Corazon, a world hidden from the sin of the modern world."

"Hmm," Ray mumbled. "Wasn't hidden that well."

Luna shot him a dirty look, and he pulled his attitude back in. "You said you wanted an explanation, so behave like it."

Ray nodded, and Benji continued. "But the new world isn't cut out for all of us. Certain people disagreed with the word of Elliot. This man took us and gave us food, protection, freedom. He rid our community of sickness and disease. The power that he has, the grace that radiates from his ever-generous soul is… it's blinding. And some were intimidated." Benji's voice grew more spiteful as he took his finger and drew a line through the chips, separating them. "Some disagreed with the way things went. Some thought things were unfair, that we should live in a democracy." Benji eased back, seemingly pleased with his analogy. "Ya see, friend, sometimes the branch misses the tree."

"What's wrong with a democracy?" Ray said, unsure of what sort of reaction to expect.

Benji smiled and looked up at him. "There's no such thing as a democracy with God."

"So Elliot's a God now?" he asked with a hint of sarcasm.

"Ray, stop," Luna ordered.

Benji moved forward a bit as if he were anticipating something incredible. "You ever seen a man heal a broken arm in a matter of seconds? You ever seen someone cure sickness in the blink of an eye? Make it seem like it never even happened? You know there is something special about this place. You can feel it, I know you can. You're just too scared to admit it." Benji's glare seemed to cut right through him; finally he saw some resemblance between the two of them. "When you see these things, and know the sort of power he wields, you give him what he wants. You ask me if Elliot is a God? Wait until you see him, wait until you feel his presence, then you'll know."

There was a thick silence following his poor explanation. Benji's hands trembled with something between excitement and rage. Ray took a deep breath. "So this is the great divide? The others left?"

Luna spoke up. "They weren't just others. They were brothers, sisters, mothers, fathers, lovers. They were family. And when a family splits, it's never easy. They were former members of our family, they became The Former."

"How many were there?" he asked.

She closed her eyes. "Some say forty, some say sixty. The total number isn't really clear anymore. It all happened so fast."

Ray shrugged. "And what—they just left? Went back to the real world?"

Benji shook his head. "They were rejects, outcasts. There was no world for them to go back to. But they couldn't stay here. They couldn't be under Elliot's protection anymore. They had to leave."

"That's it then? They just left?" Ray asked, still confused.

"More like… sent into exile. You can't survive on your own out there. Not without proper supplies," Benji stated plainly.

Ray began to pick at a hole in the sheet, gradually pulling at the thick thread until he had something to grasp. "So what about you then? What's your story?"

Luna placed a hand on Benji's back and looked into his eyes. He glanced back at her and tried his best to form a half-hearted smile. "My story?" he said, looking back at Ray. "I was… I am a hunter."

Benji swept up the remaining wood chips and got to his feet with a grunt. "We had all just assumed that the Former were gone, wiped out without the protection of Mother and her true Prophet. It had been a harsh winter. There was no way they would have made it. There had been rumors, but… well, they were just that, rumors." He began to scratch at the back of his head as he began to pace the vicinity of the room. "We were getting short on meat, and sometimes the veggies just don't cut it. So I went out looking for a doe. Ended up getting hit over the head at some point… woke up as I was being dragged through the woods by our old friend, Samuel. My hands were bound, mouth gagged. That's when it all became real."

Luna stood and kept a gentle, comforting hand on his back. "We all thought they had died off," she said. "We didn't think there was any way they would have survived such conditions outside of Elliot's care. We're not saying that the people of Corazon are never wrong, but… this seemed like a safe assumption. They had no supplies, no gear. Is it true? Did they move underground?"

Benji separated from her and continued to pace. "No, they weren't underground, but they were safe. By the time we reached the outer limits of Elliot's realm, they had blindfolded me. As soon as we arrived, they kept me in a dark room but switched on these floodlights anytime they came in to feed or question me. The intensity of the bulbs alone was enough to keep me from trying anything."

"Lights? They kept you from retaliating with lights?" she asked inquisitively.

With a heavy sigh, Benji let his head hang low. "When you're kept in the dark, even a little bit of light is enough to blind you." He looked up at Ray, who kept a relatively blank stare.

"But here you are," he said as monotone as could be.

Benji smiled. "If I didn't know any better, which I don't, I'd say this sounds a bit like an interrogation, amigo."

Ray shook his head. "Just trying to put the pieces together is all."

Benji stood up and stretched. "That makes two of us then. A Disciple will be coming for me any minute now. They'll be wanting to hear my story too. But when I'm back? Then it's your turn."

Sensing the rising tension between the two, Luna cut in. "Listen, let's all just relax. There's a lot going on here. You—" she said, pointing to Ray. "You need more rest. You'll be back in the pasture come tomorrow. And—and you…" she looked over to Benji, who still lumbered back and forth where he stood. "You need to go see about where you'll be sleeping; after a month of you missing, Brooke may have taken over your hut, but I'm sure there is a vacancy somewhere around."

"Ahh, Brooke," he said in reminiscence. "I have a lot of catching up to do," he sighed.

There was a grunt from outside of Luna's hut. "Excuse me," Orwell said, poking his head into the room. "I hate to break up a reunion, but…"

Benji nodded and took a step forward. "Of course." He walked toward the exit and looked back toward Luna. "I'll come find you when I'm back. And Ray," he nodded his head toward Ray, who still sat on the edge of the bed. "I'm sure we'll find our time to chat as well."

Luna walked him to the exit and nodded her head, "Let me know what you need, and I'll have it arranged."

He smiled softly. "You're a saint, Loon." With that, he ducked under the canvas and was escorted by Orwell to further questions.

Luna took a moment as she faced the exit; she slowly turned to Ray, her hands held tight to her chest. "I suppose I should tell you a bit more about my brother."

18

Benji was there to stay. Within the hour, he had a hut prepared for him. His first few days were full of rest, but soon he was put to work, and his story was shared with the others. Most, however, were less concerned with his presence and more concerned with Samuel, the Former whom Benji had taken captive. Samuel spent his days roped to a dying tree, hidden amongst the tall wheat near the pasture. His presence raised questions as to the validity of their so-called safety. The Disciples, however, put the community's concerns to rest with a flurry of small feasts and shows put on by followers with a particular theatrical flair. All of it acting as the commune's bread and circuses.

Days seemed to fuse together as time dwindled on; nights crept so slowly they seemed to drag. Benji became more of a consistent presence, but it was in his absence where Ray seemed to learn the most. It was when both he and Luna were alone. He felt that it was the best time to try and weasel any sort of information out of her, yet she remained silent. She would only give enough to keep him guessing, saying things like *"I remember my mother's face, but the image of my father seems to be growing fuzzy."* and *"I used to love to read books.*

I would sometimes even sneak peeks at my dad's dirty magazines… You know, the ones he'd keep in the bottom drawer of his dresser…"

Tiny things like that were all he had to go off of. It was something, but barely. He put it together that she had a family, but what else? Her dad had a stash of dirty magazines; her mom loved to cook all the time. She liked to read, and she had a brother that she rarely talked about. Other than that, Ray had nothing. He wanted to know how she ended up here. He wanted to know why she abandoned everything. There were a few nights he actually heard her tossing and turning on the floor below him. She would wrestle with her inner thoughts. It was almost as if she were begging her nightmares to halt so that she may finally get a good night's sleep. He often considered waking her. It was actually painful to listen to. He was sure that she even began crying at one point. She would always apologize to someone right at the end of her nightmare, then it was all over, and he was left waiting on a verbal cliffhanger.

He wanted to tell her that he could hear her, but the information was too valuable. Plus, he himself suffered from the occasional night terror, visions of his family drowning in the toxic water he allowed to pollute his life. He would never want to embarrass her by bringing them up.

✳ ✳ ✳

Benji was a character, loved by those around him. Within time Ray understood why people seemed so happy to see him resurface. He would break into spontaneous dance. He would swoop into any conversation with a machismo flare. He would spark toasts and sneak winks in between words to passersby. He was a hot ball of energy during the day and a calming presence come nightfall. He would often establish his place around a fire by leaving either his knife or his jacket on the stump where he most preferred to sit, hours before the fire was even lit. He'd remain there, telling stories to both young and old followers, both equally as captivated by the way he phrased the most menial of tasks, molding them into something adventurous and otherworldly.

He became a presence, not only in the community but in Luna's life. Ray slowly grew accustomed to pushing his way into her hut to find Benji sharpening his knife or picking away at a meal he had reserved for himself at an earlier time. There was an inherent confidence that came with his presence, a look that he would give others, a *what are you going to do about it* type of gaze. Ray couldn't quite explain it, but it put added tension between Luna and him. Since the very moment he pranced into Corazon, Benji wasn't going to take a liking to any newcomers, especially one who had taken residence with his sister.

※ ※ ※

This tension, like many other things, seemed particularly prominent at night. Sometimes the two of them would lay awake in silence, not knowing that the other was even present. It was often a stormy night when this would happen; the lightning was usually blamed as the cause of their insomnia. They would just lay there thinking about the decisions they made that put them where they are right now. One night as they lay there staring up at the ceiling, a tired, slightly shaken Beatrix made her way through the flap of the hut and into their room. "Luna?" she whispered, almost afraid that she might wake her. "Luna, are you awake?"

Luna sat up quickly, spooked by the tiny approaching creature. It was difficult to hear her against the sound of the pouring rain and the crushing of nearby thunder.

"What do you want, Bea? Are you all right?" she said, flicking on a battery-powered lantern by her head.

Beatrix hugged herself and looked at her toes. "I had a nightmare again, Luna. The monsters, they came back for me."

Ray thought about what she was saying and how much more real it could be for a child being raised in the wild. When a child is raised in a suburban home, the idea of a monster spontaneously appearing under one's bed is ludicrous. But if you take that same monster and place it in the deep dark woods on a stormy night, it all becomes too real.

"Oh, honey," Luna said, opening her arms, welcoming Beatrix in for a hug. "Shhh. It's going to be all right, I promise you those monsters won't touch you. You're going to be just fine… shhhh, just fine."

Beatrix sobbed into her shoulder as Luna held her close, slightly rocking her side to side. "I think it's story time, Bea."

Her sobbing stopped almost immediately. Ray just watched, minorly entertained by the whole situation. Luna pulled Beatrix away from her body and looked her in the eyes. "Is that a yes for story time?"

Beatrix shook her head no, making it clear that she just wanted to be held. She definitely wanted a story, but even at thirteen, she was too proud to ask for a bedtime story in front of Ray.

"Well, hey, she may not want one, but I'd love to hear a story, Luna," he said, smiling toward Beatrix. Beatrix shot him a playful look and cracked a slight smile.

"Hey! Look at that! I saw that! You can't hide that beautiful smile from me!" he laughed as he pointed at Beatrix, who was now beginning to giggle.

"All right, all right!" Luna cut in, "Story time." She sat Beatrix back on one knee and ran her fingers through her hair. "Let's see here… How about the story of the Princess and the Farmhand?"

Beatrix's face lit up, but she tried her best to keep a cool demeanor. "Yeah, that should work."

"All right, then," she responded. 'Let's think. Where should I begin?"

"Wait," Beatrix said, sitting up. "Do you think maybe Clover can come listen? She has bad dreams, too, you know."

Luna seemed uneasy at the idea of inviting Clover into her hut. She looked at Ray with wide eyes, shocked that Beatrix would actually think to ask that of her. "Well, do you think Clover would even like the story? Don't you think she would prefer to… I don't know, dissect a worm or something?" she said with a certain sarcastic seriousness.

Beatrix seemed eager to get her friend into Luna's hut, despite somewhat knowing Luna was not okay with it. "Please, Luna? I really want her to hear this story!"

Luna threw up her hands in surrender, "Fine, she can listen."

Beatrix jumped out of bed and ran up to the flap of the hut, "Come on over!" she yelled into the night.

Within moments, a young girl with stiff brown hair and tattered clothes poked her dirty face through the entrance, peering around as if she were unsure as to whether she was truly welcome or not. Luna realized how senseless she was being, "Come on in, Clover. It's all right."

Clover made her way into the hut, looking at every crack and crevice in the rigid structure. "Hello," she said, unsure of herself. She looked up at Ray, realizing that the two had never actually met. They had only met within the stories Bea would share with her. "I'm Clover," she said, extending a hand for him to shake.

Ray smiled at her feeble attempt to be an adult despite being only a year or so older than Beatrix. He shook her hand, "The name's Ray. Have a seat, I hear it's story time."

Beatrix patted the spot right next to her on Luna's bed, signaling for her friend to come up. Clover wasted no time, quickly vaulting herself onto the mattress and snuggling up next to Beatrix. Their friendship was evident and true, a bond so bright it was blinding.

They all sat back as Luna began her tale. *"As all great stories start… There was once a young man who fell in love with a young woman."* Her eyes briefly met Ray's as she pretended to scan the room as if they were amongst an audience. "*He often saw her, and upon seeing her, would fantasize of loving her, running away and marrying her, having children, growing old, and dying alongside her as they each held each other's hand.*"

"*The beautiful part was that she, too, had feelings for him, although, just like all love stories, there were certain obstacles and difficulties placed in the way of their love. You see, he was a farm hand, and she was a princess, born of royalty. The young farmhand worked the land that her family ruled over. Every day she would look out from her terrace and watch as he worked away under the blistering sun.*"

"*The only person the princess loved more than him was her younger sister. Her younger sister was always standing by her side. She was her best friend, and nothing would ever change that.*" Luna glanced at Beatrix, who remained enraptured by her words, a wide grin spanning cheek to cheek.

"*One day, her sister grew frightfully ill, and nobody could figure out what was wrong with her. The king and queen sent for doctors near and far, but they all brought uncertain results and bad news. Nothing worked, and her younger sister soon passed away into the afterlife.*"

"*The farmhand saw how this affected the princess. She became very sad, grief-stricken in a way. She stopped coming outside and resting on her terrace, she stopped eating, and she stopped talking. She wanted nothing to do with anything. Her family begged her to stop mourning the loss of her sister, or else she too wouldn't be far behind, but it was no use. The only thing that would cure the princess was the return of her sister.*"

"*The young man decided he could no longer live without seeing her day to day. He couldn't stand knowing that she was suffering from such a loss, drowning in her own sadness. He approached the king and queen and told them that he would venture into the afterlife and save their daughter. The family thought he was unhinged. Nobody had ever gone into the afterlife and returned. The journey would surely claim him.*"

"But he saw the look in the princess's eyes when she heard that she might once more hold her beloved sister in her arms again. When he saw the happiness in her eyes, he had made his decision. He was going to go through with it. As a token of her gratitude, she promised the farmhand that if he were to make it back alive, she would gladly accept his hand in marriage so that they may finally live happily ever after."

"The next morning at sunrise, the farmhand made his way into the woods, where he ate fruit from a poisonous tree. He died within minutes and was pulled into the afterlife. He charged his way through the fiery depths of the evil parts of the underworld, which led him straight to the gates of heaven. Even the gates themselves could not stop him. Hope alone was what kept the young farmhand alive."

Ray looked at Luna with a wild eye; what kind of bedtime story was this? Traveling the underworld? This wasn't the requiem for dreams; it was the fuel for nightmares. She noticed his gaze and gestured toward Beatrix, who was now yawning as she lay curled up on the bed, her head resting on Clover's thigh, so she continued.

"These actions angered the angels. They wanted to know who this man was and why he felt that he could willingly tread onto their land uninvited. The angels could fly, and the farmhand was not yet an angel. They quickly caught up to him and chained him to a tree, demanding answers for his recklessness. When he told them why he had done all of this, they laughed at him. 'Why do all of this for a woman who you barely know?' they asked. "What makes you so sure she loves you?'

The man sighed and answered as honestly as he could. "I don't. But I can feel it. I can feel it when I look into her eyes, I can feel it when I catch her glancing at me from her terrace. I can feel it in my dreams when I think of her, and I truly hope she dreams of me, too. I don't know, but there is only one way to find out for sure."

"The angels talked amongst themselves and came to a decision. They would allow him to return from the afterlife with the girl, but he must

first carry her through the Devil's Desert, a desert in the afterlife rumored to be impossible to conquer. He agreed and was on his way."

Luna paused and looked to Beatrix and Clover, who were already sound asleep. "And I guess that's it."

Ray shook his head, "No, no, I refuse to let you leave me hanging, absolutely not. Finish the damn story," he demanded. She laughed and continued telling the story in a more dramatic tone.

"The man embarked on his journey with the body of the princess's sister slung across his back. He traveled deep into the Devil's Desert and battled scaly green creatures with horns on their heads and long, razor-sharp talons for fingers. He battled them all and was badly beaten and bruised. He bled, he cursed, he even cried, though he promised not to tell anyone about those parts. He carried the little girl on his back until they were safely back on Earth, where their souls were returned to their rightful bodies."

"As the farmhand returned to the castle to ask for the princess's hand in marriage, he looked up to her terrace and saw her standing hand in hand with another man. He hadn't realized how long he had been gone. It had been years now that he thought of it. It was wrong for him to believe she would have actually waited for him. He was crushed by this sight and didn't know what to do. Before he had time to act, he noticed a few of the angels standing behind him. They felt for him and asked him if he had any last wishes. He requested to watch one last sunset before he was laid to permanent rest. They gave him his last wish and accompanied him to his favorite hill. It was there, as he watched the sunset, the farmhand realized that he could never trust anyone as long as he lived, and well on through death as well. The end."

Ray's face was blank. It was as if he was shocked the story had ended on such a horrific note. "What the hell kind of a bedtime story was that, huh?"

Luna shrugged, "One that works," she said, gesturing toward the two girls who were fast asleep.

"But… aren't they supposed to have hidden meanings and make people happy? That story was so depressing, I mean… there's no redemption! The farmer boy literally dies for the one he loves, and she could care less. She just moved on, I mean… that's—bullshit! He did what he had to do! Who cares how long it took him!" he screamed through his breathy voice. It was quiet enough not to wake Bea and Clover.

"Ray, I tell her these stories because she needs to know that life is not all sunshine and rainbows. Not all stories have a happy ending. What, you wanted me to say they lived happily ever after? What happens in happily ever after? Do they have a kid? Do they ever fight? Do they ever mess up? All stories have to have an ending, and happily ever after isn't an ending; it's more of a beginning of a new tale of treachery than the ending of the one you just read. The more you think about it, happily ever after could mean the most tragic ending of all. What is a life without hardships? Without challenge? It's not real; it's not a life at all. We need pain, we need sadness. Without them, we're just an ignorant shell of a human being mindlessly wandering the earth in search of meaning. Before you know it, we're watching the sunset with the angels, perched atop a hill of our own, wondering what the next move will be. Will you be the one to fight on? Or will you surrender to the light of a new day?"

She shrugged. "Plus, as far as morals go, that story is the one to tell. She needs to know she can't trust people. She needs to know that there are nasty, horrible beings out there that are existing only to hurt her. She needs to know these things. I put them in a sugar-coated fairytale to hide their ugliness so that it doesn't come as a surprise to her when she figures it out for herself!" All of a sudden, the story made so much more sense. "It's all about preparing her for what's to come," she continued.

"And what's coming, Luna? Because literally everything that's happened to me in the past few months has been a shock to me, so if you think you know what's coming or if you have some ability to predict the future, please... I'm all ears."

"I don't know what's coming. Nobody does. That's the scariest part, but that's why we prepare. That's why we pray; that's why I exercise. That's why you stockpiled money and bought yourself a cabin far, far away. We don't know what's coming, but when it does, we can only hope to be prepared."

19

Beatrix panted as she frantically dashed through the woods ducking under the low-hanging branches and hopping over the exposed roots. She tripped on an out-of-place stone and dug her heel into the ground, catching herself before she fell. She then poked her head up as if she were a meerkat, listening for any signs of danger. She kneeled on the earth, her posture ever so straight, listening quietly for what was about to come.

She began to grow anxious and began running some more, this time with a bit more enthusiasm and laughter. She tripped again but quickly scurried around the broadside of a thick, sturdy tree like a paranoid squirrel. She pressed her back up against the tree, huffing and puffing away in between two big, red, rosy cheeks.

"Gotcha!" yelled a young girl as she sprung herself out of nowhere and latched her hands onto Beatrix's arm. Beatrix screamed and tried to pull herself away but ended up tripping over herself once more, just to have the girl land on top of her. The two of them scuffled around in the dirt until each of them was thrown back onto their butts. They looked at each other with dead leaves in their hair and patches of dirt littering their faces and laughed. They laughed so hard they ended up toppling backward and making "snow angels" in the leaves underneath them.

After the two of them were thoroughly tired out, they turned to each other and smiled. Both of the girls were missing some teeth, and both of them found that equally as funny. Their giggles were so innocent, so pure, so childish in their nature. "If I were a bear," Clover huffed, "you would be dead right now," she said in between deep breaths.

"Not if I was invisible!" Beatrix replied with a sly smile.

The two girls laughed some more and then eventually calmed down and looked up at the pink-streaked sky through the dark branches that acted as cracks on the window they peered through. Beatrix held up her arm, which had a small beaded bracelet dangling from her wrist. "I love it," she said in a genuine way.

Clover then held up her arm, which showed the exact same bracelet with green and blue beads. "You better! They only took me like… two hours each!"

"Okay, I don't love it *that* much!" The two girls then giggled a bit more.

Beatrix joked around, but she had something on her mind, and Clover could tell. "What's going on with you today?" she asked.

Beatrix grew quiet. "What do you think they're gonna do with the monster?" she asked.

Clover took a moment to catch on, "The man Benji brought in?"

Beatrix nodded.

Clover sighed and looked to the sky. "They say he's a Former. I don't know about all that, but whatever he did was bad. You're sure it was him that you saw?"

Beatrix once again bobbed her head up and down. "I swear it was him. He'd always just… look at me. You think he's dangerous? You think he's as bad as they say?"

"I don't know. But he's all locked up now. He can't do anything to hurt you," she said plainly. The worrisome look grew deeper as Bea sat with her thoughts. Clover quickly changed the tone. "What else is going on? You seem sad."

"Nothing. I just don't get why people have to be so mean."

"Who was mean?"

"Just… people."

"Yeah, but what people, Bea?"

Beatrix sighed out of frustration. "Just people, okay!"

Clover decided to back off a bit. "What makes people so mean?"

"They just like to make fun of me, is all. They tell me I'm ugly, and that's why none of the boys want to kiss me."

Clover sat up and leaned on her elbows. "Just because they say that doesn't mean you have to believe them, Beatrix! You're really pretty!"

She looked over to Clover with a melancholic expression, "Swear?"

Clover smiled. "Swear."

"So why don't they want to kiss me? I try to be nice, I try to give them nice things. I made Ricky an action figure I made out of sticks, and he just laughed and stomped on it until it broke. Then everyone else laughed at me and—well, it makes me feel all weird inside when they do that! I'm not a mean person; why do they wanna be mean to me?"

"Ricky did that to you? Bucktooth Ricky? Squirrel mouth Ricky?" Clover said, trying to make Beatrix laugh. When Beatrix began to giggle, she tried her best to keep it up.

"Sticky Ricky? Picky Icky Ricky? No. He has no friends. Don't waste your time making an action figure for a boy like that. He's not worth your time. Bea, you need to be whoever you want to be. That's when you'll be the happiest."

"But if I make myself more pretty then—"

"No, cut that shit out," Clover said in a scolding manner. Beatrix gasped at her use of language. Clover rolled her eyes and tried to hold her foul mouth in. "I'm just trying to show you that you don't have to be what everyone else says you have to be. If you want to be a hunter, be a hunter, and be good at it too! Look at Luna! Use her as a role model!"

"Luna is pretty cool."

"Ya see! And being cool isn't the point. I like dead things! I like seeing how the body works, that's why I like to play with all of the skeletons I find out here, I think that kind of stuff is neat! I like hanging out with you because you're not mean about it either. Do you see where I'm going with this?"

Beatrix seemed lost, "What do the dead animals have to do with any of this?"

Clover sighed and then began to giggle. "Don't change anything about yourself, Beatrix. You're perfect. Okay?"

The sun was setting and the wind began to pick up, blowing the dead leaves out of the girls' hair. Beatrix looked toward the sunset and sighed, "I still don't have my first kiss, though. I wanted to kiss Ricky, but he just… well he broke the action figure I gave him."

Clover coughed and whispered *squirrel* in between her breaths. Beatrix began to smirk. "What's the big deal? I haven't had my first kiss yet, either."

"You're only a year older than me. Plus, you don't even like boys. You told me yourself."

"So… I still haven't had my first kiss. Plus, you don't want to kiss Icky Ricky. He'll probably gnaw your lips off with his buck teeth. You should kiss someone who you genuinely care about. Don't waste it on some… loser."

"I know, I know that's what Luna said too…"

Clover looked over to Beatrix through the corner of her eyes. "It should be something where it's just sort of a spur the moment thing, I guess, you know?"

Beatrix shrugged. "No! I don't know! That's the problem here. How are the boys going to like me when I don't even know how to kiss them? I don't even know what else to do."

Clover got to her knees with anger. "You can color, you can swim, you can cook, you can garden, you can hunt, you can gather, you can worship, you can do literally anything else any boy can do except pee standing up! Do you understand me?"

Beatrix tried stifling a giggle.

Clover looked somewhat angry. "What? What's so funny, tell me!"

Beatrix took her hand away from her mouth, "I can pee standing up, I'm just not very good at it."

The two tried to hide their laughter the best they could, feeling that they were too mature to laugh at such childish jokes, but they eventually both broke out in unison. They calmed themselves and watched the sun. Clover looked to Beatrix, who remained mesmerized by the glowing ball of fire that seemed to almost present itself to her. Clover then took a moment to think, then leaned over to Beatrix, grabbed her by the chin, and quickly gave her a peck on the lips. It was so fast Beatrix barely had time to react. Her eyes widened as she remained looking forward, and Clover eased back to where she was before she made her bold move.

Beatrix's cheeks grew almost as red and as rosy as when they were playing hide and seek an hour earlier. "Huh," she said to herself, having had her curiosity piqued. "So that's what my first kiss will be like?"

"Yeah," Clover said, feeling somewhat embarrassed, "something like that." She then turned to Beatrix with an honest smile. Beatrix took a moment and then returned the smile.

"Come on," Clover said, standing up. "We need to get back before it gets too dark."

Beatrix took Clover by the hand and used it to pull herself up as well. The two began to walk with the red glow of the setting sun on their backs. They walked in silence for a while, just admiring their surroundings and the way the bugs would click and hum right before springing themselves from the ground to find a new resting place for the night.

"Thanks for being my friend, Clover."

"You got it, Bea. You got it."

20

Samuel silently squirmed about in the tall grass off to the side of the pasture. The sun had almost set, and he could feel the cold sweat of night creeping its way down his spine. He felt the cord that kept him tethered to the tree rub his skin raw, but he continued to move every which way, just hoping for some sort of miracle. Every other noise posed a threat, whether it was another Disciple attempting to draw information out of him with a fusion of knuckles and slurs or an animal looking for prey that couldn't fight back.

It had only been a week since he had been dragged into Corazon, but he knew he wouldn't see another. The glares from the other community members alone were enough to draw blood. There was a clear and present rustling amongst the wheat. Something was drawing closer, but it was hesitant. It sat there, waiting for night. He continued wrestling his restraints.

Eventually, the sun set, and the only glow of light was from the communal bonfire in the distance, the smell of roasting venison drifting through the air, tempting him with what he could not have. Still, a being lurked somewhere within the brush, motionless, silent. The only sounds to emanate from the general direction were that of the crickets and the occasional whoop or holler from somewhere around the bonfire.

Samuel didn't breathe. He just sucked in quick mouthfuls of air, hoping that it would do something for him without alerting whatever it was that had its eyes on him. Finally, it began to move, creeping along the earth's floor until all that was left to cover was the clearing he sat on. He closed his eyes and clenched his fists, knowing that nobody would think to respond to his screams.

The figure came forward and stood up with a grunt, letting his hair fall to his shoulders. A much cleaner, healthier Benji stepped into view. He brushed his clothing of dirt and looked Samuel up and down. Samuel let out a deep breath and let his head fall back against the bark. "That was you the entire time?"

Benji nodded. "Aye, I had to make sure nobody was gonna pay ya a visit, friend."

Samuel sucked in air from his nose and shook his head. "Dante came by this morning. Gave me the shiner," he said with a half-cocked smile, commenting on the bright purple color of the left side of his face. "Then one of the other Disciples came. Got a cup of beans. That was before sundown," he said, shaking his head again.

Benji nodded, biting his lower lip. "I just need a little more time to sort things."

"I don't have time, Benji. Look at me," he hissed. Benji solemnly nodded his head.

He stepped forward, "I just gotta get in good with Sterling again. He doesn't expect anything yet, none of them do, except maybe Tobias, but I can deal with him. They're all on edge about this new guy. It's a whole story."

"I don't care about any of that shit," Samuel spoke.

"We need the guns, Samuel. We can't take Corazon without the guns. Once Sterling puts me back on the hunting team, I'll tail him and figure it out, but you can't rush this sort of thing," Benji pleaded.

"*Fuck that,*" he spat, leaning forward as much as his restraints would allow. "I just want to know how she is. I want her safe. I want her out of here."

Benji's eyes widened as he held his hands in front of him as if to make a game-changing business pitch. "I know that's all that you're worried about, but it's too soon. I need to be more established before I can cover for you. You move too fast, and they might suspect I was in on things, and then the whole plan is wasted."

"Hey," Samuel said, his tone getting more desperate. "You know they're gonna kill me, right?"

Benji shook his head. "We always knew that was a possibility."

"Fuck possibility." Samuel began to tense up. "It was a bad plan from the start, Benji. They're going to kill me soon. I haven't given them anything they want, and for what? So you can just—just catch up with some old friends? I don't have long as it is…" he sighed, defeated. "At least give me the closure of having her safe. That's all I have ever asked."

"I know, friend."

"I'm not your friend. I'm your pawn," Samuel shot back.

Benji had had enough. He tossed his arms in the air and stepped back. "What? You think it was me that gave ya the tumors? Think it was me that got ya sick? I had nothing to do with any of it. I just pitched the plan!"

"Then follow through with it!" he said, growing more impatient with every passing moment.

"Look!" Benji shouted a bit too loud. "I wasn't the one who got spotted in the first place."

"You weren't the one that left your pregnant wife behind!" he replied.

"*I wasn't the one who decided to leave her behind!*" Benji said, beyond frustrated. The two remained in sorrowful silence for a moment while they caught their breath. "Samuel," he said, sounding defeated. "You know I respect ya, but if you think you're gonna just pick her up and walk out of Corazon, you're just plain insane, friend."

Samuel looked up to him with a tear-streaked face. "If not now, then when?" he asked, disgruntled.

"How about when there are fewer people? If one person screams, you'll have the whole community on you like rabid animals. I don't know how many more times I can say this, but we just need more time," Benji frantically explained.

Samuel's eyes narrowed. "You know you wouldn't have gotten back in so easily if you didn't have me leashed up. I don't have long as it is. And you know you owe it to me to let me try."

Another silence ensued, the crickets and fire talk still present. "I'm sorry, friend. I promise I'll keep an eye on her."

"That's not good enough," he replied.

Benji began to get irritated again. "You're real stubborn, you know that?"

"*You're not the one tied to a fuckin' tree,*" Samuel said in return.

Benji began to pace back and forth, as he often did under times of pressure. He whipped out a knife from his waistband. "You wanna get it over with then?"

"Benji," Samuel scoffed.

"I'm being serious. I'll make it quick. It'll be more humane than what they'll do to ya for sure," he sighed. "You know this isn't what I want."

Samuel shrugged as best he could. "I'm sorry, but you're not getting out of this that easy."

Benji crouched down, holding the knife up near his ear as he cupped his face in his palm. "You really want to go through with this?"

Samuel took a deep breath in. "If it means getting her out of this hellhole."

Benji looked up from his palm. The breeze began to pick up, pushing his hair back with the surrounding wheat. "You know if anyone sees you—"

Samuel nodded before he even finished. "As long as you're the one to do it."

Benji curled up a fist and smacked the dirt he knelt on. "So be it, friend." He stood up and walked to the opposite side of the tree, where the clumsy yet surprisingly strong knot in the rope remained tight. He began to pick away at it with his knife until there was enough of a gap to weasel his thin fingers into the loop. With a few brawny pulls, he was able to get it loose enough for the rope to fall to the ground. Samuel dropped to the ground and gently nursed the raw patches on his torso. Benji stood over him, a deep sorrow looming over them both.

"Here's what's going to happen," Benji said, trying to remain calm. "I'm going to go rest by the fire. My guess is she'll be in Luna's hut. She's been sleeping there the past few nights. Wait until everyone is asleep, then do what you've gotta do."

Samuel stretched out on the ground, enjoying the freedom while he had it. "Simple enough."

Benji shook his head, "It won't be if ya get caught."

"Yeah, yeah, yeah," Samuel huffed. "You go do your thing."

With one last glance at a bruised Samuel, Benji turned and pushed his way into the field. "Benji," Samuel piped up, catching him before he left. "It was a shitty plan from the start—but thank you."

Benji nodded in his general direction. Samuel returned the nod and continued to stretch. Benji made his way back toward the glow of the bonfire.

❋❋❋

The flames licked up the length of the logs, which had been propped together to form a teepee. Around the fire sat large stones, which kept the curious from getting too close and provided an uncomfortable seat for those who needed the extra warmth. Benji slid his blade under his belt and casually strode into the common square. He immediately locked eyes on Beatrix, who remained captivated by the intense game of tic-tac-toe she had begun with Musgo. He sat in his designated seat, a dead log long enough for him to stretch out his legs. He used a stick to draw his sloppy O's in the dirt beneath him.

Beatrix eyed the field carefully as she navigated her best plan of attack. She hesitantly sketched an X in the bottom left square. Musgo chuckled to himself and quickly circled out his final O, which won him the game. "Five for five, little lady," he chuckled.

"You are *such* a cheater," she squealed.

"Hey now, don't hate the player, hate yourself for not being better than the player," he said with a wink. Beatrix held up a fist in front of her face as she scowled.

Benji stepped in. "Hey now, Bea, play nice," he said, patting her on the back. Bea was still put off by his presence, despite the fact that Luna personally vouched for him. "Musgo's had a lot more practice than you."

"Damn straight," Musgo whispered. Bea glared at Musgo. He smiled and stuttered. "I mean, darn straight."

She shot him a cheeky smile. "That's better."

Benji smiled and nudged her shoulder. "I hear Luna is looking for ya, dear."

Bea kicked around the dirt, blurring the game's results. "Fine, till next time, Musgo," she said with an adorable amount of intensity.

"See you then, Miss Bea," he said, humored by her overall outlook. He watched as Bea meandered her way in the general direction of Luna's hut.

"What have you got planned for the evening, friend?" Benji asked, looking toward Musgo.

Musgo didn't even look up at him; he just wisely stared into the distance. "Look at me, I'm well past my bedtime."

Benji tilted a metaphorical hat toward Musgo, "Then have yourself a good evening."

Musgo nodded and rocked himself off of the log. He then shuffled toward his hut and retired for the evening. Benji looked toward the bonfire, succumbing to his desire to rest. He found a hefty rock and leaned onto his knees, letting his head hang between his shoulders. Within moments he had drifted off, nothing but the flickering of the nearby flames to fuel his dreams.

His dreams were, however, cut short by the grunting of a familiar voice next to him. Tobias's knees cracked as he, too, eased back by the fire, his bristly face glistening with sweat. "Evening," he said, making it known that he was there.

Benji rubbed the exhaustion off of his face and looked around him. It seemed as though everyone else had retired for the night, though the fire still blazed on. "Ya scared me, friend."

"Couldn't sleep." Tobias groaned.

"Lot on your mind?" Benji asked.

Tobias nodded and looked at Benji through the corner of his eyes, "You could say that."

Benji pivoted to both face Tobias and have a better view of Luna's hut. "Correct me if I'm wrong here. But it feels like you've been a bit distant lately."

Tobias smiled, "What on earth would give you that impression?" he sarcastically asked.

"That," Benji responded. "That tone, that look, that overall feeling I get when you're around. What's going on here?"

Tobias chuckled, "The feeling is mutual, *friend*."

Benji leaned in, "Is there something you wanna ask me, Tobias?"

Tobias closed his eyes and took a deep breath as he set his gaze on Benji. "I wanna know why it took you two years to escape from the

Former. I wanna know where they are and why nobody else is asking themselves these questions."

"You sure this has nothing to do with your old friend I brought back on a leash? I already answered to the Disciples, Tobias. If you want to take it up with them, be my guest," he sighed, brushing away Tobias's concern.

"I side with the Prophet. Samuel was a good friend, but he turned his back on me when he turned his back on Elliot. And stop pretending like we don't remember who you were," Tobias growled through a closed jaw. "This humble little act might fool some people, but I remember that rambunctious asshole who was so full of himself he might as well declare himself a second prophet."

Benji nodded at his detailed accolades. "Well, that's quite the description. Seems like you filled my shoes pretty well, though," Benji whispered with a wink.

Tobias felt his temper spike. Benji noticed the movement of a figure creeping through the dark as he glanced over Tobias's shoulder. He immediately recognized the crippled silhouette as that of Samuel, who remained as light on his feet as he could.

"You better watch yourself," Tobias muttered, his fists now pressed down on his knees. "The Disciples aren't the only people who can make others disappear around here."

The blade holstered in Benji's belt felt particularly present in that very moment. He held his hands up to his face and gently shook them to mimic a fearful child. "*So scary.*"

Tobias was fed up. He got to his feet, "I'm done with this. Stand up."

"You sure about this, friend?" he asked, both amused by Tobias's machismo and skittish that his aggression would attract unwanted attention.

Before he could even get to his feet, a shriek erupted from within the woods. Tobias turned, startled by the scream. Benji, however, was already halfway across the main square.

21

Moments before the shriek, it was quiet. Ray mindlessly scratched at his leg as he navigated his dreamscape. Luna, curled up under several blankets, gave way to her exhaustion and enjoyed a deep slumber. Musgo had also managed to get some rest, his arm stretched out over Maple, who hid her exhaustion well.

Tobias sat angered by the fire. Benji poked and prodded at his fragile ego. Brooke lay awake, waiting for Tobias to return to his hut. Orwell sat quietly by the stoked flames in the Disciples' quarters, an old novel fraying at the spine pinched between his large fingers. Clover assembled small figurines using twigs and twine. She worked diligently by the lantern despite Willow insisting she go to bed. Beatrix remained curled up, just a few feet to Luna's side, though she wasn't fast asleep. She was instead wrestling with a nightmare. Samuel, newly freed, had made his way through the quiet of the community, his feet moving as quickly as they would carry him without causing too much of a stir.

He carefully peeled back the opening to Luna's flap and locked eyes on Beatrix, who gently turned over on her cot. He slid inside, kneeling down over Beatrix. He looked over her flawless skin and all her youth. His hands hovered over her body as he gauged the best way to go about lifting her from her cot. He inhaled as he gently slid his hands under her body and slowly leaned back, lifting her off of the cot.

Her body twitched awake as her head left the pillow. Without any hesitation, Beatrix let out a blood-curdling shriek and struck Samuel in the eye with her tiny fist. Samuel grabbed at his eye with a stifled grunt, letting go of Bea with one hand, leaving him only with a grasp of her shirt. His approach now seemed far less gentle. Ge pulled her toward the opening, but it was too late. Luna was already to her feet and launched herself at Samuel with all her might.

Samuel caught a shoulder to the gut and toppled backward, falling out of the hut. Luna grabbed hold of a sniveling Beatrix and pulled her close. By this point, Ray had swung his legs over the edge of the bed, and other followers had been startled awake, curious as to what and who the shriek was directed toward.

Samuel frantically scrambled to get to his feet, terrified of what would quickly follow. Luna's screams for help rang out faster than he could think as she looked up to the vent and screamed, "*Somebody help!*" while still cradling Bea in her arms. Samuel darted toward the woods just to see a good deal of flickering lights as followers held their lanterns up into the night. He turned around and sprinted in the other direction, dizzied by the intensity of the predicament. He caught a glimpse of an armed Sterling, trying to trace the origin of the scream, both groggy and excited at the thought of action. Samuel weighed his options and realized his chances of survival would fare better with the unarmed followers. He turned back toward the lanterns to see that he was now surrounded, each flickering cylinder of light drawing closer and closer with every passing moment.

His throat closed as an immeasurable panic sank deep into every pore on his body. His hand floated to his chest, where he hoped to feel his beating heart. Sterling now made it into the clearing, his eyes locked on him. An ample amount of light from the lanterns lit up the area. Samuel looked around at all the frightened faces and realized Sterling had no clear shot. He held out his trembling fists as he spun around, addressing each of the onlookers. "All right!" he shouted. "We've got you surrounded. Just let me go and nobody gets—" his panic deepened as he saw the disbelief in everyone's tired faces. "Just let me leave—just—just let me leave!"

He felt the flash of a hand land abruptly on his shoulder. Samuel frightfully spun around, his eyes wide, his mouth ajar. He looked at Benji, who for a moment wore an expression of guilt. Benji's hand remained on Samuel's shoulder, frozen in time. Samuel's shoulders relaxed, and his facial features softened. "Benji… we—"

Benji abruptly raised his hand above his head; his blade shone under the light of the lanterns. He instantly drove his blade deep into Samuel's chest. Samuel let out a muffled sound of surprise. Benji slowly relinquished his grip on his shoulder, letting Samuel stagger back as he looked at the knife sticking out of his chest. A dark red ring expanded under his already filthy shirt, he dropped to his knees.

Benji fell with him and eased him onto his back, placing his free hand on the handle of the knife. He leaned down so that his mouth was close to Samuel's ear. "I'll look after her, friend. That's a promise." He then tightened his grip on the handle and jerked the knife from Samuel's chest. Samuel's face eased into an expressionless stare. His breathing was jagged and raspy as the blood quickly pooled beneath him. Within moments the breathing stopped, and his hands fell to his sides.

Benji placed two fingers on his neck, confirming that Samuel was indeed dead. He then looked up toward the onlookers, who stared back with a concoction of fear and relief.

Benji stood up and faced the crowd. "Is everyone all right?" he asked boldly. Nobody said a word. Sterling stepped forward into the unplanned circle of people and tried to think of something to say to take control of the situation. Before he spoke, Orwell pushed his way into the circle and gasped at the sight before him.

He looked at Benji, who still held the bloodied dagger by his side. "Was this you?" he asked.

Benji nodded. "Afraid so. I heard Beatrix scream; I came over to find this one lurking around camp. Figured I'd put an end to it before any damage could be done."

Orwell nodded, "And Beatrix?"

There was a whisper that ran through the circle of followers. Finally, Tobias spoke up. "She's safe. The Former tried to take her. Luna stopped him."

Dante weaseled his way into the crowd as well, joining Orwell in the middle, his face barely changing upon seeing the tragedy. Orwell looked to Dante, who was known for his brash words. Dante groaned, "Well, what are you all waiting for? Back to bed!" he commanded.

Slowly they all retreated to their huts, unnerved by what had just transpired. "Good work, boy," Dante grunted as Benji walked by him. Benji nodded toward him, recognizing but not responding.

Luna was now outside of her hut, looking at what had transpired after her cry for help. Ray remained inside, consoling a shaken Beatrix. She saw Samuel's body lying in the distance, unmoving. She saw her brother, still clutching his knife by his side. She saw Tobias speechlessly lingering by the scene. She saw Dante and Orwell bickering as to how to proceed with the mess. She saw the passing followers; some seemed to be sick to her stomach. She wanted to go up to Benji and talk to him, figure out where everything got out of hand before an investigation ensued, but she didn't. She retreated to her hut instead, joining Ray in calming Bea.

"Sterling," Dante said. "Get this thing out of here. I don't care where you put it. I don't want the corpse smelling up my camp."

Sterling nodded and grabbed Samuel's corpse by the wrists. He then trudged backward, dragging Samuel's body with him. Dante set his eyes on Benji, who had yet to move. "Proud of you, boy. I had my doubts, but… welcome home."

Benji once again nodded; this time, a response seemed required. "As long as you know where my allegiance lies."

Dante nodded and looked to Orwell, who had been listening in. "The Prophet will be made aware of this. I'd imagine a reward will be in store."

Benji nodded and glanced at Tobias, who still remained present. The two Disciples slowly excused themselves and walked away, leaving the two men and the distant fire. Benji turned toward Tobias, knife still in hand. "I'm gonna ask you again. You sure about this, friend?"

Tobias's temper was no longer present. He seemed to be more lamb than wolf as he looked at Benji's knife, still glistening with blood. His head bobbed up and down. There were no more words to say. He backed away until he was no longer visible, leaving a distraught Benji alone with his conscience.

22

Tobias left his hut just as the sun was beginning to rise. Brooke remained fast asleep, hardly aware of what had transpired hours earlier. Orwell was also awake, stoking a fire in the common square, a pot of what would soon be coffee hung just above the smoke. He saw Tobias approaching and fashioned his face into something more somber. "Difficult times. I am sorry things went the way they did last night," Orwell said, folding his arms in front of him.

"Where is he? The body?" Tobias asked.

Orwell cleared his throat. "I'll be taking care of it later today."

"I'll do it," Tobias said.

Orwell raised his eyebrow. "You're on hunting duty today, are you not?"

He shook his head. "I've been needing a day off anyhow. I'll forfeit my portions for tonight. I just—really wanna do this."

Orwell slowly nodded, looking Tobias up and down. "Once a child of Mother, always a child of Mother, right?"

Tobias didn't say a word. He just waited for the clearance he needed. Orwell seemed intrigued by his desire to bury Samuel. "You and Samuel were close, weren't you?"

Tobias looked around to see if anyone had woken up yet. "Samuel died the day he turned his back on Mother and her Prophet. Call me old-fashioned, but I think a burial is better than letting his body wash away with the river."

The fire began to catch. Orwell poked at the embers a bit more. "You'll bury him deep enough so the bears don't get curious?"

Tobias nodded, "Of course."

Orwell jerked his head toward the woods. "You're a good man Tobias, you have my blessing. I think Sterling packed the better shovels in the shack near the pasture. We dragged the body out by the tree where we kept him."

"Got it," Tobias said, "Thank you, Orwell."

Orwell looked away. "If anyone asks, I'm going to say I did it."

Tobias forced a slight smile, "I'd expect nothing less."

Orwell turned completely toward the fire while Tobias jogged off into the woods.

The good shovels were right where Orwell had said, sturdy wooden handles and reinforced collars that accentuated the true strength of the pointed tip. Tobias took his business to the oak where Samuel had been tethered, the cord that bound him still encircling the tree. His body was just to the side of it, where the grass grew longer. It was drained of all color with sickly white skin and a filthy shirt stained a deep brown by the dried blood. An army of flies buzzed about as Tobias pulled Samuel's body out of the grass. He took the shovel and poked around, gauging where the softer earth was.

Finally, he found a spot underneath the early morning shadow of the oak, the grass still covered in dew. Without any hesitation, he perched his foot on the metal step of the shovel and leaned in. The blade slid cleanly into the earth; he leaned back and hauled a hefty load of soil off to his side. Then, one load after another, he began to dig.

As he slung the soil over his shoulder, he thought back to better days where Corazon seemed pure, and Samuel was more alive than ever. He was skinny but sprite and sprung around like a caffeinated jackrabbit whenever he got excited. Tobias thought back on the evening where Samuel seemed particularly riled up and how he leaped through the woods as they made their way to the cliff that they deemed the best for stargazing.

"What's gotten into you?" Tobias asked, humorously curious as to why Samuel couldn't keep still.

"Oh me? Just causing mischief and what not. You know the deal," Samuel yipped as he danced his way through the woods.

"Yeah?" Tobias replied. "What sort of mischief were you causing this time?"

Samuel spun around and faced him. He reached into the inner pocket of his light jacket and slid out a smooth, shiny bottle of wine. Tobias froze. Samuel lit up even more. "Looks like you've seen a ghost!"

Tobias pointed at the bottle. "You stole that…"

"Damn right. Swiped it from Orwell's little collection," Samuel boasted, holding the bottle up in the moonlight.

Tobias shook his head and tried to walk past Samuel, pretending as if he never saw the bottle in the first place. "If they find out, then… you'll be on shit duty for the rest of your time here."

Samuel tossed the bottle between his hands as he followed behind Tobias. "Looks like we'll have to get rid of the evidence then."

Tobias shook his head. "I don't want anything to do with this. I think Sterling is gonna ask me to join the hunters soon. No way I'm risking shit duty for a bottle of wine."

"Oh, so what?" Samuel chimed. "We're so far away they'll never think to look out here. Plus… there are worse things in life than emptying the waste barrels."

Tobias stopped and looked over his shoulder, "No, there isn't."

Samuel ran up behind him and spoke over his shoulder as if he were the patron saint of temptation. "Let's just take the night, get a little buzzed, spot a few stars." He could see he was appealing to Tobias's desires. "Then we sober up and head back like nothing ever happened! It's the perfect crime!"

Tobias's eyes rolled about dramatically. "The perfect crime is no crime at all. No risk of punishment that way."

"Mm-hmm," Samuel chuckled. "No chance at reward either. Look, I'm not asking you to curse Elliot's name, I'm asking you to have a drink with me. It'll be our secret. I promise I won't say a word."

The two were encroaching upon the cliff they used for stargazing. "Here," Tobias said, tossing Samuel the folding knife he had in his pocket. "Get the cork out."

Samuel's body tightened and spun about as he caught the knife. A smile spread from ear to ear as he wagged his finger toward Tobias. "I knew you'd come around. Corazon is great, but every society has its flaws," he winked.

Tobias shimmied toward the edge of the cliff and let his legs dangle freely. "I wouldn't consider Corazon flawed," he stated plainly.

"Oh yeah," Samuel stated sarcastically. "Women go up to the mountain to serve Elliot and the Disciples and never come back. Nothing strange about that at all."

Tobias shrugged, "You know the things he can do. I know you've seen it. There's a magic to this place, and if having Angels up on the mountain helps keep that magic, then so be it."

Samuel pulled the cork from the neck of the bottle with a satisfying *pop*. "There have to be better, less offensive ways of keeping the magic," he said, taking a generous swig of the wine and handing it to Tobias, who looked toward the night sky.

"There might be, but why risk it? We're protected, we're safe, we're happy. Why question what's going on behind the curtain?" Tobias muttered, taking a drag from the bottle as well.

Samuel's eyes widened as he reached for the bottle. "*Because there is something going on behind the curtain!*" he both shouted and whispered at the same time. He snatched the bottle and waved his hand about in front of him. "You're not curious? You don't ever wonder what happens? This is no way to live your life, Tobias. You need to constantly question the practices around you."

"I'm questioning your practices right now. Stealing? You're above that," Tobias said, changing the subject.

Samuel took another swig of the wine and toasted to the stars. "See, that's where you're wrong. I'm not above it. But you should be thanking me because if I were, we wouldn't have the wine, would we?" Samuel winked as he handed Tobias back the wine. Tobias cracked a smile and shoved him away after accepting the bottle, of course.

"You know…" Samuel muttered, angling all of his attention back toward Tobias. "You ever think this is just a phase? This whole holy community thing?"

"What do you mean?" Tobias asked, sounding more concerned.

Samuel sighed. "You ever think you'll eventually leave? Find a nice little home and a job that pays just enough? Start a family, send the kids to school, coffee every morning, and—holidays and birthday parties and—have other people around you? Get back to the way things were before we took up with Elliot?"

Tobias was now looking Samuel in the eyes, desperately trying to gauge whether or not he meant what he was asking. After a few moments, Tobias knew he didn't want to know the answer to that question. "This wine must be stronger than you originally thought, Samuel," he chuckled, once again handing the glass bottle back to him.

Samuel also began laughing, the two of them passing the bottle back and forth between each other for the next half an hour. Samuel remained quiet and redirected his attention toward the stars, a heavy unanswered presence looming over them the rest of the night.

Tobias leaned over on the shovel, exhausted. Layered rings of sweat on his shirt told him just how long he'd been at it. The sun was high above him, his head barely visible as he stood at the bottom of the deep hole he had spent the entire morning digging. Using the shovel as leverage, he hoisted himself out of the pit. The flies had since returned and were buzzing around Samuel's body. The unforgettable stench of death began to drift through the air.

Tobias pulled his sweaty shirt over his nose and approached the body. He untied Samuel's boots and set them aside. He then grabbed the cuffs of his pants and dragged him to the hole. With one mighty tug, he felt the weight of the body shift and collapse into the grave with a sudden thump. He fell back and caught his breath, having not been this tired in years. He took a moment to catch his breath and let the sweat dissipate from his brow. Then with a grunt, he got back to his feet.

He stumbled over to where he kept his bag. He opened it and rummaged through the contents. Within seconds he recovered a smooth glass bottle, the same bottle that had kept them mildly entertained years earlier. Tobias walked back over to the grave and looked down at Samuel, whose face no longer resembled the cheery-eyed, excitable man he once was. Tobias looked all around him to ensure nobody would be able to hear his brief eulogy.

He raised the bottle and opened his mouth, "To looking behind curtains." He then dropped the bottle into the grave and clasped his hand tightly over his mouth. He felt his emotions swell deep within him. His eyes welled up with tears, and his legs felt rubbery. He dropped to one knee and gasped, tears streaming down his face. His cries came out as an airy wheeze, too distraught to keep them in, too proud to let anyone hear.

"I'm sorry," he said, speaking softly over the grave. "I'm sorry," he repeated. He remained hunched over the grave for what seemed like hours. Finally, feeling a cool breeze at his back, he reached into the grave and pulled out his shovel. He shuffled over to the mound of dirt and took a deep breath. He then began to haul the soil back into the grave. Load after load, he slung it over his shoulder, burying his memories with him.

23

Recent events began to weigh down on Tobias like an inescapable fog. Everywhere he went, it would follow him, eating away at him from the inside. The look on Samuel's face as the life left his eyes. The rigid wall that had formed between Luna and him. The skepticism surrounding Benji and his sudden reappearance. The overall uncertainty in the atmosphere—it got to him. It penetrated his will like a razor and sunk deep into his bones. Later that evening, just as he thought his wounds would heal with Samuel's burial, Brooke tore them right open again, her hands dusted in salt.

"Are you sure? Are you absolutely positive? Brooke, this needs to be... you need to be sure," Tobias said, firm and quiet as he hovered over Brooke in the corner of her hut.

She swallowed and wiped the sweat from her forehead as she shook her head. "You just know these things, Tobias. If you were a woman, you would understand. I just don't know how—"

"I did everything I was supposed to do. *Everything*. Explain to me how something could have gone wrong!" he angrily whispered, not trying to alarm anyone at the late hour.

"Well... well, I don't know, I'm not sure... Maybe um... Maybe—"

"This isn't a time for a *maybe*. You need to be sure. Are you even listening to me?!" he asked, shaking her by the shoulders.

"Tobias, stop!" She began to cry. "You're scaring me! Please stop!" she begged.

"There's another man, isn't there? There has to be. You think you can fool me into thinking it's mine? Brooke, think about this, think about how this will reflect on me! This isn't the doings of a future Disciple." He had a wild shimmer in his eyes as he held her within inches of his face. "Now, I'm going to ask you one more time. Are you sure… *are you sure?*"

"I'm nine weeks late, Tobias, I'm having mood swings, I've lost my appetite, I feel nauseous every *fucking morning*… I told you, I'm sure. And it's yours! I haven't seen anybody else I prom—"

Tobias delivered a forceful slap to the side of her head, sending her falling to her knees, grabbing at her face, and sobbing to herself. "How could you be this careless? We're going to be the talk of the whole community. You know the rules! You *know* the rules! Think about it, Brooke! Use your head! It's been years since newborns have been allowed here!"

Brooke gripped her face and continued her sobbing, remaining strategically quiet. She wouldn't dare open her mouth. Tobias was at the point where he would do anything to turn her words against herself. There was nothing she could do or say to help her odds in this scenario.

Tobias paced the room for a few moments as he scratched at his head. "I just…" He let out a prolonged sigh. "We gotta get rid of it, Brooke, there's nothing else we can do."

Brooke turned a teary-eyed face to him, "No! We have to talk to someone! Maybe one of the Disciples could allow it! The community has been doing well. We even afforded to take in an outsider. We need to at least talk to someone! Tobias, please!"

Tobias turned to her. His face was beet red, and his fists were tight. "What? What, you don't think I want this? You don't think I want a little baby boy of my own? Brooke, I tried for years! Years Brooke! You know what I got from all of it? Nothing! Shit! You can't put this on me. I want to keep it, really I do, but we need to think practically here! We are sinning! We are supposed to be in control of our love! This is just pathetic! I can't—we can't be seen as sinners…"

Brooke saw the soft spot in him and decided to go for it, "Think about it… having a little kid of our own running around… It could be bad, sure, but what if they say to keep it? What then? We could have a life! We could raise a family right here." Tobias was getting more upset. He brought his hands to his face and wiped away the sweat and tears, the confusion of it all was too much for him. "Tobias, think about it! We could do it! All we have to do is—just ask them!"

He shook his head as he wiped at his nose, "It wasn't supposed to be like this. I want this to work. I didn't know it would happen. I just…" He became very still and buried his face in his hands as he thought for a moment. Brooke didn't know what was to come of this gesture. At this point, he could spike with rage or break down and cry. It was never a given when it came to his emotions. He wiped his face and pulled at his hair, contemplating his next move very carefully. "All right, I'll fix this. I'll um… I'll talk to Orwell. He's reasonable. I can go—*we* can go see him tomorrow morning about keeping it."

Brooke smiled and rose to her feet, "Thank you, thank you so much!" she hovered over to him in an attempt to hug him. She was rejected immediately as he stormed out of her hut.

He broke out into Corazon and hastily walked through the common area where Benji sat by a fire. He regaled a few curious followers with tales from his captivity as he carefully whittled away at a stick. Benji noticed Tobias and eyed him like a hawk as he strode past the fire. "Everything all right there, friend?" he asked with a flashy smile. Tobias glared at Benji and turned away, continuing into the woods. Benji seemed to warm himself with Tobias's frustration, knowing full well that he wasn't completely welcomed back yet.

❖ ❖ ❖

The sun rose just as bright as ever early that morning, and everyone was quickly going about their daily chores. Ray scrambled to get dressed while Luna prepared for another hunt. Ray had grown accustomed to the tending of the cattle. He now had a name for each cow and even a name for the newborn calf despite Brooke's warning. He pulled his shirt on and shot her a quick glance before leaving. "I'm off to work then, dear!" he chuckled as he ducked out of the hut.

Luna chuckled, "Well, be safe then, *sweetie*," she said in a mocking tone as she cleaned the barrel of her rifle. He smiled, though. He liked their little back and forth bickering. She enjoyed it too, to a certain extent, though not nearly as much as him. She felt as though his minor immaturity was due to him reacclimating to society. He was always able to talk, but knowing that he could now convey affection verbally was reassuring to her. He wasn't as broken as everyone had imagined.

Ray made his way toward the pasture giving a series of head nods and acknowledgments as he did. He had grown accustomed to the crutches and was able to move quite well with them. The community was really beginning to accept him. He was no longer getting the glares of anger or confusion that had once plagued him a little over two months ago.

"Morning, Brooke," he said as he plopped down next to a cow he called Betsy. He clumsily threw the metal milk pail underneath Betsy so that he may fill it with as much milk as he can.

"Ray," she said, making his presence known.

He positioned his leg so that he could have enough leverage to reach the utters and began the process. He looked over at Brooke, who was simultaneously working on another cow. "Everything all right with you, Brooke? Stop me if I'm out of line, but you've been different the past few weeks." He stopped, allowing her a moment for a response. She just continued working away on one of the larger cows in the herd. "How else am I supposed to know what happens around here?" he laughed, trying to elicit a response.

She shook her head, "I'm fine, I just have a lot on my mind." She picked up her bucket of milk and got up to bring her bucket to the tank on wheels. The tank was then transported to the pasteurizer. As she turned to get to the tank, Ray caught a glimpse of her face, which was slightly bruised.

"Wanna tell me about how you got this?" he asked, pointing to the side of his face where her bruise would be.

"Don't worry about it. It was just a stupid cow," she said, quickly covering it up with her hand.

He squinted as he tried to make out her injury a bit better. "Right… right, a cow." There was nothing else he could say. He knew she had been seeing Tobias. Everybody knew that. Luna claimed that he was using her as a way of taking out his anger and frustration. He always found a new girl whenever he was having a rough time, and she always ended up broken in some way, shape, or form. He was like an angered child with a porcelain doll. Everybody knew this. However, it wasn't right to make assumptions, and even if it were, they weren't to come from him.

"How has Tobias been?" he asked against his better judgment. Brooke's entire being was now focused on her work as she remained hunched over on her stool. He kept an eye on her as they sat there, sweating in the pasture. "You know, if you ever want to talk about—"

She sprung up with surprising ferocity. "Enough!" she yelled.

Ray looked around to see if anyone else was as alarmed as he was. There was nobody else in sight. He looked back toward Brooke, who seemed to fume as she remained planted in the earth before him. Her emotions were bubbling to the surface, but she choked them back with pure and simple labor. Ray nodded his head and turned back toward the cow. Brooke eventually relaxed her posture and crumbled back onto the stool. Both continued to work under the sun; nothing but the sound of the tiny pests hidden within the wheat could be heard.

❊ ❊ ❊

While Ray and Brooke sat in awkward silence, Luna strung herself up with a rifle and made a beeline for the hunting grounds. She met up with Tobias and some other men from the community in their usual spot—a little nook in the woods where the trees and shrubbery cleared. It was fashioned in a sort of circle where all of their hunts began and ended. They would run off and go about killing any animal they could find, then return back to that patch in the woods to skin and clean the animal of any unwanted parts. They did all of this in the woods, further away from camp to prevent attracting any scavengers or predators looking for their unwanted and tainted meat.

All of the hunters stood in their usual circle to prevent any mix-up with their stomping grounds. There was never any designated area assigned, but each of them knew they had a general place to be, and it was their job alone to be there when any game was present. They were all dressed in dark greens and browns, and they were each given a long strand of bright orange tape that they strung over one of their shoulders. This strand kept all of them from being too trigger-happy. If they saw the flash of orange, they thought twice before they pulled that trigger. They all knew that most, if not all, of the animals they took as prey were usually color blind.

Sterling was the self-appointed leader of the hunters. He was a man with practically no skeletons. People didn't know where he came from or how he got there, but he had been a member at Corazon for seven years. Some speculated he was just a hunter that was recruited for the sport of it all. He saw an opening to escape into a world of his own and took it. He wasn't like the others. He wasn't into religion or anything like that, the man just liked to hunt, and he was able to do that as much as he pleased in Corazon. He wore a great big bushy beard and had weathered down features. He was known as a no-bullshit kind of man. Nobody dared to cross him, as he was also rumored to have quite the temper. Hunting, however, gave him an outlet, so his self-appointment was never called into question.

"All right, gents… and Luna," he said, correcting himself. "The plan is simple today. Usual positions, I've set up some traps about a mile north, fifty yards before the rocks, so watch yourself. Check to see if I have anything if ya stumble across 'em," he looked around at everyone in the circle as they stood at attention. "And stay alert! I've seen some bear tracks out there lately. Just remember who's smarter and who's armed. Any questions?"

Everyone just stood around scratching at their chins and rubbing their eyes. "Remember, the bigger the kill, the bigger the portion. Good luck out there." With that, everyone was off. Luna darted into the woods with speed and agility on her side. She loved hunting. It was a way for her to combine her favorite activities and concoct a requiem for all she felt uneasy with. She had been hunting more and more as of late, and she was learning to hone her skills. She was never the best shot, but she was by far the fastest, and that's what she relied on. As long as she could get to the nearest water source before the others, she would have her pick of the litter.

The other men chugged along as fast as they were willing to go. "There she goes again, boys," laughed one of the men from the back.

"You laugh," Sterling said, "but she's been our most valuable asset for weeks now. I don't know what's gotten into her, but she's putting all of you boys to shame. Now, what are you waiting for? Split up! Don't let her make a fool out of all of you again!"

The rest of them mumbled and groaned as they began to pick up the pace, slowly fanning themselves out through the woods, streaks of orange ribbon danced through the brush. Tobias picked up his pace significantly, trying his best to stay light on his toes, afraid that he might spook his prey. He needed this, too. He had way too much on his mind and could barely focus at this point. The faster he ran, the harder he found it to breathe. The more he focused on breathing, the less he thought about Brooke and his possible baby. It made him sweat more than normal. He still had no idea what he was going to do. Before he knew it, he was running full force. Swinging his rifle back and forth to gain optimal momentum, he charged through the woods like a bull.

He could now hear the rushing water, and he was sure that he was in his sector. He was quickly approaching a few low-hanging branches and tried to duck beneath them. As soon as he cleared them, he tripped up on a root, sending his heavy body tumbling down the bank toward the river. *Whack!* His body tumbled into another human being as he was flung down the embankment. The other human grumbled and yelled as they were thrown toward the roaring water. "What the hell?!" the man said quickly, scrambling to his feet.

Tobias looked up from the running water and rubbed the little droplets into his eyes. Standing before him was Otto. He looked just as angry as he did confused. Otto stood above Tobias, looking down at him awkwardly. He brushed his long, wet locks of hair out of his face and then helped Tobias to his feet.

"What are you doing? Watch where you're going, why don't ya!" Otto yelled. "You scared Sarah half to death! She was about to kill you! You can't mess around like that! Not out here!" Otto screamed, scolding Tobias as if he were a child.

Tobias had been living on Corazon for a long time, and this was the most he'd ever heard Otto speak. "I'm sorry, Otto. I uh… Wait, who's Sarah again?"

Otto rolled his eyes, "The one that just had her hands around your throat!" he said, gesturing toward an imaginary figure standing next to Tobias. Tobias had forgotten how truly out of sorts Otto was. He remembered back to when Todd brought his brother Otto to Corazon in hopes that he could escape society. Otto never stopped talking about this woman, Sarah. He treated her like a human being even though she was just a mere figment of his imagination.

"I'm sorry, Otto," he said, picking up his gun. "I'll be more careful next time."

"It's not me you should apologize to. Look at her, she's all shook up."

Tobias looked at Otto and saw the sincerity in his eyes. He swallowed his pride because nobody else could see him and looked over to a mossy rock where he imagined Sarah would be standing. "I apologize, Sarah."

Otto stared at Tobias for a moment, looked over to Sarah, and then back at Tobias. "She says she forgives you but didn't your mother ever teach you not to run with scissors?"

"Yeah," he said, slowly turning his back to Otto so that he can make his way up the other side of the embankment. There were makeshift bridges made out of plywood lying across the thin points of the river. Otto's cove was positioned right by the sturdiest one. All of them could carry a human just fine. It all came down to how much they trusted the particular plank of wood. The wood was often soggy and slick, rotting away under the erosion of the ripping rapids.

"Wait…" Otto said abruptly. He looked over to Sarah and nodded his head. "She can sense something is wrong. She wants to know if you want to stay for a little while."

Tobias looked back at Otto and whispered, "*No thanks.*" before he kept walking.

"She said she knows. She said she knows Tobias. She knows!"

Tobias crossed the river and kept walking up the embankment, trying to shake the words of Otto. He was clinically insane. It was pointless to even grant him any attention.

"No… Tobias. You didn't…" he muttered as Tobias reached the top of the riverbank. "Tobias, wait… Wait! What have you done?" he said, trying to get Tobias to stay with him. Tobias could hear the ringing of his possible baby crying in his ear. What was happening to him? All of a sudden, he didn't want to move. He couldn't take another step forward. He was stuck, standing still in time.

"Tobias… Brooke… She's pregnant, isn't she?" As soon as the words left Otto's lips, he knew he had made a big mistake. Tobias spun around and slid back down the embankment he had just conquered, crossing the river to confront his accuser. His face was pale, and his eyes seemed to grow red as he drew closer.

"Who told you?" he said in a demanding voice. "How do you know that?" he said, ordering an answer from Otto. Otto stood there looking back and forth between his imaginary friend and an approaching fiend.

"Answer me!" screamed Tobias. His voice echoed through the surrounding woods.

"I—I—I didn't do anything. It was Sarah! She heard—it was her!" Mumbled Otto as he tried to back up.

Tobias took the butt of his rifle and struck Otto in the chest, sending him flopping back into the shallow mudwater that had formed along the bank of the river. "Don't feed me any of that shit, Otto. Tell me how you know! We haven't told anybody. Now, if you care about your well-being, you'll make the right choice here, and tell me just how the *fuck* you know about the baby."

Otto tensed up and put his limp hands in front of his face. As he looked up at Tobias, he noticed a bit of commotion up on the bank above. Luna popped her head out of the ferns as Tobias menacingly loomed over a helpless Otto. "Otto, I don't think you're taking me seriously. If you don't answer in the next few seconds, you're going to force me to take this a step further, and I really don't want to do that." Tobias clenched his jaw as he readjusted his grip on his rifle.

He didn't know how to negotiate with someone who lived so far from reality. "Brooke and I only found out about the baby last night. Have you been snooping Otto? Is that it? Are you snooping around?"

Luna held a hand over her mouth as the news broke to her. She didn't want to startle Tobias, especially in the state he was in now. She decided to stay back and observe the situation in an attempt to gain more information.

Tobias stared down at Otto, who cowered helplessly at his feet. "Pl-please. I swear it was Sarah! She must've heard it fr-from Brooke, maybe?"

Tobias stepped on Otto's knee, causing him to grunt and squirm in the mud. "I'm done living in fairytale land, Otto. I'm going to give you…" he lifted his rifle from his side and cocked it. He then aimed it at Otto's throat. "I'm going to give you one more chance."

Luna began to panic. The Tobias she knew would never do this. This was an extreme overreaction, even for him. He was threatening a member of Corazon's life. He would never do that. He had always been so gentle. She looked down at her rifle and held it close.

Otto tried to plead with Tobias, but he could barely make out a word. He held his hands in front of his face as if they would actually supply him with some sort of protection. "Wait-wait—Tobias, wait!" he was shaking. "Tell him, Sarah! Tell him! He won't hurt you! Stop where are you going?! Sarah! Sarah, stop come back!"

Otto began to weep upon realizing the gravity of his predicament. He was surely dead. "I'm trying to help you out here, you—you freak!" Tobias twisted his foot into Otto's knee, causing him to scream again.

"Just do it. Just—just get it over with," Otto said, catching Tobias off guard.

"I'm not bluffing here, freak. Just tell me who told you. Just tell me!" he pushed the barrel of the rifle into Otto's cheek.

Otto swallowed and lifted his head into the barrel as he looked at Tobias with a crazy look in his eyes. "Just do it. I can feel it. I know you want to. I know you want to pull that trigger. You want blood, you want chaos. You want this. So do it."

Tobias was taken back by this sudden burst of psychotic courage, but *he was right*; Tobias wanted to do it. He knew the consequences, but he still wanted to do it. He was done arguing with Otto. He placed his finger on the trigger. "You want me to do it? Your wish is my command, Otto."

Otto tensed up, preparing to die. Tobias felt sick, part of him wanted to pull the trigger, and the other part of him wanted to run away. His grip slowly began to tighten around the trigger when a rock was hurled from above and met the back of his head with optimum force. Tobias shrieked and dropped to his knee, clutching at his scalp with his hands and dropping the rifle in the process. He took his hand away briefly to see that it was covered in blood and placed it right back where it was.

"What the *hell was that?*" he screamed.

"*Thank you, Sarah…*" whispered Otto as he kicked Tobias in the chest, sending him splashing into the water, giving him the chance to scurry up the embankment.

Tobias tried to grab his heel, but Otto was too quick. He scampered up the embankment and vanished amongst the foliage. "Get back here!" Tobias demanded as he began to regain his vision. He knew Otto was long gone.

He punched at the water and got himself to his feet, still clutching at the back of his bleeding head. "Who's there?" he yelled, hearing his echo once again. "Who's there?" he repeated.

Nobody answered. He picked up his gun and charged up the other side of the riverbank. He no longer cared about Otto. Whoever threw the rock might have heard him, too. He looked from left to right, his senses heightened. He jerked from side to side like a feral animal, trying his best to home in on what was making that sound. He heard footsteps headed back toward the main circle and quickly pursued them. His heart raced as he ducked and dodged his way around the trees, huffing and puffing like a steel train. He didn't quite know what he would do with whoever saw him when he caught them. All he knew is that he had to catch them. Then he could make up his indecisive mind.

As he wound his way around the trees, he saw wisps of the golden hair that were all too familiar. Of course, of all the people that could have caught him threatening Otto, it had to be the one that actually mattered. Tobias growled as he tried to pick up the pace. They still must've been a half-mile away from the base. He figured if he picked up the pace, he'd still have time to change things.

Luna continued to run as fast as she could. She, too, was conflicted with what just happened. He had proven himself to be dangerous, but nothing like what she just witnessed. If she turned him in, who knows what might happen? The Disciples rarely had to ever deal with violence in such extreme measures.

Tobias chugged along, panting profusely. He was so much bigger than her. It was useless to pursue her at this rate. He stopped in his tracks and thought, *I could end it. I could end it right here, I could shoot her down, catch up and finish the job. Then I could go find Otto, kill him, and claim it was another random outsider that fled… Hell, I could even pin it on Ray, say he's being hunted or something…* He shook off that terrible idea. He was no killer. He began to run again and tripped over a few loose roots within the brush. "Shit!" he shouted in a fit of rage. He stood up and brought the butt of his rifle to the side of a tree and smashed until he couldn't smash anymore, chipping away at the wooden exterior of his stock. He sighed and looked up to the sky. *Maybe Plan A wasn't so bad after all.*

He lifted his gun and aimed it at a fleeting Luna. She ran along as fast as her legs would carry her. Tobias blinked to get the sweat out of his eyes as he lined up the crosshairs with her back. His hands shook, his legs trembled, his mouth went dry, and he squeezed the trigger.

Luna screamed as a bullet whizzed by her head, followed by a loud crack as it split through the tree a foot to her left. Her eyes shot open, and she dove for the ground as another bullet whizzed over the top of her head, followed by another loud gunshot. She screamed louder than she had ever screamed before. "HELP ME!"

Her scream echoed through the woods alerting many of the other hunters who came running. She rolled herself behind a tree, assuming Tobias was still fifty yards behind her. She let out another scream, which was cut short when another bullet splintered the side of the tree to the left of her head. A few pieces of shrapnel struck the side of her cheek, sending her to the ground.

Tobias looked around, holding his rifle close with wide eyes. The screaming had stopped. Did he hit her? His worried expression worsened; the reality of his actions began to dawn on him. Some of the other hunters were now drawing in closely. "Luna!" Sterling yelled. "Luna, where are you?! Luna!" Tobias grew clammy and lowered his gun. He staggered back a few steps before turning around completely. It was Otto's turn now. Tobias took off in the opposite direction, away from the commotion.

❖ ❖ ❖

"Shit," Sterling muttered as he dropped his gun and ran over to Luna, who was lying still on the forest floor. "Hey! Hey there little lady, no time for drifting off. Get up, Luna. Get up!" he said as he shook her body lightly. She whimpered as she slowly pushed herself up and sat against the tree. The left side of her face was cut in a few different places where the wood had splintered off from the bullets hitting the bark with such force. "Mother, have mercy. Luna, what happened?"

She tried remaining calm, shocked by the events that just transpired. "Tobias, he…" She shook her head and began to cry.

"Hey! Enough of that!" Sterling ordered, "What about Tobias? Should I send out a team? What were those shots about? Did you two see the bear? Is he in danger?" he peppered her with questions, clearly not knowing what to do with his newfound anxiety.

Luna gathered herself together. "Tobias *is the* danger, he just tried to kill Otto, and when he saw me, he—" she paused and furrowed her brow. "It was something about a baby? I just—I… I don't even know him anymore. I—"

"That's enough. What direction did he head in?" Sterling asked as he rose to his feet and looked at the other awestruck hunters standing behind him.

She shook her head again. "I don't know, he just shot at me and ran."

Sterling seemed furious but hid it well behind his bushy beard and grizzly complexion. "Take her back to Corazon quickly. Get her fixed up. Find a Disciple and tell them exactly what happened. I'm going to go find him."

"He's armed, Sterling," added one of the other hunters.

Sterling looked back at him with an intimidating gaze. "As if that *really* matters."

The other hunters aided Luna in getting back to Corazon. There they found Orwell enjoying a slow day within the designated Disciple hut. He was wrapped in a thick blanket, his gaze distant. As he began to doze off, one of the hunters burst into his hut, Luna's arm slung over their shoulder. "Orwell, it's an emergency."

Orwell sprang to his feet upon noticing the blood trickling down her face. "Luna… In the name of Mother, what happened?"

"Tobias, he shot at me. He's going after Otto, too. Sterling went to stop him."

Orwell seemed confused, as if he couldn't yet comprehend the meaning behind Tobias's actions. "Let's get you taken care of," he said, guiding her toward the exit. He looked at the small troop of hunters who waited outside for guidance. "Get her to Maple," Orwell instructed. "Send out two more people to help Sterling too. Find Otto fast."

Two more hunters darted off into the woods as they carried Luna into a nearby tent. "Here, here, sit down." She eased herself back into a soft chair, still stirred up by what had just occurred. "Tell me exactly what happened… And take your time," he said, miraculously holding on to his calm demeanor.

Luna took a few deep breaths. "Well, we were hunting. We were going about our normal business, normal sectors, you know how we do it?" Orwell nodded. He was far and away the most laid back of all of the Disciples. "So I was going about my route when I heard some commotion by the riverbed. I wanted to make sure everything was all right, but when I got there… well… Tobias was standing over Otto. Otto was saying something about a baby." She froze. Even in her state of shock, she knew better than to out Brooke and her tentative pregnancy.

Orwell exhaled slowly, "Oh dear… continue."

"So Otto said something that Tobias really didn't like. He started hurting him, stepping on his knee and kicking him. Then he took his gun and pressed it against Otto's neck. I couldn't just watch. I mean… it's Otto. He would never hurt a fly," she said, beginning to tear up.

Orwell held up a hand to silence her, "Shhh, yes, I know. It's all right. Continue."

Luna swallowed the frog in her throat. "I had to act fast. I took the nearest rock and threw it at him. It hit him in the head or something. Then I ran. I didn't know what I was going to do, I just wanted to draw him away from poor Otto. You know, give him time to run or something."

"You did this willingly? Knowing that you were putting your own life in danger?" he asked, pleasantly impressed.

"That's the thing. I never thought Tobias would actually hurt me," she said, slowly stroking her own arm while one of the remaining hunters tended to her scratched-up cheek.

"Luna, this man is not the man you once knew. You cannot think with sympathy. He tried to kill you. He's currently out there and—who knows what the result of his rage will be. You do know what has to happen. We must make an example out of him."

She began to tear up, "There has to be something else you can do. He—he's in a tough situation. He wasn't thinking rationally. He was panicked."

"Listen to me, I'm sure he had his reasons for doing what he did, but followers of Mother and the prophet Elliot know better. We exercise self-control. We preach to our people about love before hate. We preach about zero tolerance for useless violence. He broke the rule, Luna. He engaged in useless violence. And this violence shall be answered with more violence."

24

While the chaos slowly unraveled, Brooke sat next to Ray in the pasture, slowly but surely pouring her heart out. Ray had learned to pick up his lost social skills rather quickly, and one thing he was good at was extracting information. Whether it was the latest gossip in high school or a secret study tip in grad school, he knew how to get what he wanted—except when it came to Luna. She was a steel safe.

Brooke, on the other hand, was nothing of the sort. He could tell she was ready to crack. He just had to hit the right emotional pressure points. "I know I did a bad thing," she said through tears. "But please don't take my child away from me."

Ray nodded, "So they seriously wouldn't let you keep it? It's one more mouth to feed... *One.*"

"You don't understand. Elliot keeps a tight ship. It amazes me that you haven't disappeared yet! That's why I think they'll let us keep our baby. I mean, they let you stay, right? *Right?*"

These words sank deep through his skin and into the pit of his stomach. What did she mean by *disappear?* He didn't need to know the answer to that question. "Right… so explain to me how an extra mouth would really matter? Honestly."

"It's hard running things on Corazon as it is. Right now, everyone has a job, and we're working tirelessly day in, day out. We barely have enough time for meals and worship. Having a baby wouldn't just be as simple as having to feed another human, but you're taking me out of the mix, too. And if you think Tobias is going to work half as well as he does with a child to worry about… forget about it. He's tried for so long to have a child. There is no way he could focus on anything but the baby. He's a good man. He just wears a mask. I know deep down he doesn't mean half of the things he says."

Ray and Brooke watched as two men sprinted across the far pasture, both carrying rifles. "Probably saw a bear again," Brooke muttered.

"Brooke, you realize this isn't right. These people should have no say in whether or not you keep this child. This can't be the first time this has happened."

Brooke nodded as she looked off into the distance. "Sierra got pregnant less than a year after it was declared temporarily unholy. There was a big debate because we couldn't prove whether or not she was impregnated before or after it was declared. She had been with men at both times."

"What happened to her?" Ray asked, eager to hear more.

"They gave her a choice. She could get it aborted, or…"

"Or what?" he asked, knowing full well what she was about to say next.

"Or else she disappears."

"This can't happen. Brooke, if you want to keep it, I see no reason for you not to fight for it. I'll say something. Maybe if… maybe if we get enough people to stand up against it, then, well, I don't know. Maybe we can change something?"

Brooke laughed. "You're talking about a riot. A revolution. People don't care about me or my filthy baby. They care about making it into the eternal afterlife where the sun shines, and the birds sing, and nothing bad ever happens. You're asking them to turn against the same principles that got them to willingly move into the middle of nowhere."

The more she spoke, the smaller he felt. She was right. There was no way he could make them change their minds. It was all up to them. Her happiness was now resting in their hands and on their lips.

He took a deep breath and shifted his body so that he was facing her directly. "My wife, she had a miscarriage once," he said in a hushed tone. "It was a little over two months in. She wasn't even showing yet. But we knew enough to tell some close friends." Ray paused, scratching the top of his head and looking toward the woods. "They say one in ten pregnancies end in a miscarriage. You just never think you're going to be that one in ten. We both knew that sort of thing was possible, but it's not something you talk about."

He shook his head, wiping the sweat from his brow. "When you know someone as well as I knew her, you see the little things. She stopped being so passionate; even if it were something as small as a little argument, she just sort of let me win. She started eating out more. I don't know if it was because she was tired or if it was because all that grease-filled some sort of void. She even stopped putting cream in her coffee. I know it sounds like I'm reading into things, but she hated black coffee. She was the kind of woman to take coffee with her sugar, you know?" The two of them let off a little chuckle, a glimpse of sun within a storm.

"What are you trying to say here? Most miscarriages happen by now. I'm pretty far along, I'll start showing soon."

"What I'm trying to say is… expect the worst. Expect the worst, and you'll never be disappointed. Expect the worst, and everything will either meet or exceed your expectations. If you expect the worst, the only direction you can go is up."

She slowly nodded as she swallowed her whimper. His words didn't affect her the way he originally hoped they would.

"It's gonna be all right," he said, trying to comfort her. She buried her face in his shoulder and cried. "It's gonna be all right," he said, knowing full well he knew nothing.

The two of them finished grooming and milking the cattle and began to head up back to the main circle in the center of the community. The sky was a deep purple with streaks of red peeking over the mountain top. Ray stopped to scratch at a mosquito sucking away at his ankle. He used his cheap crutch to scratch away at his bite. "These things usually give you problems up here, Brooke? You know mosquitoes kill more humans than sharks." He looked up and realized she was gone. Just ahead was a sizable crowd, stumbling around each other to get their fill on the latest scandal Corazon had to offer. He heard Brooke scream as he made his way toward the crowd.

He stood on the tips of his toes so that he could get a better look at what all the commotion was about. There, leaning over the large prominent rock in the center of the community, was Tobias, bound with cord at the hands and ankles. Two of the Disciples were holding Brooke back. "Stop! Let him go!" she screamed. "He did nothing wrong! He did nothing wrong! Let him go!"

Ray furrowed his brow and looked down at his feet; he didn't want to see this. He turned away and headed for Luna's hut off to the side. As he drew further from all of the commotion, he could see her head poke out from within her hut. He smiled and began to take longer strides. "*Honey! I'm home!*" he said with a bright smile, using the same flirtatious accent they had used earlier that morning. She retreated back into her hut. He saw this as some kind of cute game.

Ray pushed his way past the flap and looked over to her, leaning against his bed with her back to him. "How was your day, dear?"

he said, said, using the same ridiculous accent. She didn't reply; he decided to dial it down drastically. "Hey, Luna. How's it going?"

He limped up to her and touched her arm. She slowly spun around, revealing her cut-up cheek. Ray's eyes widened as he turned her head to get a better look at the bruised, bloodied jawline. "Jesus Christ, what happened?" he asked, sounding worried. When she didn't answer immediately, his worry turned to anger. "Who did this to you?" he said, sounding much more menacing. He was slowly putting the pieces together. Though he was far from the whole story, he had enough.

"Ray, we can't be irrational about this. We need to think. They will take care of it, I promise. Everything will—"

Ray spun around and stormed out of the hut straight for the growing crowd. "Ray, stop! Listen! Please!" She ran up to the flap and watched as he drew closer to the crowd. She wanted to go out and stop him, but she was far too embarrassed to let everyone see her like this.

Ray muttered bad things under his breath as he locked his vision onto a seemingly unconscious Tobias, still bent over the rock at an awkward position.

"Hey! What are you doing??" asked Beatrix as she popped up alongside him, jogging to keep up.

"Go inside, Beatrix," he ordered.

"Well, what are you doing? What happened to Luna's face? What's this crowd for?" she inquired.

"I said, go inside, Bea. Go wait with Luna if you have to."

"But Ray, I wanna know. I wanna know, Ray! I wanna—"

"Dammit, Bea, I said—!"

A strong hand grabbed at his shoulder. He turned around to see Musgo, looking at him with wise eyes. They were now feet away from the screaming crowd. "I know you're not about to do something you'll regret."

Ray veered away from Musgo and looked at Beatrix. She looked taken back by how he had just snapped at her and was now turning away toward Luna's tent, breathing funny to cover the sound of her whimpering. "Bea, wait. I'm sorry," he muttered, reaching a hand out to apologize to her. It was too late. She was already long gone. He looked back over to Musgo.

"I know you're angry. So are we, believe me. But he's gonna get what's coming to him. Trust me," Musgo said calmly as he nodded his head, hoping that it would make him understand more.

Ray was breathing heavily. He barely even noticed it. He slowly regained control of his breathing and released his tight grip on his crutches.

Musgo relaxed once he saw that his words had gotten to Ray. "Now I know Luna probably wants me to bring you back to the hut. But I'm gonna let you watch this. Maybe it'll make you feel better." Musgo escorted Ray up onto a small hill where the two of them could see within the huge crowd. Dante and Orwell both raised their hands, quieting the crowd almost immediately.

Orwell cleared his throat and began speaking, his calm demeanor in juxtaposition against his harsh words. "We have two sinners amongst us tonight. Let this be a lesson to all of you. We must be more careful when it comes to the act of spreading love. Even Elliot himself has limits. These two you see before you have made the mistake of creating yet another life when we cannot afford to take care of our own. Their actions now range from irresponsible…" he looked over to Brooke, "…to reprehensible." He shot Tobias an ugly stare. "Tonight, I speak before you, not as a friend, not as a peer, but as a teacher. These two weren't careful and look what has happened."

The crowd began to whisper amongst themselves until Dante held up another hand, silencing them instantly. Orwell continued to speak. "Tobias chose to hide this from us. If he were to come to us and explain himself, we would have been more merciful, but he hid from us, he lied to us. He lied to and disrespected the name of Mother! Mother sees all. We must remember that. *Mother sees everything*. She saw Tobias. She saw his whole plan. You see, Tobias was planning on going about his day-to-day business. Little did we know, he was planning to make Brooke disappear for a while."

Brooke let out a teary-eyed gasp as she looked over to Tobias, who shook his head and yelled, "Only until the child was born! I didn't want death! I just wanted a better life for my son!"

"Silence!" Screamed Dante, who seemed to relish in the overall misery.

Orwell continued, "When Otto found out about the pregnancy, he didn't spread word around like a disease. He kept it to himself and confronted Tobias while they were alone. Tobias threatened Otto with his life. He pointed a gun made to kill beasts in the face of a human. One of the other hunters caught him in the act and decided to intervene. She drew him away from Otto, putting her own life at risk. Tobias pursued her and shot at her. *He wounded Luna,* who is now in recovery. What's important is that he tried to kill one of our own. He could have come to us in the first place, and we would have talked over his situation. Instead, he acted upon violent, animalistic instincts. Look where that has led him!" Orwell gestured over to Tobias strung over a boulder.

"It burdens me to say this, but we must do what is necessary. We do not tolerate useless violence within our community." The crowd still murmured amongst themselves. This was as close to entertainment as they ever got. "But first, I must remind you all what happens when you're not careful."

Two men grabbed Brooke by each arm as she kicked and screamed and begged them to stop. They dragged her away from the crowd and into a tent that had just recently been set up. She dug the heel of her foot into the dirt, trying to slow or at least stall them from taking her away. She continued to scream for a while. The audience listened to her until they grew tired of it and directed their attention back toward Tobias.

Tobias pleaded with the two Disciples, who slowly approached him. "Please. I know I was wrong. Please. In the name of Mother and all things sacred, *please*! Please don't do this. *Stop! Please!*" The two of them restrung his restraints so that he was spread out like an X on the boulder.

Orwell went back to where he was standing while Dante loomed near Tobias, flashing his sickly black smile as the tension grew.

Dante stepped up onto the boulder so that he was high above the crowd. "We gave Tobias the option we give all of our sinners. Exile or punishment. Though Tobias is a sinner, his faith is true. He has chosen punishment in the hopes of one day returning as a member of our community." The crowd was pleasantly impressed and had seldom ever seen someone choose punishment over exile. "Tobias… for your punishment," Dante said, rallying the masses. "Elliot sees it fit that you remain silent to reflect on your actions for the next three months!"

Ray looked at Musgo in disbelief. "What?! *He tried to kill her!* How is that-"

Musgo held up his hand. "Hush now."

Dante licked his lips. "He also sees it fit, that we follow the Book of Elliot, a particular passage that reads… *He who disrespects thy law, and acts upon useless violence, shall be crippled to the extent seen fit!*" The crowd's murmur turned to a rumble as Dante stuck out his tongue and held up a thick wooden beam that had been whittled to act as a bat.

Tobias begged Dante to put the bat down, but Dante was already set in his ways. "Your punishment begins now."

Dante continued to speak, calming down the crowd. "Tobias shall have his arm broken for the horrendous acts of violence he committed this morning. However, he has done more than just bring useless violence into this community. He has disrespected the word of Elliot by not taking appropriate actions when it came to preventing the birth of his child. He then tried to hide it. I cannot express how bad this could have been," Dante's smile widened.

"Imagine what would happen when Brooke showed up to a hospital looking and acting the way she does. Imagine the questions that would arise! What would happen if she was followed on her way back here?" Dante held his arms out to the side, the bat still grasped firmly. "Everything! Everything we have would be gone. We would no longer be a secret to the world. All of our actions from then on would be exploited and put out for the world to see. We would be taken from our newfound homes! We would be incarcerated and questioned, tortured by those who made us want to come here in the first place!" His words appealed to the crowd, who nodded in agreement.

Dante stopped to catch his breath. His even temper had given way to anger and frustration, causing his face to turn red as he spewed hatred at Tobias. "Let this be a lesson to you all! Tobias knew the rules, and he broke them. According to Elliot, chemical castration is now in order."

Everybody seemed to freeze. There were no more nods or screams from the gathered crowd. Even Ray was speechless. Tobias opened and shut his mouth. He wanted to talk. He wanted to beg and plead for them to reconsider. Yet as he lay there, tethered to that massive rock, he couldn't find the words to express his regret. His eyes drifted over the crowd; all of the faces seemed to blur together, all but one. Benji leaned up against the trunk of a sturdy spruce, his eyes fixed on Tobias. Benji watched as the dread sank deeper and deeper into his face. He seemed amused as he slid a slice of apple into his mouth.

Orwell looked over to Dante, who stood right beside Tobias's helpless body. Dante had that wired look on his face; he was ready to bring that bat crashing down on Tobias's arm. All he had to do was hear the word. Orwell nodded toward Dante, giving him the go-ahead to strike.

Tobias screamed as Dante swung the bat high above his head and came down full force on his right hand, smashing it in between the bat and the boulder. He sobbed and begged like a child right before Dante took another powerful swing, landing this one on his upper forearm. His bones could be heard cracking under the force of the dense wooden bat. His arm forcibly bent into awkward directions. One last time Dante took the back and cracked it back down on his already broken hand. Tobias screamed louder and louder. Dante took the blunt end of the bat and swiftly nudged it against the side of Tobias's head, stopping the screaming instantly as his strung-up body went limp. The crowd grew quiet again as they watched Tobias slip out of consciousness. Two other male members untethered him, letting him fall limp into their arms. The two men carried Tobias's body out into the woods. Everyone safely assumed the events that would transpire from then on.

"I think I'm gonna be sick," Ray whispered, putting his hand to his mouth.

Musgo looked at him sternly. "This is what you wanted, right? You wanted to see him get what he deserves? Well, there ya go."

Ray shook his head and turned away. "I'm going to be with Luna."

Musgo continued to watch Tobias slip in and out of consciousness, lifting his bobbing head and muttering frantic, helpless phrases before he would go silent again, his body ceasing to put up a fight as he was carried further out of sight. Ray walked back into the night.

He made his way back into Luna's hut and pulled her close to him, hugging her as hard as he could. He then looked over to Beatrix, who sat pouting in the corner. He knew she was mad at him, but there was nothing a little red ball couldn't fix. He grabbed the small sphere from off of his nightstand and rolled it over to her feet. She could no longer hide her excitement. She cracked a smile and rolled it back. The three of them sat on the ground for the next hour in silence, slowly rolling the ball back and forth. It was such a simple task, but it did the trick of taking their mind off of more pressing matters.

Hours passed, and Beatrix fell sound asleep right where she sat. All was quiet now; all was right. Ray looked deep into Luna's eyes, mesmerized by the sheer power of those deep blue glassy orbs. It was so incredibly easy to lose himself in them. He would often find himself hypnotized. His face lingered a foot away from her own. He wanted to lean in, make it abundantly clear that this was no joke. But he couldn't. There were too many tiny voices in his head telling him all of the bad that could come from all this. Little did he know she was in the same boat. He stretched out his arm and brushed her golden locks back behind her ear. She smiled and looked down at the floor briefly. She then lifted her chin so that it would be level, possibly even slightly above his own. Ray delicately traced the fresh scars on her cheek with his fingertips before moving his hand to the back of her neck. He slowly moved in, inch by inch. She closed her eyes and mirrored him.

A deep sorrowful sound erupted from outside of her hut, right in the middle of the main square. The two of them were interrupted, wondering what animal could have possibly made that noise. Beatrix shot up from her deep slumber, "What was that?" she asked, sounding somewhat afraid.

Ray pulled himself to his feet and limped over to the flap. He poked his head out, and what he saw would remain seared in his brain for the rest of his days.

He saw Brooke limping out into the middle of the square under the glow of a full moon. She sobbed and moaned as she held her hands flat against her stomach. She wasn't saying words; she just made noises, the noise of an animal who had just lost her kin. It was inhuman. She limped all the way out to the middle of the square where Tobias had previously been tortured. His body had now been removed. She threw herself against that same bolder and let her back slide down it until she was now resting on the ground. She kept her hands on her lower abdomen.

Ray looked back to Luna with fear in his eyes. Luna had her hands over Beatrix's ears, cupping them tight so that she wouldn't hear a thing.

Brooke moaned and cried some more. She now had many sets of eyes on her. Benji sat by a small fire he had lit in the distance. All that was visible was the soft orange glow and his silhouette as he took in Brooke's pain from a distance, watching her without any sort of shame. She looked up to the moon and cried out one last time, two words that broke the hearts of anyone listening. As the tears streamed down her face, she lifted her head and let out one final cry. "*My baby!*"

Ray pulled himself back inside. He couldn't bear to watch anymore. Luna turned her head away. She probably would have covered her own ears if she weren't already covering little Bea's. Brooke eventually stopped crying, leaving everyone to go rest. That night Ray lay awake in the bed. The weird and wacky world he had been living in had just taken a turn to the dark side. A restless dream turned into a nightmare. Though the part he wrestled with the most was the notion that this was not the first time this community had lived through this particular nightmare… and it surely wasn't going to be the last.

25

Ray exhaled a frosty mouthful of air and watched as the wisps of silver breath dissipated in front of his face. He had his leg propped up on the bed he had grown so used to over the past seven months. It was now sometime in October. He wasn't sure of the exact date. Nobody really kept a calendar, but the leaves were turning, and there was that scent of autumn musk floating limply through the air. He had arrived in Corazon sometime in early April, and it had taken him an estimated seven months to get to this exact day. The day he would be given the basic privileges of freedom, the day he got his leg back. There had been a few storms since he arrived, in both the figurative and metaphorical sense.

When it stormed, things got bad. Flash floods from mountain range runoff were always an issue. For the past month or so, the community worked hard preparing their homes for the upcoming winter. They took thick sections of sheet metal and wedged them up against the sides of their huts to prevent water from draining inside. After the first few rainstorms, they began to figure out the patterns of the runoff. They were instructed to quickly dig a small trench to cut back on flooding. The trenches stretched from the highest points of elevation and ran along the edge of Corazon until it met the river running close to Otto's cove. The whole community contributed to it all, except, of course, for Tobias, who was ordered to take care of waste and manure disposal, the least coveted job in Corazon, always used as a form of punishment. The trench was finished rather quickly and did a good job at protecting them from short-term floods. Yet they all knew what came next. Flood season would only last for so long. Sooner or later, winter was bound to come, and when it did, it would come guns blazing.

They had already seen their first snowfall. It didn't last very long, but they were all brought short bursts of thick white snowflakes—a bit premature but welcomed all the same. People screamed and laughed as they all ran around trying to catch the massive flakes on their tongues. Ray, on the other hand, had beads of sweat running down his back.

Maple picked away at the putty she had used to bind the two planks of wood holding his leg in place. She had already cut through the dense wire that strung the structure together, but now it was just a matter of slipping the cast off completely. "All right now," she said sternly. Luna watched from over her shoulder, making sure to take careful mental notes. "You are going to feel weak. It's this thing called atrophy. You haven't been using your leg, so the muscles have been deteriorating. Luna has been instructed to take you on daily walks. We need to get some strength back into this leg of yours."

Ray nodded in agreement, "Whatever you say, boss."

"Now, I'm going to slide this cast off. As I slide, you need to lift your leg as high as you can."

He winced as he attempted to lift his leg to its optimum height. He moved it a bit, but it wasn't even close to what Maple was expecting. "That good?" Ray said, trying to keep his leg hovered so that she could take the cast off.

"It's good if you want me to scrape up your leg in the process. Luna, help the man," she ordered. Luna made her way to his side and scooped her hands beneath his leg.

"Ooh, that's ripe," she said, turning her nose away from his leg.

He smiled and looked at her, a bit embarrassed, "Well, it's not like I could do anything about it!"

"Um, well, you could have just *not* jumped off of a waterfall," she sarcastically snapped.

"Well, I wouldn't be here then, would I?" he replied.

The two of them continued in their mildly flirtatious verbal chess match until Maple butted in. "Children! We have business to take care of! Come on Luna, lift!"

Luna looked at Ray and cautiously elevated his leg. He winced and ground his teeth as she lifted his leg higher and higher.

"All right, perfect!" Maple shouted as she eased the cast off of his leg. His muscle definition had shrunk significantly, and he had red splotches running up and down both sides where the wood had been wired up.

He reached down and itched at them rigorously. Maple was quick to smack his hands. "Ah-ah! No. Bad idea. You scratch those, and you get an infection. There's not a lot we can do for you then. Just keep taking your daily dose of painkillers, and we'll see what comes of it. But *don't* scratch." Ray reluctantly pulled his hand away.

"All right now, let's get you standing. This should help take some of the tension off. The break should be mostly healed, but that doesn't mean it won't still ache." Maple handed him a stiff wooden cane.

"Damn, Maple… you got me feeling like an old man," he said, examining the cane.

"Oh, you just wait, dear," she said with a smile. "All right, Luna, you get his left, I'm on his right." The two of them grabbed an arm and hoisted him to his feet.

He wobbled for a moment before finally gaining his balance. "Ahhh. Okay, all right." He ground his teeth some more as he tried to reposition himself using the cane as leverage. "This is going to take some getting used to."

The two of them let him go, and he began to limp his way across the length of the dirt floor. He made it to one side, took a moment to turn himself around, and walked back to the bed. "Beautiful," Maple said, admiring his work as much as her own.

Benji pushed his way into the hut unexpectedly. "Morning—" he said, preparing for casual banter. He stopped as he saw Ray up and moving without a cast. "Look at you, both legs and all. Look like a new man, friend."

Ray let Benji's words roll right off of him, still not knowing what to make of him. "Feel like one, too," he replied.

Maple rolled her eyes as she looked at the two of them. "Ray, I'll be back in a few minutes. You need to get back to work quickly. Brooke needs her space, so I'm taking you off milk duty. You'll be helping me with gathering and food preparation. Sound good?"

Ray nodded, "Of course. And thank you, Maple, for everything."

Maple walked past Benji and left the hut to prepare the cooking table as Beatrix pushed past her to get inside the hut.

"Hi, Ray," she said without even looking at him. "Can I have your crutches?"

"Oh, it's a party now, isn't it?" Benji declared. He dropped to one knee and growled at Beatrix. Bea playfully jumped back and held up her fists. Benji laughed and waved her off.

Luna admired the playful nature of the two and seemed amused by it all. "Someone has found their way back home pretty quick," she sighed, winking at Benji.

He stood up. "Is this the part where I say some corny *no place like home* quote?"

Luna tossed Ray's bedsheets at Benji, who quickly caught them. "No," she said. "this is the part where you make yourself useful and wash these sheets," she stated. She then looked at Ray, "You're not the only thing that smells."

Benji shrugged, "And I thought I was the only one who noticed." Beatrix cracked up at his subtle jab at Ray, who remained silent as he tried to keep his balance.

Bea nudged Luna in the thigh. "Luna!" she said, getting her attention. "Can I use the crutches?"

"Go for it, Bea," Ray said, cutting in. "I don't need them anymore."

"Fantastic!" she exclaimed with joy as she scooped up his crutches and darted out of the room. Benji rolled his eyes and followed her out, taking the dirtied sheets with him.

"What was that all about?" Ray laughed, looking over to Luna.

"She's going through a phase…wants to be an *artist*. She's even wearing this weird little bracelet her buddy Clover gave her," she said with the slightest hint of sarcasm.

"I just don't see how that has anything to do with those awful splintery crutches…"

"Sculptures. That girl Clover has got her into making sculptures. It's funny…when I was her age, I wanted to go to the movies and head out to the mall with friends and talk gossip and get my nails done. She doesn't even know what half of that means. She's never seen a movie, she's never heard of a mall, and getting your nails done is as simple as *getting them chopped off* around here. She can't appreciate those luxuries. She never got the childhood I had, and well… she never will."

Ray shrugged, "Is that a bad thing? The girl is creative. Making a sculpture out of old worn-down crutches? That's impressive. It's smart, she's expressing herself."

"I know. Sometimes I just wish she could have had a normal childhood. All this," she said, waving her hand in circles around her head. "It's a great place but, she needs to know there's more out there. All her life, I thought I was doing the right thing by keeping her here. Keeping her safe from the corrupted 'free world' riddled with hatred. We all made a choice by keeping the children here. But lately… well, I don't know. Lately, I feel like that choice wasn't mine to make. She stays here because she doesn't know what anything else is, he doesn't know how anything else works. The children aren't like the rest of us. I'm sorry. I know I'm rambling on."

"No, Luna, please continue," he said, staggering over to her side. "This place is warped. I know you know that. Everyone can hide behind this mask of religion and good intentions and love, but at the end of the day…" He stopped and debated the harshness of his words. After little contemplation, he thought it best to just state the facts. "At the end of the day, your leaders chose to torture a man, break his arm, and get rid of his lover's baby. That—stuff like that isn't right."

She clearly had more she wanted to say but held a lot of it back. "Tobias was—"

"I know what Tobias was. I know what he did. There just seems like better options," he said, slightly angered. "Corazon has its flaws. It's a volcano ready to blow. I can feel it, a self-sustaining community only works as well as its people." He once again stopped at the risk of upsetting her too much. He took a step forward and lowered his voice. "That thing you told me when I got here, about how Elliot and the Disciples take a woman up onto the mountain? How have you never heard from her again? That's messed up. What happens up there? Do you ever stop and ask yourself these questions?"

"*All the time,*" she whispered. "I believe Elliot is doing no harm. He stays up on the mountain to meditate in hopes that he'll get another message from Mother. You would be lonely, too. He can't surround himself with men all the time. Mother is accepting of all genders. Sometimes all he needs is a woman's touch." Luna said, nodding her head as if all of it made perfect sense.

"But what do you mean by *a woman's touch*... I know Corazon practices 'shared love,' but... how come you never see them again? *Doesn't that bother you?*"

Luna shook her head, "I know what you might be thinking. According to Elliot, the mountaintop is as close to the afterlife as one can get. It's said to be *paradise* on earth. Everyone wants to get up there. The men can only see it if they are recruited as a Disciple. But there can only be fifteen, so if one Disciple dies, another one is chosen from down here on Corazon. The women are luckier. They are chosen more often. There is no limitation. I believe twenty-one women have been chosen so far. Only the best can go—the fastest, the strongest, the most attractive—all of these things play a factor. Elliot wants leaders. They all live simple lives up there on the mountain. Lives devoted to prayer and the worship of Mother and the one true Prophet. They feast, they drink, they bathe in the river, and they share their love. It's really beautiful when you think about it."

The more she spoke, the crazier she sounded. "But yeah, sculptures... that kid, she's something else," he said, desperately trying to change the conversation.

She nodded her head in agreement just as Maple made her way into the hut. "All right now, dear, time for your real test. Come with me."

Luna held the flap open for Ray as he limped out of her hut in pursuit of Maple, who waddled away toward the cooking stations. The cooking stations were essentially a series of tables under a poorly made tarp canopy. The tables had different sets of knives wrapped in cloth along with several different spices lined up along the edges. There were big wooden mixing bowls and a variety of different tools that enabled them to mix and mash their food. In the center of each table lay a thick slab of red meat.

"So, seeing as we are going to keep you away from dairy duty for a while, we figured we have no choice but to upgrade you. Now this job isn't like dairy." Maple said dramatically, shaking her finger at him as he stood hunched over, leaning on to his cane. "It isn't just squeezing and pulling at an udder, you have to be smart. You can't over-spice the meat. You can't cook it for too long. This ain't no five-star kitchen if you haven't noticed," she chuckled at herself. "Cooking over a fire is a hell of a lot different than cooking over a stove. There's also the gathering aspect of it all. I'll take you out myself and show you which plants will taste good, which plants won't taste so good, and which berries will kill ya. This is no joking around, serious stuff here Ray, serious stuff."

"You just tell me what to do, Maple. Anything I can do to help."

"Yeah, you say that now. Just wait."

❊ ❊ ❊

Within minutes Ray was elbow deep in a concoction that seemed to be made of minced and mashed deer innards. "What the hell is this, Maple?" he said in disgust as he lifted handful after handful of mashed meat out of a bucket.

Maple sat in a chair next to him, laughing away. "That right there is what I call leftovers. Ya see, sometimes there are good days hunting, and sometimes there are bad days hunting. Yesterday was a *good* day. In fact, it was so good that we didn't need to go hunting today. That's why Luna could stay back and help me with you and your *wittle weg...*" she said in a mocking tone.

"Yeah, that's great, but that doesn't answer my question. What is this?"

"Yesterday, they tagged a few does. We could have dried 'em out for jerky, but we decided to save em' and cook em' instead. There are a few squirrels and a raccoon in that bucket as well."

"Jesus Christ," he muttered as he pushed his mouth into his shoulder, attempting to choke down the vomit rushing up his esophagus. He managed to choke it down and shot her a putrid look.

"This is the hard part. That's why I got you to do it!" she cackled, making herself laugh some more. She looked at Ray and the way he cringed each time he let the meat slop from the bucket and onto the table.

"So this is life on a commune," he muttered sarcastically. After he was done taking the meat out of the bucket, he was told to put a variety of different spices on it under Maple's instruction. She was very particular.

"Too little and you ruin it; too much, and you ruin it! It's a very fine line. Make sure you walk it carefully!" She was so precise about every little detail that she was beginning to get on his nerves. Here he was, beginning to walk on his own again, just to be sat down and forced to mead powder and dried leaves into various oddly smelling meats.

"All right, that should be it," she said, nodding her head. "I'll take care of the rest. You've done a good job. We're going to do the same thing tomorrow, depending on how many the hunters bring back today."

Ray shook his head as if to shake the past hour from his memory. "So when I asked you all what I was eating, and you replied, *meat*... this is what it was?"

Maple chuckled some more as she separated the concoction from the excess fat. She then picked up bits and pieces of the longer, more slender cuts and slapped them onto a metal sheet, which she would soon prop over the open flames. "Food is *food*. You learn to get whatever you can get when you live here. Sure Todd helps out with the monthly shipments, but with over a hundred people, a truckload will only go so far. I know it's tough, I know it'll take some getting used to… but this is a test."

Maple sounded as if she were trying to hint at something a bit more philosophical than her random tangents about respecting elders, so Ray decided to remain where he was and keep her company as she cooked.

"Life is all about tests. It builds you up, it teaches you lessons." She nodded toward his leg. "It gives you opportunities, then it tests you. It sees how strong you are. You see, Mother doesn't have mercy on the weak. Mother doesn't have mercy on all those who don't try, all those who don't put forth the effort."

Ray tried to refrain from rolling his eyes as soon as she mentioned her religion. "So this is the start of my spiritual healing, is it?"

"Call it *whatever you want*, you're still in recovery. You're still sick. You're still here, so guess what? You're still going to listen to us. And right now, I'm trying to give you some advice, so I suggest you listen." She spoke swiftly and made her point clear. Maple had this mood where if she felt she was being pressured or played with in any sort of way, she would pump up her ego like a pufferfish, inheriting this wild sense of self-confidence causing her to come off as somewhat of a menace. She was normally all sunshine, except when she had to make her point.

"You're in deep with this community now. Some people care about you and your well-being, others want to see you dead, others… it doesn't matter. It's the ones that want you dead and the ones that care about you that you have to pay attention to." She sliced up thick slabs of meat as she made herself clear. Her hand holding the blade cut through the meat in a somewhat rhythmic pattern. Her hands seemed to have a mind of their own. "Make sure you know how to keep those two groups separate."

Ray looked confused, "I don't understand."

"You keep the ones that want you dead far away from the ones that care about you… because I swear on Mother and all things holy, if you so dare cause Luna or Beatrix any harm, intended or not. You'll have worse problems on your hands than death. Just remember that."

Ray grabbed Maple's wrist and pinned it down to the cutting board. She released the knife immediately. "You people are all I have. Luna and Beatrix are family to me. I wouldn't be able to enjoy anything if it weren't for them. I literally owe my life to her, and you actually have the audacity to question my ability to keep them safe?" Maple was impressed by his outright confidence. "I knew you were old, but I never thought you were this senile. If anyone were to even think about harming them, I would kill them. I would kill them right there. I would beat them until they were unconscious, and I wouldn't stop. Now remember this, remember my words, because I lost one family. I'm not losing another."

He released Maple's wrist. She looked up at him for a few moments before showing an earnest smile. "She loves you. You know that?"

"I know," he said, keeping his stern tone.

"So what's stopping you?" she said, shrugging.

"What's stopping me? I think you know just as well as I do. You're preaching to me about how I have to keep them safe? And you ask me what's stopping me?" His stern mask slowly developed into one of anger.

Maple nodded in agreement. "All right, child. You'll do anything to keep her safe?"

"Anything," Ray spoke slow and true.

Maple took up a more serious tone. "Now you know I care about you. I care about you almost as much as they do, but if you truly mean you'll do anything to keep her safe, you're doing it wrong."

"I don't understand what you're saying, Maple."

"Listen to me. When Tobias gets his arm back and is no longer being shunned, he's going to come for you. He's a smart man, and he blames you for the death of his child."

"How does that make any sense? He should blame the fucking god he worships. Or how about that so-called prophet Elliot. It's his rules, not mine!"

"That's exactly it. He won't go against his Corazon. That boy has wanted to be a Disciple since the very day I met him. But *he needs* someone to blame. We made an exception for you. We let you live even though you didn't want to. We didn't even give his child the option. And for that, he will never forgive you. To a man like him, it doesn't matter who, someone has to pay. Someone has to feel the very same pain he felt, someone just has to suffer. Do you understand?"

Ray nodded. To his dismay, it did make sense.

Maple continued. "He is a smart man. And if I were him, I wouldn't kill you. In a sick and twisted way, it would be doing you a favor, giving you what you wanted all along. No, he would hurt those you love. He would make you feel something." She took the thick strips of meat she had cut and flopped them onto the grilling pan over the burning fire. "You won't reason with him. He's too determined. Too set in his ways."

Ray looked deep into her face as she tried getting to her point. "So what do you want me to do? What are you saying?" he asked seriously. "You want me to kill the guy?"

She forced a chuckle, "No, no, that would tip Corazon over the edge."

He held his arms out. "Then what? What do you want me to do?"

"This is the hard part, Ray. This is where we travel into the gray areas. This is where things get hard for you."

He laughed, "Oh, so you're saying things haven't been hard for me so far? Because I'll tell ya, the past few months have got me *pretty fucked up*."

"Watch your mouth and come with me," she muttered as she stood up and turned to walk deeper into the wooded area behind them, the slabs of meat still sizzling over the fire.

Maple strode deeper into the woods, and Ray heavily limped close behind her.

"You're getting around pretty well for your first day," she said, looking back at him.

"I've only been dreaming about it since you first gave me those shitty crutches."

She laughed and eventually slowed down and came to a stop. Ray noticed a small green burlap bag she let dangle by her ankles. She looked him up and down and sighed.

"What? Enough of this mysterious bullshit. Tell me what you gotta say. Nobody else is around," he huffed, gesturing to the woods around them.

She sighed again. "I care about you, Ray. I really truly do. But you want to make sure Luna and Bea stay safe?"

"More than anything," he reassured her.

She nodded and stepped aside. She then raised an arm toward the open woods behind her. "This will lead you back to where you came. Perhaps even bring you back to where you really wanted to be." This cryptic message said more than Ray was expecting to hear. Maple then extended a hand, which Ray impulsively shook. "It's been a pleasure. You're a good man. I'll tell her why you left. You're doing the right thing here, Ray. Trust in yourself."

He stood there dumbstruck. "Wait," he whispered as Maple walked back toward camp. She didn't stop to ask him what he had said. "Maple, wait…there has to be another way," he said, slightly elevating his voice as he looked back to the open, dying woods in front of him. "Maple, please don't make me do this. It'll crush her."

Maple turned around immediately. "It will *save* her. Big difference."

"There has to be another way," he said.

She placed her hands on her fragile hips, "There's no other way."

He shook his head, "That's not what I mean! There has to be another—"

She shook her head violently and raised her voice. "No! You leave right now, and she is saved. Tobias wins because you're gone and he doesn't look for revenge on her or little Beatrix. Everything may never go back to how it was before, but having you gone will be a big step in the right direction!"

Ray stood there helplessly. "You don't have to do this, I can figure something else out! I can try and make things better!"

"Ray, you have brought nothing but *controversy and blood* to this community. We got along just fine before you showed up. Did we argue? Sure, did we disagree? Of course. But there was no death. No destruction. No attempted murder. Then you show up, and you put this idea of suicide into everyone's head. You make people believe that maybe we are not as off the grid as we like to think. Maybe Mother hasn't cast this invisible bubble of protection that we once thought actually existed! It sends everyone into panic mode, and then look what happens. It didn't help that you took up with Luna either."

"Don't act like this is my fault! I wanted to be left alone!" he said, echoing his earlier sentiments. "I didn't ask to be saved! Go ahead and say whatever you want. Call it fate! Call it destiny! Call it Mother sending you a message or whatever! But I'm here, right here! You said it yourself. I'm a part of this community now! I told you I would do anything to protect them… How can I protect them when I'm gone!"

Maple began to walk toward him. "Are you even listening to me? Who exactly do you think you are? I've lived here for years! You've been here for a few months, and then all of a sudden, you know what's best? I don't think so!"

"Oh, so this is it then? I don't even get to say goodbye?" Ray said, throwing his arms up in the air as his eyes welled up with tears. "What about Beatrix… she's my friend. I can't—I can't tell her how much she means to me?"

Maple sighed, "Get going while you still have the light." She then turned and continued to walk away from him.

Ray looked back out toward the darkening woods. "Are you sure? This will save them?"

She stopped again and looked back. This time she spoke, remaining much calmer. "I'm sure, Ray. It's for the best."

"You're positive?"

"Positive."

Maple watched as Ray slowly relaxed in front of her. It was almost as if she could see the two sides of his brain battling away. His eyes were truly the windows to his soul, so much conflict, so much resolution, so much war, so much peace.

She stood there and examined him, seeing if he would turn and walk from her into the fading sky, never to be seen again. He just stood there, trying to make up his mind as the red sun sank lower and lower into the sky. Tiny flakes of snow soon drifted their way into the woods surrounding them. "I don't have any food," he said as a last resort at trying to make her change her mind.

She swung the small green burlap satchel forward, tossing it at his feet. "There's some bread and a bit of jerky in there. Make it last."

He stared at the sack by his feet for a moment before picking it up and slinging it over his own shoulder. "I'm gonna die out there, Maple," he said as he started breathing deeper. "That's over thirty miles… On this leg? I won't make it. Can't I wait? Just gimme a little more time."

"If you leave now, you'll be too far gone for them to catch you. You know they won't just let you walk away. I know I'm throwing this all at you pretty fast, but it's the only way. This is what you wanted."

Ray swallowed his pride and shook his head as a tear rolled down his cheek. "I'm gonna die if I go back out there, Maple."

"Isn't that what you wanted, Ray? You wanted an end to all of your pain and suffering? Well, here you go. I'm just showing you the way." Her words rang in the back of his head. Why was she doing this? Was this truly what would be right?

The one tear slowly branched off into many as he quietly cried to himself, standing in the mulchy patch of grass as the white flakes drifted down from above. He shook his head and looked down at his toes. He then looked up to the sky with a big smile, tears still running down his face and neck. He wiped at his nose and sniffled. "I don't know if this is the right thing to do. I don't know if this will save her. I don't know why I've been put into this situation. But there is one thing I am sure of… I don't want to die."

He looked back up to Maple through bloodshot eyes. "I don't want to die, Maple." She looked back at him, trying her best to hold a straight face. He shrugged his shoulders. "I don't want to die. She makes me want to live. She makes me want to be a better person. She has changed something inside of me, I don't really understand what it is. All I know is that months ago, I wanted to kill myself. But the only thing I can think about now? Is her. And I really don't want to die. Please, Maple. Please…"

He was so focused on the task at hand that he failed to see the silhouette of the being approaching him from behind. A pair of arms abruptly wrapped themselves around him from the back. His head was pounding, and his hands shook. He slowly turned around to see the golden-haired angel he called Luna, looking up at him; her eyes seemed a little cloudy as well.

He looked at her as if she were some sort of illusion. He then turned back toward Maple, who was now smiling with the kind face that he had always known. He turned back to Luna, "What's going on here?" he said in between short breaths.

Luna hugged him and then separated herself from him, keeping a hand on each shoulder. "We needed to see if you were still suicidal. I asked Maple to pressure you into leaving. You were right. It would be a death sentence to leave in this weather. I had to know if you would actually do it or not. I'm sorry, I didn't know she would push you this hard… I could have asked you, but there was no telling if you would lie to me or not. We needed to be sure." She took her hands off of his shoulders and stepped back. "You're cured, Ray."

Ray wiped at his nose. "I... I don't want to die..." He spoke as if he himself didn't even recognize the words coming from his mouth.

"Did you mean what you just said? About... *have* you changed?"

"If by change you mean... do I want to die anymore?" he asked, feeling that the answer was clear.

She nodded, and he sighed.

"I want to live. I do."

"And you're not going to run? You want to stay?" she asked, giving him one last out.

"I want you to be safe. I will do whatever I have to do to make sure that happens."

Luna looked over to Maple, who nodded at her with a smile. "Nothing is going to happen to us. I promise."

"But Tobias..."

"Don't worry about him," she said promisingly. "He's shunned for the time being. He has been banned from hunting detail, and he can barely move his arm. He's no threat to us right now. We have time to think."

Ray was relieved that he was no longer being forced to leave Corazon. But still, something about the way she was speaking made him uneasy. Tobias was still a threat, and he was still so close to them all. He needed to go, and he needed to go fast. It was only a matter of how.

"I think I need to sit down. Process all of this," he said, turning his back to Luna, who was within inches of his face. "There are better ways of figuring these kinds of things out."

Maple supported his shoulder and began to walk him toward Luna's hut. "We needed you to be genuine. We needed to see your raw emotions. Ray. We have been working with you for so long. This was a test. This is what I was talking about. We have been building you up day after day, hour after hour. The thing about the tests of life is that you never know when they will happen… It all happens fast, and when it does, you must be ready to make the right decision. We trust you now, Ray. You are a part of our family."

He just looked at her and nodded his head, he honestly had no words, but it was no use getting angry about it. Everybody has their methods; some are just harsher than others.

"So what now?" Luna said as she supported his other arm.

He shook his low-hanging head as he limped forward. "I don't know… what needs to be done?"

"That's the spirit," Maple said, chiming in. "Always look for work to do. Unfortunately, it's getting dark, and I'm going to head off. I'll see you two in the morning. There's supposed to be a big storm tomorrow. I can feel it in the air. Make sure you both are prepared. Stock up on dry wood while you can. You'll be lucky if there are any logs left," she said, making her way off into the distance.

Luna and Ray walked side by side as they slowly approached her hut.

"Hey, guys!" Beatrix screamed as she swung down from a low-hanging branch. "What are you up to?" she asked with her usual cheerful attitude, an attitude that brought a smile to both of their faces.

"Nope!" Maple shouted from afar. "Beatrix, get your butt over here! You leave them alone tonight!"

Beatrix shouted back, "But they like to play games with me! I gotta have a little fun too, ya know!"

Maple was quick to respond, "You come have fun with me. Go find your friend Clover! Bring her over. She can play cards with Musgo and me! Leave them alone tonight!"

Beatrix frowned and then looked up at the two of them. They both were looking around, trying to avoid eye contact with her so they didn't have to see her face when they let her down, admitting they did want some alone time. Beatrix rolled her eyes as she tried to get their attention, letting them know that she caught on to what was happening.

"Beatrix! Let's go, young lady!" Maple shouted again.

Beatrix grumbled as she marched toward Maple, who put her arm around her and accompanied her back to her home.

Ray and Luna watched them fade away into the day before retiring to her hut. Luna lit some candles as the clouds rolled in, and they each sat up on the side of the bed. He looked at her and appreciated how the light flickered on and off of her face. It really brought out her deep blue eyes, the same eyes that held so many secrets.

She sighed and looked at him, "I know what I did was cruel. I know it was a tough decision that you had to make earlier… I know you have done bad things, and I know you regret those decisions. I also know you can't go back. You can't undo what has been done. I know you care for us, and I know you want to live… I know all these things about you, and you know nothing about me."

She stood up from the bedside and walked until she was nearing the middle of the hut, engulfed in candlelight. She then crossed her arms and grabbed a corner of her shirt at each hip. She turned her back to him and lifted her shirt from her body. He looked at her bare back, and all of the markings etched into her skin. She reached around her back and traced the markings with her fingers. Each one had some cryptic reading carved deep into the tissue of her naked back. There were spaces and markings that appeared to be some kind of language.

"There was once a young, innocent girl," she spoke, her voice slightly trembling. "She liked to color. She had a brother, she had a mother and a father. But boy, did she like to color. She would color every day as soon as she got home from school. As soon as her foot hit that green grass as she hopped off the bus, she ran to her house as fast as she could. As soon as she got to her house, she would find her favorite crayon box, along with her favorite coloring book. And she would sit there and dream. Her dreams would come to life, they would dance from her imagination right onto the pages of her coloring book." She paused and slid her shirt back on. She then turned to him and continued.

"Her brother would sometimes help her, although he mainly just scribbled and wore out her nice crayons. His favorite color was *green*. Her brother would always meet her at the bus stop every day and race her home. She always won because she always had the motivation. She wanted to get there before he did so she could get the better crayons. This girl was happy. She was maybe even somewhat of an airhead. She would talk to ladybugs who crawled onto her fingers, and she sometimes liked to see how long her tiny fish could hold their breath outside of their tank. She was a sweet girl, kind to everyone, even if everyone wasn't kind to her."

"Her parents were rarely home. They were always off doing something work-related, though she never really knew what they did for a living. They would disappear in the middle of the night and be gone for days on end. Her mom would always come home crying, and her father would be a drunken mess. He would hit them a lot. Her brother took the hardest beating because he liked to act out more. But she was usually just hit for the sake of being hit. Sometimes he would hit them so hard they would blackout. They would wake up with these weird markings on their bodies. Scars that were sometimes still bleeding. The scars seemed to be in a different language. The girl often worried about her scars, but then she would start to color again and all of a sudden… Her worries were gone. The scars gave her a strange sense of bravery." She stopped and felt at her back as she sorrowfully looked at the floor. She didn't want to continue. She kept this information to herself. She couldn't think of a reason she should be telling Ray other than the fact that it just felt right.

"This girl's name was Cassidy Holmes. One day... she was on her way home from the bus. She was racing her brother and began to round the corner toward the straightaway to her house. She never knew why she always went back to her house. She didn't like it there. She only liked seeing her brother and his smiling face... and her crayons, she liked those a lot too. As she rounded the corner, she ran right into a man who was standing in front of her house. He was dressed in all white and had a really kind look in his eyes. He was just standing in the middle of her yard, but..." she blinked and continued.

"The man apologized to her for getting in her way and offered her a piece of his candy. She reluctantly took it and ran inside. The very next day, that man was still sitting on the curb. He wasn't a rapist or a pedophile... He was a man with a kind face who just enjoyed talking with some of the kids from the neighborhood. He had very nice manners and smiled a lot. This man's name was Elliot, and this is the story of how I came to Corazon."

26

Ray listened carefully as Luna explained how she wound up in Corazon at such a young age. Her words were like bullets, each one being fired by her, the gun. Each of the bullets struggled to break through this invisible wall of pain that separated the two of them. He could feel it. He could practically hear the cracking of those metaphorical bricks.

"Each and every day, I would meet Elliot at the bus stop. He would walk with me for a while, he would talk with me, he would share his treats with me… Always something new too, sometimes there were donuts, other times there were lollipops. I know this all sounds bad, trust me. But when you're a kid who is being abused the way I was, and an adult shows you some respect… treats you like a human being and cares for you the way nobody has ever cared for you before, well… you develop a trust. I got my little brother to come along on our walks with us, Elliot didn't mind. He was accepting of everyone. He told us jokes and brought us to the park to feed the ducks. And there was just… this warmness around him."

"He also had this way with words… this charisma that was untouchable. He would preach about people and how we had turned our backs on nature and had become evil or corrupted. At first, I wouldn't pay any attention to his rants, I just followed him to the park and ate my treats. But then I started to notice that he was getting the attention of certain people. It was no longer just me. I was sitting by his side as he stood on a bench and proclaimed the word of Mother herself. I realized that I was one of the younger followers, but the message remained the same. He taught us that everything— even the dirt we walk upon—is a gift and that to take that gift for granted would be to turn your back on Mother."

"He talked about how he had disappeared for a while to meditate on this mountain… And when he was up there, he was given a message from this godlike being. He referred to this being as Mother and talked about all of the wonderful things Mother had to say. Most people just walked by and didn't pay any attention to him. But for those who did… they came back. And they came back again the next week, and then they started to come back daily. And before we knew it, there was a whole crowd of people standing in front of him as he screamed his word to the heavens from atop that bench. And there I sat, right by his feet. Just a little girl snacking on that day's sweet. Sometimes we had to move because the police officers would come over thinking that something might have been up, but… we were harmless *at that point*."

Ray wanted to ask what came after the point where they decided not to be harmless, but he trusted that she would eventually get to it, so he let her continue uninterrupted. "I thought that he only waited for me every afternoon on that street corner, talked in the park, and then went to bed just to wake up the next morning and sit on the street corner for me again… But I soon found out I was wrong. He's such a smart man, he really is. This guy, Elliot, would walk around town barefoot, looking like a homeless bum. He went to places where people had problems and felt unwanted. He hung outside of counseling offices. He attended regular AA meetings. He even got in with some drug dealers and found out who was trying to get clean. He would go to them and use his sly tongue and unique phrasing to get them to listen. He promised salvation, redemption, happiness, anything good in the world all of a sudden seemed so possible when he was speaking. He always had food on him, too. He would give them something to snack on so that they felt obligated to listen to him. And I realized all this after a while, but I found that I was even beginning to listen to him."

"He would talk about how people have turned their backs on the simple nature of things and how we were all sinners just looking for a way out of this corrupting world. He would point out some individuals and ask them about their day. They would go about explaining to him what they did, and then he would tear them down and point out everything that they did wrong, everything that made them a sinner. If you didn't give change to the homeless man at the train station, you were a sinner. If you didn't share your lunch with someone in need, you were a sinner. If you didn't recycle, or thank the earth for a new day, or drive a car when you could have ridden a bike. He pointed out how easy it was to be a sinner in modern-day society. He made people, whom he referred to as his followers, feel bad about how much they take and how little they give. Then he gave us the answer to a simpler life. *Just listen to him.*"

"He told us about how if we continue to live in this world full of corruption and sin, that we would rot in the deepest abyss within the afterlife, and we would have to suffer as we watched all of the pure fly high above us. People bought into this, I bought into this. He convinced me that it was my own fault that my parents abused my brother and me. He told me that I allowed it to happen, and therefore I was the one to blame."

"I'm sorry." Ray cut in. "But that's bullshit. Making you believe you're wrong for taking an unjust beating? How does that make you a sinner? That is not sinning, it's just… bullshit."

Luna nodded. "That's what my brother thought, too. He stopped coming to the preachings in the park. I tried to get him to come back but he just sort of disregarded me. He saw this whole thing as a 'phase,' and he said that I, too, would get over it. He didn't realize how deep I was. What I didn't tell him was that I was actually starting to believe in Mother."

"What made you believe in all that? Seriously?" Ray asked reluctantly. He didn't know how well she was going to take it.

"Well… I wasn't the only one starting to believe in him. Others were listening as well. I had been following him daily for about two years at this point. People were beginning to question whether or not Elliot was legit. So one day, this guy wheels over this homeless man who was sick and in a wheelchair. The homeless man was coughing up blood and was shaking and all that… it was real bad. Elliot saw this man and immediately hopped down from the bench. He knelt down before the homeless man and touched him on the legs. He lowered his head and began to chant. *"By the power of Mother and all things sacred, please have mercy on this poor man. He has done no harm, spare his life from this pain."* And all of a sudden other people started to chime in. It wasn't just Elliot. And the craziest things started to happen. It was as if this guy was getting younger right in front of us. And then, almost like the life was pulled right back into him, the homeless man shot up and began to walk. He praised Mother and the ground he walked on. It was quite a sight to behold. I'll never forget the look on his face. The look on Musgo's face."

Ray just nodded and let her continue her story.

"That whole episode shocked everyone. We were all dedicated followers from that point on. But Elliot grew weak after that encounter. As if he had given some life of his own to grant Musgo his legs back. He healed him, but nothing is ever free. We were all taken back by Elliot's kindness and generosity. He explained to all of us that he was too weak to continue spreading his word and that he needed us to help him. He picked a few of us to go out into the city and preach just like he did. We would then report back to the park and tell him what happened. He was building a religious empire on our shoulders, and we didn't even realize. I stopped going to school. I only went home when I had to. I traveled around with Elliot and his sizable troop. We would find work where we could and help rid the city of its sin. Some people hated us too. We would all get spit upon, and we had trash thrown at us, but it was all okay because in the end, we would be granted wings, and they would be tethered to a rock in the bottom of a deep pit of despair. They started calling us The Getaway People. It was supposed to be derogatory, a joke about how everyone was always telling us to *get away*. But we took it and wore it with pride."

"Just like that, we were branded. We were the undesirables. We'd stage inner-city peaceful environmental protests, and we'd all run whenever police showed up. He saw them all as armed, lethal sinners who stop at nothing to uphold our bureaucratic system. We all took it as truth too. After all, it was coming from the mouth of a miracle worker. After a while, he decided that this way of life was not safe enough. We had cultivated too much hate."

"He told us he wanted to protect us. He told us he wanted to start his own colony, free of sin. He explained it all to us. He told us that he already made a deal with an outsider so that we could all get the supplies we needed. He made it sound like this paradise with high arches and golden gates. He called it Corazon. He said that it meant *heart* in Spanish. I don't know why he chose that of all words, but it worked. We were all enticed by the idea of paradise. It was supposed to be symbolism for the love we would share amongst ourselves. We would all be equals and live together in peace and harmony. It sounded… it just sounded so perfect. But first, we had to cleanse ourselves of our sin. And there was only one way to do that."

Luna got really quiet for a few moments. "Benji caught on to what I was doing, and it's not like I could just leave him behind. He had a choice to make, either come with us and live as Mother intended or rot away back home. He chose Mother. So we cleansed ourselves of sin. And we packed up and left. Gone, just like that. We traveled by car for what seemed like weeks. We had a small caravan that took us deep into the middle of nowhere. Some of the cars still might be sitting around these parts, rotting away."

"Hold up, hold up…" Ray cut in once again. "How did you cleanse yourself? And what did your parents say? Did they know about all of this?"

"We just vanished. It doesn't matter what they thought. One night, we just packed up all of our belongings. I put some bread, a bunch of paper, and some crayons into my little knapsack, and I was gone. All within an hour. Anything that I needed to take with me was already packed up in a box aboard the caravan. Benji practically begged me not to go through with it. He tried to stop me, but… it was too late by that point. My mind was made up already."

Ray noticed that she still avoided the topic of how she cleansed herself of all of her sin. He didn't bring it up again, though. This information was too good to risk ruining the moment.

"So we arrived in this heavily wooded area in the middle of nowhere, and our lives free of sin began. We slept in the worn-down cars and under some tarp for the first year. We fished and scavenged for any plants we knew were safe. We did everything we needed to do to survive, and I'll be honest—at first, it was awful. But then we started to build. We had a few handymen who followed the Book of Elliot, and they instructed us on how to build yurts. Those yurts, along with some minor changes and personal touches, turned into what we call huts. Once we had established living spaces, Elliot began to get sick. He claimed it was because he had been trying to heal us from all sickness and diseases that might be coming our way. We just took it as it was. After all, none of us had gotten sick. He chose a few men and a few women to accompany him higher up onto the mountain so that he could rest and heal and meditate, listening for Mother and any instructions he might have for us."

"After a while, Elliot stopped coming down, and he would send for more men to come up. He drew the line at fifteen men. They started referring to themselves as Disciples. The Disciples began to dictate what was right and what was wrong, speaking through the Prophet Elliot. They would rule what happened down here in Corazon while he remained on the mountain, doing whatever it was he was doing. Todd would come by monthly and bring us the necessities. He would sometimes even come with people that he recruited from different cities. Before we knew it, we had over a hundred people living here. We sort of lost count after a while, and taking a census was pointless. We always got what we put in. Your garden, you get a good share of vegetables. You hunt, you get a good share of meat. It was a system designed so that whoever wanted to work toward the development of the community was free to live in a world without major laws. We really made it up to seem like a really big deal, and honestly, if a man were to approach you in the street and offer you a chance to live in a place where sex is exchanged like currency and all violence is outlawed, would you do it? We didn't know it at the time, but we were creating a false paradise."

"Eventually, Maple and I grew to know each other. She was always handy with her medical background. Some say she was a surgeon or a doctor of some sort. They obviously don't know her. I think I was the only one she told about how she was a veterinarian. Musgo was one of the homeless men we recruited. He has a rough backstory, but he's the most generous soul you'll find around these parts. Beatrix was born here."

"Bea's mother died during childbirth. Bea was also the last child to have been born in Corazon. After her birth, it was declared that

Corazon could no longer afford to have anyone else living with us. There were only so many animals we could hunt. There was only so much land we could use to grow vegetation. We don't know who her father is. Her mother had shared her love far and wide. When you think about it, it sounds like a sickening thing, making her look like some kind of whore. But she wasn't. She was one of my good friends. She went by the name *Blaire*. She just really took into the whole free love movement that was constantly pushed onto her.

She was really close to Tobias at the time of her death. Some thought he might have even been the father, but… well, he denies it. We all had our own reasons for coming to Corazon. Most of us came to escape the pain and corruption of the other world; the religion just gave us a reason. But she actually bought into it all. I pray, and I go to mass, and I follow most parts of the Book of Elliot, but there are some things that I feel Mother just didn't intend for me to do. I don't want to willingly give myself to a new man every night of the week because a poorly written book tells me to. I can't talk about this very often, but—I'm losing my religion. What happened to Tobias… I know what he did was horrible, but I can't help but feel for him. I-"

"Enough," Ray ordered, putting a hand up. "Do not pity that man. He got what was coming to him. He made a decision, now he has to deal with the consequences."

"I realize that, just know that we all come from a troubling place."

"That may be true, but there is no excuse for what he did. None. You cannot hold onto these feelings for him. I know it must be tough, but he is not the man you once knew. Drop it, Luna, please… for the both of us."

Luna moved closer to him, sitting right by his side. "He wants *nothing more* than to be a Disciple. That's all he's dreamed of ever since he got here. He used to tell me his plans for how he would make Corazon better. He said he wanted two water purification systems so that we could purify one while we drink from the other.

He had this idea for a tunnel system in the mountains; he wanted to connect some of the caves so that we could have a place to stay during the winter. He had all these ideas that were just too far to reach. He knew that a Disciple had to die before another one could be recruited. Once you're a Disciple, you are set for both life and the hereafter. I don't really know how to explain how I feel, all I know is that it doesn't feel good. I know that you're the only thing driving this stake in between Tobias and me. He's been so stressed since you got here. I know you see it too. It's like I'm expected to make a choice. You just don't know him like I do… like I did."

Ray got really quiet. Everything she was saying was true; he just didn't know how to respond. Did she really have to choose between the man that wants her and the man that just attempted to end her life? Her mind was warped. It must be when living in a place like Corazon, but he would never have expected her to actually debate her loyalty between the two of them. "So… do you have an answer? If you had to make a choice, who? I know this is a horrible question to ask, but… for whatever reason, I've never wanted to know the answer to anything so badly in my entire life."

Luna angled her head toward him and slowly closed her eyes. He turned to her, not knowing if he had stepped too far. She slowly pinched the chest of his worn-down shirt and pulled it toward herself. Realizing what was transpiring, he allowed himself to shamelessly slip under her control. He took his hand and stroked the remaining strands of hair out of her face. He then gently lifted her chin so that it was equal, if not slightly above his own.

They drew each other in closer and closer until their lips met. She held onto his shirt, remaining in control. He basked in the moment, keeping his eyes closed, allowing his soul to unwind, sending all of the built-up tension in his body scattering onto the floor. It felt as if his shoulders had just dropped miles as euphoria ran over his body like water. They separated for a brief moment and quickly reunited again, this time with a spark of passion that ran through them both. He didn't want to let this moment go. If he were to remain suspended there, in that moment, for the rest of eternity, everything would be just fine. This was, after all, the first time he had had any emotional contact in years. She slowly dropped her head. Keeping her eyes closed, she smiled. He, on the other hand, looked up and down her face, looking for a sign, any signal of something, be it good or bad, he needed something.

Luna stood up and calmly walked out of the hut. Ray sat still, right where she had left him. She had not answered his question. He sat there, hanging, wanting to know what that passionate embrace had just meant. Where was she going, and what happens next?

27

The winter weather slowly picked up. The snow became more frequent, and the spontaneous gusts of wind, stronger, sweeping dead leaves clean from their branches. Winter wasn't fully upon them yet, but it gave way to that deep fall weather that required that extra layer of clothing for warmth. Luna kept things interesting by sneaking a kiss now and then, but nothing ever came close to touching the moment the two of them shared that night. People became more skeptical of their blossoming relationship, but that didn't bother them; people were always skeptical. It made Ray feel as though he were in middle school again, sneaking kisses behind the rusty jungle gym in the play yard. He didn't mind, though. It was all some sort of cute game for him. He didn't see Luna the same way anyone else did. The community was so fixated on shared love and the swapping of partners that the whole idea of what love actually is had been skewed.

All he knew is what he felt for her was something he hadn't felt in a very long time. It was a warm, welcoming feeling, the feeling of having his heart sink deeper into his chest every time he saw her face. Her imperfections became her perfections, from her thin face to the slight scarring left by the incident months before.

Tobias seldom showed his face. When he did, it was only when he was needed. His punishment was a step up from an execution. After being castrated and having his right arm crushed, the community shunned him. He went from the strong, bold hunter he was to an emasculated slave called upon to do the dirty work of the community, a runt in its finest form. He wasn't even allowed to stay within the confines of Corazon. He was forced to remain cooped up in a dainty wooden shack he built for himself. The cold was a ruthless warrior who showed pity for nobody.

Sterling crept into Tobias's small makeshift shack in the woods each morning and woke him up with a bucket of ice water. Tobias jumped up and shook off the water. He threw his hands up in the air and opened his mouth, ready to scream, just as he did every morning.

"Eh-eh! Watch yourself!" Sterling said, wagging a finger in his direction. "You know the rules. Elliot says you will only find repentance if you follow his strict word. And he says you are forbidden to speak. So what was it you wanted to say to me? *Go ahead*. I know you wanted to say something!" Sterling laughed and threw the heavy bucket at Tobias's legs causing him to jump up, knocking a major beam in his shack out of place. The poorly built structure began to collapse on him; Sterling laughed as he walked away. He found some sort of sadistic pleasure in watching the strong-spirited man before him slowly wilt away. Sterling just hid behind this cloak that repeatedly told him he was doing the right thing by torturing him. He followed a true eye-for-an-eye mentality.

Tobias stood in the heap that was his shack, holding the bucket by his side, heaving with rage, yet he didn't speak. He then dressed in his damp, cold clothing; the shack only did so much when it came to keeping snow and rain out. He missed his hut, he missed his words, and most of all, he missed his connections with the people he once held close.

He stretched out his back and began to get to work. His job that day, just like most days, consisted of him taking care of the waste from the outhouses and transporting it to the compost piles. He had to use the bucket he was holding to do so, the same bucket that woke him up by slopping cold water on him every morning.

He made his way to the outhouses, which luckily were not in use at the moment. He silently shuffled to the back of the outhouses, where he pulled out the tub, which collected all of the waste from the past day. The tub was tall and wide, with thick plastic sides. His face shriveled up as he pulled it out and got a whiff of it all. He then began to violently gag and eventually vomited off to the side. After that, it was off to work.

Tobias pushed his bucket as far as he could, deep into the putrid mush. He pushed it down until he reached the bottom of the tub, then, with one abrupt, fluid motion, he dragged it along the bottom and up toward his chest. The bucket was full and had barely made a dent in the waste that was to come. He hauled his heavy metal bucket into the woods until he found a clearing that contained the compost pile for the community. It was all gathered under a huge blue tarp, which they felt kept the snow off. Tobias often wondered what the purpose of gathering compost in the winter was. It was all going to freeze and go to waste. But that didn't matter; his words were now worth less than the waste he collected.

He walked back over to the putrid tub of waste and continued his work, trudging back and forth for what seemed to be hours. Sometimes he broke down and cried. He would push his face into the dying grass and scream. He wanted to talk to someone, have them assure him everything would be okay, but he was shunned for lack of a better word. There was nothing he could do here. He knelt, cast down to the very bottom, lower than a slave, lower than he had ever been before.

He was angry at himself more than anything. He thought back to that late summer day where he decided to ruin his reputation in Corazon for life. He thought back to how he had imagined it a good idea to kill Luna, as if that would have taken care of any of his problems. He didn't want her dead; he loved Luna. He truly loved her. The two sides of his brain were battling each other. Meanwhile, he trudged along, overcome with guilt.

Sometimes after he was done filling up bucket after bucket of slop, he would go for a walk to find plants or bugs that would allow him to survive for the night. He missed the community meals. He missed the pungent taste of venison in his mouth. He missed the flame-cooked vegetables and ripe berries that always seemed to be so plentiful. He even missed the cheap prepared foods Todd brought in for them in bulk on a monthly basis. He missed it all. He wanted nothing more but to go back and change what he had done, but it was far too late. He was too far gone.

As the weeks dragged on, he began to lose weight. He was so hungry that his stomach would sometimes go numb. He even resorted to eating questionable plants and rotting fish along the riverbank. His beard began to grow scraggly and in patches. He barely even recognized himself.

"My! You could kill a small animal from miles away with that odor!" Sterling would proclaim as he splashed Tobias with the freezing water from the waste bucket. "You need to wash up! This morning ritual obviously isn't doing it for ya!" he yelled right before he began to laugh at his own statement.

Tobias just took it all in and put one knee to the earth so that he could have a little extra support with getting himself up. He used a sizable branch to leverage himself to his feet. From there, he sighed, picked up the waste bucket, and went about his daily routine. Hours later, after he had finished, he went for his mid-evening walk under the cold pink and blue sky. He meandered his way in between the dying trees and managed to only step on the dead leaves, thus avoiding the growing patches of snow. His breath was icy and dry as he exhaled wisps of smoke into the nighttime air.

Eventually, he wandered into territory all too familiar to him. He had managed to walk along the riverside, forcing him to come face to face with Otto, sitting silently where he always sat, admiring the icy currents as he ate away at a couple of fish he had just caught and cooked over an open flame. Otto looked up to Tobias with a certain kind of sorrow in his eyes as he wiped the grease from the corners of his mouth. "Not too scary without a gun, are ya…"

Tobias lumbered there, just looking at Otto, thinking about how all of this might not have happened if only that sickly man were to mind his own business. He wanted to beat him; he wanted to kick Otto in the stomach and get on top of him and punch until even his own hands were bloody stubs. He wanted to hurt Otto so that maybe, just maybe, he would feel the same pain that he felt at this very moment.

Otto nodded as he turned his attention from Tobias and back toward the river. "The river, it calms me," he said, staring endlessly into the light current. "I don't know why, it has something to do with the current. It goes and goes and goes, and it can be tampered with. Obstacles can be put in its way, but nothing will stop the current from flowing. Sarah and I, we watch it for hours," he said, nodding his head to a small stone next to him. Otto set down his plate of fish and picked up the stone. He tossed it in his hand for a moment and then cast it into the river. "Ya see… the stone disrupted the water. But the current was more powerful. It made sure the water kept moving forward. It made sure the water didn't lose control."

"I've never understood currents. But I understand what they do, I don't need to know why. All I know is at that moment, the current felt it had to overcome that stone, so it did. And I can appreciate that." Otto said with a meek smile as he looked back at Tobias.

Tobias was beyond confused. He couldn't pick up on any symbolism of any sort. Was he the current? Was he the rock? Or was this just a lesson on how Otto likes currents?

"Sit down," Otto said, patting the ground next to him. "You must be hungry." He then took the fish he was eating and placed it aside. "I've got extra tonight, and you look like you need a break."

Tobias's mouth watered as he stared at the smoking leftovers Otto had set aside for him. Was this some sort of trick? A trap, perhaps? Or was it a testament to this man's true generosity? Tobias stumbled over to the fish and hungrily devoured it, picking away at the flesh of the fish's ribs with his trembling fingers. All manners were out the window. He tore away at the fish like a feral animal. As he wiped the grease from the corners of his mouth, he looked up to Otto. He didn't know whether or not he should speak. He knew he was being shunned, but it didn't seem as though Otto was upholding those particular standards.

Tobias sat back and picked away at the bones of the fish, pinching away any last bits of meat he could. Otto just pleasantly watched him, occasionally looking to the current or up to the pink sky as the crisp breeze ran through his hair. Why was he doing this? Tobias had threatened him with his life, yet here he was, offering his enemy some leftover food. A white flag of sorts.

"I'm not your enemy," Otto muttered as he picked up another stone and threw it into the current. "I didn't do this to you," he nodded toward Tobias's arm. "*They* did this. They crushed your arm. *They* took your manhood. They did all of that, not me." Tobias looked to Otto with a look of sorrow and regret plastered upon his face. "I will admit… I, too, was snooping around camp when I overheard you and Brooke talking about the baby. I wouldn't have said anything to anyone. I know what happens to babies around here. I… I could have approached you better. I only wanted to help. But you lost control of yourself, and… and *they* did this to you. I'm sorry, Tobias. I just want to live a simple life with Sarah here in my cove. I get all the necessities I need from Corazon, and that's it. I want nothing to do with their politics or religion. *Nothing*."

Otto picked up another stone and tossed it from one hand to the other, admiring it with his two crazy eyes. "You do what you have to do with this information. But if you take one thing away from this… know that I'm not the enemy." He once again threw the stone into the river and looked back over to Tobias, who nodded in agreement. Otto was right—the man sitting before him was not the enemy. He had lost control, and now he was paying the price.

"I know you want to be a Disciple, I know that's all you've wanted since you got here. You want power. I know you, Tobias. But you have to let that go… you have to see what's wrong here. We're living in some kind of dream world, and it's time to wake up." Otto said, looking at him with understanding eyes.

Tobias swallowed the last of his fish and looked at Otto. He opened his mouth and tried to talk, but all that came out was a squeaky breathy sound. His vocals were still shredded by the amount of screaming they had done a while ago. He cleared his throat and tried to talk again. Otto waited patiently as he tried to find his voice.

"*Th-thank you.*" Tobias squeaked as he wiped away a tear to prevent it from running down his cheek.

Otto nodded. He seemed very pleased with himself. "Don't thank me, thank Sarah. She talked me into this."

Tobias cracked a smile and awkwardly nodded in gratitude to the space next to Otto. Otto smiled and looked at him, "She says, 'You're welcome.'"

The two of them sat by the riverside and watched the reflection of the sunset in the current. Eventually, Otto got to his feet and went into his personal cove that he had dug himself into the side of the embankment. He lived there. He had gas lamps for warmth, and Sarah was all the company he needed. He seldom left his little cove.

He came back out with a heavy blanket. "Now I'm not sure what it's made out of, but it'll keep ya alive, so…"

He extended his arms, holding the blanket out for Tobias to take. Tobias used a dried-up piece of driftwood to pull himself to his feet. He stumbled over to the blanket, and Otto wrapped it around him. Tobias cherished the newfound warmth as he closed his eyes and took it all in. It was a simple pleasure, which he now regarded as a luxury.

"Now go. It's getting dark. I'd let you stay here, but… well, Sarah isn't all that welcoming," he said, waving him away. Tobias looked back and opened his mouth again. "I know, I know! Get going before they come looking for ya!" Otto whispered, throwing his hands away from him, gesturing for Tobias to hurry up.

Otto scurried back into his cove, and Tobias limped away, disappearing into the night. He eventually made it back to his makeshift shack where Sterling was waiting.

"Well, look who decided to show up!" he said in an obnoxious tone. "I was about to send a couple guys out looking for you, you're damn lucky you came back when you did."

Tobias continued to walk, avoiding eye contact with Sterling. "Get inside, boy. I've got a little surprise for you!" Tobias considered turning right back around and going the other way. Maybe he should run away… Maybe anything would be better than what he was doing now. Nevertheless, he trudged on and pulled back the flap on his shack. He stopped dead in his tracks as the blood drained from his face.

Standing before him were two women from Aria's entourage. He looked back to Sterling, trying to shield his view from the women presented before him. Sterling laughed, "What's the matter, lad! Get in there!" he ordered as he forcefully pushed him further into the small shack causing him to drop to his knees. His new blanket was pulled off of his back and thrown into the damp, muddy corner.

"I remembered how much you loved women. Oh, you were with a new broad every night!" Sterling stopped to laugh. "Anyhow, I know you've had it rough for the past few weeks, so I decided to reward ya!"

The two women reluctantly surround Tobias, who tried to avoid looking at them. They placed their hands on him and eventually began to massage his shoulders. One leaned down until she was right next to his ear, kneeling directly beside him. She whispered sweet, dirty, nothings into his ear. His face quickly turned from one of determination to one of pain as he began to buckle.

Sterling laughed, "What's the matter there, boy? Having trouble performing?"

Tobias looked up at him with hatred in his eyes. He wanted nothing more than to get up and bash Sterling's head in, but if he ever had the slightest chance at becoming a Disciple, he had to take the punishment and do as he was told.

"You ladies stay here and keep him company through the night. You can leave in a few hours." Sterling ordered, glaring at the two women on either side of Tobias.

Sterling left the tent giggling at himself. Tobias squeezed his eyes shut and laid back, trying his best to block out the physical temptations surrounding him. His body ached and stung as they kept their hands on him. At that very moment, he wanted to die.

The soft torture continued over the length of the next few hours. Tobias tried his best to sleep, but his company had strict orders not to let that happen. Eventually, the two of them stopped taunting him and left the leaking encampment. He sighed in relief and rolled over, allowing himself to quickly slip into a deep sleep.

Sterling watched all of this go down as he stood behind the flap, holding the waste bucket full of icy water. He lurked behind the flap, waiting to make sure Tobias was deep into his sleep before ripping him out of his dream world. After giving him a few minutes, Sterling pushed past the flap and sent the water cascading onto his chest and face.

Tobias shot up and screamed. Sterling laughed, but Tobias didn't stop. He continued to scream and scream and scream, pausing briefly in between to catch his breath. Sterling slowly backed away as Tobias pulled himself to his feet and started hobbling in his direction.

Sterling backed up into the woods, and Tobias followed, still screaming. It was a frightful sound, hearing a grown man scream in such a way. As he drew closer, Sterling struck him in the neck, shutting him up immediately. Tobias dropped to one knee as he grabbed at his throat.

Sterling looked him up and down, fully knowing that he had pushed him too far. He contemplated giving him the day off, but he couldn't; it was all too much fun. "Pull yourself together and take care of the waste. After that, I want you to set the grizzly traps. I saw a couple of them about five miles out."

Tobias just knelt there, holding his throat.

"Do I make myself clear, boy?"

He looked up at Sterling and nodded.

Sterling left and went about his daily activities, which included hunting, hiking, laying traps, and eating copious amounts of food.

Tobias slowly got to his feet and lumbered over to the outhouses, where a new day began.

❄︎❄︎❄︎

The snow began to slowly pick up. There were now regular dustings upon the ground every morning; other days, the flakes would drift down through the trees as well. There was always a fire in every hut. It kept everyone warm and safe. If a fire was too difficult to start, they were allowed one cup of lighter fluid upon request of the nearest Disciple. The two designated Disciples had their own hut. Nobody was allowed inside, but the Disciples seemed more than comfortable.

Beatrix visited Luna's hut frequently to check up on things. She would often stop by right before she went to bed every night so that Ray might share with her a tale from the old world.

He would tell her about simple things, like clowns, Ferris wheels, and going to the movies.

"So that's what people call a clown," he would say, reflecting on how truly absurd his description had just been.

"Why does he have a red nose?" she would ask.

"Well, it's not a real red nose, it's fake. It's because it makes people laugh," he answered.

"Why does he wear a fake nose?" she asked.

"It's fake, but it's funny. It's funnier when it's fake."

She didn't seem sold. "Why is fake funny?"

"It's like a fairytale… if Luna were to tell you another one of her fairy tales but replaces the green scaly monster with a short man with green hair and a big red nose that tripped on his shoelaces all the time… wouldn't that make it funnier?" he asked, trying his best to sound like he was making sense.

She giggled and nodded in agreement. "So back to TV? I still don't get it."

Ray found her confused expression quite interesting yet sad at the same time. Before him sat a growing girl, on the verge of becoming a teenager, who had virtually no idea what television was. He scratched his head and tried thinking of a reasonable answer. "Well… A TV is a box. You set the box somewhere, and… the box has a glass front so that you can see inside of the box. And when you turn the box on, a light turns on in the back, and that light allows you to see little people and animals and stuff."

"How do the people and animals get inside the TV?"

"Well, they're not actually inside the TV. It's just a picture of them," he explained.

"And the picture moves!"

"Yes! Well, no… It's um… It's kind of complicated. It's like someone has puppets, but those puppets are much more… I'm sorry, Bea, I can't really explain it to you well."

"But everybody uses the TV?"

"Everyone."

"And when you watch TV, you can't run around and play? Can't you go outside? You can't carry the TV with you?"

"No, you can't. It needs to be connected to an outlet. It needs electricity to keep the TV on."

"Wow… what's an outlet? What's electricity?"

Ray panicked a little bit, knowing full well he had dug himself an even deeper hole.

"All right, Bea," Luna said, cutting in. "I think it's time you go to bed. Where are you sleeping tonight?"

She thought for a moment, "I'm hanging out with Clover for a little bit, then… I'm gonna go talk with Maple. Maybe she can tell me more about TV?"

Luna laughed, "Oh, I'm sure she can! Be careful with Clover, don't get into any trouble!"

Beatrix giggled in a suspiciously innocent manner as she skipped off into the night, leaving Ray and Luna behind. He turned to her with a perplexed look upon his face.

"TV, of all of the things a girl her age should know about… I don't know. It makes sense. It's just…"

Luna smiled and touched his shoulder. "How could she know? When you are born and raised in a society like Corazon, you don't think about entertainment. Entertainment can be found all around! Call back to the birds, go hunting or fishing, try your hand at art or sculpting!"

He nodded, "Right, but you don't see anything wrong with that?"

"Wrong with what?"

"You don't see anything wrong with keeping her from the real world?"

Luna seemed taken back; she removed her hand from his shoulder and lowered her gaze, making her seem slightly more intimidating. "And what is real?"

"Luna, come on, don't do this."

"No, answer the question. What is real? What makes your world more real than mine?" she asked, sounding somewhat offended.

"Luna, I'm not saying that."

"No, you *are* saying that," she said sternly. "That's *exactly* what you're saying. So in order for me to answer your question, I need to know… what makes your world more real than mine, Ray?"

Ray ran a hand down his face and looked up to the open exhaust hole in the ceiling. "In my world, in the *real* world, people pay taxes. In the *real* world, there is an *established* government that doesn't make rules up as they go. In the *real* world, people don't hold a crippled man captive. In the *real* world, children can go see *movies* and go to the *mall* and *order some pizza* on a Saturday night with their *friends*. In the real world, there are set relationships, there's marriage, and there's divorce, and there are unspoken rules about sleeping around with other people. In the real world, people *work to earn money* so that they can spend it on supplies they need and not wait to get a monthly shipment that *rarely* lives up to expectations. That's the real world."

"So tell me, what's wrong with my world then, Ray? In my world, love is found around every corner. In my world, we teach our children principles and moral values at a very young age. We teach them to hunt and fish and treat elders with respect. We outlaw violence, and we don't tolerate abuse. We treat the sick, and we accept the homeless. We don't cast the mentally ill out onto the streets. We don't walk around like mindless zombies with our faces in a screen all day. We don't need the idea of television polluting the brains of our young. Sure we keep stuff from them, but they are the children of the future.

They are going to be leaders one day; we only teach them what is right."

"And who are you to say what's right? What makes you the judge of that? You're so used to this way of life that you can't seem to grasp the idea of going back!"

"Why do I need to go back! I love it here! You're just scared! You're scared of accepting something into your heart that you don't believe in. Well, news flash, we outnumber you. There's a saying I learned long ago, the nail that sticks out should be hammered down. You're that nail, Ray. I don't know how long it will take, but someone's going to come with the hammer."

He winced and looked at her in disbelief. "Was that a threat?"

She shook her head, "It was whatever it had to be."

"You see, this is what's wrong with Corazon. You think you need to fix me. *I'm not looking to be fixed*. In the real world, people don't worry about others' problems. In the real world, you mind your own damn business," he shouted, pointing a finger at her face.

"There is one thing that you have here that you could never have in the real world," she said, backing up slightly.

Ray sighed and set his temper to the side. "Listen, Luna… I just don't want you to think that I'll stay here for the rest of my life. This, what is happening between us is great, but I… I just don't agree with everything that goes down here. Beatrix, Clover, all of the other kids here… they deserve to know what it's like. They deserve to make their own choice. You people exiled a man for mistakenly having a baby. Hell, someone was murdered a while ago—it isn't safe here, and there's nothing you can say to make me believe anything else."

Luna closed her eyes and brought her hand to her forehead. "This is not a democracy, Ray. The rules are set in stone, bound within the Book of Elliot. Nothing is going to change. You need to accept that. Just realize that you have the power to leave now, and you still haven't. So what does that tell you? If you have a great life to get back to, then by all means… Go run along back to your "real" world. But until you figure things out, you're here, and as long as you're here, you are going to play by the rules. End of discussion."

Ray put his hands up in surrender. "Message received. I was just trying to express my opinion. I guess that's something I can't afford to have in a place like this."

She sighed. "Well, I know you have a point. I know that. I'm not saying you're 100% wrong. I'm just trying to say that you can't call the shots right now. That's it."

"I understand," he said willingly.

The two of them sat in silence for a few moments right before Luna went over to the corner of the hut to partake in her nightly prayer ritual. Ray listened in, as he usually did. There was never any set script for her prayer; it varied day to day, night to night. The only thing that never varied was whether she said them or not.

As she knelt on her small mat and kept her face hovering above the small wooden bowl of water, she whispered… "Oh loving, oh kind, oh merciful Mother. Thank you for blessing us with the gift of a new day. Protect our hearts, our minds, our friends, and our sanity. Grant us with a new day that we may continue to give you our endless praise and love through the one true prophet, Elliot. Thank you for your endless gifts." She then lowered her head to the water dish and lightly splashed her face, a way of self-acknowledging her prayer, the water baptizing her for the day to come.

She then rose to her feet and stretched. "I'm going to bed," she said plainly as she turned to him, sitting on the edge of her bed.

He smiled, "Don't mind me. I might head off too, pretty tired actually." He yawned. He brought his legs up onto the bed, and Luna sat down on the floor beside him. "Luna, please sleep in your bed tonight. I'm not even hurt anymore. Hop on up here."

She looked up at him. "You want me to… sleep with you?"

He looked confused. "Not—not like that, you know… just sleep in your own bed. I don't have to stay here. I'll take the floor tonight."

She stood up and leaped over him, curling up in the covers upon impact with the mattress. He looked up to the ventilation hole in the ceiling and smiled. It was about time. He thought about reaching over and touching her on the waist, maybe even going in for a kiss; all of the possible outcomes were running through his mind.

"Thank you, Ray… good night."

And just like that, he was content.

28

The very next day, Maple took both Ray and Beatrix out to gather. "Gathering is just as important as hunting if you ask me," she boasted. "Sure, we all need meat to eat, but what happens when we get sick of it? What happens when we want something light or even flavorful! These woods bear some of the freshest, juiciest berries. And I intend to pick every last one of them before they die out. You'll find mostly blackberries, a few strawberries out here. But we need as much as possible. Apples are always welcome, too."

Beatrix and Ray took careful mental notes. Maple showed the two of them certain types of flowers and leaves that people enjoyed too. She would say things like, "Never pick the ones with thorns or spikes on them… bad news." They quickly caught on that Maple didn't really know what she was talking about, but she knew enough to get by, and that's what mattered. She knew what sort of plants would kill you, and at the end of the day, the taste wasn't the top priority.

No matter how stern or annoyed Maple came off, she was always looking out for the community's best interest. She looked out for Ray, and she treated Beatrix like the granddaughter she never had. "So Ray," she said with a smile as they walked through the woods.

"Beatrix was asking me about television last night. She seems quite intrigued."

Ray laughed and looked at Beatrix, who still seemed flustered. "I just don't get it! I don't understand! I talked to Clover about it all night last night. It just—I don't know. How can they fit all those things into the box? Clover said you're just making things up."

"Listen, Bea. I promise, one of these days I'll show you a TV. I'll bring one here so your little bud Clover can see too, or I'll take you with me so you can see one yourself."

"Wait, so you're leaving?" Bea asked, sounding worried.

Maple raised an eyebrow and looked over to Ray. He sighed and patted her on the back of the head. "No, not yet. But I don't know if I'll stay here forever."

Maple cut in, "I don't know if I would go around saying that too much, Ray. If the wrong person hears you, well… It could be bad."

"I don't see what's so bad about wanting the best of both worlds. Todd does it."

"Todd has an agreement with Elliot and the Disciples." Maple stated.

"Well, then let me up on the mountain. I'll go talk to them, work something out."

"It's not that easy. People can't just go onto the mountain. You have to be invited."

"Well, I have just as good of a chance as anyone else in my opinion," he said, shrugging.

Maple shook her head. "Only Disciples go up onto the mountain. Nobody knows what it's like. They keep it secret for a reason. They need their peace and quiet for meditation. They live a simple life free from distractions. How else is Mother supposed to talk to them?"

Ray couldn't stand the absurdity of her words. He quickly changed the subject. "Okay, Bea, name something else that you want to know about. Something easier than a TV."

She thought for a moment and then spoke carefully. "I think I want a bike. A machine like a car but with two wheels and no motor? It sounds pretty cool."

"Oh, they are pretty cool. My friends and I used to ride our bikes around everywhere. It was awesome. I can probably get Todd to bring a bike in, right?" he asked, looking at Maple.

She rolled her eyes. "We'll see, I guess, won't we?"

Ray ignored her pessimistic attitude. "I'm going to get you that bike, Beatrix. And when I do, we are going to ride around these woods and have a great time."

"You mean it?" she asked, wide-eyed and rosy-faced.

"You better believe I do."

Beatrix tried to hide that giddy little grin she got when she was excited, but she wasn't very successful. The three of them laughed for a while as Maple and Ray swapped stories about the old world they lived in. Maple never gave too much though, she, just like many people on Corazon, kept her past bound to her chest.

"Come here, the both of you," Maple said, waving them over to the side of the beaten path. "I want you two to see this. Ray, this really concerns you, but Bea, it won't hurt for you to learn." She held up a handful of blackberries. "You see these? Know them. Know how they taste on your tongue, know how they feel, know how they look. Know everything about them, or else I'll haunt ya."

Ray looked over to Bea for a bit of assistance, but she was just as confused. Maple continued to speak. "So normally, I do the picking. I oversee some of the gardening, but the scavenging is usually my job. I know these berries by sight, so you need to as well. Don't ever confuse them with these." She moved her body and held up a hand to a bush with strikingly similar berries on it. "These right here, these are *not* blackberries. These are what I like to call *sickberries*. Sickberries are the devil's gift to the world. They have paralytic effects. You know what that means?" she asked, looking at Beatrix.

Beatrix shook her head quickly, intent on learning what Maple had to say.

"It means that they mess up your nerves. They make it nearly impossible to move. These berries stick around a little longer, they stay strong right through the winter like blackberries. You need to know the difference. I accidentally ate a single sickberry once, and the experience nearly killed me. I couldn't move a muscle, but I felt everything. There was this one mosquito that almost bled me dry that couple of days. It just kept pricking away, and I could do nothing about it. I couldn't even talk. Good ol' Musgo wouldn't leave my side for weeks."

"Jesus, Maple," Ray said, examining the sickberries closely.

"Just be careful. Look for the signs. See how these leaves are edged out a bit more? They aren't as smooth as regular blackberries. The berries themselves aren't as bumpy either. See what I mean?" She held the two berries in her hand and allowed the two to examine them. "Just remember this, I'll usually be with you so I can look over the berries myself, but just in case. *When in doubt, go without.*"

"Yes, ma'am," Ray said, sounding a bit concerned. He didn't want to be the one making that mistake, but it was either that or working out in the pasture with a mentally broken Brooke, so he decided it would be best to take his chances gathering and cooking with Maple.

They continued on their walk, picking up berries as they did. It wasn't until Ray noticed the large boxed-off structure that he stopped out of pure curiosity. "What the hell is that?" he asked, staring at the refrigerator-sized hunk of dark metal in the middle of the woods.

Maple trotted up beside him and placed her hands on her hips. "That is what we tell the kids to stay away from. They call it the *hunting chest*," she said, emphasizing the importance within her words.

Ray approached it cautiously. As he grew closer, he realized that *hunting chest* was just another word for *gun safe*. It was a thick metal safe with a dial on the front of it and a sturdy handle to its right. He grabbed hold of the handle and gave it a tug, feeling the true weight of the chest in its lack of sway. "Why's it all the way out here?" he asked, looking at Maple.

"Because guns are only safe when they aren't in the hands of others. And very few venture out this far. Only the hunters have access to this, and they don't even know the code."

"Why not?" he responded.

She kept her hands pressed firmly against her hips. "We have a pretty strict system around here if you haven't noticed already. Sterling oversees the weapons, and the only other person who knows the code is the only other somewhat decent hunter we have."

"Luna," he said, not needing to ask her who it was.

She nodded. "The girl hasn't told a single soul."

Ray kept his eyes on the hunting chest, still floored by its size. "How many guns does this thing hold? It seems a bit excessive, no?"

Maple began to walk away, looking at her surroundings to help guide them toward the greenhouse. "Just because we're safe doesn't mean we don't like to be prepared."

He followed slowly behind, still fixated on the chest. "And what kind of things are you all preparing for?"

"The worst kind of things," Maple said, fully aware of how her vague response would bother him for the rest of the day. "But never mind all that, the greenhouse is right up here," she said, a hint of excitement in her voice.

They came upon the greenhouse garden under the cliffs of the mountain briefly to examine and possibly harvest any of the spouting vegetation. The greenhouse was set up perfectly. It was built up on a higher level than most of the other facilities to prevent flooding, plus the cliffs above it kept the rain and snow from bombarding the thick plastic roof. It was also positioned in such a way so the sun would hit it without being affected by the overhanging shadows for most of the day. "Onions, garlic, spinach, and beans!" she said proudly. It'll be a *good winter,* that's for sure. So far, they're coming along real nice." She held a sprouting garlic plant to her nose and breathed in really deeply. "Ahh yes… here, take a whiff," she said, holding the large pot in Ray's face. Beatrix scampered outside, making a sound as if she were going to throw up, making it obvious she was not a fan of garlic.

Ray smelled the pungent sprouting cloves and allowed the aroma to consume him. "Damn. That's something," he said, not knowing how to respond to the smell of garlic.

She nodded and looked at the garlic with her mouth slightly ajar. Her eyes were wide and her smile even wider as she set the pot back on its respective shelf. "Nothing like a bit of garlic to add some good flavoring, huh?!" She nudged him in the arm with her elbow.

He let out a fake laugh. "Ha, yeah."

Ray looked around the greenhouse, which was bigger than any hut, but a tad cramped due to the volume of plants. There was a peace that came with the greenhouse, a quiet that remained unmatched by any other place in the vicinity. He felt a calm wash over his body. "Is this place always open, Maple?"

Maple smiled, "Only to the ones I choose to show it to. Come on now, we should go get Bea."

The two of them made their way back outside, where Beatrix had just run off. "Bea!" Ray lightly shouted. "Bea, come on, we're heading back to camp! We got enough for now!"

There was no answer. His voice echoed through the whispering woods. "Bea! Come on now! We're heading back!" Again, no answer. He and Maple looked at each other and began to cautiously walk, looking side to side for any sign of her.

"Bea? Where are you?" he shouted. There was still no answer. It was moments like this that made Ray sweat, a simple question gone unanswered under the wrong circumstances.

Maple began to chime in as well. "Bea, where are you? Bea, come on out!" Hoping that she was playing some sort of hide and seek.

They caught a glimpse of her long curly hair along the wall of the cliff fifty ahead of them. Ray ran for her, worried about why she was not answering.

"Bea. Bea, why didn't you come over here? You made Maple and me worried. You were supposed to stay close!" Ray said as his jog morphed into a quick walk. She stood with her back facing him. She seemed to be looking right at the wall. She was still, unmoving.

"Bea, what's wrong?" Maple said as she caught up with them. Bea remained still.

Ray went up to her and placed a hand on her shoulder, "Bea, Maple asked you a—"

He now saw what she was looking at. On the ground before them, right at the base of the cliff, lay a rusty metal plate with a long prong-like extension jutting out from the middle. It was a worn-out satellite dish.

"Wh-what is it?" Bea asked curiously.

Maple peered her head over both of their shoulders to get a glimpse of it all.

Ray stared at it, more confused than ever. "... It's TV."

"Can I touch it?" she asked, amazed.

"No," Ray replied, staring up at the cliffs and then back down to the satellite, trying to figure out how it ended up there.

"Where are the moving pictures? I thought it was a box. Ray, how did the TV get here? Why is there no sound? I have to turn it on! How do I turn it on, Ray?!"

"Bea, Bea... hold on. It's not—It's not a T.V... It's what brings the images to the T.V... It's... it's complicated. Let's bring it back to camp. We'll figure things out there."

"Can I hold it?" she asked, trying to remain calm.

He waved his hand toward the dish as he turned around, and she eagerly scooped it up using both arms. He looked at Maple, still thoroughly confused. "You were saying they live simply up there?"

She just kept her mouth shut as her eyes remained glued to the satellite dish.

As they stomped their way through the woods, few words were spoken. They made sure everything was okay back at the greenhouse, packed up their berries and a couple of cloves of ripe garlic, and began heading back to camp.

"We'll go right to Luna's hut. Maple, you drop the food off."

"What's the grand plan here, Ray? Study the damn thing? It's a satellite. Not much we can use it for when it's not connected…"

"It's not the satellite. It's what it means. How did it get there? Who was using it? Do they want it back? Do you know what this means for Corazon? Whatever they were using this for, you can use it too. Do you know what that means? Knowledge. It means opening up everyone's eyes to what the real world is like."

"Ray, I think we should just *leave this alone*," Maple said hesitantly.

He stopped in his tracks. "You *really* don't understand. This could be really important, it could mean—"

"I understand what you're saying… it's just…"

"What?" he said, throwing his hands up in the air. "It's just, what?"

"It's just maybe there is a reason we don't know about it," she said, a bit uncomfortable with his attitude.

"That's the problem, Maple. Something weird is going on here. Something's up. Please just—just set aside your beliefs for one moment. *One damn moment*. Look at the *bigger* picture here!"

"I am," she said quietly.

"And what? What do you see?" he said, stepping toward her.

"I don't see it ending well for you," she said, stepping toward him as well.

He stared Maple down as best as he could, but she was a firm lady who didn't take well to pressure.

"Do whatever you want. But remember who's been here longer. Remember who knows better. Remember where you stand," she said, putting her hands up in surrender and backing off.

Beatrix just admired the satellite and scratched at the rust encrusted on its curves.

Maple and Ray set aside their argument for a different time as they approached Luna's hut, carrying the satellite dish as if it were a regular occurrence. They didn't want to draw any attention.

Luna turned to them as they entered the hut, "Good morning, you three! You all must have gotten up pretty early! I didn't even hear you–"

Beatrix walked toward her with the dish in her hands. Luna paused and stared at it for a moment before snatching it from her hands. "Where did you find this?"

Maple spoke up, "Under the cliffs of the mountain, right by the greenhouse."

Luna nodded. "Did anyone see you bring it back?"

Ray shook his head.

She looked down at the dish in her arms and contemplated her next actions. After a moment of thought, she looked up at them with a worried look. "Let's get rid of it."

"What?" Ray said in shock. "What is wrong with you people! This is your ticket to information, to knowing what's going on outside! You can use this to prepare for storms! You can use this to reference the web, you can have an infinite amount of information! This could help you all so much. Why the hell do you want to get rid of it?"

"Some people don't want to know what's going on in the other world. Some people prefer to live in the dark. That's why they came here," she replied.

He ran his hands down his face. He couldn't believe how stubborn the two of them were being. "Keep it here," he said, giving up.

"At least keep it here for a while. Let's… let's just look over all of our options first."

"No," Luna spoke quickly. "I'll ask one of the Disciples what they want me to do with it. I'll take care of it… don't worry."

"That's exactly what I'm worried about, Luna. I want you to use this. We can set this up, maybe get some kind of signal out here. We can pirate a connection, I did it all the time when I lived alone."

She held the dish and examined it carefully as she spoke. "I said I'll take care of it. You three, go. Get your chores done for today. I'm sure Maple needs help preparing meals, Sterling just tagged a buck." She looked over to Maple, who nodded and nudged Ray in the arm, signaling him to follow her. The two walked out of the hut, and Luna followed closely behind with the dish, squeezing it between her arm and body as if it were a dirtied bowl in need of a clean.

Beatrix went to go find someone else to talk to. She usually ended up with Musgo, who cut wood all day. He didn't mind hearing her talk; he was half deaf as it was. Maple brought Ray back to the spice table, where she spent most of her working time. There were two long slabs of bloody meat laying across the table. She ran her hand along all of the different spices and wiggled her fingers, trying to decide how she would concoct tonight's meal. Ray stood back and silently watched as Luna approached the closest Disciple in the middle of the square surrounded by huts. He was standing close to the bonfire in the center of the community. It was a gathering pace that became more crowded as the winter season dragged on.

She spoke to him slowly and made hand gestures demonstrating what they had found. She then pointed back to her hut. The disciple nodded his head understandingly and then accompanied her back to her hut, where they both disappeared from view.

"You guys don't realize what you're giving up. You aren't grasping what this means."

Maple shot back quickly, "You aren't grasping the fact that maybe we don't want to know. If it ain't broke, don't fix it. Now hand me the pepper."

He reluctantly gave her the plastic pepper shaker. Maple kneaded the spices into the meat while Ray prepared the fire. He lit match after match, trying his hardest to get the kindling to start. He furiously repositioned the lumber and tried again. This was far too tedious of a task for him at this point. He needed something to let his anger out on. He needed to scream. He needed some form of clarity.

"Hey there. Need a hand?" A deep, burly voice said from up above. Ray craned his neck and looked up at the huge figure staring down at him. The figure looked over to Maple and began to speak. "Maple, I need to borrow this one. That all right?"

"You'd be doing me a favor!" she scoffed.

"That settles it then!" The man chuckled. "Come on son, I've got something for you to see! The name's Sterling."

Sterling helped Ray to his feet and tugged him by the shirt sleeve into the woods, away from Maple.

Ray pushed him off as soon as they were out of sight. "What the hell do you think you're doing?" he asked in a commanding tone.

"I'm saving your ass. Show some respect, boy," Sterling said, throwing Ray into a pile of dirty snow that had yet to melt away.

Ray got up and pushed at Sterling's chest, making him stagger back a few inches. Sterling laughed at his abrupt actions. "You're really feeling right at home, aren't ya, boy? Don't forget-" He grabbed Ray's collar and forcefully pulled him closer. "You're nothing in Corazon. I may not be blinded by all this religion bullshit, but I'm still higher on the totem pole. Everyone is. Know where you stand."

He set Ray down and began walking deeper into the woods. "What now?" Ray asked. "What-what I'm supposed to follow you?"

Sterling laughed. "You do whatever you want. But if you want the answers you're foolishly asking around for… you best follow me."

Ray froze for a moment and weighed the pros and cons of following the intimidating stranger promising him answers into the woods. After a moment's thought, he jogged to catch up.

Sterling talked without looking at him. He knew he was the top dog, and he was trying to hold his head up as if to declare it to the trees themselves. "I know these woods like the back of my hand. I came out here about… well, I don't know how long it's been. But the system works. I hunt and fish, they give me a roof over my head and women to please. And believe me—I please em' all!" He laughed at his own statement and elbowed Ray in the shoulder.

Ray let out an awkward half-laugh as they continued to walk.

"I've seen a lot of things since coming to Corazon. Strange things. Things that make you question what it is we're doing here."

"And what *is it* we're doing here?" Ray asked eagerly.

"We're here to worship, to promote love. To stop the spread of evil and hate by starting with our own secluded community, but I'm sure you've heard that plenty of times already. The thing is… There's no cure for evil and hate. *As long as there are people with desire, there will always be evil and hate. We just do a better job at hiding it.*"

They continued to walk until they reached the river's edge, "What I'm about to show you has to remain between us. Not for the safety of you, or me… but to protect *him*."

"Him? Who?" Ray asked.

"Who else lives all the way out here?"

Ray thought for a moment and whispered, "*Otto…*"

The two of them came upon Otto's little cove, burrowed into the side of the embankment. Otto poked his head out and stared at the two of them.

"Otto, I told ya before… you gotta move this cove up a bit. If we have a string of bad storms, you'll be flooded out. We don't want that now, do we?" Sterling stated as if he were a father looking down on his disobedient son.

Otto looked from left to right and ducked back into his little cove. A few moments passed before he popped back out and said, "Sarah says we'll take our chances."

Sterling rolled his eyes. "Right… listen, Otto, you mind if I show Ray our secret collection?"

"*Now?*" Otto whispered.

Sterling slowly nodded his head.

Otto brushed back his long, hanging hair and waved them both in. Sterling got to his knees and crawled through the tiny opening. Ray followed closely behind.

The cove was much more spacious than he had imagined it would be. There wasn't much room for standing, but that wasn't even necessary. There was a fire burning near the opening of the cove and numerous lamps scattered throughout. There was what looked like a bed stuffed with cotton and bundled in some material that resembled burlap. Next to the bed lay a pad of paper with elaborate sketches of people and landscapes elegantly drawn upon the pages; there were other sketches laying all around the room. Some masterpieces, others looked as if they were created by a four-year-old.

"Otto, did you draw all of these?" Ray asked, tracing the fine line of an ocean wave with his finger.

"Yes. Well… Sarah teaches me. The credit is not all mine." He giggled and blew a kiss toward his bed.

Sterling cut in, "Listen, Otto, let's focus on the task at hand. Where is our secret collection?"

"Oh!" he said as he scampered over to one of the lamps in the opposite corner of his room. From out of the dark, he pulled a plastic bin. A bin that the community usually uses for the storage of canned goods and necessary dried-out products.

"Bring it here," Sterling ordered.

Otto dragged the bin over and popped the lid open. Inside were tiny bits and pieces of metal and plastic. Sterling reached in and removed a couple of objects. "Hopefully, this sheds a bit of clarity on your world."

He handed Ray the first of the two objects, a long thin, smooth piece of yellow-white plastic. It was bendable and sharp in the areas where it had been edged off. "This is siding… the stuff you put on the side of a modern house."

Sterling smiled and sarcastically spoke, "You don't say! Tell me, detective, what do you make of this?" He handed Ray the second of the two objects. A fluffy pink cotton-like substance.

Ray took it in his hands and squeezed it. "Insulation?"

"You guessed it," Sterling replied.

Otto broke into their conversation. "This! This is my favorite!" He held up a few broken spindles connected by a small crossbar, the very end to the brush of a rake.

"The storms blow the things clean off of the overhang. They try to recover them, but sometimes they'll miss a few. Otto and I are usually the ones that end up finding them. What you found today, the satellite. That's a big deal. That proves to all of us down here that the Disciples are doing a little bit more with their time than just 'meditating' and 'living simple lives.' If they thought that we were catching on to them, they would get scared. And when people with absolute power get scared, bad things happen."

Ray focused on the insulation and eventually looked up to Sterling. "So what now?"

He laughed. "What do you mean *what now*? We leave it alone. That's *what now*. We don't want to push these guys. We don't want to ask questions. We want to accept everything as it is. End of story."

Ray shook his head. "I don't know if I can do that."

Sterling began to get a little irritated. "What, you think it's been easy for me? I've had to watch countless women be taken up onto the mountain. Every year a few more disappear. And do they ever come back? No. You really expect me to believe they're living out their days in happiness? Come on… It's not easy to live with when you're not brainwashed by their religion. But it's necessary; we have to."

"Says who? What happens to us if we go against the grain? Huh? What happens if I question the system? Is Elliot gonna have me killed?! *Oooh, so scary!*" he said sarcastically.

"No. No, no, no. If you ask questions… your little girlfriend Luna disappears. She'll just vanish." Sterling snapped his fingers. "Just like that. Gone. And you will never know what happened to her. You won't know if she's dead or alive, you won't know if she's healthy, you won't know if they took her or if she willingly went with them. You won't know what happened, and you never will. What you *will* know is that it's all your fault."

Ray sat back and thought about that while Otto talked to himself on the bed, pretending to gaze into Sarah's eyes. "Come on," Sterling said, taking the pink fluff from his hands. "Let's go." He nodded toward the opening of the cove.

The three of them crawled out of the cove. Otto immediately went to check on his fish that were skewered over an open flame.

Sterling got really close to Ray. "I'm telling you all this to scare ya. You're a bold man, I can tell. It takes one to know one. Don't push your luck. Remember that around here, you'll always be walking on thin ice. *Always*. If I were you, I would always look over my shoulder before you pull the sheets up at night. Bad things tend to happen when we least expect them."

Ray licked his lips and nodded. "I get it. I understand. Thanks."

Sterling began to turn around. "Yeah, don't mention—" He stopped dead in his sentence. Standing twenty feet in front of them was a crippled Tobias, holding his broken arm in a makeshift sling.

"Just what the hell do you think you're doing here, boy?!" Sterling erupted, throwing his hands over his head.

Tobias jumped back with fear in his eyes. He had no idea Sterling and Ray were going to be here.

Otto quickly intervened. "It's all right! It's all right! It's all right, fellas! It's all right!" He waved his arms frantically in the air, desperately trying to redirect the attention on himself as he scampered his way in between Tobias and Sterling. "It's all right! I told him he could have some of my fish this evening!" Otto held out a plate with a half portion of grilled fish all cut up on it. "He can just take this and leave. It's all right."

Ray bit the side of his cheek, trying to control his anger. Tobias looked at the three of them like a timid beast.

Sterling relaxed his muscles. "You want the fish, Tobias?" he asked, taking the plate from Otto's hand. "You want the fish from the man you attacked? From the man you tried to kill?"

Otto butted in again, "It's okay, Sterling! I *forgived* him, Sterling! I forgived him! He can have some fish. I got extra so he could have some! Sarah isn't hungry tonight!"

Sterling set the plate down on a bed of round rocks bordering the river. He then backed up. "It's 'forgave,' Otto. And if that's true, then… go ahead, Tobias. Take the fish," he said maliciously.

Tobias limped back, afraid of what would happen if he accepted Sterling's offer.

"Take the fish, Tobias. You must be hungry. *Eat… go on…*"

Tobias slowly crept toward the plate resting on the round pebbles. With every half step he took, Sterling became that much more intimidating.

"There ya go…" Sterling said, curling his lips into an evil smile.

Tobias reached the plate and tried to pick up the grilled fish with a trembling hand. Sterling let out a pitiful laugh and raised his arm, throwing a round stone at him. The stone hit Tobias in the neck and sent him squirming to the ground.

Otto screamed at the sight of this treachery. "No! No! No, stop! Stop that, Sterling!"

Sterling laughed and hurled another stone at Tobias, striking him in the ankle. He yelped again.

Sterling found great humor in this and looked to Ray, who didn't laugh but made no effort to stop him. Sterling extended a hand toward Ray and offered him a stone, a gesture he first declined.

"Come on, boy!" Sterling barked at Ray. "This is the man that tried to kill Luna! He tried to kill Otto here too! You just gonna let him do that?" He threw another stone, hitting Tobias in the shoulder blade, sending him back onto the ground.

Ray lightly shook his head. "It's fine… you go nuts, but I'm—"

Sterling grabbed hold of his collar and pulled him closer, shoving a stone into his hands. "Be a man for once in your life, why don't ya!" He released Ray and pushed him back. "Do it! Hit him! Make him really feel it! Throw the damn rock, coward! Do it, I said!"

Tobias got to his feet and tried to flee as fast as his blistered feet would carry him.

"Do it, throw it now! Hit him!" Sterling commanded over Otto's cries.

Ray hesitantly raised his arm and threw the stone toward a fleeing Tobias, hitting him in the back of the head, sending him crashing toward the ground again. Sterling laughed harder and harder and nudged Ray, trying to prompt him to laugh, too. He only cracked a slight smile. The thought of Tobias trying to hurt the ones he loved helped him follow through with the action.

Otto quickly ran over to Tobias and helped him up. "Tobias, here… here, take this. Get up and take this!" he pleaded as he aided Tobias in getting to his feet while simultaneously trying to force the remaining fish wrapped in cloth into his hands.

Tobias got up and clutched the back of his head, his palm was coated in blood. He whimpered as he wiped the blood on his shirt and quickly accepted the fish, fleeing into the evening. Sterling slung another few rocks in his direction, laughing as he did, even when he missed, while Ray sheepishly kept to himself.

Otto ran back into his little cove, occasionally poking his head out and shouting, "Leave us!" Sterling just giggled and hawked a mouthful of mucus into the river.

"I'm gonna head back," Ray said, rubbing the back of his head. "It's getting late, and Maple might need help with dinner."

Sterling smiled, "You just remember what I said. If you care about them, leave it alone, boy."

Ray nodded and went on his way, hiking back through the darkening woods, using only the smell of charred venison as his compass. He eventually found his way back to camp, where he immediately went to Luna's tent. She sat there with Beatrix and Musgo picking away at some venison and salad of some sort. She set her plate down and got to her feet upon seeing Ray standing in the doorway. The two of them went outside and began to chat.

"I heard Sterling picked you up earlier today… what's going on?" she said, sounding worried.

A Disciple dressed in white slowly walked behind the two of them, acting as if he were on a late-night stroll. Ray and the Disciple made brief eye contact. Luna looked over to him and nodded her head. "Evening Constantine," she said, bowing her head a bit more than usual.

He returned the gesture. "Evening, Luna," and continued to walk.

Ray waited until he was out of view to begin speaking again. "Sterling just wanted to talk is all, nothing too special. He needed help getting the tin siding up against the north wall of his hut."

Luna nodded but kept a skeptical eye aimed at him; she by no means bought it completely. But there was nothing she could do to get it out of him at this point. She stroked his arm. "You look a little shook. Everything all right?"

Ray smiled. "Yeah, just tired, really… that's all."

Luna ran her hand down until it met his and grasped it. "So Maple and I talked for a bit… I realize that everything you've been through and seen in the past half-year must be a shock to you and all, but… I don't expect you to understand, but when it comes to the satellite dish, I can't—"

"What satellite dish?" he asked plainly.

She looked at him, confused. He maneuvered his hand so that she let go. He then looked away and walked back toward her hut, leaving her alone under the late fall moonlight.

29

Luna peeled back the flap of her hut and poked her head in, looking for any sign of life. Ray leaned up against the side of her bed as he shed his dirty clothes like a second skin, stripping down to his boxer shorts.

She pushed past the flap and made it evident that she, too, was in the room. He looked up at her with a modest smile. She approached him with an earnest worry. "Everything all right with you? You aren't the same."

He coughed lightly and excused himself to go pull on a pair of pants. "I'm not the same at all. Nobody's ever the same. You aren't the same person you were two years ago. Maple isn't the same person she was when she was younger. Am I not allowed to change?"

Luna eyed him peculiarly again. "What's wrong, Ray? You know that's not what I'm saying. You seem a little *off*, is all."

He shook his head. "Don't worry about it," he said, turning to her. "I'll be fine."

She continued to look at him, trying to figure out what may be wrong through any body language he may be giving off. "You know, when I get tired of the way things are going here, I like to do things to make me forget I'm here. I like to… lose myself in something, get busy, color, or dance, or I don't know… do anything to take my mind off of what's bothering me."

Ray scooped up a handful of water from a clean bucket by the nightstand and splashed it onto his face, shaking off the remaining beads. "And what do you recommend?"

Luna leaned back and thought for a few moments before turning around and ducking her head below her bed. She then pulled out a large plastic tub and cracked open the sealed lid. She picked up the first item, a small pink box. She lifted the lid and turned to Ray, revealing the different pastel powders and brushes she had within her make-up kit. "*You feeling pretty?*" she asked sarcastically. It brought a slight smile to his lips, but that wasn't enough. She set her pink box aside and retrieved the larger wooden box with the metal clips on it.

She set the bulky wooden box aside and unfastened both clips. Within the box sat a smaller, plastic CD player, along with an array of various CDs and spare batteries for when her radio didn't get any signal. She ran her fingers over the plastic-edged cases of all of her precious discs. "This is for special occasions only."

Ray peered over her shoulder to get a glimpse at the precious cargo she seemed to be handling. "What's the occasion?" he asked curiously.

"You tell me," she replied, inserting the thin disc into the slot and shutting it tight. She stood up and turned back around to face him. "When I was packing up to run away for the last time, I barely even took any clothes with me. But my CD player and my personal collection was a must. It was the first thing I grabbed. Cheap pink plastic, battery-powered, even picks up a radio signal from time to time."

Ray stepped closer and ran his fingers over the cheap buttons. "Will we get in trouble if we listen to it?" he asked eagerly, realizing it had been years since he heard a recorded song.

"*Not as long as we're quiet,*" she whispered as she took him by the hand and pressed *Play*.

The machine clicked and made a light whirring noise as it tried to identify the particular disc. "So what does Luna like to listen to? Jazz? Classical? Hip hop?"

She smiled and shook her head. "Depends on what mood you catch me in."

"And what mood are you in?"

"How about you listen and find out?" The machine finally recognized the CD and began to play.

The song started with light chords being played on what sounded like an electronic keyboard. A deep voice quickly chimed in with perfect harmony and began speaking of lost moments in time, how to shape your life for the better, and seeing love for the last time. It was definitely some sort of low-key indie rock concoction that proved to be a unique choice. He couldn't quite figure out what it said about her mood, though.

Luna pulled herself closer to Ray so that their bodies were now touching. She placed his hand on her lower back and grasped his other hand in hers. The two of them slowly began to teeter back and forth, remaining light on the tips of their toes. Ray's movements proved to be far more robotic, but she held him close and took control.

The soft voice continued, detailing the writer's long-lost lover and the beauty within her eyes. Ray looked down into Luna's eyes, as deep as they were mysterious, like an ocean abyss. He held her closer as they began to move more freely as the keyboardist took more liberties, breaking away from the original tune and weaving a beautifully sorrowful melody of its own. Luna looked back up at Ray and smiled, showing her straight pearly teeth.

Ray's eyes began to grow irritated. He didn't know if it was the power of the moment, the feel of a woman's touch, or the wonderful tune. "Luna… you know we can never—"

"Shhh," she whispered as she rested her head on his upper chest. He closed his eyes and allowed himself to be swept away in the moment as the two twirled around her hut, lit by candlelight.

The tracks played and played as Luna and Ray refused to let go of each other. They continued to dance as the night grew darker and their legs weaker. The voice on the speaker sang of dancing, silent, secret, moments in the dark and the failure that sometimes accompanied it. He sang of insanity and safety. Topics that could otherwise be seen as disturbing if it were not such a soothing voice delivering them.

The final track slowly came to its pinnacle point as Luna moved her hand slowly from his side to the lower part of his neck, pulling him slightly closer as she angled her face up. Their eyes gently drifted shut as their lips met. The moment seemed to last forever in between the threads of time.

They separated for a brief moment, long enough for Luna to whisper, "I've never felt this way about anyone before."

They then drew closer and locked lips again, this time holding it longer. "Stay here with me. We can have a life together, we can raise Beatrix, we can have a family… We can do it right. We can be happy, Ray… I love—"

She lost track of what she was saying as a flash of panic and skin darted into her hut. The being kicking up dirt and scurried into the corner like a rat. Ray pushed Luna behind him, shielding her. The dust settled, revealing a curled-up naked human, shaking and bloody. Ray pushed Luna back more as his eyes widened.

"Ray… Ray let go of me—" Luna said, sounding petrified. Ray slowly released his tight grip on the front of her shirt. Luna took the quilt on her bed and hesitantly walked toward the being, whimpering in the corner. She grew more fearful with each step.

The being quickly turned to her, revealing itself to be a female, beaten and bloodied. Luna dropped the quilt and staggered backward.

"Oh, my—I don't—I—" She began to cough and tear up herself. The gears began to slowly turn in her head as the woman reached out and grabbed the quilt, quickly wrapping herself in it. "This isn't r-real." Luna stuttered. "It-it can't be…"

Ray took her by the arm. "What is it? Who is she? Luna, who is she?!"

The bloodied woman looked up at the two of them with swollen eyes. "Luna—I… I di—I didn't know where else to go…" She said frightfully.

Luna dropped to one knee as her fearful assumptions had just been confirmed. "*Aria… What did they do to you?*"

30

Luna grabbed a half loaf of stale bread and some leftover cold stew and quickly brought it to Aria. She accepted Luna's offerings and hungrily tore at the stale bread before she slurped away at the remaining broth. She then gestured for some water, which Luna was quick to retrieve. Ray sat back and watched it all go down, eager to find out what had happened to her.

Luna aided Aria's trembling hands in getting the cup to her mouth so that she could sip at the water. "Shhh. It's okay... It's okay, Aria, sip at it. Just sip at it easily. *Shhh*," she assured her as Aria began to get choked up as she sipped at the water.

Aria finished with the water and took a deep breath in. Luna quickly began tending to the bruises and abrasions upon her face.

"Aria... who did this to you?" she asked as she backed away from her cheek, realizing her bruises were those from a fist.

Aria began to get worked up again, and Luna had to calm her down. As soon as she was able to speak, she cleared her throat and tried to find the words.

"Th-thank you," she said, trembling.

Luna shook her head. "Never mind that now. Who did this to you? How did it happen?"

Aria peered over Luna's shoulder to get a look at Ray. Luna noticed what was going on rather quickly. "Oh, no, don't worry about him. I'll explain later. Trust me on this," she assured her again.

Aria nodded and took another deep breath in. "Okay..."

"Aria, you need to tell me what's going on. Why are you not on the mountain?"

She swallowed what she had in her mouth and looked directly at Luna. "The mountain... the Gateway, the Disciples... Elliot and Mother... All of it... It's not what you think," her hands still shook uncontrollably as she continued to speak.

"As soon as I got up onto the mountain, I knew something wasn't right... things were different. They weren't like everyone had claimed they were. Everything and... everyone seemed so nice down here. But as soon as we all got up there, out of sight, well..." She began to tear up again.

Luna looked back at a horrified Ray as she cradled Aria's head.

"They made me take off my clothes. I had to walk around like that. *Naked*, and—and I wasn't allowed to wear anything. They all just—looked at me. They *touched* me and—and when I tried to resist... They would—they would tell me how Mother wanted them to be rewarded for all of their work and that Mother chose me to reward them because I was... because I was *strong* and *beautiful*... After that, if I resisted, they would—I never resisted after that." She stopped to swallow her up-and-coming cry of pain. "They would... *force themselves on me*. I would scream and yell for help but—it was like nobody listened. They were all okay with it."

Luna paid close attention, bobbing her wide-eyed head up and down as Aria explained in explicit detail the events that occurred.

"So you ran away? You had enough, and you ran away?"

"It wasn't that easy... They keep us all on a leash at night. They tied us up and made us sleep on mattresses in the basement. They kept us locked up down there and only came to get us when they needed to... let off some steam or use us for whatever reasons..."

"Us? How many people are up there?"

Aria shook her head. "They've recruited twenty-one so far... but there are only eighteen of us left."

Luna fell back onto the floor. Her knees turned to instant rubber, not knowing how to react to such news.

Ray quickly spoke up. "We *need to* let someone know. We need to spread the word. We need to—we need some sort of justice here!"

"No!" Aria shouted with a breathy gasp. "No! We can't take on something this big... we are talking about turning hundreds of people against their beliefs. It doesn't just work like that!"

"We have you, though! We have first-hand experience! We have your cuts and bruises! Aria, we can use you as—"

"They'll *kill* me!" she said as she shook in fear for her life.

Luna grabbed her by the shoulders and tried to calm her down. "Shh. Aria, please... tell me more about what happened. We aren't going to act just yet."

Aria tried to gather herself together. "Dante was always the worst... he has this thing for me... He always summoned me. He always hit the hardest. He sometimes did other things to get himself off, too. He did—he did sick things. He would burn me with wax and cut me with that knife of his... he even shoved a gun in my face a couple of times... he always lets loose when he goes back up onto the mountain. He does anything and everything his twisted little mind is capable of thinking up..."

"Aria... I'm so sorry... I had no idea that—"

"So one night," she continued, "he grabbed me out of bed like he usually does. This time was different, though. He was angry about something. I could feel it in the way he pushed me. We went to his room, and he started to hit me. He said that... he said that Mother was acting through him to punish me for my sins.... he said that Elliot allowed it. When he brought me to the bed, something just... something snapped. I just reached my breaking point." Her hands began to tremble and shake again.

"He hit me harder and harder, and I knew if I didn't act fast, I... he's a *sick bastard*..." She wiped away some of the tears running down the sides of her face.

"When he brought his hand up again... I grabbed his knife from his sheath and just shot it right back up at him and... and I *stabbed* him." It seemed as if everyone stopped breathing at the same exact moment. They were all frozen in time, trying to calculate how her actions had just drastically changed the course of their lives on Corazon forever.

"He—He made this gurgling sound and rolled off of me. As soon as he looked down at the knife, he began to scream. He sounded like a woman, I swear... he tried standing up, but I took the lamp next to the bed and hit him in the head... that shut him up real quick. I don't know if he's dead. I crawled out of the window and ran while I had the chance. I just... I left him there, bleeding out on the floor. He—I might have killed him, I don't know..."

There were still no words spoken. Ray just sat back, stunned by what he had just heard. Luna was struck by the story in a way both sad and terrifying.

"When they find Dante, they're going to come looking for me... Luna I... I didn't know where else to go! I didn't know who else to go to! I'm—I'm so sorry, I didn't want to bring this to you. I just—I have nobody else to go to..."

Luna closed her eyes and began to think. Aria rocked back and forth as she carefully watched Luna, trying to dial in on her train of thought. Ray came up behind her and placed a hand on her shoulder.

"All right," she said, looking up at Aria. "First, I wanna say I'm sorry this had to happen to you. Nobody deserves that, *nobody*. But they're going to come looking for you, and when they do… you can't be here."

Aria grew noticeably more scared as Luna continued to speak. "And Luna… Elliot. He's not like they say—not anymore, he's—"

"I'm not giving you up," Luna blurted out, hiding behind the urgent nature of the ordeal to avoid Aria besmirching the name of her Prophet. "We need to find you somewhere to stay while we figure things out. Somewhere the Disciples wouldn't look."

The gears within Ray's head started turning quickly. "I got a place. You might not like it too much, but it'll work."

Aria nodded, "Anything. Just name it, anything."

Ray looked at Luna and whispered, "*Otto?*"

Luna looked down at her feet. "We can't put Otto in a situation like that. He's fragile enough."

"But think about it, Otto is perfect. Nobody ever bothers him. Most people forget he even exists. And if the Disciples do find out, they wouldn't kill him; Todd would stop delivering to Corazon if they did. Otto's perfect."

Aria looked back and forth between the two of them, hoping for a concrete answer as she wiped the sweat from her face.

Luna thought long and hard before closing her eyes and saying. "Go get Maple and Otto…"

Ray quickly left the hut in search of Maple while Luna did her best to console a mentally crippled Aria.

Aria looked up at her through teary eyes. "I'm so sorry, Luna."

"It's okay, I'm going to—"

"No, I'm sorry for before… before all of this happened, I didn't treat you the way you should've been treated, I… I don't know why. I felt like I needed to prove myself to people. I only cared about what the Disciples and the men of Corazon thought. I didn't even show my little posse the respect they deserved. They were all weak, just looking for a leader to follow. I knew that if I went to one of them, they'd give me up like that if they knew it was a chance for them to get some recognition from the Prophet himself.... I was such an idiot. I was just—I'm sorry."

Luna nodded her head as she held a broken Aria in her arms. "It's okay... You're safe for the moment."

Luna kept her calm, cool, and collected composure as best as she possibly could on the outside. Little did anyone else see, her mental state was eroding far faster than she could handle. Her whole infrastructure had just tumbled at the hands of Aria. She wanted to call her a liar. She wanted to kick her out and refuse to believe her lies. But she could tell there was no deception in the air, and the bruises and cuts on Aria's body each carried a story of their own.

Winter was now upon them. The winds blew heavy, saturated snow down on them from the mountain above, and the slush was accumulating faster than they could keep up. There was no way they would be able to flee Corazon under those conditions. It was at very least thirty miles away from any form of civilization. None of them were fit enough to brave the cold that would accompany them on their journey, and Aria was the only one who needed medical attention. The rest of them could at least turn a blind eye to the horrors going on behind the scenes until fall.

At the same time, she wanted to do something; she wanted to act. She wanted to go up onto the mountain and free all of the Angels being held against their will. Trapped in an abusive system, yet still looking for redemption. Once Aria had fallen fast asleep in her arms, Luna allowed herself to weep uncontrollably.

Maple soon made her way into the hut, immediately followed by a paranoid Otto. "In the name of Mother and all things sacred what—"

"Stop," Luna said, carefully lowering Aria to the floor, where she continued to rest. Luna stood up and wiped her face dry. "I don't want to hear that right now."

Maple examined her and gave her a sobering nod. She then approached Aria and quickly began tending to her wounds, dabbing them softly with a wet sponge.

"Ohh…" Otto said, shaking. "Ohh, no. No, no, no, I don't like this. I don't like this! Sarah won't like this either! Oh… oh no! Oh no! Oh no!"

"Otto, enough!" Luna snapped. "Quiet down, someone will hear you. She needs our help. Otto, you and Sarah are the only people that can help her. She needs to hide, understand?"

Ray, too, looked over to Otto and tried to adjust his tone so that it would come off as calming. "Otto, she needs to hide from people that want to hurt her… like how Sterling hurt Tobias."

Otto jumped up. "You threw a rock, too! You hurt Tobias, too!"

Luna shot Ray a dirty look, knowing full well Otto was practically incapable of lying.

Ray cleared his throat and continued to talk, disregarding Otto's jab. "And we need to keep her from ending up the same way. Nobody can know she is living with you. Luna, Maple, and I will check in regularly. You just have to trust us, Otto…"

Otto nervously shook his head back and forth in a repeating pattern. His sweaty locks of hair sticking to his forehead. "I don't like this at all. What if they find me? What if they hurt Sarah? I-I—" He stopped and squinted, trying to force the difficult words out. "I-I can't have anything happen to her. *I don't want to die.*"

Ray grabbed Otto by both shoulders and looked him directly in the eyes. "I will not let anything happen to you. Do you hear me? Nothing. But you need to help us out. Please, Otto."

Otto looked around, panicking as he noticed everyone directing their attention toward him.

He sighed and whined for a couple of moments, trotting in place like a toddler ready to blow. He then turned and pretended to take the hands of Sarah, who was just so conveniently standing next to him. He whispered some things in her ear and then sighed some more before turning to the rest of them. "We need to hurry. The sun is coming up soon. She can stay with us until she's feeling better."

Ray looked at Maple, who had stopped tending to Aria. Maple nodded her head and looked toward Luna. Luna took a deep breath in and looked back at Ray as if she were expecting a decision. They didn't have the time to play such games. "Good enough, let's move," he said as he began to pack for her, grabbing some more leftover bread and a cup for water and stuffing it in a sack. "The sun will be rising soon. Luna and Maple, you guys stay here. It will be easier to go undetected with fewer people. I'll get her to Otto's cove, and then… well, he'll take care of the rest."

"No chance. I know these woods better than anyone. I'll take her. Your leg is still healing, and I'm the fastest one in Corazon. I can get her there and back like that," Luna said, snapping her fingers.

"We're not going to get anywhere arguing. Luna will take her, end of story. Now go! Hurry!" Maple silently demanded.

Otto scurried out of the hut and frantically looked from left to right. For all he knew, the monsters that were responsible for her misery were now lurking around every tree and bush, gazing at him with eyes that saw him as prey. Luna pulled Aria closely behind. She was still weak and groggy from her daring escape. The three of them quickly bolted into the thick of the woods.

Otto whispered to himself as he obnoxiously ran through the woods with long, goofy strides. Luna and Aria kept quieter, stealthily moving on the softer, wet ground to avoid crunching any sticks underneath their feet. "*Otto! Hush up!*" Luna would whisper anytime they came close to passing a nearby hut.

The sun was beginning to peak over the horizon when the three of them reached his hidden cove. Otto zipped right in and dove underneath the covers. Aria then let herself in as well, followed closely behind by Luna.

Luna gasped as she looked around, shocked as to how much space there was. "Otto… this is incredible."

He stayed hidden under the covers and pointed to the short-walled side of the cove where there was a small mat sitting contently by a gas lamp. Aria swallowed her pride and got on her hands and knees, crawling over to where she would soon be sleeping. "May not be the best… But I'll be damned if it's not better."

Luna gave her a reassuring nod and slowly began to back out. "I'll be back, I'll come with food and more clothing. I'm going to figure this out, Aria. I'm going to figure this out, okay?" She backed out of Otto's home without hearing an answer. Once outside, she got to her feet and began making her way back to her own hut. Her brisk walk turned into a swift jog, which turned into an all-out run. She didn't want to be stopped or questioned at all at this time of day, plus there was no telling who would be looking for Aria. Because of this, she tried her best to stay away from snow. She didn't want to leave any obvious tracks for someone to follow.

Her strides stretched out long and true as she breathed in a slow and steady rhythmic pattern. She had to stay stimulated, or else all of the horrors of the past few hours would come crashing down on her head like burning embers.

She tried to pick up the pace but decided to slow it down, not wanting to cause any ruckus that may wake the other community members.

She took a deep breath in and held it in between strides so that she got a bit light-headed. She closed her eyes as she exhaled, trying her best to expel all of the negative energy from her soul.

As soon as she opened her eyes, she gasped and tried to slow up, but it was far too late. She tripped over her legs and accidentally flung herself right into the large silhouette of a man, just happening to lumber into her path.

The man grunted as he hit the ground, and she let out a slight yelp, startled by the sudden action. She got to her feet and picked up the smallest hand-held stone she could find. She put up her fists in front of her face, prepared to defend what was coming. To her surprise, it was not a bloodthirsty Disciple, hell-bent on revenge. It was instead Tobias, looking up at her with confusion.

She let out a sigh of relief and bent down to help him up. Her help was quickly dismissed as he rolled away from her, seeming frightened by her generous actions. He pulled himself up by the root of a tree and recovered his blanket, which had been slung over his shoulders and was now sopping wet as it lay face down in a puddle. He struggled to wring it out with his one usable arm, the other one dangled limply within its sling.

"Tobias…" She muttered as he tried to get away from her as fast as possible. He stopped in his tracks upon hearing her voice. She was hesitant to approach him but did so anyway, gently placing her hand on the back of his shoulder. "*Tobias… What have they done to you?*" she asked as she circled him so that she could look upon his face. The first thing she saw was his crippled arm, still hanging loose and awkward. She then looked upon his dirt-encrusted face and eventually found his eyes, bloodshot and sorrowful. She touched his cheek and wiped away a tear as it slid effortlessly down his face, darkening the dirt patches along the side of his cheek.

"I am so sorry for what they have done to you. This isn't right… none of it," she said, reflecting on their past interactions. She had so much to say and so little time to say it. It was only a matter of time before Ray came out looking for her. "I know what you did was wrong. But I know you were in a bad place. And I'm sorry this is happening to you. This is not how things should be dealt with. I'm going to fix this. I promise." She took a step back and looked at him; the dirt patches were now streaking.

He tried to avert his eyes, but she angled her head to look at him. He had been completely humbled to the point of emasculation. He stood there, unsure of what to do.

She took him by the hand and shook it rapidly. "*Talk to me. Speak, Tobias.*"

He looked down at her hand grasping his, and then back up at her frantic face. She was troubled, and he could tell. He opened his chapped, cracking lips and forced himself to speak.

"Tobias? You out here?!" An angry voice shouted from a distance. It was Sterling, stumbling through the woods with a fading gas lamp. "Tobias! You better not be playing no games!" he warned him in a savage tone.

"*Go,*" he whispered in a panicked tone, pushing her off toward her hut. She began to run, knowing that there were more pressing matters at hand. She ran all the way back to her hut, thinking of what Sterling had in mind for Tobias the entire time.

She entered her hut and immediately looked toward Ray, who remained leaning against her bed, a surprised, somewhat smug look on his face. The look that screamed *I told you so* without flat out saying it.

Luna remained still. She nervously maneuvered over to her designated corner to sip at some water.

"Hey, are you all right? Maple went back to her hut. My guess is she's going to tell Musgo about all this."

Luna nodded her head. "We can trust Musgo," she spoke without blinking. She slowly turned to her bed and walked over to it, jumping up and pulling the covers over herself. "You ever think your past catches up to you? Like karma or something?"

Ray turned to her and brushed her arm. "God, I hope not."

"Violence is always met with violence. You learn that after a while."

He tried to look into her bloodshot eyes, but she avoided looking at him, ashamed of what he might see. "We don't have to answer with violence… we can just leave. You and me, we'll get out of here. We'll alert the police or something. We can save everyone up there! Aria wasn't the first, and she won't be the last." Luna turned away from him completely. Ray wasn't going to give up so fast. "She said it herself. We can't expect others to act when they don't even know what's going on! You—all of your people—you're all living in some delusional state of denial!"

Luna shook her head. "You don't understand… I can't leave. Almost nobody here can leave. It's more complicated than you may think. I know you don't understand, but… just accept it for now. This isn't the violence. This is the answer to the violence," she said, pulling the covers up to her neck and burrowing her face in a pillow.

Ray tried to find the words to comfort her, but he couldn't; the message was too cryptic as if she was trying to foreshadow what was to come.

The two of them just lay there, Ray staring up at the closed roof hatch, anticipating what the next morning would bring.

31

The sun did come. The birds did sing their ritualistic hymn of dawn, and Luna did manage to get some sleep. The same couldn't be said for Ray, who had disappeared, leaving her hut quieter than usual. Luna awoke to a light and a repetitive itch on her cheek.

"Wake up, Luna! Wake up! I have good news!" Beatrix gently spoke, trying to ease her into consciousness as she poked at her cheek.

Luna sat up, feeling groggy still. "Hey, Bea... what are you doing here so early?"

Bea wore a huge smile that spread from ear to ear. "I have great news. Come on! Get up, get up!" She was practically shaking in her shoes from all of the excitement as she pulled at Luna's arm, trying to get her out of bed.

Luna wiped the crust from her eyes and slumped out of bed. Examining the room and coming to the conclusion that last night was more than just a horrific nightmare. She looked at the bloodstains in the corner of the room; it would be an easy clean-up she would have to take care of quickly. She was just thankful Beatrix hadn't seen them yet.

"Luna, the Disciples have come down from the mountain! A whole bunch of them!" she declared cheerfully.

Luna nearly sank to her knee as her legs went numb and her stomach dropped; she instead leaned back on her bed for support. She held a hand over her mouth and looked toward the ventilation hatch on the roof, hoping that gravity would hold her fear back. She managed to ask Bea one thing through a cracked voice as she came to a grave realization. "Is—that why you're all dressed up?"

Bea nodded vigorously. "Come on, we need to get you pretty! Can I have some makeup? I'll do yours if you do mine!" she said as she twirled around in her white lace dress.

"Bea, I think that maybe we should—"

"Come on, Luna, please———" She begged, standing on her tiptoes.

Luna tried to think fast. She couldn't have Bea looking this way in front of the Disciples. It would be better if she weren't seen at all.

Two familiar voices came from outside the hut. "You take Luna's hut, I'll check up on Tobias's. It's supposed to be empty. Quick in, quick out. We'll ask questions later." One of the men was Constantine, one of the kinder yet more aggressive Disciples. The other one she recognized as a Disciple but had forgotten his name. They were approaching the flap quickly.

Luna slid onto the ground near the fire pit. She scooped up a handful of water from a nearby bucket and let it drip into the cold ash left from the previous night's fire. Beatrix, who was hopping up and down from anxiousness, continued to pester her about her makeup. "Luna, what are you doing? Get off the floor! Makeup, Luna! The makeup!"

"All right, Bea, I dropped the key to my makeup case! Come down here and help me find it! Fast!" she said in a hurried panic.

Bea hesitantly got on her knees and hobbled over to Luna's side. As soon as she was within reach, Luna scooped up a handful of ash with her wet hand and turned to Beatrix, quickly smearing the wet, black ash down the side of her face and all down her lacey white blouse. Beatrix squealed and shot backward as Luna quickly took her hand away, already feeling horrible about what she had to do.

"Wh-why'd you—Luna—my dress! This was my second favorite dress!" Bea cried as her eyes welled up with tears, and her face began to shrivel. "My second *favorite* dress," she said as she held the black smudged dress out in front of her, examining it shamefully.

"I'm so sorry, Bea—I'm so, so sorry, I—" Luna tried to find the words to say, but the betrayal and confusion on Bea's face kept her from saying anything.

Constantine pushed back the flap and poked his head in. "Morning Luna, morning Beatrix. How are you two this morning?"

Luna slowly stood up, watching him as he looked around her hut, most certainly looking for any sign of Aria. Luna purposefully stood in the way of him and the bloodstain. "We're just messing around, Constantine. Please forgive us."

Constantine looked at her, slightly amused. He then directed his attention toward Beatrix, who still sat sobbing on the floor. "And you, Miss Beatrix? How are you doing?"

Beatrix looked at him through teary eyes. Constantine took a double take and blinked rather hard. "My… what happened to you, dear?"

She pouted and turned away. Constantine, not used to being ignored, took on a new tone. "Get yourself up. Come on, right now!"

Beatrix got to her feet and turned to him, her face embarrassed and splotchy.

"Now go get yourself cleaned up! Have a little respect for yourself. How do you expect people to take you seriously when you can't even keep yourself clean?" he stated.

His words cut right through her thin skin like a knife. Her eyes began to flow even more, even though she tried her hardest to muffle any cries.

"Come on now, get going! You're in the presence of Disciples. Act like it," he demanded.

Beatrix wiped the snot and ash from her running nose and walked out of Luna's hut without saying a word. Constantine watched her as she passed by.

"*Bea, I'm sorry,*" Luna mentioned one more time before Beatrix disappeared from view.

Constantine looked at Luna and shook his head with a slight smile. "Children these days, they don't have that built-in respect. They need to know what's acceptable and what's not. They need a firm hand, they need to be set straight. You've tried to teach her, but sometimes they just need that little extra push. I've found that—"

"Why are you here?" Luna inquired.

Constantine seemed taken back by her abrupt question. "What? I can't visit this community I have worked so hard to build under the hand of Mother and Elliot?"

"Well, it's just you said there were more Disciples. Why so many? We've been good lately."

His pleasantly false smile faded as he allowed himself to come all the way in. He thought carefully about what he was about to say as he drew closer and took her by the hand. "I fear we have a traitor among us," he said, playing his free hand on top of hers.

Luna tried to pull a very puzzled face as he gazed into her eyes from inches away, perhaps looking for any signs of lies. "What do you mean, traitor?"

Constantine licked his lips and began to speak again, still unsure of himself. "Well… Aria. You remember Aria? She was chosen to come up to the mountain with us. Chosen by Felix after he was promoted to High Disciple?"

Luna nodded. "We never really got along, but I remember."

Constantine nodded, "Yes, yes… you see, you've always been a good judge of character. It's always been something I've admired in you. You've always been able to see someone's true colors. And well... I wish we could have had this conversation earlier. I-I'm trying to find a good way to tell you this..."

Luna wanted to react so badly. She had mapped out exactly how she would put her hand to her forehead and drop her jaw in shock, but first, he needed to say it.

"Aria is sick, she... she's not thinking straight. She... well, she tried to murder Dante," he took a step back, and she quickly picked up the hint. She brought her hand to her forehead and somehow got the blood to drain from her face.

"What? I-I just don't understand..." she muttered softly. Constantine placed both of his hands on her shoulders.

"Yes... she has run away and is on the loose. She could be anywhere..." he looked from side to side, really examining the cracks and crevices of the hut.

Luna fluttered her eyelids as she looked back at him. "Wait, you said she—*tried?* She tried to murder Dante?"

Constantine smiled and nodded his head. "It seems that Dante will cling to life, though he is in bad condition. We are having Todd come up earlier this month. He should be by sometime today with emergency supplies. He told us he would also bring winter apparel. But don't let me stray from the good news. Dante should *live*! We just need to find Aria before she tries to take another life. You really don't know what someone as sick as her is capable of," he said somberly.

Luna nodded as she looked off to the side. "I'll be on the lookout then..."

"Good... very good. I'll see you outside in about twenty minutes then. We need to make an announcement."

"See you then," she muttered, still looking off to the side. Constantine exited the hut, and she remained sitting there, trying to calm herself as fast as possible.

She quickly pulled herself together and got dressed for the day, pulling on all grey or brown garments, nothing too flashy.

She cleaned up the bloodstain on her floor before exiting her hut. The outside world was much more chaotic than usual. Confused members of the community were waking up and being rounded up before they could even clear the cobwebs from their heads. "Wait! Wait! In the name of Mother, just please explain to me what's going on!" One man pleaded as he guided his son forward while being corralled by a Disciple at the same time.

"Just a quick meeting is all. No need to worry, Sam," the Disciple reassured him as he repeatedly nudged him on the back.

Everybody seemed to be gathering in the usual meeting area, the center of the community near the large boulder that Dante had previously loved standing on to proclaim his given messages to the masses. She begrudgingly followed the crowd, calmly looking all around for Ray as she did; it wasn't like him to leave without telling her.

"How are you holding up, Loon?" Benji asked, clapping her on the back.

She tried not to act as startled as she was. "Benji—you scared me."

He nodded. "Quite a lot to be scared about today, huh."

She nodded. "You heard?"

Benji sighed, "You know Constantine can't keep his mouth shut. I'd say half of Corazon knows about Aria by now."

"And what do you think?" she asked, keen to who else was listening.

Benji shrugged. "I know you were never a fan of Aria, and to be honest... I was never a real fan of Dante."

Luna gasped and looked at him. He shook his head, "Oh please. The guy had breath that could kill a cow. I'm not saying he deserved what happened to him, but—yeah."

Benji wasn't the most orthodox of followers, but his words more than often blurred the line between faith and fiction. His lack of empathy for the situation was not entirely shocking. "Besides," he said, removing an apple from his pocket. "Corazon has had enough drama."

She pushed his cheeky remarks aside and directed her attention to the rock where Constantine was now helping Orwell climb.

The two Disciples helped each other up onto the rock and looked over the confused crowd before them. Orwell cleared his throat and yelled, "Attention! May I have your attention!"

Luna was startled when Ray grabbed her from behind. She was obviously shaken by the entire situation. "Where have you been?" she whispered.

"Shh," Ray said, giving her a nod that said *It's nothing, I'll tell you later.* They both then directed their attention forward to Orwell and Constantine. They stood out more than any other Disciples, but there had to have been at least eight more Disciples scattered amongst the crowd.

Benji glared at Ray before swatting his hand off of Luna's back. Ray looked over to Benji, who looked at him with disappointment. "Come on now, friend," he whispered, not wanting to see anyone with their hands on his sister. He, too, looked toward the Disciples after his nasty glance.

They breathed heavily, and their breath seemed to linger in the air around them. A light dusting of snow was falling upon them all. Constantine stepped forward as the crowd began to quiet down. "Good Morning everyone, praise be to Mother for this beautiful day!"

"Praise be to Mother," the crowd echoed.

Constantine looked back at Orwell, who seemed to like being in his shadow. He then turned to the community and spoke again. "We have very, very unfortunate news. Last night, when most, if not all of us were sleeping soundly in our beds, a previous member of this community, Aria… attempted to murder Dante, one of our more cherished and beloved Disciples."

Everyone quickly gasped. The gasps were followed quickly by whispers and then silence when Constantine made it clear he wasn't finished.

"Dante is hanging onto life as we speak, and we ask that all of you keep him in your prayers. On another darker, more terrifying note, Aria is still out there. She left the shelter on the mountain sometime last night in fear of the consequences that would surely follow her actions. We weren't able to track her very far, but we can see that she made it down here, to Corazon."

More whispers quickly ensued. Someone let out a slightly fearful whimper.

"I shouldn't have to say this!" Constantine yelled, getting everyone's attention. "I shouldn't have to say this! But she is now a criminal and must face punishment for her actions. She is mentally sick and dangerous, making her a liability. Elliot promised all of you protection, and as long as she is at large, your protection is not promised… Our Prophet will not be a liar. His words are never flexible, never up for debate. If any of you are sheltering her, now is your time to come forward without any consequences…"

People looked around, looking for any signs of guilt or and hints of suspicion. Ray quickly found Otto and kept a steady eye on him, watching to see if he had any signs that may give them away. He stood back in the brush, deep enough to be concealed but close enough to see. Otto just stared blankly into space, occasionally whispering to the non-existent person to his left.

Constantine grew noticeably angrier as he realized nobody was going to come forward. "I cannot stress this enough. This sick woman is confused, senile. She will tell you anything to get you to believe her. Aria is smart. She is going to do whatever it takes to sell her story, to give you a reason to believe her. The truth is, she is a sinner, and everyone must recognize that. Remember… The sinner's advocate shall be punished just as much as the sinner themselves! A direct passage from the Book of Elliot!"

Luna took Ray by the hand and squeezed it tightly. Benji slowly strode away from the two of them, deep in thought.

Constantine cleared his throat and took a less accusatory tone, "I realize some of you will not take so kindly to what I am about to say, but these are direct orders from the Prophet himself. He is under a lot of pressure lately, tirelessly asking Mother for answers. Just remember that we are doing this for your safety… from this day forward, there will be eight Disciples armed and stationed in Corazon, 24/7. We will remain here, protecting you all, until the threat is gone."

This took everyone by surprise, arming those that were supposed to bring about peace and love. The crowd slowly shrank as followers pulled their loved ones closer, narrowing the spaces between the crowd substantially.

"From now on," Constantine continued, "Sterling is to be the only person who is allowed to check out any weapons. He is the only one who will be allowed to hunt, and he is the only one to be found wandering off of community grounds. We have already placed a lock on the armory. Community members must not leave the boundaries that we have already established. We all know how that turns out." People slowly directed their attention toward Ray and Luna, seeing that they were holding hands, a sign perhaps that their relations were now public knowledge.

"There is no reason to be scared unless you are harboring our fugitive or have knowledge of her whereabouts. There will also be a curfew. Everyone must remain in their respected huts by nightfall. I also regret to inform you all that we are now rationing food until Aria is found. Seeing as how we will not be hunting nearly as much and that the greenhouse can only serve so many people, it is in our best interests to limit all of you to one meal per day. Anything extra will be on the shoulders of each individual. Other than that, we can carry on with our normal lives. We can tend to the land, take care of the greenhouse, make sure the cattle grow strong and well. We can play and dance and most of all, love. I give my word to you all that by the hand of Mother and the Prophet Elliot himself. We will find her and avenge Dante."

The mixed reactions that followed were mind-boggling. Some people cheered while others looked from left to right in disbelief—disbelief that the Disciples were now declaring some twisted form of martial law. Some people began to yell, screaming about how this was never what their

Prophet had intended. People claimed to know Aria and swore on their lives she would never have done such a thing. Some said it was all a hoax, some elaborate scheme to keep them from knowing the truth.

The furious conspiring continued until a single shot from a rifle was fired up into the air, frightening everyone, sending them sprawling to the earth in fear.

Constantine spoke up again. "That's enough. I will not take any of this doubt. It is disrespectful to my Prophet and my God and will not be tolerated. Orders are orders. You all have been told what happened, and you must accept that. I realize some may be scared or hesitant to come forward, so I have a proposition. And incentive, if you will."

Everyone slowly got to their feet. Some just sat up and gave Constantine their attention. He smiled, feeling somewhat of a power high. "Felix has told me that whoever finds Aria and brings her to us will be rewarded by the Prophet himself. If a man is to come across her, he will be accepted up onto the mountain and treated as a Disciple for the rest of his days!"

Everyone was awestruck by this drastic incentive. "And if a woman shall find her, she will be treated as an Angel! She, too, will be taken onto the mountain and showered with gifts and praise! Trust in me! Trust in your Prophet and trust in Mother!"

Constantine took a step forward and threw his hands up into the air, signifying the end of his speech. He was expecting the crowd to erupt in applause, but they just slowly dispersed, knocking his ego down a few pegs. He hopped down from the boulder and picked up his rifle. Slinging it over his shoulder, he marched into the woods, determined to hunt her down. As he walked through the woods, he noticed Tobias eyeing him through the brush. He cockily strode over to him as he carried a bucket full of human waste.

"Oh Tobias, how are things?" he said, looking at him with a smile.

Tobias looked at him with a certain hatred, riddled with a kind of respect. Constantine, after all, was everything Tobias had ever aspired to be.

"I realize you may still be hurt, but you must face the fact that you sinned far too many times for me to look over them. We had to make an example out of you." The two carried on in silence. "I'm sure you've heard the news about Dante. Yes, he was always a bit of a pain, but he didn't deserve… this." He looked over to Tobias, who still refused to look his way. "You know I have a plan, Tobias, a proposition for you, a special proposition built for you specifically. Felix mentioned you by name, actually." Constantine stopped, waiting to see if he still had some sort of control over him. Tobias kept moving, one foot over the other.

"We want to make you a Disciple. There's still hope," he said, smiling. Tobias stopped dead in his tracks and slowly turned to him. It was his way of telling Constantine to speak.

"I need you to find Aria. I know she's here, and I bet you anything someone is sheltering her. You can be my silent eye. You see more than we do. You see the earliest of morning and the latest of night. If you find her and bring her up the mountain… You can have your life back and *more*. And I do mean *more*. Felix said that he would see that you are treated as a Disciple should be."

Tobias seemed wary as he looked at Constantine with regretful cloudy eyes, not speaking a word.

"I know you, Tobias. I know that's everything you've ever wanted. We need you to get to Aria before she spreads her false messages to the rest of Corazon and pollutes their minds. Your job is just as important as any of ours. I can give you a place back in the community, I can take you out of exile and give you your life back. Mother will look upon you and bless you for your bravery and grace. You must help us, though. I cannot stress how important this is," he said as he walked toward Tobias. "Now what do you say? You scratch our back, we scratch yours?" he asked, extending a hand.

Tobias silently stared at his hand as he breathed ghosts into the winter air. He hesitantly reached forward and grasped Constantine's hand firmly.

Constantine gave him a devilish smile. "Fantastic. You have made your God and your Prophet very happy. You will be reunited with them soon, I'm sure. Good luck, Tobias." The two then parted ways, not looking back for a moment.

❋❋❋

Luna led Ray back to her hut. The two of them were followed by Musgo as he quickly limped along in his old age. He obviously wanted to be in on the action, Maple had told him enough, but he really wanted to see how deep they all were. Little did he know he was falling into a trap he had set for himself a long time ago. Once they reached the sanctity of her hut, they could all let their guard down for the moment.

Ray was the first to talk about what they were all thinking. "All right. If nobody will say it, then I guess I will," he said, breaking the thick silence. "We need to weigh our options here."

"No," Luna said, spinning around. "Absolutely not. We are *not* turning her in."

"*Listen, we might not have an option...* You heard the way they were talking out there. Luna. They're all *armed*. With weapons... Do you realize what's happening here? You need to snap out of your little fairy world and face reality before we all get killed. And I'm not leaving you, so don't even pretend like that's an option."

"She came to me for help!" Her whispers resembled whimpers.

"No—she came to you because she knew you would! She knew you were vulnerable enough to take her in, and she knew she would bring all of this danger with her! Luna! Look around! There are Disciples with *guns*... They are rationing our food for no reason, trying to starve us all into turning on each other! There is no way out of this. Constantine said he'd give us a pass if we turn her in soon."

"Oh! And you believe him?" she shouted back a bit too loud. She held herself back and calmed down before speaking again. "She is a citizen of Corazon. She is supposed to be protected just as much as all of us are."

"You call this protection? We are living in a prison camp! There's no *fucking* protection! Look around!" Ray barked, getting angrier.

"I can't do it, Ray, I can't—I can't have her blood on my hands."

"Fine, let me do it then. What do you think happens *when* they eventually find her? What happens *when* they torture her to make her talk? She's going to crack, and then it'll be our heads on the line. It's not a question of *if* anymore, it's *when*. We'll be labeled as the traitors."

"You act like she's going to be caught! You act like this is bound to happen! She's safe for now! Nobody is going to look for her at the cove. Mother will give us all the strength we need to get—"

"Mother!" Ray shouted in amazement. "After all you've heard in the day, you are still relying on Mother?" He began to laugh in astonishment. "Luna—Luna, let's think for a moment." Luna began to shrink into herself, realizing what Ray was getting to. "Mother is some God, huh? Mother—she really is something else. She gave people power all right. She gave those fuckers up on the mountain the power to *rape* and *beat* and *torture* all of the women that are chained up against their will. Oh yeah, she really gave them *power* all right. It seems to me that power you're looking for is a little unevenly distributed, don't you think?"

Musgo took a step forward, seeing that Ray was making Luna upset with his harsh words. "Hey now Ray, leave the girl alo—"

"Shut up, Musgo," Ray ordered, looking at him with a scowl. He took a deep breath and then looked back over to Luna. "Ask him. Ask him, Luna."

She pretended not to notice Ray, but he was making himself too big to go unnoticed. "Ask him. Do it, Luna. Prove me wrong, I want you to prove me wrong. Ask Musgo what you've been wondering for so long, then come talk to me about power." He stopped when she held a hand up to his face. He then slowly faded into the dark of the corner.

She looked down at her toes and then over to Musgo, who stood silently watching the argument unfold. She let her gaze linger on him longer than she should have, causing him to grow uncomfortable.

"What? What do you want me to say, Luna?" he said in his raspy old-timey voice.

She took a deep breath and paced the room. "I think it's time I ask you something I've always been afraid of asking you, Musgo." He looked at her as if she had three heads as she continued. "Now, as you have said before, you're my friend. And if you want it to remain that way, you'll tell me the truth. Understand?"

"Luna, what in the world?"

"Understand?" she hissed, looking at him with hate.

He slowly nodded his head, showing a glimpse of the fear he was feeling. It was apparent he knew what she was getting to. Ray didn't know what was coming but stood by the door just in case an unwelcome intruder was to pay them a visit.

Luna continued with hesitation. "My whole life, at least… the one I choose to remember, has always been based on faith and faith alone. Never once did I question whether or not one day I would die in my sleep and see nothing but black for eternity. Never once did I question free will or the meaning of my existence. I was taught to take evolution as a theory and nothing more, I was taught to believe in Mother, to praise Mother, to love for Mother. To fight for Mother. And that was based on what? Faith."

Musgo shook his head, "Luna, don't—"

"I was taught this way of life on a street corner and sitting on park benches. I learned everything I ever believed in from a stranger in the park, and what credibility did he have? Nothing. Until one day, he brought in a homeless man in a wheelchair and claimed that he could summon the power of this God he worshiped to make this man have the ability to walk again."

Musgo lifted his face from his hands and stood tall, readying himself for what was to come.

"That homeless man was you, Musgo," she said, flapping her arms up into the air. "As soon as I saw you rise from that chair, well… I was sold. A lot of us were sold. Some people came here for the unity, for the sex, for the whole aspect of living off the grid. Some people had nowhere else to go. But I came here because I *believed!*" she hissed as she pointed at her heart. It was obvious she was now holding back years of anger and frustration behind her thin face. She was a bomb readying to burst. Her eyes welled up with tears as she got ready to ask the million-dollar question.

"So tell me, Musgo… was I right? Did the… the Great Prophet Elliot actually heal you with the powers bestowed on him through Mother? Or were you just a party trick?"

Ray looked to Musgo, who appeared to be ready to crumble. He retrieved a chair and slid it behind his legs so that Musgo could sit. He collapsed into the chair, shaking with guilt.

"You act like I don't know pain," he said in a humbled, embarrassed tone. "You don't know how it was before, Luna," he said in between sporadic huffs. "I had nothing. And when I say nothing, I mean it. I didn't even have a street corner to sleep on."

Luna turned her back to him as she exhaled forcefully. She began to furiously wipe at her eyes.

"Luna, you gotta see where I'm coming from, please. Once I knew what I had done, I wanted to take it back. I wanted to take it back so badly. But it was too late, we were already halfway to nowhere."

She kept her back turned on him.

He tried to find the words to properly apologize, but there was no use. His lips trembled to get the next words out. "When a man— When a man gets so hungry at night, he'll eat a dead rat or roadkill. Or chew at the moldy sandwich on the sidewalk... And a stranger comes up to him and takes him to a sit-down restaurant, the type of place he was never welcomed in before, well... well, the hungry man will listen and believe just about anything that stranger says. You know how persuasive he can be. You know how he is, Luna. We had no clue we were going to just be cogs in some sexually perverse system. But at the time, it just seemed so right. Yeah—you have to forgive me, Luna."

Ray looked at the two of them in astonishment. This revelation was enough to bring her to her knees.

Luna seemed just as shocked as anyone else, despite expecting what was to be said in the first place. She shook her head from side to side as she stared into the distance with furious wide eyes. "My whole life, gone. And *for what?* Because some criminal bought another homeless man a *hamburger?*" She shook her head in despair.

"Luna, please, you have to listen to me. You have to see my side of the story, see where I'm coming from. I beg you... please, please believe me. Words can't describe what I feel."

She looked over to him through watery, bloodshot eyes. Watching him with his arms stretched out, trying desperately to portray how sorry he was. She shook her head. "I don't know what to believe in anymore..."

Musgo's head sank below his shoulders as he let his shaking body go limp.

"I need some time to myself," she muttered with a soft voice.

Ray approached Musgo from behind and placed a hand on his shoulder. Musgo slowly rose to his feet and looked over to Luna one more time. He opened his mouth and got ready to speak; Ray simply patted him again and shook his head, trying to tell him that it was no use. The damage was already done. It was the kind of wound that only time would heal.

Ray escorted Musgo out of the tent, leaving Luna alone with her thoughts.

Musgo looked up to Ray as he hobbled along. "Please, you have to understand, I never meant for any of this to happen. You just—you have to go with your gut and believe me. I have nobody else to—"

Ray cut him short. "You believe in redemption, Musgo?"

Musgo paused and touched Ray's arm. "What do you need me to do?"

"I have an idea that might... well, I don't know what will happen. But something will change. I need you, though. You're respected, you're liked," he said, holding his stare as best he could.

"Just tell me what I need to do, Ray. By the hand of Mother, I'll do it—I'm sorry, uh... anything I need to do to fix this. I can't have Luna think of me as some monster. I can't live with that on my conscience."

"Well, it's not that simple. Something bad is going to have to happen first. Something that angers people. We are gonna need a spark of some sort," Ray said, his voice simmering to a whisper as they walked along the wet earth.

Musgo went into deep thought for a few moments as the two of them continued to walk. "I don't know what we could possibly do that hasn't already been done. This is a system we're talking about… it's not like we can just snap our fingers and make something happen. This has been something years in the making. I have no clue how we can make people change their way of life. You got any ideas?"

"I do… unfortunately. But they have to believe that they had the idea on their own, if they knew we had anything to do with it, it would defeat the purpose. They need to discover this revelation out of their own free will."

Musgo shook his head. "We don't believe in free will, we believe in predestination. You know, fate and shit. Nobody's gonna bite."

"That's why we need to make them believe they discovered it on their own. It's going to mean freedom for everyone here, freedom of choice, freedom from the corrupt hand that guides them," he said as he watched Otto skip away through the woods. "But it's gonna cost us."

32

Otto skipped along from tree to tree, making it back to his hidden cove rather quickly. He had left before the entire speech was over. He didn't see any point in staying. In his mind, the speech was over long before it even began. He even managed to grab a bit of leftover bread and a hunk of venison before he left. He ducked under his tiny hole in the earth and gracefully slid into his dirt-layered home. Aria remained cowering in the corner, watching his every move very carefully.

Otto nervously looked at her and gave her the bread and venison before running about his home and picking up small sheets of paper. "Gotta find a pencil. Gotta find a pencil. Gotta find a pencil. Where's the pencil? I can't find it. Where did I put it? Where did you go?" he said frantically as he darted about the room.

Aria slowly moved forward, "Wh-what are you looking for?" she inquired softly.

He looked at her with wild eyes. "My pencil. If I don't have my pencil, I can't draw. If I can't draw, I can't think. If I can't think, I'll freak out, and if I freak out, Sarah will get mad, and if she gets mad, then I'll—"

"Otto, Otto, it's all right, settle down… here," she said, reaching behind her and presenting the sharpened pencil she held onto for protection. He quickly snatched it from her and started sketching away at one of his crumpled-up pieces of paper.

She retreated back into her corner, where she sat and observed him. He would sometimes make noises corresponding to his drawings. The floor was littered with old sketches of houses, people, and places from his memory. The details were always so vivid, never bleak. The pictures seemed to come alive as if the characters inhabiting them were smiling at you. They seemed to know you, recognize you. They peered right through the thin lining of the paper page and directly into your soul.

She even found herself a bit spooked by the images. They seemed to know her. They seemed to know all of her little secrets and lies. They looked at her as if they were all simultaneously chanting *I know what you're thinking*. The scariest pictures came when Otto strayed away from his memories and delved deeper into his mind to find the ridiculously twisted creatures that he loved to give names.

There was the Nooksnog, a hairy, guinea pig-like beast that weighed well over 400 pounds and stood on two powerfully muscular hind legs. The Nooksnog had razor-sharp teeth and eyes like a vortex, eyes so deep it mesmerized its prey long enough so that it could pounce and claim its next meal. He also had beasts like the Gurblewarp, a mix between an albino tree frog and a rhinoceros. It was a very dangerous creature who would stand up to nearly any other animal unless it crossed paths with a pack of Forest Cats.

He loved to think up fuzzy reptiles and cattle with lizard skin. He would spend hours, sometimes even days, trying to perfect the texture or feel of his new creation's skin. He also liked to take the time to explain to Aria the advantages of having a bear with an exoskeleton or a fish with human-esque appendages. Over time he grew more and more comfortable with her presence.

As the weeks rolled into one another and the snowfall picked up considerably, the two found themselves huddled close around his gas lamps. He tried to stay away from open flames seeing as how it might attract the attention of some unwanted Disciples. He even slowly stopped talking to Sarah. He only mentioned her here and there in the midst of his real conversations but seldom asked for her opinion on the topics.

He was surprisingly gentle with her, given his jittery and rather fluctuating persona. He was very conscientious of the fact that she needed medicine every night, and he was always to be the one to give it to her. It was almost systematic. He would return to his home every evening when the sky turned pink so that he would give her the medication. He would watch her take it, too, forcing her to open her mouth and move her tongue side to side.

She returned the favor by holding him on the nights where there were storms, the nights where he got all riled up and couldn't seem to calm down. He also got this way when he would come across a Disciple scouting out the woods around his cove. They would often put him on the spot as a means of entertainment.

"Where you heading, Otto?" Orwell would ask.

"B-back to the camp," he'd reply.

"You seem like you're in a rush? Everything all right? You need me to walk with you?"

"No-no-no, Sarah, Sarah can keep me company. We have fish waiting for us. Fish um... we should go now—"

"Well, let me come with you, ya never know what you might find… we can't be too careful with a wannabe *murderer* out running around," Orwell would say with a smirk.

Otto would then have to think on his toes and really capitalize on the clinically insane card that he kept so well hidden up his sleeve. He would sometimes drop to the ground and start crying or hit his head repeatedly against a tree. He even began to undress on some occasions and roll around in the snow like a madman. Really anything that could make the armed Disciple uncomfortable enough to leave him alone for the time being. After all, he was just Otto, just the village idiot.

At times like these, he would come home, scared of what could have happened. She would take him in her arms just like she had when there were bad storms. She had this method of gently stroking his head while whispering soothing words into his ear while he shook senselessly in her arms.

She now saw Otto for the extremely brave man he was given the conditions, and the more she thought about that, the more she regretted her prior behavior toward him. She recalled days where she would completely disregard his advances at friendship, calling him a *retard* or *halfwit*. She often wondered if he remembered any of her slanderous remarks toward him. She wondered if he had the capability to hold a grudge. Everything seemed so passive in his eyes. He still gave food to Tobias every night when he limped over the frosty landscape in search of a requiem to his barking stomach. Aria was sure to keep extra quiet every time he came around. She considered perhaps poking her head out to see the sunshine, but she knew even that would be risky.

One night, when she lay back, warming her hands by the gas lamp and observing Otto as he frantically sketched away at a crumpled piece of paper, she decided to ask him a question that had been on her mind for quite some time. "...Otto?" she asked hesitantly, afraid that she might be disturbing him.

He answered immediately without missing a beat, barely even lifting the pencil from the paper. "Yes?" he huffed.

She thought about how she was going to phrase this question carefully and then spoke. "Why are you doing this? Why are you... helping me?"

He stopped drawing for a split second and focused on his train of thought. "You needed help," he replied as simply as possible.

She rolled her eyes, yearning for an answer that could maybe bring her some sort of closure. "But I was always so mean to you. Do you remember that? I called you names and wouldn't even give you the time of day… now you open up your home to me and—and *risk your life* for me… for someone that barely even considered you human. I am so sorry, but—I just don't understand…"

Otto continued to draw while making faint, minorly hurt facial expressions.

She looked at him, hoping that her words would get some sort of rise out of him. "Well, say *something*. Give me a reason, please. I—I am so, so grateful, but I just—"

"I draw with a pencil," he muttered fast, the words tumbling out of his mouth like dice.

She looked at him more confused than ever. She opened her mouth to possibly further the topic, but there was no need; he continued without hesitation.

"I draw with pencil. Not pen. I could get pens. But I draw with pencils." He stopped drawing and nodded at his work for a moment, allowing her to see the more accepted human side of him as he actually admired his work. "Pencils are the best. The pencil has an eraser." He held the pencil up and pointed to the tiny pink nub on the end. She nodded slowly, not sure as to what he was getting at.

"I like the eraser because I make mistakes. *Everyone* makes mistakes. *I* make mistakes, *you* make mistakes. The eraser helps us *fix* our mistakes. Correct our mistakes. You made a mistake. I will be the eraser."

He took the paper he had scribbled on and crawled over to her side. He then turned the paper over and handed it to her, revealing a stunningly accurate portrait of her face.

"It's-it's beautiful," she said, putting her hand over her lips as she was taken back by the accuracy of the portrait.

He sat back and admired again. This time he wasn't examining his work but the happiness he so generously bestowed upon his damsel in distress.

"Thank you so much," she said, touching the top of his hand.

He quickly leaned in, taking her gesture as a notion to act. He closed his eyes and puckered his lips as a small child would. She pulled back and held her hand to his chest, stiff-arming him, preventing him from coming any closer. The two of them looked at each other in disbelief.

He wanted her to explain her actions. She could see it in his eyes. She looked away from him, trying her best to hide her sheer embarrassment with the wrongly read situation.

"I'm not ready... not yet," she muttered sorrowfully. She peeked at him through the corner of her eyes as he quietly sat back.

He nodded lightly, "Yes. Of course. It's your turn now."

"Pardon?" she asked, her tense shoulders relaxing.

He nodded more vigorously as he looked right at her. "It's your turn now. Your turn. You get to be the eraser now..."

The two of them shared in that awkward encounter for a few more silent minutes as they listened to the last of the crickets chirping away. Aria soon laid back and closed her eyes, falling into what was perhaps the best sleep since her escape. She now felt a strange protection she had never felt before, as if Otto would fight to his dying breath to save her. It was an idea that both warmed and shattered her heart simultaneously. Otto, well, he dreamed of fuzzy Nooksnogs and friendly Gurblewarps.

33

Benji had a way of slipping in and out of conversations undetected. One moment he would be fully engaged, debating Maple on how to best season the venison. Next, he would be referencing the nature of love and how it was, in his eyes, a recipe for heartbreak and jealousy. His audience always varied. He would amp up his intellectual vocabulary whenever a Disciple was near and tone down his intense thoughts whenever dealing with one of the younger followers. He was a chameleon, able to adapt to any sort of social situation with ease. It was as if he had rehearsed each one of his lines hours before the conversation had even begun.

To those who thought they knew him, it was always the same ol' Benji. But to his sister, it was a simple facade. He was different, not in the broken way that one might expect a prisoner of war to be, but in a way in which he appeared rejuvenated. He had caught his second wind and was going to ride it as long as it lasted.

He knew it, too. He knew that Luna saw right past his carefully woven veil, and he was curious as to what she thought of the man behind the tulle. He would periodically duck into her hut, patiently waiting for her to return from a hunt. This would always catch her by surprise, especially in the moments where she looked forward to having a fraction of a moment to herself.

He had a way of moving in complete silence, the soles of his feet barely gracing the ground with each step. It was a skill that was both impressive and slightly unnerving to those who noticed it. It gave him the ability to float around Corazon unnoticed, a stark contrast to his personality, which seemed to be displayed under a perpetual spotlight.

The one thing he couldn't keep silent about was his love for apples. He always had one on him. It came in handy when he both grew hungry and needed a moment to formulate a quick-witted comeback in his head, mid-conversation. The crisp crunch of the apple was always a giveaway. That's why Luna took a moment to collect herself before entering her hut after washing off in the river.

She ducked under the tarp and stood up, making direct eye contact with Benji as he leaned against the side of her bed. Her wet hair was pulled tight behind her head in a ponytail; a towel was fastened tight under each of her arms, leaving nothing but her naked shoulders exposed. "You can't keep showing up like this without telling me," she said, aggravated. "I could have been naked."

He nodded as he finished chewing the apple in his mouth. "I assure you I'm more than capable of holding a hand in front of my eyes," he replied, miming the gesture.

"That's not the point," she said, pulling out her clothes from a bin she kept by her prayer corner, one hand remaining on the knot of the towel. "It's about privacy. I don't like walking into my home not knowing if someone is going to be there waiting for me."

"So you don't welcome family, but a suicidal stranger?" he asked, raising an eyebrow.

Luna straightened her posture and looked at him, placing her free hand on her hip. "You really want to go there?"

He smirked. "I'm just looking out for you, Loon. I'd hate to see you get your heart shattered."

"Mm-hmm," she huffed. "Well, you can look out for me without sneaking into my hut."

Benji took a moment and looked around her hut, debating on another bite of apple to prolong the time he had to think. He decided against it and stood up, taking a step toward Luna. "Crazy time for Corazon, isn't it?"

She had her back turned to him as she resumed picking out clothes. "I don't know what you mean," she muttered, pretending to be lost in concentration.

"You don't know what I mean?" he chuckled. "I mean, it's crazy about Aria, trying to kill a Disciple and what not. You know anything about that?"

Luna spun around and took on a new demeanor, not wanting things to turn into an interrogation. "Do you really think I care about what happens to that bitch?" she asked, sounding hostile.

Benji smiled, "Oh, I'm not insinuating you do. I just wanted to hear your thoughts," he said, backing up. "I'm not saying Aria was a pleasure to be around, but… I'm certainly not saying Dante was either."

"He's a Disciple," Luna stated, her arms crossed.

"And how does that make him different from any other man here?" he asked, throwing an arm up in the air. "I know Aria was less than pleasant at times, but I find it hard to believe she'd attack the man for no reason. She was a bitch, yes, but she wasn't stupid."

Luna remained crossed, still showing her discomfort with his sudden appearance. "I don't know what you want me to say."

"I want you to admit that something is off around here, Loon," he said, trying to convey his frustrations. "What happens up there? And why was it flawed enough to allow something like—like this!" he shouted. He drew back into himself, realizing that shouting wasn't going to be the best way to communicate. "This is why they had to leave. This is how the Former were made, a lack of explanation. These girls, they go up there and—and what?"

"Those aren't questions we ask," she stated.

"*But why?* Why aren't those questions we ask? This is what the Former warned us about. They knew the word of Elliot was being twisted, and when they spoke up, they were exiled."

Luna remained silent, not wanting to reflect on his words.

Benji continued. "Elliot, and the land that Corazon rests on. It's sacred. Nothing is going to take the sacrality away, but—we can't allow it to be tainted by the actions of those abusing the word of Elliot and Mother herself. This land belongs with the people who will uphold the original teachings of Elliot. It belongs to the people who will *do good.*"

"*You sound like one of them,*" she whispered under her breath.

Benji shrugged as he took a leap of faith. "And so what if I do, Loon? Maybe they were onto something."

As much as she hated to admit it, her brother was making sense. If Aria could be used as any evidence—bad things were happening on the mountain. Everyone saw it, but few acknowledged it. "And what if you're right?" she asked, debating whether or not she would let him in on the small circle of people who knew about Aria's whereabouts. "What if things aren't the way they used to be. What can we do about it?"

Benji smiled and stepped forward again. "*We can take it.*"

"Excuse me?"

He nodded, "You heard me; we can take it. Reclaim what was ours in the first place. Corazon is nothing without its followers, and if we can get enough people to open their eyes… we can reclaim what is rightfully ours. This sacred land, and the Prophet that made it all possible."

She hesitated, worried as to what he would say next. "What do you mean, *take it?*"

He paused, then looked back up at her. "We demand answers; we demand change. If we find enough people to agree with us, then it's completely reasonable."

"It sounds like you're setting the stage for another split," she replied. "What if the Disciples refuse?"

"Then… we take it," he said again, this time sounding more hesitant.

"You're talking about a coup," she stated, her eyes narrowing.

"I'm talking about making things right again, re-establishing the community we once had. Taking back the land that is rightfully ours, and living in peace, just as the Prophet always intended. It's possible. We just need a little help," he said in a hopeful tone.

Luna squeezed her eyes shut, not sure if she wanted to know the answer to her next question. "We?"

Benji took a moment to himself as he stepped down from the stone of righteousness and took on a tone more based in reality. "I mean you and me. Beatrix, Maple—*the good guys.*"

Her skepticism didn't fade. She shook her head. "I think things are typically more than just good guys vs. bad guys."

"What do you mean?" he asked, cocking his head to the side.

She sighed. "We're told that there are two sides to everything. Good and bad, left and right, up and down. But there's more to all of it. Not everything is so black and white."

Benji was still. His eyes remained fixed on Luna, like she was a puzzle he was actively trying to piece together. "Right. No, of course. Forget about it," he said, scratching the back of his head. "Did you ever ask Sterling about getting me back on the team? That's why I came by. I um… I've got that itch again. I'm ready to get back out there."

She nodded, "Did Orwell clear you from the gathering team?"

He shrugged. "Not yet, but I was always cut out to be a hunter, you know that. It runs in our blood," he chuckled.

She nodded. "I'll run it by Sterling again, but he won't budge until Orwell gives him the go-ahead."

Benji nodded. "I thought that much. You and Sterling run things well with the other hunters. They say it's all real organized."

She nodded again, "We try," she stated. "Not much room for disorganization when you're handling firearms."

"Mm-hmm," he said. "Listen, I really just need to blow off some steam. All of this…" he waved his hand around in the air. "It's got me stressed. I'm going to get out for a quick hunt before the sun gets any lower. What's the code?"

"What do you mean?" she asked.

"The code, to the hunting chest? I'm sure Sterling gave it to you, that's what the other hunters have told me, at least. I just need a gun, nothing too fancy," he said.

Luna clasped her hand over the knot in the towel again. "I don't have the code, sorry. I need to get changed. You should leave."

Benji held his hands out to the side, a smile spread across his face. "Come on now, Loon. I know you have the combination. They all told me."

"I'm not allowed to give anyone the code. It's for Sterling and me only," she stated. "Now, please, I'm getting cold."

Benji seemed as though he were getting irritated, his half-cocked smile nowhere to be found. "Loon, it's me, all right? I just want to feel like I'm doing my part around here. Picking leaves and berries all day? That ain't me. Just give me this. I'll return the rifle back to the hunting chest by sundown, promise."

She remained stoic. "I'm not giving you the combination," she stated. "If you want it so badly, talk to Orwell."

He shook his head. "Orwell won't clear me, and you know that. Listen —just give me the combination," he said, his words taking on a more threatening tone.

Luna heard it; there was no unhearing it. He knew there was no chance he would be getting the combination now. She seemed confused but concerned. "There's a lot of hate in your heart, Benji. There always has been. I can feel this anger inside of you, and it's frightening. What happened? What they did to you, it changed you."

"You forget that *they* were friends and family. Now you dismiss them as *the other*. You've turned them into some sort of nightmare."

"Benji, I am done having this conversation. Please leave," she said, growing equally irritated.

"Loon, listen to yourself. This land should be for everyone! All who believe in Elliot and Mother. Not just the ones that are all right with Disciples doing whatever they want!"

"Benji, I said *leave*."

"The combination, Luna. What is the code?"

"Get out!" she demanded, pointing toward the exit.

His ego quickly deflated as he lowered his arms and stepped toward the exit. He looked back to her and opened his mouth as if he were ready to say something else when Ray entered the hut. He looked at the both of them and sensed the thick tension following her alarming outburst. "Everything all right in here?" he asked.

Luna nodded, "Benji was just leaving."

Benji looked at Ray and smiled. "Peachy keen, friend," he said with a flourish of enthusiasm. He then walked past Ray, turning to glare at Luna just before leaving.

Ray kept his eyes on Luna, who had yet to change out of her towel. "You okay?"

She shook her head. "What are we going to do?"

He didn't need to question her further. He didn't need an explanation. At that moment, what he needed was to act, whether she approved of it or not. He folded his arms and sighed. "We're going to figure it out."

She gingerly reached for the towel knot by her shoulder and pulled on the tag, causing it to slowly unravel. Ray turned away, rejecting any sort of advance. He walked back outside, finally giving her the alone time she had been searching for.

34

Ray trudged out into the snow so that he could welcome an incoming all-terrain vehicle with the rest of the community. Todd sat behind the wheel and tried to remain in control of the vehicle, veering from left to right. He pulled up and brought the massive black vehicle with thick wheels to a halt.

"God, you wouldn't believe the shit I had to go through to get here. I cut myself a path out here a few years back so that it would be easier to get here during times like these. Would you believe it's already being taken over by ivy?" He shook his head and sarcastically laughed as he hopped out of the driver's seat and unlatched the trunk. People quickly flocked to the back of his truck, removing all of the boxes and bins they possibly could. Inside were used coats and heavier winter jackets. He also had bins brimming with new socks and some old boots with holes in them.

"Hey, we really appreciate it," Ray said modestly, trying to hold in the fact that Todd clearly knew what was going on up on the mountain. In fact, the more he thought, the more it made sense. Why else would Todd make a special trip up there every month? It was clear to him that it wasn't Otto that kept him tethered to the community the way he was.

"Just doing my job, pal. Not much else left out there for me. The World's gone to shit."

Ray chuckled.

"You laugh, but I'm not joking," he said as he lugged a plastic bin off of the bed of his truck. "These folks must've known what was coming. If you could see the way things are out there, it'd make the whole living in the woods thing not seem too bad after all. It's always one side versus the other out there. Nobody's allowed to just *exist* anymore. Rumor has it there's this new virus working its way through Italy right now, scary stuff. Sometimes makes me wish I lived here for good. But somebody's gotta be on the outside."

Ray scratched at his now bearded chin. "You're kidding me."

"Well, you've been gone longer than you think, having been cooped up alone for so long. People are changing, politics are… I guess you could say they're more corrupt than you could ever imagine. The lower class sinks lower, and the rich keep getting rich. They got these camps now, for the homeless… work them till their fingers bleed for a meal and a half a day, and they call it 'freedom and equality.' And this isn't stuff from some third-world outsourcing company. This is stuff happening right here in the good ol' U.S. of A."

"Interesting," Ray whispered, reflecting on how the world carried on just fine without him.

Todd looked around, tilting his head toward the sun like some ancient Greek hero for a moment, basking in his own glory. He saw himself as a savior to Corazon. He had, after all, aided in the building of it, and if it weren't for him, they wouldn't have half of the necessities they had at the moment. "I guess it's not all sunshine and rainbows up here, though. I got a call from Elliot himself, asking for some uh… some special supplies?" Todd whispered as he nudged Ray and pointed to a metal case in the backseat of his truck. "I mean, he's requested some weird things before with that pirated signal he's got, but… he actually called me for this. It sounded like an emergency… I also got an order in for a ton of meds, and… well, I gotta know. What's going on here?"

Ray peered skeptically into the truck, directing his full attention on the silver-plated case in the back. "What type of stuff do you have in there?" he asked.

Todd examined his face for a few moments before shaking his question off. "I'll, uh, I'll show you on our way back." He clicked a button and locked the truck from the outside, stuffing the key deep inside of his pocket. "Take me to go see my brother, yeah?"

Ray nodded his head and gave a faint smile. "Sure, let me just grab a couple jackets first." He then snapped back into reality and made his way to the winter jacket bin. Maple had already retrieved a jacket for Luna and Beatrix, but he was going to try and snag two for both Aria and himself. He approached the bin and removed two sizable jackets. He then turned around to come face-to-face with Felix.

"One jacket isn't enough?" he asked, his words oozing with a malicious curiosity.

Ray thought on his toes and quickly responded as best as he could. "Little Beatrix returned hers. She's a growing girl. It's about time she has a proper fitting jacket."

Felix nodded, seeming ashamed that he hadn't thought about the fact that Beatrix was a growing girl. "Very well then, on your way."

Ray began walking without any sort of goodbye acknowledgment to Felix. In his eyes, Felix was the one running the show, or at least the one that mattered. He had inherited this aggressive persona that he deemed necessary in this apparent time of crisis. He was the one dishing out orders with little to no regard for Elliot. It was now his time to shine. He was the one holding the reins to Corazon in Elliot's prolonged absence, and everyone seemed to recognize it.

Ray made it back to Luna's hut, where she lay still in bed, just as she had upon realizing her way of life was a lie. "Luna, you gotta get up, we gotta do something. You can't just waste away here like this. It's not healthy."

She simply pulled the covers up even further. Beatrix sat on the floor and looked up to Ray. She had that concerned look on her face that only an innocent child could bear.

"Luna?" she asked sweetly. "Luna, I'm not mad at you anymore… I forgive you for staining my dress. I know you didn't mean to…" she said in a softened voice. Beatrix knew Luna had purposefully done it, but she couldn't for the life of her figure out why her best friend would ever do something like that.

Luna remained still in bed.

"Bea, why don't you hop up there with her, stay warm. I'm gonna go see about something, I'll be right back." Ray said, gesturing her up onto the bed.

Bea leaped from her seated position right up onto the mattress and nuzzled her head up under Luna's arm. Luna then accepted her request to cuddle and opened up her arms for a warm, drawn-out hug. This brought a smile to all of their lips right before Ray went back out to see Todd.

❋❋❋

"So you wanna tell me why there are a bunch of holy men walking around with guns?" Todd asked as the two of them walked through the woods away from Corazon.

Ray shrugged. "Ask them, it's a complicated story."

Todd looked up the incline and saw a silhouette of an armed Disciple outlined by the sun in the distance. "They really watch ya all the time, don't they?"

"Like you wouldn't believe," he replied.

"Somebody really messed up somewhere along the line. This seems pretty serious. Goddamn," Todd muttered in a tense tone that saturated the air now weighing on him.

"Yeah, I guess you could say that," Ray said, looking at the same Disciple in the distance.

"It doesn't have anything to do with Otto, now, does it? That boy's been misunderstood since day one, I'll tell ya. I'm lucky I found him a place where rebels and rejects could live together in peace. I don't even care if he doesn't talk to anyone else. He's made himself up that Sarah girl, and that's all he needs. As long as he's staying out of trouble, I'm okay with just about anything," Todd said, smiling.

The two of them moseyed to the cove by the river. The cove now had a thick fur flap that sheltered it well. Todd looked at Ray and laughingly pointed to the fur flap. "He's a smart one," he whispered.

Todd then began to creep up alongside the entrance. "I'll just pop my head in and surprise him," he whispered with a childish grin plastered across his face.

Ray, all of a sudden, felt extremely light-headed, realizing Todd might see Aria and put the pieces together. He quickly mustered up a fake sneeze and roared as loud as he could. Otto poked his head out just in time to confront Todd at the entrance. It was apparent Otto was caught off guard and extremely nervous upon seeing how close things had come to falling apart.

"Todd—" he croaked, scrambling to his feet while hugging the wall, making it impossible for Todd to see past him. Todd took his actions as a genuine surprise and broke out in laughter. Otto made it to the outside of the cove and gave Todd a big hug, pushing him away from the cove in doing so.

"Whoa there! Where's all this coming from, Otto?" Todd asked.

"Just—nothing. Just—happy to see you," Otto replied.

"Well, I'm happy to see you, too. Look, I gotcha a nice jacket and some of those super processed cake things you like," Todd proclaimed, holding out a large plastic garbage bag.

Otto's smile quickly turned from one of fear to one of a young child on Christmas day as he accepted his brother's generous gift. "Ooh—yes, I like these. I like these very, very much. Thank you, brother!"

Todd looked over to Ray and pointed at Otto. "What have you guys been feeding him?"

Ray shrugged again. "Berries, venison… any kind of vegetable Maple deems acceptable. Oh, there's always bread."

Todd looked at Ray differently, finally noticing the uneasiness in the air. The three of them lingered there in silent tension for a few moments before Todd decided to take charge. "Must be something in the water then," Ray felt a tingling in the bottom of his spine after hearing Todd say those words.

❊❊❊

Inside of Otto's cove, Aria had wrapped herself in one of the larger blankets and was listening to the muffled conversation outside, not knowing whether or not a Disciple was going to storm the small space at any time and drive a knife through her throat.

Just like Otto, she had no idea Todd was going to be paying a visit on this cold afternoon. He had been called in on an emergency run from the mountain, something that had never happened before.

She listened as the three of them talked and caught up with long, drawn-out silences in between micro conversations. It was the silences that were the worst. They seemed to suffocate her as she waited for what was to come.

"Well, I guess that's it then. I better get going. It was nice seeing you, Otto. You've changed," he said, wagging a thick finger at his brother. "You seem real well and, well, I don't know. Keep up the good work, I guess."

Todd stopped and laughed for a moment at the absurdity of his own statement. He then wiped at his nose and looked back to Otto. "But seriously, I, uh… well I love ya brother. Take care, and be safe, all right?"

Otto nodded, "Yeah, be safe, yeah. I love you, yeah. Thank you for coming. Thank you for coming, Todd."

Todd nodded and then looked at Ray. "All right then, let's head back."

Ray nodded toward Otto before turning back toward the woods.

Otto then crawled back into his cove to find Aria still rolled up, clutching the tiny knife that made her feel so strong. He laughed and shook his head in relief as he leaned up against the wall.

Things weren't the same for Aria and Otto. They both ran by a different code. Things were colder out by the river all alone. The nights were darker, and the animals sounded more vicious. The closest thing Aria ever got to daylight was seeing it through a crack whenever Otto threw back the flap to go into the world. She began to grow tired and weak. Constantly in fear for her life, she would shake at night, partially from the cold and partially from the metaphorical demons that lurked behind every twist and turn of her dream world.

She sometimes dreamed of things the way they used to be. She often considered praying to Mother to take things back to how they were. She then realized she was fueling the system that abused her and quickly reconsidered her actions. She wanted to go back and relive so many of the events that brought her to this place. Some nights she even considered just getting up and walking as far as she could, leaving Otto behind, though she knew there was no way she would make it that far in the current winter weather.

❋❋❋

Tobias slowly lumbered about Corazon on the prowl for any sign of Aria or suspicious acts. He knew Aria well before all of this had transpired. They loved together and often enjoyed each other's company in the early morning hours after the love had ended. It was difficult for him to comprehend just how much things had changed in the past year.

He limped over the icy earth using the worn-out boots Otto had so generously gifted him. It was people like Otto that made Tobias regret his former way of life, walking the earth as some supreme meta-human. It was times like these that made him realize how normal, if not, inferior he truly was in the grand spectrum of things. The late-night hours when everyone else was fast asleep was when he felt most alone. Even when everyone else had turned their back on him in exile, there was something about the dark and silence, drowning in a sea of his own regret.

"*Hey,*" a voice called from the thick of the woods.

Tobias jerked around like a frightened animal.

"*Come here. Yeah, you… Come here…*" The raspy voice called out again.

Tobias took a couple of steps forward. Could this be the devil come to test him?

"*Come on, we don't have much time!*" the voice silently urged him.

Tobias warily took a few more cautious steps toward the thick of the woods where the voice called to him. He clenched his fist, preparing for a fight.

All of a sudden, a hand reached out and gripped his jacket, ripping him from sight and into the darkened brush. He lost his balance in the dark, and his body landed on the ground with a heavy thud. He thrashed about, throwing handfuls of snow in every direction and grunting as he flailed his fists about.

"*Hey! Control yourself! I said, control yourself!*" The whispering voice demanded.

Tobias kept on fighting as hard as he could with one arm, briefly making contact with the side of what felt to be a human's ear.

He was quickly brought to an immediate halt upon feeling the smooth edge of a sharpened blade pressed against his throat. "*I just want to talk to you,*" the voice said.

Tobias froze and ceased all attempts at escape. Whoever it was who held the knife to his throat had played dirty and clearly had reason to speak with him. He held his hands out to the side in surrender; he could feel the presence of the man who lumbered over him, the cold steel still pressed to his neck. "Stand up, slowly," the man said.

The blade left his throat, and the hand that held him loosened, allowing him to move freely. He flattened his back against a tree and used it as leverage to shimmy himself to his feet. He then looked up at his captor and slowly tensed up as a chill ran up his spine.

"*I need your help,*" Ray whispered with dismay.

Tobias looked at him with anger, confusion, and pity all rolled into one.

"Yeah... I need your help," he repeated.

Tobias nodded and made a gesture for him to continue.

"You don't have to be all quiet around me, I'm not going to rat you out. I don't care. I don't believe in any of this shit. I need you to speak so that I know you understand."

Tobias nobly held his stare, showing Ray that he didn't care if he refused to believe. Tobias was still strong in his ways and would uphold his side of the punishment.

After a moment of no answer, Ray shook it off. "So be it," he said, once again wondering if this was all one big foolish waste of time. He debated storming off and scrapping the idea altogether, but there was no saying whether he would get another chance. He dragged a hand down his face and shook his head before looking right back at Tobias. "What if I told you I could get you, Aria…"

The muscles in Tobias's face tightened, and his breathing became shallow.

"Would you be able to deliver her? Would you take her to the Disciples and claim that you found her wandering around?"

After a moment of thought, he nodded his head in determination. Here was his enemy handing him everything he needed for redemption.

Ray then looked side to side, "I can tell you where you might find her, but first, I need you to promise me something. I need your *word*, Tobias…"

Tobias nodded again, this time more serious.

Ray swallowed the little pride he had left and cleared his throat. He then took a deep breath and looked directly into Tobias's eyes. "Promise me Otto won't get hurt."

Tobias, all of a sudden, felt dizzy. How had he been so blind for so long? Otto, the man he realized he had underestimated for so long, had been harboring a fugitive, all while treating him as a charity case.

"I need your *word*, Tobias!" Ray demanded, pushing him against the tree. "They'll kill me and hurt Luna and Bea if I do it. They'll take it out on the community if anyone else does it. But you, you're already a reject. If you claim you found her, then… well you heard Constantine, it's only up from here," Tobias nodded his head; his face seemed confused. Ray quickly made things clear, "I'm doing this for them," he stated, pointing in the direction of Luna's hut. "Understand? This is for them, not you," he repeated.

Tobias nodded again. It was clear that he understood.

Ray took one more foreboding step closer. "I just wanna make something clear. *This is not an alliance.*"

Tobias clearly understood. He remained in place, leaning up against the tree, the threat of a man he once was no longer visible. Ray nodded and started to back away. He did so until he was shrouded in night, no longer visible.

Tobias remained there on the tree, carefully contemplating how he would proceed with his newfound information.

35

Ray made it back to Luna's hut, where he lay down without any startling noises. Beatrix and Luna were fast asleep, exactly how he had left them. He didn't sleep that night. He wrestled with the idea that he had, for the first time, gone behind Luna's back to do something he saw as the greater good. The tiny voices of conscience in his head scolded him for his actions, but his ethical mind tried to tell him differently.

Tobias floated along silently with the wind, winding his way through the trees and hopping over the snow-covered roots. He found his way to Otto's cove and looked around. He had to find a place to observe. He wasn't going to risk his blossoming relationship with Otto on the word of someone he couldn't trust. He had to know for sure. He slung the broken extension cord he had grabbed before he left over his shoulder and ducked off to the side. He laid down on the embankment and waited for morning for when he would see her. Sterling would surely be looking for him, but if he could get Aria up to the mountain before sunrise, Sterling would be under his control. *He* would be the one dragging buckets of waste through the snow.

Tobias watched carefully, occasionally being distracted by the current. This was his final chance at redemption, according to Felix, and he wasn't going to let it slip through his fingers.

Aria tossed and turned within the confines of her heavy blanket. She threw it off of her and sat up, pulling at her hair out of frustration. She looked over to Otto, who slept like a baby, with one arm hanging off of his makeshift bed. A faint gust of wind blew past the animal skin flap and caught the side of her arm, giving her goosebumps and bringing a smile to her face.

She eyed the entrance for a few minutes before getting to her knees and taking the decision more seriously. "*Just enough to feel alive again,*" she said, assuring herself that a breath of fresh air would surely do not harm, trying to coax herself into biting the bullet and getting to feel the great outdoors again. "*Just a taste…*"

She lowered the gas lamp level so that Otto might slip into a deeper slumber. She got to her hands and knees and quietly waddled over to the entrance. She could, for the first time in a month, hear the wind and the roaring of the nearby current. The mid-winter moonlight hit her face and dilated her pupils as the crisp air filled her lungs with life. She smiled as she looked out to the moonlit landscape that she had once roamed as a free woman.

One by one, she placed her hands further out into the night. She slowly inched up until she was completely submerged by the glow of the moon. Her senses overwhelmed her, and she sprang to her feet with joy. She gave a breathy scream into the air so that no sound was able to resonate as she jumped up and down and jogged in place, finally getting to move her entire body. She sent snow flying in every direction as she leaped with joy.

She leaped from one foot to the other, trying her best to space out her footprints so that they would be that much easier to cover up. She made her way to the river, where she let the current run over her smooth skin. The feel of the frigid water against her hands forced goosebumps to shoot up her legs. She was finally feeling something.

Tobias watched her from a distance. His fears had been confirmed. He watched her dance in the night, knowing that it was surely the last time she would be able to move so freely. He watched as she knelt below the river and scrubbed at her dirtied body with the chilled water. He slowly began to creep in her general direction. He wanted to let her enjoy the moment. He, too, knew how it felt to be in this situation. By his side hung a cord, which he had fashioned into a lasso of sorts. He drew close enough to toss the cord behind her; it landed softly in the snow, barely making a sound. She had still yet to notice him.

She brought the crystal water to her lips and sipped from her hands. She then splashed the remaining water onto her face and looked up toward the moon. She took a deep breath in and exhaled into the night. She stood up and turned around. As soon as she saw Tobias, she knew what she was in for. Her jaw dropped halfway, and her eyes floated down as if she were ashamed, as if she should have known this would happen.

He looked at her understandingly. She knew what he was here for; she lightly shook her head, hoping that it would somehow convince him to rethink his decision. He gave her a nod of resistance, and her face slowly began to crinkle. Tobias quickly put a finger to his lips, warning her not to make any noise. He didn't want Otto to wake up and begin resisting her arrest. She, too, realized what could come of that, and it was clear they both wanted what was best for Otto.

He gestured toward the cord that lay at her feet. She picked it up and began to sling it around her wrists. Tobias slowly approached and aided in restraining her properly. Once the cord was tight enough to cut off the circulation to her hands, she looked up at him in silence, her eyes welling up with tears. Her face was attempting to plead with him one last time before the decision was made.

Tobias looked into her eyes and wiped the tear that ran down her cheek. He then brought her head closer to his so that their foreheads were touching. The two of them shared a quiet moment of mourning for the sins they had committed for the reasons they were now in this predicament. He gently lifted his face and kissed her on the top of her head. They then separated from each other; Tobias slowly drifted apart, further and further, until the cord was pulled tight and she was forced to accompany him on his way toward the mountain.

The two of them walked in silence, reflecting on the decisions that brought them to this point. They soon left the river's edge, and after that, left the walls of Corazon, embarking on the path toward the house of the Disciples. The path was cleared, having been made smooth by the countless trips the Disciples made back and forth over the years. Tobias marched forward with discipline and determination while Aria was silently guided along by her hands bound in cord. She didn't put up a fight; she didn't even make a noise as the two silently walked through Corazon. The two had made it up the path to the house on the mountain within the hour.

It was still dark and rather hard to make out the details, but Tobias could tell it was a sizable two-story house with what seemed to be plenty of windows. He looked at the house with two gleaming eyes, hoping that he may soon call it home.

He pulled Aria over to the cliff, which overlooked Corazon. Sitting near the edge, he gestured out toward the view. The tiny huts seemed even smaller from this point of view. A few fires had been lit by the less sociable night owls in the community, and the backdrop of the crystalized stars and swelling moon proved to be a beautiful scene.

Aria walked over to him and sat down by his side. She, too, looked over Corazon, admiring the beauty. After a while, she spoke up, "Do you remember how this all started, Tobias?" she asked him as the two of them sat still near the edge of the cliff.

He looked at her with a plain face. She quickly began to grow upset. "Please just answer me," she begged. "Please," she repeated as she began to cry. "Please just answer me."

She tried to pull herself together, shaking her head from side to side to expel the tears. "You got me here. You did what you were told. All I ask is that you talk to me. I—I don't wanna die surrounded by strangers."

Tobias looked at her with a slight alarm. The alarm subsided, and he gently nodded as he placed a hand on her shoulder. "*Okay.*"

She looked at him as if he were a new person. "*What have they done to you? This is not the Tobias that I know.*"

"I was a sinner, and I was punished. I got what I deserved," he stated as if he had rehearsed it time and time again.

"Don't say that. You talk like you owe these people something. Look at me. *You don't owe these people anything.* You work for them. You kill their food. You harvest their vegetables. You protect their citizens. They owe you. Don't ever let them tell you differently."

He wore a scowl. "How could you say something like that. Mother will see us all when we ascend into the—"

"Fuck that. Look at me. Look at yourself. Does this look like something Mother would let happen? I don't care how many sins we've committed. It's up to her to judge us, not them," she hissed, waving her arm toward the fortress behind them. "I am broken. Mother let me get raped. Mother let me get hit. She let them cut me with knives and burn me with candle wax. Mother let them pull my hair and slap me around like some sort of animal. Mother let that happen. Our God, our salvation, let that happen. How am I supposed to believe in something that allows so much pain to come my way?"

Tobias shook his head. "You'll regret—"

"I'll regret what? I'll regret what I'm saying when I'm on my deathbed? Well, here I am! And guess what? I don't feel a damn thing. I don't feel her salvation, I don't feel her warmth or courage filling up my soul. You wanna know what I feel? I'm cold, and I'm wet, and I want nothing more for this moment to be over. *I was supposed to be the chosen one.* Felix came down and chose me to accompany him up on this Mountain. *Me.* He made me feel like I was special."

Tobias saw the heartbreak in her eyes. He recognized that yearning for *specialness*. He saw it as exactly what he had been chasing the entire time.

Aria continued to pour her feelings out before him. "He made me feel like I was loved, like I was more important." She wiped at her nose and looked down, trying to stifle a cry. "When I finally met Elliot, it all made sense," she sighed, deflating like a balloon. "Well, look at me now," she said through a cracking voice. "I'm certainly special, aren't I?"

Tobias took her hand in his. "I'm—I'm sorry," he said sullenly. "I should have never brought you here."

Aria let out a sound concocted of both a laugh and a cry of pain. "You were always some smooth talker, weren't ya?" The two of them gazed at the top of the red sun as it slowly peaked over the horizon. "You were never this manly man looking for redemption when I met you. No, you were a silent little nobody. Before all of this shit, before you convinced me to come here before you fell in love with Luna… before all of this…" She shook her head and tried to find the words. "You know, when you took me out on our first date, I thought you were a shy little bookworm. I thought it was adorable how, when we were sitting in that booth down at Marco's Diner, your foot accidentally brushed up against mine under the table, and I could see the embarrassment in your face. I could tell that you were just a scared little transfer looking for some company."

Tobias fell into a flashback that she constructed like some sort of guilt trip. All of a sudden, he was there. He could feel the smooth plastic seat of the booth he sat at. He could see her flawless, brightly smiling face. He could make out the dimples in her cheek that she would get when he said something dorky. He could feel her leg against his.

"I remember how you were afraid to ask me out on another date… how you kept choking on your own words. I really liked you, but you didn't quite know it yet. You were just that weird, emotionally broken kid that everyone felt bad for. Everyone had heard of the boy who lost his parents in a house fire, I just never thought *I'd be the one* taking him out on a second date."

He remembered his stuttering. He remembered the way she twirled her foot into the ground when she got nervous, and it was oh so clear she was getting nervous as she waited for him to say the words.

"I remember our first kiss. You accidentally—" she giggled. "You accidentally missed my lips and ended kissing right below my nose!" Tobias even smiled as she spoke of this incident. He remembered their awkward first encounter vividly.

"How you would always ask me to come watch a movie with you. You said it was because you didn't have any other plans, but I knew it was because you only wanted to see me. I remember our long, sophisticated talks as we walked through the park. I remember how you would always give any spare change you had to the guy who slept on the bench."

He could hear the clink of the coins in the brass mug; he could feel the warmth of her hand around his. He felt the ridges of her neck on the tip of his nose whenever he nuzzled his head into her shoulder pocket like a tiny bear cub when he was trying to be cute.

"Oh, and the conspiracy theories! The government's out to get us this, aliens that! I could've written a book and had a feature-length film on all the bullshit you talked about. I remember how you would sometimes get together with that "Elliot" guy who showed up in the park every so often. I remember you talking up this place called

Corazon! And how wonderful it sounded. *A place without laws or limits! It's all based on love! Hate and violence are literally prohibited!"*

He thought back to how excited he would get when the man in the park injected his well-thought-out ideas about how society was crumbling and how much sense it made in the moment.

"I remember how you practically begged me to come with you. I was so in love, you could've told me to jump right off a bridge, and I would have… I probably would have been better off, too. I remember how scared I was leaving everything behind. I remember how confident you seemed. *"This is our new life!"* you would say. The excitement in your voice alone… I felt so happy for you. And it really was quite perfect in the beginning. But then… you had to go falling in love with Luna, and I was all of a sudden put on the back burner."

Tobias thought back to the first time he ever laid eyes on Luna. How she was so beautiful as she sprinted through the woods, her golden blonde hair flying in the breeze as she pursued a deer on foot.

"You left me like I was some broken toy. And I was forced to fend for myself in a society where sex is the only currency. I made my living as best as I ever could. I cooked, I cleaned, and I got passed around like a dirty dish towel. You and Luna, you two were just lovebirds, weren't ya? But you couldn't get me out of your head. You'd come see me to check up on me like we never even had this past, and Luna wonders why I hated her so much."

Tobias was at a loss for words as she picked apart his wrongdoings from the very beginning.

"Soon, she even got sick of you sneaking around to come see me and your other women of the night. You just got too proud and cocky. You got carried away with the shared love idea… and before I knew it, we had lost you. I only had one thing to fall back on. It was this so-called 'religion.' Before you ask me why I didn't run, think real hard. I had nothing, I was a ghost in the real world, I was the girl that went missing and was never found. If that's not enough, getting out of these woods alive… forget it."

Tobias's eyes watered up as he stared at the rising orange sun. "I had no idea…"

"Oh, please. Spare me. You knew exactly what you were getting us into from day one. Now look what you've done," she said, looking at him with hateful eyes and a friendly smile.

Tobias stood up. "Come on, let's go… we need to leave right now—"

She let out a melancholic, drawn-out moan that sounded like that of pitiful laughter. "You and I both know it's too late to run."

The sun was now rising higher and higher, and there was commotion from within the house of the Disciples. Within thirty seconds, three men dressed in purple came running out of the house with rifles in their arms. They each pointed theirs at Aria.

Tobias looked at her in panic. She just sighed and looked toward the sunrise. "Beautiful, isn't it?"

Tobias licked his lips and looked from left to right as he began to realize the gravity of the decision that he had just made. He didn't want Aria to die. He let his own desires outshine her bare necessities. The Disciples eyed him suspiciously. He wasn't allowed to talk now. According to them, he was still being shunned.

"Get off of me, I can do it myself!" yelled a nasty voice from within the house. A boot kicked open the door leading to the stairs that brought them down to the walkway. Dante slowly limped out of the doorway, using steel crutches to propel himself forward.

"My, my, my… look who's back…" He hissed, showing off his blackened teeth. Aria refused to turn around and look at him. She knew what was in store for her. Tobias stood by the wayside and held his head high, pretending not to be fazed by the act that was about to unfold, though even his stoic expression couldn't prepare him for what came next.

"No! No, wait, stop! Stop!" a mousy voice called out from nowhere. Everybody froze and looked around, trying to pin where the sound was coming from.

"Please stop!" The voice panted again. "Please don't hurt her!"

Within a few moments, Otto's head was visible, bobbing up and down as he ran along the ridge of the mountain.

"What is *he doing?!*" barked Dante as he continued to limp his way toward Aria.

"Aria, don't worry! I came to protect you!" he yelled, holding out the small pocketknife he kept in his cove as he ran in between her and the Disciples.

Tobias began to panic even more, wondering what he could possibly do to avoid any harm coming to his generous hero of a friend.

Aria began to cry, knowing full well that none of them would leave this situation alive unless Tobias decided to act.

Dante pushed two of the Disciples aside, coming face to face with Otto. He stared at a frantically sweaty Otto for a few moments before directing his attention toward Tobias. "Otto was sheltering her?" he asked with a look of pain on his face. Tobias could see the bloodstains on his garments seeping right through the bandages on his stomach.

Tobias stood still and didn't move his face whatsoever, trying to capitalize on the fact that he was being shunned.

"Speak, Tobias. I'm ordering you to speak!" Dante yelled, spewing a concoction of hatred and spit on the feet of everyone present.

Tobias took a deep breath in and held his mouth shut.

Dante tried to hold a stare but quickly looked away, pulling a revolver out from behind him. "I think it'd be in your best interest to answer me, Tobias," he said, pointing the gun at his chest.

Tobias began to breathe heavier and heavier. His heart rate escalated, and his hands got sweaty. Dante pulled back on the hammer, still pointing the gun at Tobias. "I said speak, boy." Tobias bit his tongue and closed his eyes, not knowing what he could say to spare Otto's life.

"Dante!" one of the Disciples called out, stopping him before he made any rash decisions. Dante turned to look at the Disciple behind him. The man was looking toward the house, where an older gentleman had wandered out onto the porch. He looked at them with confusion and worry.

Dante growled and lowered his revolver, quickly concealing it within his robes. He turned to face the concerned man and held out his arms. "Good morning, my Prophet! How are you on this fine day?"

Tobias looked at Aria with doubt. The man he saw on the porch was no angelic being. He was old and beginning to develop a hunch. His head was shaved bald, and he had a grey beard that hung slightly off of his face. He was dressed in a white shirt and tan pants and seemed to shuffle from place to place. He took small steps off of the porch, his expression of worry remaining stuck to his face. "What is going on here? Who are these people?"

Tobias dropped to his knee and bowed his head. "What is he doing?" Elliot asked as he hobbled closer.

Dante was quick to respond. "Nothing, my Prophet. He is just lost. We will find him a home. You should get back inside and get some rest," he said as if he were speaking to a child.

Elliot's eyes were misty and full of concern; he looked each person up and down as if they were strangers. "Can I help you?" he asked, gripping the cuff of one of the Disciple's robes. The Disciple nervously looked toward Dante, who jerked his head toward the house.

"Come with me, Prophet," the Disciple said as he slowly guided Elliot back toward the house.

"No, what are you doing? Let go of me!" he demanded. The Disciple continued to gently guide Elliot toward the house. "I said let go!" Elliot demanded. The Disciple jumped back and once again looked to Dante, who seemed to be growing more and more aggravated.

The door to the house swung open again. This time, Felix walked out. He seemed well groomed and ready for the day. "What's going on here?" he asked. The other Disciples seemed to stand at attention.

Dante rolled his eyes. "Elliot doesn't want to go back inside. He's concerned for our… guests," he said, snarling.

Felix nodded his head, "Yes, all right," he said, making his way off the porch and approaching Elliot. "Good morning, my Prophet, how are you?"

Elliot looked at Felix, and his discomfort was quickly extinguished. "Felix! Yes, thank you. Who are these people? What do they want with me?"

Felix set a gentle hand on Elliot's shoulder. "My Prophet, they are just visitors. They'll be leaving shortly. Here, let's get you something to eat. Conrad and Traver will set you up with something nice."

Elliot touched Felix's arm, "Conrad and Traver?"

Felix whistled to two of the Disciples who held rifles. He snapped his fingers, and they immediately reported to him. "Yes, they're friends of yours. They will make sure you are well fed, okay?"

Within a moment, Elliot began to nod, "Yes, yes, that sounds nice," he muttered, a smile slowly forming on his face.

Felix clapped him on the back, "Great, just follow them inside, I'll be there in just a moment or two."

Elliot nodded his head and allowed the two men to guide him back up onto the porch and inside the house, the screen door snapping shut behind them. Felix saw the entire thing over, then slowly set his eyes on Aria, Tobias, and Otto, who were cornered by Dante, the remaining other Disciple, and the cliff's edge.

Felix slowly strode toward the three of them while Dante removed his revolver once again. "He hasn't always been like that, as I'm sure you remember," Felix spoke, his gaze falling on Aria. "A few years ago, he began saying things that—didn't quite make sense. And not in the religious sense, in the reality sense. In fact, one might say his mind has come to resemble Otto's more than anyone else's," he said.

Tobias got up off of his knees, and Felix sighed. "It's a common thing, really. Happened to my grandfather. Though—I will say, it's quite ironic that the one man who protects all of us, can't even protect his own state of mind. It seems that Mother has different plans for him."

Aria seemed angry, having a disposition about her that made it seem as though this weren't the first time they had argued about the matter. "He's sick, Felix. The man needs to be in a home with people that can properly look after him."

Felix chuckled, "And what do you call this?" he asked, waving his hand toward the house. "Because I'd call it a home with people who look after him. Besides, what do you think will happen to all of us if Elliot's grace can no longer protect us? If he leaves, disease, famine, and violence will surely seep back through the cracks and into our lives, just as it has with the old world."

"And what if he dies?" Aria spat.

"The Book of Elliot says that The Prophet's grace will be bestowed upon a worthy successor. Seeing as how I have been appointed the High Disciple, it is only fitting that the successor be me. Until that point, he will continue to perform the miracles we all take for granted. I'm sure Mother will see it so."

Aria shook her head, "Holding your own Prophet captive just so you can make the rules and keep control… Disgusting."

Felix's smile faded, "No good deed goes unpunished, Dante."

Tobias stood up and spoke what he knew may be his last words. "Felix—" he said, directing attention toward him. "Please, as the High Disciple, I beg you to have Dante reconsider his actions. There has to be a better way."

Felix began to walk toward Tobias while Dante held Otto and Aria at gunpoint. "You're the one Constantine promised redemption to if you were to bring her to us, correct? A life alongside the Disciples on the mountain?"

Tobias glanced at a broken Aria, then sheepishly nodded. "Yes."

Felix looked at Tobias for a prolonged period of time, relishing in the misery that came with the uncertain stakes. "Well, then, child… welcome to the Disciples." Felix then spun around and placed a hand on Dante's shoulder before continuing to walk toward the house.

Dante looked at the remaining Disciple, who swiftly placed his hands on Otto and viciously ripped him from in front of Aria, tossing him to the ground. Tobias watched as everything seemed to unfold in slow motion. Aria screamed as she looked at Otto sprawling to the ground. She looked back just in time for her to stare down the barrel of Dante's precious revolver. Dante smiled with his blackened teeth one more time before he squeezed the trigger, sending a short burst of light erupting from the tip of the barrel. Aria's body jolted, froze, then fell limply to the earth.

❊❊❊

Reality itself seemed to slow. Tobias, rattled by the sudden thunderous crack, homed in on a noise, a guttural, feral noise that came from the lips of Otto. With no hesitation, Otto leaped from where he lay and jabbed his pocketknife into the leg of Dante, just above the knee. Dante squealed like a pig right before catching a thunderous knee to the mouth. He flopped back onto the ground, clutching at his mouth and rolling about in the dirt.

Otto growled and turned to face the remaining Disciple, who alone stood no chance. Within seconds the screen door snapped open, and the other two Disciples scurried out, rifles at the ready.

Tobias was frozen, crushed by the fact he just witnessed Aria's execution and worried about Otto's retaliation. One of the Disciples brought the butt of his gun to Otto's collar bone with force, but Otto remained standing. He instead struck another Disciple with his pocketknife, making them scream and yell as they cupped a hand over their face. His knife wasn't going to kill anyone, but he was determined to do as much damage as he possibly could before it was his time.

Dante took a pause from writhing on the ground to look up and yell "Kill the bastard!" through his broken, bloodied teeth.

The Disciples scrambled to recover from Otto's attacks. They all managed to find a position, creating a circle around him, each of them pointing a rifle at his torso. None of them, however, wanted to shoot. They all recognized the outcry the community would have if they found out Otto, of all people, had been shot. Aria was a ghost. She was expendable, but Otto was different. He had connections; he had heart. People would notice an absence like that. Otto took one last look at Tobias, a look that begged for help. The look quickly turned from that of help to that of disappointment when the first shot rang out, causing everyone to go white.

Dante held his revolver out as he propped himself off the ground. Otto froze and touched his stomach, realizing he had been tagged. He quickly shook it off and began to growl again. He charged Dante, who shot him again, sending a red mist out the back of his shoulder blade, staining the muddied snow behind him with a red as deep as the rising sun. Otto staggered back before once again shaking the pain off. He yelled as he charged them. This time one of the Disciples shot off a round, tagging him in the arm, then another one shot him in the hip, and another round went beaming into his chest. Tobias looked away with agony.

Otto mindlessly stepped back, holding his pocketknife that now had blood trickling off the blade. He kept backing up and backing up. Consciously stepping over Aria. He got down to one knee and scooped her up in his arms, baring his teeth and straining all the muscles in his neck as he did. Otto was breathing heavily and fast. The Disciples just watched as he kept trying to pick her up, growing more and more frustrated with each attempt. Dante seemed entertained with his will to live. Otto finally scooped her limp body up in his arms. He looked down at her flawless face and brushed a silky lock of hair out of her eyes. With a soft smile, Otto closed his eyes and shifted his weight, rolling backward right over the edge of the cliff.

Dante, upon realizing what was happening, quickly got to his feet. "Somebody grab him!" he hurriedly spat.

It was too late. Otto had rocked his body back enough to clear the cliff's edge, holding Aria's body in his hands as he did. If he didn't die by the time he hit the ground, the fall would surely kill him.

Dante screamed as he cast his revolver aside and pounded his fists into the ground. "Do you know what this means?!" he asked as he eyeballed all of them. They all looked at him with uncertainty. One of the Disciples helped Dante to his feet. "Who's stationed in Corazon right now?" They all looked at him as if he were out of control. "I said who the hell is down in Corazon right now?" He screamed as hard as he could, spewing brown fluid from his mouth.

"Orwell!" One of the younger Disciples replied hastily. "Orwell and—and Constantine and—and-"

Felix pushed past the door and stumbled down the porch, worried as to what chaos had ensued since he left. He looked at Dante with darts in his gaze. "Where are they?"

The other Disciples looked toward the cliff. Felix closed his eyes and ground his teeth. He pointed at the remaining Disciples. "Get down there now! I'll radio Orwell and see if anyone has noticed. Find those bodies before anyone else gets to them or Mother as my witness. I'll kill you myself," he muttered, holding a hand to his forehead.

Dante took a step forward, "What happens if—"

"GO!" Felix boomed. The remaining Disciples jumped in place and scurried toward the path to Corazon, rifles over their shoulders, sweat running down their faces. Dante hobbled up to Felix, looking at him as if he were about to be scolded. Felix refused to look at him as he hobbled his way onto the porch and inside the house to tend to his new wounds.

Felix sighed and set his eyes on Tobias, who remained where he originally stood, still trying to comprehend the events that had just unfolded before him. "You," he stated.

Tobias didn't look at him, his eyes fixed on the ground, his breathing shallow. Felix turned his back to him and began walking back inside. "Come with me."

36

Having woken to the sound of gunshots, the citizens of Corazon were up and about, eager to see what the commotion was regarding. Luna forced Bea to stay inside while she went to explore the source with the rest of the community. The crowd was filled with whispers, saying, *What do you think it was? Is everyone all right? Maybe they found Aria? Did she kill again?* The questions were continuous and met with doubt.

They all trudged through the snow with haste. Ray came up behind Luna. "Everything all right?" he whispered, all of his scripted responses planned out in his head.

"Yeah, I'm worried, though," she replied, completely unaware of what he had orchestrated.

Ray nodded, "I just, um… well, I just checked in on Otto. Not there, neither is… you know."

Luna gave out a worrisome gasp. "Footprints?"

"Three sets of them, no sign of struggle, though," he said, appearing worried but feeling as though a massive weight had been lifted from his shoulders.

Luna struggled to gather her thoughts. "Well, maybe… maybe they went for a walk?"

Ray looked at her with pity. She saw his face and prepared for the worst.

"Has Todd left already?" she asked.

"He left earlier on last night. He said he had a job to do or something, I don't know. I got Aria an extra coat. I thought it'd help Otto out a bit, you know, so she could stop using his when she got cold?"

"That was nice," she said with a blank face, too concerned to show that she was pleased with his actions. The two of them trudged along, knowing full well what they would eventually find. Ray decided to say something to perhaps lighten the mood, even just for a moment.

"Beautiful day today," he muttered as he walked forward. Luna just peered at him through the corner of her eyes.

They soon heard the screams from way up ahead and ran toward the commotion. They quickly came upon the brunt of the crowd and pushed through until they could view the horrific scene for themselves.

There before them lay Otto, his arms still wrapped around Aria's body. People gasped and cried at the sight of the two bodies. Benji barged in between people and stumbled over to the two bodies. He hesitantly put his two fingers to Otto's neck. His head dropped, and he looked toward Luna. "They're both dead," he said, his voice trembling. He noticed how the accumulating crowd hung on every word. He decided to capitalize on his moment. "They've been shot! Both of them! Two of our own, shot by the only people who carry guns," he said, his anger beginning to bubble. He got to his feet just in time to see Constantine and Orwell pushing through the crowd as quickly as they could. Orwell held a radio in his hand.

"All right, everyone away! Clear out! All of you!" Constantine demanded, knowing full well that the questions they would have would be of the realm he could not yet answer.

Nobody moved, though. They were still dumbstruck by what they saw, not knowing what to think of it just yet. The collecting crowd murmured and spoke, questioning the meaning of it all. *Who is it? It can't be—Otto? Otto and Aria? Where did they come from? Why is he bleeding so much? Where was she hiding? Who killed the two of them? What happened?*

Orwell panicked and looked to Constantine, hoping that his response would be better than his own. Constantine rolled his eyes. "Everyone back up! There has been a terrible accident!"

"Nobody is shot by accident!" Benji yelled. The crowd slowly began to pick up, not seeming to disagree with his observation.

"Otto wouldn't hurt a fly! He was crazy, but he would never hurt anyone!" he stated again, his voice rising. Somewhere in the crowd, a child could be heard crying profusely.

"He's got holes in him!" one man proclaimed.

"I count five at least!" the woman next to him screamed out.

Constantine slung the rifle from over his shoulder and fired a shot into the air out of panic that he would lose the growing crowd's attention. Everyone jumped, Benji nearly hit the ground. "I said that's enough! Everyone, get back to work! As you were!" Constantine yelled.

Another man cleared his throat, unsure of the ground he was about to tread on. "What? Is that a threat?" The crowd began to murmur again; this made Constantine back up and look to Orwell for support. Orwell simply put his hands up in denial. He had no idea how to proceed.

Orwell's walkie-talkie began to buzz with static. The voice of Dante was quickly heard throughout the surrounding crowd. He burst in and out of frequency with much static surrounding his voice, "Get those fucking—bodies—back up here, damn it! Don't let those ignorant people—hold you up! Hurry now—Before—they see it, dammit!"

"Just tell us what's going on!" Maple shouted from the back.

"We deserve to know!" Another woman chimed in.

"What happened to them? You said you would punish Aria. You never said anything about Otto!" another shouted.

The crowd began to close in, forcing Constantine and Orwell into a closed space surrounding the two bodies. "That's close enough!" barked Constantine as he accidentally backed up into Otto's body.

Orwell tried to hush everyone, holding out his hands as if they were sacred barriers. "Let's all just think about what we know! Two of our own have died, yes questions need to be answered, but we don't have those answers right now. What we need is to go back to our huts and prepare for a proper night of mourning. Why doesn't everyone just turn around and slowly—"

"Don't you dare touch his body!" A woman screamed. "We need to clean him! Prepare him and Aria for a proper burial!"

"People! People of Corazon!" A loud, elderly voice spoke out. Everyone directed their attention to Musgo as he gently pushed his way through the crowd.

Maple grabbed hold of his sleeve as he passed by. "What are you doing?" she asked with fear in her eyes. "*Get over here!*" she said, hoping her stern words would keep him close.

Musgo pulled her closer and kissed her gently on the cheek in passing. She held onto his sleeve, afraid of what would happen if she let go. The crowd soon absorbed him as he proceeded to move forward, leaving Maple alone with a horrified expression on her face. He slipped into the middle, accompanying both Orwell, Constantine, and Benji, who had moved off to the side to give Musgo the floor.

"People of Corazon!" he said again, gaining the attention of almost everyone. "We have lived for so long free of sickness! Free of death and free of agony! Today everything changes. Today we wake up."

Constantine pulled Musgo back. "What's the idea here, old man?" he growled.

"Your odds aren't lookin' too good, young fella," Musgo whispered into his ear. Constantine looked around at the people that surrounded him and slowly relinquished his grip.

Musgo cleared his throat. "Elliot, the man up there on the mountain… he preaches to us and tells us of a world where Mother controls everything. Mother prevents us from fatal sickness and old age. She prevents animal attacks and helps spread the love to us all. For so long, our lives have been in the hands of Mother, the great and powerful Mother!"

The crowd whispered, "Praise be to Mother."

"But I am here to tell you, *no*. To show you that there is no God." His statement was immediately followed by the growing rumblings of the soon-to-be mob around him.

"There is no God. No higher power, no judge, jury, or executioner. For years we have relied on a man whom we barely see to give us the answers we barely understand. I can't live like this any longer. Elliot claims to be all-powerful, to be the word of Mother himself. He claims he can heal. He claims he can prevent sickness and violence! Well, what do you call this?" He screamed as hard as he could as his voice began to crack.

"*Follow me and I shall rid your pitiful lives of the temptations of evil, violence, and signs to the gates of hell! Follow me and I shall give your life prosperity, love, and infinite meaning! Follow me and you will be whole again!* A direct quote from the Book of Elliot! Does this make you feel safe? Does this make you feel whole? Does this seem like an act done without violence or harm?" he shouted, nearly out of breath.

"No," Willow muttered, bringing her fingers to her lips. She turned and quickly scanned the crowd for Clover and Beatrix. The two of them were lost amongst the sea.

"Otto was my friend," stated a weeping boy as he stood behind the leg of a man.

Musgo nodded, taking things to a more somber tone after captivating those around him. "We were told that Aria was a sinner. We were told that she did horrible things to a man whom we all know to be sick and perverted in his ways. Do I have to paint the picture for all of you? Aria was raped! And Otto tried to keep her hidden! He tried to do the right thing! And this is what happens! Look what has become of them!"

Ray observed Musgo from afar as he carefully kept an eye on the path leading up the mountain. Within a moment's time, a band of armed Disciples would clumsily parade down, looking for the crowd. It would only be a matter of time before they found them all.

Ray quickly joined up with everyone else.

Musgo continued on his rant. "We have a choice! We have the power! We are not controlled by the hand that feeds us! We tend to the land! We hunt the food! Now they are trying to say we don't deserve all of it! They try to take that away from us! They kill those who step out of line! They rape the women, and they castrate the men who don't comply! Open your eyes! I am a sinner! You are a sinner. We are all sinners for turning the blind eye as long as we have. Our sins are in the past, but we can at least try to redeem ourselves by not allowing this madness to go on any longer!"

Constantine felt a change in the tide as the people began closing in. Musgo cracked a smile; his words were getting to them. Constantine gripped the stock of his rifle tight. Musgo now held everyone captive. It would no longer be a matter of who was in charge but who held the better point. He knew deep down he couldn't let that happen. Constantine glanced back at Orwell, who seemed to have shrunken into half the man he was at sunrise, nervously picking away at his fingers as his eyes darted around the crowd. He then noticed the flash of purple garb in the distance and was immediately washed over with a feeling of temporary relief. With one hefty sigh, Constantine hurled his arms up and brought the stock of the rifle upside the back of

Musgo's head. Musgo winced and clutched at his head as he dropped to his knees. "That's enough out of you," he whispered, worried about where Musgo would have gone with his glorified tirade.

The Disciples swarmed the questioning crowd, poking and prodding with the barrels of their guns in order to get through. They quickly surrounded the bodies of Otto and Aria while everyone else began to quickly theorize about Musgo's short speech.

Musgo continued from where he knelt, his hand still clutching his pounding head. "Look! Watch them as they take away everything that could prove me right! Otto and Aria were not punished! They were murdered! And they'll do the same to us if we question the meaning of all this! They'll kill—"

"I asked you nicely!" Constantine hissed out as he brought the stock of his gun down hard on the top of Musgo's balding head.

Musgo froze as the light left his eyes. He felt the shock of the impact run up and down his spine as a single rivulet of blood ran down the bridge of his nose and over his lips. He looked deep into the crowd, trying desperately to find Maple with his lifeless eyes. She broke through the people who were now screaming at the use of Constantine's unnecessary demonstration of force.

Maple ran up to Musgo but was immediately held back by two other Disciples wearing purple. She sank to her knees as she screamed Musgo's name. He still knelt where he had just taken the blow and smiled an ever so slight smile. He had finally redeemed himself in an irreversible way. He limply fell forward, burying his bloodied head in the dusting of snow.

The Disciples shouted and barked at people to stay back, claiming that Musgo was senile and not to be trusted, claiming that Aria had brainwashed him. People couldn't help but watch with teary eyes as Maple frantically tried to claw her way toward Musgo, who remained unmoving, his head still bleeding.

Luna tried to run up and assist her but was pulled back by Ray with the help of Benji, who knew her involvement would only exacerbate the matter. She fought as hard as she could, but they fought just as hard back. Ray tried to wipe away the tears with his hand; she screamed and begged him to let go of her. He just kept apologizing as he knew the damage had been done.

"Easy there, Luna, it's gonna be all right," Benji said through a deepening scowl. Ray let go of her leaving Benji with all the work. He pushed his way toward the center of the closing circle. The Disciples who tried removing the two bodies were now unable to escape. People demanded answers. They demanded clarity and closure, all of which they were sure they wouldn't receive.

Ray quickly made himself apparent by waving his arms up and down. Once he had the basic attention of a good portion of the crowd, he yelled out, "Musgo had an idea! He had a theory! Musgo did nothing to harm anyone! Just like Otto! Just like Aria! Are we not allowed to act in self-defense?" Two men dressed in purple quickly approached Ray. "And if you kill 'em, you just prove my point! Take it from an outsider! This is not the way things have to be! Musgo was my friend!" he said, trying his best not to let himself go. "Otto… he was my friend! And I didn't have to know Aria to know she didn't deserve what happened to her! Look at what we are turning into!"

He looked around to make sure everyone was still captivated. A Disciple approached him from his left, but he drew a knife on him, and the smaller man in purple slowly backed away. "Is this what you thought a society based on the foundation of love would look like? You are not controlled by this God you worship! Make up your mind! Stand with me! We have the people! We outnumber them! We can take back what you were promised, but I need you! I *need* you."

Constantine fired his gun up in the air again and looked from right to left. Ray gripped his chest in relief, thinking that was the bullet meant for him. Constantine began to speak up, "The next person to step forward will be shot, by the Power of Mother and all things Holy… look what we have become, listening to a fool, an outcast, a defective human… We should be listening to the only voice that matters, the voice inside of us all," he said as he wagged his finger in the air like a southern preacher. "The voice of Mother!"

"I am not the murderer here!" Ray screamed, pointing at Aria and Otto. "If you want to listen to the voice inside of you all, that's fine! But just know that voice is your conscience, not your God! You all have the power to choose what happens next."

Benji sighed as he kept Luna restrained, "Your little friend is suicidal after all, isn't he, Loon?"

Constantine erupted, letting all of his anger pour out of him. "You want free will?! Is that what you want?! Bring her here!" he roared, pointing at Luna.

Luna elbowed Benji in the ribs, freeing herself from his restraint. She shoved the others to the side and lunged for Constantine. Orwell, thinking on his feet, snatched a handful of her hair and pulled her to her knees. Without missing a beat, Constantine held the barrel of his rifle to her head. Everyone screamed and backed up a good measure. Benji unsheathed his knife and followed in Luna's steps just to be blindsided by the remaining Disciples who pinned him to the cold earth under their weight. Certain followers quickly evacuated, taking their children and fleeing to their huts to hide from the blossoming madness. The more curious followers, the ones who had been caught in the crosshairs of the chaos, remained still.

Constantine raised one brow. "The man wants free will? Well, being the generous human I am, I'll give him what he asks for. He now has the power to choose. Leave us as he found us and protect the one he loves or stay and face the consequences of his actions. We were fine before he showed his face. Now we're at each other's throats… like savages from the old world! We have brought shame to our Prophet and to Mother! Now we get to watch this sinner practice what he preaches! What will it be then, Ray?"

Constantine was set in his ways, and it was clearly making people uncomfortable. This was no bluff.

"Constantine," one man said from the crowd. "I don't think Elliot would—"

"Shut up!" he barked back. "Do you see Elliot here? Do you see Felix here? No! I'm here, *I'm here*. Make up your damn mind, Ray!"

The crowd parted as a woman began to make her way to the inner circle. The woman was sobbing as she stepped up and stood before Constantine and Ray. Everyone gasped as they looked upon the broken face of Brooke, staring at Constantine like an animal. "If you *kill* her…"

Constantine froze, not knowing what to say to the woman whose baby he had aborted in the name of Mother.

She stopped and looked up again. "She has done *nothing* wrong. You cannot punish her for something she has no say in."

"Agreed," stated a large man as he took a step forward to accompany her. Both of them stood alongside Ray.

Constantine shook his head. "If you two don't—"

"They're right," another man said, joining the two in the middle.

A meek woman with hair as black as night stepped to Constantine's side. "We cannot disrupt the order of things. Corazon has been successful because we don't fix what's not broken, we can have a civilized talk about this later, but this type of arguing won't do any good."

Another follower stepped forward, standing next to Orwell as he held Luna's hair tight. "Mona is thinking clearly," he said, nodding toward the woman with the jet-black hair. "We can't afford to have such fundamental differences. We have to preserve our way of life, the life Elliot worked so hard to craft."

"No," stated Willow as she pushed her way into the center. "This is not what Elliot intended."

Soon a variety of different followers stood before Constantine and Luna, each giving their two cents as to how to proceed. Constantine slowly lowered his rifle, intimidated by the growing crowd. Orwell let go of Luna's hair, and she crawled to her feet, standing by Ray and the others.

Some followers accumulated around the two of them, while others gathered around the Disciples. The Disciples who had pinned Benji to the ground stood with the others. Benji dusted himself off, knife still in hand. It was evident that there was a rift. The community slowly separated into two sides.

"So this is what you want? War?" Constantine asked as he looked around. The community was unequally split; those that favored Ray and Musgo's argument of free will outnumbered the rest, but the opposing side had weapons, a luxury none of them would be lucky enough to afford in this scenario. "This is where you take your stand? This is what you lay down your life for? Mother will not have any mercy on you… You will not be remembered! Your family! Your legacy! It will be nothing! This is what we've been working toward for all these years… and here you all are, ruining it."

The larger group of people standing shoulder to shoulder, protecting Ray and Luna and harboring the bodies of Musgo, Aria, and Otto, stood strong.

"This is your last chance! You will blindly follow what this suicidal maniac says to you?" He eyed all of those who were staring him and his small militia down. He then shook his head slowly. "So be it." Constantine took a few steps forward so that he was now standing apart from both groups. He turned to his followers and raised his rifle. "Men and women of Mother! If these sinners do not take a knee in the next ten seconds…. Kill them all."

Orwell gasped. "Constantine, you can't be—"

"Ten!" Constantine commanded.

The people surrounding Ray and Luna looked to each other for guidance, but everyone was just as lost as the next person. Constantine walked back to the followers of Mother and looked back to the rebels. "Nine, eight." His mouth widened ever so slowly as he spoke, allowing his eager tongue some room to lick his chapped lips. The crazed look was back in his eyes as he continued to count down. "Seven... six..."

Some individuals on the rebel's side began to drop like flies, bowing to one knee and crying to Mother for forgiveness, looking for a certain redemption that was never going to come.

"Five... four..." Constantine's lips began to curl outward, a deranged smile thirsty for blood plastered on his face.

"Enough!" Luna demanded from inside the circle of rebels. She pushed her way out into the un-established no man's land and stopped halfway, signaling Constantine to come and meet her in the middle. He lowered his rifle as he walked out to meet her face to face.

"What's it going to be then?" he sighed, obnoxiously looking her up and down.

"I have a proposition for you," she said as the rebels who dropped to their knees quickly scurried across no man's land to join the followers. She tried to find the words as her lips moved without sound. She was having a deep internal conflict as all eyes remained glued to both of them. "I know you don't want bloodshed... I know you want things as they were..." She muttered into the air softly so that nobody could hear her.

Constantine nodded. "Go on..."

She struggled to find the words again. Everybody watched her carefully, trying to pick up on any hints or mannerisms she might have been trying to give off. She just stood very still as she spoke. Constantine seemed to agree with what she was saying as well. After a few minutes of unheard conversation amongst the high tension, he turned and headed back to the followers. Luna remained still for a brief moment and then turned to the rebels. They took her in, allowing her to go right back to where she was positioned before by Ray's side.

"What's going on? Luna, what's the plan here?" he asked, grabbing her arm in anticipation for the worst.

She bent over and ran her hand along the snow-dusted earth. "It's over, Ray... it's over."

He looked up to the followers as they all began to turn away and head back toward the center of Corazon. "Wait, what did he say to you? What happens now, I mean—where do we—?" He turned to Luna just in time for him to see her swinging a sizable stone against the side of his skull. He jolted and hit the ground as his face went numb. Everybody turned to the two of them in shock.

"L-Luna w-what-wha—?" he spat as he looked up to her, holding his arms out to shield his face.

She raised the stone above her head in one swift motion. "I'm so sorry." She then swatted his arms out of her way and brought the stone down hard, making flat contact with the same side of his head.

Everything went black as Ray slipped out of consciousness. Falling deeper and deeper into the splotched stars that flew around within the confines of his daydreams.

Everyone quickly backed up, giving Luna her space as she sat on Ray's stomach and took deep breaths as she looked toward the sky with her eyes closed. One hand curled into a fist, the other holding a bloodstained rock. Benji looked at her in awe, both impressed and terrified of her actions.

Three Disciples then approached the rebel group. Two of them lifted Ray's body from the earth with a stretcher and began to walk him into the woods. The third one remained looking at them with a rifle in his arms. "Show's over... back to it."

Everyone looked around, confused as to what had just transpired. "All of you! Let's go!" The Disciple ordered as he loaded his gun. The crowd before him quickly dispersed. Benji approached Luna as she breathed heavily, still kneeling on the ground.

"Loon?" he asked, putting a hand on her shoulder. She quickly stood up and stormed off, leaving behind Benji, the lone Disciple, and Maple as she mourned over Musgo's lifeless body.

37

Ray came to as he lay on a soft bed of snow, swaddled in the warmest blanket he had ever felt. His face throbbed from the bottom of his jaw to somewhere near the top of his head. He could practically feel his temples pulsating. As he blinked his eyes, the fuzzy images before him grew ever so clear. Luna looked down on him in pain as Constantine and Orwell stood silently by her side.

Ray brought a hand to his face and felt the massive lump protruding from his head. He winced in pain as he sat the rest of the way up, grinding his teeth as he straightened his posture and looked up at the three figures before him. "So this is what I'm worth."

Luna lent him a hand in order to help him up. He disregarded her gesture of aid and turned to help himself up. "So what, you give me to them, and they let the rest of you live? Is that it?"

Luna shook her head. "There was no way we were winning that fight."

"We outnumbered them two to one!" he growled.

"They had guns. They had guns and the power of Mother behind them. People want to die for a cause… what cause do you have when you figure out that your entire existence is a lie? I did what was best for us… for Bea."

Ray winced in pain again as his head began to pulsate once more. "So what now? They put a bullet in my head? Gut me like a pig? Tie a cinder brick to my ankle and throw me in the river?"

Luna stepped forward and grabbed his arm. He quickly jerked away from her. She looked at her feet and then back up at him. "I wasn't going to let anything happen to you. But we all knew you were the problem."

Ray looked deep into Luna's eyes, hearing the irony within her voice. "*Problem*," he said, raising his eyebrows in disbelief.

"You were starting trouble, making people question their beliefs. Look what happened. Ray, Musgo's dead," she said as her eyes began to well up.

"He knew the risks. Luna. He did this so that you would forgive him. He got you into this mess, and that was his way of getting you out. Proving to all of you that violence can and will be used again if someone didn't stand up. And you're just going to let that go to waste? He dies for this, and you're just giving up on him."

"No, fuck you," she said, wiping the tears from her eyes. "Fuck you, Ray. You were always about the plan. You always wanted that big plan. You thought you could solve everything, didn't you? Well, guess what? Some things are too complicated to just talk your way out of them. When you got here, everything worked, we lived in peaceful ignorance, now—"

"Are you even listening to yourself!?" he yelled right before wincing again. "You realize you are doing exactly what they want you to do! You don't understand that when I leave, nothing is going to change! The women will still be chosen, and raped, beaten, and killed. Nothing is going to stop this cycle unless we act!"

"What happens then? Where do we go then, Ray? We act, we win, we take over. What then? Do we just go home? There is no home for us. This is it; this is all we have, and you thought you could prance right in and change that. Think about Bea!"

"Yes! Yes, let's *think about Bea*! What happens when she gets older and Elliot decides that she would make a nice addition to his collection? What then?!" he roared, throwing his hands up in the air. Ray ran his hands down his face, wiping the cold sweat away from his brow. He slowly calmed himself down before speaking up again. "You know… You know I really *loved you*. I really truly loved you. You made me feel like—like I belonged. You made me feel like I had a family for one last time. You changed me, you really did, Luna… You think after all this time, I would be smart enough to see the real you," he said, looking her right in the eyes.

She held his stare for a few moments, finally seeing the true soul within him. She saw a purpose, she saw a reason to keep living, and here she was, ripping that away from him. "Here," she muttered, throwing a thick green burlap sack at his feet. The bag clanked and clunked on the ground, telling him all he needed to know. "These are all the tools and food you'll need. We won't kill you, but you can't stay here. Not anymore."

"Luna, you know I'll—"

"My job here is done. Your leg is healed, right?" she asked, looking him up and down.

"It was never about my leg, and you know—"

"Your leg is *healed, right?*" she asked again.

"So nothing else ever mattered? All of this was some sort of act? You can't tell me you don't mean the things you say. You can't really look me in the eyes and abandon me here…"

She shook her head. "I told you before. To heal you physically, I needed to heal you spiritually and mentally. I did what I had to do to achieve that. What did you think was going to happen? We'd fall in love and live happily ever after? Living off the fat of the land? Have a couple children of our own? My work is done, and you need to leave and *never* come back. If you do, they will kill me, they will kill Beatrix, they will kill Maple, Clover, *everyone*."

He picked up the burlap bag and slung it over his shoulder. "*Yeah,*" he muttered with malice. "*Yeah, my leg is fine.*" He then took a few steps forward and then a couple more, bringing him face to face with Luna. He looked at her with a form of pity and disgust, betrayed by the one person that dared to show him compassion.

He looked into her icy blue eyes one last time before moving on past her and glaring at Constantine and Orwell. They gave him a cute little nod before he looked on toward the darkening desolate woods. "You found your way here, you can find your way back to wherever you crawled out from." Constantine chuckled.

Ray just kept moving, not even giving him the attention he craved.

"Ray!" Luna shouted. He turned back to her with the slightest glimmer of hope in his eye. She flicked a small silver object in his direction. He caught it with one hand and looked down at his palm to see the face of the silver medallion reading *something more*. He looked up at her, astonished that she had kept it for so long, thinking that it had gone missing the day he tried to end his life. He wanted her to say something, leave him with some form of hope. She just turned her back and walked back toward Corazon, leaving him alone. Orwell and Constantine soon accompanied her.

Ray made his way deeper into the woods, eventually losing sight of all of them. He walked until he grew tired and decided to open up the bag that they had so generously supplied him with. Inside of the heavy burlap sack was a knife, a compass with a note saying to head southwest, a prepared meal, and a lighter along with a small plastic bottle full of what he thought was lighter fluid. He slumped up against a tree as he watched the snow drift down from above, still wrapped in the extremely warm blanket he had woken up in. He listened for any of the creatures of the night lurking around him in search of their next meal. He rubbed his hands together to promote friction. Even inside of the thermo-blanket, the cold would still nip at his extremities.

"All right, all right…" He spoke under his breath, trying to soothe his anxiety. After all this time, after all these years, he found himself feeling truly alone, and more importantly, scared. "You're gonna be fine… You're gonna be fine…" He said as he curled up into a small ball. "Tomorrow morning, you wake up, and you walk southwest. Keep the pace, make it back to the cabin before midnight. Just focus… focus… *focus*…"

❉ ❉ ❉

While Ray lay curled up in the woods, Corazon became further divided. Those who sided with the Disciples took on the name *Believer* and were granted a purple ribbon, which they were instructed to keep tied around their arm at all times.

Those that attempted to think for themselves were quickly put down, hammered into submission. Luna began to bargain once again, this time with Constantine and Orwell back at Corazon. Luna spoke calmly and without the sacred respect she had once used. "He's gone, now keep up your end of the bargain and leave us be," she hissed at them inside of her hut.

Constantine smiled; his calm demeanor had returned since the de-escalation of the tentative coup. "Luna, you've done well, but let's not forget how you promoted him for so long. You did, after all, instill in him this… *rambunctious spirit*. You were the one to take him in."

"And I was the one to cast him out. I did as Mother would want and saved his life," she said, trying her best to reason with his irrational outlook.

"How's that going for him?" Orwell laughed. Constantine quickly joined up with him.

"Enough," she said sternly. "He's gone now. What's done is done. Now make everyone lower their weapons. I don't want a war. We don't have enough people to afford that."

"Here's the thing," Constantine said, taking a step forward. "Your little friend didn't just cause a scene… no, he had an idea, and idea's spread. He polluted the minds of so many of our citizens… That doesn't make Elliot very happy."

Luna scowled. "Constantine, we had a deal, and you will uphold your end. Orwell—you know this is only what's right."

Orwell remained silent, intimidated by Constantine's sudden burst of rage from the day before. Constantine smiled. "Oh, I will, dear, don't you worry. But you did take responsibility for Ray, and now you have to clean up the mess he has made."

"How do you want me to do that? You said it yourself; it's an idea. You can't just get rid of an idea."

"You need to drill it into their heads. Tell them all how Ray was delusional. Tell them all how he was losing it, how he is not to be trusted. Make sure they all know that Ray was the one who killed Aria and Otto, and Ray is the one they should be mad at. Turn him into a symbol for all things evil. Make them hate him, make them gag at the very mention of his name. Make them see how all of this is his fault and that we can go back to the way things were if we really try," he said, stroking her shoulder.

"You want me to turn him into some sort of monster… I'm not doing that. Let them think what they want to think, let the people make a decision for themselves instead of cramming it down their throats with fear. Do the right thing for once," she said, moving away from his grasp.

"Oh, I am doing the right thing. I am restoring the good to the community. We cannot have differing ideas in a place like Corazon. The system only works when everyone is on board. You need to do this, you have no choice."

Luna scoffed. "You can't kill me, I am the only link between them and you. They see me as a leader now. I'm too valuable. If I die, they riot."

Constantine laughed, "That's why you're going to help us. They love you, Luna. They listen to you for reasons I still don't quite understand."

"I'm sorry," she inquired sarcastically. "Why exactly do you think I'll help you?"

His smile grew even wider. "You see... I was really hoping you would ask that... we're ready for you!" he called out toward the hut flap.

Two long slender hands protruded from the opening and peeled back the canopy. The High Disciple Felix looked toward the fading firelight with a bright yellow smile. "Good evening Luna."

She nearly froze where she stood; she wanted to choke and praise him at the very same time. She stuttered as she tried to find the right words... "Felix, I—I don't—"

"Luna, Luna, Luna, my sweet child, no need to worry yourself at this moment. I come in peace. We just want to sort this whole... miscommunication out," he said in his signature calming voice. "I want you to know that we are not the enemy, dear... We are simply dealing with the... repercussions caused by this stranger in the woods. We don't want to bring harm to you or the community." He looked back at the Disciples and raised his brow, gesturing for them to nod their heads in agreement. "We just want things to go back to the way they were. We want people to bow their heads in Mother's name again. We want them to live their happiest, healthiest lives. We can't do that when those individuals who look up to you run around with rebellious thoughts within their brain... so you're going to help us. We need you to be the shepherd, lead the sheep back to the herd, Luna..."

"*I can't,*" she whispered as she clenched her jaw, looking off to the side.

Felix clasped his hands together in front of him. "You know I spoke with Elliot about our dilemma. He isn't pleased; he expected more from such an upstanding follower," he sighed.

Luna's head dropped. "Tell the Prophet I am sorry, but—I just don't know what to believe anymore."

Felix's smile slowly faded away. "Well then, I cannot force you to believe again. I can only hope that you see the light that will guide you toward the right path, the true path…" He bowed his head in silence for a moment. He sighed and looked back up at her, his eyes narrowed. "And as a reminder of the importance of finding that path, I want to show you one last thing."

Felix turned to the hut flap and called out for someone, "Come in, sweetheart!"

Luna looked confused, wondering who would possibly respond to such a demeaning remark. Her jaw quickly dropped as she watched Beatrix innocently skip in through the flap, her smile bright, her mind completely oblivious to the evils around her.

She hopped from one foot to another. Luna watched as the ribbons in Beatrix's hair flowed with every leap; her new silky white dress and touches of makeup made her seem that much older.

She looked over to Luna, and her face lit up, though she didn't say a word in fear that she may be disrespectful in front of the High Disciple. Luna had purposefully tried to keep her in the dark for so long, afraid of what she might think if she knew the truth. Beatrix smiled a bright, toothy smile as she looked over to Felix, who bent down and patted the top of her head.

Felix smiled and glanced at Luna before looking back toward Beatrix. He placed his hands on her petite shoulders. "Look at you…" He whispered, brushing her hair back behind her ear.

Luna couldn't hold herself together, "Don't you *dare!*" she screamed abruptly.

Constantine grabbed her from behind and buried the barrel of his revolver in her back so that Beatrix couldn't see what was going on. Beatrix looked toward Luna, all confused. She then licked her lips and slowly directed her attention back to Felix, who remained rather calm.

"Beatrix..." he whispered. "I haven't forgotten about you... Mother sees everything, you see. And I am a very busy man up on the mountain... You know Elliot came to me the other night," he said, tilting his head toward her, her eyes were gleaming with excitement. "He says that you've been quite the good girl and thinks that you deserve a reward. How does that sound to you?" he asked kindly. The excitement could be felt ruminating from Beatrix's body. All of a sudden, an opportunity she had never foreseen herself achieving was now lingering at her very fingertips.

Felix lifted her chin and looked deep into her eyes. "Beatrix, my dear... I don't know how to say this. We usually never initiate anyone this young, but... Elliot has spoken, and he wants *you* to accompany the Disciples and me up on the mountain. What do you say, child?"

"Yes!" she screamed, a bit too hyper. She quickly grew shyer and held herself together. "Yes. Yes, Felix. By the power of Mother and all things holy, yes." Beatrix began to tear up out of pure joy. Luna, meanwhile, shared in tears of different emotions.

Felix stood up tall and faced Luna with a wide smile, smoothing out the wrinkles and minor scars upon his face. "Well, that concludes my business here, Luna. I thought you might want to witness Beatrix's initiation. I know how close you two have become."

Luna just glared at him through a tear-stained face. Beatrix walked up to her, still confused as to why she was crying. She lifted her tiny hand to Luna's cheek and wiped away some of the droplets.

"It's okay. Luna, I'm a pretty girl… I'm beautiful now… Elliot wants me! *Me, Luna!*"

Luna shook her head from side to side, looking up at Felix, "*Please don't do this.*"

Felix took Beatrix by the arm and guided her toward the exit. Beatrix took one last look at Luna before exiting the hut, thoroughly confused. All her life Luna had been encouraging her to try to make it up on the mountain. Now that the opportunity had finally come, she'd try to prevent it from happening.

Felix then made his way back to Luna and lifted her chin as she cried profusely. "Listen here, child… listen here," he whispered.

Luna blinked, draining her eyes for the time being. She looked at him with rage and despair.

He sighed and straightened his posture, "You protect us, and we protect her. Do I make myself clear?"

She wiped the mucus from her nose with the sleeve on her shirt as Constantine let go of her, forcing her onto her knees in front of Felix. He grabbed her by the backside of her head, pulling her hair so that her face was angled up toward his own. "I said, do I make *myself clear?*"

She quickly nodded, "Yes—y—yes, yes, you make yourself clear."

Felix smiled and looked down at her. He then bent over her and pressed his lips firmly against her own, indulging in every single moment of it all; Luna put up no struggle whatsoever. He pressed harder and harder, pushing his tongue further into her mouth. After a putrid ten seconds of this, he backed off and placed his hand on her forehead. "Elliot and Mother bless you, child. I hope you make them happy."

He let go of Luna's hair and strode out of the hut. She listened as he once again kindly greeted a confused Beatrix before heading on their way.

"Good evening, Miss Beatrix. Are you ready to take a trip up the mountain?"

"Oh boy, I mean—of course, Felix…"

"Oh, don't you worry about your tone, young lady, and The Prophet will accept you all the same."

"Yes, Felix…" she squeaked.

Constantine removed the gun from Luna's back. She crawled to one end of her hut and pressed her ear up against the tarp so that she could hear more of their conversation as the two voices faded away.

"You're going to love it up there with us, Beatrix. Everything is just so perfect. Mother will look down upon you favorably!"

"Praise be to Mother!" she yipped.

"That's right, praise be to Mother," he said as they walked off into the distance.

Constantine and Orwell pulled on their coats and looked around Luna's hut. They began to search high and low, opening drawers and rummaging through bags.

Luna got to her feet and ran her hands down her face. She sniffled as she asked them what they were doing. "What's the problem?" she asked, confronting them directly.

"Well, ya see," Orwell stated, "we need to check the place, make sure there are no more remnants of your little boy toy. You know, *propaganda*, stuff that might make people second guess themselves."

Luna pulled a funny face. "What do you expect to find? He came here with absolutely nothing! What the hell do you mean propaganda?"

Orwell pulled out her bin from underneath her bed. "And what do we have here?" he asked sarcastically as he snapped the lid off.

"Just leave that stuff alone, it's all mine, I swear," she said, eyeing the both of them.

Constantine, who was rummaging through her clothes, picked up a bra and held it to his nose. "That may be so…" He said with a smile. He inhaled deeply and exhaled with a smile as he lowered her bra from his nose and stuffed it in his pocket. "But ya can never be too careful."

She looked away in disgust and focused on Orwell, who had removed the wooden box that contained her CD player in it. "I told you to leave that stuff alone!" she yelled. "Please!"

Orwell removed the CD player and placed it next to him. He looked at the device and then up at her to see the way the expression on her face changed when he fiddled with the buttons. She would grow noticeably more worrisome with each button that he pressed. "Yeah..." He grumbled as he stood up. "I should probably take this in for examination. Ya never know what kind of hidden messages the outsider could have recorded on this." He chuckled at his own absurdity as he picked up the CD player and walked toward the hut's exit.

Luna growled and lunged for the CD player gripping it with both of her hands and yanking on it as hard as she could. She got ahold of his thumb and quickly twisted it until she heard a *pop*. Orwell squealed and jerked his free elbow into her nose, sending her sprawling to the ground, cupping a hand over her nose. Constantine ran up alongside her and kicked her in the stomach, forcing her to flop around the ground like a fish.

"Know where you stand, girl!" Constantine screamed, pointing a fat finger in her face. "Don't forget what happens when you cross the line! All it takes is one radio call, you can use your imagination as to what happens after that. Little miss Beatrix is counting on you, whether she knows it or not!"

Constantine then pushed Orwell out of the hut, taking with them her CD player and a handful of underwear. She lay flat on her back, her face caked with blood, tears, and dirt. She curled up into a small ball and rocked back and forth, thinking of a simpler time.

38

Maple sat still in the corner of her hut, hearing the believers bark orders at the rebels outside. She hugged herself and rocked back and forth as pangs of memory would shoot through her like lightning, making her see the stock of the gun landing on top of Musgo's head over and over again.

"Hey there, it's okay, darling." A low, raspy voice whispered into her ear. She turned to see a much more youthful Musgo wiping her tears away. *"Everything is going to be okay."*

She blinked and wiped at her eyes, wondering if all of this was reality. He just remained still and smiled at her. She licked her chapped lips before speaking. "C-can you stay?" she asked, knowing full well that this was her illness taking over.

The young Musgo smiled and gently stroked her cheek with the back of his fingers. *"You know I can't…"*

His words seem to cut even deeper into her mourning. "What do I do?" she asked. "Everything is so… so backward. I don't know right from wrong, I—I need your help, I need you back here… with me."

"I know it hurts. That's okay. It's good to hurt. It means I meant something to you, just like you meant something to me," he said with a certain

ghostly whisper. *"You just have to stay strong. Do what you have to do to survive. Things will sort themselves out."*

She pulled Musgo close and locked him in a deep embrace. She nuzzled her head deep into his soft chest. He closed his eyes and put his arms around her as well. *"You know what you have to do,"* he said reassuringly.

She pulled him in even closer. "I don't know if I'll be able to go through with it."

"You can't think about it, you just have to act. You may not be able to take out the head of the snake, but you will sure as hell do as much damage as possible to the body before we meet again. Promise me you'll fight, Maple. Promise me."

She began to silently cry as she pressed her cheek against his worn-out jacket. "Can you stay for a little while?"

He let her remain suspended in time without an answer, but eventually, he had to tell her. *"I'm sorry, honey."* The hug lasted a few more moments before Maple's arms caved in and met her chest. She looked up to an empty, cold room.

After a minute or two of self-reflection, she got herself up and slung a heavy cloak over her shoulders. With that, she stormed out into Corazon like a woman with a plan. It was time to make a change.

"Maple! Just the woman I was looking for!" Constantine shouted from across the common area after having declared himself the immediate leader in the community. "Bring yourself over here, Maple. Let's put ya to work!" he said pleasantly as if he were doing her a favor. She looked around at all of the believers who kept a steady eye on her. The believers weren't forced to work; they got a free pass for keeping their faith while all of the rebels were worked to the bone. The more work, the less conspiring.

She shuffled over to Constantine, who looked her up and down with pity. "Where were you off to?" he inquired.

"Just going for a walk," she said blandly.

"Well, that's not very productive now, is it? Why don't we get you back into the kitchen? I really miss that stew you make. What is it again?"

"Beef stew?"

"That's it! Beef stew."

The two of them held a stare for a bit until Maple confronted him with a problem. "Well, I hate to rain on your parade, but I cannot make the stew without the proper ingredients, and all of the proper ingredients are in the woods. I'm the only one who knows what to get, and—and well, you're not letting me do that now, are you?"

Constantine was taken back by her abrupt response. "Well… I'll have Orwell accompany you. He can help you find whatever you need," he said with a cheeky smile.

She nodded her head. "Very well then."

Constantine waved Orwell over to them and explained to him that he needed to keep a sharp eye on Maple to ensure that there was no funny business. Orwell nodded and went along with her, deeper and deeper into the woods until they had reached the greenhouse.

"So what goes into the stew?" he bellowed.

"Get me some onions, and garlic, and… carrots if there are any left."

A grumpy Orwell growled as he listened to her order him around like some sort of farmhand. "Onions, garlic, and carrots," he repeated to himself as he scanned the greenhouse for any signs of those particular vegetables and spices.

Maple observed him from the corner. She watched as he gathered everything they needed and came back to her like a dog. "Good boy," she said out of spite.

The two of them then made their way into the woods again. "I need some blackberries if you can manage to find them, too," she said as they trudged through the snow.

"What do you need blackberries for?" he growled. "You best not be putting blackberries in my stew, Maple."

"Your job is to make sure I stay in line, not complain. Now find me some blackberries. Who's the chef here?" she replied.

He turned to her and got right in her face. "You better watch yourself, *widow*."

She immediately shut up and continued to walk. He followed close behind. After a few minutes of silence and intense searching, she found what she was looking for.

"There!" she shouted, pointing to a nearby bush littered with blackberries.

Orwell glanced to the bush speckled with small black orbs. The bush was behind a wall of roots and thorny branches. He sighed, "Well, get to it then."

"What? You won't help me?" she asked.

"Lady, if you want those precious blackberries so badly, you can go get them. I'm not putting my ass on the line for some fucking berries. I don't even *like* berries," he begrudgingly moaned.

She rolled her eyes and dropped to her hands and knees. She slowly pushed forward, past the jagged branches that began to cut into her skin and pull at her hair. She extended an arm and tried to grasp them. The bush was a mere inch and a half away from her grip. She winced in pain as she used her left foot to push herself in even farther, forcing the thorns to open up cuts on her face and arm. Orwell looked at her in horror as she removed herself from the patch of thorns, holding out an arm with a handful of blackberries.

"What is wrong with you, woman… they're just blackberries," he said, in shock at what he had just witnessed.

"You need to," she heaved. "You need to enjoy the little pleasures in times like these. You wouldn't understand." She then slid the blackberries into her pocket and began to walk. Orwell examined the bush once more, confused, and then tagged along.

The two made it back to Corazon, where Maple was immediately put to work. She positioned herself over the large pot over the fire and began to add all of the chopped-up and diced vegetables. She then added all of the meat and flavoring she would need to feed all the community.

Orwell remained hovering over her shoulder in fear that she might poison the stew. For safe measures, Constantine ordered that all rebels shall get a half serving for every full serving a believer received. The believers could tell themselves apart from the rebels by a purple tag that hung from their upper arm. Things began running much differently in Corazon, and few people seemed to enjoy the abrupt change.

Everywhere you went, there was always some sort of heavy religious presence, be it a Disciple with a rifle or a group of self-proclaimed believers with their clubs and jagged-edged blades. The believers took it upon themselves to enforce the word of Mother. They paraded around Corazon like royalty and began to skip out on their daily chores, forcing the rebels to pick up their slack. Anyone who refused was either beaten or cut. Most people chose the beating in fear that the cut administered to them may get infected and result in a more serious problem. The curfew had changed, too. All rebels had to report to be within their designated hut before sundown or else they would be reprimanded. If they wished to spend the night with the company of another, they had to check in with a Disciple first and make it public knowledge. If any rebel was caught sneaking around at night, they would be cut. Within a week's time, almost every rebel had received a batch of fresh bruises or a festering wound to the arm or leg. Some took it as a punishment for turning their back on Mother. Others took it as a form of pride, proving that they would not crumble under the pressure and pain, claiming that they would somehow find a way to get out alive.

Luna slowly gave in, fearing that Beatrix's well-being was now completely in her hands. She began to hold daily meetings that all of the rebels believed were being held in *secrecy*. Little did they know it was all a show designed by the very people that got them into this mess. Things began to get confusing when Luna began to preach about sin and how it was corrupting them all. She began saying things like, "Turn back to Mother before you completely succumb to this way of life." She even claimed that Ray was mentally unhinged and was not to be trusted.

"Ray was a monster. A man looking for an easy path to power. He saw us in our vulnerable state of mind and made us turn against the one thing that unified us all. Faith. He's gone, yet his word lives on… why have we let him do this to us? Look at how we are living. Does this seem like we are unified? Our peers are physically hurting us for sneaking around at night just to see loved ones. What happened to the community founded on love? We can have it all back, but we must rid ourselves of this hateful sin that consumes us!"

Constantine was usually listening in on the other end of the canopy that separated them, and Luna knew this. The gathering before her would usually savagely question her, asking her how she could turn her back to a man that wanted nothing but the best for her. She usually chastised them in return.

"How dare you make that assumption," she would spit. "You have no idea what you're talking about. The man you speak of would abuse me. He would put on a front and claim to be this humble drifter, but we all know what he was deep down. Don't be fooled by the act. I was, and look where I am now."

These sorts of remarks would usually bring her accuser to silence. They had no idea how much Luna actually worried about Ray, not knowing if he had made it back to his quaint cabin in the woods or if he were somewhere along the route, having frozen to death. The thoughts would rot into her mind all through the night and continue to decay during the day.

❊ ❊ ❊

Ray drifted away into the vortex that was his fever dreams. He would float into this black void that contained all of his deepest secrets and darkest regrets. He saw his father crying over something he did. He saw his mother looking at him as if she didn't even recognize him. He saw his wife and child being pulled away from him, ripped from each other's grasps by forces unknown. He saw Luna, surrounded by the croaking frogs that he had dreamed of so many times before. He saw Beatrix walking along the edge of a cliff, balancing herself on one foot, a sight that nearly gave him a heart attack.

"Where do we go now? All the lonely souls who wander the earth, with no purpose?" the ghost of Musgo whispered in his ear as he floated by in a gust of frigid wind.

Ray gasped as his eyes shot open and he sat up. He had stopped to rest at the base of a large pine tree for the night, but it was now midday, judging by the sun's placement. He had no intentions of sleeping that long. His body was slowly shutting down. It had now been days since he had left Corazon. He wasn't sure which direction was right, the compass seemed to be accurate, but his home was nowhere in sight. It was so much easier to navigate during the spring when the ice had melted. But here he was, lost in late winter, enough food for another day at most.

He kept pushing forward, one leg over the other. He would often repeat that, telling himself, "One leg over the other… Left, right, left, right, left, right…" just to hear a voice at times.

His hands were barely working. He often wrapped the blanket Luna had sent him off with on his hands alone. It was there where he had practically no more feeling at all.

"No... No, no, no..." Musgo would whisper in the wind. *"Keep your heart warm, throw that blanket back over your shoulders, warm up the chest, let your heart do the rest. It's when you lose feeling there that you should be scared."*

Ray shook his head, trying to rid his mind of the guilt and anguish that was most likely causing these hallucinations. He tried singing songs, but his chapped lips grew more painful with every passing minute. The water Luna had given him was now frozen over, and all of the wood he had searched for in wanting a fire was far too wet to use. This left him with some dried fruit, a lighter, and some lighter fluid.

He sometimes held the lighter under his hand, touching the flickering light to his skin until he actually felt a pang of feeling. Sometimes it took a few seconds, sometimes longer. The more he pushed forward, the more he began to doubt himself. He wanted to stop. He wanted all of this to just end. The demons that once polluted his mind began to creep back in and fill his head with dreadful ideas.

Eventually, he stumbled upon a tree with its roots raised significantly from the ground due to some form of erosion. He decided that it would make for a nice home for the evening and nestled under its massive structure for some protection from the roaring winds surrounding him. He quickly collapsed and slipped into a shallow slumber, just to be woken by the curious bugs every half hour. It quickly became apparent to him that he would not find salvation for the night under that particular tree and decided that it would be best to just keep moving.

Breaking down out of pure exhaustion became an hourly occurrence. Once his knees hit the icy landscape, he would simply remove some of the dried fruit and meat and chew on bits and pieces of them, trying to muster as much energy as he possibly could from his little snack. After a few minutes of an attempted cry that came out as long, drawn-out, whispery moans toward the ground, he would get to his feet and keep moving.

His muscles burned more than they had ever burned before. His legs went numb, his underarms got really red and bumpy, a concoction that proved to be rather painful as he swung his arms back and forth to keep up the momentum. His leg that had been out of commission for so long began to feel brittle and overused due to the atrophy that had occurred throughout his recovery. His vision was blurry, and his face grew red splotches on it from the blistering cold.

After what seemed like a lifetime of moving, he finally dropped to his stomach, letting the snow slowly blow over his body. He took one last look up at the world as he was slowly engulfed in white. As he allowed the icy hands of mother nature to slowly pick him apart, he looked up to a very strange sight in the distance: a bush engulfed in flames. The flames burned strong and true but were not ordinary in their appearance. The long tongues of fire licked up the trunk of the rather sizable bush and bore colors of vibrant blues and greens. He had never seen a fire like that before in his life. He admired in and all of its beauty, quite the sight to leave the world with. He even thought about the blinding light everyone saw before they died and if this was what they were referring to. The flames slowly engulfed the bush, standing alone in the middle of an icy landscape. That's when Ray noticed the figure beside the bush that seemed to be huddling close for warmth. He wanted to scream for help, but it was far too late; his voice had completely left him hours ago. The figure then moved abruptly as if it noticed that Ray was watching.

A strange figure seemed to trudge toward him from his side. As it drew closer, he could make out the face of a grizzly bear. This scared him greatly. He tried to muster up the strength to kick and scream, but he only managed to wiggle around his left foot in a strange pattern and exhale a breathy whimper from the bowls of his frostbitten lungs. The bear was tiny and seemed to be disfigured. It also walked on its hind feet with immense ease. It grew closer and closer, up to the point where the sizable animal was only a mere few feet away from him. That's when he saw something that would save his life.

The bear shed its skin right there in front of him, revealing a much smaller frame cloaked in black. It was a human, a small human that had fashioned a coat out of the bear's skin. The human removed a dark blue thermos and unscrewed the lid. The human then held the spout of the thermos to his lips and allowed him to drink from the lukewarm contents inside. The soup tasted awful, but Ray's tastebuds were so damaged from the cold that he barely even noticed. The soup surged through his body, lighting up every organ with its warmth. The human then set down their thermos and maneuvered themself so that they could help Ray up. He latched his hands onto their arms and used them as leverage to pull himself out of the snow that was quickly engulfing his body. The human made a dramatic arm wave and shouted, "Come on!" at the top of their lungs. They then pointed into the distance.

As he looked up to the sky, he noticed how the snow blew in awkward directions, about a quarter of a mile straight ahead. It almost seemed as though there was a barrier preventing it from doing its job. He mustered every ounce of strength in his body to push himself to his hands and knees. Just over the pure white slope was a darkened blocklike structure. His face seemed too frozen to even smile. He simply crawled, now putting one unmovable hand in front of the other, pulling himself closer with every dramatic arm flail. The human scurried to his side and pushed him upright, trying to get him to stand as quickly as possible. He managed to use the human as a crutch and get himself to his feet. The two of them then began to quickly trudge toward the oncoming structure.

The closer he got, the more familiar the darkened structure became. He had at long last found *his cabin*. The door was unlocked just as he had left it. He managed to twist the knob and fall in through the front door. The human pulled the rest of his body inside and swung the heavy wooden door shut using their foot. Ray then lay in the center of his previous home, defrosting on the ground. The cabin was in no way warm, but it was a dramatic difference from the temperatures outside, and as soon as he gained feeling in his body, he would start a fire, and everything would be all right, if not just for a moment. He then let himself slip effortlessly into a deeply deserved slumber.

He awoke the next day with a pounding headache. His skin, heart, and head seemed to pulsate as well. It took him a moment to realize it was his body adjusting to the heat. He looked down at his feet, which were swollen, having doubled in size. His toes were pudgy and were swelled to the point of deformity, which made it extremely difficult to take his boots off. It came to the point where he had no choice and had to cut around the hardened leather and mesh plastic with a knife that he kept in the upper desk drawer in the common area of his living room. *What had happened last night?* He thought to himself. He vaguely remembered being rescued but couldn't put his finger on what had happened or who had saved him.

Once the boots were cut off, he looked around, appreciating all that he had a bit more now that it had saved his life. The cabin was separated into two rooms. As soon as one enters the front door, they are walking into the common area where there is a couch facing a rather large television to the left. Ray had gotten his friend to set up a satellite that linked onto a far-off signal giving him access to a lot of channels, though most of them would come in speaking Spanish. Some TV was better than no TV at all; he used it for the background noise mostly anyhow. The common room also included a kitchen unit with a functioning sink and a very large freezer unit. The kitchen unit also contained an outdated stove and a cabinet that housed all of his cooking utensils.

The other part of the cabin was closed off. It contained his bedroom, where he slept alone for many years. His bedroom was small and not grand by any means. It contained a small twin-size bed for one, a lockbox he kept his personal information in, and a locked cabinet with his rifle and ammunition in it. As far as going to the bathroom went, he had a shovel he kept leaned up against the back of his cabin that allowed him to make a bathroom anywhere he wanted. When there was no snow on the ground, there was a garden that could be seen in the back. The garden supplied him with a lot of the food that kept him going for so long. It was either that, soup, or any animal he had managed to catch or trap.

Things felt strange, being in the home that had held him for so long. This seemed to be the only place the world would ever welcome him. A fugitive on one end, a troubled philosopher on the other. It was here where he could escape from it all. This was his realm where anything he said goes. There was a certain relief that came with that, a certain relief that allowed him to let go of all of the troubling thoughts that cluttered his brain.

The cabin door flew open, and the human dressed in black shed their bearskin again, throwing it onto the nearby couch. The human had two armfuls of lumber, which Ray quickly assumed was for the woodstove. The being walked over to the stove and let their arms go loose, causing the wood to tumble from their grasp and into a messy pile on the floor. "There's a pre-cut pile out back," they said in a low, muffled voice.

Ray looked at the person with admiration and astonishment. "I know... it's my house."

The human looked at him through their blackened ski goggles and nodded. "Nice place you got here."

Ray couldn't take it any longer. He held it in as best as he could. "Do I know you?" he asked, straining his eyes as if it would help him see past the deep black scarf that covered their face. The being brought a hand to the tail end of the scarf and pulled at it, slowly unraveling it, letting it fall lightly to the floor. It was a young-looking face, a flawless face from the nose to the chin. The being then lifted the goggles from their eyes. It took him a moment to recognize the hazel eyes with a hint of green. "Oh my God…" He said, trying his best to find the words that escaped him. "Clover… what are you doing here?"

Clover slowly discarded the numerous jackets she had stolen from Corazon before following him on his journey. "I knew exactly what was going to happen. They were going to lead you out into the middle of nowhere and give you instructions on how to get home. I was done with Corazon. I hate the way things are going there. I didn't know where to go. I thought that maybe if I followed you, you could lead me back to the *real* world. I thought you would lead me to safety. It wasn't long until I figured out you didn't know where you were going either." She removed her hat and tossed it to the side. "I decided to break off without letting you know, and I eventually came upon this cabin. I stayed here overnight, but… I just couldn't sleep knowing that I might have left you for dead. I went out and looked for you the next day and well… you know the rest. I had no idea this was your cabin. You were heading in the right direction the entire time, I was just… lucky, I guess."

Ray stroked at his beard and rubbed his hands, trying to bring feeling back to them. "Clover, you shouldn't have done that. You could—you could have died."

"And you *would have died*. You're lucky I came around when I did! You would have frozen to death, no more than a half-mile away from your safe haven too!"

"All right, all right. I'm sorry… thank you, Clover. But, but what about everyone else? What about Beatrix and Meadow and all of your friends back home? I mean, did you think about them?"

"Friends? I don't have any friends. Beatrix was the only one I actually gave a shit about, and even she was blinded by Elliot and all of his bullshit."

"Watch your mouth," Ray muttered.

"No fuck that!" she rebutted. "I've been through *a lot of shit* in the past month or so. You're not the only one that suffers, *okay, Ray?* I can swear as much as I damn well please. You wouldn't even be here if it weren't for me! I just saved your *fucking* life! So don't slink around acting like you're some *high and mighty* adult who thinks he actually has the authority to tell me what I can fucking say and not say! Get that through your *fucking head,* man!"

Ray paused, finding himself once again at a loss of words. "Okay, then," he said calmly.

"Okay?" she asked, seeming surprised.

"Yeah, you're right. You're growing up, you can say whatever you want. I'm sorry."

She smiled, seeming rather proud of herself.

"All right now, potty mouth, help me get to my *fucking* feet," he said with a smile.

She grasped his hands and tried to pull him up, yet as soon as all his weight was on his feet, it felt as if he were standing upon a floor of needles, slowly pushing themselves into his defrosting feet. He quickly sank back to his sitting position. He huffed and winced as he grabbed at his feet, feeling the red veins that seemed to pulsate at the touch.

After a while of sitting in the dark rubbing his feet, the circulation began to slowly return, filing his feet with semi-warm blood and bringing life back into the tips of his toes. Eventually, the swelling began to settle down. He kept the blanket slung over his shoulders and approached the wood stove he had to the side of his television. There were still dry, dusty chunks of lumber he had yet to use, just sitting there, waiting for him. Clover began to search his cabinets for useful supplies.

She inserted the wood into the stove and then searched for some old newspaper to act as kindling. Eventually, she found some spare paper in a basket of remnants from Ray's past. Articles that had headlines like "CROOKED MICROBIOLOGIST POISONS ENTIRE COUNTY" and "COUNTY WATER INSPECTOR; MICROBIOLOGIST OR MURDERER?" He examined the articles for a while, slingshotting him right back into his past. It had been so long since he'd actually *read* in general. Each article outlined the numerous crimes he had committed in terms of conspiracy, covering up his tracks, and inadvertently fatally poisoning fifty-six individuals, including women and teens. The articles brought a tear to his eye, but before he could conjure up the rest of his emotion he had kept locked up for so long, he had Clover, who remained very quiet, stuff the dry articles in between the logs of wood piled up in his woodstove. The paper quickly caught fire and began to heat the cabin, filling both his cabin and body with the warmth of light and life.

"What are they?" Clover asked as she wedged the paper between the logs.

"I'll tell you if you tell me the story behind that… pretty bracelet you got there."

Clover lifted her wrist up and jingled the green and blue beaded bracelet around on her arm. "Made one for Beatrix and me. She has the exact same bracelet, exact same color. It's, I don't know. It's our little thing. It makes us a part of the club."

"Can I be a part of this club?" he asked.

"Nope!" she said with delight. "There's only room for two. But seriously, what are these things? Books?"

He looked at her with some sort of pity, "They're newspapers. They tell people what's going on in the world. People write things and print them onto thousands of them and give them away to people who want to know what is happening."

"Okay," she said, expecting more.

"That's pretty much it…"

"What do they all say?" she asked.

Ray wanted to respond but didn't know what to say. All this time and he had never even thought about the education the children of Corazon received. "You don't know how to read," he gasped, wondering why he hadn't come to this conclusion sooner.

"Nobody ever taught me," she said. Ray took a deep breath in and sat back. "So are you going to tell me what they say?"

Ray shook his head as he gazed into the firelight. "They talk about a bad man making a big mistake."

"Like a fairytale!" she exclaimed, sounding proud that she drew her own conclusion.

"Not quite," he said with a slight smirk. He quickly saw the enthusiasm fade from her face. "But yeah…" He said, trying to correct himself. "It all sorta works like a fairytale."

The next few days were somewhat of a dreary existence. It consisted of Ray sleeping and eating while staying curled up next to the fire in his heavy blanket while Clover scurried about the cabin, cleaning and snacking on whatever food she could find. Ray wore the blanket like a second skin, letting the cotton fibers cling to his body like a web. He would occasionally rise to get food as well. The cabinets in his kitchen were cheaply made of warped wood, and pests had consumed most if not all of the open bags of food he had so foolishly left behind. He luckily always kept dehydrated prepared meals piled high by his sink. They were all prepared and ready to go in off-brown airtight bags, they didn't taste too divine, but that hardly mattered anymore. He tore through the heavy plastic outside and snacked on whatever he could find, usually a dehydrated meat sample with a side of crackers and a vitamin. His favorite part came with the hard candy that each package was mandated to have. It reminded him not so much of a simpler but easier time.

Slowly, the feeling returned to his body, one appendage at a time. With Clover's assistance, he was able to walk somewhat normally and could now move every single one of his fingers. He was capable of making a fist with his hand and wiggling the base of every finger. It was the fine motor skills that suffered the most and would surely come back in good time. Whenever Clover was looking for someone to play with, which was very rarely, she would toss a crumpled-up ball of paper to him. He tried catching it but wasn't too successful the first few times. After a while, the tiny paper ball was bouncing back and forth between the two of them.

39

"Dinner is served!" Orwell shouted as he waddled over to the main dining table, where he would serve the rest of the community. He carried a heavy bowl of Maple's stew in his arms, the stew sloshed from left to right, spilling onto the ground with every step. "Come get it, people!"

Community members, rebels and believers alike, quickly assembled to form a line in front of Orwell, who dished out the portions of Maple's stew. Those with a purple tag on their sleeve got a hefty helping, while the rebel group got half of what they were promised. They didn't dare say anything, though, as a lot of them were slowly beginning to come around to feeling as though they had been tricked by both Ray and Musgo. All of the rebels continued to attend Luna's meetings, where she spewed hatred toward Ray and his corrupt ways. The rebels began to quickly lose their fire, believing her more and more with every gathering. After the gatherings, Luna would always meet with Constantine to ensure that Beatrix had not been harmed whatsoever. Some nights he was reassuring, promising that as long as she held up her end of the agreement, Beatrix would be fine. Some nights he would simply reply with a nasty black smile, wanting to see her suffer.

Felix and Orwell also began paying Luna regular visits, taking things from her each time they came. Sometimes it was makeup; sometimes it was a blanket; sometimes they would just touch her, making her feel uncomfortable and vulnerable, knowing full well she wouldn't dare fight back.

Maple just worked relentlessly, slaving away over the fire. She was the best cook Corazon had, and they were going to work her until she collapsed, which she sometimes did. The believers were given special privileges. They were allowed to have weapons on them at all times, allowing them to dictate what the rebels could and couldn't do. It grew to the point where the rebels were never alone, always having an eye on them. There was always a believer in their hut, always a believer at their table, always a believer in their bed if they were a woman, even if they hadn't requested the company.

❊❊❊

While everyone slurped up the remnants of Maple's stew down below, things were beginning to change up above. The mountain had surely seen better days, but order was still ever-present.

Dante, who was still in recovery from his numerous stab wounds, removed a rather large bird from the oven.

"Gentlemen!" he proclaimed, looking around the table at the withered, hairy faces of the older men sitting around him. "And ladies…" he said with a smile nodding his head toward Beatrix, who wore a dress and sat silently at the end of the table. She quietly played with a red ribbon dangling from her hair. Dante set the bird down and began to cut away at the meat. Once the bird was properly carved, he nodded toward them all, "Please, help yourself."

Tobias sat off to the side and watched as all of the men tore away like savages at the meat in front of them. They also eyed Beatrix in all of her youth. They looked at her like starving, greedy cannibals ready to attack. Tobias kept a watchful eye on Dante, knowing that he was far and away the most ruthless, lacking the most morals of the bunch.

"Beatrix…" said one of the men in purple as he wiped away grease from his lower lip. "Why aren't you eating, child? We need some meat on your bones! We need to fatten you up for next winter!" The other men laughed obnoxiously, but this made Beatrix want to huddle up deeper into her metaphorical shell.

"I'm not all that hungry," she replied politely.

"Not all that hungry!" one of the men shouted, slamming his hands down on the table. This abrupt action made the Disciples laugh some more. They were all clearly intoxicated.

"Aye, leave her alone," Tobias muttered from the corner. "Can't you see she's scared?"

The Disciples all turned and looked at Tobias with hatred in their eyes. Dante was the first to speak up. "And what are you gonna do about it? Why don't you go… pray to Mother for answers! That's what you came up here for, right?" They all began to laugh at him. "Sixteen Disciples! Did you actually take that to heart? You little mangy fuck up!" The laughter continued. Tobias slowly curled up his fists and closed his eyes. Trying his best to absorb the judgment. His cast had been removed, and he found it hard to fully grip his fist, but he continued to try over and over again.

Tobias stood up, allowing his natural fight-or-flight mechanism to take over. He looked at Beatrix and jerked his eyes toward the other room. Beatrix quickly excused herself from the table and accompanied him in walking somewhere private.

"Aww, come on, Tobias! At least let the girl have a proper meal! You can't abuse her like that!" Dante yelled in between, chewing his meat.

Tobias ignored him and pulled Beatrix into a room off to the side. The room was painted a light violet and had a beaten-up green futon in it. In front of the futon lay a small green rug and a television mounted on the wall.

"Hello, Beatrix," he sighed as he sank down to one knee and placed both of his hands on her shoulders. "How are you feeling?"

She rubbed her eyes and yawned. "Ray told me I'm not supposed to talk to you."

This seemed to hurt Tobias greatly. He paused and looked toward the ground. "Ray had his reasons for saying that at the time. But—Bea, I want you to stay away from those men, okay? If you need anything, you can come to me. Can you do that?"

"What do you mean? They're Disciples! They're the best men Mother has to offer!"

"No! Listen to me. You stay away from them, do you understand?" he said, gripping her shoulders harder.

"But Dante said he would even give me a place to sleep, he said I could use the prayer corner in his room and that he'll start giving me daily communion! That means I can be considered a woman in the community, Tobias!"

Tobias nearly fell backward. "Do not take anything from that man. Stop taking the communion too. You're not ready, not yet. You stay far away from him. You need to sleep here, all right? Right here in this room, I'll keep an eye on you. And look! You can watch TV too! You like TV?"

Her eyes shot open, telling Tobias all he needed to know. "I've never really watched TV before. I've never even seen one, really..."

Tobias smiled. "Perfect, that's perfect, have a seat, I'll get it set up for you."

Beatrix hopped onto the couch and glared at the flat black void that was so perfectly positioned on the wall. Tobias began to fiddle with the buttons on the side. "You know, I used to watch TV *all* the time."

"Really?" Beatrix said, amazed.

"Oh yeah. It was one of my favorite things to do. But just remember…" The television flicked on, and Beatrix was immediately submerged in a cartoon world where animals could talk and drive cars. Pure laughter followed almost instantly.

Tobias chucked at the sound of her laughing. She was so mesmerized; she soaked up every single detail of the television, seeing every color, every tiny pixel. He sighed and scratched his head. "Just remember that too much ain't good for ya," he said with a smile. She completely ignored him, of course.

Tobias looked up to see a figure looming in the doorway. Elliot gazed at them from the hallway, a pleasant smirk positioned promptly under his nose. He gave Tobias a kind smile and held out a hand, summoning him.

Tobias reluctantly left Beatrix for a moment and accompanied Elliot to another room. Elliot was dressed in loose white garb. He looked more tired than usual as well. "I apologize for disturbing you, I um—well—"

Tobias took Elliot's hand in his own. "What is it, my Prophet?"

Elliot looked toward the room where the blue light of the television flickered against the violet walls. "Remind me of your name again?"

"Tobias," he said with a hefty nod. "How can I help you, Prophet?"

Elliot's eyes remained glued to the room where Beatrix sat. "Why is there a girl in my house?" he asked, sounding concerned.

Tobias looked toward the dining room, not knowing how to answer the Prophet's question without stepping over an unspoken boundary. "Felix wants her to stay here for the time being."

Elliot nodded as if that all made perfect sense. "Yes, yes, of course. And—what is her name?" he asked, an almost childlike curiosity in his voice.

Tobias smiles, "Her name is Beatrix."

Elliot nodded, "Yes, of course. Beatrix, I remember."

Tobias looked into Elliot's clouded eyes. His eyes carried with them a certain mysterious hue, a look that spoke to him, a look that said he could see what was happening; he could see the before, the after, and the forever more. It was a feeling beyond wisdom, beyond clairvoyance. It was both the look of a Prophet and the look of someone in need of help. But the look saw him, and to him, that meant everything. It was now clear to him that there was no malintent within Elliot's mind, just the clouding of old age and the regret of losing control of the community he founded. "Would you like to speak to her, Prophet?"

Elliot quickly nodded, "Oh yes, that would be lovely."

Tobias took Elliot by the hand and guided him into the violet room, where Beatrix, too captivated by the cartoons, failed to notice the significance of the moment. "Beatrix?" Tobias said, disrupting her cartoon fix. "This is our Prophet, Elliot. He would like to sit with you for a bit, is that all right?"

Beatrix looked Elliot up and down with awe. That awe slowly faded to that of normalcy, to something more reminiscent of disappointment. The so-called "Prophet" that had been held to angelic standards her entire life was now presented to her as a normal, if not slightly less than normal, man.

Elliot, on the other hand, seemed more excited to be in the presence of such youth as she did to be in the presence of such royalty. "Hello, Beatrix," he said softly. "Would you mind if I sit with you?"

Beatrix looked to Tobias, who tried to remain neutral. She then looked back to Elliot and nodded. Elliot shuffled over to her and took a seat next to her. Everything he did seemed to be gentle and well thought-out. Beatrix looked at him, and he looked at her. "It's nice to meet you?" Beatrix said, her words curling into something that sounded more like a question.

"Yes, oh, it is nice to meet you too, young lady," he replied, sounding exhausted. "What are you um… what are you watching here?"

Beatrix didn't know quite how to respond to the man. Tobias stepped in, "Beatrix was just starting to watch some cartoons; you can watch them with her if you'd like. If not, you can come with me, and we can find you something else to do."

Elliot nodded, "Cartoons, yes. Cartoons it is," he said with a chuckle.

Tobias remained fixed on Elliot, the eccentric, fast-talking, quick-witted man who had convinced an entire community to follow him into uncertainty was now reduced to the confused, aging mind he saw before him. Nevertheless, he was captivated by her youth and seemed to relish in the little time he had to watch cartoons with her.

Tobias now leaned on the doorframe and watched the two of them, reflecting on the odyssey the past year had become. He felt a light tap on the shoulder. He turned around to see a naked woman with red, curly hair looking him up and down. "You're new," she said, her tone slightly flirtatious. Tobias quickly moved her to the side so that Beatrix wouldn't notice.

"What are you thinking? There's a child in there!" he scolded her, trying his best not to stare.

"Mm-hmm," she said, rolling her eyes. "Age is just a number out here…" she paused, allowing him to speak his name.

"Tobias," he sighed.

The woman smiled, "Well, Tobias, you look a little stressed. What do you say we go find a room of our own and… I can show you a few things."

Tobias removed her hand from his arm, knowing that his duties lay with keeping an eye on Beatrix. "Sorry, I'm busy."

The woman didn't seem to listen. "You sure? You seem stressed, nervous. I can take care of that for you—"

He held up a hand out of frustration. "Look, lady, I said I'm busy so—"

She didn't expect his abrupt outburst. Her face was no longer that of a sexy, slender seductress but a vulnerable human trying to do her job. "I apologize for upsetting you. Can I get you anything?"

Tobias simmered down. "No need to be sorry, I'm just—what's your name?"

Some humility slowly returned to her face, "I'm June, I remember you. I was one of the Angels picked years ago."

He nodded. "I'm sorry, my memory isn't as good as it used to be," he said, trying to cover for the fact that he genuinely didn't recognize her.

She scoffed, "You're not the only one whose memory isn't as good as it used to be," she said, nodding toward the violet room.

Tobias's eyes narrowed, "How long have you been up here?" he asked, his voice growing quieter.

She shrugged, "Short enough to see the rise and fall of a Prophet, long enough to know not to talk about it…"

Tobias nodded his head. "Yeah…" he muttered half-heartedly. "It's a well-kept secret."

June leaned her head against the wall. "From what I remember, we were too busy surviving to notice the difference. By the time he really started to lose it, all the community needed was a friendly wave of admiration from the top of the cliff. It's amazing, really."

Tobias crossed his arms; he clearly didn't know how to react. "When did all of this start?"

June lowered her tone and stepped closer to Tobias. "About three years ago, he started calling people by the wrong name. He remembered Felix for whatever reason, so… just like that, he's the chosen one. Then it would be little things, forgetting to wash his hands, leaving the stove on, sleeping at odd hours of the day, shifting the topic at hand mid-conversation."

"That bad?" he asked, concerned.

June shook her head. "There is nothing left of the Prophet you once knew. Once the Disciples caught on to what was happening, they took hold of the reins. They realized that if they could keep Elliot out of Corazon, they could make the rules up, and—well, that's when Angels started getting hurt. It hasn't been the same since."

"You ever try running?" he asked, realizing he too was speaking with fear.

She turned so that her back was to the wall, her eyes fixated on the dining room where the Disciples licked their plates clean. "How'd that work for Aria?" she muttered. Tobias felt a surge of shame run from the top of his head to the soles of his feet. He choked back what he thought would be a whimper and said nothing. "There's nowhere to go. The community would never believe us, the Disciples would punish us, and hypothetically, if we did make it out—we're already rejects. There's no going back after the cleansing. Maybe this is what we deserve."

"I came after..." he said solemnly, as if he had missed both a triumphant victory and a speeding bullet.

She looked back at him, eyeing him up and down, trying to get a read on what his angle was. "One of the lucky few, aren't ya?" Tobias remained silent. He had gotten used to silence in the past few months, finding that often, the absence of words said even more. June just sighed and clasped her hands together, "I get it," she said, matching his mood.

"June!" A voice boomed from down the hallway. Felix's head poked out from one of the doorways. "Oh, I'm sorry, did I catch you at a bad time?" he asked, leaning further into the hallway to eye both of them.

June shook her head, "No, Felix, how can I help?"

Felix flashed a smile. "Oh, just a little project," he said as he walked toward the two of them. "Run along, I'll see you in my quarters in a minute," he said with a nod.

June took a moment and looked at her toes. She then inhaled an immense amount of strength and walked away, turning into the room where Felix had just left, the door shut behind her. Felix clasped his hands together and looked at Tobias with a ruddy complexion. "Tobias," he stated, shaking his head as if he were thoroughly amused. "How are you adjusting?"

His mouth opened and shut. It seemed as there were no appropriate responses to such a question. Felix chuckled, "Speechless, yes. Everyone is at first. There really aren't words to describe the reward for years of dedicated service to Mother, is there?"

Tobias tried to relax. "I suppose there aren't."

Leaned up against the wall where June had just been, his gaze still fixed on Tobias. "I realize your introduction to us may have been a little harsh. And I won't make any excuses, what happened happened, and now we move past that," he said, nodding. "But it's important that you know there is an order to things, even up here, on the mountain. We are wolves; they are sheep," he said, jerking his head toward the window where Corazon was barely visible. "Every wolf pack has the alpha, the leader, the one that makes the decisions," he said, swatting Tobias on the shoulder. "And as much as the alpha tries to control the pack, sometimes those rambunctious pups get out of hand."

Felix shrugged. "It's the nature of the wolf. The wolf pushes boundaries, the wolf takes what is his. The wolf sometimes steps out of line, but… the wolf still maintains order because it is a part of a pack."

Tobias was confused, not knowing whether he was expected to contribute to the conversation. "I'm not following you, Felix."

Felix sighed. "Don't fear the alpha, Tobias. If you stay in line, the alpha won't bother you. Fear the rambunctious pups. They're the ones you should be worried about."

Tobias clenched his jaw, weary of how Felix might react to his next words. "Why not sort out the good pups from the bad, then?"

Felix remained as still as stone. His eyes drifted toward the ceiling as he thought. "Well, that's the alpha's job, not yours. You can try to make it your job, you can… but just know that the alpha might see that as a threat, and if the alpha feels threatened? Then the pups are the least of your concern."

Tobias nodded, "Understood."

Felix smiled; his eyes narrowed. "Good. Now, if you'll excuse me…" his words lingered in the air as he turned around and strode back toward his room, shutting the door firmly behind him.

40

Ray sat atop the icy roof of his cabin, ever so delicately adjusting his satellite dish. If he angled it in the right direction, he was able to get a few fuzzy stations from stray signals. He had the volume on his television cranked all the way up so that he could hear whenever there might be a blip of hope. Clover stood inside and yelled at the top of her lungs, telling him to move it in whatever fashion got rid of the most static on the screen. A millimeter too far left or too far right, and the signal was gone. He scratched at his beard, which was beginning to grow quite long as he pondered the different ways he could go about it. With his luck, he'd be on the roof of the cabin for hours.

Luckily for him, Clover helped him guess the positioning within the first few minutes. He slid down the ladder and easily climbed down until the fourth from the last rung, which he decided to skip altogether. He let himself indoors and fed the woodstove a couple more logs. Clover had recovered an ax from the shed out back and decided to split some more wood to keep the cabin warm and to keep herself busy. Ray lay the heavy cloak Luna had left him with by the stove to dry. He had worn it more than his actual winter coat, which he had left back at his cabin when he started this short journey of his. Clover soon adopted the coat and took it up as her own, wearing the heavy, extremely oversized coat on top of her smaller light blue jacket. She fiddled with the television, trying to find one of the three news channels that Ray always used to tune into. He stood over her shoulder and glared at the screen intensely. To his dismay, all of the news channels had resorted to static black and white or a ringing blue screen that had a small banner telling the viewer that the station was no longer available.

He cursed his signal and settled with a spaghetti western that brought back fond memories from his childhood. "This…" he said, waving the DVD back and forth in his hand. "This is what you call a movie." He opened up the case and removed the small shiny disc.

Clover's face lit up. "Hey, that's what Luna used whenever she was getting sad!"

Ray had a quick flashback to the night he and Luna and danced together to the sweet sound of the CD player that made him feel alive again. He smiled, but it was only to cover up the pain he felt deep inside of him. "Yeah, sort of… but this has pictures on it, moving pictures." He looked at her and recognized the face she was making. It was the same face Beatrix would make when she was thoroughly confused about something Ray was trying to describe. "Just—you'll see. Have a seat."

He popped the disc into the DVD player and sat back on the couch. The television hummed with energy before the pictures sprang to life. Clover was blown away by the advertisements alone.

"Wow," she said, her jaw hanging open.

Ray just lay back and folded his arms behind his head. He thought about how it was nice being the smartest person in the room. He was now playing the role of God in Clover's eyes. She saw his abilities to make the television light up as other-worldly.

Clover was thoroughly amused and wasn't going anywhere. He observed her for a moment, watching her, taking in all of the wonders. He could see the hope and aspirations aimlessly floating around within her green eyes. She was so preoccupied it hadn't occurred to her to eat, and it wasn't until her stomach was growling where she decided to bring it up.

Ray approached the cupboards and removed himself a package containing "Beef and Chicken Fajita Roll-ups." He tore through the heavy brown plastic with his knife and moved the powdered chemicals to their assorted packages, letting them steam and fizzle until his gourmet meal was done cooking. He took a rusting fork from one of the drawers with a broken handle and began to mix and swirl the contents of his "Fajita Roll Up" within the package. He smelled his homemade concoction and quickly backed away. He had grown so used to the taste of fresh vegetables, bird, and venison that he forgot how awful the dehydrated meals really were.

Nevertheless, he put one forkful after another into his mouth and swallowed as fast as he possibly could. He picked up the packet and moved toward the television, though it wasn't the pixelated platform that caught his attention. Instead, he began to move closer to the stove, focusing on the blanket Luna had given him. The underside of the blanket, the side he kept pressed up to his skin, had some strange black markings on it. They seemed to have been etched out in coal and covered the area of the blanket. He curiously circled the blanket until he now had his back to the stove and was looking at it straight on.

His jaw dropped almost as quickly as the back containing the soupy remnants of his fajita hit the floor. He stared down at the blanket marked up with coal and finally understood the message Luna was trying to send him. Written on the underside of the blanket in thick, bold, black print were the words **BRING HELP**. How had she known he would have seen that? How did she know he would have even made it back alive? And how on earth was he going to bring help? The more he thought about it, the more it made sense. The Disciples surely inspected everything she had put into the bag, the one thing that seemed innocent enough was the blanket she had wrapped his unconscious body in before they even had a chance to inspect it.

"What's going on? What are you doing?!" Clover yelled, snapping out of her trance.

"The blanket. Luna, she sent a message! Look at the blanket!" he exclaimed excitedly.

"What?"

"Look at it! Come here and look at this!"

Clover hopped off of the sofa and ran to his side. She gazed at the smudgy black letters that covered the area of the fuzzy inside of the blanket. "What does it say?"

"It says to *bring help*. They expect me, they expect *us* to bring back help, Clover!"

Clover, who seemed far less enthusiastic, took longer to respond. "Please, I bet you they already forgot about me. They don't care that I'm missing, I doubt they think I'm going to go back for them!"

"Clover, listen, we have to. They are all depending on us," he said as if he were still trying to piece the puzzle together.

"No, they are all depending *on you*. And when all is said and done, you're going to be the one they thank. I did my part. I saved your life, and I never want to go back there again! I don't care how much they need me. They treated me like shit, like I was some sort of—sort of *diseased animal*. They don't deserve my help. If you want to risk your life by trying to make the trip back, there be my guest, but I'm staying right here."

He knelt down so he could look her in the eyes. "Think about Luna, I mean—"

"*Fuck Luna*! She never even liked me! Hell, you never gave a shit either until you were stuck between these four walls with me!" she spat.

"Clover, don't—"

"No, *admit it!*" she shouted. "Admit you don't really care about me! You just want to go back there and pretend like everything is all right by saving the day so that you can play house with Luna and Beatrix. I was just some freak you picked up along the way! Admit that you don't care about me, Ray! I know I was never part of the plan, I know I wasn't supposed to follow you—"

"But I'm sure as hell glad you did!" Ray said, grabbing her by the shoulders with force. "Listen, I never got to know you at Corazon, and I am *sorry*, okay? *I really am*. But that's in the past. We are talking about the here and now. These people *need us*, Clover. They need as much help as we can get. Yeah, you might have been an outcast but guess what? None of that matters anymore. What matters now is that people need help. *Innocent people*. And if you want to stay back and let them die, then so be it. But that's on your shoulders, and that makes you no better than the people who abandoned you."

Her bottom lip quivered as she looked at Ray through a shallow stare. "I don't owe anybody at that *fucking hellhole* anything… *nothing*."

"Even Beatrix?" Ray said, knowing that this final rhetorical question would pack more than just a punch. She stood her ground and remained silent. He walked away to his bedroom and slammed the door. It wasn't as if he could just prance back into civilization and request military assistance. He was pinned between a rock and a hard place, and there was no easy way out. His answers, unfortunately, were going to come a lot sooner than he had expected.

"You need to do something," Ray said to himself as he began to pack. He didn't know where he was going, but he knew he had to do something and fast. It was only a matter of time before things spun out of control in Corazon, and he had already wasted enough time by not getting her message soon enough. He found all of the ammunition he could possibly carry and packed it into the smallest backpack he could find. He wanted to remain light so that the journey wasn't as bad as last time. The snow was now melting as spring grew closer and closer, but that would make for a damper terrain giving him even more of a reason to pack light. He decided that it would be best to sleep on it, feeling that his next move would be crucial, and required some serious thought. Little did he know his next move was not entirely up to him.

Ray lay back on his bed for hours, hoping that some sort of clarity would naturally fall on him. As he lay there, somewhere between his dreams and reality, he caught a peculiar flash of light through the window, the light of what appeared to be a lantern. Within moments there were three of them, then four. Before he knew it, his cabin was surrounded by light that seeped in through the windows, stripping away any privacy provided to him by night.

"Clover?" he called out, his voice filled with worry.

There was no answer. He quickly grabbed his rifle and darted out into the living room, where he saw the shadow of Clover staring out from behind the blinds at the mysterious lights outside.

"*Clover!*" he demanded, signaling her to get away from the windows. She looked at him, and he quickly waved her to come toward him. She casually left the window and walked over to him. Ray pushed her behind him and looked all around, listening carefully for any other noises.

The lights slowly faded, then there was nothing. A pure silence, saturated in anxiety. Then there came the delicate crunch of feet as they covertly maneuvered themselves over the snow.

"*Come here,*" he whispered in her ear as he pulled her by the arm into his bedroom. He swung open the doors to his closet. "*Come on, in ya go!*" he whispered, trying to rush her as best he could. She hopped into the closet and looked back at him with fear in her eyes. "*You stay right here. And do not open this door at all. For anyone. I will come and get you. Just stay here, got it? Stay here,"* he said, grasping her firmly by the shoulders. She nodded, and he closed the doors on her.

He looked toward the door and pulled back the bolt handle on his rifle as slow as he could. There was a dull shimmer of a bullet in the chamber. He slowly eased the bolt handle back forward until he heard the discrete *click* telling him the rifle was now loaded.

He crouched, trying his best to stay light on his feet as he moved toward the living room. He stationed himself behind the couch and aimed the rifle toward the door. Aside from windows, there was one way in and one way out of this cabin. His intruder was going to have to go through him first.

His mind began to race as the silhouettes of what looked to be at least ten people surrounded his cabin. All of whom seemed to be armed, with long objects propped up against their shoulders. He immediately suspected the Disciples. Thinking it was Felix sending some rogue community members to murder him when he least expected it.

Then his thoughts took a far darker turn. His mind began to race, thinking of how perhaps his previous sins, before Luna, before the Disciples, before Corazon—that had now caught up with him. All of a sudden, the shadows weren't rogue squatters but armed government officials ready to take him to federal prison. How had they found him? He had been so careful to cover up his tracks. Either way, one thing was for sure, he was not going to be able to fight them.

All of a sudden, a flashlight beamed through his window, making contact with his face. It shone down his body and then made its way back up to his face, temporarily blinding him. He held up his rifle to the light, and it quickly vanished, leaving him temporarily blinded and flustered. Ray was breathing heavily. He didn't want to die, not like this.

"All right!" yelled a coarse voice from outside. "You need to put the rifle down, boss! We didn't know there were any cabins out this way. We just need to talk, is all!"

Ray tightened his grip on his weapon. He didn't recognize that voice. "Let's talk then! But you're not coming inside."

Faint laughter could be heard from outside once he said that. "Listen, we all know I've got you outgunned... I'm not a violent woman, but if you don't let us into your home, well... I'm just gonna have to insist."

Ray wiped the sweat away from his brow and tightened his grip on the stock. The woman was right; there was no way he could shoot his way out of this.

"Sometime tonight, my friend. My men are getting cold!" she shouted.

Ray panicked as he stood up and slowly moved toward the door. "How do I know you won't just kill me as soon as I open up?"

The woman laughed. "I coulda killed you whenever I wanted. I don't need you to open the door for that."

Ray looked all around him and noticed the shadows outside of his windows. Everyone had their sights on him. "Okay... okay! I'm—I'm unlatching the door."

"Gonna have to ask you to put your gun down, too," the woman said calmly.

He slowly lowered his gun and set it up against the wall. Once his gun was lowered, he unlatched the lock mechanism on his door and quickly backed away.

The door cracked open, just enough for the woman to slip her fingers in between and curl them around the edges of the door, pushing forward, letting herself into the cabin. She stood in the doorway and looked at Ray through the dark. "You got any lights in this here cabin? Or are you some sort of albino?" she chuckled.

Ray gestured toward the panel to the large woman's left. The woman slinked along the wall, still keeping a steady eye on Ray. Her hand reached the light panel and flicked the switches up, lighting up the dusty room. The woman looked at Ray and smiled in surprise. "Now that's a bright light!" She was tall and had broad shoulders that nearly filled the frame of the door. Her hair was cut short, and she held herself with an almost condescending confidence.

Ray stared at the giant woman who stood in his doorway. She was dressed head to toe in thick denim and what appeared to be various sweaters; holstered at her side was a black object. She unsnapped her holster and removed the object. Ray winced, fearing the worst. She looked at him and all of his fear and chuckled. "We're clear," she stated into the object. The room then buzzed with empty air static. She lowered the transceiver and clipped it back onto her belt. Soon the doorway was filled with shadow and the faint outline of curious faces.

"The name's Ruth," she said, stepping forward. "You must be Ray."

Ray kept his distance, the two of them separated by a couch and a small table. "How do you know my name?" he asked, not sure if the answer would bring him any peace.

She looked around the room and nodded her head in admiration. "Word travels a lot faster around the woods than one might think," she stated. "Is anyone else here with you?"

Ray shook his head, trying his best not to let his eyes flicker toward the closet in his room. Ruth nodded her head again. "Ray, we have a problem. This problem has been an issue for quite some time, and we have reason to believe you can help us with it," she said, leaning up against the windowsill. The bodies began to shift and whisper outside. Something was clearly happening.

It seemed as though the breeze had stopped; not even the frigid air could piece together the thick atmosphere around them. "What do you mean *we have a problem?*" he asked, desperately wanting the entire encounter to turn out to be a feverish nightmare.

"No!" commanded a voice from outside. "Enough of this." A familiar face pushed his way into the cabin and looked at Ray with danger in his eyes. "We're taking over Corazon, and you're going to help us," Benji stated, a desperately furious look on his face. "Welcome to The Former, friend."

41

Benji paced about the room like a psych ward patient, running his hands through his long sweaty hair as he shook the cold off of him. The shadows who lingered by the door slowly moved in closer, the light bringing their facial features into view. Benji signaled for them to come inside as he continued to pace. "You're an interesting one, aren't ya, friend?"

"Excuse me?" Ray asked, still trying to comprehend what was going on.

Benji wagged a finger at him. "I thought you were the law for a good while, I'll be honest."

Ray blinked a couple of times before reiterating himself. *"Excuse me?"*

"The law," Benji said, stressing each letter. "The feds, the heat, the FBI, CIA, TSA—*whatever*. I thought you were undercover," he stated, slightly amused by the idea of it now.

Ray still hadn't let down his guard. Each new body posed a new threat as they slowly shuffled into his cabin. "No, I'm pretty far from anything related to the law."

Benji shrugged, "Well, I know that now, don't I? As skeptical as I was, your story is starting to pan out," he said as he craned his neck, looking around the cabin.

Ray straightened his posture and eyed the rifle he had leaning up against the wall at the far end of the room. Ruth's enormous body lingered directly to its right, her eyes fixed on him. "I'm done playing any games, Benji. Why are you here?"

He smiled and spun in place. "Fair enough, friend. I'll try my best to keep it snappy." He smiled, though his brow remained stern. "My sister loves ya. She does. She did what she had to do to keep the peace, but… she loves ya, Ray. And I suppose that requires me to care for you a bit, too. You know, look out for you and such."

"This," Ray replied, nodding toward the small troop of ragged individuals standing just inside his door. "This is not looking out for me. This is pressure, this is you looking for something."

Benji shrugged again, "All this time, I thought you never even knew me. Suppose I was wrong."

"Benji gets to the fucking point," Ray snapped, sick of the word games.

Benji's smile faded, and he made his way over to the wooden chair Clover had been using up until Ray shoved her into his closet. There was now a heavier tone as Benji let his head hang for a moment. "Corazon has to end. What they're doing to their people is… it's wrong on every level."

Ray forced a nod to show Benji that he was listening.

"You saw what they did to Aria. She wasn't the first, and you know she won't be the last. And what happened with Otto, with Musgo? They were two of the purest souls I ever had the chance of meeting." Benji stopped and held a hand to his mouth as if to muffle a whimper. He set his hand aside and looked up, a hint of anger in his deepening scowl. "They held a gun to my sister's head. They take what they want when they want it, and they profit off of the followers' belief in Mother. Corazon is no longer what it used to be, and something needs to change."

Ray nodded again. This time it was more genuine. "You saw what happened. Luna almost got killed. Change isn't going to happen in an instant. Your best bet would be to go in there and walk away with whoever is as disgusted as you."

Benji sighed. "Once upon a time, it might have been that easy. A few years back, they might have just sent the non-believers into exile and labeled them as Former. But now they know that the Former are alive and well, thanks to Samuel. He couldn't stay away. He got so fixated on getting his daughter out that he mucked it up for everyone else."

"His daughter?" Ray asked, surprised.

Benji nodded, "I figured the gossip would have gotten to you after a while. Beatrix, that's who he was after. The genius tried to snatch her up right out of the hut you were sleeping in. He wanted to get her out of there before she was old enough for the Disciples to—well, I don't need to explain it to you. You know what they do."

"You killed Samuel," Ray stated. The other Former standing in the room either shifted their attention to the floor or set their eyes on Benji.

"It was a mercy kill, friend. He knew the risk. He'd rather die by my hand than theirs."

Ray shook his head, "You do whatever you're looking to do, but count me out. I'm going for Luna and Beatrix. I'm going at night, and I'm walking out of Corazon without causing a stir."

Benji chuckled. "Not an option. Everyone is walking on fucking eggshells right now, afraid of what might happen if they speak their mind. Corazon is no longer a community. It's two groups—right, and wrong. And the right currently has a foot on the wrongs' neck. It's a prison camp," he said, gripping his throat.

Ray took a deep breath in, fully expecting that to be the case. "Then I'll be extra quiet."

Benji stepped forward; his voice seemed more desperate. "You're not hearing what I'm saying. You won't be leaving with the two of them. You won't be leaving at all. These people—these followers or believers or whatever you want to call them... they're so deeply seeded in belief that they'd kill their own child if it gets them Mother's blessing. They won't hesitate when it comes to proving themselves, it's been done before, and it'll be done again."

"What do you mean it's been done before?" Ray asked, intrigued by Benji's desperation.

Benji nodded toward the couch. "You should have a seat," he looked back at the troop of people standing behind him. "Warm yourselves up, get comfortable, we're staying the night."

"*Yeah, please, make yourself at home,*" Ray sarcastically hissed.

"Please..." Benji pleaded, "have a seat."

Ray obliged him and carefully sat on the sofa, a coffee table still separating the two of them. Benji sighed, "How much do you know about the cleansing?"

Ray shrugged, "Rite of passage, right? Luna told me everyone had to do it before they came to Corazon."

"Yes," Benji stated, "but do you know what it entails?"

"No," Ray said quietly.

Benji adjusted the cushion he sat on and leaned in. "Elliot is capable of extraordinary things. The control he has over his followers is... unmatched. There's this look he gives you, I can't quite describe it, but when you see that look for the first time... you know there's something special happening. Everyone can tell you where they were the first time they saw the look. It touches something inside of them. It gives them clarity, it—well, it's special, and you'll know it when you see it," he said, nodding his head. Before we all up and left for Corazon, he was garnering quite a bit of attention. The feds don't take well to secret meetings, mass gatherings, and preachers yelling about sin on park benches. The following was getting too big, and he needed a way to weed out the true believers from those who were just playing along," Benji said, rubbing his hands together. Ray was already completely captivated.

"Elliot's whole idea was about not only ridding yourself of sin and worshiping the Earth and love Mother bestowed upon her children, but also pushing that idealism on others. It was aggressive, his followers were known to harass people who they felt were living in sin. It didn't help his case with the feds. Rumor had it they were setting up a sting. They were gonna take him in on inciting violence or something. I guess Willow had gotten into it with some civilian and—well, it doesn't matter. The point is, they knew the power Elliot had was dangerous, and Elliot knew his time as a free man was limited. He was angry at the world. He tried to foster this utopian community where love was abundant, and his followers only lived off of what they needed. It sounds perfect on paper, but apparently, the community around us didn't think so. So that's when he decided to initiate the cleansing."

Benji leaned back. "Elliot and Felix made this plan. They'd buy a plot of land, they'd truck up any necessary resources for building a small community, and he'd sort out who was destined to live their life away from the old world with an initiation. The cleansing. In order to cleanse yourself of your sin, you had to find another sinner, someone worse than you, and rid the world of their sin. And because people were hesitant to pledge their allegiance to a self-proclaimed Prophet in the park, the only way to do that was to kill them."

Ray choked on his own saliva as he sat up straight. "I'm sorry, what—"

"I said 'kill,'" Benji stated plainly. "Elliot ordered his followers to go out into the world, find a sinner, and kill them. He said it was your way of proving yourself to him, that it would separate the believers from the nonbelievers. It didn't matter who, it didn't matter how, but you had to take a life. Anyone who lived in Corazon, any of the first group—they're all killers."

Ray thought of what he could possibly say in response to such a claim. "What about Luna, Maple, and Mus—"

"Everyone, friend," he said, still as stone. "Every single one of them took the life of a stranger. And after that, they were wanted. Elliot had an iron grip on all of them, he knew they were his forever, he knew they would never return to a world where they were murderers. Then, with the grace of Mother in his sails, he took all of us, and he vanished."

"What do you mean?" Ray asked, a cold sweat breaking out on his forehead.

Benji snapped his finger in the air. "What I mean is… when I say there's something special about that man, I mean it. He took over 200 people who murdered in his name and left with them before anyone knew any better. The bodies were eventually discovered, the hunt for *The Getaway People* ensued, and nobody was ever found. Do you know why?"

Ray decided to play along. "Why?"

"Because as much as I hate what Corazon has become, as much as I despise how the rules have been twisted and altered, as much as I wish things would have just stayed the way they were—sitting around a crazy preacher on a park bench… I believe Elliot is the one true Prophet of Mother. The things that man has done and continues to do are otherworldly, and I'm not alone in that belief." Benji sat back and rested as if he had just finished an exhausting sermon. He took one more breath in and spoke again. "So when I say you won't be walking out of Corazon without a fight, I mean that. People can live with love while still being friends with death."

"I don't believe you," Ray said. "Not Luna. She wouldn't hurt—"

"I saw it with my own eyes, friend. My own sister, wielding a knife like someone who had never held a weapon before," Benji stated, his eyes beginning to well up. "And all of us? Everyone here in this room right now? We're no exception. We fell to the same story."

Ray tried his best not to show the fear he felt as he looked around at the various individuals sitting around his cabin, leaning on his walls, rummaging through his cabinets. All of them relatively unfazed at the fact Benji has just outed them all as murderers. He couldn't yet tell whether Benji was threatening him, asking him for help, or something in between the two. "So why go back at all? Why not leave well enough alone?"

Benji leaned in, his eyes still misty. "Because there's still hope, friend. Because Otto, Aria, and Musgo had to have died for something. Because people like Luna, Beatrix, Maple, and many others *still have a chance at redemption*. They can still live a life of love without the corruption that Corazon has succumbed to. We just need to rid Corazon of its corruption."

Ray threw his hands in the air. "Great! What a great idea! Why didn't I think of that?"

Benji was clearly insulted by his outburst. "I don't appreciate your sarcasm."

"Well, what the fuck were you expecting, Benji? Huh? You drop all this information about murder and redemption, and your plan is to just—just rid Corazon of corruption? Stellar, really, that sounds like the perfect plan."

"Enough, Ray," Benji said, growing irritated.

"Then tell me exactly how you plan on de-corrupting an entire community? Please, I have to know," Ray said, his temper reaching its bubbling point.

"Because!" Benji shouted. "Because the corruption is killed with the corrupted," he said calmly. "Corazon has many corrupted followers. They'd be the ones who sided with the Disciples while standing over Otto's body. They'd be the ones who now wear a purple ribbon on their arm like a badge of honor. They'd be the ones that allow the Angels to be taken, beaten, and raped. They'd be the ones that have to be killed. Once they're gone, the corruption will be too, and Corazon can thrive as the community it once was, again."

"So this is what this is all about?" Ray asked, gesturing toward the others who sat around his cabin. "This is your army? Your freedom fighters?"

Benji smirked. "We were able to surround your cabin and take it over within minutes. You only saw us because we wanted you to see us. We tracked both you and Clover here."

Ray's eyes darted toward his room. "It's okay," Benji said, holding a hand up. "We don't care about her. My point is, we were able to do all of this *without guns*. Just imagine what we could do if such a luxury were available."

"You want my rifle?" Ray asked, confused.

Benji shook his head. "Your rifle is your own. And one long gun is of no use to us. We need more, we need to get into the hunting chest. That'll give us as many guns and ammo as we'd need to do what we have to do."

"Do what you have to do?" Ray questioned.

Benji nodded. "We both know I don't have to explain things to you."

"You're talking about killing everyone," Ray stated.

Benji seemed very at ease now. "I'm talking about killing murderers. Murderers who will murder again to protect a system they're too brainwashed to realize is corrupt."

"No," Ray stated, shaking his head. "I don't want any part of this. Even if I did, Sterling guards the chest like a hawk."

"We'd take care of Sterling," Ruth chuckled from back on the wall.

Ray began to speak to both of them. "Even if you did, the chest has a code. You won't be able to get in without it. Especially after what just happened."

"That's where you come in, friend," Benji said with a smile. "You and I both know Sterling gave Luna the code to the hunting chest. She won't give it to me. Believe me, I've tried, but you? Her secret vice? Her little passion project? I bet you could get it out of her."

"This is crazy," Ray said, standing up. "I'm sorry, but I can't help you. You and your troops need to leave."

Benji clapped his hands together as he, too, got to his feet. "Troops! That's a good one. You hear that, gang?" he chuckled, glancing back at the group of misfits behind him. "That won't be happening, Ray," Benji said, seeming almost apologetic.

"Benji, don't be a—"

Benji crossed his arms. "This isn't the first time we've visited your cabin, friend. We've known about it for months now. I put out a search party to find it as soon as I heard your story," he tapped the transceiver that was clipped to his belt. "They found the articles. Looks like you're quite the fugitive yourself."

Ray's shame kept him silent. Benji knew he had him dead to rights. "There's no going back for you. But you can still have a somewhat honorable life with people that will take you in, care for you, and treat you as one of them. But that's not happening unless you help us. If we found this cabin, they can too. I'm sorry to say this, but you're backed up against a wall. You're *going* to get that code for us if you ever want to feel human connection again. And if you refuse, I'll have no choice but to gut you myself, friend." His words stung and carried with them a certain punch. Benji wasn't one to bluff, and the killing of Samuel was a testament to that.

It was now evident that his ask was more a threat than a favor. Ray tried to hold himself together. "When are you planning to—do all this?"

Benji began to pace again. "We need to be smart about it. We need to find a way to pick out the good from the bad, and we need to keep Elliot alive."

"Why's that?" Ray asked.

Benji placed his hands on his hips. "We're talking about the holy land. Sacred grounds. It's only sacred as long as a Prophet stands. The Book of Elliot says that a new Prophet is appointed at the time of the current Prophet's passing. But if he dies, there's no telling who that will be if they manage to avoid us—well, then Corazon is all just dirt and leaves. Word around the pines is that Felix has geared up to take the throne. We need to make sure that doesn't happen. We need Elliot alive."

"Wait—what? You're telling me you still buy into all that stuff?" Ray asked.

Benji nodded, "You don't need faith to feel the presence of Elliot. Just because his practices have been corrupted doesn't mean Mother is nothing more than a fable. I believe, and you should too. You don't want to meddle with power like that, friend."

Ray was silent, shocked at the fact that Corazon's number one opposition still held on to the belief that Elliot was a prophet, that the man who started the entire nightmare was the one that could bring it back to a dream.

Benji allowed Ray to revel in his astonishment. He continued hashing out a plan. "I could send out a few scouts tomorrow morning, assuming everything goes as planned, we could take Corazon in a day or two."

Ray's eyes widened. "That seems rushed," he replied, still shook to his core.

Benji held out two arms. "We're the Former. We've spent years in the shadows, carefully working toward this day. Believe me, this is anything but rushed."

Ray felt light-headed, still reeling from the revelation that Luna killed in the name of Elliot. He wiped the cold sweat from his forehead. "Look, I've got to get some sleep. Send out your scouts, do whatever it is you're going to do, let's just talk more about this tomorrow."

Benji crossed his arms again and sighed. "Time is wasting, friend. We need to do this as soon as possible. I can give you a day or two, but what needs to be done needs to happen soon."

Ray shook his head. "Fine, give me a day or two, but this…" he said, signaling to the others in the room. "Can't happen. You know where I am, you know how to find me, so respect my home for what it is."

Benji bore an overdramatized frown. "I suppose that's fair. But you'll understand if I leave Ruth to oversee things. Not that we need her. If you run, we'll just track ya, not all that hard in the snow," he chuckled.

Ray glanced at Ruth, whose massive body was still leaning up against the wall. Her playful short hair in direct juxtaposition to her overall foreboding demeanor. "I'll keep an eye on him," she said with confidence.

"Whatever gets everyone out of my home faster," he said, giving up all negotiations.

Benji nodded his head, "Of course, friend. Welcome aboard," he said with a wink. Benji then turned to the other individuals and whistled. "You heard him, everyone up. Beeline for camp, we're staying there tonight. Regroup tomorrow morning at sunrise," he ordered. Everyone was up on their feet again, strapping on various backpacks and heavy jackets.

They all began to march out the door from which they came, quickly disappearing into the dark. Benji stopped before crossing the threshold. He turned to Ray and held out a transceiver. "You'll be needing this, friend." Ray was hesitant to take it. Benji held it forward a bit more. "When the time is right, you'll press the big button and tell us the code. We can take care of the rest. I'll be by sometime tomorrow to fill you in on the rest of the plan, but familiarize yourself with this. It's your ticket back." Benji flashed a smile and pushed the transceiver into Ray's hands. "Give Clover my best," he muttered, shutting the door between them.

Ray took a moment to breathe, not realizing how claustrophobic Benji had made the atmosphere. He looked over to Ruth, who was remarkably silent given her stature. "I'm off," he said, nodding in her general direction but purposefully avoiding eye contact.

"Sleep tight," she said, repositioning herself on the wall and closing her eyes.

Ray slipped into his room and quietly shut the door. Even though it was no longer a secret, he hesitantly opened his closet, careful not to make any additional noise.

Clover sat at the bottom, a flannel shirt draped over her head. Ray lifted the shirt off of her frizzy hair. She was petrified, scared both of what she heard and what might happen to her when the speaking stopped. Her youthful hands shook, her eyes fluttered, her skin was hot and clammy.

"Are you all right?" he whispered.

She slowly grasped his hand in her own. "They're gonna kill everyone, aren't they?" she asked.

Ray squeezed her hand tight. "Clover..." he said, trying to figure out his next move as if he were playing chess. "Not if we can do something about it, but we need to go." There was a rustling coming from the other side of his door—the sound of what he could only imagine was Ruth adjusting herself for a good night's sleep. "Do you know where the gas is?" he asked her.

Clover nodded. "It's by the firewood, right?"

He nodded. "Yes, all right, listen. We are leaving tomorrow morning, and you're going to help make a distraction, all right?"

She nodded, very wary of the coming obstacles. He could see the panic in her face. "Hey," he said, snapping her out of her trance. "We're gonna get Bea out of there. You and me, all right?"

She took a deep breath and tried her best to relax. "All right."

42

Back in Corazon, things slowly began to get back to the way they were. There was still a dramatic power rift between the self-proclaimed believers and those who harbored doubts, but the believers were not constantly pushing their presence and dominance upon them anymore. Things slowly but surely returned to normal, and everyone began to dissipate into the black and white followers they once were. Luna stopped giving daily lectures about the dangers of doubt. The Disciples stopped taking her things, though Orwell made it a point to make his presence known. Other community members witnessed a lot of it but decided not to intervene, seeing it as some sort of righteous punishment.

Luna remained quiet and allowed herself to be thrown around like a rag doll for the safety of Beatrix. She missed her so much, and Beatrix missed her as well, but there was literally a mountain between them, and Felix's instructions were clear. Stay away, or bad things will happen. Luna didn't even think for a moment that Tobias would be protecting her. She, after all, had no idea where he had gone. She had seen him the night before Otto and Aria's body were recovered, but nothing past that. Truth be told, she slowly began to forget about Tobias. There were much more pressing matters at hand.

Night after night, Maple would prepare meals for the community. Everyone had to eat from the same cauldron or carcass so that she wasn't able to tamper with it at all. She would often grow lonely, especially as the snow began to melt and cause the ceiling of her hut to leak. Those were the nights where Musgo would have fashioned some sort of adhesive from mud and sticks as a quick fix to the distracting leak. It was the little things that hung on her, the things she took for granted, the leaks that could not be mended. Her hut was positioned under a grouping of trees and was often subject to a lot of damage when high winds tore the branches from the trunks and sent them cascading onto her roof. The runoff water would then leak in through the cracks and crevices.

During the late cold nights, she would curl up in tight little balls and rock herself to sleep. The caretaker had now become the one in need of care. She knew that with her aging body, she wouldn't last much longer under the semi-extreme conditions of Corazon during winters such as the one that had just passed. More than anything, she wanted to hold her beloved Musgo in her arms and squeeze him tight just one last time. She had lost most forms of human contact. Musgo was gone, and Luna barely saw her anymore with the way the Disciples treated her, constantly keeping her busy with menial, manual work. The dynamic of Corazon had drastically changed yet still claimed to be a community under the cloak of love. Everyone knew it, but nobody dared say the words; Corazon had lost its soul.

One night she decided to go out walking. The snow had been melting, creating soft, damp ground for her to tread upon. She slowly walked through the torch-lit common area. She looked around, taking in her surroundings while breathing deeply. She gazed up to the mountain where the faint sight of lights could be seen. She thought about Beatrix and what sort of hell she was bound to endure up there. It saddened her, it infuriated her, it made her want to act, but as she stood in the middle of that common square, doing next to nothing. She knew that there must have been twelve sets of eyes on her, watching her every move and seeing it as suspicious.

"Maple, I must commend you for this excellent stew," Constantine said, trotting toward her from the shadows. She turned to face him and nodded.

"I'm glad you like it," she said as plainly as possible.

He kept walking toward her, slurping away at the bowl he held up to his lips. "Tell me your secrets! Come on, what sort of spices do you put in here? I mean—it's absolutely *incredible*," he proclaimed with so much enthusiasm some might have taken it as sarcastic.

She looked at him as if she had never seen him before. Where was all of this curiosity coming from? She knew just as well as he did that he didn't give a damn.

"Oh well, a little bit of this and a little bit of that," she said blandly, not wanting to engage the maniac in conversation.

"Ah, well, whatever it is you're doing, it's scrumptious," he then stopped and stared at her with a smile, expecting her to engage him.

She felt uncomfortable at the moment and decided to break the silence. "Constantine, I've been meaning to speak with you lately, but… but I haven't really found the time. Would you mind?" she asked, gesturing toward her hut.

"Of course, Maple, anything for you," he said, accompanying her back to her hut. He placed a steady hand on her back and guided her through the night. There was an uneasy presence in the air; the both of them could feel it. He peeled back the flap and allowed her to go in first. He then ducked under and stretched out his arms. "I must say Maple, you do keep this place quite tidy," he yawned, looking around at the pristine interior of Maple's hut. There were two beds and two desks draped with a white cloth with accompanying chairs. Upon one of the desks were a variety of different candles.

The candles surrounded a rag that Musgo always carried around with him. It was the signature red flag that was always hanging off of his belt. Upon the rag was his heavy multi-tool, which he also always carried with him. The pair of items acted as somewhat of a shrine to him, a symbol of what was right. On the other desk sat a wooden bowl full of dried berries.

Constantine ran his long slender fingers along the cloth and multi-tool surrounded by candles. "You know, I never wanted to hurt him… but I had to make an example. Whenever the sheep step out of line, it's the shepherd's job to whip them back into the herd. I'm sad to say Musgo was one curious sheep. Admirable, but curious." He noticed Maple's somber tone as she held her trembling hands behind her back and looked around her hut, attempting to see the place with fresh eyes in order to take in the details he currently saw. "I was acting through the power of Mother, I really hope you understand," he muttered, gracing her shoulder with his fingers.

She kept her back to him, "Yes… of course."

He looked at her with pity, knowing that she was most likely crying. "Maple, you can't blame yourself for what happened, you didn't know this was going to happen, so you should feel no guilt. He was in the wrong. He deserved what was coming to him."

She spun around quickly. He was expecting retaliation but received the contrary. She was dry-faced and wore a faint smile. "You're right. Can I get you anything while you're here? Some water? An after-stew snack, perhaps?"

He politely declined. "I'm all set. I do appreciate your hospitality, though."

She made her way over to the bowl of dried berries on the table. "Are you sure? If the stew was too salty, this would surely even things out. Mother, forgive me, but I always fail to deliver dessert to those who deserve it the most. I picked and dried them myself. Blackberries are always in season, you know."

Constantine eyed her with a hint of suspicion. He had tried to elicit some sort of emotion, yet here she was, more chipper than he had expected.

She held the bowl out toward him. He looked down at the berries and then up at her. He reflected on the pain he had caused her for a brief moment and saw the hope in her eyes. All she wanted to do was please him; it was a look he had seen so many times before. He gave her a quick, bright smile. "Well, I'm glad to see you're turning your views around." He took a couple of berries and tossed them into his mouth. "I gotta admit…" He said as he chewed. "I didn't quite know how you were going to react with the whole Musgo thing and all. But I'm glad to see you're doing better. We need that old-fashioned Maple spirit back in the community!"

"Well, I'll try my best," she said sweetly.

"Say, these berries are pretty good. I like how you dried them out; it keeps the flavor without making them too overbearing. You do have a gift, Maple. There is no denying that!" He casually tossed a quick handful into his mouth and chewed away.

"I can't say I don't miss him," she said, looking toward the small shrine she had made him. "But one day at a time. Things are going to get better soon."

"That's the spirit. We need to return to our loving way of life, and it all starts with people like you," he said as he swallowed the glob of berry and juice he had pulverized in his mouth.

She gave him a modest smile. "Please, where are my manners? Have a seat." She then walked to one of the desks, removed a chair, and pulled it toward the back center of the room between the two beds. Constantine sat down, looking pleased with the respect he was getting.

"Common courtesy is so important these days. I do appreciate it," he said, moving around, trying to get comfortable. He brought a hand down to his stomach, which seemed to be hurting him.

Maple pulled out a chair for herself. "So… enough about me. How are you feeling?"

Constantine now had a peculiar expression on his face; he looked rather disgruntled. "Goo-" he said, licking his lips obsessively.

"I'm sorry?" she replied, looking confused.

"Good," he said bluntly. Slowly raising a hand to his lips.

"All right, you look a bit pale, is all," she whispered as she leaned forward, her slight smile deepening.

His hand dropped from his quivering lips. He tried to make a fist but was unable to. He just looked at her like a scared child with his mouth slightly ajar.

"Constantine?" she asked, standing up and going to his side. "Constantine, what's wrong?"

His eyes drifted over so that he could look at her face. He made a breathy noise with his mouth, but no sound was resonating whatsoever.

"Speak to me, Constantine," she demanded as she grabbed his arms urgently.

He tried his hardest but was unable to say anything whatsoever; a jumbled concoction of airy syllables fell from his lips.

The look of confusion on Maple's face slowly transformed into a malicious look of pleasure. He realized quickly that he had fallen into a trap and tried to flee. His attempt resulted in him stomping his feet on the ground; he had been so preoccupied with the fuzziness in his lips that he hadn't even realized the numbness in his legs.

Maple disappeared behind him and returned with a chord, which she used to bind him to the chair, restricting his movement even further. "You can freak out if you want, it's useless at this point. You see, Constantine, what you just ate a few minutes ago were not blackberries. They were something I like to call *sickberries*. They have paralytic effects on those who eat them, I should know. Years ago, I had a run-in with them myself. I could barely move or talk all through the night, I probably would have died had Musgo not helped me through it. It was incredible what a single berry had done to me. I'm looking forward to seeing what a handful does to you."

He began to sweat profusely, blinking to keep the beads out of his eyes. Maple rubbed his shoulders before leaving to fetch the cloth and multi-tool she had acting as a shrine to Musgo. She unfolded the multi-tool, folding out a pair of pliers. Constantine panicked internally, knowing full well what was in store for him.

"You're right, you had to make an example out of him, didn't you? And I guess now it's my turn to make an example out of you... Before we begin, I just want you to know where this is all coming from." The look of pleasure evaporated, leaving one of anger and remorse. "Musgo was old, innocent, and he may have made his fair share of mistakes in the past, but haven't we all? He was harmless, and you clubbed him over the head, putting him down like some sort of diseased animal. He had no way of defending himself. You took the coward's way out."

Constantine wiggled the last of his fingers before they too were taken over by the infectious tingling feeling that was coursing through his body.

"So I'm going to do what has to be done. I bet you're *scared*... I bet you're wondering if anyone is going to *save you*. I bet you want nothing more but to scream and cry and *beg*. Musgo didn't get that chance, so *neither will you*. The only difference—as I understand it, he must have passed quickly. I'm afraid you won't have that luxury."

Maple picked up his stiff hand and rubbed it with the tips of her fingers. "I guess we can start here. You know, a little test. You ever wanted to know how high your threshold for pain is?"

She took the pliers and placed each prong on either side of his finger, right where the center knuckle was. She positioned the tool and then looked into his eyes. His pupils kept drifting back and forth from the pliers to her face as if he were begging her to stop. She placed her free hand on his arm for leverage and squeezed the pliers as hard as she could until she heard a *pop*. The sound of his knuckle being crunched under her sheer force. Constantine let out a measly whimpering sound as if he wanted to scream but couldn't. His jaw was thoroughly locked in place.

"Hmm," she said, repositioning the pliers. "Looks like it's pretty high." She placed the pliers on the knuckle of his middle finger and paused, looking him in the eyes right to take in every ounce of misery that spilled out of his eyes. She took a deep breath and looked back toward the pliers in her hand. "Let's try this again."

Outside of her hut, the crickets chirped. The people slept. The moon shed a silver glow over the land. Nobody heard a thing.

❊❊❊

Luna awoke that morning to the sound of robins chirping away near the ventilation hatch on her ceiling. It was a surprisingly peaceful sound that made her feel a certain ease that she hadn't felt in a very long time. She hadn't had a good sleep since Bea was taken from her. She couldn't keep her mind off of what might be happening up on the mountain. She also thought of Tobias and where he had ended up, if he was still alive or not. Not to mention Ray and whether or not he had even made it back to his cabin, wondering if he even received her SOS message. It was these kinds of thoughts that would keep her lying awake at night.

She slugged herself out of bed and looked at her prayer corner, where the bowl of water and prayer rug she had used for so long were now accumulating dirt. She wanted to ask Mother for answers, but she knew it was just feeding the endless system of evil she had helped create. On days where she wasn't forced to work, she would just sit around her hut and stare at a fire, she wasn't eating nearly as much as she should have been, and her all-around health was slowly deteriorating. Some saw her as giving up on life; she saw it as a means to an end.

"Luna?" a sweet, elderly voice whispered from the outside of the hut flap. "Luna, are you here? I'm coming in…" Maple pushed past the flap and let herself into the warm, darkened environment that had seemed to be stripped of the life it once had. She looked at Luna, who still sat on the side of her bed. Luna seemed drained of all of her hope. She was no longer the sarcastic, confident woman everyone knew her as. She was a broken, hollow shell of the human she once was, doing whatever the Disciples told her to without question.

"Luna, are you all right?" Maple asked, "I'm worried about you… how long has it been since you've seen the light?"

Luna drearily looked toward Maple with pale, bloodshot eyes. "I don't know, I… things are changing. I, um..." She found it very hard to find the words she was looking for. She was growing used to only speaking when spoken to. "I can't feel it anymore, it used to mean something, but I just can't feel it anymore…"

Maple let herself come further into the hut, putting a hand on Luna's shoulder and sinking to her level. "What are you talking about, dear? What do you mean you can't feel it? Can't feel what?"

"The sunshine… I can't feel the sunshine. It used to feel like something. It used to feel like hope, the start of a new day, the end of yesterday. It felt special, it told me that I had a purpose, that I mattered… Now it's just warmth on my skin. But I can't truly *feel* it. I can't see the sunshine in all of this Maple. It's all so dark, all the time."

Maple placed a hand on Luna's cheek. "Hey now… don't speak like that child. Things are going to get better. You just—you need to believe in something."

"Like what?" Luna blurted out. "Like Elliot? Like Mother?"

"If not Mother, then *something*. You need to have a purpose, a reason to push on. The silent revolution is only beginning…"

"Silent revolution?"

Maple slowly nodded. She hesitantly took Luna by the hand and led her outside.

"Wait, Maple, stop. I'm barely dressed. Let me at least—"

"Hush up!" Maple ordered. "We don't want to attract any unwanted attention, understand? Pull on a pair of jeans and let's go!"

Luna did so without hesitation; Maple had more than gotten her attention. She followed her outside into the daylight, which seemed more blinding than normal. Passersby looked at her as if she were a complete stranger. They all knew what was happening to her, but they were far too afraid to ask any further questions. She held a hand up to shield her eyes from the sun and her face from the public. She just watched the back of Maple's heels so that she knew where to go. Maple led her into the woods to the more secluded area that Maple preferred for her hut.

"Now listen," she said very bluntly, looking left to right. "I need your help. But if you want nothing to do with this, you can turn me away." She stopped and snapped her fingers. "Just like that! I just, I need some guidance."

"Maple, you're scaring me. Just tell me what's going on." Luna said, still squinting from the sunlight.

Maple took a deep breath in. "I'll show you. Get inside."

Luna ducked under the entrance of Maple's hut to see all of the furniture moved to the side. In the center of the room sat a stout structure with a black sheet draped over it. Luna also realized there were plastic bags split open and folded so that they covered most areas of the floor beneath them. Maple went up to the fixture in the middle of the room and grasped ahold of the top fold. "Last chance…"

Luna nodded, signaling Maple to pull it off. Maple cranked her hand down to her side, causing the sheet to float up into the air and fall to the floor rather quickly.

Luna swallowed, trying her best to stifle her scream. Before her sat Constantine's pale, lifeless body. He remained sitting in the chair, his bald head slumped down, forcing his chin to touch his chest.

"He bled out, just so you know. Real slow, Luna. I made him feel every last drop. *Every* last one." Maple said with pride.

Luna lowered her hand from her mouth. "Maple… *what have you done?*"

"I did what needed to be done! Nobody else is doing anything. You all just stand around and wait for something to happen, but… I'm done waiting!" she said, stomping her foot on the floor like a child. "I'm done waiting," she repeated.

Luna went up to Constantine and gingerly lifted his chin from his body; she jumped back upon noticing his throat had been cut. His head fell limply back on his chest. Luna placed a hand over her mouth, unsure as to whether she was about to vomit or not. She suddenly felt dizzy and reached for the table for support.

She took a moment to gather herself. She clenched her jaw tightly as she leaned hunched over on the table, not wanting to look at Constantine's body for a second longer. "I won't condone what you've done here," she said, slowly turning to face Maple. "But I also won't say he didn't have it coming. I just don't know what we can do now, I think maybe—"

"We need to bury him. I've got the bags. I can remove any appendages that won't fit! All we have to do is drag him out a few hundred yards away from the community, hide the smell! I've already started digging a pit."

Luna ran her fingers through her hair, a sign that she was already feeling the weight of the situation on her shoulders.

"*Luna.*" Maple said calmly. "Luna, it's okay! The ground is still cold enough to mask the smell!"

"That's not the point, Maple… What if—what if someone sees us! What happens when they come looking for him? What happens when it rains, or things are flooded and his body washes out of the earth? It's just—what were you thinking?!"

"What was I thinking?" Maple gasped. She felt her emotions swell and stepped closer to Luna, her arms stretched out in front of her. "I was thinking Musgo didn't die for nothing. I was thinking that we need to get out of this place. I was thinking that this was our chance to start making a difference!" she said, growing louder. We can't just run away, Luna. You wouldn't be able to let Beatrix go, and the Disciples would have no problem shooting us in the back to save their own. There is no hope. Do you understand that? There is *no hope*." Maple aggressively stated. It was evident now that something had broken deep within her. She was not the Maple Luna had come to love; she had evolved into something far more disturbed. "The only thing we can do is *destroy it from the inside*, go down fighting. So are you going to help me or what?"

Luna stopped and glared at Constantine's carcass for a moment. "Okay. But if this goes south… I can't risk it, Maple. It's all coming back on you."

"I would expect nothing less." Maple said, nodding understandingly. She walked to the corner of her hut and picked up a shovel. She then tossed it across the room to Luna, who grasped it firmly. "Walk about 200 paces south—past the really tall spruce. You'll see the hole I started earlier this morning."

"And where will you be?" she asked, wanting to know every step in Maple's plan.

Maple pulled out a hacksaw from under her bedsheets. "I'm going to make things a little more manageable," she nodded, a deranged look in her eyes.

Luna lifted the shovel and swung it over her shoulder; she was done asking questions. She turned to leave and began to exit Maple's hut.

"And Luna!" Maple said before she left. "Make sure you have a story to back yourself up. If a Disciple happens to see you, you're going to want to have a solid explanation as to why you're digging a grave."

"Got it…" She said right before she exited the hut.

The air was brisk outside of the hut, and it nipped at the tips of her fingers. She marched out into the woods so that she could avoid any interaction with unwanted individuals. She marched until she passed the tall spruce Maple had referenced. Within moments she had located the pit. She wasted no time jabbing her shovel into the frozen ground, sending small chunks of dirt flying in every direction. Eventually, her jabs turned into all-out swings. An ax would have been a better tool. She spent an hour chipping away at the earth until she had made a hole about four feet into the ground. With little hesitations, she decided that a shallow grave would have to suffice and began to pry her way out to the sides using her shovel as leverage. Within another hour, she had made significant progress resulting in a hole large enough to fit his body in at awkward positions. "That'll have to do," she said as she climbed her way out of the small pit.

By the time Luna had made it back to Maple's hut, Maple had already set three different burlap bags off to the side of the room. What was left of Constantine was now no more than a stain on the earth where he previously sat.

"It's done," Luna said, almost giving Maple a heart attack in the process. Maple slowly calmed herself as she lowered her hand from her chest and stepped aside so that Luna could see the progress she had made. "You've been busy," Luna said, gesturing toward the brush and pale of water Maple had used to scrub away the last of the evidence.

"Looks like I could say the same for you," Maple said, noticing the dirt running up Luna's arms.

Luna crouched down and placed her hands on her knees. She was tired. All the digging had taken a lot out of her, and Maple could see that. "Go get some rest, child. I'll take care of it all from here."

Luna shook her head. "We don't have the time to waste, just let me take a bag and—"

"Nonsense. You said it yourself—this is my mess, not yours. You've already helped more than you know. You've saved me an immense amount of time, and for that, I am grateful. You know… you know I've always looked out for you, dear, right?"

"Maple, I—"

"I know these circumstances have gotten rather out of hand… but just know that you have always been my number one priority. I can see the good inside of you, Luna. You may have done horrible things, but that doesn't take the good out of you. A lot of these people lost that long ago. But you've still got that, and I need you to hold onto that for as long as you possibly can… Understand?"

"Maple, you don't have to—"

"*Understand?*"

"…yes, yes, I understand. Thank you."

Maple pulled Luna in for a hug. She squeezed her harder than she had ever squeezed her before. "Now go. Get out of here and wash yourself up. I don't want any sort of evidence they can use against you. Take the path back to your hut with more coverage. Let nobody see you and once you wash, stay in your hut. Come out under no circumstances."

"You're worrying me, Maple," she said, looking puzzled. "I don't want you to do something stupid, I—"

"*Just*—go…" Maple instructed, pursing her lips together as she spoke. Luna took the hint and did exactly what she was told. She ran along the edge of Corazon with the most foliage to cover her tracks. She ran in the perfect median, far away from the public eye.

She slipped into her hut and quickly washed herself the best she could with the limited water supplied to her. She removed her shirt so that she could wipe down some of the dirt that had managed to creep its way onto her shoulders. She scrubbed hard, removing any remnants of the dirt she had just collected. She scrubbed until her skin was red and irritated, thinking that somehow, she was scrubbing the sins right off of her.

She heard a shout in the distance and looked toward the flap like a deer in headlights. She quickly resumed scrubbing, waiting for another sound, a gunshot, screaming, anything. But it never came. She finished cleaning herself and then sat quietly on the edge of her bed, waiting. For what, she did not know.

43

As everything was slowly unraveling, Beatrix sat legs crossed, pleasantly perched upon an old couch in the house on the mountain. She clicked her heels together as she watched the cartoon cat and mouse run aimlessly through the house, hitting each other with all sorts of blunt objects. The reception would fade in and fade out, but it didn't seem to bother her. Tobias sat back, leaning against the back of the sofa, keeping his eyes on the doorway, trying to fend off unwanted individuals with his protective stare. Next to him sat June and all her beauty. She leaned her head up against his shoulder and rested her eyes, occasionally looking up at him to smile.

Tobias began to doze off. He had been on watch all night and hadn't even realized how tired he was. His head bobbed up and down as his mind tried to fight his body from the urge to sleep, but it was no use. Within minutes he was deep within a lost slumber. June blinked as she adjusted her eyes to the light. She sat up and saw that Tobias was sleeping. This made her happy. She knew how hard he was trying to stay awake, but the fact that he couldn't made him seem more human. She kissed him on the forehead and stood up. As she stood up, Beatrix spun around, sitting on the couch with her knees and staring at June in all her nakedness.

"Why are you naked?" she asked without hesitation.

June paused, not knowing how to explain the results of a soul-crushing patriarchy to a girl of her age. "Because… I lost my clothes," she replied, unsure of herself.

"Oh," Beatrix said, not knowing how to proceed. She stared June up and down, examining every slight curve and bruise on her body. She then reached across the couch and grabbed ahold of the corner of a blanket that she had been using to keep her warm. She held it up in the air and raised her eyebrows ever so slightly.

It took June a moment to realize that this was Beatrix's way of offering her coverage. She smiled and accepted her offering, wrapping herself in the blanket and taking a seat next to her. "So what are you watching?"

"TV."

"Well yeah, but—you've never seen a television before you came up here, have you?"

"Nope! First time."

June shifted her positioning on the couch to face Beatrix directly. "How old are you, Beatrix?"

Beatrix didn't take her eyes off the screen. "Thirteen… I think."

June brought a hand to her mouth to hide her shock. "Do you like it here? On the mountain?"

"I miss my friends," she said, eyes still glued to the television. After a moment of thought, she looked away, craning her neck toward June. "I miss Clover and Luna… I don't know, I wish they could just come up here and watch TV with me. But Tobias won't let me leave him. He says it's safer that way."

June placed her hand on her shoulder, "Well, he's right," she muttered, fearful that she might say too much. "Tobias is a good guy. Tobias is…" she thought for an example. "Tobias is a mouse!" she said, referring to the television screen in front of them. "He takes care of the other mice. All he wants to do is eat cheese and have fun with the other mice—ya get it?"

"Then who's the cat?" Beatrix questioned.

"Well, the cat could be anyone. That's why people like us have to stick with the mouse. The mouse is smart. The mouse will *protect* us other mice," she winked.

Beatrix let out a dramatic *oohhhh* that told June that she wasn't nearly mature enough to understand what she was trying to convey.

"You know," Beatrix said, resting her hand on her face. "This isn't all that great. I really don't think I want to be up here. I want to be back with my friends. I like the television and all, but… well, something is missing."

June pulled her close and put her arm around her. "Don't worry, we'll be out of here soon enough, I'm sure."

The brief moment of tenderness for each other was cut short when the shuffle of feet swept its way into the room. "Good afternoon, children." They both turned around to see Elliot standing idly in the doorway. "I heard the television. It all sounded so familiar like it was cut directly from a dream," he said, his hand floating up to the atmosphere surrounding his head as if he were about to pluck something out of thin air. June seemed sympathetic. She saw the remnants of wisdom that lay hidden within his clouded attempts at conversation.

"Good afternoon, my Prophet!" Beatrix excitedly stated as she turned to him with great enthusiasm.

"Ahh yes," he said, recognizing her excitement. "And how are you, Penny?"

"What?" Beatrix asked.

June quickly tapped Beatrix's shoulder and addressed Elliot. "She is doing just fine, my Prophet. We both are."

He moved into the room a bit more; his fingertips touched one another as he held his hands in front of him like a timid teenager. "And how are you two enjoying your stay?" he inquired, sounding like a concierge.

"It has been very nice!" Beatrix piped out. "The food is so good, and the TV is so big, and the people—well, they all seem to get along, I guess. I do miss my friends, though."

"Friends," Elliot muttered. The two of them couldn't tell if it was a question or a statement. He seemed lost in thought. He looked back up at June. "I'm sorry, dear, but I seem to have forgotten your name."

June nodded. "June, my Prophet."

Elliot nodded, his fingers still pressed up against each other. His face was concerned as he clearly wasn't saying what he came there to say. Tobias remained passed out on the sofa, barely moving. "And June, your little friend..."

June nodded again, picking up the remnants of his sentences and piecing them together. "This is Beatrix."

"*Beatrix*," he said, tracing her words with his own. "Yes, Beatrix. I understand now."

There was a sudden *thud* that came from a room upstairs. It sounded as though someone had toppled a dresser or vanity. All of them looked toward the ceiling; Elliot seemed more concerned than the others. Tobias remained sleeping. This both amused and worried June at the same time.

"Beatrix," Elliot said again, directing the attention back toward her. "I was wondering if I could have a word with you, child."

June stood up and quickly went to his side. She began to feel up his shoulders and whisper in his ear. "Wouldn't you rather have a word with me, my Prophet? I'm a good listener—" she said, placing a hand on his forearm.

Elliot stepped away from her, alarmed by her sudden need to put her hands on him. She had forgotten, in her panic, that Elliot was not one who enjoyed being touched by hands other than his own.

He looked at her with disgust and maneuvered himself so that he was free from her grasp. "In the name of Mother and all things holy!" he shouted while still somehow holding his soft tone.

"I'm—I'm sorry, my Prophet," she said, bowing her head.

He eyed her suspiciously. "Go pray that Mother may forgive you for your misjudgment," he said, seeming to be fully cognizant of her intentions.

"Yes, my Prophet!" she shouted in hopes that her words would wake Tobias. He remained unfazed. June began to move on down the hall, leaving Beatrix and Tobias behind. Tobias still slumped back in a deep sleep.

Elliot smiled at Beatrix and held out his hand. "Come with me, I want to show you something."

Beatrix hopped off of the couch and tiptoed around Tobias's body. Elliot held out a warm hand, which she generously accepted. He seemed at peace, very content with how things were going as he guided her down the corridor. "Right here," he said, gently pulling her into a room.

Once in the room, he gently shut the door so that he wouldn't make any noise. "Please, have a seat, my child," he said, gesturing for her to sit on his bed. She hopped up and took a seat, smiling at how bouncy the springs were beneath her. He shuffled over to a chest at the other end of the room and looked back at her with excitement.

"I have something to show you… do you like toys?" he asked, hoping that she would be more enthusiastic in her response.

"Well… I had a ball that I liked to throw around with Ray back in Corazon. That was a whole lotta fun!" she chuckled.

"I'm afraid I am not familiar," Elliot said as he lifted the cover of the chest up. "Is he visiting as well?"

"I don't know," she said, afraid that that may still be the case. "I know he was going to leave at first, but he might stay and wait for me to come back. He told me that he would teach me how to ride a bike and that he'd be like my dad, just like Luna is like my mom, and then—"

"Yes, yes," Elliot said as he clenched his jaw together, a vein appearing near the top of his temple. "I remember those," he said in regard to her mention of *bikes*.

She remained still as she began to pick up on the gaps of time he seemed to miss. All of a sudden, she had a dreadful thought, a thought that begged the possibility of her never seeing Luna or Ray again. The Prophet was certainly not the being she assumed he would be. Her face, though she tried to hide it, showed her fear.

"Hey now," Elliot muttered as he sank down to one knee and reached under his bed. "None of that, dear. There is no sadness here, not with us. Mother is watching us all; she would hate for you to be sad in her kingdom… you don't want to disappoint Mother, do you?"

"No! No, not at all. Praise be to Mother," she recited.

Elliot grinned. "I have something for you," he said, removing his hands from under his bed. He brought up two dolls. One with long blonde hair, and the other with long brown hair. "Here. They are yours now."

Beatrix took the dolls in both of her hands and held them up to her face. "They're tiny people…"

Elliot snickered. "Tiny people, yes," he said. He quickly noticed how she held them in her hands as if she didn't know what to do with them. "You can make them move and make them talk using your own voice. It's—I knew a girl who had great fun using them."

"Like when Clover makes the puppets out of dead animals she finds?"

"I'm sorry?" he asked, sounding disturbed.

Beatrix backtracked, "Nothing. This one here—this one looks like Luna," she said, holding up the blond figurine.

"Like this," he said, disregarding her mention of Luna. He took the dolls in his hands and shook them around as if they had a mind of their own. "*Ohh, hello there. My name is… Penny! You look very pretty today!*" he chirped in a high pitch.

He then took the other doll and raised it slightly higher, signaling that it was now her turn to speak. "*Oh, hi Penny! My name is Debra! Thank you very much! Did you remember to say your prayers this morning?*" He then paused and reflected on how embarrassing this would be if he were caught doing this by any of the other Disciples. Beatrix seemed amused, though, and that's all he cared about for the moment.

She giggled as he handed the two dolls over to her. Right before her hands were around their waist, he pulled them back. "You're special, Beatrix. I can feel it," he said with the utmost clarity. He looked into her eyes as deeply as he could. "Something is happening here, in Corazon, on the mountain. Something… is coming," he said, darkening the mood of the room. "I need you to be by my side when it arrives, understand?"

This was the sort of rhetoric she had expected from the Prophet. She nodded, not knowing whether she should accept the dolls or not. Elliot relaxed and relinquished his grip on the plastic figurines.

She looked up at him with wide eyes. "Of course, my Prophet," she said, trying her best to show her dedication.

He let the dolls ease back into her hands. "You have fun with these, child." He then stood up and began to leave the room.

"Prophet?" Beatrix asked, not wanting to be left alone. "Whose dolls were these?"

He released his grip on the doorknob and sighed. "A girl who would have been a little older than you, child. They were hers."

"Why aren't they hers anymore? She doesn't want them?" she asked, not knowing the sort of territory she was encroaching on.

"She…" He didn't really know how to go about explaining this. "She was taken from this earth. These were her dolls. Her name was Penny. You remind me a lot of her, child."

Beatrix held the dolls on her lap and didn't move them at all, not knowing how to react to Elliot's ominous words.

"You enjoy those dolls, child. Just put them back when you're done. *I love you…*"

This made her feel rather uncomfortable. She decided to go with the response that was appropriate for every situation. "Thank you, my Prophet! Praise be to Mother!"

With that, he gave her a faint smile and shut the door.

44

Flames licked up the sides of the stockpile of firewood incredibly fast. A thick black smoke rose into the air at a pace that could only be described as sluggishly quick. The plumes of nauseating smoke were thick and overwhelmed Ruth, who had woken first to the smell, then the heat. She jumped up and frantically looked for the sources of the fire, her body glazed in sweat. "Hey!" she shouted, hoping that someone would answer.

With no regard for his privacy, she launched her shoulder into the door leading to Ray's room. "Fire!" she shouted, attempting to alarm him. But there was no Ray, the bed was made neat, and the rifle was gone. "Fuck!" she yelled, slamming the door against the wall so hard one of the hinges popped. She removed the transceiver on her belt and held it to her mouth. "He's gone," she stated, looking out the window at the flames that were engulfing the firewood.

The transceiver buzzed with static. She shook her head and ran outside to face the flames. She quickly began to kick snow at the base of the pile, hoping that it would do something; her efforts were less than fruitful.

"We can see it from where we are!" the radio buzzed. *"Put it out now! It'll only attract attention!"*

She held the transceiver up again. "Did you hear what I just said? The man and the girl are gone! They must've left before I woke up." She looked around for footprints but was too distracted by the size of the growing fire.

"PUT THE FIRE OUT!" Benji boomed from the other end of the transceiver.

Ruth cursed as she clipped the transceiver back on her belt. She looked to the cabin. There was a shovel propped against the exterior wall. She darted for the shovel, picked it up, and charged the firewood like a madman. She swung the shovel at the pile over and over again until a log was dislodged, allowing the entire pile to recklessly roll to the earth, spreading out the fire and thinning the smoke.

She then quickly tossed as much snow on the now independent logs as she could, casting the white powder over the hungry flames. Within ten minutes, she had gotten it under control, and ten minutes after that, she had smothered the rest. She lay back in the ash-stained snow, exhausted and angry.

"It's out," she stated into the transceiver.

It took a moment for Benji to respond. "You better hope nobody saw that smoke. How long of a lead does he have?"

She sighed and winced with embarrassment before responding. "I don't know. The fire was blazing by the time it woke me up. If I had to guess, they've covered an hour's worth of ground."

Benji once again hesitated to respond. On the other end of the line, he was grinding his teeth and trying to soothe his newly discovered headache. It took everything he had not to hurl the transceiver into the brush. He tried his best to hold himself together. Not only was Ray blatantly disobeying him, but the whole operation would be at risk if he were to let their plans slip before they had surrounded Corazon. He pressed down the PTT button, and the static stopped.

He held the transceiver up to his face, the antenna narrowly missing his eye. "Just get back here as soon as you can. We'll regroup and head out. I'll get everyone ready. We're taking Corazon with or without the guns."

Benji sighed and closed his eyes. Adam, a younger boy whom he had recruited to The Former while he was still living his life as a sleeper within Corazon, watched him carefully like one would watch an atom bomb as it was carried to the drop zone. Benji switched the transceiver to a different channel and paused before he spoke. "I thought I told you to stay put," he said into the radio. He waited for Ray's response.

Ray's transceiver repeated Benji's words. Ray stopped walking and snapped his fingers at Clover, who trotted along right beside him. She stopped and leaned up against a shallow-rooted tree, seeing it as a place fit for a well-deserved break. Trudging through the melting snow was no easy feat. Ray took a moment to respond to Benji, "Last time I checked, I wasn't taking orders from you."

"They'll string you up from the mountain, friend," he said, brimming with frustration. "And she'll be the one to tie the knot."

"Ah, come on now, Benji," Ray said, overcome by the burst of confidence following the successful evasion of Ruth. "Give your sister a little more credit."

"You don't know what you're getting yourself into." Benji barked. "And when you figure it out, you'll want us to be the ones with the guns."

"Mm-hmm," Ray passively hummed into the radio. "I think I'll take my chances. Best of luck to you and your boy scouts, though," he said, right before switching the transceiver off.

Clover eyed him as she retrieved an apple from her backpack. "Now you're just pissing him off," she said plainly.

He shrugged, "It won't matter as long as we get in and out before they do."

She polished off the apple on her jacket and looked at him. "You're still just tossing gas on the fire."

He looked off toward the trail ahead and squinted. "The fire is already out of control. No going back now."

"What do you think happens to us when we die?" Clover asked, still slumped up against the mossy side of the tree as she crunched into the apple. She looked at Ray as the juice trickled down her chin. He was standing upright, using a broomstick as somewhat of a crutch. Though he wouldn't admit it, his leg was still less than healed.

He stretched his back and twisted from side to side as he glared into the distance. "Do you think this is the right way?" he asked, completely ignoring her question.

"Yeah, we're going the right way. That's the rock that looks like it has all the diamonds in it," she said, pointing at the mossy rock with rather large deposits of glassy quartz minerals. "But you didn't answer my question," she said, nodding toward the large rock.

"How does Todd even get here? There are no tracks." Ray said, scratching his head. "You would think that there would be tracks. Have you seen the truck he drives?"

"Ray!" she shouted, finally getting his attention. "What do you think happens to us when we die?"

He sighed and jabbed his makeshift staff into the ground. "That's the cause of all of this. That question right there, *what happens to us when we die?*"

"And?"

"And? And I don't know, Clover. I've never tried it before," he said, mildly frustrated.

"But what do *you think* happens? What do *you* believe, Ray?"

He threw his back against the tree right next to her. He carefully thought of his next words as he ever so slowly slid down the wet bark.

"You know Clover…" He took in a deep breath and looked up toward the sky. "There was a time when I thought there was…

something better. There was a time when I thought there was some sort of being in the sky that… that watched over us all and protected us from evil. There was a time where I thought about all of that stuff. I was a good kid, raised in a good family. We went to church every Sunday. The only time we ever missed a week was when my mom got pneumonia and Dad was stuck holding up her hair as she was hunched over the toilet." He thought on the moment with fondness as a smile instantly flashed across his face.

"Yeah, things were nice, simple. But you grow up, and you question the nature of everything, thinking that you're some sort of *philosophical mastermind* capable of seeing things on a different level than everyone else. Then you grow up a bit more, and you realize that your philosophy is all bullshit. It's always been every man for himself, and it always will be. But for whatever reason, when I married my wife and we had our little boy, I started going back to church. There was this calmness to it all. It was warm and welcoming, a lot like the masses you went to in Corazon. After a while, I started going every week, even when my wife would stay home with Marty. It was just second nature for me."

Clover looked at him from the corner of her eyes. "Did you go to mass when you poisoned all those people?" she asked timidly.

Ray looked over at her with his mouth hanging open; he was so caught off guard. "How do you know about—"

"I was sneaking around Corazon one night when I heard you talking to Luna in her hut. I know I shouldn't have listened to you talk, but… you were a stranger, and I was just curious about what it was like in the real world. Once I heard you mention it, I couldn't stop myself from listening."

Ray looked away from her for a moment, "No, it's okay… Some people think that believing in God is some sort of fast pass to happiness. Just because someone goes to mass doesn't make them a good person. There are good people that do bad things and bad people that do good things. It doesn't have to make sense. It just happens like that."

"So what does all of it mean?"

"All of what?"

"All of this—why I am here if not for… Mother or whatever you want to call it?"

"People just want a manual to tell them what the right thing to do is. The one thing that was made to unite us all is the biggest obstacle in our way. There's nothing you can do."

"I don't understand…" Clover said, tucking her knees up to her chest and resting her head against the bark.

"People aren't thinking for themselves because they're so fixated on the idea of belonging to something bigger."

Clover smiled as she wiped the juice from her chin. "Hmm… deep," she said with a sarcastic smile.

He shot her a smile back. "Come on, kid, we've got some land to cover," he said, digging his walking stick into the ground and pulling himself up with a grunt. Clover was quick to hop to her feet, half-eaten apple in hand. The two continued walking deeper into the woods. Ray looked around and tried to remember landmarks he used to get to the watering hole, which he intended to call his final resting place last time, while Clover, on the other hand, relied on more recent memories.

The two walked on in silence for a while, admiring the wilderness for what it was while simultaneously covering their tracks as best they could. Every mile or so, the two would backtrack their steps, splitting into different directions to throw off any of The Former that would surely be hot on their trail. The moments of tension-ridden silence would be punctuated with lessons on how to distinguish the difference between fox, bear, and deer tracks, courtesy of Clover. Giving Clover the opportunity to teach was a treat in itself—as she seemed to really enjoy it. These brief lessons were often followed by more silence.

"So what's the plan here?" Clover asked, looking over to Ray as they hiked along.

"What do you mean, plan?" he asked, sounding a bit irritated.

"Well, what's the plan? We're going to find Corazon eventually. I know we're on the right track. I see the way you talk to yourself when we take our little rest stops. I can tell you're nervous, so… I don't know, maybe I can help."

"Yeah… that's the thing," he said, sounding a bit grim. "Once we find Corazon, I need you to stay back. I'm sure they've noticed you're gone, and they might put two and two together. I need to scope things out, see what's going on. If it's too dangerous, I'm going to grab Luna, Maple, and Bea and get out of there. Us five will have to get back to my cabin, and then… well, let's see if we make it that far first."

"So I'm just supposed to sit back and watch? What if you get caught?" she replied, sounding worried.

"If I get caught? They'll kill me. They'll look for the people that might have been in on it, too. When you show up out of nowhere, they'll immediately assume you were with me. You have a choice. If I get caught, you can go back to Corazon, risk being hurt. Or you can just turn around and head back. Try to navigate your way back to the cabin. There is enough food to last you for a while. There are maps lying around too. Take what you can and try to find your way out of here," he said, gesturing to the wilderness around them. "I'm not going to tell you what to do. Like I said, you have a choice. One is just a hell of a lot better than the other."

"Ray, I want to help. I don't want to just stand around and watch. What if something goes wrong and people start getting hurt. I can't have that happen! I can't—"

"It won't! All right? It won't! I don't know what I'm doing here, you got me! I haven't known what I've been doing for the past eight years, Clover! I have no plan, I have no backup, I have no nothing. The only thing I can think of is Beatrix, Luna, and Maple and how I can get them out safely. That's all I got. I am more than welcome to suggestions, but if you're thinking we're just gonna run in there guns blazing, then… you're fucking wrong. I'm scared, all right? I am seriously scared. So if I go in there and something bad happens… knowing that at least someone got out and can let others know about what's happening in here… well, that makes me feel just a little bit better. Understand?"

Clover got really quiet and let her head sink down so that her chin touched her chest.

"Hey, come on, don't do that to me…" Ray said, trying to get her to cheer up. "Come on now, Clover, you're all I got right now. You can't just shut me out," he said, tossing his arms in the air. She glanced over at him briefly but then remained silent.

Ray sighed and kept on walking. She repeatedly glanced in his direction to convey her anger with him. He began to rummage through the deep pockets of his jacket. "Okay, listen, I was going to save this for you right before I left, but I guess it wouldn't really do any damage if you have it now." He pulled out a long slender item wrapped in a shiny metallic wrapper. Clover examined the item as Ray dangled it from his fingers. "This here is what we called a candy bar. It may be pretty stale, but… well, it's better than anything else I can offer up right now." He then held it out in her general direction.

She eagerly reached out and he pulled it back really quick. "What do I hear?" he asked as his eyes began to widen.

"Please?" she questioned in a muffled, reluctant voice.

He gave her a genuine smile and handed the candy bar over. She quickly tore through the wrapper and examined the sleek chocolate exterior. She then nibbled and nibbled until she made her mind up that it was indeed the most delicious delicacy she had ever tasted. Her face quickly went from mopey to excited right before Ray's eyes. He decided to hold his words and let her enjoy the moment.

He took the time to wonder how he had never really noticed Clover before. She had always been present. She was just *there*, hidden in the shadows somewhere. She was just as curious and lively as Beatrix, but for whatever reason, she was neglected. Clover dared to ask the questions that Beatrix wouldn't. She was the one who didn't care how the others viewed her. She was always herself, and everyone, including Ray, subconsciously persecuted her. As he examined her chowing down on the sugary goodness of the treat he had given her, he felt a sadness he had never felt before. Why was it that nobody paid attention to Clover? She had been denied a childhood, and everyone just allowed it to happen. It was almost cute how Beatrix, the beloved child of Corazon, and Clover, the forgotten one, had managed to become such great friends. Clover had to have been thinking about her; she usually just kept quiet about it, though. No matter how little she spoke or how little she actually showed her emotions, Ray knew she missed her best friend.

"Hey, do you hear that?" Clover asked, snapping him out of his daze.

"What? What do you hear?" he asked, his state of mind abuzz with fearful excitement.

"Water… rushing water."

"I don't hear anything," Ray snapped in ignorance. He was rather grumpy; the extremely long hike had taken a lot out of him. Slowly but surely, his face began to change. "Water… that's water!" The two quickly began to pick up the pace, trying their best to locate the source of the running water. Clover spotted it from afar and took off further into the woods. Ray tried his best to keep up. He found her jumping up and down as she pointed to the river. The very same river he had used in an attempt to end his life over a year ago.

The two of them admired the river in all of its beauty for a few moments before they continued. They sat down and watched as the ripping rapids tore through the earth and leaped over the rocks. The river was truly beautiful. It could be extremely calm one moment and wild the very next. Ray knelt down and dipped the tips of his fingers into the water. "Wow… I don't remember it being this cold…"

Clover kept looking left to right. "We've been walking for a while, and this place seems really familiar. So if I were looking at us from the other side…." She turned around and looked at what was behind her. She looked at the different trees and their roots. She looked at how the setting sun shed its orange glow on the wet earth. "I know this place… I know this place! This is where I had my first kiss!"

Ray hadn't the slightest idea on how to respond to that. It seemed like Clover was still trying to figure something out. She whispered under her breath as she kept looking at the natural structures around her. "Yes… yes! Follow me!" She then took off down the riverbank. Ray barely had enough time to catch up.

"Where are you going?" he huffed as he used the broomstick as a third leg to lean on.

"You'll see! Come on! And try to keep quiet."

He immediately shut his mouth and looked around, expecting to see a wild animal of some sort. All of a sudden, Clover came to a screeching halt, digging the heels of her worn-out boots into the muddy surface below her.

"Do you see it?" she whispered as Ray bent over, trying to catch his breath next to her.

"See—see what?" he wheezed. She pointed directly forward. All he could see was mud and sticks, but she was right. There was something oddly familiar about this place. Then, as if everything clicked all at once, he saw what she was looking at. There, built into the side of the riverbank, was his old friend Otto's cove.

"Oh my God…" Ray said as he hurriedly ran toward the entrance. He dropped to his hands and knees and crawled into Otto's cove. Clover was close behind. Once they both knew they were out of sight, the two of them flicked on the remaining lamps that still harnessed enough oil for a warming glow. The warmth quickly brought Otto's cove to life, illuminating the dark and revealing to them all of the artwork he had scattered throughout his hideout.

Ray began to laugh as he looked around at all Otto's cove had to offer. "Leave it to Otto," he said, resting his rifle against the side of the wall.

"I never really talked to him…" Clover said, reflecting on how uncomfortable she would get whenever Otto came around. "I had no idea he was this… talented," she said in awe as she picked up one of his drawings.

"He was something else," Ray replied, thinking back to the last time he saw Otto alive and how happy he was to see his brother Todd. He wondered if Todd had been back yet, if he had returned with his monthly supplies to find the Corazon he thought he knew reduced to madness. He wondered what sort of lie they had told him as to why he couldn't find his brother anywhere. Before he could think anymore, he was parallel with the beaten-up mattress Otto had smuggled into his hideout, and his head was drifting toward the pillow. He hadn't realized how truly tired he was.

He quickly looked toward Clover, who was already dozing off on a thick blanket somewhere in the corner. He knew that this might very well be the last time they would get to let their guard down. He felt safe, he felt secure, if not just for a moment.

Within moments he was sleeping, sliding down the slick slope that would bring him to his darkening dreamscape. He had arrived, standing outside of a suburban home, saturated with color. There was something wrong; the atmosphere was cold and unforgiving. An unknown force kept pushing him toward the door, begging him to grab the brassy knob and see what waited for him inside.

He looked around him at the plots of mowed grass, the boxed houses with plastic siding, and the unnerving absence of people. It was all wrong; there was something amiss. He twisted the knob and pushed past the door. Inside the home remained the same feeling of uncertainty. There was a carpeted staircase, a living room to his right, and what appeared to be an office to his left. Ray hesitantly stepped into the living room, the television was fuzzy with black and white static, and the cushions belonging to the furniture were thrown about the room. He continued, carefully stepping over the cushions and what appeared to be broken glass.

Then he saw the tiled floor of the kitchen, and it was clear he was not alone. He moved forward until he saw the figure standing breathless in the center of the kitchen. She had blond hair and a fragile yet might frame. There was not a doubt in his mind he was looking at Luna. She remained with her back to him. She continued to breathe heavily. "Luna…" he said, continuing to move forward.

She didn't respond. That's when he saw it. As he took his final step into the kitchen, he noticed the three lifeless bodies sprawled out on the floor. In her hand, she held a knife, a thick red rivulet of blood trickling down the blade. He froze, not wanting to move any closer. "Luna," he stated, hoping that this was all a twisted misunderstanding. "Luna, what's going on?"

She continued to do nothing but breathe. With a mighty burst of courage, he stepped over the bodies and placed his hands on her. She let her head hang low, and her hands trembled. He wrapped his arms around her and tried to get her to look up at him. Usually, by this time, his dream had ended, and he was snapped back into reality, but for whatever reason, this dream turned nightmare refused to end. "Luna, Luna, it's me. Let's go! Luna, we need to go! Let's go! Luna, look at me!" he frantically shouted as he tried to get her to simply angle her head upward. There was a sudden urgency in the air. He knew they had to leave, or something far worse would be in store. Slowly her head raised so that he could look upon her face. She seemed lost, her eyes were glassy and weak, and her entire body was now trembling in fear.

Her lips opened as they shook, but she had barely enough strength to whisper. "*Ray…*"

He was quick to respond. "Hey there, beautiful. That's right. It's me, let's go, we need to leave. Now."

She opened her mouth once more, this time with slight undertones of regret and anger. "*What have you done, Ray… what have you done…*"

He held her by the waist as her body began to sink to the floor. "What? What do you mean? I'm here! I came back! Come on! What are you doing? Stand up!"

Small rivulets of blood began to run from her nose and mouth. This made Ray try even harder to get her to her feet.

"Luna, stand up! Stand up, damn it!" he screamed as her body continued to fall, pulling him with her like a bag full of rocks growing heavier by the second.

He looked down to where she was falling; her body was disappearing right before his eyes, her clothes crumpled upon the floor. He let her go altogether, letting her disappear into the madness. He quickly backed up until his back was against the cold, dark presence he was running from in the first place. He felt a cold hand on his shoulder, the hand of fear itself. He closed his eyes as the tears began to stream down his face.

"Just do it already!" he screamed at the fear behind him. "Just get it over with!"

Before he could even conjure up another sentence, he felt a shadow-like blade slide through his body and eject out of his chest. He dropped to one knee. He could feel the blade being raised above his head, preparing itself to crash down violently onto his skull. He closed his eyes as he could feel the force of it all coming down on him.

All of a sudden, he woke up, startled by what was happening within his dream. He yelled out and gripped the sides of Otto's bed. His teeth were clenched together, and his body was covered in sweat despite the rather cold weather. He slowly released his grip on Otto's mattress and looked up. That's when everything changed.

Crouched down under the entrance was Clover, who was huddled up behind Luna. She looked at him with concern. He tried finding the words as Luna ducked into the cove and crawled toward him. "Hey there," she said quietly through misty eyes.

He reached his hand out so that he could gently touch the side of her face. She felt different. Her complexion had changed. It was as if she was now a completely different being now that he knew he was touching the face of a murderer. He had no words; he simply pulled her closer so that he could embrace her tighter than he had ever embraced her before.

"You scared *the shit* out of me," she said with a smile as the two rocked back and forth.

Ray pulled her away quickly. "*Me?* You're lucky I got your message!"

She shook her head, "They checked the bag to make sure I didn't put anything in it... the blanket was the best option. How's your head?"

He sighed, "Getting beat unconscious with a stone never felt good."

She bit her lip, knowing full well her feelings of apology were beyond words. "It was the only way you were getting out of there alive. They've been looking for a reason to get rid of you since you showed up."

"Guess that means you've saved me twice now," he muttered.

Her hands remained glued to his shoulders, "I was more worried about the cold than anything else. It looks like the worst of it has passed, but I stayed awake at night wondering if you made it back to the cabin or not."

He nodded, trying to think of a better way she could have gone about things. "You're lucky our little friend found me when she did. I would have frozen to death in my own front lawn."

Luna looked back to Clover, who stayed huddled in the corner. She examined her with kind eyes and a welcoming smile. "She told me… she's a brave little girl. We owe her a lot."

Ray shook some of the metaphorical cobwebs out of his head and slowly began to focus on the situation at hand. "Bea. Where's Bea?"

Luna's head sank to his level as she dropped to both knees so that she could tell him without breaking down. "You need to remain calm. Tobias came to see me yesterday. He says she's all right. He says she's safe for the time being."

"Tobias? What do you mean, Tobias? He—why is she with *him*?" he said, expressing slight alarm.

"She was taken up onto the mountain. They're using her as some sort of collateral to hold over my head," she said, her face riddled with distress. "They told me they'd bring her back once things got back to normal, but there's no fixing a rift like this."

"Wait, what? You let them take her up onto the mountain? Luna!" He got to his feet and looked toward his rifle as if he were ready for war. "How could you let this happen?! That was—that was our little girl! That was—"

She closed her eyes and tried her hardest not to lose herself. She let go of him and fell backward, sobbing. "I can't do this anymore, I—I can't do this, I'm so—"

He pulled back his yearning to lash out and crouched to her level. "Luna, hey—we're going to figure this out, all right?" The transceiver clipped to his belt felt particularly heavy at that very moment. He could feel it weighing on him, knowing full well that it could bring about the end of Corazon as they knew it. He looked at the mess of a woman he had created and thought about how her life would have been lived in blissful ignorance had he had never intervened. "We need guns," he stated.

"You have a gun," she said, wiping her face clean with her sleeve.

"No, we need more. You need one, Maple needs one, and I'm running low on ammunition," he said, watching Clover as she stood idly in the background.

She shook her head. "That's a fight we're going to lose," she stated.

"I don't want a fight, I just want reassurance. I know about the hunting chest," he said, wanting to get right to the point. She looked up at him in surprise. "I stumbled across it when Maple and I were gathering a while back, the day we found the satellite. Sterling trusts you. You've told me yourself. If you know the code, then we—"

"I can't give up the code," she said as if she were a disobedient child.

Ray was growing angry; his voice took on a new tone. "Listen to me. Every second we waste here is another second Bea is up on the mountain. If we're going to get out of this thing, we at least need a fighting chance. We're done here, Luna. Corazon, everyone here—they don't matter anymore. If this goes right, then we'll be gone before anyone notices, but if this doesn't go right? Then the least you could do is give us the tools we'll need."

His words were stern and clear. She no longer saw the suicidal man sleeping in her bed. She saw a man willing to do anything to get out of Corazon alive. Luna took a deep breath and folded her arms tight. She looked down and muttered the code. "*3842, you have to twist the dial in the opposite direction every time you hit the number,*" she said, having given up the secret she swore to protect.

He nodded and mouthed the code under his breath a few times before moving for his rifle.

"But you need to know something," she said, stopping him again. "The Disciples made me speak to the other followers just in case you decided to return. You have no allies here. Not anymore."

"What?" he asked, the fuse to his temper growing shorter every second.

"They told me that if I wanted Beatrix back unharmed, I needed to turn them against you. You know, untie the knots you fashioned within the community. These people—they've been trained to hate you. Everyone in the community has been debriefed. They know that they need to alert the Disciples. Otto's cove is safe for now, but sooner or later, they will come for you."

His face loosened significantly as he hid behind his hands, tuning out the world around him. "I knew it wasn't going to be easy."

She ran her hand through his hair. "If you want to turn back now, forget any of this ever happened. Forget about me. Forget about Beatrix, Clover, Corazon, the Disciples, Elliot, everything… If you want to forget about all of that and live the rest of your days out then, then that's fine. I won't stop you." After what was nearly a full minute of silence and contemplation, she pressed her forehead against his as she looked down the bridge of her nose as if it were a sight on a gun. "I'll always love you, Ray. *Always.*" She then stood up and proudly walked toward the exit. As she began to make her way through the exit of the cove, he spoke up.

"If I were to leave you all here, like this… and live out the rest of my so-called life. It wouldn't be a life worth living." He stood up and slung his rifle over his shoulder. "I'm going to go up the mountain, and I am going to get Beatrix. And if anybody gets in my way, they'll have to kill me because I won't stop breathing until all of us are safe and far away from this place."

He then looked over to Clover, who felt he was only referring to Beatrix and Luna. "*All of us,*" he said again, this time emphasizing it as he looked at Clover with a sense of admiration and care. She tried her best to hide her smile, but deep down, they all knew she had already become a part of the family.

Luna slowly drifted back inside, and the three of them linked up for a moment of calm just before the storm. Everyone knew Luna was one for making a plan, but it all seemed relatively straightforward. She touched the two of them on the shoulder and spoke carefully. "I'll get Maple. I think I know where she is. Clover, do you have anyone you need to leave with?"

Clover shook her head, "Just Bea."

Luna nodded and directed her attention toward Ray. "She's in the house on the mountain. It's not a long hike, but you need to stay off the trail. If any Disciples are coming down for the day, you'll run into them." He nodded, having understood her instructions. "Tobias is not our enemy," she said calmly. "If he wants to help, let him. Clover, you go get supplies, food, water, and anything else you can fit into a backpack or two. Everyone regroups back here, then…"

"Then we'll leave," Clover said, finishing her sentence.

Ray understood what was being asked of him, but there was something still sitting in the pit of his stomach that he had to get out. "There's something else," he said. The words he wanted to say began to ball up in his throat. "It's Benji," he stated. "He's—"

A single gunshot rang through the woods, alerting everyone within range. Luna's eyes shot open. "Maple!" she screamed in panic. She quickly grabbed her jacket and tore out the exit. Ray ran after her. She stopped mid-track and turned to him, grabbing him by his collar. "You need to get Beatrix! If this is Maple—everything is about to go to hell. I don't have time to explain! Go and…" she saw the fear in his eyes begin to spread. He, too, sensed that this may very well be the last time they ever touched. She shook off the emotional feelings quickly. "You need to go. I'll see you again. One way or another."

He thought about her final words and what they could have possibly meant. "*One way or another,*" he repeated with certainty as they pulled each other in for a final kiss. They separated, and Luna took off running faster than she ever had, ducking and dodging her way through the foliage.

Ray turned back, still trying to process what had just happened. He quickly ran back to Otto's cove where he picked up his rifle and the bag with all of the ammunition, he had no intention of going to the hunting chest, but he quietly repeated the code to himself as he gathered the necessary belongings. "*3842, 3842, 3842, 3842.*"

Clover grabbed him by the hand and begged him to tell her what was happening. "What's going on?" she asked, concerned. "Getting supplies will take no time at all. I'm not staying here alone. I'm coming with you!"

"No!" he ordered as he turned to her and stuck a finger in her face. She jumped back, surprised by the sudden aggression. "You stay here. I will come back for you, okay? I will come back for you."

She refused to let go of Ray's arm. "No—you. You can't go! Ray, you're going to die! You'll die up there! You can't—you can't go!" she cried as the tears began to flow down her cheeks.

Ray now saw the influence he had on Clover. He now realized how much he truly meant to the very same girl he had completely disregarded for so long. He was the only positive male figure she had in her life, and because of this, she had already adopted him as a father figure, the only man and only person next to Beatrix she had ever allowed herself to grow close to.

This, of all things, really brought him close to tears but still wasn't enough to stop him. He sank down to one knee and held her close. "I have to go, Clover. I have to go, or we may never see Beatrix again. We could be a family! All of us! You, me, Bea, and Luna! We could be a family and live in a house of our own, and we could all be happy one day! Do you see it, Clover?" he said as he looked into her eyes as she continued to cry uncontrollably. "I'm gonna fix this, okay? I'm gonna fix this," he said as he tried to once again remove himself from the clinging child.

She scratched and tried to fight him as he forced her off of him. "I'm so sorry," he said, trying his best not to get emotional. "I'm so sorry."

With that, he gave her one final push, sending her falling back toward the dark corner of the cove, buying him just enough time to grab his rifle and bolt out of the cove. He ran as fast as his legs would carry him, occasionally looking behind him to make sure Clover didn't pursue him. He ran until he was all out of breath, causing him to slow down and lean against a nearby tree. He looked up toward the mountain, then zeroed in on the very cliff that held the house where Beatrix would be—the cliff that overlooked Corazon, the cliff on which Otto and Aria had mercilessly been executed. Ahead of him was a thick brush that gave way to the trail leading up the mountain. As he peered through the trees and saplings that partially constructed his view, he could see the sway of a purple robe swinging in the breeze.

He lined up his crosshairs with the billowing robe to see if action would be required. It was a Disciple. He swayed through the woods with no destination in mind, cigarette in his mouth, rifle on his back. Ray set the Disciple in his sight and peered at him through the crosshairs, ready to pull back on the trigger should the man's attention be directed toward him.

The Disciple stepped forward and took a generous drag from the cigarette before casting it aside, his eyes still fixed on the sky. "Mother, forgive us," he said aloud as he expelled the smoke from his nose. With that, he continued moving forward toward Corazon. Ray looked up from his sight and watched the man walk with more purpose. He was no longer an obstacle, and no blood was shed. He knew full well that the man would not be the last Disciple he would come across that day.

45

Luna leaped her way through the woods, hoping to find the source of the gunshot, worried about who it was fired by and for whom it was meant. A scary idea kept creeping into her head of what she might find when she came across the source of the gunshot, but she tried her best to keep the bad thoughts at bay. She was en route to the place where Maple had buried Felix. If she had made a mistake, that's where it would be.

She huffed harder and harder as she tore through the woods. "Maple!" she yelled as she let the thoughts take over. "Maple!" she screamed again. She tripped over herself just as she bolted into the clearing where they had buried Constantine's corpse. She panted as she helped herself to her hands and knees. She looked up and screamed, throwing herself backward in fear. A few feet in front of her lay a bear who seemed to be wounded and breathing rather shallowly. She clamored to her feet without taking her eyes off of the massive beast.

The bear was heavy, with nappy, thick fur, and a vicious snarl. It lay there panting; a bloodied patch lay where it had been wounded.

"Luna!" a voice called out in a scolding manner. "What in the name of Mother are you doing here?" Orwell asked from across the clearing on the opposite side of the bear. She looked around her and quickly tried to think of a reason she could give to him to explain her presence. He held the shotgun close to his chest as he delicately tiptoed closer to the beast between them. He looked up at her, noticing how she was sweating profusely. "I was following the tracks," he said, nodding toward the bear. "This mama bear almost made it into camp, managed to avoid all of Sterling's traps. I was just out patrolling, and… I saw her from afar. Started following her until I had a clean shot and… boom."

Luna looked down at the bear, "Obviously, not clean enough," she said, alluding to the fact that the bear was still breathing.

He shook his head in disappointment as if he was mad at the bear for not dying quicker. "Yeah," he said, agreeing with her. He then chambered another shell and took aim at the bear's head. Luna braced herself for the noise. Orwell pulled the trigger and blasted the bear in the head with a hefty slug, causing it to stop moving completely. "How's that for a clean shot?" he asked with a straight face, looking up at her.

She began to wipe the sweat from her brow as he slowly approached her. "What brings you out here, Luna? Last time I checked, you were supposed to remain in your hut."

"I wanted to make sure everyone was all right…"

He flashed a crooked smile as he spoke, "Well, why wouldn't everything be all right?" He held his arms out, gesturing to the world around them. "We're in paradise, don't ya know?"

"I'm sorry, Orwell, I'm just going to get back to my hut now. Didn't mean to disturb you," she apologized, getting to her feet.

Orwell grabbed her by the wrist as she turned to leave. "Well, hold on now… I just killed that bear. I'm a hero now." He took a deep breath in as he closed his eyes and exhaled into her face. He then pressed her hand against his chest. "My heart is beating so damn fast. That bear coulda really hurt someone if I didn't do something, you know?"

She tried to slowly bring her hand away from him, but he wouldn't allow it. "You're right, very brave… Th-thank you."

He then began to step forward, closely examining her neck and face at an awkward angle. She still tried pulling away. "Well, hold on now, I don't get a reward for my heroic deeds? Last time I checked, the hero always gets the girl." He then sloppily kissed her neck, breathing heavily. She pulled her hand out of his grasp and turned away. He raised the gun and cocked it again. "Do you really wanna know how this ends? You're not supposed to be out of your hut right now. So do you want the pleasure? Or the punishment?"

She glanced over to where Constantine was buried. The dirt had been overturned and proved to be darker and richer than the other surrounding soil. She quickly looked away, not wanting Orwell to notice where she was gazing. "Fine," she said as she allowed him to grasp her arm more forcefully.

"I want you to say it," he hissed through his yellowing teeth.

"What?" she asked, scared.

"You heard me. I want you to say it… I asked you a question, it's only polite to receive an answer," he said, clenching his jaw together, flecks of spit landing on Luna's face. "So answer the question."

She swallowed and took her time to reply. "I want the pleasure," she said, defeated.

"Say it again, slower this time," he growled, taking in every ounce of the discomfort he made her feel.

"Let's go over here, it's… softer, more comfortable," she said, grabbing his free arm, trying to lead him away from Constantine's shallow grave.

He calmly began to follow her. Just when she thought she was in the clear, Maple dashed into the clearing with a knife grasped firmly in her hand, practically stumbling onto the bear's carcass. Luna tried to direct Orwell's attention away from her by moving in for a kiss, but it was too late. Orwell turned around and held his shotgun up at Maple.

"And just what the hell are you doing all the way out here?" he barked, "How is this gunshot any less alarming than the others? I'd expect thicker skin, especially from a hunter," he said, glaring at Luna.

Maple froze and tried to conceal the knife behind her back. "I apologize, Orwell, just going for a walk," she said, trying to cash in on her elderly charm.

Orwell wanted none of it. "The hell you are. Put it down."

"Put what down?" she asked innocently.

He held up his gun so it was level with her face and began to approach her. "Put the weapon down, or I'll blow you all over the trees."

She tossed the knife aside and quickly glanced over to Luna, the bear, then the grave.

Orwell followed her gaze and noticed the splotches of blackened dirt upon the earth. He grew a perplexed look on his face as he began to approach the grave, not yet knowing what to make of it.

Before he got any closer, he turned to Luna, who had now gotten closer to him. He didn't quite know what was going on, but he knew he was in danger, and that caused him to act out. "All right!" he yelled, trying to beef up his dominance using the shotgun. "Both of you, on your knees!" he screamed. Luna slowly walked over to Maple. The two of them then slowly got to the ground and knelt in the dirt.

He then directed his attention back over to Maple and smiled. "All right, chief. Your time to shine. Get over here and start digging. Can't wait to see what treasures we find," he sarcastically spat.

Maple began to stand up but was immediately pushed down. "Crawl," he ordered her. He then gestured to Constantine's grave with the stock of his gun, keeping the sights on her at all times. Luna just watched in horror, not knowing what to do. Orwell kept his hand on his transceiver, not knowing whether or not it was appropriate to call for backup at this point. Now that Constantine was gone, he had to take up more responsibility. He felt the need to prove himself to the rest of the Disciples, and alerting all of them for no apparent reason would just be an embarrassment to all involved.

Maple began to dig her fingernails into the ground, pulling back handful after handful of dirt as she stared down the barrel of Orwell's shotgun. He kept repeatedly glancing back at Luna to make sure she was still.

After what seemed to be an eternity of digging, he ordered Maple to stop. He had no clue she had been purposefully stalling so she could buy Luna some time to hatch a plan. Little did she know Luna's mind was on other things as well, whether Ray would make it up the mountain unharmed and whether Clover was actively gathering supplies.

"Pull it out," he said, looking at the plastic strings of a bag smothered in dirt.

Maple tried her best to discourage him in what could be her final moments. "Orwell, I don't think—"

"Pull the fucking bag out, Maple," he demanded, sounding as if he were on his last string. Maple began to tug and pull at the bag. Orwell looked back over to Luna. "You stay right there, ya hear me?"

Luna just slowly nodded, paler than a ghost.

Maple continued to tug and pull at the plastic until the upper half of the bag tore, sending her sprawling onto her back. Orwell jumped back out of excitement from her sudden gestures. He then tightened his grip on the shotgun and slowly inched forward.

As he got closer, he could make out the rotting remains of a corpse that had been stashed there. He turned away with a look of disgust plastered across his face. The putrid smell of rotting flesh was now evident after the plastic ripped. He then pointed the gun at Maple, who remained helpless on her back. "Is it, you know… him?"

She bobbed her head up and down, "It is. It's Constantine."

He held a sweaty hand over his mouth, trying to stifle what was on its way out, but it was no use. He vomited off to the side of the hole, looking at Luna with bloodshot eyes as he did. Once he finished, he wiped away at his mouth and the corners of his lips. He wore a sneer on his face like none they had ever seen before. It was ugly and terrifying at the same time. He kept the shotgun pointed at Maple. "This was supposed to be a place of peace, you *sick* fucking animal."

Maple was quick to speak up. "Luna had nothing to do with it! I swear! It was all me. It's what the bastard gets for what he did to Musgo!"

"That's enough!" he screamed as he lifted the walkie-talkie to his face. "They won't want me to kill you. No… they're going to turn you into a lesson. The both of you will suffer, I'll make sure of it." He then pressed down the button on the walkie-talkie, and the static picked up his voice. "I need all back up immediately. Half-mile south of Maple's hut. Emergency, I repeat, emergency."

Maple looked over to Luna, who remained frightfully still as Orwell spoke. Maple looked at Luna with those kind eyes she had grown to know and love, those high risen cheekbones that drew wrinkles every time she smiled at her, and the lips that spoke the sweetest, most reassuring words she had ever heard. Maple also took in Luna and all her greatness. The two stared at each other, absorbing each other's glow, knowing that someday, they would be reunited again.

"Go," Maple mouthed without using her voice. She gestured the word to Luna, who remained still after all this time. "Go," she mouthed again. Luna looked at her with a certain sadness that only a relationship between the two of them could capture. "Go," she mouthed one last time, this time with more urgency.

Luna's face lit up as Maple threw a handful of dirt into Orwell's eyes, temporarily blinding him. He jumped back and scratched at his face, giving Luna just enough time to roll back onto her feet. With that, she took off into the distance.

Orwell clumsily fired a shot off, attempting to hit her, but it was no good, missing her ankles by a foot. He screamed out of pure rage and smacked Maple with the blunt side of his gun, knocking her unconscious. He then frantically fiddled with the walkie-talkie, trying to alert the other Disciples. The static noise took charge again, long enough for him to scream, "Find Luna! I repeat, find Luna!" he yelled out.

***

While Luna wound her way aimlessly around the woods in fear for her life, struggling to find a safe haven while simultaneously trying to concoct a plan, Ray was struggling to scale the rougher patches of trail.

His forearms burned like they never had before as he gripped onto the slippery slate rock for dear life. His left foot tried to find some sort of rough surface to use as traction, but it seemed that he had found the only spot on the slope that gave way to flat rock. He quickly removed his right hand to place it on another spot on the slope. He looked at the rock where his hand had just been. It now contained a bloody print from where the slate had split his knuckles. He then counted down from three and swung his body to a new, coarser layer of rock.

Ray made the mistake of glancing down. He was nearing the top of the trail, though still not utilizing the main path. He clung to the ridged edges and inched his way closer to the top. The lip of the overhang was now within arm's reach, yet he was at an awkward angle. If he were to move too fast, he would certainly lose his footing. He now regretted bringing his rifle and ammo along. It was just contributing to the dead weight, an expense he could not afford at this point in time.

After realizing he was growing weaker with every moment he thought about his next move, he decided he needed to act. He took what he thought could have been his last deep breath and let go of the rock with his right hand. Using his feet as a spring, he leaped up and swung his hand down on the wet lip of the overhang. His feet dangled out from under him, and his body twisted and turned in every direction, trying to even out the weight distribution. He threw his left hand up onto the lip as well, trying his best to even out the weight he had dangling. After a few seconds, he calmed himself and pulled with all of the strength he had left. He managed to throw his right elbow over the lip and used it as an anchor to swing his right leg up as well. He then maneuvered himself so he could roll his body up and onto the ledge of the cliff. He remained there, breathing heavily as he looked up to the cloudy sky. He had made it.

As much as he wanted to enjoy his moment of victory, he knew he had a mission and couldn't afford the time to waste. He extended his bloody fingers up and down, trying his best to regain feeling as he got to his feet and headed off to the side of the main path where he would remain undetected. The scattered trees gave him limited coverage, but it would be enough.

He could make out the roof of the house in the distance, perched near the cliff overlooking Corazon. The very top of the roof was now visible. He removed his rifle from around his back so that he could use the scope as a way to see what was going on in the distance. It looked as if there were three Disciples dressed in purple near where the mouth of the path opened up to the house's front yard.

Each of the Disciples was armed and chatting amongst themselves. One of them had an ax resting on his shoulder. Ray then looked over to the house, where he saw Tobias, looking worriedly out toward the sky. He lingered under the door for a few moments before turning back inside; what he was thinking about was beyond him. Ray took his rifle in his hands and squeezed it hard. The gun itself could only fire one round at a time before needing to be reloaded. There was no way he would be able to take out or even wound all three Disciples before they could react. After little consideration, he knew the only way he would manage getting out alive was if he snuck into the house without being detected.

He crept toward the house, closer and closer until he could practically feel the warmth radiating from its exterior. He kept a steady eye on the Disciples who were on guard by the entrance. It was difficult paying attention with the rather loud hum of a gas-powered generator a mere three feet away from him, a simple explanation as to how the Disciples had been living so lavishly. Once he was around the side of the house, he could let his guard down. He stood on the tips of his toes and peered through the window, which seemed to be unlocked. It opened up to the kitchen, where there were many modern utilities not in use. He did, however, see Tobias, who seemed to be speaking to another individual out of his view. He watched as Tobias's eyes followed a tall, slender, naked woman into the kitchen. He seemed to be having a completely normal conversation with her. There was nothing noticeably sexual about any of it. When it looked as if the conversation were wrapping up, they both smiled. She looked at him and began to step forward in a seductive manner, an action he preempted by holding out his hand in between them. The naked woman's smile then grew a bit more honest and at ease as she accepted his handshake as the end of their conversation. She then happily left the room.

Tobias remained in the kitchen for a little while, standing with both of his hands resting on the top of his head. A small figure bolted into the room and threw herself onto Tobias's leg like some hungry animal. Ray was taken back to find that figure was Beatrix, laughing as she pretended to gnaw away at Tobias's leg. He smiled as he shook her off. He then crouched down and put his hands up to his face, moving his fingers like the giant fangs of some larger beast as he made a grotesque roaring noise. Beatrix jumped up with joy as she then scurried out of the room. Tobias followed, chasing her throughout the house.

Ray was thoroughly confused as he watched the two run about in a playful manner. He needed to find a way to get Beatrix away from Tobias if he was going to get her out safe and undetected. He waited for a while longer, lurking in the shadows, trying to figure out if now was the best time to strike. He pressed his wet palms against the glass of the window and slowly shifted it upward. Once the window was open a crack, he pushed it the rest of the way up with the tips of his fingers and got ahold of the sill, creating a firm grip that he would use to help him scurry up the siding. He ran up the wall with his muddy shoes and pulled himself into the house, rolling onto a sink and knocking over a glass.

He quickly got to his feet and held out his arms, his hands curled into tight knobby fists as he heard the glass shatter onto the kitchen floor. He looked around with wild eyes, unsure if someone would come bursting through one of the two entrances wielding some sort of ax or sword. To his surprise, things were actually quite silent. There was a rustling coming from somewhere upstairs, and a television played some Spanish cartoon in the other room. He tried stepping over the glass, making sure he avoided the awkward crunching noise that was sure to follow. He picked up his rifle and toed around the glass, peering around the corner into the room with the TV.

He entered the room, holding the rifle out in front of him, ready to pull back on the trigger at a moment's notice. There was a Disciple passed out on the couch, an empty bottle of liquor next to his hand. Ray slowly faded away, wanting to avoid confrontation at all costs. He turned around and peered up the staircase leading to a hallway.

He was willing to bet Beatrix would be in one of the rooms that remained tucked away.

Step after step, he creaked his way up the staircase, listening carefully for any high-pitched voices. He wrapped his hand around the brass knob of the first door and gently twisted.

A scream erupted from one of the doors down the hall. Ray let go of the knob and dashed down the hall, trying his best to locate the source of the scream. It was the last door on the right. He stared at the thick wooden frame, unsure if he should intervene or not. He held his rifle tight, and the sweat began to accumulate on his hands and head. Another scream rattled the walls. This time it was surely coming from the door he stood before. He rattled the knob to the best of his capabilities, but whoever was in there had it locked. Without hesitation, he stepped back and shot his foot toward the knob, completely breaking the cheap wooden frame, causing the door to splinter inward.

He immediately held up his gun to see a half-dressed Dante holding down a naked female on the bed. He looked at Ray with a grizzly expression as he held a long slender knife above his head. The bandages from where Aria had stabbed him still present.

Ray moved inward. "Get off of her. Get the fuck off of her," he stated, trying not to yell. His finger was already on the trigger. Dante quickly rolled off of her. The frightened female leaped off of the bed and scurried out the door behind him.

Dante put his hands up, letting his gut hang below his unfastened belt. "Now hang on a second, hang on just a quick second."

"Shut your fucking mouth," Ray ordered, stepping forward.

The fear in Dante's voice was apparent. His hands shook as he held them near his head. He looked up at Ray and tried to force a smile. "What are you doing, Ray… you're no killer. You know that. You don't—want blood on your hands."

"Where is the girl? Beatrix. Where is she?" He demanded an answer as he inched closer and closer, proving more and more dominating with every step.

"Just take her! Take her and leave! We don't want this violence! We are all—we are all children of Mother here!" he said, licking his lips.

"Where is she," he muttered, his tone more aggressive this time.

"You're no killer. Put the gun down, Ray... I'll bring you to her. I can bring you right now," he pleaded.

Ray began to lower the gun. Dante was right; he was no killer. He only wanted Beatrix. The longer he lingered there, the more Dante made sense. "Take me to her now. Now," he demanded.

"Right now," Dante said as he nodded. "Right now!" he yelled with more force this time.

Immediately Ray's vision went blurry as someone threw a plastic bag over his head and pulled back with all of their might. He gasped for air, but the plastic only filled the void of his mouth, making it impossible for him to get any actual oxygen. He thrashed about as he saw the hazy figure of Dante stand up through the crinkling plastic. He grabbed hold of his captor's belt and shoved him forward, releasing the grip on the bag. He quickly pulled the bag off of his head and raised the gun without hesitation.

The gun was knocked to the side by Dante just as Ray pulled back on the trigger. The shot cracked its way through the house, sending a bullet rocketing through a wall. Ray fought off Dante as best as he could, hitting him upside the head as Dante sloppily swung his butcher knife in every which way. The fight fell into the hallway, where another Disciple grabbed Ray by the collar of the shirt and threw him into a wall, causing him to lose control of the gun, rendering it useless.

He looked up and folded his arms above his head, deflecting the giant boot that came close to crashing down on his skull. Ray kicked as furiously as he could, managing to make contact with Dante's knee, sending him yelling as he hit the ground.

"Enough!" a soft voice called out from the end of the hallway. "What is the meaning of all this madness?" Felix asked as he quickly walked up to the cluster of men panting on the floor in the hallway. Felix caught a glimpse of Ray's face and quickly stopped in his tracks. "My, my, look who's back..." He admired Ray's bravery for a split second before he looked up at Dante and the other larger Disciple. He shook his head. "Dante, Simeon, you two should know better. Do you want another protest? We need to do this quietly, without any struggle."

Dante sat up against the fractured door frame while Simeon kept his boot pressed up against Ray's chest.

Dante sighed, "Well, then get me my knife. I'll cut his throat right here. We won't have to worry about this prick anymore."

Felix shook his head. "No, no," he said, dismissing Dante's idea. "This sinner is far less deserving. A quick death is no fate for a man this... disruptive. Get creative with this one, Dante."

Dante wiped the sweat and blood away from his mouth. He looked up at Felix and gave him a malicious smile. "The tub?"

Felix contemplated his thought and then gave Dante a nod. "The tub. Get it done. Let me know when it's finished." He then turned his back to them and walked away.

Ray tried to stand up but was forced back down by Simeon's boot. He reached for the transceiver on his waist, but his arm was pinned under Dante's body. Dante noticed his struggle and plucked the transceiver from his hip. "Looks like the sinner might have brought some company with him."

"In the name of Mother and all things sacred, Simeon, get this man to the bathroom and keep him quiet." Felix groaned, clearly tired of dealing with Ray and his stubbornness. "I'll check on Elliot," he stated.

Ray was done putting up a struggle. It was pointless while under the boot of a man of such stature. Dante pulled himself to his feet with a heavy wheeze. Felix watched him with a pitiful stare as he got himself situated. "I'll help Simeon get the tub set up," he growled.

"No," Felix sighed, frustrated. "You go find the girl. And no funny business, I want her brought to me," he stated. Dante nodded his head as he stood at attention. Felix's patience with him had worn out. There was no longer any need for traditional respect. He wanted results.

"Right now," he hissed. Dante scurried down the hallway, and Simeon looked down at Ray, a twinkle of joy in his stare.

46

Luna scoped out Corazon from the outskirts of the community where the brush grew thick. She kept her eyes peeled and her wits about her. She was perched outside of the limits of Corazon but close enough to see the main square where gatherings usually occurred. She was closer to the community than the cliffs that held the house on the mountain. The very house she hoped Ray would recover Beatrix from. Every Disciple was scampering about, fully armed as they ordered people around. Screaming at the locals, believers, and rebels alike, telling them to find Luna. They wouldn't find her; even if they did, she was much too fast. She had camouflaged herself as an extra precaution. Her face and arms were now covered in dirt, allowing her to blend in with the earth around her. She needed to find Maple. There was no leaving without her.

The Disciples paced around like madmen, waiting for their next orders on what to do. In the middle of Corazon, around the rock where everyone delivered the news for the day, a structure was beginning to be made. A large structure made out of thick splintery beams of wood forming an X. Within minutes, they dragged Maple's body out of the brush. She was completely conscious and yelling things at the bystanders, who seemed confused to see a prominent figure of the community dragged through the main square. It was apparent that something bad was on the rise, and they didn't know what to do about it. Maple was the last of the wolves amongst an abundance of sheep.

Orwell dragged her up to the wooden structure and had the other Disciples bind her hands and feet to each of the ends of the X using wire and twine. Maple just allowed this to happen. She seemed to fully accept the consequences of her actions. She knew it was her time. Luna watched with horror as they hung her from the X. She couldn't do anything to save her from where she was stationed. Even if she was down in Corazon, there were way too many followers. She would be far outnumbered by those who were stuck in their ways.

Once Maple was thoroughly bound to the fixture, Orwell stood on top of the large rock in the center of the square, just to the side of Maple. The same rock Tobias had been tortured on, the same rock where all of the big news for the community was announced. "All right! This is your chance to be the hero!" he cried out.

Another larger Disciple touched him on the leg to get his attention. "What are you doing, Orwell? You're going to scare the others..."

Orwell kicked the hand off of him and glared at him with wild eyes, "She's listening, she's watching. *Trust me.*" He then looked back out into the distance and scanned the horizon for any sign of Luna. After finding nothing, he opened up his mouth again and began to yell to the masses. "This woman you see before you is not the woman you have grown to know and love!" he yelled as he looked at the gathering of people beginning to form around him. "She can cook and talk and love just like the rest of us, but let me show you all what she really does." He then hauled up one of the large trash bags so that everyone could see it. He pulled out a knife and ran the blade across the cheap plastic bag, spilling the contents out into the open. Everyone shrieked and backed away.

Orwell seemed proud to have received that kind of a reception. "The woman you see before you is a murderer. A butcher. And because of this, she is going to die." Gasps ran through the mass of people before him. "Another murderer walks amongst us. A woman by the name of Luna. I'm sure you all know her. She is hiding, but she is not gone… not yet. It is our job to find her so that we can bring justice to our beloved Disciple Constantine!" He tilted his head back as if he were trying to force himself not to cry, causing the tears to drain back into the ducts. "This was a Disciple! One of our very own! And she murdered him in cold blood! Mother will show her no mercy, neither should we!" This outcry received mixed cheers in response. Maple just looked forward, not fazed by any of it.

Orwell nodded as he got some people to cheer in Constantine's memory, a verbal go-ahead for Maple's execution. He then turned to the woods behind the crowd.

"Luna, I speak only to you now! At this time tomorrow, Maple will be burned. You have an opportunity to give her a quicker death. All you have to do is turn yourself in. Bring an end to all of this madness. We all trust you will make the right decision!" He then stopped screaming and took a few steps back onto the rock, observing his situation and how he came to be here. He had no more power than any of the other Disciples, but here he was, the quiet one, taking charge.

Luna cupped a hand over her mouth as she watched the crowd slowly disperse. There was nothing she could do. If she went down to rescue Maple, she would surely die. Then what would come of Beatrix, of Clover? She turned her back to them, seething in her rage.

❋❋❋

Ray tried to move his hands and legs. His movements were slowed and created a sloshing motion that rippled all the way back to his chin. There was a faint scratching noise coming from his left, but his vision had not yet adjusted. As he slowly homed in on his surroundings, his hands were bound by a cord and placed in front of him. His feet were also bound rather tightly and rested on the edge of a bathtub, the same tub where his body lay. His clothes were soaked in the rather cold water, and his mouth was taped shut with heavy-duty industrial tape. He looked over to his left to see Dante.

He was hunched over a sink, looking at himself in the mirror as he viciously brushed away at his black teeth. He looked over to Ray and smiled, white foam dripping from the edges of his mouth.

"Good morning, sunshine," he gurgled as he spat the toothpaste out of his mouth. "How'd you sleep last night?" he asked as he took a dampened towel and ran it down his face. He hung the towel up and grabbed his butcher knife, which was sitting in the very same sink he spat into. He then pulled up a stool and sat next to the tub, looking down at Ray with a very strange, almost endearing expression.

"I gotta tell ya, I didn't sleep too well last night," he said, bringing the knife down to Ray's shirt and toying with the buttons using the tip of the blade. "Some *maniac* came into the room while I was trying to have some alone time with my lady! Can you believe it?" he said with a smile as he flicked off the first button of Ray's shirt. "In fact. This is the same maniac that's been driving all of us Disciples crazy," he said with a very calm demeanor. "I mean, this guy… he comes out of nowhere. Literally, we have no idea who he is, but one day, he's just here. And we couldn't do anything to get rid of him. We had this peaceful way of life where nobody asked the questions they shouldn't ask, but then this maniac joins our community and starts spreading his crazy ideas all around…" he flicked off the second button on his shirt, exposing Ray's chest that much more. Ray spoke, but it only came out as muffled blurbs and not the words he wanted to say.

Dante continued. "And before ya know it, all hell breaks loose. People start believing they have a choice in what happens to them. They start believing that there are other ways to live. They start thinking outside of the box. We don't want that. We want them to live in the world we designed. We want them to stay in our box—you understand? Things run smoothly that way. Things are safer that way. But no, this maniac, he just had to fuck it all up. He just had to pull at the yarn until everything started to unravel on itself." The buttons began to pop off rather quickly. Dante then brought the knife up to his face and examined it carefully, admiring its filthy beauty.

"This maniac caused us all a lot of trouble, but now… well now it's all going to come to an end, and I'm going to make this maniac really feel for all of the trouble he put us through. Remember this pain; remember it well. It'll be the last thing you ever feel." He then brought the knife to the top of Ray's chest and dragged it down ever so slightly so that it only cut through the very top layer of his skin. Ray thrashed about, sloshing water in every direction as he winced in pain. Blood began to trickle from the wound and run down his chest until it was reduced to a thin watery red upon contact with the tub water.

"I just want you to know… one maniac to another, I like the pain. I really do. It makes me feel something on the inside, something that only comes with suffering. It's as if I feel more awake, in a way. I can appreciate you wanting to be the hero and all, I really can. But I gotta tell ya, I've never met a hero so dumb in my life," he took a moment to chuckle. "Did you really think that what—you were going to just prance in here? Rescue the girl? Run away and elope with Luna? You really thought it would be that easy? I admire your bravery, I really do. But there is a fine line between being brave and being stupid. We are talking about years and years of organization. You can't just dismantle that and send us all into chaos. But I'll admit you did do a good job at trying…"

He moved Ray's shirt to the side using the dull side of the butcher knife so that his shoulder was exposed. He then nicked him with the knife, a small cut, but deeper this time. Ray squirmed some more as he watched the blood trickle down his arm, dyeing the water as it did.

Dante laughed. "I love teasing people, I really do. You know, Aria was a tough one. She took an awful lot. I like to see how far I can push them—the Angels. It was amazing how she kept coming back to me. She kept coming back because she believed it was the *right thing* to do. It was funny, really. Cute, in a way. It almost saddened me to put a bullet in her head. And Otto… well, he just shouldn't have gotten in my way. The half-wit had it coming."

Ray tried to sit up, but Dante was too quick and had leverage on him. He grabbed Ray by the locks of his hair and forced his head underwater. The first thing he noticed was how much the water stung his wounds. They seemed to fizzle with pain. He struggled to break free, but Dante had the better positioning. He kicked his legs and folded his arms, but it was no use, it only exacerbated his desire for air. Eventually, the struggle led him to inhale through his nose, causing water to quickly clog up his airway. His vision began to dim as his heart pounded. Dante yanked him back up above the surface of the water, but he still wasn't able to breathe. His nose was clogged. He whipped his head back and forth, trying to loosen the duct tape over his mouth. Dante grabbed him by the scruff of the neck and tore the tape off of his lips with force. Ray collapsed back into the water, gasping for air.

"You're not going to get off that easy now. How does the vinegar water feel? It's an old remedy passed down through the family." Dante laughed, putting a new strip of tape over his mouth before he was even done catching his breath. "Pull yourself together!" he yelled as he lunged forward and hit Ray in the face, all five knuckles landing squarely across his cheek.

"I want you to know, us Disciples are men of our word. After I'm through with you, we're going to find Beatrix and Luna. Then it'll be their time for a bit of redemption!"

He laughed again, forcing Ray underneath the surface of the water once more. His chest and abdomen burned like never before as the vinegar in the water seeped into his open wounds. He tried his best to fight his way out of the tub, but it was no use. Dante had all the power. He let Ray soak in the concoction a few more moments before yanking him back out of the water.

Ray lay his head on the side of the smooth white tub as he once again coughed up the water he had swallowed. He slowly began to drift into an unconscious state, but a strong, firm slap from Dante woke him right back up. "Stay with me here pal, the fun hasn't even started yet."

Ray closed his eyes tight. This was it. This is where he would die. He lay there, waiting for some sort of closure, waiting for the bright light he finally realized was never coming. The situation proved so intense, he didn't even reflect on how he would, in a twisted way, have the poetic death he had been looking for all along. Drowning, trying to right his wrongs, trying to be the hero.

As he squeezed his eyes shut, he envisioned a scene where he was stepping out of a car. He was well dressed in business casual wear and was no longer sprouting a beard, a rather professional look. As he stepped out of the car, he began to walk toward a beautifully simple white house, a toad croaking on the front step. He saw himself walking up the front steps and swinging the cheap screen door open, listening for the signature *smack* it would make as it made contact with the door frame as it closed.

He didn't know where he was, but he knew exactly where he was going. He wound his way around the edges of the house. He admired the various drawings and artwork that decorated the wall, deep, beauteous, colorful art. He then entered a room where the white light shined the brightest. There he found three figures with their backs to him. There was a tall, fair, golden-haired angel dressed in white in the center. By her presence, he knew that it was most certainly Luna. On either side of her stood a smaller girl. One with darker blonde hair, similar to Luna's, the other with deep black hair. He knew right then that the little girls were Beatrix and Clover.

This scene brought a smile to his face. But it was what they were looking at which drew his attention the most. All three of them were standing in front of a white structure that was raised off of the ground. It was a crib, and as he got closer, he could hear the muffled, playful screeches of what sounded like a beautiful baby boy. His dream wouldn't allow him to get any closer. It seemed this was all he would be able to see. This was his version of heaven. This was his God. This was his eternal resting place.

"What the hell are you doing? Shut the door!" Dante roared as he looked over to Tobias, who stood awkwardly in the doorway. Ray opened his eyes ever so slightly, just enough to see who it was.

Tobias looked over at Ray, his face plastered in worry. He then looked at Dante, who had the same sickly complexion he had when he killed Otto and Aria. Ray's face was not hard to read. He had the same exhaustive stare Aria had as they watched the sunrise—it was the stare of someone who had given up.

"I said shut the damn door!" Dante screamed as spit spewed out of his mouth in every direction.

He blinked a few times and then looked directly at Dante. "Where is she? Beatrix? Where is she?"

Dante's smile grew a bit bigger. "I don't know. I'm sure she'll turn up eventually," he said with a cackle in his laugh. "Now leave us. This is no business of yours."

Tobias sheepishly began to close the door, keeping a sorry eye on Ray as he left him for dead.

Dante whipped his head back over to Tobias and pointed the knife in his direction. "I said leave or else I'll gut you right along with him!" he barked with pure hatred and rage in his voice. Tobias quickly shut the door, leaving them be.

Dante turned back to Ray, who remained barely clinging to the edge of the tub. "That man…" He said, shaking his head. "He likes to act all rough and tough, but he's just a daisy if you ask me. I won't be surprised if he's next on the list of people to rid Corazon of. He represents the weak link, the easily manipulated. Worthless if you ask me," he said, shaking his head. "All right then, let's get on with it," he mumbled, twirling the butcher knife in one hand as if it were a toy.

"Ladies and gentlemen… the final act has arrived," he chuckled as he cut away the remaining scraps of Ray's shirt. "Come on, now, wake up!" Dante yelled, sticking the point of the knife into his hand. Ray's eyes shot open as the blade slid in between his knuckles. Dante withdrew the knife and grabbed his hair, preparing to submerge him once again.

Ray was now able to be manipulated like a rag doll. He was bleeding out quickly and growing weaker by the second. He turned his head to the side, trying his best to resist Dante's force. He saw the door to the bathroom open again. This time Tobias walked right in—slowly, but with confidence. Tobias held up a finger to his mouth, signaling Ray to keep quiet and not draw attention in his direction. He held a wooden cutting board in his hand, what Ray thought was the closest object he could find that would do enough damage. Tobias crept up behind Dante as he continued to try to force Ray's head underwater.

Dante seemed to grow angrier with Ray's will to live. "Well, it looks like playtime is over then. He flicked the butcher knife up in his hand and forced Ray's head against the wall, once again exposing his neck. Without wasting any more time, he held the knife to his throat and began to press inward.

Out of nowhere, Tobias smacked Dante as hard as he could in the back of the head with the cutting board causing Dante to jolt forward and catch himself on the tub. He let go of Ray, who slowly sunk back into the water. Dante turned around as he gripped the back of his head. He faced Tobias with an amused expression of betrayal.

"Oh, look who decided to man up!" he yelled with a certain cheerful anger. Dante withdrew his revolver that he kept on him at all times. He then pointed it at Tobias, who flattened himself against the wall, not thinking the entire situation through.

"Give that bitch a big ol' smooch for me when you see her," he said, pulling back the hammer on the revolver.

Just as Dante's finger began to tighten around the trigger, Ray used every last ounce of strength he had left to force the upper half of his body out of the water so that he could wrap the rope that bound his wrists around Dante's neck.

Ray pulled back as hard as he possibly could, taking Dante along with him. Dante tried to breathe in but only got a mouthful of vinegar water as his face broke the surface of the tub water. Ray turned toward the wall, pulling Dante's body further into the tub until only his boots were left dry, kicking about in the bathroom as he clamored for air. The shock of it all caused him to drop both the knife and the gun, giving Tobias an opportunity to act.

Tobias dove off of the wall and quickly retrieved Dante's knife as Ray struggled to choke him. Dante fought as hard as he could, thrashing around like a fish out of water.

Ray used his legs to force his body up in the tub so that his head was now above the surface, and Dante's was submerged. Dante kicked hard, just enough for him to break the water's surface and get one lung full of air before he was forced under again. Tobias finally came to his senses and brought the butcher knife high above his head. He kept the knife lingering in the air for a moment before Ray's blunt words snapped him back into the ever-cruel reality.

"Do it!" Ray pleaded with him. "Do it now!"

Tobias brought the knife down hard, puncturing somewhere in Dante's stomach. He let go of the knife quickly, but it only seemed to make Dante kick even harder, once again allowing him to break the surface and let out a half-gurgled scream.

Tobias pulled the knife back into his hand and struck Dante again and again until his legs stopped kicking. After a moment of silence, Ray hesitantly released the hold he had on Dante's neck; his body remained unmoving.

Tobias collapsed to the floor in exhaustion. Dante's body floated to the surface of the tub, a terrified expression permanently fixed on his lifeless face. "Get this monster off of me," Ray heaved, gesturing toward Tobias.

Tobias stood up and grabbed ahold of Dante's blood-soaked shirt, the knife still sticking out of his chest. He then hauled the body out of the tub, allowing Ray to climb the wall and slip onto the floor. The two living men lay there breathless for a moment, not knowing how to proceed.

Ray coughed up a load of water onto the tiled floor. He lay there like a corpse, his face pressed firmly against the ground, his eyes barely open. He could feel the life slowly seeping back into his body. He looked over to Tobias, who was propped up against the wall, breathing heavily. Ray blinked a few times and gurgled a few simple words. "You killed him."

Tobias looked at Dante's body as the blood slowly drained from his wounds. He then nodded his head. "He deserved it."

Ray lifted his torso off of the floor with wobbly arms. He then propped himself against the wall as well, picking up the revolver that Dante had dropped in his struggle. He saw that there were still six rounds in the chamber. He eyed Tobias, curious as to why he saved him.

Tobias looked over to Ray, noticing he had the gun in his hand, his finger around the trigger. "So what now?"

Ray took a few more moments to catch his breath. He then set the gun on the floor and slid it over to Tobias. "Now we finish what we started. We find Beatrix."

Tobias shook his head. "She's probably with Felix, and he's either long gone or has a small army of heavily armed Disciples with him. We don't want to make a scene. We wouldn't make it three feet."

"You got any better ideas?" Ray asked, tired of acknowledging the near-impossible odds they were up against.

Tobias thought for a moment. "June."

"Who?"

"The women. The Angels. They're all in the basement, we need to help them," Tobias gasped.

"We need priorities," Ray said in rebuttal. "We need Beatrix."

Tobias had clearly formed his position on the matter. "I'm getting the Angels. They've had it the worst, and I guarantee you they'd do anything to take a stab at one of these guys. We've already got one, that leaves fourteen other men in between us and Beatrix."

"You're saying we should get them to fight for us?" he asked. "What happened to not making a scene?"

"You and I both know this isn't going to happen quietly."

Ray threw his back against the wall. "What have I gotten myself into?"

Tobias slowly forced himself to his feet and stumbled over to Ray amongst the bloody mess they had made. He extended a hand, an olive branch. "Whatever brought you up here, whatever crazy idea you had that actually made you believe you could pull this off… keep thinking about it. Keep fighting for what you want. Do that, and… we might just have a chance."

Ray still kept a hesitant eye on Tobias. This was, after all, the man who had shot at Luna out of pure rage and confusion. Now he was the only chance he had at getting out alive. Ray firmly grasped Tobias's hand and allowed him to pull him to his feet. The battle had begun.

47

Tobias removed the knife from Dante's chest and handed it to Ray. "Follow me, I know where they might have her."

Tobias cracked the bathroom door open and led with his dominant side, grasping the revolver in front of him. Ray followed closely behind. Tobias led him along the edge of the kitchen, hugging the wall as they went, being careful not to make any sudden noises. He carefully opened a nearby cupboard and retrieved a set of keys, which he grasped firmly so that they didn't jingle.

Ray kept looking behind them, afraid that a Disciple might blow a hole through their chest when they least expected it. The house was surprisingly quiet, so quiet that the Disciples who remained on watch could actually be overheard using brief, muffled sentences as they stared down the empty dirt path. They had been surprised to hear of Ray's capture and still hadn't the faintest idea of his escape.

Soon, the two of them reached a door. Tobias quickly sorted through the keys until he found the one that was able to slide effortlessly into the slot. He then swung the door open, once again leading with his gun. Ray followed quickly, swiftly shutting the door behind them.

Tobias was quick to throw on the lights, shedding light on even the darkest corners of the room. Ray looked on in shock as he stared at many naked women, struggling to adjust their eyes to the light as they sat up on their beaten, filthy mattresses lying on the floor.

The women blinked until their vision was clear. Once they saw what was presented before them, their facial expressions changed drastically. They went from a look of dread and resentment to hopeful yet distressed, a melancholic mixture of emotion. June stood up on her mattress and smiled at Tobias, who smiled right back.

He quickly went to the wall where their chains wouldn't allow them to reach. He snatched and grabbed all of the keys hanging on their designated hooks. The keys were numbered and corresponded with the same exact number sloppily spray-painted on the top of each of their mattresses. Once Ray caught on, he too began to throw each of the keys in the direction of their corresponding mattress, allowing for the women to unlock themselves and help others in being unshackled. Each of them sported a bloody ring around their ankle from where the cuff had rubbed their skin raw.

June quickly ran into Tobias's arms as soon as she let herself free. Tobias spun her around, and the two kissed as they held each other close.

"What now?" June asked once the sheer excitement had slowed.

The smile slowly faded from Tobias's lips. He set June aside and looked at all of the other women who had just been set free. "I need help. There's a girl, her name is Beatrix, she shouldn't be far from here, she may even be in the house… but I need to find her, and as soon as possible."

Ray stepped forward, trying to prove that his word was more important, "She's my little girl. Please bring her back to me."

Tobias shook his head and took another step forward. "We all need to leave as soon as possible. This is your declaration of freedom. As soon as you walk out of this room, we are going to be at war. You can stay here—stay safe, but nothing ever changes. Bad things have happened to all of you at one point or another, and bad things will happen to her unless we find her. This girl is still innocent. *She's still good*. And it's up to all of us to protect the little good that's left in this place."

A tall, skinny, red-haired woman with a scar on her face spoke up from the corner of the room. She still sat on the edge of her mattress. "And what will Mother think of all this?"

Tobias clenched his jaw, not wanting to speak on the issue. Ray quickly took command. "We need to forget about Mother. We need to forget about everything you have learned here in Corazon. It is an evil place that has made you believe you are something that you're not. Aria broke free, Aria rose up and refused to take the beatings."

"Aria also died," someone chirped from the back of the room.

"Aria did die. Yes, she did. But she died standing up for what she believed in. She wasn't going to lay down and let the Disciples walk all over her. She took a stand, and she started something that it's up to us to finish. Don't let her die in vain. She was once a hopeful, young woman like you, wanting to come up here to the mountain in hopes of having a better life. Is that what you got? This is where things change."

The naked women looked around at each other. They were dirty, some were bruised, and some had scabs. Slowly but surely, they began to step forward, inch by inch. It started with June, who walked up to Tobias and took him by the hand. She turned to her colleagues and spoke very plainly. "These are the good guys."

One by one, the women joined them, forming a small circle around the two of them. "What's the plan then?" The red-haired woman with the scar on her face asked.

Tobias was the first to speak. "Find Beatrix. If we see any Disciples… Use anything you can find—a pan, a knife, a fork, a lamp, anything."

They all gathered up near the door. The women talked amongst themselves, making individual game plans as they formed around the door.

Ray looked over to Tobias. "Listen…" he said in a despondent tone. "When we find her, I'm going to take Bea, Luna, and Clover, and I'm leaving with them. We're never coming back. I've already talked it over with Luna, and… well, you were never part of the plan."

Tobias looked away and then at the floor. "I've protected her. Beatrix, she cares for me. And to be honest, I care for her too."

"That may be true, but one more body is one more mouth to feed and one more person to worry about," Ray said. "You should know all about that."

"I can hunt for myself I can feed myself, don't worry about any of that—"

"That's not the point." Ray snapped. "You saved my life, I'm grateful for that, but you know what you did. I'm sorry, but that's the way it has to be."

"We'll settle this when we're out of this place," Tobias said, feeling that the two of them had reached a compromise. However, Ray knew there was no compromising, Tobias was not going to come away with them, and that decision had already been made.

Tobias took a moment to himself before he turned to the women behind him. "Everyone ready?" he asked, holding up the revolver and pulling back the hammer.

The women nodded and whispered words of encouragement to their friends and loved ones. For a lot of them, this was it. Tobias put his sweaty hand on the doorknob and held it there, not wanting to turn the knob, not wanting to face what was on the other side of the door. June put her soft hand on his shoulder. He looked back at her. She smiled back at him and nodded her head.

"It's okay," she whispered.

He turned back to the door and swung it forward. He dashed into the kitchen with his revolver held out in front of him. He pointed it in all directions clearing each and every visible corner. "We're clear!" he shouted, signaling for all of them to come out of hiding.

They scampered about, all taking posts somewhere in the kitchen and looting the doors of any objects sharp enough to penetrate or heavy enough to bludgeon assailants. Ray stuck with Dante's knife seeing as it was far sturdier than the kitchenware the others resorted to.

Out of the very corner of his ear, he heard laughter, a muffled laughter that was not suitable for the situation they all found themselves in. He quickly dashed to a window to see that one of the Disciples was heading inside for what he assumed to be either a drink or a trip to the bathroom. "*Everyone quiet!*" he whispered as he darted to the side of the door where the Disciple would be entering.

He decided against the knife; he didn't want to cause a scene. He was going to have to resort to hitting him and hoping for the best. He quickly grabbed the empty knife block that rested on the counter to his side and held it high above his head. Everyone seemed to freeze in time, hiding behind cupboards and grouping behind Tobias, who held the only gun out of all of them.

The knob twisted and the door opened, letting natural light pour into the room. The Disciple had his head angled down toward his boots and hardly even noticed Ray. The door swung shut. The man looked up just in time to see the knife block come down hard on his head, knocking him to the ground instantly. Ray was quick to get on top of him so that he could strike again and again until the man dressed in purple lay still on the floor with three sizable lumps on his head.

The action was swift, but as the armed man's body hit the floor, it created a thud so loud that it shook the walls. Tobias and June both looked out the window to see if the sound had alerted the other Disciples. To their dismay, it had.

Three of the five Disciples by the path began to walk toward the house, their guns in hand, one of them still wielding an ax. Ray quickly picked up the gun of the man he had just knocked out cold. This particular gun was more modern, a semi-automatic handgun holding far more than six bullets. The Disciple fortunately also carried more ammunition on him, all of which Ray was quick to loot. He looked up at all of the women, standing around and waiting for an order. "Go. Find her!" he shouted, knowing that staying quiet was no longer a necessity.

The women dashed out of the kitchen and began to search all areas of the house. A few of them darted directly out the back doors and into the wilderness, bringing with them any scraps of clothing they could find to bear the weather around them. Ray quickly positioned himself in the hallway that led to the kitchen and flattened his back against the wall so that he would have the most coverage. Tobias did the same, but he hid behind a couch. Both men aimed their sights at the door.

The door swung open but was stopped by the weight of the unconscious Disciples body. They began to push and shove and eventually moved the body away from the door and let themselves back into the house. Ray swallowed hard. He had a clear shot but didn't want to pull the trigger. After all this time, he still didn't want to kill.

It didn't take long for the Disciples to figure out what was going on. They quickly looked up directly toward the hallway, seeing a glimpse of Ray as he took off and ran into one of the empty rooms.

One of them shouted as he raised his semi-automatic rifle and began to blow holes in the wall, missing Ray by inches, the dust and drywall crumbling to the floor with every stray bullet. Tobias responded by shooting off a few rounds in their general direction in the hopes of hitting something. To his surprise, one of the shots was followed by a thud, what he could only assume was a body hitting the floor. He lifted his head to see that he had tagged another Disciple in the knee. He was on the ground, writhing around as he cupped both of his hands around his leg. The next Disciple had managed to evade the unorganized spray and was already making his way down the hallway, dragging behind him the hefty ax he had previously rested on his shoulder.

The Disciple kicked open the bedroom door. It was Simeon. He turned to his left just in time to see a coat rack fly in his direction, bashing him in the upper forehead. He roared as he responded by flailing his ax in Ray's general direction. Meanwhile, Tobias was in the midst of a shootout with the other Disciple he had tagged in the knee, who retaliated by blindly shooting toward the sofa Tobias had used as cover.

Simeon let out a terrifying war cry as he mindlessly swung his ax at Ray, who continued to back up. The ax made contact with the tip of the gun, sending it flying to the side of the room. Ray slowly backed up as he tried to figure out a way to subdue the assailant. Out of nowhere, the red-haired woman with the scar hopped on his back and began to tug and pull at his neck with a small chain she had recovered somewhere. Simeon swung around, trying his best to get ahold of her body. Ray lunged for the gun. He leaped to the side of the room just as Simeon flung the woman into a wall.

Simeon then charged at him, ax held high in the air. Ray pointed the gun at his chest and squeezed the trigger, letting off a round that caused the large man to stagger back. His chest began to bleed; he looked down and touched his bloodstained garments. He began to approach Ray again, confused as to why being shot felt no more than getting punched in the chest. Ray squeezed the trigger, and another bullet beamed out of the gun. He then squeezed the trigger again and again. Each round caused Simeon to take another step back in order to regain his balance. Simeon dropped the ax and held his hands up in surrender, his eyes locked on his robes, now running with blood. Ray angled the gun up and squeezed the trigger again, sending a bullet whizzing through Simeon's head, forcing him backward and onto the ground immediately.

The scarred woman got up and wiped a bit of blood from her mouth. She gave Ray an appreciative head nod; the nod was then returned. As she exited the room, the clap of another gunshot rang out. The woman froze, then fell against the hallway wall. The man with the wounded knee saw his opportunity and took it. Ray reloaded his weapon and went to the door, only revealing enough of his body to see the Disciple down the hall. It looked as if there was another dead, naked body by the man's feet.

Ray tried slowly inching out in an attempt to get another shot, but the Disciple kept shooting, the door panel splintering away with every bullet. It was obvious this man had never operated a gun before but found the general idea simple enough.

Ray was prepared to leap out into the hallway in an attempt to take the man by surprise, only hoping he wouldn't be prepared for a moving target. He broke out in a light sweat and his eyes were stinging. He could barely hear his thoughts under all the pressure. Right before he launched himself into the hallway, the fire was met by returning fire at the other end of the hallway. Then, just like that, the gunfire went silent.

Ray ran out and threw himself into the wall, shooting at an assailant who had already fallen. He turned around to see Tobias, who was grabbing at his side. "Got him," he said in between deep, heavy breathing. Tobias limped to his side and helped him to his feet. "I heard them saying they took this from you," he said, holding out the transceiver.

Ray looked at the small black box with the antenna sticking out of it. He reluctantly accepted it and clipped it back onto his belt.

"Where'd you find something like that?" Tobias asked, skeptical of what was to come. Ray was about to respond when screaming erupted from upstairs. With little time for rest, the two of them responded as quickly as they could.

He hobbled up the stairs, his heart nearly pounding out of his chest, Tobias waiting on the floor, hung over the banister to better catch his breath. Ray watched as three women toppled a Disciple in the hallway, each of them contributing, taking turns as they attacked him with whatever they could grab.

Tobias caught a flash of light out of the corner of his eye. The front door had swung open, the glass reflecting the harsh early spring sunlight. It was Felix, his heavy hand yanking Beatrix by the arm out into the world. "Beatrix!" he shouted, alerting the both of them as the screen door snapped shut behind them. Ray turned and saw Tobias angled toward the front door. He couldn't concern himself with the final Disciple. Bea was his only priority.

Tobias looked to Ray as he clambered down the stairs. "Looks like he's running to Corazon—" he said in passing. Ray moved past him and threw open the door. Tobias looked back up the stairs, expecting a third body. "June!" he called out. "June, we need to go!"

His mind began to race as he expected the worst. Visions of seeing June being torn apart began to cross his mind. "June!" he called out again. Another booming sound erupted from upstairs. Someone had another firearm.

June emerged from the madness and threw herself into the railing. Her body had scrapes and bruises all over as she slowly limped down the staircase. He smiled out of relief, and she flashed a pitiful smile right back at him. Just when all seemed all right, a large figure lumbered up behind her as she stepped down the stairs.

"No!" Tobias yelled. "Get down!" he called out as he raised his gun. June was fast, but she was not fast enough to escape the crippling grip the man had on her hair as he pulled her back and yanked his blade into her back. She crumbled to the stairs, giving Tobias a clear shot. With no hesitation, he pointed his gun and squeezed the trigger until all that could be heard was the click of an empty chamber. The Disciple fell back, dead, and Tobias hurried to June's side.

Tobias stared in horror at her body as it was sprawled out awkwardly on the staircase. "*June,*" he said in shock. "June, we need to go. We—we need to go—"

He held a hand to his mouth, trying to stifle his cry. He wanted to mourn, but there was no time. With a steady hand, he closed her eyes and stood up straight. He knew his aid was needed in other places. He left the staircase and pursued Felix along with Ray. Nothing would prepare him for the events to come, the results of which would haunt him for the rest of his life.

48

Tobias hobbled outside, where he saw Ray standing very still; a mere few feet had been covered since he lunged out of the door. "What?" he asked, concerned. "What happened?"

It wasn't until Tobias was closer where he saw Felix standing near the very edge of the cliff looking over Corazon. The very same cliff where Otto and Aria had met their demise. Felix's face said he was to a point beyond that of anger, beyond that of rage. His hand encircled Beatrix's tiny arm, giving him complete control.

Ray had his gun set on Felix. His hands didn't shake. His body didn't flinch. He just stared down at the sight as he looked on at the two of them.

"*I'll do it*!" Felix barked in a voice never heard by either of them before. "I'll do it! Don't fucking try me!" he roared.

Tobias hesitantly moved up to where Ray stood but no further. Felix began to speak up as soon as Tobias came into view. "Not another step! Not one more step, or I swear I'll do it!"

Tobias put his hands up. "All right!" he said in surrender. "All right, just… take it easy."

Felix's eyes twitched as he looked back and forth between the two men standing before him. "Him too!" he yelled, gesturing for Ray to put down his gun.

Tobias looked over to Ray. "Ray..." he muttered, trying to reason with him.

"I got a shot..." He said, sounding uncertain.

"They're on a cliff, that's not a risk you want to take. There may be another way just... listen to him," Tobias said, trying to get Ray to calm down. A desperado with a vengeance was the last thing they needed at that moment.

Felix yanked Beatrix in front of him, ducking low, making the chances of a clean shot much more difficult. Ray quickly held up his gun, dangling it by his finger. "Fine—fine," he said with a sympathetic, worried expression on his face. "You got me. Just let her go. I'm the problem here, and we all know that."

Felix gave him a dangerous smile and shook his head, "You just don't learn, do you? You just don't learn!" he yelled, whipping Beatrix around. She was visibly upset and frightened whenever he moved abruptly.

"Felix, listen to me—" Ray pleaded.

"No! No, now it's your time to listen!" he said, once again whipping her to the side.

Beatrix clung to Felix's leg in fear of being flung around like a rag doll again. "Ray, I'm scared," she whimpered.

"It's alright!" Ray reassured her. "Everything's gonna be alright, Bea. Don't you worry."

"Yeah, go ahead," Felix said. "Lie to her. Everything is not going to be alright. Nothing is alright, and *you are to blame*," he said, his eyes widening. "There are people dying, and *you are to blame*. Corazon is divided, and *you are to blame*. Aria and Otto are dead, and *you are to blame*. Mother is angry, and YOU ARE TO BLAME," he screamed, flecks of spit flying in every direction.

"We had a system!" he continued. "It worked! The people were happy! They loved one another and didn't ask any questions! It was perfect!" he preached. "You took that away from me, from us—with your *old-world delusions* and politically correct agenda—that never worked for these people! That's why they came with us in the first place!"

Tobias shouted back. "No, fuck you, Felix," Tobias said, sick and tired of the charade. "You took the word of Elliot, and you twisted it into something—ugly. You ruined Corazon, and for what? So that you could sleep with whoever you wanted and call it faith?"

Felix broke out in a twisted laughter. "You still don't get it, do you? All these years, and you still don't get it!" he jeered. Tobias's fists tightened as Felix spoke up again. "I was saving you people! *Saving you!* These people came to me with nothing! They were broken! I gave them food! I gave them shelter! I took their worries and I made them my own while Elliot just—stood there spouting off and collecting the praise!"

"You lied to them!" Ray yelled out. "To the Angels, to everyone!"

"I did what I had to do to sell the idea of a paradise! And look what I made!" he said, throwing his free hand out behind him. "I made a *goddamn paradise!* I did! *I made this while Elliot lost his fucking mind.* And once that old bastard finally kicks it—then it's my turn to get the sort of respect I deserve. Then you'll see what Mother is truly capable of."

"It's over, Felix. Enough about Mother, enough about paradise. Just give us the girl, and we'll leave," Ray pleaded, not wanting to see any more blood.

Felix contorted his face into something that resembled a smile again. "Am I talking to a reasonable man? Or the suicidal stranger that murdered his way up my mountain? You have no idea what sort of things Mother is capable of doing… Tobias," he said, looking directly at him. "You know it; *you've felt it*. You know it's real. All of that is over if you let this sick man convince you otherwise. We must save what's left of The Getaway People. There's no turning these people away from Mother. An idea like this lives as long as there is blood running through our veins. It won't die until every single one of us is dead and gone!"

Those words embedded themselves in Ray's mind, giving clarity to Benji's way of thought. It was true, the vast majority of Corazon was too far gone, and the killing of Felix would not sit well for those so intertwined in Mother's strings.

Felix staggered back and forth. It was obvious that he, too, was in a fight-or-flight state of mind, the emotions surging through his body were beyond comprehension as he jerked Bea around by her arm. Tobias remained speechless, not wanting to speak on the matter. Ray held his hands out in a desperate attempt to reason with him. "Look…" he pleaded, "I'm your problem, I'm the one. The *defective human being*, right? Take me, cut me up, make me bleed, anything. Just please, for the love of whatever you believe in, let her go…" he begged.

Felix relished in Ray's desperation; he finally had control over the one man who refused it in the first place. Beatrix seemed even more concerned now, her innocent words spilling right out of her. "Ray, no! Ray, I want you to take me back to Luna, I—I still want to learn how to ride a bike! I want to have a house with a TV, and I want us all to live together and be happy! Ray, I don't want to—" she pleaded and pleaded, but that wasn't going to stop anything.

"That's enough!" Felix barked as he shook her free from his leg and held her closer to the cliff's edge. She let out a loud shriek. He held up a shaking hand. It was now apparent that Felix was crying. "This is your fault!" he cried out, shaking. "All of this. However, this ends. All of the death, the blood, the destruction. *You're responsible! Never forget that. Never forget what you did here today!*" he hissed.

Then there came a certain calm, a clarity, a moment of pause before the chaos broke back into play. The screen door snapped shut, and a humble figure shuffled his way into view. "What is going on out here?" Elliot softly asked as he strode past Ray and Tobias, his eyes set on Felix and Beatrix. "What has become of you men?" he asked.

Felix was silent. He, too, felt the general atmosphere of the moment shift as Elliot walked directly toward him. "My—my Prophet, you need to get back inside. It's not safe here." Felix said, still holding Beatrix by the arm.

Elliot stepped in between the four of them, still gently making his way toward Felix and Beatrix. "I feel… this hatred," he said, his mouth slightly ajar. "Mother is not happy. I feel this hatred, and Mother is not happy," he shook his head, looking at Beatrix.

Ray and Tobias remained still, the situation still proving far too risky. Felix spoke up. "My Prophet, you need to—"

"Mother hasn't been happy for quite a while, Felix," he said, his eyes narrowing as he directed his attention to Felix. "Her heart… it aches," he said, gesturing toward the earth he walked upon. "*She has been robbed of her purity, and she is not happy. And she will rise. And she will demonstrate. And she will conquer, and she will dominate, as it was, as it is, as it will always be. And only love will restore what rubble she leaves in her wake.*"

Felix found himself at a loss of words, confused by the crystal-clear sermon of the man who he thought had lost his touch years before. "My… my Prophet…" is all he could seem to say.

Elliot knelt down and took Beatrix by her free hand, consoling her and all her fear. He closed his eyes and took a deep breath. "Are you ready?" he asked, opening his eyes. The cloudiness that had once plagued them was gone, giving way to two emerald gems that seemed to understand her fear and anxieties at that very moment.

Ray eyed Tobias, who eyed the gun that lay by his feet. He wanted to talk to him, break things down and hash out a plan, but it was clear they had reached a point where plans were no longer relevant. They were mere instructions on how to blow out a match in a house that lay ablaze.

Elliot opened his arms wide and leaned in. Beatrix accepted his embrace and squeezed her eyes shut. "It's time, my child," he said, his words dissipating into the breeze. Beatrix's fragile body relaxed. She, too, took a deep breath. Felix watched the two of them, fully aware that he was caught in the workings of something beyond comprehension.

Tobias snapped out of the trance brought upon them by the presence of the Prophet. He dove toward the gun, realizing Elliot had tucked Beatrix away, his body now acting as a shield. Felix gasped, not having enough time to react accordingly. Tobias rolled over the gun and sprung up, his aim already set on Felix. With no hesitation, he pulled the trigger. Light shot out from the barrel of the gun. A loud crack echoed through the woods around them. Everybody froze where they stood.

Elliot remained huddled over Beatrix. Ray was a statue, not fully comprehending what had just transpired. Tobias looked up from the sight and saw Felix. Felix lumbered back and forth, a hand grasping his chest, a single stream of blood trickled in between his fingers. His face seemed as though he was lost, like he was searching for the pain that came with this death sentence. He looked back at Ray and Tobias, who now understood what would surely come next.

Ray broke into a run, his eyes set on Beatrix, while Tobias sprinted for Felix.

In that split second, Felix looked toward the clouds, one hand on his heart, the other still firmly grasping Beatrix's arm. "Mother, forgive me," he muttered just before jerking his arm toward the cliff, causing Elliot and Beatrix to lose their balance and topple over the edge.

Tobias leaped for her as he watched Beatrix's tiny wisps of hair disappear over the edge of the cliff. He reached out, desperately trying to grab hold of whatever he could, but it was too late. The Prophet and Beatrix fell swiftly. Tobias attempted to slide to a stop, but the rock was smooth, and in his feverish attempts at rescue, he too slid over the edge.

Tobias hung on to the edge with what little strength he had left. Beatrix and Elliot had already met the ground with two very distinct, very gut-wrenching thuds. Tobias attempted to use his other arm to leverage himself up, but his bones, still healing, couldn't take it. His grip slipped, and he, too, fell to the earth.

Ray dropped to his knees, appalled by the tragedy that had just unfolded before his very eyes. Felix collapsed. His hand, covered in blood, fell loosely to his side as he looked off in the distance.

Ray yelled as he slammed his fists into the ground. "What did you do?" he said, angling his head toward Felix. Felix didn't move. He didn't say a word. "What did you do?" Ray shouted, approaching him like a feral animal. He grabbed Felix by the collar and held him up. He had lost too much blood and was no longer responsive. His eyes drifted back and forth.

Ray threw Felix's upper half to the ground and peered over the edge of the cliff. There, sprawled awkwardly in close vicinity with one another, lay the unmoving bodies of Beatrix, Tobias, and Elliot. Ray held a hand to his mouth and turned away, coughing up what little he had in his stomach onto a nearby stone. He turned toward Corazon and looked bitterly toward the community that had allowed such an atrocity to occur.

With little hesitation, he picked himself up and ran toward the path leading down the , tears flowing from his eyes as he desperately hoped the events that had just unfolded were no more than hallucinations brought upon by a lack of oxygen. There was nothing he wanted more than to wake up on the rocky bank where it all began and leave well enough alone.

49

While everything was crumbling around them, Luna continued to scope out areas she would remain undetected. Her hands were sweating, and her body seemed to itch all over. There was no way to stop the madness at this point. She could hear the gunshots resonating from the cliffs behind her, and the scene in front of her wasn't calming her nerves in any way. She looked up at the sun. Judging by its position, she had no longer than half an hour to free Maple. She rocked back and forth as her mind shook with conflict. She knew Maple wouldn't want her to be a hero. She knew Maple was ready to die for Musgo and everyone else in Corazon. She knew Maple wanted martyrdom. She knew all of this, but she couldn't let Maple die and live with the fact that she didn't at least try; she knew Maple would have done the same thing for her.

❋ ❋ ❋

Ray panted as he ran up to the spot where the three bodies had just fallen. Each one lay still; each one held a certain awkward position of their own. Ray stumbled as he limped toward Beatrix, who lay still on the ground. He wanted to stop, turn around and pretend like all of this was a bad dream. He wanted all of this to end. He couldn't stand the fact of thinking that Felix may have been right. All of this could have been a result of his actions.

Step by step, he approached her little body. He knelt down in front of her and gently ran his trembling hands along her fragile bones. He took in deep breaths and tried not to expel them. He didn't want to react too strongly just yet. He then quickly brought a hand to her neck, extending two fingers so that he could feel for a pulse. He brought his ear close to her meek chest as he positioned his hand again and again in hopes that he may have been doing it wrong. After realizing she had no pulse, he quickly broke out in stifled cries and began to administer CPR as best he could. Starting chest compressions as soon as possible. He counted in silence until he reached fifteen pumps and brought his mouth to hers, breathing two quick breaths into her body, causing her midsection to rise ever so slightly. He then continued with the chest compressions. He would take sporadic breaks and feel for a pulse, becoming more and more concerned with each failure.

"R-Ray—" he heard a voice whisper from behind him. He looked over to see Tobias, his leg bent in an awkward direction. Tobias was crying as well as he slowly shook his head.

Ray knew exactly what Tobias was trying to say as he lay in a mangled mess himself. Ray scooped Beatrix's body up in his arms and buried his face in her chest. He then let out a loud regretful moan, which could bring emotion to the hardest of individuals. He held her body close and cradled it in his arms as he gently rocked her back and forth, reminiscing on how he promised he would show her how to ride a bike, how he would buy her a television, how he would build them all a house so that Luna, Clover, Beatrix, and himself could live out their days as a happy family. He thought about how all of this was now rendered impossible as he cradled her little body close, swinging back and forth as he knelt on the cold, hard ground.

He then positioned his gaze to the third body, which lay sprawled out next to Tobias. Elliot, in all his mystery, had managed to survive the fall. He lay. Still, a newly spilled red stream ran from the corner of his mouth, over his ear, and onto the dirt below. He looked at Ray, his mouth moving as if he were trying to say something. He then extended a shaking arm and raised two fingers so that it appeared he was pointing at Beatrix's body. Ray held her close and shook his head.

Elliot turned his hand and moved his trembling fingers as if to summon him. Ray refused. "Enough," he breathed, tears still streaking his face. Elliot continued to reach for her. An urgency lit up his elderly eyes.

"Do it," Tobias grunted, attempting to set himself up against a sizable rock. "Bring her," he huffed.

Ray cradled Bea's body even closer, shaking his head, refusing to grant the Prophet any last wishes. Elliot continued to reach for her. Tobias piped up, expelling all the oxygen he had. "*Do it!*" he shouted before coughing to catch his breath.

Holding her body close, Ray reluctantly moved forward, treading further into the Prophet's euphoric aura. He knelt down next to Elliot, whose hands shook with a desperate excitement. He said no words as Ray placed her body next to his. Elliot grasped her hand in his own and looked toward the clouds as his breathing began to stagger.

The euphoric presence began to fade, clearing the air for the cold reality death set upon them all. Elliot held Beatrix's hand. A smile slowly spread across his face. He closed his eyes, and despite the change in atmosphere, he seemed to be at peace. His head sank to the side, he breathed a final breath, and his heart stopped beating.

An emptiness seemed to drown out the shouts and hollers in the distance. Elliot and Beatrix lay still next to each other, Ray stood above them, not knowing what to do or where to go. He unclipped the transceiver from his belt and turned it on so that he could hear the static, still staring at Bea's body with two bloodshot eyes. He wiped at his mouth and pressed down the button that allowed him to speak. The static stopped, and he opened his mouth. There was a split second, a moment within a moment, where he questioned his actions. But he remained blind by what he had just witnessed. He cleared his throat and spoke clearly. "3842. The code is 3842."

It would only take mere moments until the static ceased, and Benji piped up from the other side of the radio. "*I knew you'd come around, friend.*"

Ray looked back at Tobias through teary eyes as he clipped the transceiver back onto his belt. "I'm sorry. I'm—I'm sorry."

Tobias grew more concerned in his confusion. "What did you just do? What was that?" he asked, his upper body propped off the ground by his elbows.

Ray ignored his questions and knelt so that he could pick up Beatrix's small body again. This time, instead of merely cradling her, he turned his back on the scene and walked toward Corazon.

"Ray—"Tobias begged as he remained broken on the cold ground. "Don't—do this," he said as he coughed. "Come— back!" he pleaded.

Ray slowly limped away into the woods, traumatized by the events that had just occurred. It all didn't feel real, yet here he was, cradling the body of his little girl.

"Ray!" Tobias cried out. "You—can't leave me!" He tried to get up, but he couldn't seem to move, his leg was a broken mess, and his body felt heavier than usual. He ground his teeth together as he tried to lift himself up, yet he was just too weak. The events that had recently transpired left him useless. He knew that once the adrenaline wore off, he would be in a world of pain. There was no way he would survive the night. "Ray—help me!" he called out.

Ray kept limping away, staring down at Beatrix's lifeless face as her hair fell softly over his arms. Tobias's calls in the distance became a whisper after a while. He trudged through the woods carrying

Beatrix as he did. The trauma inflicted on him was now more apparent than ever as he wondered how he would explain things to Luna. Then an even more dreadful thought floated into his mind, forcing him to think about how he would explain things to Clover.

Before he had figured out to deliver the news, he was forced to improvise. Up ahead in the distance stood Clover, blatantly disobeying his orders as she gazed toward Corazon from the safety of a thick redwood. He hastily tried to maneuver himself into the brush in order to buy himself more time, but it was too late. Clover had seen him approaching and leaped down from the tree to accompany him. By the time she was close enough to see who he had in his arms, she was petrified. "Clover," he said, wanting her to allow him the time to explain.

She did no such thing; she backed up.

Ray stepped forward, not wanting her to flee, but knowing that would likely happen, he began to get choked up again. "Clover, I tried—I tried to—" He couldn't do it. He couldn't physically string together the guilt he so desperately wanted to convey. She backed up even more, shaking her head in disbelief. "Clover, please, you have to—"

She took off running. Where she was going, he did not know. "Clover, come back!" he called out, but she was too far away and had no intentions of turning back. He then realized why Clover was positioned the way she was in the redwood. Just beyond it, perched on the ridge on the outskirts of Corazon, was Luna. He caught a glimpse of her golden hair through the crooked, blossoming branches.

He gently set Beatrix on a bedding of leaves and arranged her arms so that she appeared at peace. Luna was still, her eyes behind a hefty pair of binoculars as she scoped out her next plan of action. Before he knew it, he was mere feet away from her, an unknown entity forcing him to walk forward, forcing him to break the news, forcing him to shatter her heart. She was far too focused on what was going on with Maple to notice his presence.

Ray stopped where he stood and tried to say something. All that came out was a faint squeak of his voice. He was beyond words at that very moment.

Luna turned around, surprised by whoever was standing behind her. Her face grew pale, and her body seemed to go limp. "Where's Bea?" she asked, wanting to express joy but not knowing if the occasion called for it.

Ray stepped aside and pointed in the direction of her body. Luna leaped up and darted in that direction. Ray waited for it, the noise, the sound that only occurs when creatures lose the ones they love. It was a deep moaning sound that could emotionally cripple even the fiercest beasts. Yet it didn't come. There was sound, but it was not the sound he had expected. There was chatter, a conversation.

He turned, expecting the worst. His jaw dropped, his knees buckled, and the nausea brought on by sheer shock returned. He fell to his knees and looked up at the scene with an expression of disbelief. There before him was Luna, hugging Beatrix tight as she, too, was on her knees. Beatrix stood there, reciprocating her embrace, her smile wide, her cheeks rosy, her eyes overflowing with life.

"Are you all right? Did they hurt you? Is everything okay?" Luna asked, peppering her with questions.

Beatrix shook her head. "I don't really remember. I just got here."

Luna seemed confused, but it didn't matter. She continued showering Beatrix with every ounce of her love. "Luna!" she giggled. "Take it easy, jeez."

Luna pulled herself away and looked her up and down. "We're gonna leave, okay? Ray is going to help us get somewhere safe, I just need to—"

Ray approached her, staring at her like she had several heads. "Beatrix…" he muttered, not knowing what else to say.

Beatrix looked back at him, not understanding his expression of disbelief. "Ray…" she chuckled in return.

He leaned in and touched her shoulder, now beginning to believe that all of it may be nothing more than a dream. "What just happened?" he asked her.

She spoke in between yawns, "I don't remember. I just woke up," she stated plainly. "Do you guys know where Clover is?"

Ray blinked, still not sold on what was currently happening. "We're going to get her, and um… then we're going to leave."

"Maple too. We need to get Maple." Luna chimed in, making the task seem deceitfully easy.

Ray stood up, his skin pale and sweaty. "Luna…" he said, "what did you just see?"

She touched him on the base of the neck. "What's the matter with you?" she asked. "You look horrible. What happened up there?"

He just shook his head, unable to take his eyes off of Beatrix. Luna pulled him closer. "Ray. What happened?" she asked again.

As he opened his mouth to answer, the transceiver buzzed with static as someone tried to break through. *"Ready to—taking positions—one minute."* said the voice as it barely broke through the static.

Luna glanced at the transceiver. "What the fuck is that?" she asked, sounding alarmed.

Ray managed to take his eyes off Beatrix for the moment and focus on Luna as she shook him out of his trance. "Ray!" she shouted, "who was that on the radio?"

He touched the transceiver and looked her in the eyes, immediately regretting his previous decision. "It's—The Former."

Luna backed away, shaking her head. "We don't have time for jokes."

"Luna…" he said, "It was Benji, they're all here," he said.

She moved past him and grabbed Beatrix by the hand. "What did you do?" she asked. "What have you done?"

He took a deep breath and moved toward the two of them. "We need to go, we need to go right now."

She once again shook her head, "We need to get Maple, we need to get Clover, we need a better plan—"

"We need to go now!" he shouted.

She stood up and pushed him away from her. "Who are you! Wh-what have you done!" she screamed out, the fear evident in every one of her words.

Ray was thoroughly confused as to what she was talking about. Something was changing within her, something that he couldn't control. "Luna—it's me. You know me. You can trust me, but we need to leave now, or else we will lose everything," he said, grabbing her hand.

She pulled it away, "The code… to the hunting chest—did you?"

He sheepishly backed away, not wanting to give her the answer to that question.

Beatrix looked at the two of them, knowing full well she was missing something. "What is going on, you guys? Where is Clover?"

Luna held Beatrix close. Her look of betrayal cut through Ray, quickly disintegrating any shrapnel of heroism he held dear. Just as he was about to respond, a bright red beam of light shot up along the other side of Corazon, near the gateway. It spurted off red sparks in every direction as it rose higher into the sky like a deep red, burning star. The three of them gazed at it, not fully knowing what to make of it until they heard the sound that followed.

The dense silence brought on by the curiosity surrounding the flare was punctured with sharp, sporadic cracks of thunder that everyone quickly recognized as gunfire. The gunfire was followed by screams and a low rumbling that one could only assume was the frantic footsteps of fleeing civilians.

Luna dashed back to her lookout spot to watch the madness unfold. Teams of Former broke through the dense brush and took aim at anyone who tried to run, gunning them down like wild game. Several Disciples quickly engaged them in a firefight, while others took shelter as best they could.

The teams were tactical, bold, and wasted no time. They pushed their way into Corazon, slowly slaughtering their way toward the center, forcing anyone who stood in their way onto the ground. They had come from every angle, squeezing the masses toward the center. They all wore thick green and brown clothing, and their faces were caked in mud and filth, they roared commands at one another and made elaborate hand gestures to signal to other teams.

Benji stepped out into the carnage and blew a whistle right before jerking his arm toward one of the larger huts. One team responded quickly, tactfully crouching as they pushed toward the hut. Within moments a flurry of followers poured out the door and fled to the woods for better cover. The team quickly tossed wet rags onto the dried straw, wood, and mud that made up the foundation of the hut. With one flick of a lighter, the rags went up in flames, setting the hut ablaze within a minute's time.

Luna eyed Maple, who remained tethered to the post at the center of the community, her captors thoroughly distracted by the explosive savagery. With no hesitation, Luna leaped of the barrier that gave her concealment and took off, running right toward the thick of the chaos.

50

Ray tried to catch up with her. He frantically chased after her, yelling for her to stop.

"Stop! Luna, you don't understand!" He grabbed her by the back of her shirt and yanked her down like a lion taking down a gazelle. She tried to fight him, but he pinned her to the ground. Beatrix shouted at them as she tried her best to keep up.

"Stop it!" she screamed, just as overwhelmed as they were.

"Look at what you're doing! Think about this!" he yelled at Luna, bits of his foamy saliva landing on her face. She now looked at him as if she barely even knew the man he was, as he sprawled himself out over her, pinning her arms and legs, restricting any sort of movement.

Her lips quivered as she tried to find the right words to say. "You couldn't save your own home… don't stop me from saving mine."

These words sunk deep into his chest and pierced his soul. It hurt in a different kind of way, a pain he hadn't felt in so long. He lifted his arms from her wrists as he lightly nodded.

She stood up and dusted herself off; he remained on his knees. "I'll meet you by Otto's cove," he huffed. "If you don't show up soon,

I'm taking Clover and Bea and finding somewhere safe," he said, using his knees as leverage to stand up.

She nodded and looked at him, debating whether or not he deserved a noble send-off. Another gunshot rang out in the distance. There were no more words to be said. She looked at Beatrix, nodded, and ran straight into the war zone.

Beatrix cried for Luna to come back, but it was clear her innocent words would do nothing to hold her back. Ray scooped Beatrix up in his arms and held her close as he trudged back to the lookout, further and further away from the madness.

Luna pushed toward the center of the community, where Maple was still strung up. Benji's people began to flank the southern side of the community, giving Luna a little more time to think. She ran up behind Maple and quickly began to work on the knots that were holding her in place.

"Luna, what is all of this?" Maple asked, fretting with anxiety.

Luna frantically picked away at the knots. "I don't need to know what it is to know that it's not good. We need to move!" she said as she untied both of Maple's wrists. Maple then began to untie her ankles herself while Luna stood on watch for any incoming threats. Sledge dashed through the center of the community and took shelter on the broad side of a hut. In his arms, he clumsily held several long guns, a secret stash in case things ever got out of hand. Two more followers were quick behind him. He dished out the rifles and whispered things to them, drawing in the air as if it were a map. With an over-exaggerated nod, the two followers dispersed, running right toward the gunfire. Sterling slung his spare gun over his shoulder and crept out from cover, disappearing into the woods again.

Maple hopped down from her structure and took a moment to regain her balance. Luna immediately ordered her to stay low as the two of them traveled hunched over, making their way to where

Sterling had previously stood. "We need to make it to Otto's cove. Ray has the girls. He's waiting there for us."

Maple nodded her head. "What's the best way to go?"

Luna winced, trying her best not to let herself go. She had run into the chaos so quickly. She hadn't the faintest idea as to how she was going to find her way out.

"Aye! Luna!" A man yelled as he bolted back into the clearing. "Get down!"

Both Luna and Maple hit the ground as an array of bullets whizzed over their heads. It was only a split second before they were able to turn around, seeing a small man, dressed in camouflage, fall face down into the mud, the knife he had been brandishing stuck up from where he had landed.

Sterling smiled as he ran up to them. "So this is what it all comes down to!" he laughed. "Had to have known The Former would come back for us eventually, huh?" he said, eerily cheerful. "When do you think Mother will come down to protect those of us who were most loyal?" he said with a sarcastic chuckle.

Luna stood between Sterling and Maple, still fully aware that the two of them were wanted by the Disciples. Sterling noticed her discomfort and addressed it immediately. "You know, you two don't seem too threatening considering…" he wagged his finger up in the air, "everything else." He looked all around him and slung his spare rifle off of his shoulder. "If you ask me, it looks like it's every man for himself," he said, handing the rifle to Luna.

She accepted it from him, "Thank—"

Another loud gunshot cracked through the woods as a bullet clipped Sterling's shoulder. He gripped it as he fell to the ground. "Shit!" He looked back up at the two of them; a deranged sparkle lit up his eyes. He turned toward his assailant and laughed at him, howling in his general direction. He got to his feet and raised his arms up high. "You're gonna have to try a lot harder than that boy!"

he then turned to Luna and Maple. "I suggest you ladies find another way out of here, I'll hold this bastard off," he said with a wink. This made them look around and realize how many lifeless bodies were scattered around them.

The two of them quickly scampered in the other direction, once again using the huts as a means of cover. Luna removed the clip in the rifle; Sterling had left her with four rounds. She looked at Maple, "Stay close, I don't have a lot of ammunition."

Maple then huddled up behind Luna, preparing for the worst.

❈❈❈

Ray stepped into Otto's hut to find Clover, quietly crying to herself over a collage of various pencil drawings. "Clover," he said, hoping for some form of acknowledgment. She just tucked herself even further into her metaphorical shell. "Clover, someone really wants to see you," he said, still unsure of how to explain Beatrix's existence at that moment.

Beatrix stepped around Ray and approached Clover. "Hey there. I still got my bracelet," she said, holding her arm out in the air so that the homemade bracelet could dangle freely from her wrist.

Clover froze and slowly spun around, looking first at Beatrix, then at Ray. Her face wore the same expression of disbelief he had experienced just before. He wanted to shrug and say how he had made a mistake, how he had somehow missed her pulse, but he knew what he had felt. He remembered the feeling of cold skin in his arms and the emptiness that followed the loss of life. Yet here she was.

Clover allowed herself to take a step forward, not being nearly as delicate as Ray was when it came to addressing the elephant. "You were dead," she stated, not wanting to get any closer. "I saw you. You were dead," she said again.

Beatrix forced a giggle. "No, I just had to leave for a little while. I was keeping Elliot company up on the mountain."

Clover took another step forward. "But after that, I saw you in Ray's arms. You were all white, and you weren't moving... you were dead."

Beatrix seemed mildly confused. "He picked me up when I was sleeping. I don't remember much before that, but the Prophet was there. And—"

Clover took one more step forward, then the threshold burst. She threw herself onto Beatrix and squeezed her, tears running down her face as she tried her hardest to hold herself together. Ray backed out of the hut, knowing that the two needed a moment to themselves. They were here, they were safe. Now it was only a matter of if they could afford to wait. "You two stay here," he said. "*I mean it.*" He looked toward Clover, who knew she had been dangerously disobedient. "I'm going to go check out the area. I'll be right back."

❋ ❋ ❋

Luna and Maple successfully slipped into the woods. It was now just a matter of staying hidden all while getting to Otto's cove undetected. The two of them crept over the roots and dry sticks on the ground. The area around them was alive—the birds were chirping, and the nearby river seemed to be roaring louder than usual. It helped significantly when it came to maintaining their silence.

The two of them walked along, only whispering what needed to be said. "*There. Straight ahead, to your left a bit,*" Maple muttered, nudging Luna. About seventy yards ahead of them stood a man in a makeshift, ratty-looking uniform. He had a military-style haircut and sprouted a patchy beard. "*Are you gonna shoot him?*" Maple questioned, curious as to why Luna was waiting so long.

"Let's see if he moves," she said quietly. "*This place is crawling with freaks like that. They outnumber us. It's better we don't draw attention to ourselves,*" she whispered.

Slowly but surely, the two of them began to head in a different direction, deciding to follow the river to Otto's cove instead of cutting through the woods. It was much more silent along the riverbed, but it left them exposed and with little cover if presented with an obstacle or adversary. Screams could be heard in the distance, followed by more high-pitched cracks of gunfire. The whole scene was quickly turning into a massacre.

The two of them picked up their pace, knowing that the longer they were out there, the more apt they were to be caught. Right when they least expected it, about twenty feet in front of them, a woman jogged her way over the top of the bank and ran for the river. The woman was dressed in white and held her arm as if she had been wounded. Maple and Luna froze, hoping that this woman had not seen them, crouching closer to the ground to better blend in with the environment. The woman nervously hopped in place as she looked upstream and contemplated jumping into the currents.

That's when Luna got a brief look at the woman's face. It was Brooke, the woman who had been seeing Tobias earlier that year—the very same woman who stood up for her when the Disciples threatened her with death. Brooke began to bend her knees, willing to take her chances with the rapids, then face a certain fate with whatever she was running from. Luna's conscience got the better of her as she shouted, "Brooke!" just loud enough for her to hear.

Brooke turned to them with a look of pain and fear embedded in her face. She began to hobble over to them. It was now evident she was being chased. One of the Former appeared at the top of the crest, where the bank began to sink. Brooke tried her hardest to run to them, but it was no match for the speed of the bullet that whizzed through her head. A red mist projected onto Luna and Maple as they stood in front of Brooke. Brooke froze, her body stiff and rigid, right before collapsing to the ground. The man looked up from his rifle, noticed Luna and Maple, and immediately took aim again.

Without taking aim, Luna hurriedly fired all four shots in the man's general direction. She opened her eyes to see the man grabbing at his neck in the distance, he staggered back for a brief moment before his front garments began to stain, and he tumbled down the bank and into the river. The current swiftly swept his body up along with it.

"Move!" Luna ordered as she began to pick up the pace. Within a moment or so, another armed vigilante was shooting at them. It was, in fact, the man they had seen just before, the very man whose life they had spared. Maple quickly noticed how he was approaching an area thick with foliage; he wouldn't be able to see them through all of the blooming greenery. He shot down at them as he ran along the embankment. Maple pulled back on Luna's shirt as soon as she was sure they were out of sight.

"He can't see us. We won't be able to lose him, but now is our time to act!" Maple said, pushing Luna up the embankment. "I'll distract him; you get him from behind."

There wasn't any time for arguing. This was the very best plan they had. If Maple didn't act as a distraction, they were sitting ducks. Luna quickly scampered up the embankment as Maple continued to jog along the river's edge. The man who had previously been shooting at them ran along the edge of the ridge, still thick with springtime vegetation, waiting for the trees to thin so that he could have a clear shot. He saw the previous two targets moving. He had not even noticed that one had dropped off.

Luna gained speed as she ran up behind the man. There was still quite a bit of distance to cover, but she needed to reach him before the tree's cleared, and Maple needed to keep running or else he would have a clear shot at her.

Luna recognized the man from behind. A former follower who went by the name of Cal. He was a dedicated follower who followed the word of Elliot to the greatest extent possible. Everything seemed to fall in line for him until his lover was chosen as the next Angel. Her name was June, and she was everything to him. After that, a crack had formed. Slowly but surely, he began having contact with other people who held their own doubts. That crack grew deeper and wider until there was nothing to fill it but hatred. He disappeared one day, the rumors said he had joined up with the Former, but they were all just rumors. He was a believer, a worshiper, a lover, and a friend. But at this very moment, he was nothing more than an enemy.

Maple and Cal were slowly approaching the point where he would have a clear shot. Luna was still gaining speed. Maple realized she had now entered a point where she was vulnerable; it was now all up to Luna to get to the man in time. She chugged along, watching as Cal took position. Within a moment's notice, he squeezed the trigger and let off a single shot, just before Luna was able to strike him in the back of the head with a stone. The force of it all sent Luna and Cal rolling down the embankment.

Luna, dizzy, crawled to her feet just to see Cal attempting to do the same. She kicked him onto his back and straddled his arms so that he was defenseless. With two might swings, she bashed him over the head with the stone, knocking him into a deep state of unconsciousness.

She rolled off of him, panting. Not having the words in her to describe how she felt.

"All right," she sighed as she sat up, still panting. "Otto's cove should be another half mile up the—"

She saw Maple holding her stomach as she sat across from her in the soft, wet dirt.

"Maple!" she cried, rushing up to her and placing her hand on Maple's wound in order to have extra pressure. Maple touched her wound and saw a handful of blood as she lifted her palm to her face. She seemed confused; she hadn't felt a thing.

"It—it's all right, dear..." Maple muttered, all of the spunk and sass she had once spoke with nowhere to be found.

"You're right, we just need to get to Otto's cove. Ray will be waiting there, he can maybe—"

Maple's face shriveled up, truly revealing her old age for the first time in a while. She wasn't going anywhere. She grabbed Luna's hand and grasped it firmly on her lap. "I still remember the way you looked when you first saw him. I knew that look, I knew what you were in for, I knew that man would be nothing but trouble in your life."

Luna tried her best to keep herself together. This was all too much to handle throughout the span of a day.

"Don't let go. Don't give up on him. Make all of this worth it," she said, clenching her jaw together tightly and nodding her head.

Luna shook her head. "I can't do this anymore, Maple—I—I just can't handle this. I can't do it anymore. She said as a spool of drool ran from her mouth as she shook her head, completely distraught.

Maple lightly swatted Luna's cheek. "Aye... now that doesn't sound like the woman I raised." She paused for a moment to readjust her positioning to lessen the pain. "You have seen it all. You are the toughest, most daring young woman I have ever had … the pleasure of loving. The stage may be bloody, but that doesn't mean there isn't more behind the curtain. You must push forward. You must. You don't have any other choice."

Luna buried her head in Maple's shoulder. "Please, don't. Maple, please…"

"Come on now. More will be coming. Give me the gun, I'll hold em off as long as I can." Maple said with confidence.

Luna reluctantly handed Maple the gun. She then kissed her on the forehead and hugged her longer and tighter than she had ever hugged before. This was her way of saying goodbye to the best and only mother figure she ever had. The only woman who taught her to fight, the only woman who taught her to love. Luna stood up, having heard some others yelling in the distance. She looked at Maple with regret one last time.

Maple shooed her on. "Go on now. I'll give Musgo your best, dear. Someday we'll be together on the other side again, Luna, trust that. *I love you.*"

Luna began to bawl as she walked down the riverbank, leaving Maple behind. "I—I love you too." With that, she picked up the pace, carrying on with nothing but a knife. She quickly made her way toward Otto's cove, afraid that the assailants were close behind. Her fears were answered with an array of gunfire 300 yards behind her. The shots were followed by two quick shots from a different firearm. Then everything went silent.

❈ ❈ ❈

Ray rocked back and forth as he stared at the closed-in space that was Otto's cove. Luna had been gone for too long, it was only a matter of time before Benji and his men showed up at the cove. He bit his lip and slapped his face in order to get himself focused. He paced the area alongside the river in order to clear his head. He couldn't bear to be in the same room as Beatrix at that very moment, his heartstrings still recovering from what he had witnessed hours before.

The gunfire was becoming more and more prominent. It was all slowly making its way toward them. He grew more nervous with every passing minute. He had no way to protect himself, no means of defending himself, not to mention the girls.

"That's it," he muttered after hearing more gunfire dangerously close to the clearing. "Clover, Beatrix. Come here," he ordered. The two girls shuffled outside. "We're leaving. Now. Get everything you need."

The two of them were quick to respond, throwing any necessities into a bag that Clover slung around her back. Even after having spoken with Beatrix, she remained uneasy and rather quiet. Beatrix seemed just as chipper as usual as she waited for Ray to give them their next order. He couldn't allow himself to reveal to them that he was now just as clueless as they were, but running away from the sound of gunfire seemed like the best plan at that point in time.

"What about Luna?" Beatrix chirped as he began to walk away from the cove.

"She'll catch up," he responded, just as nervous as they were.

Clover was next to speak up as she trailed behind him. "But what if she doesn't—"

He stopped in his tracks and knelt down to face them. "Look, I don't know. I don't know what we're going to do, but before we figure it out, we need to be safe. So let's move."

Clover remained still, "We're not leaving her."

Ray was getting more frustrated. "Clover, we don't have the time to—"

Clover spoke up before he could finish, showcasing her inner streak of rebelliousness that he had grown so accustomed to. "We'll leave a trail, something that she can follow."

He held his arms out to the side, "What do you want to use? Huh? Everything blends in out here, there's no way we—"

Clover tugged at her bracelet until it snapped off of her wrist. She then looked to Beatrix, who did the same. Clover held out a handful of beads whose colors were all different. "We'll use the beads," she stated, having solved the problem.

Ray just nodded his head and continued walking.

Clover and Beatrix followed close behind, dropping one bead every few yards.

51

Benji nearly choked on the thick smoke that rose from the flaming huts and ashy heaps of a burning Corazon. Ruth and several others approached him. Behind them, they dragged a body.

He looked at them, his eyes wide with expectations.

Ruth avoided making eye contact as she stared at the mud and twigs at her feet. "We found a body. It's him."

Benji clenched his jaw and squeezed his eyes shut. "He's dead?"

Ruth nodded while the other cowered behind her massive build. "We did find this one, though."

The others moved to reveal a tired and broken Tobias, whom they had dragged from the base of the cliff. Ruth looked at Tobias, then back at Benji. "He says he saw it happen. A few of them fell over the edge; the Prophet didn't survive."

Benji puckered his lips as he tried to contain his disappointment. He looked at Tobias, who seemed to barely be keeping his wits about him. "Bring him over there."

The Former grabbed Tobias and dragged his body over to a nearby tree, where they propped his back against the bark and tried to position his broken leg so that it was mildly bearable. He moaned as they moved it, trying his hardest to ignore the pain.

Benji slowly walked up to him with a certain elegance in his step. "Tobias, Tobias, Tobias. I thought you would have had enough of me by now?" he said, crouching down so that he was eye level with him.

"Sorry about Samuel," he muttered. "The guy had a bloody death wish, though. We found tumors in his neck back at the camp. He came up with this whole plan where I bring him in, acting as the prisoner who freed himself and managed to take his captor hostage in the process. And let me tell ya, I deserve a fucking Oscar for that performance, friend."

Tobias held his gaze, not intimidated in the slightest. Benji continued, "I wanted to stick to the plan, ride things out as long as possible, but you savages would have torn him to shreds before a proper plan could be made. Besides, he only wanted little Beatrix. After the split broke him and his Mrs. up, she was all he had left. It hurt me to stick him, it really did." Benji stated, seeming somewhat remorseful. His words had clearly gotten to Tobias, who was now breathing heavily as he sat up against the tree.

"So what happened up there, huh? How come you and the Prophet went tumbling down the mountain?" he asked, raising his brow.

Tobias didn't say a word.

Benji smirked, "Tobias. I know we've never really gotten along, but I'm holding all the cards here, friend. Either you tell me what happened, or…" Benji nodded toward Tobias's leg. "I can see what I can do to fix your leg, but trust me, I'm no doctor."

Benji placed a hand on Tobias's leg and looked him in the eyes. "What happened on the mountain, Tobias?"

Tobias winced in anticipation, "It was Ray. He came and—and tried to get Beatrix, we unlocked the Angels, caused a big stir…"

Benji nodded, "Good work, much more than I'd expect from a man like yourself. Go on."

Tobias reluctantly continued. "Felix took Bea out to the cliff; he was using her as collateral. Elliot—he came out and hugged her. It didn't make that much sense. But I saw a shot and I took it. I got him, but not before he pushed the two over the edge. I ended up going over too when—I tried to grab her."

Benji seemed impressed with the way things had gone down. He looked over at Ruth, who was on standby. "And the girl?"

Ruth shook her head. "Wasn't there."

He looked back to Tobias, who shook his head. "Ray took her body with him."

Benji rolled his eyes. "Of course he did."

Standing up, Benji began to pace, trying his best to piece things together. "So Elliot, he died. But the Book says—"

"I know what the book says," Tobias said through clenched teeth.

"Mother has to speak through someone, yes? If not Felix, then who? Elliot must pass on Mother's touch to someone new, it must be so." Benji said, eagerly awaiting a response.

Tobias forced a smile. "And what if it was me?" he asked, sounding cheeky.

Benji still seemed mildly amused. "Then you'll be coming back to our camp with us. And you'll protect us with your presence, just as Mother truly intended. But it's not you. I'd feel the presence. Besides, Elliot would never bestow his gift on someone so—filthy."

Tobias shrugged, "Looks like you'll have to take me there and find out."

Benji chuckled. "No, Tobias. You'll be staying right here with the rest of the waste Corazon manufactured. You had your chance at salvation, and you chose punishment. How silly," he winked. "Where's Luna and her dog?" he asked, taking on a new, more menacing tone.

"Ray?" he asked.

Benji nodded, "That's the one."

Tobias coughed, not knowing what sort of information would prove valuable. "Long gone."

Benji took a deep breath in. "We'll see about that one, friend," he looked toward Ruth and changed his tone. "This one isn't worth the ammunition. Go round the others up and give me a gun."

Ruth tossed Benji a rifle, which he swung under his arm. He looked back at Tobias with a whimsical expression. "Till next time, friend."

The Former then spread apart. Benji snaked his way into the trees, leaving Tobias crippled in the ashes of Corazon.

52

Benji had his rifle at the ready as he wound his way through the wilderness. Other Former passed him as he crept through the trees. They nodded toward him or whistled or made some sort of elaborate hand gesture, but it was all silent. They could tell he had an agenda.

It wasn't long before he came across the mouth of the woods, where the river ran fast and the trees thinned out. All the adrenaline had tired him out. He knelt by the water and drank, quenching his thirst in an instant. It was there where he saw the tracks. The result of pacing, back and forth through wet ground. Benji stood up and examined the tracks, finding that they led directly to Otto's cove, a place he was aware of but had tried to avoid throughout his time in Corazon.

He then saw little prints dashed in amongst the mud. He followed them until he found the point where they all came together, blending into some sort of messy connection of footprints right before the land began to dry. He looked up toward the trees for any sign of life. There was nothing, no movement, no noise. But there was a bead. A single, blue bead.

Benji bent over and picked it up. Its color proved to be in stark contrast to the natural landscape around them. He squinted and made out what he believed to be another bead, a green one. He walked up to it and once again picked it up. He narrowed his gaze and looked up again toward the woods. He scanned the dirt until he found another blue bead. This one, he left alone. He had gotten the message.

His walk turned into a jog, which quickly turned into a run, a skill he shared with his sister. Within no time, he was hot on their trail, tracking each bead with every few steps he would take. It wasn't long until he spotted them, a hazy outline of what appeared to be a man and two girls in the distance. He kept a distance between them but never let them out of his sight. After a few minutes, he had confirmed that the three of them had no real direction and were relying on hope alone to guide them through the densely wooded area. He slowly moved in, rifle still out in front of him.

"All right, friend," he said from twenty yards away, the stock of the rifle already nuzzled in his shoulder.

Ray turned and pulled the two girls behind him. Benji had them pinned. There was no destination they could run to. They could only split up and hope for the best.

"End of the—" he stopped speaking as soon as he saw Beatrix poke her head out from behind him. Benji lifted his head from his sight and stared at her for a prolonged moment. "Are you trying to jerk me around?" he asked, looking at Ray.

Ray didn't know what to say. He was tired of bartering for his life. Benji seemed to be paranoid. He looked all around him and then focused back on Ray. "Where's Loon?" he asked, sounding concerned.

Ray shrugged. "She went back for Maple," he stated.

Benji nodded, still concerned. "Well, my people know what to do if they find her. Is everything all right, girls?" he asked, looking toward Clover and Beatrix.

The two of them just pulled themselves closer behind Ray, who stood helplessly at the end of a barrel. Benji continued his makeshift interrogation. "I heard the little one croaked. Why is she standing right behind you?"

Clover held Beatrix close.

Ray kept his hands up in surrender, his hands far away from the knife sheathed behind him. "I don't know what happened. I missed her pulse."

Benji chuckled as he shook his head. "No, no, you won't be fooling me. I feel it too."

"What?" Ray asked.

"I feel that warmth. That um—that happiness, the joy. It's like—victory, it's like…" he stared at Beatrix. "It's like you're in the presence of a God."

Ray could feel Clover's fear from behind him. She was shaking. There was something about Benji that terrified her. There was a certain unhinged quality that seemed extremely prominent at that very moment.

Benji's eyes narrowed. "Mmm-hmm. Girls, come over here."

They didn't move.

Benji was getting angry. "I said get over here!" he demanded.

There was still no movement.

He sighed and reinforced his grip on the rifle, setting his sights on Ray's head. "Look, if you don't get over here right now, I'll blow his brains all over these woods, and I'll just take you both with me. Now get over here."

Benji seemed disappointed. He looked down from his gun one last time. "Last chance, ladies."

He then looked back at Ray. "I tried."

Taking sight, he pulled back on the trigger. The bullet exploded from the barrel and went hurtling right toward Ray's chest. The shot echoed through the woods. Ray clutched at his chest, wincing as he expected the worst. Benji looked up as the blue of the smoke cleared. Ray remained standing there; nothing had changed.

Beatrix slowly relinquished her clutch on Ray's upper thigh. "Ray?" she asked.

He looked down at her, expecting to be dead. There was no blood, no wound, no hole in his shirt or body. Beatrix looked up at him with two hopeful eyes.

"Yes?" he responded to her.

"Just checking," she said in reply.

Benji looked at the three of them in bewilderment. He ejected the casing from his gun and loaded another round, not taking his eyes off of them in the process. "Incredible," he said in awe. "Just incredible."

He slowly approached them, his gun still set on them, Ray still clutching his chest. He maneuvered his body and swung his rifle, bashing Ray to the side. He grabbed Clover by the hair, screaming. Beatrix jumped onto his legs, but he managed to kick her off. "Let's put 'em all to the test!" he shouted, casting Clover into a patch of leaves and taking aim.

Beatrix let out a loud cry as she reached for Clover. Ray scrambled to get to his feet. Benji pulled back the bolt handle and watched it spring back into place. He then aimed it down at Clover. But something stopped him from pulling the trigger.

An animalistic shriek cried out in the distance, causing Benji to lower his sights for a moment. He looked in every direction, making sure to direct his attention back toward Clover. There was movement nearby, the pitter-patter of feet sprinting across the earth's surface. Just as he raised his gun again, Luna came sprinting down the pathway. She pushed forward so furiously that Benji hadn't the slightest idea what was going on. She leaped onto a nearby tree and used it to propel herself upward. As she reached the pinnacle of her leap, she raised her knife high above her head. Using gravity to her advantage, she wedged the blade of her knife deep within the crevice of Benji's shoulder, bringing him down with her in an instant.

He screamed and threw an elbow backward, knocking her off of him. Benji grabbed at his gun, but Luna leaped on top of it, preventing him from raising it. Instead, he squeezed the trigger, firing his last round so that they couldn't use it against him. The reverberations of the weapon send shock waves running up and down her spine as she lay on top of it, pinning the weapon to the ground. As soon as the bullet had torn through nearby foliage, she spun around, grabbed hold of the knife, and pulled on it, worsening the gash in his shoulder. He once again elbowed her off of his back and pulled the knife out of his shoulder. The two of them circled each other, waiting for the other to strike like two alpha predators waiting to strike.

"You crazy *bitch*," Benji spat, his face still mildly amused. "You know you can end this all right now, come with me. We'll take the girls, go back to camp—happily ever after."

"Not a chance," she growled, waiting for him to attack.

Ray grabbed the most sizable stick he could find and swatted Benji over the back of the head. He was quick to turn around and slash at Ray's arm, slightly cutting him. Clover saw this and leaped to her feet, grabbing the hand with which Benji wielded the knife, preventing him from coming back on Luna with it. This gave Luna time to once again jump onto his back, pulling him away from Clover.

Benji booted Clover in the stomach, forcing her backward into Ray's arms. Luna kept pulling until he fell backward, flattening her against his back and the earth, knocking the wind out of her in the process. He swiveled around and raised the knife. Ray once again grabbed hold of his arm, trying to get the bloody knife out of Benji's hand. He kneed Benji in the rib cage just as Luna bit the wrist that was holding her down.

Benji fell to his knees, giving Luna an opportunity to escape. She began to crawl away, reaching for a nearby rock. Benji grabbed her ankle and pulled her back, driving the knife into the meat of her upper thigh. Luna screamed like she had never screamed before, so hard that birds fled their nest.

Ray threw himself onto Benji. Not the best of ideas, but the only one that came to mind. He flailed his fists about in the air, making contact with whatever he could. A discombobulated Benji forced him off and began to wale on him as hard as he could. Clover and Beatrix watched as Benji hit Ray again and again and again, all while Luna writhed in pain as she bled from her leg, rolling back and forth on the ground.

Beatrix ran to Luna's aid while Clover once again tried to intervene. Picking up a stick as she approached Benji. She punched him in the back of the head. When he turned to swat her away, she jabbed him in the eye with a stick. He shot backward and grabbed at his eye. Ray lay still on the ground. Clover quickly ran over to him, trying to wake him before Benji decided to strike back.

"Wake up, Ray!" she said, shaking him. "Wake up!"

Benji rolled around in the mud for a few moments before slamming his fists into the earth, letting out a war cry. Luna knew what this meant and examined the scene around her. It was going to be Clover against a fully grown man if she didn't act fast. Against her better judgment, she began to tug on the knife, trying her hardest to dislodge it from her leg. She screamed as she slid the knife back out from under the tissue and muscle. Beatrix cradled her upper half as she did this. Luna sat up and used all of the strength she could muster, both mental and physical, to remove the jagged blade.

Benji got to his feet and looked around with the only eye he could see out of. Clover began to throw stones at his head, distracting him from finishing off the others. He growled like a rabid beast as he tried to catch her, shielding his face from the stones at the same time. Ray slowly began to cough, bringing life back into his lungs. One eye was already beginning to swell shut. He tried to see what was happening, but the earth was spinning around him.

Luna screeched as she pulled out the tip of the knife. She was beginning to see spots, her vision blurry, most likely due to the blood pouring out of the gash in her upper leg. She tried to stand, but it was no good. Any pressure on her leg would cause her to collapse. Beatrix held her arm, trying her best to keep Luna from losing consciousness. Ray looked over and saw this as Benji was still fixated on getting his hands on Clover. He noticed the knife in Luna's hand and how she was trying her best to move closer to Benji.

Clover quickly noticed the trap that was forming and knew she had to act fast. She hurled more stones at his head, confusing him further and driving him backward toward Ray, who remained on the ground. She threw the rocks harder and harder, driving him back a bit more each and every time until he was now inches away from Ray's feet.

With one last mighty throw, Clover slung a hefty stone, striking Benji in the lower chin. He stumbled backward enough so that Ray was able to stick out his leg, causing him to trip and fall to the forest floor. Luna wasted no time. Now that Benji was within range, she lifted the blade and jabbed it directly into his side. His eyes shot open as he gasped for air. The veins in his head were popping and extremely noticeable against the beat red complexion on his face. He tried to stand up in an attempt to flee. He got to his knee and sloppily yanked on the handle of the knife, sliding it out while trying to keep his spare hand cupped over his wound. The blade kept getting caught on a new piece of flesh or tissue, forcing him to yank harder and harder on the object protruding from his side.

He tore the blade out of his side, and a thick flow of blood was quick to follow. It ran right into his hand and slipped out from in between his fingers. He kept his hand on his wound, bewildered by the fact that his sister had actually done it. He limped a few feet, still trying his best to keep a firm hand on his deepening gash.

He moaned as he hobbled forward. Clover slowly approached him from behind with the largest piece of wood she could find—a limb from a nearby tree. With one mighty blow, she swung, making full contact with the back of his head. Her dried-out staff splintered upon contact. Benji's body went limp as his hand fell loosely to his side, allowing his gash to bleed freely. His eyes rolled back into his sockets as his head fell back onto the ground. Clover backed up, keeping a steady eye on him to ensure he was not getting back up. She then fell back onto her butt, casting the branch aside, completely out of breath.

The four of them heaved on the ground. Luna propped herself against a tree and tried desperately to put pressure on the hole in her leg. She sniveled as she pushed down on the tender gash. Ray slowly forced himself into a crawling position and crawled over to her side. She lay her head on his shoulder and allowed herself to finally break down. Every muscle in her body quivered, every bone shook as she let the pain of the last twenty-four hours sink into her soul. Ray pushed on her wound as well, noticing that she, too, was losing copious amounts of blood. Beatrix, worried that she was not being useful, began to stroke her on the shoulder—anything she could do to improve the situation.

Clover came over to them both, looking at them like some sort of scared, lost animal. She had no idea where to go now. Were they going to be forever hunted? None of them could find the words to say to one another. There was no *feeling better* from all of this. Corazon had been torched. They had no shelter; it was now the four of them against the wilderness.

The sun was setting, sending a deep pink springtime glow to shine on all of them through the branches. Ray held onto Luna tight, slowly muttering "*Shhh.*" in a soothing tone as she sobbed away the last of the air in her lungs. "I've got you," he said, remembering how those were some of the first words she ever spoke to him when she pulled his body onto that riverbank. "*I've got you,*" he whispered again.

Luna just buried her head in his shoulder and cried for what seemed to be hours. The sun sank lower into the sky. They all knew they were far too weak to cover any actual ground; they were just going to have to soldier it through the night. Luna soon fell into a deep sleep as she used all of the energy she had left to purge the pain from her body. Ray held her until he, too, was fast asleep. This left Clover and Beatrix alone in the dark, in a wooded area full of things that wanted to hurt them, human and otherwise.

53

The two girls sat still, slowly digesting all that they had seen that day. Clover looked toward Beatrix, who had remained remarkably calm throughout the entire endeavor. "Are you all right?" she asked her, genuinely concerned upon noticing her lack of distress.

Beatrix nodded, "Just fine," she stated. "Are you hurt?"

Clover lifted her shirt and showcased the bruising on her stomach, deep splotches of purple and blue. "Could be a lot worse," she said, looking toward Luna, who grew more peaked with every passing moment.

Beatrix once again didn't appear too concerned with Luna's physical state, Clover had assumed she'd be a wreck, but instead, she sat in front of them, seeming fully rested and completely calm.

"Hey," Clover said, wanting to keep the conversation afloat in order to keep herself awake. "Do you remember a while back? We were playing in the woods. You had told me about how you had never had your first kiss?"

Beatrix nodded. She smiled, bringing some life to her demeanor. "Yes, that was around the time I gave you—" she picked a bead out of the dirt to her left and held it in the air. "Our bracelets."

Clover returned her smile. "I don't think I told you this at the time, but—that was my first kiss, too," she said, curious as to how Beatrix would react.

Bea held her smile. She nodded in approval. "It was a good one," she said as if she were a connoisseur on the topic.

Clover pressed her hands against each other as she started to nervously rock back and forth. "I um... I don't want it to be my last."

Then Beatrix realized that her friend's recollection of their special moment was coming from a place of fear. Clover had her knees tucked to her chest, and her eyes were the eyes of someone who had seen something they shouldn't have. Beatrix inched forward until they were close enough to touch. She could see the tears in Clover's eyes by the way her eyes were glinting in the moonlight.

"Clover," she said, taking her friend by the hands. "Do you trust me?"

She nodded, "More than anything," she whimpered. Clover leaned forward and rested her head on Bea's shoulder. Bea maneuvered so that the two of them could huddle together for warmth.

"Good, because you need to trust me when I say everything is going to be all right, okay?" she said, sounding sure of herself. Clover didn't respond. "*Okay?*" she repeated.

"Okay," she replied blankly.

The back and forth between the two withered away until all that was left was the sound of crickets around them. Clover perked up. Just before shutting her eyes to sleep, she looked over to Bea, who still remained in her state of Zen.

"Beatrix?" she said, trying to prepare her for what was to come. "I think I love you."

She smirked, "You think?"

Clover paused and spoke with more certainty. "I love you."

Bea's smile widened, "I love you, too."

Clover took a deep breath, a sigh of relief. She closed her eyes and escaped into the confines of her dreams within minutes, her head resting peacefully on Bea's chest. Soon Bea would fall asleep as well. The two would dream of a life far from where they were at that very moment. A life out of the woods, a neighborhood, a house with siding, a television, and friends. But no matter where they were, they were together. The two of them remained like that for hours. In fact, all of them remained in that resting state for some time.

It wasn't until she felt a bug crawl its way up her wounded leg where Luna jolted herself away, swatting at the bug while simultaneously trying to keep herself from screaming. Ray jumped in place and addressed it immediately. "What is it?"

She took a moment to find herself, then looked at him, scared. "Was it all a dream?"

He shook his head, "I'm afraid not."

She nodded and looked at Bea and Clover as they sat there resting. "There's no way I'm gonna make it out of these woods," her free hand still clutching the wound on her leg.

"Don't talk like that," he said, leaning in. "You're going to be fine. Come sunrise, I'll head out, find something, *someone*. They can send help, a helicopter or something—don't talk like that."

"Not like that," she said, tenderly nursing her wound with her fingers. "I'm not gonna make it out there," she gestured to her right, to where she assumed they would find civilization. "It's not for me. I don't know that world anymore. And it doesn't want me back."

He repositioned himself on the trunk of the tree and kept his eyes on her. "You don't have to. We can find a place—something like my cabin. It'll be small but quiet, away from everything else. We'll make it work for us."

She paused; there was something in his words that stuck out to her. "Us?"

He swallowed his pride and tried to elaborate further, but all he could string together was, "You know... *us*."

His words were followed by a tense silence. "Why do you think there will be an us?" she asked.

"After all this, I just—I thought—" he tried to recover from his assumptions.

"All this..." she scoffed. "And by all this, you mean..." she looked toward the night sky, spotted with stars. "You mean how I rescued you? And how you repaid me by overturning everything I believed in?"

Ray desperately searched for the words he could use to make things right, "Luna, I—"

"Corazon did a lot of bad," she said, her demeanor hardening before his eyes. "We let things happen that shouldn't have happened. We lived in blissful ignorance, and for that, we'll be held accountable..." She shook her head, finding it difficult to look at him. "But Corazon also did a lot of good. It took the rejects in. It gave them a place to call home, it got them clean, and it gave them purpose. It made them feel like they were a part of something bigger. Like they actually belonged." Her fondness for what Corazon was to her began to peek through.

"We had our issues," she stated. "But they were *our* issues. Not yours. You had no right to get involved. But you did, and now people are dead."

"That was him," Ray responded in defense of himself. He gestured toward Benji's body, which lay a few yards away from them. "He did that. Not me."

Luna remained still, "The Former was always just a rumor, nothing more. We knew they were out there, but they weren't a threat. I always had my suspicions about him," she said, nodding toward Benji's body. "But he was harmless without a weapon."

She choked back her emotions and continued, taking a more accusatory tone. "You never went to the hunting chest, did you? The code was never for you, was it?" she asked, eyeing the transceiver still clipped to his belt.

Ray tried to defend his actions. "You wanted me to get help—"

"I wanted you to get help. Not send an army," she said, losing the battle with her emotions. "Just tell me… did you do it?" she asked, looking back at him. "Did you give them the code? Did you arm The Former?"

He looked her in the eyes and saw the raw emotions swelling beneath them. He knew his simple answer wouldn't do him any justice. He could see the yearning within her, the need for closure, the need for someone to blame. "No," he stated, holding her gaze.

She stared at him for another moment, giving him the chance to change his answer. He remained silent and stoic. She looked for the truth in his eyes, but there was nothing to be found. With a simple nod of her head, she directed her attention back toward the girls, who remained sound asleep. "Every decision from here on…" she muttered. "It's for them, not for us."

Ray knew this was no time for trying to reason with her. She was right; it was about keeping them safe. Everything else had been reduced to an afterthought. "I agree," he replied.

Luna cracked a smile as she looked at the two girls, thankful that they had made it out of the chaos with more than just their lives. "Wake me before you leave," she said, her eyes slowly falling shut.

He nodded, not sure if she realized his arm was still around her. "Of course," he said. Then he felt it again, the feeling he had felt a few times before. The need for confirmation that everything would be all right, the validation, the warmth of embrace, the simple pleasure of acknowledgment, the tender nod of affection that remained disguised as a simple term. "Good night, Luna," he said, ensuring that his words would be heard.

There was silence, a longer silence than usual. The night was alive with all other sounds—the wind in the trees, the chirping of bugs, the sounds of slumber, but there was no reciprocation of his send-off. Of everything he had experienced in the last few days, it was the absence of her words that cut the deepest. He felt a numbness somewhere within him as if a fire had been extinguished.

He wouldn't sleep for the rest of the night. He'd just close his eyes and breath, hoping that by doing so, he'd find some comfort. That wasn't the case. He opened his eyes to find Bea awake again. She had separated herself from Clover, who remained asleep. The early morning sun's fiery glow peeked over the horizon, striping the landscape with shadow.

Bea was pacing around Benji's body. Ray woke up in time to see her search one of the many pockets on his pants. She pulled her hand out and examined the contents —a tiny handful of beads.

"What are you doing?" Ray asked, still groggy.

She looked at him, then back to her beads. "I'm going to make our bracelets again, I need the beads," she said, stating her business exactly how it was.

He leaned forward, placing his elbows on his knees. "That doesn't bother you?" he asked.

"What?" she replied, looking back at him.

"The body. It doesn't bother you? Seeing a dead body?" he asked, glad that his resting place was far away from the cadaver.

She meandered her way over to him and sat down in the dirt in front of him, counting her beads in the early morning light. "It's not the body people are scared of. It's the death," she stated. She looked up at him with easy eyes that seemed to be unfazed by recent events.

"Sorry, what?" Ray asked, noticing how her way of speaking had changed, dismissing it as a concussion.

"A dead body won't hurt you," she muttered as she finished fingering through the beads in her palm. "That's not what people are scared of. It's the death that scares them," she said, looking back up at him to see his reaction.

He was now fully awake, completely caught up with what she was saying. "And why doesn't it scare you?" he asked, the bruising in his face now much more prominent.

She closed her tiny palm over the beads and slid them into her pocket. "*Because it's not as bad as people think,*" she whispered.

Her little words had confirmed it. He was no longer looking at the girl he once knew. She was now something completely different. He could feel it in the air around them. He had felt it since the very moment Elliot had placed his hands on her dead body. It was in her demeanor. It was in the way she moved; it was in her very essence. It was clear to him now that as long as she was there, they would be safe, and they would be protected. It was the feeling that countless others had tried to explain.

Her eyes carried with them a certain mysterious hue, a look that spoke to him, a look that said she could see what was happening. She could see the before, the after, and the forever more. It was a feeling beyond wisdom, beyond clairvoyance. It was both the look of a Prophet and the look of someone who knew what was coming.

She stood up and placed a hand on his shoulder, easing him back onto the sturdy tree trunk. He felt his emotions surge beneath his overwhelming exhaustion. "I tried to—" he gasped, ashamed that his attempts at heroism resulted in all of them setting out in unfamiliar territory. "I just wanted to do the right thing. I didn't want—I didn't mean for—" he shook his head, unable to coherently express his sorrows. "She shoulda left me there."

She nodded her head. "The path forward isn't always cut with good deeds."

He swallowed his emotions and angled his head up at her. "Who told you that?"

Beatrix nodded toward the sky as a gentle breeze brushed by the both of them. "She did."

Ray looked at the sky, then back to Bea, who watched his every move. "By her, you mean…" he held his hands out, palms facing up. His lips trembled; he couldn't say the word.

Beatrix nodded. "Yes."

The two remained there, eyes locked. Ray's hands shook, his lips quivered. "Is it too late?"

Beatrix knelt before him and took his hand in her own. It was cold to the touch and shook within her grasp. "It's never too late, Ray. But if we're going to get out of here, I need to know you're with me."

He closed his eyes and squeezed out the last of his remaining tears. Closing his hand on hers, he slowly nodded his head. It was as if the task itself was painful. He looked at her again, this time with a molecule of hope.

"I need to hear you say it. *She needs to hear you say it.* Mother says you can still be saved," she stated. "Believe in me—*believe in us.*"

"After all this?" he asked, his face pale and expressionless.

Bea nodded her head, still holding his tired gaze. "After all this."

He clenched his jaw and let his head sink back onto the bark. After all of the lying, the lust, the vengeance and death—to request belief seemed too much to ask. He took a deep breath and looked at her with certainty in his narrowing eyes. "I don't believe in you. But I believe you."

Beatrix smiled softly. She pulled her hand away from him and stood back up. It wasn't clear to him how she had taken such a response. "We have a long way ahead of us. It's time for you to rest," she said, looking down at him. He slowly nodded; she was right.

He couldn't think of anything to say that hadn't already been said. Luna's breathing became abundantly present. He turned and looked at her, somehow still gracefully sleeping under such brutal conditions.

With the limited energy he had left, he shifted his body, leaning his head onto her shoulder.

Within seconds his eyes were closed. The gentle breeze lulled by, the sun fully peeked over the horizon, and the quiet of the early morning engulfed them all. Despite everything that had happened since he had been brought to Corazon—there, sitting against the tree, Luna, Clover, and Beatrix by his side, he finally felt what he had been searching for all along. He had found his peace.

If only for a moment.

About the Author

Liam Cuddy has always had an affinity for the things he couldn't explain. Having grown up in the small town of Auburn, New York, most of his days were spent hiking, biking, or sitting on the shore of Owasco Lake drumming up ideas for stories that had yet to be written. He found the time and inspiration to complete his debut novel throughout his four years at Niagara University. He is currently pursuing a master's in communication, while working on various other creative endeavors. To contact the author, or to order both current and future work, visit liamcuddy.com.

Made in the USA
Middletown, DE
20 July 2021